MARVEL

A CLASSIC MARVEL OMNIBUS

WOLVERINE

WEAPON X OMNIBUS

NOVELS OF THE MARVEL UNIVERSE BY TITAN BOOKS

Ant-Man: Natural Enemy by Jason Starr

Avengers: Everybody Wants to Rule the World by Dan Abnett

Avengers: Infinity by James A. Moore

Black Panther: Who is the Black Panther? by Jesse J. Holland

Captain America: Dark Design by Stefan Petrucha

Captain Marvel: Liberation Run by Tess Sharpe

Civil War by Stuart Moore

Deadpool: Paws by Stefan Petrucha

Spider-Man: Forever Young by Stefan Petrucha

Spider-Man: Kraven's Last Hunt by Neil Kleid

Spider-Man: The Darkest Hours Omnibus by Jim Butcher, Keith R.A. Decandido, and Christopher L. Bennett (forthcoming)

Spider-Man: The Venom Factor Omnibus by Diane Duane

Thanos: Death Sentence by Stuart Moore

Venom: Lethal Protector by James R. Tuck

X-Men: Days of Future Past by Alex Irvine

X-Men: The Dark Phoenix Saga by Stuart Moore

X-Men: The Mutant Empire Omnibus by Christopher Golden

X-Men & The Avengers: The Gamma Quest Omnibus by Greg Cox

ALSO FROM TITAN AND TITAN BOOKS

Marvel Contest of Champions: The Art of the Battlerealm by Paul Davies

Marvel's Spider-Man: The Art of the Game by Paul Davies

Obsessed with Marvel by Peter Sanderson and Marc Sumerak

Spider-Man: Hostile Takeover by David Liss

Spider-Man: Into the Spider-Verse – The Art of the Movie by Ramin Zahed

The Art of Iron Man (10th Anniversary Edition) by John Rhett Thomas

The Marvel Vault by Matthew K. Manning, Peter Sanderson, and Roy Thomas

Ant-Man and the Wasp: The Official Movie Special

Avengers: Endgame – The Official Movie Special

Avengers: Infinity War – The Official Movie Special

Black Panther: The Official Movie Companion

Black Panther: The Official Movie Special

Captain Marvel: The Official Movie Special

Marvel Studios: The First Ten Years

Spider-Man: Far From Home – The Official Movie Special

Spider-Man: Into the Spider-Verse – The Official Movie Special

Thor: Ragnarok – The Official Movie Special

A CLASSIC MARVEL OMNIBUS

WOLVERINE

WEAPON X OMNIBUS

by
Marc Cerasini
David Alan Mack
Hugh Matthews

TITAN BOOKS

Wolverine: Weapon X Omnibus
Print edition ISBN: 9781789096026
E-book edition ISBN: 9781789096033

Published by Titan Books
A division of Titan Publishing Group Ltd
144 Southwark Street, London SE1 0UP

First edition: December 2020
10 9 8 7 6 5 4 3 2

This book is a work of fiction. Any references to historical events, real people, or real places are used fictitiously. Other names, characters, places, and events are products of the author's imagination, and any resemblance to actual events or places or persons, living or dead, is entirely coincidental.

Special thanks to Lou Aronica, Lucia Raatma, Eric Fein,
Danny Fingeroth, and Julia Molino.
Original trilogy edited by John Betancourt & Keith R.A. DeCandido.
Cover art by Marko Djurdjevic.

FOR MARVEL PUBLISHING
Jeff Youngquist, VP Production Special Projects
Caitlin O'Connell, Assistant Editor, Special Projects
Sven Larsen, VP Licensed Publishing
David Gabriel, SVP Sales & Marketing, Publishing
C.B. Cebulski, Editor in Chief

A CIP catalogue record for this title is available from the British Library.

Printed and bound in Great Britain by CPI Group (UK) Ltd, Croydon, CR0 4YY

Book One
WEAPON X

by Marc Cerasini

1

PROPHECY

RAIN. Gouging thin canals through soiled windowpanes. Night. Bending from black to phosphorescent green. A sickening hue, like alien pus.

Liquid all around me. But not drowning.

Neon hummed beyond the glass. Twisted tubes. Huge letters spelling out a single word etched in blue-white light: PROPHECY.

The word seemed apocalyptic. No. That isn't right. It was part of the apocalypse. Some drunken bum down the hall had clued him in.

"The apocalypse is coming"—that's what the geezer said. "When all the secrets will be exposed."

No more secrets, no more running.

"Hell is comin'…"

That's what he said. He spit when he said it, too. Then the old guy just stopped breathing.

Air. No air here. But breathing still.

It happened a lot at the Prophecy. Old guys. And not so old. Keeling over. Dropping dead.

Trapped inside. Like floating in a coffin. But not dead. Not yet…

The water from the sky was as old as the earth. Logan watched it fall. The same water. Billions of years. Over and over. Fish crawled out of it. Man crawled out of it, too.

Then I crawled out.

Trapped inside. Liquid all around. A vile chemical. But not water…

Dinosaurs fed on plants, drank from lakes. This rain was part of those lakes. The wells of villages. Warriors, barbarians, samurai. The water they drank went up and came down. The same water. Trapped in a cycle.

Everything, even the earth, has its limits.

A shock of lightning scratched the night. Logan's eyes shined through the glass—feral-sharp, scanning streets lit by shards of bone-white brilliance.

Another strike, a tree split. The energy sundered it. Like a warning of things to come.

"Storm's comin', and it's a big one. *The* big one. The one I've been looking out for."

The road. He remembered the road. The cold steered the wheel. Black woods at night. The far north. Endless wilderness. Soon he'd be back. Soon he'd be home.

Beyond the glass now: wet concrete, rusty Dumpsters, graffiti-scarred alleys, haunting tenements, emptiness. *They haven't found me. Not yet.*

Logan turned from the window, crossed the stained brown carpet. The room was as small as a cage, empty bottles like stalagmites spiking the floor, spiking his brain.

A week-old newspaper ripped under his booted foot, meaningless events. Day after day. He collapsed on a couch, spring-cushioned by a tabloid spread over it. His massive fist tightened, crumpling the newsprint, hurling the ink-black words at the blank TV.

Useless headlines. Day after day after day.

Nearby, a Seagram's bottle, shimmering with many promises. Half-empty. No. Half-full. He poured a healthy swallow into a glass, always grateful.

Ripples of electricity scratched the night.

Searing bolts stab his brain.

Logan winced in shock, retching as a salty trickle rolled down his throat. Then the pain vanished, leaving only the coppery taste of blood—a familiar tang. He touched his throbbing temple, but found no stain. Only beads of salty sweat moistened his fingertips.

He swallowed again, and the metallic sting was gone, too. Were his senses off? Or was the alcohol awakening demons of past mayhem, forgotten violence?

Forgotten...

"The apocalypse is here. Time to write home, to make peace with somebody—"

Peace? With whom?

He remembered the saloon, a dozen milling bodies. The usual fog of burning tar. The air had felt frozen. But his muscles, beneath the flannel, had been warm enough. He'd lined up the bottles on the bar in front of him, green pickets. Glass pillars. His fortress.

Time to write home.

"Dear Ma—ya goat-headed, misshapen, walleyed witch. Got some news for ya. The secret is out! Signed: yer son with the hairy paws."

As if he knew who his mother was. Everybody's got one, right? Or two, maybe. Secrets, that is. Logan had a doozy. A serious mother lode. Hard hiding it sometimes. But he got by.

Another shot of whiskey straight from the bottle. But no oblivion. Not even a rush, until he noted its absence. Then the sensation arrived as if he'd conjured it. He sucked his cigar.

Gagging. Tissue rips. A ravaged throat.

Maybe the apocalypse has already begun.

This place where he was hiding, this Prophecy, it was a tenement transformed by the faithful into a refuge for fallen Christians. He'd been a Christian once, a long time ago. He still remembered enough of the lingo to lie his way through the door. It was a dump, of course. But it was free—for the fallen. So he'd qualified.

Warm whiskey dribbled past Logan's wiry, raven-black chin stubble, onto his sweat-stained T-shirt.

Choking. Then a voice. But who?

"Enough of the stuff to stun an elephant…"

Alcohol alters the flow of electrolyte ions through brain cells. He remembered reading that somewhere—part of his black ops training, maybe. Whiskey slows the speed at which neurons fire.

"But I'm not drunk. And I want to be… I need to be…"

Alcohol suppresses the production of a hormone that keeps the body's fluid reserves in balance. Without that hormone, kidneys begin to steal water from other organs…

"Steal water?"

The storm continued to rage, intensifying.

The rain continued to pound on the windows.

Liquid all around. But not drowning.

The brain shrinks as a result.

Logan snatched the bottle again and spilled the dregs into the bottom of his glass. But he paused before shooting it back. Cradling the drink in his heavy fist, Logan slumped into the battered couch.

Violent images flowed over him. A dispute he'd had with a nickel-and-dime crime boss. The idiotic bravado.

"Stupid. He should have known better..."

It happened after he'd become an outcast again. This time he'd been booted from a secret branch of the Canadian Intelligence Service. The infraction had been trivial compared to the heinous acts he'd performed in the line of duty. But Logan sensed his peers were happy to rid themselves of the enigma in their midst.

Secrets. I had plenty. More than any man should bear.

Not long after, Logan found work. His reputation became a two-edged sword. An unending line of young punks or fading old-timers always there to challenge him. But that meant jobs were easy to come by.

This time around, it had been Logan's "associates" who'd executed the double cross.

That day, Logan recalled, had gotten off to a bad start. He resented the trip to the gunrunner's garage to collect his cut of the profits. But when he saw the sneer on St. Exeter's face, Logan knew things were about to get much worse.

The gunrunner leaned against a crate of fragmentation grenades, his cashmere sweater, Prada pants, and Gucci loafers incongruous in the junkyard setting.

"I didn't think you'd have the guts to show up here, Logan. Not after your connection failed to deliver the goods."

St. Exeter pushed back his hair with a delicate, manicured hand.

Logan met the man's cool gaze. "You're spewing crap, René. I know for a fact that those air-to-airs are already in the pipeline to your 'clients' in Latin America."

"Perhaps. But the weapons were of... inferior quality."

"The Pentagon would be surprised to learn that, considering they were all state-of-the-art Stinger missiles."

As Logan spoke, two of St. Exeter's bodyguards entered the garage behind him. Two more, in greasy coveralls, climbed out of a repair pit to flank him.

Half smile in place, René stared at Logan with eyes like black empty holes.

"You're not gonna pay," said Logan. It was not a question.

Suddenly, the grease monkey on Logan's left pulled a wrench out of his stained coveralls.

Stupid.

Logan hit the man with enough force to drive his jawbone into his brain. A grunt, and the mechanic crumpled. Logan snatched the tool from his dead hand before the man struck the ground.

Dodging a bullet fired at point-blank range, Logan spun and hurled the wrench at the man who'd pulled the trigger.

A crunch of bone, a splash of red, and the shooter's head jerked back. As he fell, his Magnum dropped at Logan's feet.

Logan ducked a wild shot, then snapped up the weapon. He fired without aiming—a lucky shot. The bullet clipped the second bodyguard's throat. Gurgling, he fell to his knees, clutching at his neck in a widening pool on the concrete floor.

Finally, Logan's luck ran out. The last of René's bodyguards charged, in an attempt to push Logan into the repair pit. The pair fell in together. At the bottom of the deep concrete well, both scrambled to their feet. A shadow fell over them. Logan looked up in time to see St. Exeter toss an object into the hole.

"Catch, *mon ami*."

Logan snatched the grenade out of the air. When the bodyguard saw it, he lunged for the ladder.

"Where you goin'?" Logan grabbed the man by his collar, spun him around, and jammed the grenade into his gut.

Wheezing, the bodyguard folded around the explosive and Logan released it, then dove for the opposite end of the pit. Heat and gore washed over Logan as the muffled blast slammed him against the concrete wall.

Bleeding from a patchwork of wounds, Logan crawled out of the pit that had become the bodyguard's grave, only to discover that René St. Exeter had fled the scene.

Logan caught up with him a few days later, on a public street in the heart of Montreal. The final confrontation occurred amid a dozen gawking witnesses, but Logan didn't care.

Some things, like payback, were too damn important to delay.

Even after the rage had passed, Logan felt no regret—only anger that he was forced to move on. Later that same night, he planned to hop a freight. His destination: the Yukon. As far north as Logan could go, to the very edge of civilization. He'd leave behind everything—a Lotus-Seven, some worthless possessions, his past.

With a bit of luck, Logan could start over.

Start over?

"Good place to start over, eh?"

The voice—familiar—came from years past. Back when Logan was still with the Defense Ministry. Back when he operated out of the Ottawa branch of the CIS.

Logan had been hunched in a corner, honing his blade, when the stranger approached. He'd looked up long enough to see past the big man's proffered hand, to the name tag tacked onto his broad chest: N. Langram.

The screech of metal on tortured metal resumed as Logan sharpened the edge of his K-bar knife.

The sandy-haired man reluctantly withdrew his hand, then slumped down on a weight bench across from Logan's.

The training area was empty but for them. Minutes before, they'd been told that their training had ended, that their first assignment was at hand.

"I think it's a great place to begin again... the CIS, I mean," continued N. Langram. "I've been to a lot of places, done a lot of things, legal and illegal, and I'm happy to forget my past and bury it forever."

Langram slapped his knees. "To my surprise, after all my mischief, the Defense Ministry and the CIS decided to let bygones be bygones and offer me a second chance."

"Good for you," said Logan.

"I figure they've done the same for you, eh?"

Logan fingered the tip of the blade. A drop of blood dewed his fingertip. He tasted it.

"My name's Langram... friends call me Neil." This time, the man didn't offer his hand.

"Logan."

"Quiet one, eh?"

Logan spun the knife and plunged it into the scabbard. Then he crossed his arms and stared into the distance.

"I've been wondering why they paired us. You and me. We're

strangers and we've never even trained together. So I'm trying to figure out the angles…"

"What have you deduced, Langram?"

Missing Logan's sarcasm, Langram tried to answer the question.

"Odd parameters for this mission, don't you think?" he began. "I mean, why not a simple HALO jump? The CDM has hundreds of soldiers who've trained for High Altitude Low Opening insertions, and hundreds more qualified for reconnaissance infiltration of hostile territory. Which means they don't need either of us. We'd be considered overqualified for this mission, except that the men in charge decided to do a few things the hard way."

"Like?"

"You have to admit that there aren't too many operatives in the CIS— or even the CDM—who are proficient in the use of the HAWK harness," said Langram.

The HAWK, or High Altitude Wing Kite, was a specialized piece of "personal aerodynamic hardware" developed for use by the Strategic Hazard Intervention Espionage Logistics Division—and S.H.I.E.L.D. didn't give lessons on how to use their high-tech flying suits to just any soldier.

"Maybe the top brass thinks the HAWK is the best means of insertion," said Logan. "With a HAWK we can control our own speed and angle of descent, and when and where we land. And we can fight back—even while we're airborne—if it becomes necessary."

Langram nodded, conceding Logan's points. "I know all that. I've used the HAWK before. And so, apparently, have you, Mr. Logan."

"Your point?"

"Maybe you and I crawled through the same mud," said Langram. "Or maybe we just have some of the same friends… and enemies."

Logan sat in silence.

"Secretive one, too, eh?"

Secrets. I've got plenty. Too many for me to handle sometimes.

"That's okay, Logan. I won't pry."

"You already have."

Langram refused to take offense, and they sat in uneasy silence for what seemed like a long time.

"I know the geography pretty well," Langram said at last. "The Korean Peninsula, I mean. And the area where we're going, too."

"Nice place?"

"If North Korea is a prison, then the region around Sook Reservoir is solitary confinement, a cell on death row, and the gallows all rolled up into one ugly bastard of a package."

Logan shrugged. "Sounds delightful."

Langram studied the other man. Logan avoided his gaze.

"So that's my expertise," Langram said. "And since you don't appear to be a nuclear weapons specialist, I figure you know either the local lingo or something about the guys we're chasing."

"Right so far."

"And since you are very skilled with a blade, and you ain't Korean, I have to assume you know plenty about Hideki Musaki and all his Yakuza thugs, and about the weapons-grade plutonium they hijacked on its way to that top secret government laboratory up north—the one processing weapons of terror."

Logan nodded once. "I know Hideki Musaki... personally. But we're not tight."

Langram smiled for the first time since their meeting. "So you've wandered the Far East, eh? Somehow I knew it. Seeing you reminded me of a place... a dive called Cracklin' Rosa's. And a man, too. A fellow known in those parts as Patch. He had a proclivity for the blade... just like you."

Again, Logan did not reply.

Langram glanced at his watch, then stood.

"Got to go, Logan," he said. "But we'll be seeing each other a lot in the coming days. In the meantime, remember what I said about the CIS being a good place to start over. To ditch your past if you want to... not many get a second chance."

Langram turned to go.

"Hey, Langram."

This time, Logan was on his feet and facing him.

"I'll watch your back if you'll watch mine. And when this mission's over, if we're both still alive, I'll buy you a drink..."

Another drink. And another. But never enough to bring release. Wait. What was I thinking about?

Like wisps of mist, the memories of that first meeting with Neil Langram slipped away.

Reduced by a creeping amnesia to dazedly pondering the drink in his hand, Logan watched as the whiskey morphed from clear brown to cloudy green.

Nauseated, he looked away.

On the other side of the window, the word PROPHECY glowed with ghastly phosphorescence. An acrid, chemical stench assailed his nostrils, and battered couch springs dug into his flesh. But despite his physical discomfort, Logan's head lolled and his eyes closed.

Sleep came, but Logan's dreams were no different than his waking life. He longed for escape while he continued to run, his legs pumping on a perpetual incline, stretching farther and farther into the future. At the top was the humming neon of the Prophecy sign, waiting there, waiting for him.

Suddenly awake, Logan bolted upright, crushing the glass in his grip. Thick red blood pooled in his palm, but he felt no pain.

Logan staggered to his feet, impatient now to flee, to escape before the apocalypse swallowed him up.

He tugged the flannel shirt over his wide shoulders. He pondered the predictability of his nightmares. Visions of pain and bones and spikes. Of vile stench and horror. And of dagger hands…

Searching for the keys to his car, Logan rummaged through a pile of yellowing newspapers. He noticed a headline on a grease-stained tabloid: MERCY KILLER "QUACK" ELUDES FBI.

Under the headline, next to the story, a grainy black-and-white image. The photograph of a portly, bearded man with a bland, unremarkable face.

The picture and the headline vaguely troubled Logan, but he didn't know why. When he tried to snatch the memory threads to connect them, they dissolved like streams of vapor in his increasingly clouded mind.

Lightning cracked the sky, split another tree.

Another warning.

Storm's comin', and it's a big one. The *big one. The one I've been looking out for.*

Logan pocketed his money and his keys. He left the Prophecy without a backward glance. His last memory: the neon sign blinking steadily in the rain.

Suddenly, Logan was sitting on a bar stool, hunched over a stained counter of a dingy gin mill. Outside, through filthy plate glass, the rain had stopped. A blanket of dirty snow covered the broken streets and sidewalks.

When did it snow?

Hands shaking, Logan reached for the bottle at his arm. He swallowed, wondering if all the booze had finally caught up with him and induced some kind of mental blackout.

Logan had no memory of the drive, yet through the big window he could see his Lotus-Seven parked in the lot.

Did he drive through rain, then snow? Had hours passed? Or days? Had he missed the freight train… and with it his only chance to escape?

For the first time in Logan's memory, panic welled up inside of him. Another swallow of whiskey took care of it, but left confusion in its wake.

Logan regained a certain measure of control by observing his surroundings—the bartender calmly washing glasses while watching a muted television tuned to a soccer game. Another man seated at the opposite end of the bar, drinking quietly. Logan sniffed the air, and his nose curled at the smell of rank booze and stale tobacco.

Tubes like worms. Boring their way into his ears, nose, his mouth, his brain.

Outside, a lone traffic signal switched from green to yellow to red and back again. There were no pedestrians on the sidewalks, and the clock on the snow-covered steeple down the block was running backward.

We travel into the future every second we live, but no one can go back in time, according to Einstein. Which proved the old geezer wasn't so smart after all.

In the shadows, under the dartboard, Logan spied three men with long coats and sunglasses, hats pulled down over their faces, drinks untouched in front of them. They sat at the edge of darkness. Waiting. Watching.

Time to go…

Logan rose, tossed a wad of bills on the bar, and headed for the door. The shadow men ignored him… or seemed to. Their inaction gave Logan hope, but not much.

Outside, his heavy boots crunched the icy snow.

Boots. Like a soldier's. Like mine. I was a soldier once. No, twice. I fought in two wars. Both of them a long time ago.

Logan looked down to find his boots gone, his feet no longer clad in hard leather, but swathed in soft moccasins. There was still snow. Everywhere. But this covering was pristine and virgin white. The reflective snow of his youth. It coated trees and blanketed rocks. It shimmered with frost under a pale winter sun.

The tavern, the parking lot, the shadow men had disappeared. Logan padded alone through a silent mountain forest.

Home? Could I be home already?

Hoarfrost crunched under the balls of his feet. The chill seeped bone-deep into Logan's wiry, teenaged frame. But despite the frigid air, the darkening sky, the deepening snow, Logan slogged ahead.

It was the burning rage that pushed him, maddened him—an unreasoning need for vengeance that drove Logan farther and farther into the wilderness.

Through calf-deep snow, Logan followed the spoor, moving quickly in a painful effort to catch up to his elusive quarry. Numb fingers clutched his father's long knife, ready to strike, ready to stab, to rend.

Eager to kill.

At a rocky precipice cleared of snow by the relentless wind, the footprints Logan had tracked ended abruptly. Frustrated, Logan scanned the forest, then sniffed the air, hoping to locate his prey by scent alone.

Harsh winds stung Logan's face—a face raw from the bitter cold and bruised from the beating he'd received at the hands of Victor Creed, the bully known to the local settlers of this region by his Blackfoot Indian name, Sabretooth.

I know Creed hates me. But I don't know why. More secrets, deeper and darker than the forest around me.

Sabretooth had turned up at the door of Logan's log cabin hours—or was it days?—before, just as he had every year around this same time. There was neither rhyme nor reason to Creed's visits—only that they always occurred when Logan was alone.

Logan had walked beyond the boundaries of his father's homestead, inside the tree line where he gathered firewood for the cold days and nights ahead. He was alone again. His father had been gone for weeks, fur-trapping up north.

To guard his son, his meager possessions, and the precious furs he'd gathered during trapping season, the elder Logan had left behind his hunting knife and a fierce husky named Razor.

Returning with a heavy bundle of dry timber, Logan had heard Razor's frenzied barks and angry howls, muffled by distance, by snow and by trees. He'd tossed the firewood aside and hurried back to the cabin as fast as he could run.

He found Razor's blood and brains staining the snow, and the Blackfoot helping himself to the pelts Logan's father had left to dry under the winter sun.

Through tears of rage, Logan stared down at the murdered animal while Creed's taunts battered his ears. Then, with the savage cry of an enraged beast, Logan hurled himself at his tormentor, to land on the man's back. Logan clawed at Creed's face and tore at his throat with his teeth.

With a fierce growl of his own, Sabretooth dashed Logan to the frozen ground.

Stunned, he sprawled in the snow next to his dog's stiffening corpse. As he fought for consciousness, Logan saw the Indian loom over him. Heard the man's stinging laughter ringing in his ears. Felt the torrent of kicks and blows that rained down on him.

Finally, the blackness rose and swallowed him up.

Much later, Logan bolted upright, his body numb from the cold. The sun had crossed the sky, the day fading. Logan's memory returned, and with it a murderous rage.

Racing to the cabin, Logan snatched the hunting knife from its place over the mantle. Without regard for the elements or the waning daylight, Logan set off, determined to hunt down Sabretooth and end his enemy's existence once and for all.

Within the first hour, Logan lost Creed's trail, then picked it up again. Now the Blackfoot's spoor was mixed with another's. A bear's. A large one, by the size of the prints. Like Creed, the animal was moving up a crude mountain trail toward higher ground.

Minutes later, as Logan nearly crested a hill, a dark figure rose up from behind a boulder. The grizzly roared a challenge, and Logan reared back in surprise.

Lumbering forward on its short hind legs, the mammoth grizzly towered over him. The animal weighed at least four hundred pounds. When it roared again, hot spittle splashed Logan's cheek. The creature's steaming breath rolled over him.

For a moment, Logan felt paralyzed. Then he raised his knife and let loose with a howl of his own. Moving forward, the blade slashing back and forth, Logan prepared to face the creature's massive onslaught.

The bold, unexpected move startled the bear. The beast halted, eyes wide, ears twitching—just out of the blade's reach.

Legs braced, Logan prepared to charge. His rage clawed his heart and he longed to slash and stab this creature—any creature. Nothing could threaten him.

Time seemed suspended as man and beast eyeballed each other very cautiously and carefully.

Then, from somewhere behind the grizzly, Logan heard a snort, followed by a terrified bleat. In the back of the looming grizzly, Logan spied four black eyes peering at him from under a tangle of low, snow-laden pine branches.

Black fur rippling, brown snouts wet and steaming, the frightened cubs emerged from cover, only to cower behind their mother.

Seeing the helpless pups, Logan lowered his blade. With wary eyes locked on the angry grizzly, he took a single step back, then another.

The bear snorted, her fur bristling, as Logan continued his careful retreat. Even in his harsh world, Logan believed that not everything that was a threat should be destroyed.

"Go in peace. You are not my enemy and I am not yours," Logan whispered softly as he continued to walk backward, down the trail.

The bear sensed Logan's intent. She dropped on all fours, then turned her quivering back on the human.

Slapping the cubs with her front paws to move them along, the grizzly plunged between the snow-covered trees.

Logan watched the creature retreat, her hide dusted with snow, two cubs scurrying at her feet. When the bear had moved out of sight, Logan closed his eyes and leaned against a tree, heart racing from the aftershock of the unexpected encounter.

When he opened them again, Logan found himself outside the tavern, in the middle of the snow-covered parking lot.

The night had grown much colder—unseasonably cold, unless Logan had lost weeks or months since his time at the Prophecy, instead of mere hours.

But he had no time to worry about that now. Not with the shadow men so close…

With a stab of relief, Logan spied his Lotus-Seven. The top was down—absurd in this weather, even for someone who did not feel heat or cold like everyone else.

Logan found his keys and slid behind the wheel.

The throbbing roar of the engine reassured him. But before Logan could throw the vehicle into gear, figures emerged from the darkness. Then a man spoke.

"Mr. Logan?"

Logan looked up just as something hard, cold, and sharp struck his shoulder, stabbed through muscle and ribs, and pierced his lung.

A hot gorge closed his throat. Wheezing, Logan struggled to rise, as toxins surged through his body, sapping his strength, bringing his mind to a standstill.

Helpless as a dishrag, Logan was dragged from the car. He lashed out—only to be pummeled to the cold ground by vicious, unseen fists. With the last of his waning strength, Logan fought back. But as the powerful tranquilizer took effect, the dark and the pain devoured him.

Just before consciousness slipped away, Logan felt an odd sense of relief. There was nothing more he could do now. Days of running and nights of hiding were over. Escape was no longer possible.

The apocalypse has begun.

2

THE HIVE

BEHIND angular eyeglasses that gleamed in the dim light, the Professor watched the medical team labor over their patient.

A dozen physicians and specialists crowded around a naked figure cocooned behind the thick walls of a translucent tank. Inside the Plexiglas coffin, "Subject X" floated in a greenish chemical soup comprised of interferon-laced plasma, molecular proteins, and cellular nutrients, along with a kind of synthetic embryonic fluid of the Professor's own devise.

A few ounces of that murky liquid were more valuable than those technicians could ever imagine. Worth more than the average North American skyscraper—and far more to the elite few who actually understood its purpose.

The Professor's thought was interrupted by a flashing light on his console. The team leader was informing him that the delicate preparatory process was nearing completion.

Like Subject X's airtight coffin, the Professor's own chamber was hermetically sealed—an electronic realm of steel and glass, fiberglass cables and silicon chips. Inside this chamber, computers purred and processors hummed. Polished adamantium steel walls dully reflected scrolling streams of data on flickering monitors and banks of high-definition TV screens.

The Professor's rail-thin body sat erect and motionless on his ergonomic throne, his pale flesh stretched taut over prominent cheekbones. Coolly, he appraised the medical procedures as they played in real time on a large central monitor.

A rare smile curled his lips as he observed the team's progress. Despite wearing somewhat restrictive environmental hazard suits, cumbersome helmets, and bulky air-scrubbers, the medical staff performed their assigned duties quickly and efficiently—so efficiently that Subject X would be ready for the first experiment tomorrow, well ahead of the original schedule.

The preliminary work had gone splendidly, the Professor decided, and his staff had performed with exemplary efficiency.

And why not? Had he not trained them himself, demanded the highest degree of professionalism, commitment, and self-sacrifice from every last one of them?

The Professor touched a button. On a different level of the compound, a blinking light alerted a second medical team that their skills would soon be needed. He manipulated everything that went on inside the immense research facility from this command-and-control center. Via constant digital recordings, the Professor knew of every action, every sound that transpired within its walls.

Billions of bits of data traveled to the Professor through hundreds of miles of fiber-optic cables—an information network that snaked its way through every room, every vent, every wall.

Poised like a spider in a technological web, the Professor surveyed his domain from the center of the vast complex. From behind sealed doors and coded locks, he could access any accumulated data, observe any experiment, and issue commands with the flick of a switch or the utterance of a spoken order.

What interested him now, of course, was Subject X.

Through the monitor, the Professor viewed the arrival of the second medical team. With a hiss, a pressurized door opened, and the group moved in to replace the preparatory staff. The members of this new team were clad in the same bulky environmental suits, not to protect them, but to shield Subject X from the threat of contamination—a necessary precaution.

The task of this second team was to fit Subject X with a variety of biological probes designed to monitor bodily functions, along with hollow injection tubes sheathed in Teflon. These tubes were crucial to the success of the adamantium bonding process.

The Professor's long-fingered hands—the hands of an aesthete, he liked to think—played lightly across a custom-made ergonomic keyboard only he could decipher. Abruptly, the ubiquitous whir of air-scrubbers and the constant hiss of the climate-control systems were drowned out by snatches of conversation and ambient sounds transmitted from the medical lab.

Scrolling data vanished from the supplemental view screens, to be replaced by images of men in protective suits crowding around the simmering, transparent coffin.

Dr. Hendry, the team leader—his environmental hazard suit marked with a broad green stripe to signify his status—studied Subject X through the opaque fluid.

"Who shaved the patient?"

At Hendry's side, a man raised his hand. "I did."

"What did you use, poultry shears?"

"What?"

"Look at the man." He pointed to the lone figure in the clear, rectangular tank.

Behind his faceplate, the other man seemed perplexed. "That's really weird. I shaved him twenty minutes ago, and he was as smooth as a billiard ball…"

"Could have used a haircut, too," observed another member of the team.

The physicians and specialists took their positions around the Plexiglas, gazing mutely at the figure inside. The pale pink male form was swathed in bubbles. His raven black hair drifted around his head like a storm cloud.

A flexible steel breathing tube looped down from a wheezing respirator to a mask that completely covered the subject's nose and mouth. This technological umbilical cord also contained various sensors, tubes that supplied nutrients, and needles to administer drugs, if necessary.

The silence was broken at last by a trundling medical cart pushed by a nurse clad in the same bulky gear worn by the others. On the cart's antiseptic surface sat an array of surgical probes resembling medieval torture devices more than any modern medical implement. Each gleaming probe was comprised of a hollow, razor-sharp stainless steel spike—some as long as six inches, others as short as an inch. A long, flexible tube was attached to each spike's base, along with wires to channel biological information to various monitoring devices.

Many of these probes would be used to measure and evaluate the subject's mundane bodily functions—heart rate, blood pressure, basal metabolism, body temperature, electrolyte balance, respiration, hormonal activity, digestion and elimination, and brain functions. Others would be used for more arcane purposes.

As the Professor remotely observed the procedure, the team leader began to attach the first probe. Reaching into the simmering stew, Dr. Hendry plunged a slender four-inch spike directly into the brain of Subject X through a hole drilled into the cranium above the left eye.

A flurry of movement erupted inside the tank. The medical team was taken by surprise when the subject jerked once, then opened his eyes and stared up at them, seemingly aware.

"Back away from the subject," Dr. Hendry commanded, even as he stood his ground.

The subject's eyes appeared focused and alert, though the pupils were dilated. Subject X tried to speak as well, but the sounds he made were muffled and incomprehensible behind the bubbling respirator and whirring machinery.

"The goddamn tranquilizer is wearing off." The neurologist's tone was critical.

"We pumped enough into him to stun an elephant!" said the anesthesiologist defensively.

"I can't believe it, either, but look at his brain wave patterns."

The neurologist stepped aside to display the encephalograph's readout to the rest of the team.

"You're right." The anesthesiologist could hardly believe it. He had never seen anything like it. "The subject's still in a fugue state, but he's regaining consciousness—despite the sedatives."

"Okay, I want Thorazine. Four hundred and fifty CCs. Stat." Dr. Hendry extended his hand for the hypodermic gun.

His surgical assistant lifted the injector, loaded a plastic vial of the powerful drug into the device, then hesitated.

"Are you sure about the dosage?" the assistant asked weakly. "Thorazine is going to mess up his brain functions something awful, and 450 CCs…"

The timid voice trailed off, but the meaning was clear. The serum could kill the subject.

Dr. Hendry gazed through his faceplate at the ghostly silhouette thrashing inside the coffin-shaped tank. The subject's chest was heaving, his jaw moving behind the breathing mask.

"If he comes around, he's going to mess us up something awful," Dr. Hendry replied.

"But that's a huge dose—enough to finish him, maybe…" The anesthesiologist's voice wasn't as weak as the assistant's, but it faded, too. He'd felt obligated to say it, though he knew it didn't matter. Not with Hendry in charge.

Watching from his sealed chamber, the Professor grunted in irritation and keyed the intercom. When he spoke, his sharp tone thundered inside the medical lab as well as the team's environmental hazard helmets.

"Administer the Thorazine at once. In the dose Dr. Hendry prescribed. The patient must not awaken. Not again."

Hendry snatched the hypodermic gun away from his assistant and plunged the injector into the churning tank. The hypodermic hissed, and Subject X tensed as a violent spasm wracked his thick frame. Soon, however, the subject's eyes closed and his respiration and heart rate slowed.

"He's out," said the neurologist.

"Blood pressure normal. Heart rate normal. Breathing is shallow, but the respirator will force sufficient oxygen into his lungs," the anesthesiologist noted with relief.

Inside the helmet, Dr. Hendry tried to shake the perspiration out of his eyes. "For a second there, I thought we were going to have to release the cyanide."

"Then we'd know how good these hazard suits really are," someone quipped.

The attempt at humor broke the tension of the moment, but the laughter was forced.

"Continue the procedure," the Professor's voice commanded.

Dr. Hendry lifted his eyes to the ceiling as if searching for the invisible cameras that recorded every step of the delicate process. After his assistant slapped a long probe into his gloved hand, Hendry reached into the boiling mixture and plunged the needle-sharp skewer directly into the subject's abdominal cavity.

Again, Subject X tensed as tremors rocked his muscular frame.

The Professor keyed his intercom. "There's been another spike in brain wave functions," he said, observing the data on his private touchscreen monitors.

This time, Hendry backed away from the tank with the rest. "What should we do, Professor?"

"I want you to use the biodampeners to inhibit Subject X's brain functions…"

The anesthesiologist spoke up again. "But Professor, we've already administered enough Thorazine to—"

"—stun an elephant, yes. But the sedative does not seem to be effective," the Professor murmured. "As you can plainly see, Subject X is hardly… placid."

Hendry signaled another member of his team. The man stepped forward, cranial probes in hand. The rest of the staff retreated to allow the specialist enough room to work. But before he attached the probes, the psychiatrist spoke.

"If you wish, we can activate the Reifying Encephalographic Monitor. Interface with the brain should be very simple while the subject is unconscious…"

"That won't be necessary," the Professor replied. "The dampeners will suffice, for now."

The psychiatrist accepted the answer without argument and went to work.

"Will you be joining us in the medical lab, sir?" Hendry asked.

"Shortly, Dr. Hendry. Shortly…"

Within a few minutes, all the cranial probes were in place and the devices activated. The readouts indicated that the biodampeners—tiny devices that emitted low-level electromagnetic waves to short circuit brain activity—had done the trick. Subject X would not awaken now. Not until they wished it.

"You may proceed," said the Professor.

Satisfied that the preparatory procedures were at last back on track, the Professor switched off the audio feed, though he allowed the video images to continue to play across the monitors.

As he shifted in his chair, the Professor's arm accidentally brushed a bulging personnel file, which sent a stack of yellowed newspaper clippings fanning across his desk.

MERCY KILLER "QUACK" ELUDES FBI, read the sensational headline emblazoned across one clipping. Next to the headline, a grainy black-and-white photograph displayed a bearded man with a round, almost cherubic face. The caption read:

DR. ABRAHAM B. CORNELIUS NOW A FUGITIVE FROM JUSTICE.

With a weary sigh, the Professor stuffed the clippings back into the file and set them aside. Keying a recording device built into the console, he began to dictate in a slow, clear voice.

"This is a memo to the attention of Director X. Date, current... I have met with Dr. Cornelius at the designated location..."

Designated location? The Professor found himself musing. *A ridiculous euphemism for the sinkhole of urban blight where the fugitive scientist had fled in an effort to avoid capture, imprisonment, and perhaps execution.*

"The meeting was cordial..."

If one can call the threat of blackmail cordial.

"... and Dr. Cornelius expressed an interest in our project and its ambitious goals..."

In truth, Cornelius was desperate to escape punishment. In the United States, the authorities dealt harshly with murderers—especially those who'd taken the Hippocratic oath.

"Dr. Cornelius has willingly agreed to our terms for employment, and seems grateful to be of further service to the science of medicine..."

As if he had a choice.

"However, I question whether Dr. Cornelius is the optimum candidate for such a critical position in this experiment. In the past he's demonstrated a disturbing propensity for independent thinking, as his crimes suggest.

"I also doubt his expertise will be required. There will be no tissue rejection, of that I am certain, and Dr. Hendry concurs. My bonding technique will be sufficient to sheathe Logan's skeleton, I assure you."

Ridiculous of the Director to equate Dr. Cornelius's skills with my own. There is no comparison. I am an architect of the flesh, an artist, a visionary. Cornelius is merely a skilled practitioner of a single discipline. Can Director X not see the difference?

"Surely other researchers in the field of immunology are equally qualified and have much less... questionable backgrounds?"

The Professor keyed off the microphone. With a frown, he carefully reconsidered his statement and paused with a thought.

If I object too strongly, Director X will question my motives, even my loyalty. Perhaps it is better to be gracious and diplomatic, to accept this interloper as I accepted Ms. Hines. They can both be disposed of later, when their services are no longer required... In the end, only results matter.

The Professor keyed his microphone.

"Erase memo back to the word 'employment.'"

The recorder hummed, reversing itself.

"I feel that Dr. Cornelius will be a valuable addition to this project," the Professor continued. "His credentials are impressive..."

But he's certainly not a genius...

"... I am sure that he will be able to assist me greatly in the coming months..."

Though I neither want nor require an assistant, no matter how qualified Director X feels this man is. Did the artist Michelangelo require an assistant to paint his vision of The Creation on the ceiling of the Sistine Chapel?

"... This project is far from completion, and there is much work to be done..."

Did God require an assistant or additional help to fashion the universe? I think not.

"And, of course, Ms. Carol Hines, formerly of NASA, has also proved herself to be a valuable asset..."

The woman is acceptable, even if Director X thrust her upon me. To her credit, Ms. Hines required no additional training, and has assumed her duties immediately upon arrival.

"She comes highly trained by the National Aeronautics and Space Administration, and is proficient in the use of the REM technology—one of a few capable specialists in the world..."

Better still, the woman is malleable and easily led; the type who would provide an invaluable service and expect little in return. Best of all, she would ask no questions—the perfect drone, a worker bee. Certainly not a queen...

"Both individuals have arrived at the facility, and are settling in."

And Dr. Cornelius had better hit the ground running, or he is less than useless to me, and to the experiment... I'm already impressed with Ms. Hines's dedication and her considerable skills. But I shall reserve my judgment of Dr. Cornelius until I observe the man in action...

"I shall file an additional progress report of success or failure, after the adamantium bonding process is completed. Until then..."

The Professor added his cyber signature, then keyed off the microphone and slumped into his chair. His thoughts were troubled.

If only men were as predictable, as tractable as the elements.

As a scientist, the Professor knew with certainty that the molten adamantium bubbling in the vats below him would melt at a precise temperature. He also knew that the same substance would harden with the tensile strength greater than a diamond when cooled. He knew the precise composition of the resulting alloy on the molecular level. He understood how the various elements would bond and what configurations the electrons would take as they circled the atoms. Yet he could not predict with any kind of certainty how one of the lowliest animal wranglers in his facility would behave under the precise circumstances for which he'd been trained.

The Professor leaned back in his command chair and gazed, unseeing, at the flickering monitor.

Meanwhile, inside the medical lab, activities continued apace. The technicians had finished placing the probes and were draining the coffin-shaped container. The valuable fluid would be pumped into a stainless steel vat, where it would be cleansed of impurities and stored for use in subsequent procedures.

Subject X would spend the night in a carefully controlled holding tank, in an electronically induced slumber. His vital signs and brain activity—what there was of it—would be monitored by a medical staff separated from the subject by an impenetrable wall of Plexiglas. Chemical compounds, fluids, and basic nutrients would be added intravenously as needed.

On the console, another flashing light indicated that the procedure had ended. The Professor watched the medical team file out of the lab, stripping off their environmental hazard suits and mopping their sweating brows.

His console buzzed and the gray, patrician features of Dr. Hendry appeared on the central monitor.

"The probes are in place, Professor. No indication of infection. No threat of rejection. Vital signs are all quite positive."

"Very good," the Professor replied. But the team leader did not log off.

"More to say, Dr. Hendry?"

The man on the monitor cleared his throat. "I spoke with the new immunologist," he said.

The Professor raised an eyebrow. "And?"

"I'm impressed by his work, but not by the man. Dr. Cornelius's theory is sound, and he seems to have solved one of the most intractable problems of the bonding process…"

"I sense more than hesitation in your tone, Dr. Hendry. You may speak candidly."

"He's a common criminal," Hendry said, agitated. "He's violated the ethics of his profession. Can't we utilize his work without actually employing him?"

"The procedure is experimental, much can go wrong. It's better to have Cornelius here in case unexpected complications arise."

"But—"

The Professor cut him off. "It's out of my hands."

Hendry frowned. "I… understand."

"Very good. Carry on."

With a touch of a button, Hendry's face vanished, to be replaced by an endless parade of scientific data crawling across the monitor. The shift in focus pleased the Professor.

The certainties of the physical world and the comprehensible workings of advanced technology are infinitely preferable to the unpredictability of human thoughts and behavior.

Illogic and ambiguity had always troubled him, and the Professor longed to purge humankind of useless emotions and wanton desires. Control of the human mind was the key—but absolute control had never been achieved. Until the development of the Reifying Encephalographic Monitor, it had never been possible.

Until now, the limits of the REM device had not been explored, not even by its inventors. NASA used the innovative device for training purposes, or to stage virtual reality drills. But the Professor knew the machine was capable of so much more.

They call themselves scientists, yet they behave like children, playing with a loaded weapon, never realizing its potential…

"Sniveling cowards, the lot of them…" the Professor muttered.

With the REM device, mastery of the human mind was within his grasp—no thought would remain secret, no desire hidden. Every hope, dream, fear, or rage could now be monitored, controlled, measured, and evaluated. Memories could be erased, personalities altered, false recollections implanted to replace real experience.

In the Professor's own estimation, the genesis of the technology behind the Reifying Encephalographic Monitor became a testament to the timidity, the lack of imagination, and myopia, which plagues the scientific community.

Brain Factory, a video game company in Southern California, pioneered and marketed the first, primitive REM as a novelty device. However, early product testing proved too dangerous for human subjects. The Consumer Products and Safety Administration stepped in and banned the use of REM technology for any entertainment purposes and other commercial usages.

Several researchers in the fields of psychology subsequently recognized the potential of the breakthrough technology in the treatment of mental disorders. But instead of embracing this area of study, the American Council of Concerned Psychiatrists spoke out against the REM device being used "until such time as further testing could be completed."

Of course, no further testing would be possible without funding, and psychiatrists and academics—fearing obsolescence should the device live up to its vast potential—blocked any grants for research projects using the Reifying Encephalographic Monitor.

At that point, Brain Factory fell into bankruptcy, and made a bargain basement deal with the United States government. With a new infusion of cash, Brain Factory went on to produce *It's Clobbering Time* and *Fing Fang Foom*—two of the hottest computer games in the world. In exchange, the Central Intelligence Agency, S.H.I.E.L.D., and the National Aeronautics and Space Administration received exclusive rights to the use of the Reifying Encephalographic Monitor for "research and training purposes."

Though he did not know how the CIA or S.H.I.E.L.D. ultimately utilized REM technology, the Professor discovered that NASA had squandered the greatest scientific breakthrough in the history of brain research by using the REM as a teaching tool. Instead of tapping the machine's mind control powers to exert total mastery over its astronauts and NASA researchers, they limited themselves to using the device as if it were a textbook, for simulations and training exercises.

The Professor would not be fettered by the same restraints. In the coming months, he fully intended to test the limits of the REM machine's untapped potential on Subject X. It was not enough to transform the subject's body. His mind must be restructured as well. The ultimate mastery of Logan became the Professor's goal. He knew it was only a matter of time.

The Professor knew that the physical form had certain limits, vulnerabilities. Bones—even ones sheathed in adamantium steel—had limits, too. And chemically enhanced muscle and sinew could still tire or fail.

But a mind reduced to a beast-like state of consciousness—devoid of fear and doubt and desire, stripped of memory and emotion, and unfazed by the dread of personal extinction—would never waver. In its pristine purity, such a mind would experience no pain, suffer no discomfort, feel no remorse.

Burn away the chaff, rip away the superficial layers of humanity and unleash the savage, unreasoning animal that lurks behind the civilized facade of every human being.

Then I will mold that animal into Weapon X—the deadliest implement of war ever forged.

But unlike the Supreme Being who gave humanity life, I will not make the mistake of bestowing free will on my creation. Weapon X will be nothing more than a tool to do my bidding. An extension of will, yes. My own.

3

THE WRANGLER

THE man pulled the leather parka snug around his neck as a chilly blast whistled through the pines. With every step, the autumn snow crunched under his boots. Rabbit tracks crisscrossed the trail, and overhead a raptor cawed as it drifted in lazy circles on the thin mountain air.

The trail he followed ended abruptly, with a five-hundred-foot drop. In the river valley below, the rushing waters churned blue-green foam and the skeletal brown trees wore an uneven dusting of white. From a distance, the snowcapped peaks of the Canadian Rockies shimmered orange and yellow in the hastening dawn.

For a long time, the man stood on the precipice and gazed at the breathtaking vista. His blue eyes shone in the morning sun, face ruddy from the cold. Sandy hair ruffled under a wool cap, obscuring a gauze bandage that covered a two-inch gash across his forehead.

Too soon, the peace of morning was shattered by an electronic chirp. The man grabbed the communicator tucked next to a holstered Colt in his belt.

"Cutler here…"

"Playtime's over, Cut. You have to come home now."

Cutler ignored the jibe. "What's up?"

"Deavers wants you in his office ASAP."

"Roger that."

"Looks like the major's got a job for you—"

Cutler cut him off and pocketed the communicator. He turned his back on the dawn and without a second glance, retraced his own footprints along the trail. Through tangled brush and dense pines, he noticed barbed wire and electrified fencing—the first indicator of civilization. Soon he was close enough to read the bright yellow signs posted every few yards:

NO TRESPASSING

DANGER!

The signs were printed in English and French. A few were even printed in Blackfoot Sioux, the dominant language of the Native American population in the region. No one was permitted to approach this complex. Few even knew it existed.

Cutler followed the fence until he reached a security gate, where he slipped his identity card through the magstripe reader and entered his code on the keypad. Above his head, face-recognition technology confirmed his identity while a retinal scanner photographed his right eye. Two seconds, three, and Cutler heard the beep. The gate opened.

Inside the compound, no guards were in view—only more security cameras, X-ray sensors, and magnetic scanners. As Cutler crossed a barren stretch of frozen ground, an animal stench floated down from the pens. He heard snorts and grunts, too. Mercifully, the wolves had stopped howling soon after the sun showed itself.

Hiking beyond the concrete kennels and steel cages, Cutler headed toward a modern glass-and-steel structure that dominated a low rise. The four-story building was topped by conical microwave towers and spidery satellite arrays. Beneath were five levels of steel-lined tunnels, laboratories, workrooms, and storage chambers—including a moderately sized adamantium smelting facility on the deepest level. The underground maze had been bored out of solid granite, expanding beyond the limits of the deceptively modest surface structures. So extensive was the complex that an on-site fission reactor had been installed to provide for its energy needs.

Pushing through the glass double doors, Cutler found himself flanked by an armed security team—the same men he saw every day. Per established security protocol, they checked his ID and scanned his fingerprints.

"Out for your morning constitutional?" a guard asked.

Cutler nodded.

"I think nature boy was writing poetry. Sunrise, purple mountain's majesty, and all that crap," said another, his tone less friendly. "Makes me wonder how the hell a guy like Cutler gets Class A security clearance in the first place."

"Same way you did, Gulford. I won a contest."

A few moments later, Cutler entered Major Deavers's sparse office. The major's back was to him. He swiveled from his computer terminal and brusquely waved toward a cushioned chair. He wore a tense look on his face.

"I'll stand," said Cutler.

Despite their differences in rank, neither man saluted. Technically, they were no longer in the Canadian Defense Forces, so the acknowledgement of rank was not required.

"You're the security chief as of this morning," Deavers told him. "At 0830, Subject X is to be moved from the holding cell on Level Three to the main laboratory."

Cutler silently cursed.

"The subject is sedated and ready to go," the major continued. "Anticontamination protocols are in place, so please wear your environmental hazard suit. Don't bother with a weapon, though—Subject X is down for the count, and guns make the docs nervous."

Deavers rose. The man was ten years older than Cutler, and a head taller, too. Salt-and-pepper hair, always cropped short. Jawline smooth as a baby's ass. Even his khaki green coveralls, standard issue around the compound, appeared crisply pressed.

"And clean up your act, will ya, Cutler? Shave, comb your hair, take a shower. The Professor is going to be in the lab today and he likes his staff to look sharp."

Cutler turned to go.

"One more thing," said Deavers. "Take Agent Franks with you—"

Cutler stared for a moment. "Why do I have to break in the new guy? I'm no tour guide."

"Because there's no one else available," Deavers replied. "Most of the staff is tied up with this morning's experiment. The Professor's ordered double security for the rest of the day, and Erdman's still in the infirmary from that altercation in the parking lot the other night—"

"Couldn't be helped, sir."

"—and Hill was medivaced out of here last night. Gutted by a cougar that escaped from its cage. Docs give him a fifty-fifty chance to pull through. Either way, he won't be back anytime soon."

Cutler blinked. "I didn't know."

"Look," Deavers said. "Agent Franks is a real bright kid. You'll like him. He's friendly and eager and a born volunteer. Rice just briefed him on data retrieval and security protocols, and Franks got high marks. Show him the ropes and he'll lighten your load."

"Is that all, sir?"

"No. Keep the new kid away from me. I can't stomach Boy Scout types. Got too much on my plate to babysit a newb."

"Yes, sir. That's my job."

Deavers turned his back on Cutler, his gaze returning to the computer screen. "Get out of here!" he barked, not looking again in Cutler's direction.

Dismissed, Cutler showered, shaved, and hooked up with Agent Franks in the ready room. The fellow had a boyish face and wide brown eyes. He wasn't too obvious as he checked out the cuts and bruises on Cutler's face.

As they suited up, Franks peppered Cutler with questions.

"Is it true the guy I'm replacing was mauled by a grizzly bear?"

"Don't worry," Cutler replied with a slight smile. "That was a few weeks ago, before we worked all the bugs out of our animal control procedures. Now we've got professional animal handlers on staff, so we don't have to deal with bears anymore—"

"Thank God."

"—just the big cats."

"Cats?"

Cutler's smile widened greatly. "You know about them… lions. Tigers. Leopards… cats."

"Cats? Bears? Who needs all these wild animals, and why?"

Cutler's grin disappeared. "You'll find out soon enough."

Many minutes passed in silence as the men donned their complicated environmental hazard suits.

"Big turnover rate around here?" Franks asked at last, lifting his helmet and testing the communicator.

"They come and go," Cutler replied. "This place has only been up and running a year, and the research they do… well, let's just say it keeps changing direction. And like I said before, there are a lot of bugs to be worked out."

Franks pointed to Cutler's bruises. "So what kind of 'bug' ripped into you?"

FROM the very moment Cutler and his group brought Logan in, the medical team complained about "the subject's" condition. Nobody seemed worried about Erdman, though. He was only coughing up blood from a broken rib that had pierced his lung.

Cutler and Hill had barely placed the unconscious Logan in the tank before technicians swarmed all over him. A man in a doctor's smock shaved the subject while a vile-smelling, antibacterial immersion fluid was pumped into the decontamination tank. Then the doctors began their preliminary examination.

The chief physician appeared the most displeased. "Looks like your boys got a little enthusiastic," said Dr. Hendry, frowning as he indicated the subject's swollen jaw and bruised throat. He gritted his teeth in annoyance.

Major Deavers nodded. "He put up some resistance when my men brought him in last night."

"And your thugs saw fit to rough him up, eh, Major?"

Cutler, fresh from the infirmary where his forehead had been sewn shut, worked his jaw, teeth grinding up his obscene reply.

"They had to jostle him a bit," said Deavers, not even glancing in Cutler's direction.

Cutler turned and left the lab. It was bad enough Hendry and Deavers saw fit to talk about him as if he hadn't been standing right there, as if he were one of their research animals, incapable of comprehending human conversation—though he should have been used to that kind of treatment by now, especially from the academic types crawling all over the compound. But he'd be damned if he was going to stand there and listen to Hendry call him a thug.

What I am is a professional, as much of a pro as anyone else in this damn facility.

For more than a decade he'd trained to become a soldier, one of a very few highly-skilled professional warriors who possessed both a background in special operations and field experience in both spy craft and unconventional warfare. As a former member of Canada's Joint Task Force Two, Cutler's military and counterterrorism training had lasted longer, and been far more comprehensive, than the commonplace schooling of these degree-heavy eggheads that cluttered up Department K's labs, cafeterias, and dormitories. And Cutler was willing to bet that his expertise was far more valuable, too. Especially these days.

Hendry and his fellow quacks wouldn't even have their prize "Subject X" if Erdman, Hill, and I hadn't risked our necks bringing him in. And I'd sure love to see Dr. Hendry try to take down a mark as tough as Logan without messing up a hair on the precious subject's head.

To be fair, Erdman and Hill did more than mess up Logan's hair. They'd almost killed him. Cutler touched the bandage on his forehead and wondered how such a routine assignment could have gone so wrong…

○————————————○

A simple shoot-and-snatch. "Spy school stuff," the Major had called it. Three agents on a lone mark. "Pop him, pack him, bring him in—and don't let any damned civilians see you do it," he said.

They'd caught up with Logan the night before, outside a church-run dive on the edge of town. They followed him to a local gin mill and waited in the bar while their man consumed at least a fifth of whiskey in under an hour.

A lesser man would've been intoxicated—if not falling-down drunk. Cutler had been impressed when Logan walked a straight line across the icy parking lot without a single stumble.

As Logan climbed into his car, they made their move. Hill was handling the tranquilizer gun. Erdman and Cutler were responsible for the snatch. It was Hill who'd pulled a Murphy when he alerted the target to their presence by uttering his name.

"Mr. Logan…"

Hill said later, in the debriefing with Major Deavers, that he'd wanted a clear shot.

You were standing, like, five feet away, Cutler thought in disgust. *How much of a clear shot did you need?*

From behind the wheel of his convertible, Logan looked up just as Hill pulled the trigger. The dart struck him in the shoulder as he attempted to rise. A moment later, Logan's legs gave and he toppled out of the seat.

Erdman caught Logan before he hit the pavement, then grunted under the man's weight. "Help me with him. He's real heavy for a little guy."

Suddenly, Logan's eyes opened and he lashed out. The blow sent Erdman reeling back with two broken ribs. When he landed, his head cracked against the ground.

With a roar, Logan tossed Hill out of the way, then leaped onto Erdman's chest. As he pummeled the helpless man, Erdman curled into a defensive ball.

"Get him off of me!" he howled between pain-wracked coughs.

Cutler grabbed Logan's hair and yanked his head back to expose his throat. A blow to the jaw, followed by another to the solar plexus, knocked some of the fight out of their mark. As Logan folded, Cutler loomed over him, fists raised, waiting for an opening, or for the sedative to take effect.

He thought he was alert, but Cutler never saw the blow that got him— only an explosion inside his head, and his own blood staining the snow.

As Cutler went down, Erdman rose, cursing and spitting. He leaped onto Logan's back and wrapped his powerful arms around the man's throat. Gritting his teeth, Erdman squeezed.

"Didn't you get him with that stupid stun gun?" he growled at Hill through blood-flecked lips.

"Of course I did!" Hill cried. "Point-blank."

Cutler stumbled to his feet. Through a bloody haze he saw that Logan was weakening—either from the sedative or from Erdman's choke hold. Though Logan purpled from lack of oxygen, he fought on relentlessly.

Hill hefted the stun gun. But instead of reloading, he turned the weapon around and used the handle to pistol-whip the struggling man to the ground.

"Wait!" Cutler shouted. "If you kill him, he's useless."

But Hill was full of adrenaline—too pumped to stop now. He hit Logan again and the man's head lolled.

"Major's not going to like this," Erdman wheezed. "He said no body damage."

"Sure," said Hill. "But the major didn't say what a tough son of a bitch this guy was gonna be!"

Hill raised his fist high, but Cutler blocked it. "Enough, Hill. He's out cold."

Logan slid to the icy ground. He didn't move again.

Cutler pocketed the gore-soaked stun gun and shook the blood from his eyes. He checked out his partners. Erdman, ghostly pale, was doubled over and clutching his side, his breath a gurgling wheeze. Hill was still twitching from the fight, a ball of raw energy. Cutler tried to calm him.

"Let's get Logan into the van before someone sees us and calls this in."

He and Hill carried the listless body to the waiting van. Erdman limped at their side, pausing to spit a wad of blood and saliva.

Then Erdman spoke, his weak voice a wet wheeze. "This one here... watch him, Cut... he's trouble... and a whole lot tougher than he looks. He's one vicious son of a bitch."

o———————o

"LET'S pressurize the suits," said Cutler, tapping the control pad at his wrist. "You first, Franks."

Cutler's voice boomed inside the other man's helmet, and Franks adjusted the volume. Then he tapped the keypad on his own wrist until tiny red digits appeared, counting down from ten.

At zero, Franks heard a sharp hiss and his ears popped. The environmental hazard suit seemed to tighten around his waist, armpits, and shoulders as the joints vacuum-sealed. The surge of claustrophobic, suffocating panic passed quickly as the rebreathing system kicked in and cool air filled his helmet. Before proceeding, Franks waited patiently for a second digital readout to verify the suit's integrity.

"Sealed," he declared when the light flashed green.

Cutler sealed his own suit, then both men stepped through a Mylar quarantine barrier into an adamantium-lined holding cell. Once inside, Cutler introduced Franks to Subject X.

Logan—scalp freshly shorn, unrecognizable—drifted in a swamp-green chemical solution behind the translucent walls of the holding tank. An oxygen mask covered his face, intravenous tubes snaked into both arms. His head wasn't the only part shaved—not a hair remained on his entire body. Follicles had been replaced by hundreds of probes that projected like porcupine needles from Logan's arms, legs, torso, throat, and groin.

Long copper needles penetrated the corners of his eyes, which were taped shut. Many more spikes pierced his ears, nose, and even his brain through holes drilled into the temple and at the base of the skull.

"Cripes, he looks like a goddamn pincushion," Franks said as he circled the tank. "Who the hell is he?"

Cutler paused. "A volunteer," he said.

Franks studied the silhouette bobbing in the tank, then shook his head. "There isn't enough money in the whole wide world to get me to volunteer for this shit."

"Maybe he didn't do it for the money."

"You're right," said Franks. "This guy's probably a soldier, just like us. Maybe he's a hero or something—an astronaut, maybe. He looks like a bodybuilder to me. Check out those arms and that chest. He's one tough-looking guy. A freaking gorilla on steroids…"

To Cutler, Subject X seemed smaller now than last night in the parking lot. A lot less formidable, too.

As Franks paced the length of the holding cell, he noticed a team of technicians in lab coats observing their actions through a Plexiglas window overhead.

"We're supposed to move this guy, right?" said Franks, trying to ignore the audience. "So how are we going to get him out of that stupid tank?"

"We don't, Franks. We load the whole tank—subject and all—onto a flatcar."

"A what?"

Cutler opened a wall panel to display a stainless steel vehicle that resembled an armored golf cart. With a whine of servomotors, Cutler guided the flatcar out of the battery-charging unit and over to the bubbling tank.

It took several minutes to show Franks how to operate the flatcar, and where to hook the tank's life-support systems during transport.

"I sense you've done this before," said Franks.

Cutler nodded.

"So hero here isn't the first volunteer. There were others…"

Franks was fishing. Cutler wasn't biting. Not until he knew the guy better, trusted him not to shoot off his mouth.

"He's the first human," said Cutler.

Franks grinned. "Mystery solved… That's the reason for all those wild animals."

"Drop it, Franks. We've got work here."

Under Cutler's supervision, Franks backed the flatcar under the holding tank and activated the electromagnetic clamps that held it tightly in a magnetic grip. The tank settled in, the flatcar groaning under its weight. As the vehicle rumbled to the exit, fluid sloshed inside the crystalline coffin and the subject bumped against its transparent walls.

Cutler glanced at the digital readout on the flatcar's control panel and noted with satisfaction that life support was working normally. Then he checked his watch.

"I've got twenty minutes to get Subject X down to the main lab, so I'll see you later, Franks."

"Can't I go with you? Where are you going?"

"That's 'need to know.' And you don't need to. Your security clearance ends at the elevator, so turn around and follow the yellow signs back to the changing room. Don't open any other doors or you'll violate security protocol, and you wouldn't want to do that on your first day—makes a bad impression."

"No, sir… I mean, yes, sir…" Franks turned to go, little-kid disappointment on his face.

"Hey, Franks. If you're bored, go see Major Deavers. I'm sure he'll find some action for a Boy Scout type like you."

○———————○

THE main laboratory sat one level above the adamantium smelting plant in an area approximately the size of an airplane hangar. Typically, only a small portion of the massive space was in use at any one time, with the rest of the level dark. However, when the elevator doors opened, Cutler was astonished to find the enormous floor fully illuminated. The entire lab had become a hive of frantic activity.

Flashing red lights hit Cutler's eyes as he exited the elevator. WARNING. ZONE UNDER QUARANTINE. Red-light procedure required environmental hazard suits be sealed and pressurized before personnel entered the area. Cutler was all set.

He moved forward into the steel-lined, dome-roofed cathedral—a space hollowed out of solid bedrock. At least fifty physicians, medical assistants, computer technicians, and various specialists, all clad in the same pressurized suits as Cutler's, crowded around an enormous holding tank in the center of the floor.

That tank was empty now, but it was easy to guess who the guest of honor would be. Cutler squired Logan forward, guiding the rolling flatcar toward the center of the lab. When the medical team saw him, they rushed him like sycophants swarming a red-carpet celebrity.

His escort duties fulfilled, Cutler was shuffled aside, the hardest shove coming from his favorite scientist—Dr. Hendry, the same doctor who'd called him a "thug" and complained about Logan's condition when they'd first brought him in.

In a hurry to check the subject's medical status on the display panel, Hendry's voice sounded shrill over the headsets. "Heart rate, normal… Respiration is normal… Blood pressure is normal. Okay, people, let's get him to the tank, stat."

A team of technicians wheeled the flatcar to the base of the mammoth tank, where a waterproof hatch on the larger vessel yawned. Using a Plexiglas sluice, the medical team attached the smaller holding tank to the larger vessel.

Finally, a bubbling green biological soup was pumped into the larger tank. After a few moments, the level in both containers was equal. As the fluids merged, the technicians literally floated Logan from his holding tank into the larger container.

A specialist squeezed through another hatch—a neat trick in a bulky EH suit—and splashed into the containment tank beside the unconscious man.

First, he attached Logan's intravenous tubes and respirator to the systems built into the larger tank. Then he used a handheld sensor to check the status of the hundred or more probes piercing the subject's body—one probe at a time. The process took many minutes, and several probes were flagged and replaced by another specialist who had also squeezed into the tank.

Finally, the two men gave the doctors a thumbs-up and climbed out. The hatches were sealed behind them and more fluid flowed into the tank until it was near to brimming with a bubbling green liquid. As the two technicians headed for the changing room, small robots scooted across the polished metal floor, cleaning the chemical trail the men left in their wake.

Banks of computer terminals clustered around the central containment tank hummed and ticked as their systems began to interface with the probes in Logan's body. Consoles surged with energy and monitor screens began crawling with indecipherable data that flowed endlessly.

Moving unnoticed among the sea of physicians, technicians, and specialists, Cutler spied some new faces in the observation booth—an enclosed gondola ringed by catwalks that hung from the high stone roof over the center of the lab.

Behind a glass partition, a short, stout, middle-aged man with a full brown beard and thick glasses watched the containment procedure with interest. His hands were thrust into the pockets of a stained lab coat. From a distance, Cutler read his name on the security clearance tag: DR. ABRAHAM B. CORNELIUS.

The name sounded familiar, but Cutler—a news junkie—just couldn't place it.

Next to the middle-aged man sat a petite young woman in a pale green smock. Though she had plain features, even from this distance Cutler could tell she was intelligent and intense.

Or, more likely, compulsive and driven, like most of the eggheads around here.

As she punched keys on a small handheld computer, the woman pushed a wisp of straight, brown hair away from her elfin face with an impatient gesture.

Yep. Compulsive and driven, Cutler decided.

He turned his attention to the ceiling, where a two-ton metal cap alive with arcane technology was lowered by stout steel chains. As the heavy lid clanged into place, technicians climbed aboard to connect yet more pipes, tubes, and sensors.

"The containment tank will be sealed in five seconds," a disembodied voice warned. "Four… three… two…"

With a roaring hiss that reverberated throughout the vast domed chamber, the airtight seal was activated.

"Containment tank sealed and pressurized," declared the disembodied voice. "Venting now…"

Rushing air ruffled papers and buffeted the staff as the atmosphere in the main lab was sucked away, to be replaced by pure, filtered air. The vented gasses exited into biohazard tanks that were disposed of in accordance with the rules and regulations of Canada's Environmental Protection Agency.

In a few minutes, flashing red lights shifted to green. The voice spoke once again: "Main laboratory decontaminated. You may now depressurize your suits."

The group immediately broke their pressure seals and removed their helmets. Many began to strip away their protective clothing as well. Amid sighs of relief and celebratory laughter, they inhaled cool, fresh air, mopping sweat from their brows or scratching some persistent itch that had been tormenting them.

Cutler removed his own helmet and gloves and tossed them onto a conveyor belt. Others did the same. The belt carried the gear over to a dumbwaiter, which transported the contaminated clothing to a sterilization room on another level.

Suddenly, Dr. Hendry's voice hissed a warning to his staff. "Heads up, gentlemen. The Professor is arriving."

Cutler had never seen the famous Professor up close. Curious, he turned to watch the Professor glide into the lab. Already, Dr. Cornelius and the anonymous woman had exited the booth and moved to the main floor. Now they watched with the others as the master of this facility, and the genius behind this experiment, moved among them.

"How is the patient?" the Professor asked.

"I'm told he has a few injuries," Dr. Hendry replied haltingly, his tone deferential.

"Is he severely damaged?"

Hendry shook his head. "Not at all."

"Any deep cuts? Abrasions… We can't afford leakage."

"I understand," said Hendry with a nod. "We plugged him up pretty tightly. Teflon patches around all the probes, sealing the entry wounds. The subject's mouth, nostrils, ears, and anus are all surgically sealed, and a catheter is blocking his urinary tract."

Abruptly, the Professor turned to address another. "Good morning, Dr. Cornelius. Are we set to begin?"

As they spoke, Cutler noticed that the Professor treated Dr. Cornelius with a measure of respect—a deference he apparently reserved for a select few. Dr. Hendry was one. Now, apparently, this Dr. Cornelius merited equal treatment, which both surprised and impressed Cutler.

As the conversation degenerated into technobabble, Cutler shifted his attention to the woman. She listened in rapt attention to the two eggheads as if she were listening to the spoken word of God.

Cutler shifted his feet in an effort to catch her attention, and the woman turned her forest green eyes in his direction. He locked stares with her, gave her a polite nod, a small smile.

To his surprise, the woman looked right through him, as if he wasn't there. Something about her unblinking, almost vacant gaze disturbed him.

Finally, the Professor dismissed most of the staff.

"Everyone not a part of this phase of the experiment is to depart the lab immediately," he commanded.

Most of the milling crowd quickly moved toward the elevator. Cutler joined the crush.

As he pushed his way into the crowded car, he couldn't help wondering just what the Professor and the rest of these mad scientists had in store for that poor sucker floating in the tank.

4

THE FUGITIVE

SOMEONE *is watching me. I can feel the eyes. Curious. Penetrating…*

For many minutes, Dr. Abraham B. Cornelius resisted the urge to wipe his forehead, beaded ever so lightly with sweat.

Just like on the courthouse steps… all those camera lenses pointing… reporters barking questions…

The dampness increased. Dr. Cornelius could feel all in his caramel-brown beard, his mustache, his eyebrows. And worst of all, his forehead felt slick now with perspiration. *Obvious perspiration.*

Is that what they're looking at? Or are they thinking the same thing as the people in that courthouse crowd, the ones who'd pointed and whispered, "That's him. That's the one. Cornelius, that doctor who murdered his wife and child."

Dr. Cornelius could hardly stand it. Dipping into a pocket, he pulled out the handkerchief he always carried—the one his wife had embroidered in the corner with a delicate C. Pretending his glasses needed cleaning, he made a show of wiping the bottle-thick round lenses, then, ever so casually, he dabbed the sweat away, offhandedly, indifferently.

Eyes watched me then. I could feel them. Like I can feel them now. But perhaps they're only speculating. Perhaps they don't know. Or if they do, they don't know everything…

Hands thrust back into the pockets of his wrinkled white lab coat, Cornelius put back his treasured handkerchief and surveyed the faces of the men and women around him in the pressurized observation booth.

Which one of these people is staring? Or are they all watching? I need to know…

On his left stood Carol Hines. No M.D. following her name, no title of any kind. Yet after watching the frenzied pace at which she'd been working for the past few days, Cornelius could only assume her expertise was vital to the success of the experiment.

The petite Ms. Hines had a smallish face and wore her hair in a severe, almost boyish style with thick, straight bangs. She might be described as attractive if her features weren't constantly pinching with impatience and dissatisfaction—nothing like his tall, slender wife, a dedicated scientist who had an easy laugh and whose face, even when working intensely, had reflected exhilaration, enjoyment, even delight.

At the moment, Ms. Hines's intense green eyes were fixed not on him but a large liquid crystal display panel of a handheld device. Unblinking, she tapped the keypad with robotic efficiency, her face an agitated frown.

When Dr. Cornelius was introduced to Ms. Hines several days ago, she'd hardly even glanced at him, and she'd barely looked in his direction since.

Clearly, she's not the one...

Cornelius next turned his attention to a medical technician hunched over a terminal near the observation window. The man had hardly taken his eyes off the monitor since Cornelius arrived. He seemed transfixed by the medical data streaming into his terminal from the lab below.

Abruptly, the man looked up. Cornelius steeled himself to meet the recognition, the accusation—but the technician looked past him to the digital chronometer on the wall.

Cornelius shifted his attention to another technician, this one wearing a headset and microphone. The man was on his feet, dividing his attention between two ticking digital display panels on the console and the activity on the other side of the glass.

Until a moment ago, the main laboratory had been filled with a lethal antiseptic gas that created a germ-, virus-, and bacteria-free environment with near-genocidal efficiency. This draconian measure was performed to protect Subject X from the threat of contamination during the prebonding preparation and transferal period. Now that the subject was fully immersed in a sterile suspension fluid, the lab was being vented of the toxic gasses.

As the technician watched, his digital readout measured the rate and amount of sterilized air being pumped back into the massive space. The display next to it measured how much poison was being sucked out. When both displays glowed green, the technician spoke into his headset.

"Main laboratory decontaminated. You may now depressurize your suits."

Cornelius joined the others at the window to peer down at the laboratory floor. The relieved medical staff were stripping off their bulky environmental hazard suits, then tossing them along with their helmets and gloves onto a fast-moving conveyor belt.

Among the group, Cornelius spied a stocky, powerfully built young man with dirty blond hair and attentive blue eyes. His ruddy face upturned, the young man was openly staring into the observation booth.

He's the one... the one who's been looking...

Cornelius sensed intense curiosity behind the man's stare, but no hint of recognition, accusation, or emotion in his neutral expression.

He's some kind of policeman, though... after a year on the run I know the stare of the law when I see it. A fed, or ex-military, maybe. Or he's a private security guard. But not a clock puncher.

Cornelius knew he was right. A year on the run gave him a sixth sense for such things.

Suddenly, an alarm bell sounded inside the booth.

"Depressurizing. You may now proceed to the laboratory floor."

Behind them, a heavy steel hatch opened with a sharp hiss and Cornelius moved to the exit with the others. Outside the booth, a narrow catwalk with a mesh steel surface ran for many meters; under it, a drop of fifty meters or more.

Cornelius noticed that the air had a faint chemical taint. It stung his nostrils, and he wondered briefly if the lab had been thoroughly purged of the toxic disinfectant, or if there was a fatal malfunction in the venting system.

Have I traded the possibility of one gas chamber for another? A lethal injection for a lethal atmosphere?

White-knuckled hands clutching the guardrail, Cornelius followed Carol Hines along the catwalk, then down a steep flight of grated steel steps to the main floor.

Moving among the doctors and technicians, Cornelius felt more at ease—hidden in plain sight, anonymous in a sea of earnest faces too wrapped up in their work to pay much attention to him.

Then, like a royal herald, Dr. Hendry spoke. "Heads up, gentlemen. The Professor is arriving."

Along with everyone else, Dr. Cornelius turned to greet his master, his keeper, the man who'd promised him protection from the law—as long as he gave his all to this unprecedented undertaking.

Walking erect as a proud general surveying his militia, the Professor moved among the members of his staff, meeting their eager, respectful gazes with an air of polite but indifferent superiority. Occasionally, the Professor paused to address a technician about a specific issue. His face remained impassive as he listened to the reply, and he usually moved on without comment when he'd heard enough. The Professor did not waste words.

It was the same the first time I met him. Why is he treated with such reverential awe by these people? I know what power he holds over me, but what about all the others? Can they all be volunteers? Did they all willingly commit to this bizarre experiment?

Before being "recruited" himself, Dr. Cornelius had encountered the Professor only twice before, yet each chance meeting came at a crossroads in his own life.

Their first encounter occurred many years before, when Dr. Cornelius was poised on the brink of professional triumph and personal happiness.

It seemed so long ago now... like another lifetime. No. Like another man's life...

○————————○

WITH a wide grin, the dean of the medicine department greeted Dr. Cornelius at the door, pumping his hand like a lost brother. Before a hundred colleagues, he gave a glowing introduction to an internationally diverse audience that included Cornelius's former teachers and fellow pupils from his medical school days.

It was simply the most gratifying moment in his career. To return to his adopted country, to his alma mater, to present to the world his successful results after years of struggling—years that in many ways had already been rewarded, in Cornelius's own estimation, by the beautiful woman who watched him from the front row.

"As a researcher, and an esteemed member of the academic community both here in Canada and in the United States, Dr. Cornelius is known to us all as a revolutionary thinker within the field of immunology," the dean declared. "But Abraham Cornelius refused to allow his accomplishments to end there. He returned to his native country and received a degree in molecular biology and the first-ever doctorate in the field of biomedical nanotechnology."

Amid all the cheers and applause, Cornelius felt humbled by the effusive outpouring of support from his peers.

"On this momentous day," the dean continued, "Dr. Cornelius has returned to our school of medicine, to outline a series of new techniques and technologies for the suppression of the body's immune system during transplant procedures previously considered impossible. It is my privilege and pleasure to introduce to you, Dr. Abraham B. Cornelius."

Cornelius rose, nodding at the warm applause, then, standing before an international audience comprised of specialists in the fields of transplant surgery, neurological function, and bionic limb replacement, he presented his theories.

"I believe that the threat of tissue rejection that followed many transplant procedures will soon be a problem of the past…"

For the next eighty-five minutes, he discussed several nanomedical devices that he'd developed—along with innovative surgical procedures that would open up new avenues in the repair and replacement of damaged organs, muscles, even nerve tissue.

"Soon, programmable microscopic devices injected inside the human body will fight infection, destroy cancerous tissue without damaging healthy cells, and wage battle against the body's own immune system after transplant surgery."

When the seminar ended, practically every member of the audience rushed the stage to extol the limitless potential of Cornelius's groundbreaking research. Many, including the dean of medicine himself, urged Cornelius to begin testing human subjects as soon as possible.

"Oh, well, that will have to wait," Cornelius told the audience during an impromptu question-and-answer session. "I'm not sure I'm ready for clinical trials quite yet. Perhaps in a year. More likely two. I'm still trying to complete the animal testing. Then I'll have to correlate my findings, write a new paper, and present what I hope will be positive results. Of course, there is also the ever present issue of funding—or the lack thereof."

His colleagues smiled at that, having faced the same hurdle. Then Cornelius touched the shoulder of the woman who stood at his side. She smiled and wrapped her arms around his waist.

"And because my former assistant, Dr. Madeline Vetri, has just consented to be my wife, I will also have to pencil in a wedding and a honeymoon. I'm told by the bride-to-be that attendance at both is mandatory."

Madeline laughed and poked his arm.

Opposites attract, they say, and Dr. Cornelius and his fiancée could not have seemed more different. She was French-Canadian, he a U.S. citizen of Irish-Jewish descent. Plain-faced and slightly paunchy, no one would ever mistake Abraham Cornelius for a movie star, while Madeline Vetri was easily the most attractive woman in any room. Her long, lustrous hair was raven black, in contrast to Cornelius's own tangled brown mop, and she was as slim and tall as he was short and stocky—even in low heels she stood nearly a head taller than him. And while his manner was quiet and reserved—a harsh critic might even say dull—Madeline's every gesture brimmed with grace and vivacious energy.

More applause and more congratulations greeted the joyous announcement—then ceased abruptly. At the entrance to the auditorium, a buzz of excitement erupted.

"It's the Professor," someone murmured and all eyes turned.

"Welcome, sir…" called the dean with a respectful nod as the man they called the Professor glided down the center aisle.

It was as if the Red Sea parted. Physicians, researchers, academics—all stepped back in quiet awe as the Professor passed. Finally, the man halted in front of Dr. Cornelius.

"I've read your paper," he said without preamble, and without extending his hand. Behind his angular glasses, the Professor's eyes were unreadable, dead flat.

"Your work shows potential, Doctor. And much promise for future scientific pursuits. But I must concur with my colleagues—"

The Professor's cool gaze took in the woman at Cornelius's side.

"—when they say you should put aside any… distractions… you may have in your personal life and concentrate solely on clinical trials. Anything else would be counterproductive, a waste of time."

His declaration complete, the Professor licked his thin lips. To Cornelius, the gesture seemed vaguely reptilian.

At his side, he felt his fiancée tense. He squeezed her hand, turned his head to meet her eyes, reassure her. The Professor's statement was galling—but when Cornelius turned back to demand an apology, he was gone.

"Good God, who was that ridiculous man?" Cornelius asked the dean, who guided him away from the others before answering.

Dr. Cornelius was shocked to learn the Professor's identity. Forgiving the insult to his fiancée would not be easy, yet he couldn't help but feel uplifted. His research had just been endorsed by one of the most brilliant scientists since Albert Einstein.

○———————○

"GOOD morning, Dr. Cornelius. Are we set to begin?"

Revived from his reverie, Cornelius managed a wan smile. "Good morning, Professor. Yes, I believe everything has gone quite smoothly. It certainly looked that way from the observation booth."

The Professor stood, emotionless and unreadable, his hands clutched behind his back. "And your nanochips are ready for injection?"

Cornelius directed the Professor's attention to the tank.

"Right there, Professor... inside that blue container."

He pointed to a teardrop-shaped metal jar roughly the size of an average household aerosol can. It was attached to a long injection needle situated among a cluster of them located on the ceiling of the holding tank.

"Should we begin the process?"

"Whenever you are ready, Professor. The nanochips will be injected directly into the heart simultaneously, so the microscopic devices will be dispersed throughout the body quickly. The chips should fuse with the subject's bone in less than a minute."

The Professor barely nodded, then drifted away to interrogate another member of the team. Like yes-men around a winning candidate, the crowd followed. Only Carol Hines remained at Cornelius's side. For the first time since they'd met, she showed a glimmer of interest in something that did not involve her REM machine.

"An injection straight into his heart?" she asked. "What are you pumping into Subject X, anyway?"

"A silicon-based chip with a coded memory—several million of them, in fact. Each one creates a microscopic valve that will adhere to the tiny sinuses in the bone. The valves are self-sustaining and can even use nutrients absorbed by the body to replace the ones that malfunction or wear out."

"You mean they reproduce?"

"Precisely."

"I see… And your goal with this?"

"Well, the first objective is to sheathe the subject's skeleton with adamantium steel, to increase bone mass and tensile strength. But because bones are living organisms—and vital organs in their own right, since bone marrow manufactures blood—they cannot be completely coated with steel, or the bones would die and so would the subject."

Carol Hines nodded. "You need pores—holes that will allow blood to pass through the steel barrier?"

"Exactly."

"And the nanotechnology creates these pores?"

"More accurately, it replaces them," Cornelius explained. "Human bones already have tiny pores that permit fluids to pass. My chips will seek those out and replace their function once the adamantium bonding process has been completed."

Despite his reservations about the project and his suspicions about the Professor, Cornelius was astonished to find that the work of the last few days had stimulated some of his old love for scientific discovery. And it didn't hurt that the usually reserved Ms. Hines had suddenly taken an interest in his area of expertise. It had been so long since he felt needed.

"Well, I have my doubts," said a loud voice in a decidedly hostile tone. "In fact, Dr. Cornelius, I fear your technology will do more harm than good. Why are you so certain that these nanochips of yours will not degrade the integrity of my adamantium bone sheathing?"

Dr. Cornelius met Dr. Hendry's skeptical gaze with a very stern one of his own.

"For one thing," Cornelius replied, "my nanochips can withstand the destructive power of white-hot molten adamantium because they are actually three times more resilient than the steel itself. So the question you should really be asking, Dr. Hendry, is will your adamantium degrade the integrity of my nanotechnology?"

Hendry stood his ground. "What do you conclude?"

"An unequivocal no. Why? Because these two very complex processes are complementary—"

"Complementary or contradictory?" snapped Hendry.

"—which means that despite their obvious differences, the two technologies will work together to achieve a single goal—to make the subject's bones virtually indestructible."

"I'm reassured to hear you say that," Hendry replied, his tone still skeptical. "Some of us here in Department K have devoted years of our lives to this project. We want nothing more than for the Weapon X project to succeed."

Cornelius raised an eyebrow. *There* was the resistance. Right there. He was the new guy, the star exchange student from lands unfamiliar. He had come into their midst with little warning, carrying a briefcase of breakthrough research—and they resented it, to a man.

"Surely, you understand our trepidation," Hendry continued. "After all, we wouldn't want our efforts—all of our hard work—to be jeopardized by the use of a reckless and untested technological process devised by a... a newcomer."

Cornelius tried not to laugh out loud. *Newcomer, indeed.* "The Professor has expressed the utmost confidence in my technology," he said evenly.

Hendry moved to reply, but was interrupted by a booming voice from a loudspeaker.

"The bonding process will begin in thirty minutes. All personnel take their positions and commence prebonding procedures."

Dr. Hendry instantly wheeled around and strode away. Dr. Cornelius had intended to escort Ms. Hines to her workstation, which was located next to his. But when he turned in her direction, he found nobody there.

○———————○

IN truth, Cornelius wondered why he even had a workstation during this procedure—and so close to the Professor's own that it made him uncomfortable. It was like having the front row seat in a class taught by a particularly exacting teacher.

It's not like I'm drowning in work...

It had taken Dr. Cornelius all of five minutes to interface his computer with the biological monitors embedded in the subject's body. Now, with nearly twenty minutes to go before the bonding process commenced, he had absolutely nothing to do.

For Cornelius, most of the really intensive labor took place during the distillation of the liquid silicon solution, and the chemical processing that crystallized the substance, which helped encode the programming onto the molecules themselves. Once the nanotechnology was formulated and vacuum-sealed in a sterile vessel, Cornelius's job was pretty much over.

After the nanochips were injected into Subject X, they were out of anyone's control. In the bloodstream, their internal programming would take over. All Dr. Cornelius could do at that point was monitor their progress.

So why am I here? Not even the inestimable Dr. Hendry—the Professor's own right-hand man—has such a choice seat for this critical experiment.

Of course, Dr. Cornelius was aware of one skill he possessed that would prove useful. If his nanochips completely failed, he could unleash a synthetic hormone of his own invention into the subject's body. This substance would essentially "kill" the nanochips, which would then be filtered out of the body by the liver, to be eliminated like waste matter. If that happened, it would spell certain doom for the experiment—and for Subject X.

Without holes in the poor bastard's bones, he will die. Slowly, painfully, his skeleton will asphyxiate while the rest of his body withers from a dearth of whole blood.

But why dwell on the negative?

Cornelius never wanted to be a part of this research. His intention always had been to help humanity, to cure disease—not to create some kind of superweapon. Not to turn a man into a killing machine. An unstoppable tool of war.

Unconsciously, Cornelius began to massage his temples as a pain bloomed behind his eyes.

How the hell did I end up with these people? Doing this kind of work? Trapped in this place?

○——————○

AFTER the triumphant conference at McGill University's School of Medicine, Cornelius's time had been absorbed by his intense research and, of course, his wedding. He had put the unpleasant encounter with the Professor out of his mind until the second day of his honeymoon, when a very expensive bottle of Taittinger's Blanc de Blanc was delivered to his stateroom aboard the cruise ship *Delphi*.

"BEST WISHES FOR A HAPPY MARRIAGE," read the card. It was signed by the Professor.

Recalling the man's negative reaction to his pending marriage, Cornelius was surprised to learn that the Professor was capable of such a magnanimous gesture.

He considered mentioning the gift to Madeline, but the memory of the man's distasteful conduct at the conference stopped him. Cornelius tore up the card and flushed it down the toilet. Later that night, they celebrated their marriage by finishing the Professor's bottle of champagne in a single sitting.

During that extraordinary week, Madeline Vetri-Cornelius conceived their only child. A boy was born nine months later, christened Paul Phillip Cornelius after Madeline's father, a noted architect in his native Quebec.

Then came the agony, and there began a downward spiral. A disease that robbed him of all his joy, and the madness that resulted in murder...

Half a year later, after the indictment on a charge of double homicide had been handed down, Cornelius, rather than face a prison cell or executioner, became a fugitive. His lawyer had convinced the judge that bail was uncalled for, that an esteemed member of the medical community was not a flight risk.

But Cornelius fled just the same.

Months later, he'd begun to live what he thought was an anonymous life in a small trailer park outside of Syracuse, New York, when he received a package. No stamps on the outside, no postmark, either—which meant that the plain brown manila envelope had been stuffed into his mailbox by hand while he was working the graveyard shift at a local medical supply warehouse. The label was addressed to Ted Abrams—the name he was living under at the time—but when he peeked inside, it became obvious that the unknown sender knew his true identity.

Cornelius's first impulse was to hide from the truth. He hurled the envelope into a corner. With shaking hands, he brewed his morning coffee, toasted two stale slices of bread. Temporarily soothed by the caffeine, he retrieved the envelope and spilled all of its contents on the table next to his plate.

Inside were more than a dozen newspaper clippings culled from wire service stories that had been filed over the past eighteen months. The stories all covered the same subject—the phenomenal rise and precipitous descent of Dr. Abraham B. Cornelius, from esteemed immunologist to fugitive double-murderer.

The envelope also contained a note written in large, almost childlike block letters:

YOU ARE BEING WATCHED. AT 11:00 P.M. TONIGHT YOU MUST BE WAITING IN FRONT OF THE MAIN MUNICIPAL LIBRARY IN BUFFALO, NEW YORK. IF YOU ATTEMPT TO FLEE BEFORE THIS MEETING TAKES PLACE YOUR LOCATION WILL BE LEAKED TO THE AUTHORITIES. IF YOU FAIL TO ATTEND THIS MEETING YOUR LOCATION WILL BE LEAKED TO THE AUTHORITIES. IF YOU AGREE TO THESE TERMS CALL THIS NUMBER NOW.

A telephone number had been scrawled in red ink below the message. Of course, there was no signature.

Is it blackmail? But why not just demand money? What's the reason for this secret rendezvous crap? Why the hell do I have to drive to Buffalo for a goddamn shakedown?

He stared at the remains of his morning coffee, cooling in the cup, the butter congealing atop the dry bread on his plate. Hesitantly, Cornelius lifted the receiver and dialed. A phone rang once. Then a male voice answered with two words.

"Wise decision."

The line went dead. Cornelius slammed the table with his fist. Enraged by the crass manipulation, and at being treated in such a disdainful manner, he immediately redialed the number.

This time, he got a recorded message stating that the number was no longer in service. He tried a second call, a third, a fourth—with the same results.

That afternoon, as wan yellow rays streamed through the dirty windows of his trailer, Cornelius tossed and turned in his narrow bunk. At five o'clock, he rose. Plenty of daylight was still left in the summer afternoon, and Cornelius weighed his options over another pot of coffee.

Finally, decision made, he showered, shaved, packed a small bag with a few necessities, and left the trailer without a second glance. He was due at his warehouse job in an hour, but he would not show up tonight, or ever again. Cornelius knew that no matter what happened at this forced meeting, he would never return to Syracuse.

As he drove to Buffalo, Cornelius noticed a storm was brewing in the darkening sky. By the time he arrived, the clouds had cut loose and the city turned gray under the gloomy downpour.

While waiting under a lamppost in the rain, Cornelius heard the clock on a nearby steeple strike eleven. He looked up to see a figure emerge from the watery curtain. Cornelius wondered if it was the person he was supposed to meet, or just a bystander.

Maybe the man should have given me a code word or something, so I'd recognize him as the genuine blackmailer.

Despite his misery, Cornelius managed the slightest chuckle.

A secret code. How ridiculous. And wouldn't that make this absurd espionage melodrama complete?

No code word was necessary, as it turned out. The man walked right up to Cornelius and lifted his head. As a brief waterfall ran off the tan wide-brimmed hat, Cornelius recognized the sharp refined features of the Professor, his square glasses speckled with raindrops.

"Professor, I—"

"Don't speak. Just listen carefully. I have a proposition for you. Do not tell me how grateful you are. Not now. Not ever. For what I offer you is not charity."

"What do you want from me, then? I have no money, no reputation. What can I possibly—"

"I have need of your special skills," said the Professor. "That is all you are required to know for now."

"But—"

"If you accept my proposition you will be spirited across the Canadian border within the hour," the Professor continued. "If you turn me down, you are free to go with the assurance that I will not expose you to the authorities. But bear in mind, doctor, that it is only a matter of time before the Federal Bureau of Investigation catches up with you."

The Professor paused to let his words sink in.

"By the way, congratulations are in order." The Professor's eyes were empty, dead flat as on the day Cornelius had first met him. "Did you know that you have made the FBI's Ten Most Wanted list? The press release was issued just yesterday."

The news had not yet reached Cornelius. His guts twisted at the very thought.

The Professor leaned closer, until Cornelius could feel the man's breath on his cheek. "And did you know that the Syracuse branch of the FBI has been alerted to your presence within their jurisdiction? They staged a raid on that trailer you call a home... and at that warehouse where you work. If you weren't here with me, you would be locked up in a cell by now."

Cornelius felt the panic quickly closing off his throat. He needed air. The Professor was crowding him, pushing him.

"What's your offer?" Cornelius snapped back. "I want to hear all of the details before I accept your, or anyone's, job. I'm going with the highest bidder."

The Professor seemed surprised by the doctor's obvious ploy—an attempt to regain a measure of control. A small smile lifted the edges of his thin lips. Under the glare of the street lamp, the Professor's grin reminded Cornelius of a bone-white skull.

"Come, come, Dr. Cornelius. Don't be ridiculous... Do you really believe you have any choice in the matter?"

○━━━━━━━━○

"PROFESSOR? Dr. Cornelius? We can begin the procedure now."

The Professor nodded to Dr. Hendry, then faced Carol Hines. "Has the REM interfaced with the subject's brain?"

"Interface has been achieved, Professor," she replied crisply.

"Dr. MacKenzie, deactivate the brain dampeners."

With the flick of a switch, the psychiatrist cut off power to the generators, and the steady stream of ultrasonic energy, precisely tuned to a frequency that paralyzed Logan's brain, abruptly ceased.

"I detect a slight spike in the subject's brain activity," Dr. MacKenzie warned immediately.

"It's an error," said Carol Hines.

"You're sure of that?" MacKenzie shot back, the shock of red hair on his head bristling. "There can't be a glimmer of brain activity—not even dreaming—or the subject may be able to cling to certain facets of his personality even after conditioning."

"It's an anomaly," Hines insisted. "I've seen this phenomena before. Spikes occurred with test subjects at NASA, usually when their sleep was interrupted."

"What could cause such brain activity?" replied MacKenzie.

Hines shrugged. "There are several theories, Professor," she replied. "We might be seeing random electrical activity inside the hypothalamus—the area of the brain that controls bodily functions—or continuing chemical reactions within the pituitary stalk. But, of course, that's only conjecture."

The Professor seemed satisfied with her explanation, though Dr. MacKenzie remained unconvinced.

"The waves I saw on the monitor suggest activity in the cerebral cortex," the psychiatrist insisted. "Most certainly not random electrical or chemical activity."

MacKenzie glared at Hines, who stood her ground. It fell to the Professor to break the impasse.

"What do you see on the encephalographic monitor now, Ms. Hines? Dr. MacKenzie?"

"Interface with the REM has been achieved," said Carol Hines. "As of now, there's no brain activity we don't control."

MacKenzie hesitated, then nodded. "The screen is blank... now. Perhaps Ms. Hines is correct in her assumptions."

The Professor waved his hand. "Very well, then. Proceed."

"Stage One, people. Prepare to inject the nanochips," Dr. Hendry said, eyes on Cornelius.

Dr. Cornelius tapped the keyboard and his program sprang up on the monitor. Hunched over the terminal, he entered the code that released the injector.

M-A-D-E-L-I-N-E

The screen blinked: CODE ACCEPTED.

Then: INITIATING INJECTION PROCEDURE.

Finally, the monitor flashed: READY FOR INJECTION.

Cornelius reached for the control, then paused, his beefy index finger poised over the release button.

A moment passed. Then two. Still Cornelius held back.

Suddenly impatient, the Professor rose out of his chair. "Doctor... proceed."

Cornelius felt the man's eyes on his back—staring... always watching—and he punched the key.

A hydraulic whine from inside the bubbling tank, and a razor-sharp needle came out of its sheath like a cat's claw. Down it came until the tip caressed pale flesh.

Then the pointed tip plunged through muscle and bone, deep into Logan's beating heart. The figure in the tank jerked once, then thrashed about in a long, continuous spasm—an unanticipated reaction that set alarms ringing on a half-dozen monitors.

Specialists and physicians darted between terminals and the lab filled with excited voices.

Then Cornelius heard it, or imagined he did. A human cry that tore at his insides. A wail that drowned out the alarms and the shouts of the medical staff. The tremulous screams of a pain-wracked child, shrieking in uncomprehending agony.

5

THE MISSION

LOGAN was falling, tumbling through a black void. A sustained blast of frigid wind battered his body and roared through his mind. He reached for memories, something to hold on to.

Nothing there.

Panic rushed in to fill the void.

The storm has me. The whirlwind.

He moved his fingers, toes, and found himself enveloped in a smothering technological cocoon. He heard the rasping noise of his own breath, hot behind an oxygen mask that muzzled nose and mouth. He turned his head—to bump against the walls of a climate-controlled cybernetic helmet. On the other side of the visor, only darkness—and then a blinking cursor, flashing an inch from his left eye.

Logan watched as the computerized Heads Up Display cycled through its initiation sequence, then interfaced with a geopositioning satellite in Earth's orbit. Two seconds later, the HUD projected a map grid of the terrain below on the inside of his visor.

Logan recognized the grid, the map, the all-too-familiar terrain, and his memory flooded back with crystal clarity.

Must have bumped my head… knocked me for a loop…

As the parameters of the mission poured back into his mind, critical data scrolled across the visor. Wind velocity, airspeed, external temperature—a chilly seventy degrees below zero—his rate and angle of descent, longitude and latitude. The altimeter told Logan that he was in free fall from an altitude of thirteen thousand meters.

Somewhere above him—and probably miles away by now—the unmarked MC-140 he'd jumped from was on afterburners in a race for the border. They probably had a couple of North Korean MIG-22s chasing their tail, too. Logan silently wished the pilots luck getting home.

Only sixty-three seconds of free fall to go. At six thousand meters, the wings of the High Altitude Wing Kite harness would automatically deploy and the repulsors would fire to slow his descent. Until that time, Logan would continue to drop like a stone.

He noted the local time: 0227—the middle of the night.

"Terrain and objective," he said in a voice dry and raspy from the pure oxygen he was gulping.

The grid shifted. Outlined in sharp detail, Logan saw the digital silhouette of rugged hills and a narrow road that wound through them. To the north, an artificial lake restrained by a concrete dam. At the foot of the dam, a hydroelectric plant surrounded by double and triple fences, watchtowers, several wooden structures with detached latrines—probably barracks—and an antiaircraft gun emplacement.

Finally, Logan spied his objective—a collection of circular structures on the banks of a shallow river created by the dam's runoff. The three- and four-story structures appeared to be fuel storage tanks. But why store fuel near a hydroelectric plant? It's the water that turns the generators; no oil was needed.

More ominous, reports confirmed that dead fish had been turning up downstream, where the runoff from the dam flowed into a larger river. JTF-4 Intel believed that a toxic substance was the cause—a chemical, biological, or possibly nuclear pollutant. Intelligence concluded that the pollution came from the supposedly innocent power plant, which meant it was generating more than electricity. The North Koreans were probably producing weapons of mass destruction at that site as well. Canadian Intelligence wanted to know what types of weapons, and in what quantities—which is why Logan and his partner had been sent on this mission.

On his visor, hovering over the glowing map, Logan saw a second blip. Invisible to the naked eye, another figure plunged through the night not so very far away—Neil Langram, Logan's partner. The two men would come down in separate landing zones, then rendezvous on the ground.

A muted alarm sounded inside Logan's helmet, and his training kicked in. He stiffened his spine and threw his arms over his head as if he were high-diving into the dark, shining waters far below. Spine rigid, he spread his arms and legs wide to form the letter X.

The second alarm. Logan braced himself, muscles tensed, as the readout counted down.

FOUR... THREE... TWO... ONE...

With a sudden jolt, the "wings" deployed. Leatherlike membranes of a frictionless fabric burst out of hidden seams under Logan's arms, along his torso, down his legs. Flexible ribs inside those wings instantly filled with compressed air, giving the membrane shape and creating an airfoil.

But by design Logan was still falling headfirst, as his rate of descent had hardly slackened. If Logan tried to catch wind and level off now, the HAWK harness would be ripped away by the stresses and he would plunge to his death.

A blinking cursor. Digital numerals. Another countdown.

Then the Stark Industries Mark III Repulsor units kicked in. Each of the six saucer-sized, disc-shaped devices was capable of firing three one-second bursts before their energy supply was exhausted—more than enough to slow Logan's descent.

But when the units fired, Logan felt a sharp, stabbing pain, like a knife plunging into his heart. He folded in agony and fell even faster. Alarms sounded in his ears, and the noise merged with the wind's howl. To Logan, black night seemed to turn a phosphorescent green.

Suddenly, an explosion in his head—a red haze of pain. A moan was ripped from Logan's lips. Through the agony, he wondered if his harness had somehow malfunctioned.

Soon, the anguish receded and Logan was able to concentrate. He fought for more control of the now-aerodynamic full-body flying suit against the shifting air currents. After some effort, he managed to level off at about two thousand meters. He was gliding parallel to the horizon at roughly three hundred kilometers per hour.

"Target."

Instantly, a flashing pipper appeared on the map grid, highlighting a point on the slope of a low hill above the dam and the hydroelectric plant. Logan was still several kilometers away. He switched to infrared mode and suddenly he had a rouge-tinged panoramic view of the surrounding countryside.

"Telescopic mode... magnify... magnify... stop."

His telescopic night-vision visor revealed every detail on the ground below. Though he was still far away, Logan could make out vehicles parked near the top of the dam and a previously undetected security gate.

And in the valley below the dam, Logan could see guards manning the watchtowers, and other uniformed men with dogs walking the perimeters on both sides of the fence.

Moving his arms, he slipped into a descending glide, occasionally adjusting for wind shear or updrafts caused by the hills.

To Logan, this was the only good part of a HAWK harness drop— flying like a bird on fluttering wings...

As he approached his target, Logan knew the fun was about to come to an end.

His plan was to buzz the facility in an effort to determine the quality and strength of the security forces. Then, if all went according to plan, Logan would find his landing zone, land without detection, make his way down the hill, across the dam, down the valley, over the fence and into the hydroelectric plant—all while avoiding contact with the guards, the dogs, and any minefields or electronic surveillance systems that might be installed around the complex.

"A freakin' cakewalk," Langram had called it.

Roger that.

Logan noted that the other blip was above and behind him now— Langram, still on target. Logan knew his partner would soon break off, to land on the opposite side of the lake. That way, if one of them were caught or killed, the other could complete the mission.

He and Langram would maintain a strict radio silence during the entire operation. They would not meet until they were among the storage tanks, or maybe not until they reached the extraction point after the mission was all over.

Of course, if things go really bad for either one of us, we won't be meeting at all.

Suddenly, a powerful updraft pushed Logan several hundred meters off course. Logan manipulated the HAWK's twin repulsion jets—activated by sensors in his gloves and a button in the palm of each hand—to compensate for the wind shear. Within seconds he was back on course. His computer control system took over to keep him on target.

Logan marveled at the quality of this new device, and how user friendly the next generation of HAWK harness had become.

Not like the bad old days.

Logan recalled that the first prototypes of the High Altitude Wing Kites were exactly that—powerless gliders made of leather, canvas, and spandex, deployed from standard form-hugging S.H.I.E.L.D. battle suits. Those early models were not very reliable and lacked the amenities of the improved versions. Logan wondered how he'd gotten by without a pressurized helmet, heating unit, HUD, wireless computer control, GPS system, infrared night-vision visor—or even the repulsion units.

The current HAWK even eliminated the threat of radar detection. Sheathed in nonmagnetic, wave-absorbing composite material—a flexible version of the coating used on stealth aircraft—Logan and Langram were invisible to all forms of electronic detection and hi-tech surveillance.

Of course, one improvement had yet to be made. No one at S.H.I.E.L.D. R&D had devised a way to make landing a HAWK harness easy. Logan hadn't used one in a couple of years and regretted it, for as the ground hurled up to meet him, he began to wonder if he still had the chops to pull off a smooth touchdown.

"It's easy to land a HAWK. Even a four-eyed yahoo can find the ground in one of these birds," Nick Fury once told him. "It's making that landing without cracking up that's tough."

A smirk tugged his thin lips. Logan could almost smell Fury's cheap stogies.

You'd think a guy neck-deep in covert ops could get his hands on some contraband Cuban Monte Cristos.

Logan concentrated on his approach. After calibrating the wind and angle of descent, the HUD displayed the flight pattern to the landing zone. But, first Logan wanted to make that reconnaissance pass over the power plant.

Like a silent, invisible wraith, Logan dived lower and lower. Finally, he raced parallel with the horizon, less than sixty meters above the ground. He passed over a steel fence and shot over a guard tower—low enough to see inside. He observed a few tired guards, teacups, and a knot of men playing dice.

Tempted to land right now… these guys are hardly awake. I could drop down and find out what's in those tanks within five minutes… but that would be wrong.

Logan had his orders. He was to land in the hills, bury his suit, and make his way down to the facility on foot.

Anyway, if it's too easy—where's the fun?

Racing silently over the hydroelectric plant, he noticed that a hangar-sized double door was open, a cluster of workers lounging just inside the pool of light. Beyond the plant, the area around the storage tanks was dark. Even in infrared mode, most of the details were lost in shadows.

Finally, Logan banked and headed for the gray, featureless wall of the dam. He bent his head back and spread his arms as wide as he could, to create more wing surface and lift. Then he fired the repulsion jets.

He rose like a bottle rocket over the dam. He spun in the air, then zoomed low across the dark water, his black suit shining like sealskin under the spray.

Logan fired the repulsors one last time, cleared the shore, and raced up the slope. Ahead of him, the designated landing zone—a barren stretch of brown Korean hill that had been deforested to make way for power lines still under construction. As he approached the LZ, Logan noticed thick stumps sticking out of the ground and several fallen trees blocking his path.

In preparation for the landing, Logan bent the harness to slow his airspeed. At eighty kilometers per hour, he loosened the harness so that he'd be ready to punch out of it the second he spotted a fairly level piece of real estate.

Landing in a HAWK harness was roughly the same as jumping out of an airplane with a parachute, then unbuckling that chute about ten or fifteen meters above the ground and falling the rest of the way. The landing tended to be hard, and you didn't always end up on your feet. Most guys curled into a ball and rolled until they came to a stop.

Not Logan.

As his visor ticked off the altitude in meters… 50… 40… 30… 20… his airspeed was reduced to less than forty kilometers per hour.

Logan threw his legs forward and punched out of the harness. The wings disengaged, folding like a crushed butterfly in his wake. He hit the ground running, rolled three times, and hopped to his feet. But the momentum he'd built up in the descent was still pushing him. Ahead, Logan spied a fallen tree in his path. Just as he leaped over the obstacle, a silhouette—human—rose from behind the log.

It was too late for Logan to stop. He slammed into the stranger and heard a muffled cry. Hurling out of control, they both tumbled down a steep slope in a cloud of dust.

○━━━━━━━━○

THE alarms had been silenced. Calm had been restored. Subject X now drifted motionless, the spasm subsided. Technicians and doctors moved about the room, recalibrating instruments and rebooting key computer systems.

"We'll lose a little time, Professor. It's unavoidable," Dr. Hendry said, face grave. "The technicians will have to get the computers back online. Restore function in some of the probes. But for now, Subject X has been stabilized."

The Professor barely nodded before facing Dr. Cornelius. "The nanotechnology. Is it functioning?"

"The process is complete, the silicon valves are working like the real things," said Cornelius. "You can see them on this full-body ultrasound... the tiny black specks on the skeleton..."

The Professor glanced at the image, then raised an eyebrow. "And you are absolutely convinced that your nanochips did not cause the subject's seizure?"

"Not a chance," Cornelius replied with more confidence than he had ever felt.

"Then we must turn to you, Ms. Hines," the Professor hissed. "What is your theory? What do you think went wrong?"

Carol Hines swallowed nervously. "I... I still believe we're dealing with random electrical impulses in the hypothalamus. It's man's basest instincts— the 'lizard brain'—fighting for survival in the very face of extinction."

"Poetic rubbish," Dr. MacKenzie scoffed. "There was obviously brain activity going on somewhere in the cerebral hemisphere. The subject was experiencing random memories, a total recall of some past event, the pangs of birth—whatever."

"Nothing like that showed up on the monitors," Hines insisted.

"We both saw the spike," MacKenzie replied, "only you dismissed it as an anomaly."

The Professor lifted his hand to silence the argument. "What does it mean, Doctor?"

MacKenzie faced the Professor. "The REM failed to completely interface with the subject's mind. There was a hole in the system, a flaw in the program. Some of Logan's—I mean, the subject's previous personality was exerting itself."

MacKenzie turned his back on the Professor to face the man in the tank. He tapped the glass as if it were a fishbowl.

"Something was going on inside that head of his. Subject X is not ready to surrender his identity… not yet," MacKenzie stated. "I'd stake my reputation on it."

The Professor placed his hands behind his back and paced around the laboratory. "This presents us with a small dilemma. Two of my associates disagree about a critical phase in the Weapon X program. We are at an impasse. How are we to proceed?"

MacKenzie stepped forward. "I've done everything in my power to keep Subject X under control. We experienced no difficulties until the brain dampeners were deactivated. I suggest we go the chemical route— Pheno-B. Three-point first dose, more if needed."

MacKenzie stared a challenge at Carol Hines. She met his gaze, then faced the Professor. He was staring at her, too.

"I'll reboot the REM mainframe," she said. "And start the interface from scratch. It's possible… maybe it's possible… that a step was overlooked."

MacKenzie, smug in victory, turned his back on the woman.

"The reboot should take about an hour," Carol Hines continued. "And we can try again."

"One hour, then," the Professor replied. A moment later, he was riding the elevator to an upper level.

With the Professor's departure, Dr. Cornelius approached Hines's workstation and touched her arm.

"Don't feel too bad," he said. "Stuff happens… delays… mistakes… errors in calcultion. Nobody's perfect. Bet this kind of thing went on at NASA all the time."

Carol Hines tapped her keyboard without looking up.

"Anyway, the Professor was in a quandary, and he went with Dr. MacKenzie… you can't blame him for—"

"For what?" she interrupted, looking up at him. Her thin face was flushed under her severe haircut. "For listening to the person with the most letters after his name?"

Cornelius shook his head. "You've got it all wrong, Ms. Hines. The Professor went with the technology he trusts, not the man. His decision had nothing to do with advanced degrees, or the fact that MacKenzie's a doctor. It's just that he's used Pheno-B before, but never the REM."

He could see he'd reached her and that she was paying attention to his words.

"If you'll recall," he continued, "the Professor was looking to blame my nanochips for Subject X's strange reaction."

Cornelius was relieved to see the lines on her face soften.

"And in case you haven't noticed before," he whispered conspiratorially, "there's a certain Dr. Hendry who's got it in for me. So don't feel too persecuted just because the project's headshrinker doesn't like you. I'm beginning to think everybody involved in this project is up the proverbial creek without a paddle."

6

THE EXPERIMENT

FROM his chair, the Professor lifted a pale hand. "Let's make history."

The clatter of keys and the echo of voice commands came next. Inside the massive space, scientists and technicians had set to work.

"Feed."

The command came from Dr. Chang, a metallurgist known for his work with special alloys. Chang was hunched over a full-body monitor beside a two-tiered portable pumping station set against the bubbling tank.

"Conductive feed," said the tech assistant seated right below the metallurgist, at a second workstation.

Behind leaded glass at the base of the pump, steam hissed as liquefied adamantium flowed from the holding tank into the feeder tubes that snaked into the subject's containment unit.

"Steady… adamantium breakdown twenty-nine in one, sir," Dr. Chang warned. "I'll compensate."

The Professor shook his head without an ounce of concern. "It'll reduce. No problem."

Chang nodded. "Feed."

"Steady…"

"Feed."

"Cardiotach?" asked the Professor.

Carol Hines was about to glance at the heart monitor when Dr. Hendry barked, "High. Higher than we expected."

The tank looked like a simmering glass kettle; the figure inside bobbed as a cork would in boiling liquid. Subject X would either make scientific history or die a burning death.

Dr. Cornelius watched the procedure with tense anticipation. The room smelled more like a steel smelter than a medical lab or a makeshift operating room. An odor of burnt metal hung in the air, and in the last few minutes the temperature on the floor had increased several degrees. The reason for both: the holding container at one end of the room, glowing crimson-hot behind a thick wall of leaded glass. Inside, hundreds of pounds of molten adamantium steel were pressurized and primed to pump into the subject's body.

Cornelius knew that adamantium was the hardest substance in the universe. Developed in the 1940s by Dr. Myron MacLain, a United States government metallurgist, the alloy was created using a mixture of several top-secret resins including an infusion of the mysterious substance vibranium. In its liquefied form, adamantium was only malleable for approximately eight minutes, and only if maintained at a constant temperature of fifteen hundred degrees Fahrenheit. After four hundred and eighty seconds, the alloy would not bond to any other substance. This meant that any interruption during the critical pumping stage would be catastrophic.

Around Subject X's tank, the team supervised all facets of the process at computer terminals and medical monitors. One sound rose above the white noise of whirring machinery: the beep of the machine that measured heart rate, breathing, body temperature, and other body functions.

Dr. Chang's hands continued to play on his keyboard. Inside the leaded glass, the cloud of steam dissipated. "Steady…"

"Feed…"

"Suffusion enacting… now!"

The activity in the tank increased exponentially. As molten metal filled the feeder tubes, they superheated, then quickly transferred that thermal energy to the fluid inside the tank. In seconds, Subject X was totally obscured by a boiling chemical stew.

"Steady…"

"Feed."

At the monitor, Dr. Chang watched the molten adamantium seep into the subject's skeleton. On the ultrasonic image, it appeared as if the ghostly gray-white bones were being coated with black paint.

On his own display panel, the Professor magnified that same image several hundred times to observe the surface of the right femur. It was clear from the ultrasound that the nanochips were protecting the delicate fissures in the bones as well as the veins and capillaries that ran through them.

Cornelius watched the same data on his monitor and felt a mixture of triumph and relief. A few years ago, he believed that the process he just witnessed would be impossible. But the sheer vision of the Professor, the immense scientific progress of the program, and its vast resources made anything seem possible.

"Steady…"

"Things are going well, Doctor. I'm pleased."

It took a moment for Cornelius to realize the Professor had addressed him.

"Feed?"

"Suffusion?"

"Steady. Both steady," Dr. Chang replied, pushing a shiny black strand of hair away from his face.

As Cornelius watched, living tissue was being bonded to a metal alloy to create the world's first truly bionic organism. It was indeed history in the making, and Cornelius was moved to speak.

"This is an extraordinary experiment, Professor. I'm honored to be a part of it."

The Professor's thin lips curled into an expression more like a sneer than a smile. "Of course you are, Cornelius."

"Cardiotach?" This time it was the metallurgist who called for an immediate update.

Hendry shook his head. "Not good… I guess it's ANS."

"Feed."

Dr. MacKenzie spoke for the first time since the bonding procedure began. "Let's up the Pheno-B. Two points… no, one. Any more and he'll have beans for brains."

"Is there any reason for concern?" The Professor directed this question to the psychiatrist, but it was Hendry who answered.

"I don't believe so, Professor. You chose Subject X for his rather remarkable stamina. What we're getting here is his autonomic nervous system kicking in. He's a hard fellow—even unconscious."

"Chelation beginning," said Dr. Chang.

The mass of roiling bubbles around Subject X expanded outward as he began to thrash violently, bumping up against the glass walls.

"What was that?" the Professor demanded.

"Resistance, sir," MacKenzie replied.

"He's pulled a feeder tube!" the metallurgist cried. "Cut the flow to tube Nineteen B, use backup tubes A and C to compensate."

"Compensating."

"Maintain."

"Damn... resistance. More resistance," said Hendry, anxiously.

"Equalize."

"Feed."

"Impeded."

"Feed backup channel."

"Balance imminent," spoke the metallurgist. "Steady... steady... balance achieved."

The thrashing subsided. Molten steel continued to be pumped into the subject's twitching flesh.

"How's the REM interface holding up?" asked the Professor.

"It's at one hundred percent," Carol Hines replied. "I upped the amps to short out the subject's autonomic nerve functions. I believe that has corrected Dr. Hendry's ANS problem."

"Hendry... ANS?"

Hendry looked up from his monitors. "Subsiding, Professor. Nearly normal."

"Cardiotach, Miss Hines?"

She hesitated before answering, surprised that the Professor had called on her again. "Rising rapidly, sir. As of now, the heart rate is 198 per minute and increasing."

The Professor gritted his teeth. He found the subject's accelerated heart rate troubling.

"Diagnosis, Dr. Hendry?"

"Sir, I believe the nanotechnology is at fault—"

"Now, wait a minute—" Cornelius protested.

The Professor lifted his hand. "Clarify, Dr. Hendry..."

"On the ultrasound monitor, you can see gray flecks covering the skeleton which Cornelius tells us are his nanochips. Well, look at this—"

A magnification of the subject's heart muscle revealed the same gray-black specks lining the interior of all four chambers.

"I believe Dr. Cornelius's programming was incorrect. The nanochips treated the dense heart muscle like bone, with predictable results."

Cornelius was speechless. *Could I have been so wrong?*

The Professor frowned and spoke tersely. "Ms. Hines, would you please access the subject's medical profile and history? I studied it long enough, but I could have missed something."

"On-screen, sir," Hines said.

"Detail any cardio-abnormality."

"None, sir."

The Professor gazed in silence at the figure adrift in the tank. When he finally spoke, his tone was rueful. "You're really letting me down here, Cornelius. Why didn't you prepare for this in advance?"

Cornelius stared at the image. His nanochips still clustered around the valves—doing who knows how much damage to the subject's heart—when they should have been long gone.

Hell, they were long gone a few minutes ago. Why did some of them end up back inside his heart muscles?

"I thought I'd prepared for everything, Professor. But who could have foreseen this?"

The metallurgist interrupted them. "Sir, the rate of adamantium absorption should be twenty-four in one—"

"Of course."

"It's fifty-three in one, sir… and increasing."

For the first time since Cornelius met him, the Professor appeared baffled. He immediately called for an explanation from Carol Hines.

"It seems that Subject X's highly accelerated heart rate is draining the adamantium reservoir at three times the estimated speed of absorption," she explained.

An alarm sounded, interrupting them. Dr. Hendry analyzed the problem without looking up from his monitor.

"The subject's thrashing again. And there is some leakage in the tank. I detect trace amounts of adamantium."

"The damaged tube?" Hines offered.

"No," Hendry said at once. "The leak is coming from the subject's pores. He's passing adamantium through his sweat glands."

The Professor was suddenly alarmed. "Rejection?"

"More likely… elimination," Hendry replied. "His liver, his lymph nodes—they're dealing with the metal as they would a bacterial infection or a toxin. Some of the alloy is being filtered out, passing through his skin. Not enough to worry about, but…"

"This guy's liver functions must be phenomenal," said Dr. MacKenzie. "So efficient I doubt our boy can get drunk even if he wants to. That could also explain his resistance to drugs."

"My God! It might also explain the nanochips lodged in his heart," Cornelius declared.

"Explain, Doctor," said the Professor.

"The subject has phenomenal stamina, right? And we can see that his immune system is amazing, too—"

"Your point?"

"Those chips didn't travel to his heart on their own, and their programming wasn't flawed. They were forced back into the bloodstream by the subject's immune system!"

Cornelius whirled to face Hendry. "What's the white blood cell count inside the subject's heart?"

Hendry tapped his keyboard. "Elevated… Abnormally high, it's as if—"

"As if he's battling an infection." Cornelius faced the Professor. "That means his immune system was strong enough to kill a percentage of my chips, which are now being passed out of his body like waste matter, through the sweat glands."

The Professor digested the information. As his mind turned, his glasses seemed to dance with reflected light.

Dr. Cornelius glanced at the cardiotach, noting that the heart rate had stabilized.

"I can assure you that there'll be no further problems, Professor," he said. "Subject X's heart rate can't possibly go any higher or he'd be… well, a superman or something."

The Professor's head jerked as if stricken by Cornelius's observation. His pale flesh turned bone-white, and though he didn't speak, the Professor's jaws moved behind thin lips.

"We're going to pass the equalization point, sir. We'll have to compensate on every channel," Chang's assistant warned.

Dr. Hendry was also perplexed. "So soon?"

"Astonishing," said Cornelius.

The technician paused, looking to the Professor for a decision. But Cornelius could see that the scientific genius was paralyzed, unable to take action, unable even to speak.

Cornelius stepped forward. "Refeed, then," he commanded.

"On every channel."

Dr. Hendry blinked, but said nothing.

Guess I'm in charge—for the moment, Cornelius thought. *And if that's the case, I say we push the envelope... to the max. If this guy Logan can swallow so much adamantium without so much as burping, who knows what else he can do?*

"Feed?" the technician asked for confimation.

"Feed on all channels," said Dr. Chang, glancing at Cornelius.

"Compound feed. Maintain at Level Two."

"What's causing this, Doctor?" The speaker's hand dug into Cornelius's shoulder like a talon.

"Your guess, Professor, is as good as mine," Cornelius replied. "We've pumped enough Thorazine into the subject to drop a bullock, so the problem is obviously more than a cast-iron constitution or an auto-nervous anomaly."

"Doctor?" It was Carol Hines, her green eyes looking past the Professor to Cornelius. "I've some interesting data for you."

Cornelius—with the Professor in tow—approached the woman's terminal.

"According to Medfax, Subject X has been shot at least five times and survived each attack. Four to the trunk, one to the leg. He's also suffered a number of grave injuries."

Cornelius shrugged. "Tough geezer... We know this, Hines."

"But the bioscans, the ultrasound, show neither epidermal nor internal scar tissue. None whatsoever."

"Cornelius, didn't you say that the subject was hurt last night?"

"Yes, Professor." *Well, Hendry actually said it. I only saw some of the injuries.*

"Then where are his wounds?"

That gave Cornelius pause. He glanced at the figure in the tank, too shrouded in bubbles to make out details... only pale flesh, black hair drifting like a tattered banner.

"Hines, do you have any readings?" Cornelius asked, still staring at Logan.

"I have a trace," she said. "Some clotting around the mastoid. But an hour ago he had a dislocated jaw, cuts, abrasions. Now there's absolutely nothing."

Cornelius and the Professor mulled over the information as Carol Hines continued her report. "On the board there's a direct linear equation between the phenomenon and the intense cardio-activity. And…"

She hesitated.

"Well, I don't know how important this is… Seems silly. But Mr. Logan's hair has almost entirely grown back again in just twenty minutes. We shaved him a number of times. This anomaly was attributed to the tank's synthetic embryonic fluid."

The lab became very quiet as all eyes shifted to the subject in the tank. Only the steady beep of the biomonitors broke the silence.

"We seem to be in the midst of something unprecedented," Cornelius declared in an almost reverential tone. "Our Mr. Logan is somewhat more than human."

"Okay, I have to rethink this fast," said Dr. Hendry, who had joined the huddle. "If the patient's wounds are now healed, his heart rate could drop—be prepared to de-escalate at a second's notice. That's option one."

"What if the heart rate starts to climb again?" Hines asked.

"We go to option two," Hendry said. "If the rate continues to rise, pump equivalent noripenephrine to its ratio… but keep me informed of all changes."

Nobody was talking about killing Subject X anymore, Cornelius noted. *Probably because it's clear that whatever we do probably isn't going to hurt the guy, let alone kill him. At this point, I'm not sure anything we do can harm him…*

"Dr. Chang, Ms. Hines? Is the adamantium reservoir sufficient for all this… additional activity?"

"Sufficient at the current rate, Dr. Hendry."

Hendry slapped the console. "Not good enough. Go to reserve."

Carol Hines shifted her gaze to the Professor. "I'll need authorization from—"

"You have it, madam. Go to reserve adamantium, now."

The Professor's command was shouted over his shoulder as he strode to an access door leading to an auxiliary lab.

"Professor," Cornelius called. "I could use your advice on…"

The door closed shut. The Professor left without a word.

Dr. Cornelius scratched his bearded chin. "How do you like that?

We're in the middle of a crisis and he walks out."

What in blasted hell could be so important?

○————————○

THE Professor seethed. *That fool Cornelius wants my advice? Has he forgotten that he's here to give counsel, not receive it? I am the master here.*

Inside a small containment area off the main laboratory, the Professor closed a heavy hatch and activated the magnetic clamps to lock out the rest of the world. Behind him, a terminal automatically sprang to life. He began to punch a code known only to him into the desktop communicator, but suddenly paused. The Professor noticed his hands were shaking.

Absurd to be this rattled, he told himself. *I haven't been this unsteady since I began pulling the strings instead of being pulled by them.*

He completed the code and waited as a satellite picked up the feed and scrambled the communication.

"Speak." The voice on the other end echoed faintly, mildly distorted by a constant electronic hum.

"It is I," the Professor began.

A split-second delay as the transmission was coded. "You risk much by contacting me, Professor…"

"Yes, I know. But I have something to say—"

"What is so important that you choose to break established communications protocol?"

"The operation is proceeding right now—"

"And going well, I trust?"

"Yes—"

"Subject X will survive the bonding procedure?"

"Of course he'll survive it," the Professor stated, his agitation increasing. "That's the point. You knew that Logan was a mutant."

Silence.

"This fact comes as quite a surprise," the Professor continued, his voice tight. "Why did you not inform me?"

"This conversation is risky, Professor. For both of us."

"No one can hear me. I'm in a sealed lab down the hall—"

"You should be with your patient."

"I can see the operation on a monitor. I must insist that you hear me out—"

The Professor sensed the Director was irritated by his call, but he had to press on. "Logan is a mutant. He has a superhuman power to regenerate damaged tissue. He is practically immortal, and yet you don't inform me of this important factor?"

"That information was available to me, it is true. But Logan's mutant status was classified—on a need-to-know basis—and you, Professor, did not need to know."

"I'm in there with that backwoods Cornelius and my staff, and this, this girl—practically a typist—discovers the truth about Logan by pushing a few buttons on her blasted computer!"

"Your point?"

"It makes me look like I don't know anything. I had to leave the operating room in case they asked me any questions about it. I felt like a fool!" The Professor hated himself the moment he'd confessed it. His voice betrayed him as a whiny child and he was repulsed.

The Director chuckled. "You sound angry, Professor."

"Yes…" He forced the calm back into his voice. The control. "You could say I'm a bit put out."

"But according to you, the procedure is going as planned."

"You don't understand… I'm supposed to be in control of these people. How can I give even an illusion of that if I'm not thoroughly briefed by you?"

Silence.

The Professor sought to quell his anger. He knew Director X did not like emotional displays, nor did he respect weakness. When the Professor spoke again, his voice was steady, devoid of expression.

"Do you not trust me?" he asked, then immediately regretted asking the question. *Damn it!*

The Professor hardly listened to the reply, for the Director's response was unnecessary. Of course Director X did not trust him. The mere fact that the Director withheld such critical information about the subject spoke volumes to the Professor regarding Logan, the experiment, the Director's priorities, and the Professor's own place in the scheme of things.

"I see," said the Professor at last. "Then I have one last question."

"Yes?"

"What else do I not know about Experiment X?"

This time, there was no reply. The Director had ended the call.

○———————○

BACK in the laboratory, the rate of adamantium bonding had increased threefold. Dr. Chang suggested that a leak might be the culprit, so Carol Hines and Dr. Hendry searched their monitors for evidence of one.

"The channels are sufficient, Doctor, but there's an excess drain at… wait a moment… at the *flexor brevis—minima digiti* section."

Cornelius's first-year anatomy classes were too far behind him. "Plain language, please, Ms. Hines."

"Sorry. The hands and wrists, sir."

Cornelius stood behind the woman, gazing at the monitor. He glanced at Hendry, hoping for answers. But the man's angular face and square jaw were tense. It was clear he didn't know what to make of the alloy leakage, either.

"Not much of this so-called leak is showing up in the tank," Cornelius observed. "Less than one part for one hundred thousand. But the adamantium has to be going somewhere. It can't be collecting at his wrists—what would it bond with?"

Cornelius shook his head. "We're going to need some advice on this… Anybody know where the Professor is?"

Blank stares.

"No? Have him paged, then."

After a moment, loudspeakers boomed with an exasperated voice. "Cornelius? What is all the fuss?"

Cornelius looked around for a communicator, then spoke. "Professor, where are you?"

"What do you want, Doctor?"

Cornelius realized that the Professor could hear everything. *This lab is obviously bugged. How many other rooms are wired? Are they watching us right now?*

"We have a new problem," Cornelius began. "Could you return to the operating room?"

"I'm busy… What is the problem now?"

"There's an excess adamantium drain to the *minima… flexor*—the hands and wrists. We can't account for it and we're unable to stop it from occurring."

A long silence followed.

"Uh, Professor? Did you hear me?"

"Of course."

"Well, then—"

"It's all part of my program, Cornelius. Do you think I don't know what I'm doing?"

"No, sir. Of course not—"

"Continue with the procedure, and the wrap-up when the bonding is completed."

"Then you won't be returning to the lab?"

Another long silence. This time, Cornelius realized the Professor had cut him off.

Carol Hines looked up at Cornelius. "And the leak, Doctor?"

"It doesn't appear life-threatening, nor is it interfering with the procedure, so we're going to ignore it. Let's finish this up, shall we? We'll try to find out what happened with the leakage in the post-op examination and evaluation phase."

○———○

THE intercom buzzed, the sound filling the cramped quarters, waking the man in the bunk. Cutler sat up and punched the button. "Cutler here," he said, rubbing his eyes.

"Your Boy Scout has been camped outside my office for the last few hours," Major Deavers barked. "Your idea, I presume?"

Cutler chuckled a bit. "Just wanted Agent Franks to familiarize himself with all the personnel and procedures around here."

"Franks is on his way to the main lab to pick up Subject X. Meet him there. This time, you won't need EH gear."

"So the operation's over?"

"And the patient has apparently survived. Go get him, then escort Subject X to a new holding facility—Lab Two."

Cutler nodded and keyed the intercom. "No containment facilities there. That means the patient's out of the soup?"

"Yeah, for good. He's going to maximum security biomonitoring cell for post-op surveillance. Some technical types will be there to meet you and hook him up."

"Roger that. Out."

Cutler stepped into his standard-issue green overalls and brushed back his hair with his hand. Then he exited his quarters and rode the elevator down to the main laboratory.

When the doors opened, Cutler noticed that the huge tank was completely drained of fluid. Wires lay coiled at the bottom of the tank. Like fairy dust, twinkling silver specks of hard adamantium dotted the inside surfaces of the Plexiglas walls.

Next to the tank, in a powered wheelchair, Subject X slumped, head tucked into his hairy chest. Logan was naked and still damp from the post-op chemical bath. His hair hung down in wet ringlets.

Cutler did a double take. *Wasn't he shaved the last time I saw him? Strange.*

Agent Franks stood over the subject, a look of disgust marring his young face.

"Sickened?" Cutler asked as he sidled up to the young officer.

Franks shrugged. "Kinda, I guess. He's still got all those probes and wires sticking out of him. That's gotta hurt."

"Doesn't look like he's feeling much pain. Bastard's zonked. Out like a light."

"Geez, look at this," said Franks.

Cutler circled the chair to find thick wires coiled around a hook on the seat back.

"All those wires are still plugged into him," Franks said.

Cutler nodded. "Let's get the subject to Lab Two. The medicos are waiting. Maybe then we can call it a day."

7

THE MUTANT

A thousand nails grinding into my back. My arms. My legs. Gouging. Slashing. Burning...

Logan slid helplessly down the crumbling slope.

Roots and jagged rocks shredded the flight suit and ripped into his flesh. Loose stones battered his helmet in a clattering wall of noise. His cracked visor shimmered with psychedelic light—bright visual chaos from his malfunctioning Heads Up Display. And in his grip, tight against the skin of his tattered stealth suit, Logan clutched the black-clad stranger in a bear hug.

Blind, deaf, and unable to stop his precipitous tumble, Logan risked losing his captive to rid himself of the useless helmet. But when he let go, the stranger hung on, arms around his neck. Logan's fingers fumbled with the latch at his throat. With a hiss, the helmet detached. Blinking against a tide of dirt that pummeled his eyes, Logan spied a tall shape looming in the darkness.

He seized the handle of the Randall Mark I at his belt. As he tobogganed toward the tree, he tore the all-purpose knife free of its Velcro scabbard. Then he stabbed outward.

A hollow thud as the seven-inch blade bit deep into the wood—then a jolt that nearly tore the handle from his grip. The earth disappeared under him in a shower of rocks and dust. Logan's feet dangled over an abyss. Hundreds of feet below, the man-made lake shimmered in the pallid moonlight.

Logan gripped the knife with both hands while his captive held on to him. Muscles straining against their combined weight, he hung for a moment—long enough to feel a warm, wet stream of sweat course down his ravaged back. Then Logan slowly hauled them both onto a ledge formed by the tree's twisted roots. As he swung his leg over the edge, his captive squirmed up over his shoulders and around the tree. Turning, the shadowy figure helped pull Logan the rest of the way, then collapsed into a heap at the base of the tree. Panting from the strain of saving both their lives, Logan lay on his side. When the figure rose, Logan reached up and closed his fingers around the stranger's arm.

"You. My prisoner," Logan snarled in passable Korean.

To his surprise, there was no resistance. Instead, the stranger used the other hand to pull away the dark commando mask. Logan stared up at almond-shaped eyes filled with concern.

"Are you hurt?" the woman whispered, kneeling at his side.

Logan recognized her accent and hissed a reply in the woman's native tongue. Japanese. "*O-namae wa?*"

"English, please, Mr. Logan," she said in a voice barely above a whisper. "General Koh has deployed hundreds of audio sensors in these hills. If we are heard, better to be in your language than mine. Many of Koh's agents understand Japanese."

Logan grunted and rolled onto his back. Then he winced and sat up. Even in the dim light, the woman could see the dark stain on the ground where he'd collapsed.

"You're hurt... bleeding."

Logan shook her away. "Give me a minute and I'll be all better." His tone was edged with bitterness, and the woman gave him a curious stare, her small, round face washed in the moonlight.

Then she rose, and Logan watched as she inspected the harness and belt that circled her trim, formfitting night camouflage suit. A lot of equipment had been hung on the woman's diminutive frame, and from the expression that marred her dainty features, some of it had been lost.

"You still haven't answered my question. How do you know my name, but I don't know yours?" Still on the ground, Logan cautiously unzipped the sheath of the Heckler & Koch G36 strapped to his leg. The woman detected the move and drew her own weapon—a sleek black USP 45 Tactical.

Big toy for a little lady.

She noticed his reaction, and a smile touched her full lips. "I am Agent Miko Katana, Japanese National Police, Tokyo Prefecture."

Logan blinked in surprise. "A cop? You're a cop!"

"Hardly a cop, as you say," she replied. "I'm a member of the Special Assault Team."

"You're still a cop. So explain to me, Officer—what the hell is a Japanese detective doing in the middle of North Korea?"

"The same thing you are doing, Mr. Logan."

"And what would that be?"

As he spoke, Logan freed his automatic rifle and placed it on the ground—far enough away to gain some trust but close enough to grab if he needed to. Miko understood the gesture and holstered her Tac.

"Truce, Mr. Logan?" she said, brushing aside straight hair that fell around her pixie face in a silky black curtain.

"Maybe," he replied, rising. "But only if you'll tell me where you got my itinerary."

"Itinerary? That is very funny."

"Cut to the chase or I'm cutting you loose, Agent Katana," growled Logan, no longer amused.

Miko frowned, then spoke. "French intelligence has been operating a deep mole inside of Canada's military community for a number of years. At times they share information with SAT. Nothing of much consequence, usually. But two days ago, a GIGN operative in the South Pacific tipped us off to your mission, provided the details—"

"What kind of details?"

"We know there is another operative involved," she replied, "Agent Neil Langram. We know the location of your landing zones, your time over target, and your final objective. We also know how and where you'll be extracted when the mission is concluded."

Logan considered her story. *The woman could be bluffing, but I doubt it.*

France's Groupe d'Intervention Gendarmerie Nationale was one of the most active counterterrorism forces in the world. Unfortunately, they weren't always on the same side as the Canadians, and it bothered Logan that the French learned about his mission, then passed on the details to a third party.

"What you just told me is a keg of political dynamite waiting to explode—if it's true," hissed Logan.

"Why would I lie?"

"Why would you tell the truth?"

"Perhaps as a gesture to gain your trust, Mr. Logan. Perhaps because I require your help."

Logan picked up his G36, twirled it, and thrust it back into its holster. "Now, why would I help you?"

"Does it matter to you that lives hang in the balance? That an entire nation may be at risk?"

"Probably not."

The woman's expression hardened, her tiny hand caressed the handle of her automatic.

"Mr. Logan, I do not care how you feel or what you believe. You must help me get inside the complex below before it is too late… if it is not too late already."

○━━━━━━○

"ABE… Abe, please… Please, wake up…"

Dr. Cornelius heard his wife's plea, but her voice—like her image—seemed spectral and very far away.

"It's Paul… he's crying again. His fever is raging. I'm afraid he'll burn up," Madeline cried. "We have to take him to the emergency room. We must go now!"

Over the sound of his wife's sobs, Cornelius heard the agonized scream of his infant son. Suddenly on his feet, Cornelius found himself moving in slow motion, his legs hindered as though he were running through an ocean of glue.

"I'm coming!" he pleaded, pushing against the clinging tide.

But no matter how he struggled, how he raged, Cornelius's every step forward seemed to carry him back. His heart pounded against his rib cage, threatening to burst. He redoubled his efforts, yet his legs failed to carry him to his child.

Finally, Cornelius burst through the sea of milky fog to reach his son's bedroom. The colorful wallpaper glowed in front of his eyes like a hundred computer screens; the toys hanging over the crib looked ominous, twisted—long steel spikes, six-inch hypodermic needles, blood-flecked surgical probes.

When Cornelius stared down into the crib, Paul Phillip, his son, was gone. In the boy's place, Subject X—his flesh pierced with a thousand steel thorns—lay on bloody sheets.

Cornelius heard a scream and bolted upright. A pen slipped from his limp hand and clattered to the floor. He reached up to adjust the mashed glasses on his face, then tossed them on the keyboard in front of him. Rubbing the sleep out of his eyes, he pushed himself away from the computer terminal.

Must have been more tired than I thought… Passed right out.

The intercom buzzed only once. On his monitor, Cornelius saw the pinched face of an earnest young technician who was manning the observation booth adjacent to Lab Two. Cornelius didn't know the name of the young technician working "status tech" and it didn't matter, anyway. Wearily, the doctor pulled on his glasses, then punched the key.

"Cornelius here… Status?"

"Resting, Doctor. But he's on the ground, not on his cot."

The technician tapped a key, and the view from Lab Two filled the monitor. Cornelius saw Logan sprawled out on the floor on top of a bed of coiled tubes and wires—eyes closed, chest heaving. Body hair now covered the subject's chest, arms, legs, genitals. On the right-hand side of Cornelius's screen, a toolbar supplied real-time data on the subject's temperature, respiration, blood pressure, heart rate, and electrolyte balance.

"S'okay. Anything to report?" Cornelius could see the young man was concerned about something, though the readings were well within the normal range.

"No, sir… except…"

A complication? Absolutely impossible. Subject X was making a remarkable recovery.

"What?"

"Well, you know," the technician began. "Looks like this guy's really been through the mill."

"Uh, yeah," Cornelius replied.

What does this technician want me to say? Cornelius wondered. *That I feel bad for the subject? That I think it's wrong to put another human being through this kind of torment? That the Professor is inhumanly cruel? The Weapon X program misguided and sick?*

"Keep a close eye on him," Cornelius said before ending the transmission. *So I don't have to.*

Dr. Cornelius glanced at the digital clock. *It's three in the morning. Jesus. No wonder I'm so exhausted. Maybe I should call it a night?*

He rose and stretched his back, which had been bent over the computer terminal when he'd fallen asleep. He reached out to power down his workstation when the intercom buzzed again.

Stifling a yawn, Cornelius answered.

"Doctor? He just woke up." This time, the technician sounded nervous.

"How does he look?"

"Like cow flop, Dr. Cornelius."

Logan appeared on Cornelius's monitor. Subject X seemed to be in the same position as before, only his eyes were open and staring blank and unseeing, at the opposite wall.

"Is he moving?"

"No. Just staring."

Better leave my terminal active, Cornelius decided. *Just in case something really does go wrong.*

"Okay," Cornelius told the younger man. "Keep monitoring. Call me if anything happens. Out."

Cornelius kicked off his shoes and stripped off his lab coat to drape it over his chair. Then, still fully clothed, he stretched out on the bunk, tucked his glasses into his shirt pocket, and closed his heavy eyes.

Almost immediately, he slipped into a deep, dreaming sleep...

o———————o

"SO, Clete. You've seen the results. What do you conclude?"

"Do you really need a second opinion, Abe?"

Dr. Cornelius nodded. "I'm a research scientist. You're the practicing physician. Now, what's your diagnosis, Doctor?"

Dr. Cletus Forester pulled thick bifocals from the pocket of his pale green lab coat. Holding them to his face without opening them, he studied the results of a battery of tests he'd performed. Unfortunately, they mirrored the first set of charts provided by the child's pediatrician.

"The, er... patient's white blood cell count is far higher than normal, even for a child five times the boy's age," Dr. Forester began. "If you didn't know this from your own work, your pediatrician probably told you that children have lousy immune systems—which is why they're sick all the time."

"But not Paul?"

Forester shook his head. "Your son is different. His antibodies are through the roof, and they're busy little bastards, too—killing everything in sight. Persistent generalized lymphadenopathy is present—"

"Those lumps on his neck, under his arms?" Cornelius asked.

Forester nodded. "The groin, too. The lumps haven't shown up on the boy's skin yet, but they will soon. Only a matter of time. You say the fever is chronic?"

"Above one hundred at all times—but spiking to one hundred and two or even one hundred and three at night," Cornelius replied.

"Night sweats?"

"Every night, practically. Some mornings the sheets are soaked. My son..."

Cornelius paused, biting back emotion. When he spoke again, his tone was neutral. "Paul sheds fluids as fast as I can pump them into him. When the bad bouts occur, he's on an IV constantly. Even then, his electrolyte balance is totally shot to hell."

"There are signs of connective tissue disease," Forester added.

"Systemic lupus erythematosus?" Cornelius said, surprised. "So Paul's crying might be related to joint or muscle pain... damn... I never considered the possibility of lupus."

Dr. Forrester slowly shook his head. "Not lupus. Not precisely. Something like systemic lupus erythematosus. Something we've never seen before."

Cornelius, lost in thought, rubbed his chin. "I was reluctant to use painkillers, but now..."

"Use painkillers. Alleviate the boy's suffering," Forester said.

Cornelius looked up. "But there must be more I can do... a treatment to reverse the organ damage? Maybe a synthetic antibody to fight the antibodies he's producing..."

"Look, I'm sorry to tell you this, Abe," Forester said. "But, to be blunt, you're grasping at straws. You've obviously arrived at the same conclusion I have, or you wouldn't have sought a second opinion."

Cornelius looked up as if stung. "What are you saying, Clete?"

"We... we both know that your son's condition is fatal... that it's only a matter of time."

Cornelius looked away. "I haven't accepted that prognosis."

"Come on, Abe!" Forester cried. "Paul's immune system is forming antibodies that are attacking the cell nuclei. His DNA. RNA. Cell proteins. Phospholipids. It's only a matter of time before the organs are degraded and fail... one by one. Maybe three months. Four at the outside."

Behind his bottle-thick glasses, Cornelius's eyes burned. "I haven't given up. Not yet."

"But there's no cure—"

"I'll find one."

"—And probably there will never be a cure," Forester insisted. "In any case, it would take years, maybe decades, just to isolate the underlying cause of the condition. And more years trying to find a treatment to alleviate the suffering, never mind a cure."

Forester placed his arm on Cornelius's shoulder. When he spoke again, it was as a friend, not a physician. "Abe. Listen to me and accept what I'm telling you for your own good.

"The patient... your son, Paul... doesn't have decades, or even years. Prepare yourself for the worst. Grieve when the time comes, and get on with your life."

○━━━━━━━━━○

IT seemed as if he'd just closed his eyes for a moment when the intercom buzzed again.

Cornelius rolled off the bunk and stumbled to the terminal. He keyed the speaker, then fumbled with his glasses.

"Doctor?"

The same technician, now looking positively frantic.

"Yes... Status. What is it?"

"He's moving now."

"Violently?"

The technician paused. "He just leaned forward a bit."

You woke me up for that? Cornelius thought.

"Status..."

"Yes, sir."

"You don't have to tell me every time the patient shifts weight."

"Yes, sir... sorry, sir." The technician vanished.

That's it, Cornelius concluded. *After twenty-two hours on my feet, I need some rest.*

Cornelius stooped over the keyboard and pounded out a short message instructing the status tech to direct all inquiries to the Professor for the next two hours.

If the tech wants to go into panic mode before his shift ends, Cornelius figured that the Professor can deal with it.

But before he could power-down his terminal, Cornelius received yet another call.

"Status?" he answered.

"The patient's fine, sir. But he seems alert now."

Cornelius was suddenly wide awake. "He's aware?"

"He's just staring at his hands."

"Hands?"

"Yeah. The wires on his hands."

Cornelius recalled that Dr. Hendry put post-op bioscan monitors on the subject's hands in an effort to find out where the extra adamantium ended up collecting. Both Hendry and Chang feared that Subject X would lose mobility in his hands if too much adamantium accumulated around the delicate bones of his fingers.

"I'd better come over," Cornelius told the man. "Call the Professor. Have him meet me there. Out."

○――――――――○

"I have desperate need of your help or I would not ask, Mr. Logan," Miko Katana said. "Lives hang in the balance—"

"So you mentioned," Logan replied. "But you'd better preach to the choir, 'cause I'm not buying."

"Please, Mr. Logan, hear me out before you judge."

Standing on the ledge that hung over the dam and the man-made lake, Logan faced the woman, eyes level with hers.

"Two weeks ago, a Japanese research scientist was kidnapped while visiting Seoul. SAT intelligence uncovered evidence that the man was snatched by agents working for General Koh because of the knowledge the scientist possessed."

"Knowledge of weapons, no doubt," said Logan. "It's no secret that the North Koreans have a nuclear program up and running. It's a delivery system they lack—rockets and missiles. So let me guess—the missing scientist is a rocketry expert? A whiz at telemetry? Is that what you're hinting at?"

"I am not at liberty to discuss the doctor's work."

"Lady, you're not giving me squat."

"I am telling you what you need to know—nothing else."

"So basically you want me to help you get inside that facility—but you won't tell me why beyond some bullshit about people in danger. Then, once we're inside, we're supposed to find some guy who has been kidnapped, but you won't tell me who he is or why he was snatched. And you keep talking about some guy named General Koh, who has a hand in all of this—yet I never heard Koh's name in any of my intelligence assessments. Who is this Koh?"

"General Koh is a Japanese problem that does not concern you," she replied.

Her answer didn't surprise him. "Look, babe, I've got to know a bit more."

But Logan's demand was met with a wall of silence and an unwavering stare. Time was ticking by. Logan would soon be behind schedule—and his tardiness would jeopardize the success of the mission, putting Neil Langram at risk, too.

"Okay, you win," Logan said at last. "You can come with me, but only because I'm lonely."

And because your team obviously has better intelligence than mine. And in the spy game, knowledge is power—the kind that can save your life.

"Thank you, Mr. Logan. I promise I will not compromise your mission, even if it jeopardizes my own."

"Fair enough."

Miko Katana reached for a pack at her belt. "Before we start, let me patch you up. You must be in terrible pain."

The woman stepped around Logan and examined his blood-stained back. But when she began to clean his wounds, Miko got a huge surprise.

"I… I do not understand. A few minutes ago, your back was covered with lacerations. Now your wounds are nearly healed!"

"It's like I told you," Logan replied. "Give me a couple of minutes and I'll be all better."

"This is not normal," Miko replied.

"Yeah, tell me about it."

"But how do you do this?"

"Good genes," Logan said with bitterness.

Miko accepted his explanation and set out to clean the wounds that remained. When she was done, Logan tore off the remains of his high-tech stealth suit, then popped open a metal canister that had been hooked to his belt. He dumped a tight black bundle the size of a bar of soap into his right palm. As he worked it in his hands, the bundle expanded until Logan finally shook it out. When the formfitting camouflage suit was completely unfurled, Logan stripped off the rest of his gear and donned fresh clothing.

While he changed, Miko shyly averted her eyes. She cautiously crawled to the very edge of the cliff to observe the dam through miniature binoculars.

"See anything?" Logan asked as he snapped his utility belt around his waist.

"Just normal activity. The North Koreans do not seem to be aware of our presence."

"That's great," said Logan as he hefted his G36 and fed a round into the chamber. "Because I've had just about enough surprises for one night."

8

UNFORESEEN CONSEQUENCES

DESPITE the hour—nearly dawn—sleep eluded the Professor, as sleep always had, since early childhood. He sat rigid and alert on his ergonomic throne, grateful for the timelessness of his command center, where he could ignore the twenty-four-hour cycle and utterly dispense with the sleep ritual—at least until physical and mental exhaustion forced him to retreat into dreamless slumber.

Fortunately, that happened with less frequency. In the past few months, as the Weapon X project came to fruition, he marveled at how much more he was able to accomplish without the need for sleep. How uncluttered and crystallized his thought processes had become without the uncontrolled fancies of dreams or nightmares.

The entire Weapon X program would have been impossible without my sacrifice, my constant vigilance, the Professor reflected. *All I ever wanted was success—which is why the Director's reckless action is such a betrayal.*

Flickering unseen on his central monitor were images from Lab Two, where Subject X lay in a post-operative stupor. The laborious procedure had gone well—so well that the Professor didn't need to look at the medical data to know that his patient would make a full and rapid recovery.

That issue was never in any doubt. The patient was destined to survive because Director X stacked the deck to ensure success. *Perhaps I should thank him... Thank him for jeopardizing the project, years of work. Thank him for his lies, his treachery.*

But no thanks were possible. The Professor felt only a huge burning rage.

Why did the Director exclude me from such a critical decision? Why risk a rigidly structured experiment by adding a wild card—a mutant? Who knows what variables have been added to the equation? What surprises might be buried in the subject's DNA? What unforeseen consequences may arise?

As a scientist, the Professor understood that the most important factor in any experiment was total control of all its aspects. Nothing could be left to chance.

But with his careless decision, the Director has wrested that control from me.

The Professor's intention was to develop a procedure to turn human beings into weapons of terror—the first step toward creating an entire army of mindless supermen under his rigid control. But now he didn't even know if his process worked on humans, because it had only been attempted with a mutant.

The only way I can salvage what remains of this project is to seize control of the reins once more—find a way to reassert my will, my vision of the Weapon X program... which means I will have to take complete charge of the psychological conditioning phase of Subject X through my own surrogates.

Of course I will have to push aside Hendry, MacKenzie, and anyone who has resisted my ideas and questioned my vision.

The Professor clenched his fists in a vain effort to still his quavering hands. He couldn't keep them still.

Look at me now, he thought without a trace of self-pity. *I am incapable of controlling my own reflexes. How can I hope to regain control of the experiment? Of this facility? Of Weapon X?*

The sudden buzz of the intercom startled him, shattered his intense concentration.

On the central monitor the image of Subject X—now conscious—was abruptly replaced by the apprehensive face of a very young technician, eyes wide behind delicate glasses.

"Uh, Professor, sir? This is the status tech worker at Lab Two."

"Yes, what is it?"

"Dr. Cornelius asked me to—"

Suddenly the youth on the monitor began to babble. "Oh God! Oh my God!" he howled, eyes wide.

"What is it, man?" the Professor demanded, jumping to his feet.

"Blood," the technician gasped. "Something's happening... oh God. More blood—it's spurting out of his hands!"

BEHIND double panes of three-inch-thick Plexiglas, a technician frantically pounded a keyboard. His mouth gaped, his jaws moved, but his shouts were muted by the observation booth's soundproof walls.

Inside Lab Two, Subject X thrashed on a bed of tangled wires and coiled tubes, writhing in paroxysms of relentless, stabbing torment. What began as a dull ache in his wrists had rapidly detonated into intolerable agony. Now Logan's hands twitched uncontrollably, and the thick muscle that sheathed his wrists burned and quivered under bruised, tortured flesh. On his corded biceps, veins bulged until they threatened to burst.

Teeth gritted, an animal moan escaped his blood-flecked lips. His arms jerked in violent spasms that yanked a battery of medical probes from his flesh. Sparks rained down from shorted monitors and shattered probes. Logan's arms flailed wildly, splattering a crimson spray on walls, ceiling, Plexiglas panes.

As he staggered to his feet, beads of sweat appeared on Logan's forehead and neck, to run in rivulets down his torso. He reeled at his first halting step, his joints afire.

Heart pounding at an inhuman rate, the veins on his forehead, neck, and forearms swelled and then throbbed. Blood started from his gums, his nose. Red stained his cheeks, as blood flowed like tears.

Finally, Logan dropped to his knees and threw back his head. His mouth gaped, and in a spray of blood-foamed spittle he unleashed a howl of mortal anguish.

"STATUS... where is Cornelius?"

As he spoke, the Professor attempted to pull up images from Lab Two, but something—probably the subject's thrashing—had shorted out much of the system. The only camera he managed to activate projected a red smear—its lens splashed with blood.

"Oh God, sir! I need help here. I'm all alone. I'm not trained for this."

"Listen to me, man!" barked the Professor. "Patch me into your monitors. I want to see."

"Yes... yes, sir."

A moment later, Subject X appeared on the Professor's monitor.

Logan was on his knees, probes ripped free to dangle from the ceiling, the walls, like chains in a dungeon. A hundred wounds seeped black blood. Shattered probes protruded from his spine like porcupine needles.

Despite the horrific tableau, the Professor dispassionately observed that the subject's mouth was open in what he presumed was a sustained scream.

How tragic that the sound system has failed. I must remember to view the surveillance tapes later… listen to his shrieks… assess the level of pain he experienced.

The panicked voice of the tech interrupted his thoughts. "Sir… should I go in there and help him?"

"Uh—" *Intriguing idea.* "No. Not yet, Status."

"But he must be in terrible pain, sir."

The Professor smiled. "Yes. I think you are right."

On the monitor, Logan was still on his knees, his face buried in his chest, fists clenching and unclenching spasmodically. The subject screamed again and stared in dazed horror at his own wrists.

Suddenly, the Professor's ears were battered by Logan's inhuman howl. Impressed that the anxious technician had managed to restore the sound as well as the visuals, the Professor quickly lowered the volume, then looked back at the screen.

The image came as a shock. Awestruck, the Professor cried out. "Look at that!"

At Logan's wrists, on the backs of his hands, anguished flesh began to bulge and stretch. He doubled over, the movement tearing out the last remaining medical probes in a fountain of blood. As the subject's cries intensified, the Professor lowered the volume again—thankfully not enough to miss the wet, ripping sound of three razor sharp points bursting through the epidermis of the mutant's hand.

Over the auxiliary monitor, the Professor heard the technician scream like a child.

"You said you're all alone in Lab Two, didn't you?" asked the modulated voice.

Pause. "Yes, sir."

"I'll summon a security team." The Professor opened the glass hood that covered the emergency alarm, fully intending to alert Major Deavers to the potential crisis. But as his finger hovered over the red button, the Professor discovered that his formerly shaky hands were now as steady as a rock.

"God! He's got... nails... spikes coming out of him. Right out of his hands! What do I do?" the technician gasped.

"Stay calm. Help is on the way."

The Professor's eyes remained locked on the figure in Lab Two. Three clawlike appendages—a total of six of them now—protruded from each of the subject's hands. About thirty-one centimeters in length, slightly curved, and coated with adamantium steel, the claws appeared to be sharp-edged.

Where did they come from? How firmly are they rooted to the subject's skeleton? Does he control the deployment of his claws, or is their extension a reflex action?

So many questions...

One thing the Professor knew for certain. *Those... claws... no doubt caused Subject X excruciating agony as they extended.*

"God, Professor, more blood. He needs help, right now."

"Listen to me," the Professor commanded. "Do you... do you have access to the patient's cell from the observation booth?"

"Yes, sir, I do."

"And you're sure the subject needs medical assistance?"

"God, he must!" the technician replied.

"Then you should go in there and try to help the poor man."

A long pause. "Yes... I'll do that, sir. If... if you say so."

"I believe you should," said the Professor. "And be sure to close the security door after you enter the cell. Just to be safe."

On the auxiliary monitor the Professor saw the technician nod, his face ashen.

"Good lad... run along."

○——————————○

DR. Cornelius stopped at the dispensary for a cup of coffee before heading down to Lab Two. As he waited for the pot to brew, he attempted to contact the observation booth on the wall intercom.

"Status? Status? This is Cornelius. Come in..."

No reply, so he beeped the booth again.

Come on, Status, you've been bothering me all night. Why won't you pick up now?

Cornelius began to worry after three attempts went unanswered. At the very least, Status Tech was violating the project's protocol by ignoring his call.

Cornelius spun on his heels and hurried out of the dispensary without his coffee. The aroma had attracted two members of the security team, who were due on the outside perimeter for the sunrise shift change. Both were swathed in Kevlar body armor, though the older man neglected to don his helmet.

"You and you!" barked Cornelius. "Come with me!"

"Yes, sir," Franks replied crisply.

"Something wrong, sir?" asked Cutler.

Cornelius shrugged. "Could be. I don't know for sure. Please just stick close."

The guards followed him into an elevator. They rode down to Level Two in silence, though Franks and Cutler exchanged anxious glances when they discovered their destination. They'd been on Level Two hours before, delivering Subject X to the technicians.

Sure enough, Dr. Cornelius led them to Lab Two, though he paused at the security door.

"The lab worker here, what's his name?"

"Not sure, doc," Cutler replied. "Cal or Cole or something."

"He's new, sir. Just met him today," said Franks.

"New?" Cornelius was perplexed. "If he's new, then he shouldn't be in this section."

Cornelius punched the security code into the keypad and entered the observation booth, Cutler and Franks bringing up the rear. The doctor was surprised to find the booth empty, the power off save for dim emergency lights. The monitors were blank, and a smell of ozone and burnt plastic hovered in the air. On the other side of the Plexiglas wall, Lab Two was pitch-black.

Cornelius bit back a curse. "If he left without authority, I'll have that kid's hide for a drum." He scanned the console, searching for a light switch. Cutler found it first.

As the lights came up, they heard a sudden scream that ended abruptly in a wet gurgle.

On the other side of the Plexiglas, in the center of the lab, the missing technician lay sprawled on a bed of coiled tubing, shattered electrodes, and twisted wires. Blood spurted from his mangled throat. The man's eyes were pleading, his arms and legs twitched as his lifeblood pooled around him.

Hunched over his victim as if he were watching him die, Subject X stood—bloodstained and naked. His corded arms outspread. Protruding through bloody holes in both hands—six curved adamantium steel claws.

"Good Lord! What the hell happened here? This is horrific!" Cornelius exclaimed.

"He's dead, he's dead!" cried Franks, averting his eyes.

Only Cutler kept his senses. He triggered the alarm and activated the security system, which sealed all the doors between levels. But even through soundproof walls, the men in the booth could hear the Klaxon's wail.

Franks slowly backed away as the figure on the other side of the Plexiglas locked eyes with him. "Is that him? Is that Subject X?" he stammered.

"It's Subject X!" Cornelius cried. "That's my patient, but God… what's happening to him?"

"He murdered the boy," said Cutler. "He's covered in blood. Used those knives coming out of his hands."

Behind his thick, round glasses, the scientist's eyes narrowed curiously. "They look like claws."

"He looks like a rabid animal," Cutler shot back.

Franks stepped up. "Sir, we'll get guns and blow the thing away."

"Too late for that," said Cornelius. "Too late for anything."

"You're right," said Cutler. "It is too late. That son of a bitch is about to come right through the panel."

Cornelius snorted. "Ridiculous. That's four inches of Plexiglas. He's tough, but—"

The clear plastic wall exploded outward, showering Cornelius, Cutler, and Franks with a pelting crystalline hail. From the middle of the whirlwind, a howling figure leaped into the observation booth to face them. Cutler heard an angry snarl as Subject X dropped into a crouch, ready to spring.

o———————o

ON his central monitor, the Professor watched the chaos in Lab Two with joy. The frantic cries of Cornelius and the security men were music to his ears.

"It's Subject X! But God… what's happening to him?"

"He murdered the boy… covered in blood. Used those knives… out of his hands."

The auxiliary monitors scattered around the console provided real-time windows to the manic activity in other parts of the facility. From Level One Security, Major Deavers and a team of wranglers hurried to the elevator. In the OR, physicians and technicians assembled to deal with the emergency medical needs of Subject X.

"... look like claws..."

"He looks like a rabid animal..."

"... get guns and blow the thing away..."

"Too late for that. Too late for any—"

The Professor touched a button and cut the audio, his hand as steady as the finest surgeon on his staff.

Weapon X is already a success, the Professor realized. *The subject has more potential for mindless violence than even I imagined or ever could have hoped.*

Logan's primary instinct... perhaps his only instinct... was for destruction. When he viciously slashed that technician's throat—an innocent who only tried his best to alleviate the subject's pain—Weapon X acted on instinct, unclouded by mercy or reason. In a word, the subject's performance was...

"Magnificent."

o———————o

"OUT of the booth!" Cutler cried as he threw himself between Franks and Cornelius and the rampaging Logan. Franks dived for the exit before the last pieces of Plexiglas tinkled to the floor. But Cornelius froze, eyes wide with surprise behind bottle-thick lenses, and Logan whirled to face the bearded scientist.

With a guttural roar, Logan raised a clawed hand to strike Cornelius down. But before he could deliver the fatal blow, Cutler leaped on his back, locked his legs around Logan's neck, and seized his clawed arm with both hands.

"Move!" Cutler roared as he struggled to take Logan down.

Transfixed, Cornelius didn't budge. As Logan strove to free his upraised arm, Cutler felt his grip on the madman slipping. With a roar, Logan reached up and yanked the man off his back. Spinning helplessly, Cutler rolled over the computer terminal and through the remains of the shattered window. He landed on his back, hard. He tried to rise but fell again, his head lolling against the bloody carcass of the murdered technician.

Logan advanced on Dr. Cornelius. Face-to-face, their eyes locked, and Cornelius braced himself for the fatal strike. It never came. Instead, Logan's legs gave out and he reeled. With a final moan, Logan tumbled to the steel floor and lay still. Cornelius dropped to his knees beside the subject and touched his wrist to check for a pulse—only to recoil as the adamantium claws retracted, vanishing under folds of the subject's flesh.

The security door burst open. Weapon drawn, Major Deavers rushed in. Backing him up was Agent Franks and a team of animal handlers, electroprods crackling in their gloved hands.

Cornelius raised his hand to stop them, then placed two fingers on Logan's throat. "The subject is alive—barely. But all of his life-support systems have been torn away. We have to get him to the OR, stat, or we'll lose him."

To the doctor's surprise, the wranglers pushed him aside and seized Logan with rough hands. Using wires and tubes from the shattered medical probes, the guards hog-tied the unconscious man, ignoring Cornelius's protests.

Finally, the scientist spied the tag on Major Deavers's body armor. "You! Are you in command?" Cornelius barked.

"Yes, sir," Deavers replied gruffly, his voice echoing behind the clear face mask.

"I want you to take control of your boys, then take Subject X to the OR for evaluation. Time is of the essence. With his life support gone, he doesn't have long."

Deavers looked past Cornelius to the mangled corpse on the floor. "What about him?"

Cornelius faced the technician, then lowered his eyes. "There's no hurry… he's gone."

Deavers's eyes burned, but he bit back a response. Then he turned to face his men.

"Put him on a gurney and take the bastard to the OR," Deavers commanded. "Restrain him well. And if he wakes up—or even snores— shock him with your prods."

Two burly handlers tossed Logan onto a gurney, strapped him down, and wheeled him out. Meanwhile, Major Deavers and Agent Franks entered the lab to check on Cutler.

"He's out," said Deavers. "Doesn't look bad, though."

Deavers slapped Cutler awake, and when the man opened his eyes, the major shook his head in mock sympathy. "On your feet, hero," said Deavers, offering his hand.

Cutler took it, pulled himself erect, and shook his head to clear it. "What hit me?" he moaned. "And do I look as bad as I feel?"

Major Deavers directed his attention to the corpse sprawled on the floor in a darkening pool of his own blood.

"You look a hell of a lot better than that guy."

———o———————————o———

"IF I had known what you were really up to, Professor, I might be very upset with you."

Cornelius sat in the shattered observation booth among shards of Plexiglas and smashed consoles, cradling a cup of lukewarm coffee in his trembling hands.

"Possibly," said the Professor. "Though I never hid the true nature of the project from you. Rather, you chose not to discuss the more controversial aspect of the program with me. Thus, I felt you were not ready to accept certain... ugly realities."

"I thought you were trying to create some kind of superbeing. A... a supersoldier or something. Surely you've heard of that program, back in the 1940s?"

"Of course."

Cornelius put the cup to his lips and gulped loudly, draining it. He wiped his mouth with his shirtsleeve, then frowned. "I've helped you to create a monster, not a superbeing..."

"No, not a monster exactly—"

"To hell with that! It's a mindless, murdering animal."

"Well, yes. But we can make him behave."

Cornelius almost laughed. "Behave? Good God, Professor. It slaughtered an innocent boy in there."

Without looking, he pointed to the dark stain on the floor of the now-empty lab. "Then it came after me and the guards—straight through that blasted window as if it wasn't there."

In an uncharacteristic gesture, the Professor laid a comforting hand on his colleague's shoulder. "You must have been terrified, Doctor," he crooned sympathetically.

"You don't know the half of it."

Oh, but I do, the Professor silently countered, bowing his head to hide the slightest of smiles. *And I'm delighted by your reaction. I can only imagine how those who confront a fully trained and conditioned Weapon X will feel! No nation, no power, could stand up against such might.*

The Professor withdrew his hand. "But in the end you weren't hurt, Doctor, so let's not overindulge ourselves, hmm?"

Cornelius placed the cup to his lips, found it dry, and set it aside.

"Logan could have killed us all. I met his eyes for a second... filled with hate and fury. But I couldn't tell if it was some animal bloodlust, or horror at what we have done to him."

All we've "done to him" is free the untamed, unchecked beast inside, thought the Professor. *A beast that will soon be trained like a circus animal to perform on cue.*

The Professor watched as Cornelius rose and crossed the booth, to replenish his cup from a near empty pot. "And then what happened, Doctor?" he asked encouragingly.

"Then, with his life supports torn away, Subject X went down... collapsed. Those terrible knives—"

An extraordinary adaptation, those claws, the Professor privately marveled. *A dazzling evolutionary leap—*

"—sunk back into his body."

Stealthy. Lethal. The perfect weapon for Weapon X.

"And I thanked God for my good fortune."

A pity I hadn't thought of such an innovation first. We might have been better prepared for it...

The Professor shifted impatiently. "Well, you have survived to tell your tale. Now we should consider—"

"But the boy is dead, Professor."

"Yes, it's very tragic. Whatever could have possessed him to leave his booth?"

Cornelius shrugged. "I don't know. He must have seen the danger. But still, we have to answer for it."

The Professor frowned. "How so, Doctor?"

"Well, the police, obviously… and what about the boy's family?"

"Surely you do not want the police involved? Asking questions? Prying into people's lives? Your life? Why, if that happened, I'm not certain I could ensure your safety, Dr. Cornelius."

"That hardly matters now," Cornelius replied, surprised because he meant every word. After facing Logan's wrath, his terror of imprisonment had evaporated.

The Professor studied his colleague, puzzled by his change of attitude. "And I thought we'd won you over, Doctor. Convinced you not to squander your scientific knowledge. Impressed you with our steadfast dedication."

Cornelius lowered his eyes. "I've had enough."

Not until I say you have. But finessing is obviously required. How very tiresome…

"Fortunately, I don't believe police involvement will be necessary," the Professor replied, ignoring Cornelius's statement. "The boy's relatives can be compensated. Secured, let us say."

Cornelius wasn't listening. He fumbled with his coffee, the bitter brew staining his lab coat.

To vent his impatience, the Professor swept the Plexiglas debris from the top of the computer monitor. "Doctor. I realize you must be feeling a little estranged from me just now, so perhaps it is time to induct you further into my program…"

Cornelius looked up. "Program?"

Always the soft touch, then the iron hand.

"Yes… but first I will require your explicit trust. Do I have that, Dr. Cornelius?"

The doctor's jaw moved a second before a sound emerged. "I… I don't know. There's a lot—"

"That I will explain."

He's disoriented, the Professor observed. *Looking for direction… leadership. Now the iron hand.*

"Your trust, Doctor," the Professor repeated. "I require it. Offer that trust and I shall accept."

"Well," Cornelius said in a whisper. "Okay, then, if you want… I trust you."

The Professor licked his lips. "Thank you for that."

"You're welcome, sir."

"Tell me, Doctor, are you familiar with the term *Homo superior*?"

Cornelius shrugged. "As in master race or something?"

"To some extent. But no… I mean mutant." The Professor paused to reactivate the blood-flecked monitor. "Mutants aren't human, Dr. Cornelius, they are *Homo superior*. Subject X is not human. He is, therefore, *Homo superior*. Look here—"

The Professor replayed the final moments of the status technician's life. "What do you see?"

Cornelius was repulsed, yet scientific curiosity compelled him to watch. "What do you think?" he said angrily. "I see a wild beast that was once a man."

"Very well, Cornelius. I accept your assessment. Yet I see a man as ever he was, but with his subconscious stripped bare. Cut from his very soul and scored to the bone. Our friend has come into his own at last. For that we should rejoice. We are transforming him—architects of Logan's mind, body, and soul."

Cornelius scratched his chin, unnerved by the Professor's thin smile. "The experiment. The adamantium bonding process. Are you saying it mutated him into this infernal thing?"

"No, Doctor. You must understand that this 'infernal thing' is what the patient has always been. A determinedly violent individual pummeling his way through a purposeless life."

As the Professor watched the endless replay loop on the screen, his eyes were filled with something that resembled pity.

"Imagine such a life, Cornelius? One day distinguished from the next only by the changing patterns of bruises and blood from last night's drunken fight. But then, inexplicably, the wounds are healed and gone before noon and his first beer…" The Professor shook his head. "How sad. Why, I doubt if he even suffered hangovers."

The intercom buzzed.

"The diagnostic tests have been completed, Professor," Dr. Hendry reported. "We are assessing the results now. It will be a few hours. Perhaps by noon."

"And the subject?"

"He's been placed in maximum security. Lab Five, Level Five. A team is monitoring his activities."

The Professor's delicate hands tapped the keyboard and the murderous scene on the monitor shifted to a real-time image of Logan in another cell, awake and struggling against the bonds that restrained him from head to toe.

"Think of it, Dr. Cornelius," the Professor continued. "All his years, Logan has endured this... madness. Suffering a destiny that tore at him from his guts outward. Battling a fate decreed him by nature—a curse not unlike the scourge of lycanthropy in the Middle Ages. Do you even know Logan's history?"

"No," Cornelius replied. "Only..."

"Only that he was kidnapped for the purposes of this highly advanced experiment, correct?"

Cornelius nodded.

"Yet that did not trouble you?"

"I... I thought he was a criminal or something. I figured that the REM machine was part of the process... to rehabilitate Logan. To make him a better man."

The Professor threw back his head and laughed. "You have stumbled upon the truth, Doctor, for it is my intention that Mr. Logan be fully rehabilitated."

Cornelius could not tear his eyes away from Logan on the screen. "You were saying... his history, Professor?"

"Logan became a government agent and was ideally suited to the dangers of his activities. He had nothing to lose—not even his godforsaken life." The Professor faced Cornelius. "You saw the Medfax yourself, Doctor. Shot several times. Stabbed and beaten in the course of duty. Recklessly seeking the honor of dying for his country. How pitifully desperate he must have become."

On the monitor, Logan managed to free his arms. As they both watched, he began to tear at the thick cables that circled his waist.

"But now his demon is free," said the Professor. "Released by the intervention of Project X. His double identity—tormented mutant and secret spy—has been eradicated by the REM device. It's been supplanted by the superego, and all of Logan's primal instincts are focused and resolved. Do you understand?"

"I'm not sure I—"

"Before he became clay in our hands, it was as if Logan did not exist, anyway. He had no family. His body never aged, he carried no scars to remind him of past mistakes. Only his memories told him he was alive at all, and those memories caused him nothing but pain and endless suffering."

The Professor moved closer. "Logan's curse was to live on, while past friends, lovers, wives—perhaps even sons and daughters—aged and died before his eyes. Imagine such loneliness?"

"Yes…" Cornelius answered without a moment's hesitation.

Of course you can, the Professor recalled, then continued.

"How many times must he have considered suicide? Yet even death was denied him. No wonder he sought escape in alcohol. It's as if Logan understood that a retreat from the ego—the death of the 'I' and all of its memories—was his only chance at salvation."

"Yes, I do see, Professor."

"Of course you do, Doctor. And what you're looking at right now is Logan stripped of ambiguity, of emotion. What you see is the most formidable tactical weapon ever conceived."

"The knives, then, in his hands," said Cornelius. "Pure adamantium…"

"They're not knives, Cornelius—they're claws! And already Logan knows how to use them."

As they watched, Logan extended his talons and severed the last of the cables restraining him to the bunk. He sat up, claws fully extended.

"Are they asleep in that booth?" the Professor muttered as he punched the intercom. "Security!"

"Security here."

"We need the gas now, in Lab Five."

"We're waiting for Dr. Hendry's authorization…"

"You have mine," the Professor cried. "Haste! Haste! He's almost on his feet."

"Copy."

As Logan rolled off the bunk, a cyclone of yellow gas was blasted into his face from nozzles hidden in the walls, the floor, even the ceiling of the cell. Choking, he went down on his knees and clutched his heaving chest.

"Oh my God," gasped Cornelius.

Logan's mouth gaped, and a green bile erupted from the back of his throat. He hit the floor facedown, but twitching arms and legs quickly tossed him onto his back. Finally, Logan gagged like a beached shark. As he slipped into unconsciousness, the claws slowly retracted into his flesh.

Cornelius sank into a chair, transfixed by the image.

"A necessary action, Doctor. You saw what happened."

"Yes… but… I mean…"

"Spit it out, man. I'm open to suggestions."

"Can't we treat him better than this? He's still human, isn't he?"

The Professor considered his words. "In some way, perhaps. But your earlier description was more apt. 'A mindless, murdering animal,' I believe you said."

"Yes… I suppose so…"

"And this is why I am depending upon you, good doctor." The Professor rested his arm on the other's shoulder in what he imagined was a paternal gesture.

It made Cornelius's skin crawl.

Cornelius closed his eyes to banish the image on the screen, only to find Logan's face seared into his brain like an afterimage, as if he'd stared at the sun too long.

"In truth, Subject X is not so very different than your amazing nanochips," murmured the Professor. "He was created for a specific purpose. Now he must be restructured. Trained. Then programmed."

Cornelius opened his eyes. Logan seemed to stare up at him through the screen.

"You can do all of this," uttered the Professor. "Manipulation of the mindless, Dr. Cornelius. It is your calling."

9
REVELATIONS

CAROL Hines traced the curved adamantium blade with her left hand.

Magnificent.

In her mind, this was an unprecedented achievement.

The Professor had created an entirely new biological defense mechanism within the subject organism through the use of technology—totally bypassing the vagaries of the natural selection process. Amazing.

She shifted her wide green eyes to a second X-ray, this one taken laterally. It revealed a mysterious knot of muscle and cartilage in the forearm that held the claws in place. The muscle also served as a sheath when the blades were not in use.

Amazing architecture.

The claws appeared both lethal and efficient. To Carol, this configuration alone was a testament to what could be achieved when total discipline and a single vision were imposed on a scientific community in unison.

A true triumph of the will.

Like a patron of the arts, she moved from image to image, studying each of more than a hundred X-rays and ultrasounds wallpapering the medical conference center. Behind her, more personnel began to file into the room, answering the Professor's summons, as she had, to attend this emergency meeting.

Carol Hines paused as a particular image caught her eye—an electron microscopic photograph of the surface of the subject's unbreakable steel claw.

No sword-maker in ancient Japan could have forged so perfect a blade.

At a magnification of more than one hundred thousand times, not a flaw, not a ripple could be found in the sleek, glassy surface. And the subject's claws were twice as dense as tempered steel.

Virtually indestructible, thanks to the adamantium alloy...

A resin replica of the subject's blade configuration had been cast while he was unconscious. It now hung from surgical wire in the center of the wall display.

Carol Hines couldn't resist the urge to touch one shaft of the three long, slightly curved blades, to imagine the cold-cast resin's dull edges were really a steel alloy and sharper than a razor.

I had my doubts about the Professor, Carol admitted to herself, *especially after he seemed to freeze in panic during the bonding process. But it's obvious he truly had a vision of what Subject X was to become. And that vision has come to pass...*

"Pretty remarkable development, eh, Ms. Hines?"

She turned to find Dr. MacKenzie, the staff psychiatrist, standing at her side.

"I never imagined such a thing was possible," she replied, awe in her voice.

"If I were a Freudian, I could make much hay out of this particular configuration," MacKenzie chuckled as he rubbed the side of his red beard. His face was florid, his shock of red hair uncombed. The doctor had obviously been up much of the night, along with everyone else. But the lack of sleep hadn't affected his jovial nature.

Carol Hines offered MacKenzie a reserved smile. "What is your discipline, doctor? Which psychological theory do you expound?"

"In my golden youth, I was a student of Alfred Adler—a fact you probably could have deduced yourself."

"That seems intended as a very witty remark. I'm sorry, but I don't understand the reference."

"Well, Ms. Hines, Adler believed that the sense of inferiority rather than the sex drive is the fundamental motivating force in human nature. Feelings of inferiority, conscious or unconscious, combined with defense mechanisms are often the cause of all psychopathological behavior, in Adler's opinion."

"I still don't understand."

"Since you arrived with that magic machine of yours, my services as staff psychiatrist are no longer deemed important. Hence my own feelings of inferiority."

"I'm sorry, but—" Ms. Hines began again.

MacKenzie threw up his hands. "No, no, please don't apologize.

You misunderstand me. I readily surrender to your expertise, Ms. Hines, and truly hope that you assume all of my responsibilities in the very near future. To be frank, I've had my fill of the Professor. And of Project X."

After MacKenzie's impromptu admission, they stood in silence for a moment, viewing the images as others moved around them.

"Any idea why this meeting's been called?" MacKenzie asked when they were more or less alone.

"I was about to ask you the same question," she replied. "Perhaps it might have something to do with the violent incident last night in Lab Two."

"Possibly…"

MacKenzie sounded doubtful. In her heart, Carol Hines harbored doubts as well. Something was in the air. A whiff of change that she had sniffed before. She sensed the same tension, the same confused feeling she'd experienced at NASA after the last space shuttle accident—a feeling of chaos, mingled with the knowledge that certain individuals had lost power and prestige within the organization while others had gained it.

The difficulty for me, she recalled, *was trying to figure out whose star was on the ascent, and whose was falling like space junk.*

Institutional chaos and ambiguity eroded one's sense of purpose, fostered doubts, diminished productivity.

No one is immune. Not even a scientist like my father—his doubts led to alcohol abuse and worse.

Carol believed in focusing on the task, not the politics swirling around it. Better a worker bee than a queen. Better to keep one's head down than get it chopped off—like my father's, when a drug he developed failed to pass Federal Drug Administration approval.

The drinking, the violence got much worse after that. But at least the beatings stopped when I reached adolescence, won a few science fair prizes. Yes, the beatings stopped, but not the abuse…

A cluster of technicians jostled them, and MacKenzie and Hines moved to a quiet corner to continue their conversation.

"Quite impressive how you reasserted control over Logan after last night's incident," MacKenzie told her.

"It was very simple," she replied. "Subject X has already been conditioned to accept the REM interface. It gets easier each time you use the device."

"I did notice the same spike in brain activity during the initial interface—more chemical activity?"

"I don't believe Logan was on a trip down memory lane, if that's what you mean."

"You're certain, Ms. Hines?"

"I think we've covered this ground before, Doctor."

MacKenzie grinned, relishing the verbal sparring. "Anyway, Ms. Hines, that machine of yours has turned out to be the only means of controlling the subject. Drugs like Thorazine and Pheno-B, technology like the brain dampeners, even knockout gas have all proven ineffectual in the long run."

"Yes. Dr. Hendry did mention that the subject was gassed."

"Indeed." MacKenzie frowned. "A whopping dose, too. Enough to subdue an elephant for a week. Subject X woke up in twenty-eight minutes. By then, you had your machine attached and the interface put him down for good."

"Actually, I doubt Subject X was ever really 'awake' or 'conscious' as we understand the terms. His individual consciousness—his ego—has been completely eradicated. His memory, all traces of his former personality have been wiped away. The subject is a blank slate."

"Someone smashed up Lab Two, Ms. Hines."

"More like some*thing*. Subject X was acting purely on instinct—lashing out as even an insect will do if its survival is threatened."

"Hmm. I wonder if Logan felt threatened…"

Carol faced him. "I've heard whispers that someone—one of the status technicians—got injured. Flown out to a hospital this morning. Needs intensive care."

"Interesting…"

"You don't think so?"

MacKenzie shrugged. "I was outside this morning. I try to get out every morning—even we pale-skinned academics need a little sunshine now and then."

Carol Hines raised an eyebrow. "And?"

"We had quite a bit of snow in the last couple of days. A few inches at least. This morning the helipad was still covered."

The sharp whine of electronic feedback interrupted them. Then the amplified voice of Dr. Hendry called the meeting to order.

"Can we all take a seat, please? The Professor would like to brief us on some... recent developments."

"Excuse me, Ms. Hines," MacKenzie said. "I must join the rest of my staff in the orchestra pit."

The clatter of folding chairs filled the room until everyone found a place. Carol Hines sat alone, surrounded by empty seats.

Despite the post-operation incident in Lab Two, there was a general feeling of confidence among the staff. When the Professor stepped up to the microphone, he was greeted by a wave of applause that he immediately swept aside. As he began to speak, two men stood with the Professor—Dr. Hendry on his left and, on his right, Dr. Cornelius.

"As we move into Phase Two of this experiment, I have found it necessary to reevaluate the core members of the team and shift some of the responsibilities to other members. This new hierarchy I have formulated will be permanent..."

Suddenly, the room felt very uncomfortable. Colleagues exchanged puzzled glances, wondering about the long-term ramifications of the unexpected managerial shake-up. Only Carol Hines appeared completely unfazed. She alone was not caught totally by surprise.

"As of today, Dr. Cornelius will assume overall responsibility for the next phase of the operation," announced the Professor.

A wise choice—the best the Professor could make, she thought. Hendry had neither the proper attitude nor true dedication to the project. He questioned every idea that was not his own and spent too much time defending his sandbox to be an effective leader.

"Dr. Hendry will move into a support staff role, though he will still be responsible for the subject's overall health as well as the future physical conditioning of Subject X."

Murmurs intensified until the Professor paused, waiting for complete silence.

"Dr. MacKenzie, our staff psychiatrist, will retain his current title. But he and his staff of psychologists will now report to Ms. Carol Hines, our REM technician."

Carol blinked in surprise. Then her eyes met Dr. MacKenzie's. The man offered her a sly smile and a salute.

"This change is necessary for the success of the psychological conditioning process and is in no way meant to impugn Dr. MacKenzie's reputation as a physician or his participation in the experiment. This change was only made because the REM device will play a critical role in the next stage of Project X—the retraining and reprogramming of the subject—and Ms. Hines is our resident expert in that technology."

The Professor paused to scan the sea of anxious faces.

"Now I will turn over the floor and this meeting to Dr. Cornelius, who will outline the next stage of our ongoing experiment in much more detail…"

o————————o

"HAVE a good lunch, Cutler?"

"Yes, sir. Thanks for asking."

Cutler stood at attention before the major's desk. He'd shown up in his boss's office wearing crisp new overalls, fresh from Supply. He chose overalls because they were the only regulation gear bulky enough to cover the bandages that swathed his torso.

The major glanced at the after-action reports he was holding, then tossed them aside and rested his hands on his desk.

"Good work, Cutler. Both Franks and doctor-what's-his-name said you saved their bacon. But you should have called for backup before entering Lab Two, not after. Next time you might end up with considerably more than a few stitches."

"A dozen stitches, sir. And I won't make that mistake again."

"No, you won't. You're on light duty for a week."

"Come on, Deavers—"

"Seven days. Starting now."

"What do I do, sweep the halls?"

"You're going to review all current security procedures, double-check the cameras and motion detectors, test the alarms, and then implement a complete lockdown of the entire complex by midnight."

"Now, why would I implement a lockdown, Major?"

"Because the Director ordered one, that's why. All personnel, without exception. Until further notice."

"What happened? World War Three?"

"Management happened," Deavers replied. "I got the coded message this morning. Supplies come in, nobody goes out. End of story."

"Why do I get my day ruined?"

Deavers laughed. "Hey, you're not the only one. Rice is working on a complete communications blackout, including Internet and phone access—you should hear the egghead's bellyaching. And poor Franks is on perimeter duty, walking the fence in the snow and freezing cold for the next ten hours."

"Yeah, the lucky bastard," said Cutler.

THE thoughts played through his mind in an endless loop as Cornelius lay sleepless on his bunk.

Beast... once a man, but scored to the bone... animal now, no longer human.

Dr. Cornelius had fallen asleep listening to the jumbled, chaotic voices recorded during and after Logan's violent episode in Lab Two. Now they mingled with his own conflicted thoughts.

He has claws, but he's still a human being... No, not human. Homo superior. *Logan must be superior. With those spikes embedded in his cheeks, the corners of his eyes, his brain. He'd be dead if he wasn't a freak of nature... a mutant...*

Cornelius sat up and deactivated the recorder. Chest heaving, heart pumping, he found himself doused in a cold sweat. He fumbled for his glasses, then he checked his watch.

Quarter of seven... but is it morning or afternoon? In this damn place, there's no way to tell. Been days since I saw the sun...

He rolled off the bunk and crossed his tiny quarters to the computer terminal. Next to the black screen, a digital clock read 0647, military time.

"It's early morning," he groaned. His voice sounded strange as it echoed in his ears.

His movements had activated the room's overhead lighting, and the computer terminal also sprang to life. The intercom buzzed a moment later.

"Cornelius here..."

"Good morning, Doctor," said the status tech. "The Professor wanted me to tell you he will attend the experiment this morning."

"What time?"

"0800 in the main lab."

"What about the HDTV screen?"

"Up and running. Ms. Hines is going through the checklist now, but the screen has already been connected to and interfaced with the REM. Everything should be a go."

"Thanks, Status. Out."

Need some coffee… have to fortify myself for the day ahead. The day I play Dr. Frankenstein. The day I create a monster…

But instead of hurrying to the cafeteria, Cornelius sat down at his desk and reviewed the latest data on Subject X.

The indications are all positive. No sign of rejection—Logan's superimmune system was overridden long enough for the bonding to take place. Now that system has reasserted itself, and Logan has made a recovery in record time. No aftereffects, no scars, no wounds—except where our probes remain in place.

He rifled through pages and pages of information to find the blood test he'd ordered yesterday. He found the results near the bottom of the file, and eagerly scanned them. At first glance, Cornelius was disappointed. Logan's blood was unremarkable in every way. Type O negative. Normal white blood cell and platelet counts. Plasma normal, too—a little heavy on the trace minerals, but that could be due to the massive amounts of adamantium being pumped into him.

All normal… and yet Logan's blood can muster itself into a bacteria- and toxin-fighting substance as powerful as the Professor's cherished Weapon X.

Cornelius was ready to toss the blood test aside when he noticed something unusual about Logan's white cells.

As an immunologist, Cornelius knew that normal humans had several different types of white blood cells. But one type—neutrophils—is dominant. Neutrophils are quite good at attacking invading bacteria, but that's pretty much all they do.

Another type of white cell, the lymphocyte, is more powerful and much more versatile, though there are far fewer of them. Lymphocytes fight more than bacteria—they battle all foreign substances, including poisons, and work with the immune system to combat infection in a manner not yet fully understood.

While Logan's overall white blood cell count was within the normal range of one to two percent, his lymphocyte count was off the charts.

Not only that, but the hematologist had noticed certain anomalies in the shape and size of Logan's lymphocytes. They were larger and had some "additional structures as yet unidentified," according to the man's cryptic notations.

Could this be the secret of the subject's phenomenal immune system? Cornelius wondered. *Could it be something so simple? So basic as a white blood cell? If so, then vaccines for a hundred—no, a thousand diseases might be isolated and synthesized through a thorough study of Logan's unusual blood.*

Only then did the realization come. *This... this is a seminal find. As fundamental as the discovery of penicillin.*

Cornelius suddenly found himself shaking with raw emotion. He tore off his glasses and tossed them onto the table. Then he covered his eyes.

Good God... if I'd had access to Logan's blood a few years ago, I could have easily synthesized a vaccine for my son's disease. I've found the secret—the cure—too late to do any good.

If only I'd found Logan then, Cornelius despaired, *everything would have been different. My son's suffering would have ended. Paul could have lived a normal life, and my wife, Madeline, would be alive today.*

His hands came away wet with tears.

Maybe they were tears of hope, because if Cornelius's work was successful in the past, no one would have had to suffer like Paul—ever again.

Yes, the Professor will have his monster, his killing machine, his goddamn Weapon X, because I'll be the one to create it for him.

But in return—for my own part in this hellish, twisted experiment—I will pick the Professor's brain for all his knowledge, his techniques, and then use Logan as a guinea pig in an effort to alleviate human disease and suffering, to find a panacea, a universal elixir that will cure every single disease forever.

Cornelius prayed that the ends justified the means.

<hr />

CARDIO-INHIBITOR, MS. HINES...

When he heard the booming voice echo through the night shrouded valley, Logan melted into the shadows under a tall pine, dragging Miko Katana down with him.

"What is it?" she mouthed silently.

Logan tapped his ears like she was crazy. Surely she'd heard it, too. How could she miss that sound?

They scanned the woods around them, which were fairly thick now that they'd reached the base of the hill. They had moved close enough for Logan to smell the water, though the lake and the dam beyond were still invisible through the dense foliage.

Cautiously, Miko drew her infrared lenses—Logan's had been destroyed with his helmet—but after a careful scan, she saw nothing.

"Sorry," Logan whispered as softly as the wind in the trees. "Thought I heard a voice or something. Maybe I hit my head harder than I realized."

"No problem, I could use a rest."

Miko drew a pocket sized GPS system. But before she activated it, he stopped her. "The dam is that way—less than a kilometer," he gestured with his thumb. "The road's over there. Maybe five hundred meters. Beyond that, the lake."

"How do you know this?"

"Brought up on the frontier. Didn't have GPS. Not even a compass. Just the sun. Moon. Stars. And instinct."

"Your 'instincts' are well honed." She tucked the device away. "To the road, then?"

"Let's parallel the road until we get to the main throughway over the dam, then it's back into the woods. Then we head to the complex right below."

When they set off this time, Miko took point, weapon drawn. Logan let her go.

After my foul-up back there, she'd rather trust her own ears, he thought ruefully. *Or maybe she's got something to prove.*

Though Miko's Tac was equipped with a noise suppressor, if she actually had to pull the trigger, no amount of shooting would save them— they would be hunted down like imperialist running dogs. It had happened to Logan before.

Fifteen minutes later, they reached the road—a wide dirt trail sprayed with oil tar to keep the dust to a minimum. On one side of the road ran a drainage ditch deep enough to hide in if they had to. On the other side, a sharp drop to the lake below, where moonlight shimmered off the rippling black water. Across that lake, a black ridge rose as high as the one they'd just ascended.

There was no sign of traffic along the winding road, or the dam beyond. There were only the aircraft lights twinkling on the pinnacle of the dam's tall superstructure.

Miko pushed forward, but Logan stopped her.

"I presume you think your missing scientist is inside that complex, am I right?"

Miko looked at him through a curtain of hair. "What is it your American celebrities say? No comment."

"That's Hollywood. I'm Canadian."

"I cannot tell you because I do not know, Mr. Logan," she said.

"Fine, because if you did plan on rescuing him, think again. Unless the guy has sold his services to the North Koreans, and then faked his own kidnapping—"

"An impossibility, Mr. Logan."

"—he's not cooperating with his captors. And that means the North Koreans had to soften him up a bit... so that he'd see things their way." Logan paused to let his words sink in. "Chances are good that even if you find him, he'll be in no shape to travel—let alone make a break."

Miko walked silently for a few steps. Then she whirled around to face him.

But as she opened her lips, Logan silenced her. "Listen!"

At first, she heard only the water. Then a flapping sound—a steady beat that echoed off the hills.

"Go! Get down," Logan whispered, pushing her into the ditch. She landed in thick grass and a shallow puddle of stagnant water. Logan dived in next to her.

The pounding became a steady roar as the helicopter rose over the ridge on the other side of the lake. Miko cautiously peered above the edge of the trench, then used her night-vision binoculars to identify the vehicle.

"An MD-500 helicopter," she told him. "North Korean military markings... North Korean Special Forces, to be precise."

"Damn."

"Something is suspended from its nose. Not a weapon but—"

"Get down!" rasped Logan, pulling her back into the ditch just as the spotlight stabbed through the darkness. But not in their direction. Instead, the spotlight played across the opposite slope. "Don't like the look of that," snarled Logan.

The chopper hovered over the hill, shaking the branches as the spotlight probed the ground between the trees. Soon, a second helicopter roared across the lake, joining the hunt. And on the road at the base of the hill, more activity—a convoy of vehicles raced from the dam. The helicopters still hovered in place. Several armored cars and a Russian-made armored personnel carrier rumbled ahead.

"Langram. They're looking for my partner," said Logan, face grim. "Hope he makes it."

Then a new sound—more beating rotors—this time coming from behind. They ducked their heads as two more helicopters roared over the ditch, bright white lights tracing the ground, following the road.

"They're on to us. They have to be," said Logan. "Must have tracked us as we came down. Don't know how, but—"

"Logan, more vehicles on the road!" Miko shouted. "They're coming from the dam, driving right for us!"

10

ILLUSIONS

"CARDIO-INHIBITOR, Ms. Hines."

Tapping, and then she looked up, bright green eyes on Cornelius. "Activated."

They all stood in the west corner of the main lab, which was now dominated by a digital screen the size of a wall. In the middle of the room, Subject X lying naked on a technological "table" mounted atop an array of computers and diagnostic machinery. Carol Hines sat at a terminal, inches from Logan's head.

"I don't understand the point of this twenty-four-hour delay, Doctor," the Professor grumbled. Hands in his pockets, he leaned over the edge of the massive medico-diagnostic tub. Logan lay in its sunken center, sprawled on a bed of wires and tubes.

"Ms. Hines and I have determined that all of Dr. MacKenzie's conditioning techniques will most likely fail," said Cornelius. "We have decided to take a different approach using the REM device."

"But it took MacKenzie years to develop his data, formulate effective surgical techniques," countered the Professor.

"His data was based on human subjects. Logan is *Homo superior*, which renders the good doctor's advance research moot."

"Surely Logan has the same psychological makeup as anyone. The psyche is formed by experience and conditioning. He probably thought he was human until he discovered the truth."

Cornelius shook his head. "Dr. MacKenzie was relying on brain surgery, detaching the hippocampus, rewiring the prefrontal lobe, severing the hemispheres. But with Logan's healing abilities, it's possible he could regenerate the damaged brain tissue—"

"Preposterous!" snorted the Professor.

Carol Hines spoke up. "But Professor, with all due respect, we've already learned that Logan can regenerate damaged nerve tissue—something impossible with a normal human being. Why not total restoration of his brain functions, too?"

"And there are also risks of side effects," Cornelius added. "The hippocampus is particularly sensitive to global oxygen deprivation. Epilepsy could result."

"I see." The Professor rubbed his chin. "Logan would certainly not be a reliable or effective weapon if he suffered chronic seizures."

Cornelius nodded. "Worse than that, there's the possibility of anterograde amnesia. How could Logan accept conditioning if he lost the ability to form new memories?"

The Professor's eyes remained focused on the subject. Cornelius sensed he was still unconvinced.

"There are other factors," Cornelius warned. "The subject is still aggressive despite ego eradication."

"Reason?"

"Chemical reactions have been ruled out. No metal poisoning is present, no schizoid chemical imbalances we can detect."

"Perhaps it has something to do with pain," said Carol Hines.

Both men faced her.

"What if the organism itself were experiencing a kind of recognition—a memory, if you will—of the pain experienced during the bonding process?"

The Professor scoffed. "Memories reside in the brain, Ms. Hines, not in the individual cells."

"Whatever the cause," Cornelius declared, "his brutish impulses have become greatly exaggerated since the adamantium bonding process began."

"And this... treatment... will correct that situation?"

"No, Professor. Hardly," Cornelius replied. "But it should give us a real knowledge of Logan's mental stress dynamics and a better understanding of his current capabilities, such as his retention of language skills, his recognition of symbols..."

The Professor's eyes narrowed. "I hope this isn't a waste of my time, Cornelius. We should've begun reorientation by now. What's the point of this weapon if we can't control him?"

"But we can control him, somewhat." Cornelius handed the Professor a spidery headset and microphone. "Use this. It's a direct link to his cerebral cortex."

The Professor seized the device with greedy hands. "With this I can speak to him? Control him?"

Cornelius shrugged. "Suggest, perhaps. Control? I don't know."

Carol Hines tapped her keyboard. Cornelius threw various switches. The console on the medico-incubator activated with beeps and dings as vital signs were monitored.

Cornelius directed the Professor's attention to the giant HDTV monitor, now rippling with silent static.

"Ms. Hines has interfaced successfully. The REM is digitally coding the electrical impulses inside of Logan's brain, and will translate them into digital images."

"Remarkable."

"Indeed, Professor. We can actually watch Logan's dreams," Cornelius told him. "What you'll see on the big screen will be in direct relation to your spoken words. Tell him he's eating, and you might see a sizzling steak. Tell him he's flying, and you may see the image of a bird, an airplane—"

"I understand, Doctor," the Professor barked impatiently as he raised the microphone to his lips. "Logan," he began in a commanding tone. "You are in my control, Logan…"

"Yes, like that," said Cornelius. "Speak clearly and slowly. But you shouldn't use his former name, sir. It probably wouldn't mean a thing to Subject X at this stage, but we are trying to eradicate the previous markers of his life."

"Yes. Quite so," the Professor replied.

"Ms. Hines, we'll need an exacting flow of adrenergics as soon as possible," Cornelius cautioned.

"It's all in the system, sir," she replied. "I programmed it myself. For the most part, it was pretty straightforward."

"Splendid."

They looked up when they heard the Professor's sonorous voice.

"You are a beast," he said. "You are an animal born to serve…"

Cornelius and Ms. Hines exchanged glances.

"You have one master—and it is me. You will do anything I say—"

"Uh, Professor?"

"Yes? What?" snapped the Professor.

"We… We haven't begun yet, sir," Cornelius explained. "The link hasn't been activated."

The Professor pursed his thin lips. "Then please get on with it already, Doctor."

Cornelius gave Carol Hines a signal, then ran down the checklist in his head. "Set three of six in post-adamantium cell-bonding process. Stress and engram block and block complex. Language and symbol comprehension scan. Feed interface with the monitor. Two way communication. Have all that?"

"Yes."

"Proceed, Ms. Hines…"

She tapped the keyboard with machinelike precision. Cornelius stepped up to the Professor, who watched the whole process with predatory eyes.

"Pardon my suggestion, sir," he began, "but it might be advisable to avoid any directives to the patient during these tests. The psychotechnics of the situation warrant caution, as—"

The Professor cut him off. "Thank you for your suggestion, Doctor. Have you any more?"

"No," Cornelius replied. "I guess not."

A sudden pop, then Carol Hines's console sparked. "Oh!" she cried, jumping back. Smoke and more sparks emerged from behind the faceplate of her terminal.

Then a thunderous, crackling roar—screeching like feedback magnified a hundred times—as the electronic systems overloaded and shorted out one by one.

The Professor tore off his headset, but the noise was filling the lab as well. He howled and covered his ears.

"Overload!" Cornelius cried, his voice lost in the racket.

The fire extinguishing system blasted flame-smothering halon gas that quickly doused the electrical fire brewing inside of the computer, but the damage had already been done.

"Hines! Do something!" Cornelius cried. "Cut off the power!"

"I'm trying," she said as she pounded the keys. Finally, she located the audio cutoff and the deafening noise ended as abruptly as it began. Only an insistent fire alarm could be heard reverberating through the corridors outside the sealed laboratory.

Another electronic pop, then a crackle of static—this time from behind the massive HDTV monitor.

"What was that?" the Professor cried as the wall screen sprang to life. Projected on it, a roiling purple haze, like psychedelic smoke. "And what's that on the screen?"

Carol Hines glanced at the monitor, then down at her smoldering terminal. "We're getting some sort of internal feedback, sir," she reported. "The interface is—"

She squealed and pulled her scorched fingers away from the console. "The imaging is so powerful, it's burning circuits," she cautioned. Her statement was followed by another automatic blast of frigid halon.

On the wall screen, three curved, bone-white spikes rose into the frame. Each structure had a raw, jagged, unfinished look. Several times the digital image froze and began to break up, only to reconstitute, sharper than before.

"Something's wrong here," said the Professor as he stepped back from the monitor.

The spikes became ribs that morphed into spinal column, hip bones, a skull. Then a booming voice filled the lab with a single word: "PAIN!"

Cornelius tore his eyes away from the screen. "Okay. Shut it down. Shut it all down. We'll clean up the mess, check the data preps and find out what the hell went wrong."

A sudden, incomprehensible scream of baffled rage echoed off the walls.

"Ms. Hines, I said shut it down!" Cornelius cried.

"I… I can't, sir. There's no response!"

"I'M HURTING… PAIN!"

On the screen, the image of a skeleton was fully formed. Wild eyes glared with hate from dark sockets. Gnashing teeth turned to fangs as spikes sprang from every bone, every rib.

"WHAT HAVE YOU DONE TO ME?"

"If you can't cut the monitor, will you please cut the damn audio so I can hear myself think?"

Carol Hines met Cornelius's angry glare with a look of fear. "The audio feed is not activated, Doctor. It's malfunctioning. I shut it down already."

CUTLER was manning the security command center when the fire alarm went off in the main lab on Level Five.

As per established protocol, he sealed off the floor from the rest of the underground complex. With the clatter of keys, the fireproof hatch closed automatically, the ventilation system shut down, and the elevator cars ascended to the surface and disgorged their passengers before powering down.

Cutler was about to alert the emergency response team when they contacted him.

"Anderson here. I've got a halon gas release in the main lab. Heat sensors indicate the fire is extinguished, but there's smoke so I'm dispatching a security team."

"Who's with you?"

"Franks and Lynch."

"Arm yourselves with tranquilizer guns. Sidearms with live ammo, too. Kevlar body armor. Helmets and visors."

"Come on, Cut. It's a fire, not a war."

"Don't be too sure," Cutler shot back. "There's another experiment going on down there. The Professor and his team are working on Subject X."

There was a pause before Anderson replied. "Okay, I'm calling for immediate backup."

Cutler grinned. "Great. I'll be right down. Over."

Cutler was halfway out of his chair when a firm hand pushed him back down. Another reached over his shoulder and keyed the intercom back on.

"Major Deavers here. Listen up, Anderson. I want you to call Rice or Wesley if you need help. In the heat of the moment, Agent Cutler probably forgot that he's been assigned to light duty. Over…"

o———————o

THE Professor stared at the monitor, transfixed. A grinning death's head stared back at him.

"PAIN! WHY PAIN?" the voice raged.

"This is unbelievable, Cornelius," the Professor cried, hands covering his ears. "You must stop it. Stop it now!"

"I can't. We're not sending. We're receiving." Cornelius looked up at the screen. "*He's* in control."

Then he turned. "Hines. Can you get Logan under control?"

Green eyes wide, she glanced away from the horrific image on the screen, hand covering her heart. "No, sir, Dr. Cornelius. I... I can't do a thing."

When Hines looked back at the screen, the bulging eyes seemed to stare back at her. Fearfully, she slowly stepped away from her console. She bumped against the diagnostic table.

A thick, muscled arm shot out of the high-tech sarcophagus, fingers curled into a grasping claw.

"PAIN!" roared Logan as he reached for Carol Hines.

"Doctor—help m—" Her frantic plea was cut off as Logan's fingers closed around her throat.

Still clutching the helpless, choking woman, Logan tore an intravenous tube from his neck and stared into Hines's terrified face.

"YOU! YOU GIVE PAIN TO ME..."

Her frail fingers clawed at Logan's hand, nails breaking as she tried to pry open his grip. Logan shook her as she pleaded for her life with gasping sobs. "No... oh, no... oh God, no..."

"PAIN..."

While Cornelius called for a security team, Logan struggled to rise against the wires, tubes, and restraints that held him to the diagnostic table.

The sound of the fire alarm mingled with the loud howl of the security alert, creating a chaotic cacophony. Suddenly, a very stern voice broke through the clamor.

"Logan! Leave that woman alone, you animal."

It was the Professor, eyes burning behind his square lenses.

He's mad, thought Cornelius. *He hasn't seen what Logan can do...*

"This is your master! You are in *my* control," the Professor bellowed. "You have no will but to serve me! Your master..."

A guttural snarl rumbled in Logan's throat. He locked eyes with the Professor and tossed the woman aside like a rag doll.

Carol Hines sprawled to the floor, unconscious or worse. Despite his fear, Cornelius dropped to his knees at the woman's side and dragged her back, away from the raging wild man.

"Stay where you are!" the Professor shrieked as Logan reared up from the table, tearing away the last of his restraints and ripping out tubes and wires. As he crawled off the recessed slab, a security team burst through the door, tranquilizer guns ready.

Before the Professor could retreat, Logan vaulted. Fingers reached for the man's throat, and the Professor fought in vain against Logan's choking grip.

"Guards, tranquilize Logan now!" Cornelius cried, still cradling Carol Hines in his arms.

But Agent Franks hesitated. "We might hit the Professor."

"Just shoot, damn it! SHOOT!" screamed Cornelius.

With the Professor still struggling in his grip, Logan spun around to face the guards. Hair wild, eyes wide, Logan howled and stomped his feet at his new foes, snarling like a trapped animal.

A third guard—Anderson—barked a command from the corridor. "Fire! Fire now!"

The shots were not loud—just a sibilant hiss accompanied each gas-propelled tranquilizer dart as it burst from the tube, followed by a wet smack as it impacted. The darts peppered Logan in the throat, chest, face, and belly. But he did not go down.

More shots, Anderson adding to the volley with his own dart gun. Finally, without a sound, Logan fell backward, into the incubator tub. His legs twitched as powerful nerve suppressants made their way into his bloodstream and then dispersed throughout his body.

Carol Hines lolled on a chair, eyes fluttering. Then she coughed and held her head in her hands. Cornelius faced the others. "Professor," he called. "Are you all right?"

Cornelius saw the man stumbling to his feet, clutching his throat. His face was ghostly pale, and Cornelius feared the Professor was about to collapse, too.

"I didn't hit the Professor, sir," Franks babbled to Anderson.

"I know it."

The Professor coughed, then his eyes focused on the now unconscious Logan and he snapped.

"Kill him!" he shouted. "We must kill Logan now!" The Professor lunged at Franks and tried to tear the tranquilizer gun out of the agent's grip. "He's a wild animal! We cannot control him!"

Franks pulled away and the Professor spun around and lunged at Anderson, trying to rip the automatic pistol from his holster.

"Give me that gun," the Professor demanded as they grappled for the weapon.

"I can't do that, sir," cried Anderson, trying to fend off the man without hurting him. Suddenly, Cornelius threw himself between the two men.

"Professor, calm down now. You don't know what you're saying."

Wild-eyed, the Professor clutched the lapels of Cornelius's lab coat. "That beast tried to kill me. Didn't you see?"

"Yes. Yes, of course," said Cornelius. "But you're just in a state of shock right now, that's all."

The Professor muttered something unintelligible, and Cornelius grabbed his arms to steady him.

"Guard," Cornelius called over his shoulder. "Get some medical staff in here. Stat."

"Yes, sir."

"Doctor!" The cry came from Carol Hines, standing near the diagnostic table.

Cornelius raced to her, the Professor following reluctantly. They watched in awe as pinpricks of blood spouted from Logan's forearms. Then, the adamantium claws slid out from their sheaths, to gleam bloodstained-silver in the lab's dim light.

SNIKT! The sound of the claws silenced all.

"It's alright. He's totally sedated," Cornelius whispered. "That's some sort of random impulse we're seeing—a reflex. Good thing it didn't happen when he attacked you, Professor…"

"Oh God!" gasped Hines. "Look at the screen!"

Logan's violent thoughts flashed on-screen. Framed in splashes of clotted crimson, the face of the Professor dominated the digital frame—mouth open in a frozen shriek, glasses pierced by razor-sharp claws, the eye sockets gaping, bloody pits.

Cornelius looked away. "Well," he said in a weary voice. "I guess we've all had enough for today. Turn off the monitor, Ms. Hines…"

○————————○

SHE winced when his hands touched her throat.

"Sorry to startle you, Ms. Hines, but I must examine the injury."

"Of course," she replied, staring straight ahead as he circled her, fingers probing her neck, shoulders, ribs.

At last, Dr. Hendry removed his hand. "No soft tissue damage on your neck. Just some bruising. Nothing a little makeup wouldn't hide, eh?"

"I don't wear makeup."

"Yes. Quite. That bruise on your rib may smart, but nothing is broken."

He stepped over to the sink and washed his hands. She pulled up her green smock to cover her nakedness. Hendry dried his hands, then opened a glass cabinet filled with plastic bottles. "I'm going to give you a mild painkiller, and an analgesic to reduce the swelling."

"Thank you. How is the Professor?"

"Resting comfortably, I hope. Dr. MacKenzie is handling his treatment. Most likely all the Professor needs is rest. He's a workaholic. And speaking of sleep, would you like something to soothe your nerves?"

"I'm fine. I can't take a nap now, I have duties to perform."

"You seem to be holding up well, Ms. Hines. It must have been quite a shock—Subject X attacking you like that."

"I thought he was going to murder me… and the Professor."

"Yet I doubt that was Logan's intention, at least in your case. If he wanted to kill you, Logan could have broken your neck with one hand, as easily as you or I break a pencil."

She faced him. "Thank you for that comparison, Doctor. It's an image I'll cherish."

Hendry laughed. "A sense of humor, Ms. Hines? Who knew?"

She slid off the diagnostic table. "Can I go now?"

"First I'd like to ask a question. You don't have to answer if you don't want to."

She raised an eyebrow, but said nothing.

"I couldn't help but notice old scars on your abdomen. They look like chemical burns. And you've had a surgical procedure, too. One not listed on your charts…"

"Chemistry set. I was accident-prone as a child."

"I… see. And the surgical procedure?"

"Emergency appendectomy when I was fourteen. I guess I forgot to list it when I filled out my personnel file."

"Not to worry," Hendry replied. "I'll fix that oversight right now."

"Then I can go?"

Hendry nodded. "Light duty for a day or two. Cold compresses to relieve the swelling. And if you have trouble sleeping, give me a call."

After she left, Hendry went to the computer and pulled up the personnel file for Carol Hines. On her health chart, he entered the results of the examination. Then he scrolled down to the "Past Medical History" section of the woman's profile. Under "Prior Surgeries" he deleted "none" and then typed: *Surgical procedure, approximate age 14. Cesarean section?*

○────────○

"YOU'RE gonna fall out of your seat, Cutler!" Deavers barked.

Cutler straightened up in his chair and took his feet off the terminal where they'd been propped, then spun to face Deavers. "They teach you that in management school?"

"What?"

"Sneaking up on people."

"I've got my eye on you, Cutler, if that's what you mean. And I think you're enjoying this light duty thing way too much. Consider yourself active—as of now."

"That screw-up in the lab last night got you spooked, too? Should have let me get in the mix."

Deavers closed and locked the security command center hatch, then sat down across from Cutler. "You got that right, Cut. Since I lost Agent Hill, this place has been going to hell. Last night, Lynch and Anderson behaved like amateurs, and Franks is as green as grass. Nearly dropped the Professor with the tranquilizer gun instead of the resident menace, Logan."

"Sorry I missed it."

"Well, you won't miss the next mess, because you're back on the active list—as head of tactical security."

"I don't want Hill's old job," Cutler shot back.

"Why not?"

"Because I don't want to end up in intensive care like Hill. I am not an idiot, Deavers!"

Deavers leaned close and spoke barely above a whisper. "Listen, Cut. Things are only going to get messier around here, and soon. We've got a house full of mad scientists and one very dangerous monster. I need your help to keep this place together."

"No way, Major."

"Come on, Cutler. You're the best I've got, even if you are an insubordinate son of a bitch with a chip on your shoulder. You also seem to be allergic to authority."

"Nice to see you drop that 'big boss' facade, Major. Makes you seem almost human. Did you give the same pep talk to Rice?"

"Rice is no longer my problem. He's been transferred to data control and information security, permanently. Orders came down from the Director."

"I love management."

"So what will it be, Cutler? Are you gonna do the right thing for once and stop being a pain in my ass?"

Cutler spun in his chair. "I'd really hate to leave this here comfy security booth, but I've got to tell you the truth, Deavers."

"What's that?"

"You had me at 'son of a bitch.' And I do love to wear those spiffy Kevlar battle suits."

○———————○

AFTER her examination, Carol Hines hurried back to her cramped quarters in the section of the complex known as the Hive.

By the time she'd reached her room, her heart was racing. She didn't calm down until she'd locked the door behind her and curled up on her bunk.

I certainly handled that badly, she thought. *I'm sure Dr. Hendry is a capable enough physician to know that my scar isn't from a simple appendectomy.*

She tore off her smock but tossed it in the corner, then stood before the mirror, examining her wounds—new and old.

I do everything I possibly can to forget my past, and my own body betrays me. It's like a map that leads perfect strangers to long-buried nightmares.

She covered her ears in a vain attempt to shut out the voices in her head that had been echoing for years.

"Your medical history has revealed a… psychological malady that forces us to decline your application for top secret security clearance, and deny you a position at the National Security Council. Very sorry, Ms. Hines…"

"Dear Ms. Hines: We regret to inform you that the National Aeronautics and Space Administration only considers applicants in top physical condition for astronaut training. Your prior condition forces us to remove you from consideration."

"Anyone who has attempted suicide—even in the turmoil of early adolescence—probably won't pass the stringent criteria of the United States Air Force Space Command..."

The fools. I never attempted suicide. I was young. Afraid. I only wanted to be rid of the... thing... in my womb. I never intended to harm myself... only it.

Yet her past dogged her for years, denied her opportunities within the research community. And when she finally did land a job at NASA, it was as a low-level training specialist, not the position she most coveted—astronaut.

It's not as if I didn't have the intelligence and the skills. I was an honors student by the time I was twelve. My father used to call me his "little scientist."

My father treated me special, too. Stopped beating me. Started to take an interest in my studies, my science projects.

Life became tolerable after I brought home that first science fair prize in third grade—almost idyllic, until... the accident, a few years later.

That's what my father called it. The accident. Like it was nobody's fault. Like it just happened—sort of like a storm, or an earthquake.

But if it was an accident, why did I blame myself?

In spite of her resolve, Carol felt a wetness on her cheeks. She wiped her eyes with the palms of her hands and buried her head in her pillow. As she slipped into a troubled sleep, she thought she heard the voice of her long-dead mother...

"Your father is going to be so proud," Mrs. Hines said. She held a report card in one hand, her third drink of the day in the other. "My goodness. Only fourteen and already a whiz in advanced chemistry."

If my mother wasn't already half-tanked, she might have noticed that I was as pale as snow. But Mom only concentrated on the slip of paper.

"Can I go to the garage now?" Carol asked.

"Not until you get out of your school uniform, young lady—you just about burned the color out of your last smock with those chemical experiments of yours."

"Yes, Mother."

Upstairs, Carol stripped away her clothes and studied her reflection in the mirror. She imagined that her belly already protruded—her mother had even remarked at breakfast that she seemed to be gaining weight.

A neat trick for someone who throws up practically every morning...

It wasn't as if she was too young to know what was happening to her body. Even if she didn't grasp the truth at first, Carol Hines was an honors student and knew how to do research. As soon as she suspected the truth, she went to the library and took out every book she could find on the subject.

She knew every aspect of the biological process she was going through. And more, so much more, too, because "Daddy's little scientist" had studied heredity. She found out that if the parents were a near genetic match, if the bloodlines were too closely related—cousins, perhaps—then there was a much higher probability of genetic abnormalities and inherited diseases. Cystic fibrosis. Down's syndrome. Friedreich's ataxia. Hemolytic anemia. Hemophilia.

The thought of having a disabled child horrified her. *How could Daddy's special little girl give birth to something that was malformed? Defective? Imperfect?*

Daddy loved perfection—didn't he tell her that himself? The night he was drinking while helping her with her homework. The night she sat too close to him. He always told her to keep her distance, but that night she felt her father's perverse love...

She carried a monster in her belly.

So before her father came home, before supper with the family, Carol Hines went down to the garage and mixed up something special with her junior chemistry set.

"Do what you oughta, add acid to water," her father used to say with a big laugh.

That night, in the garage, she mixed the acid but dispensed with the water. Instead, she used the corrosive on herself in a desperate, misguided attempt to burn the abomination she carried out of her womb...

A buzzing inside her head—the intercom—made Carol Hines bolt upright in her bunk.

"Hines here."

"Ah, so you *are* at home," Dr. MacKenzie said jovially.

"I went to see Dr. Hendry. And I felt a bit tired after... after what happened this morning."

"Understandable," MacKenzie replied. "Unfortunately, we have need of your skills. Subject X is thoroughly sedated, but the drugs are quickly wearing off. Dr. Cornelius has attempted an interface with that machine of yours, but he does not have your deft touch."

"Problem?"

"We're getting those pesky brain spikes again. And with all that happened today… well, you see our dilemma."

"I'll be right there. Over."

More responsibility… But I never, ever wanted to be in charge. Just do my job, keep my head down, so it won't get cut off.

She rose and dressed in one of her array of identical green smocks. Without glancing into the mirror, she left her quarters and followed the maze of corridors that led to Logan's cell.

A maze… this place is becoming another maze, just like NASA. The Professor promised me a place where pure scientific pursuit was the goal; a place free of judgment, petty bureaucratic politics.

But it was all lies.

Already the bureaucratic infighting has started, and Dr. Hendry is snooping into my past—no doubt in search of ammunition he can use to destroy my career, destroy me.

I wonder. Have I traded one maze for another?

Carol Hines felt lost.

11

PREY

"**I** count two four-wheeled APCs and a big job—looks like a knockoff of a Soviet BTR-60. Eight wheels, searchlight on top, maybe six men inside with a driver. You can count on a dozen soldiers coming right for us."

Logan crawled back into the drainage ditch and handed Miko the night-vision binoculars. Behind them, the sound of beating blades echoed off the hillsides as twin helicopters with searchlights scoured the valley.

"We can't go backward, either. It's only a matter of time before those 'copter jockeys figure out I've made it to the road. They'll hunt us like a pack of wolves."

"So we are trapped."

"*I'm* trapped," said Logan. "I'm betting they don't even know you're here."

In the moonlight, he saw her frown.

"Why do you say that?" she asked.

"Because all the leaks are coming from my end. You knew about the mission. Why not the Koreans?"

She couldn't argue with Logan's logic, so Miko didn't try. "What do you have in mind?"

"Can you find that clearing in the foothills where we rested?"

"*Hai*, easily."

"Meet me back there in two hours."

"But what about the helicopters? Surely they will be searching the hills as well as the road."

"They won't be looking for me by then."

Miko shook her head. "You are not thinking of surrender?"

Logan laughed. "No way. I'm not crazy. I've got a better idea. I'm going to let them kill me."

She blinked. "Are you insane?"

"I don't like this any better than you. I've been shot before—didn't much care for the feeling. But this is the only way out that I can see—for both of us."

Realization dawned on Miko's face. "This is wrong. You could really die."

"You saw the way I recovered from that fall down the hill. I can heal, faster than any... human."

"But machine guns, bayonets... won't they finish you off or capture you if they find you are alive?"

"They won't get near me. I'll show my face, let them pop off some shots, then I'll tumble into the lake. If they're still looking for me tomorrow, they'll be dragging the pond, not scouring the hills, where we'll be safe."

"And after we rendezvous?"

"Face facts. No matter what, the mission is over—"

She tried to object, but he cut her off.

"—because we lost the element of surprise. They're going to double security. Triple it. And it's worse if they managed to grab Langram. They'll beat or drug the truth out of him in a couple of hours, so the extraction plan is compromised. If that happens, we'll both have to take your ride out of here."

Miko's face was grim. "Can we not stay together?"

"And risk both our lives?" Logan shook his head. "This is a much better plan."

He peeked over the edge of the trench. "They're less than a minute away. Get down into the ditch and crawl on your belly until you can make a clean break for the tree line."

He turned away to watch the road.

"Logan... I—"

"You got something to say?"

"Good luck," Miko whispered. Then she was gone among the tall grass. The rustling sound of her retreat was soon drowned out by the noise of the vehicles bumping along the rough road.

As Logan scrambled up the side of the trench, he freed the G36 strapped to his leg. A man seated in the top hatch was playing the searchlight in the ditch ahead of him. Logan carefully averted his eyes to retain his night vision. When the searchlight stabbed upward, into the tree line, Logan noticed a glint of moonlight off glass, and smiled. The BTR's armored windshield visors were up, the bullet resistant windows exposed. He quickly switched magazines.

These guys seem pretty cocky. But a Teflon-tipped titanium shell should ruin their day—and punch a huge hole right through that windshield.

As the eight-wheel personnel carrier rumbled closer, Logan suddenly lost his nerve. His heart palpitated, he broke out in a cold sweat, and doubt flooded his mind. When he threw the safety, his hands seemed unsteady enough to spoil his aim. Logan felt short of breath as he beat back rising panic. For the first time in a month, he had the urge to drink himself into a stupor, to sink back into a bottle, where he'd lived for far too many years.

Beat back the fear. Swallow it. You can take a bullet, you can live with the pain, Logan told himself.

But another part of him wanted to turn tail and run like a rabbit, to dive back into the ditch and crawl away from this place on his belly.

He started to rationalize his thoughts. *It's not fear, it's what you do with it. No matter what, I'm in control of the situation and I'm not running.*

That thought seemed to calm him, and Logan took several slow, deep breaths as the BTR rolled within range. When he glanced down at his hands again, they were as steady as a statue's.

Now the ten-ton personnel carrier was close enough to shake the ground under his feet. Logan saw that it had raced a little too far ahead of the other two vehicles—a break for him. Logan rose out of the ditch and stepped into the middle of the road.

The man in the top hatch was busy scanning the woods to the side, so it was the driver who spotted Logan first. The vehicle slowed, and its driver barked something to his comrade in the hatch.

Logan stood, left hand raised in mock surrender, right hand hanging at his side, the G36 tucked behind his leg. He slouched his right shoulder, hoping they'd think he was injured. The man in the top hatch swiveled the searchlight to frame Logan in its beam.

Bad idea. You die first.

Logan's arm shot up and the G36 coughed. The titanium shell exploded the searchlight into a shower of glass and fiery sparks. The man behind the light flew out of the hatch the instant the nearly expended shell caught him under the chin. His entire head disappeared in a shower of blood and fractured skull pieces. The headless corpse dropped onto the back of the BTR like a bag of dirt.

Logan could see the pale, frightened face of the Korean behind the wheel, illuminated by the dashboard light.

Now you.

Arm outstretched, Logan pumped off a second shot. The windshield splintered into a spiderweb, splashed dark crimson.

Suddenly, the BTR lurched forward as the driver's dying spasm punched the gas pedal. Eight tires squealed and dug into the dirt as the vehicle shot forward, an electrical fire streaming from the broken light on top.

Logan hesitated for a fatal instant and the armored frontal plate struck him full on, lifting him off his feet and tossing him halfway through the now-shattered windshield. As two Korean soldiers tumbled out of the rear hatch, the BTR-60 lurched off the road, bumped down a sharp incline and over a low cliff. Engine running, wheels turning, the vehicle hit the lake with an enormous splash.

o———————o

CUTLER doused cold water on his pallid face. Cheeks stinging, he wiped away the last traces of shaving cream and studied his reflection. With his index finger he traced the scar that divided one eyebrow with a faint white line—the result of his scuffle with Logan the night he, Erdman, and Hill snatched the man.

Seems like a lifetime ago.

Time, Cutler knew, passed slowly in lockdown.

The last six weeks seem to have stretched time to the point that I can't remember when I wasn't living in this Hive, doing this same rotten job day in and day out.

He pulled a comb through his damp, sandy hair—noticing for the first time a touch of white at the temples. He turned away from the bathroom mirror and reached for his uniform. A piece of paper fell out of the pocket and drifted to the ground. Cutler picked it up and read it.

MEMO FROM THE DIRECTOR TO ALL PERSONNEL
RE: Security Measures

DUE TO SECURITY CONCERNS AND SEVERAL DANGEROUS EXPERIMENTS THAT WILL SOON BE CONDUCTED INSIDE

THE ABOVEGROUND FACILITIES, ALL PERSONNEL ARE TO MOVE TO QUARTERS ON LEVELS TWO AND THREE OF THE UNDERGROUND COMPLEX, EFFECTIVE IMMEDIATELY. PLEASE BE ADVISED THAT YOU HAVE TWENTY-FOUR HOURS TO PACK AND PREPARE FOR THE MOVE. SEE YOUR DORMITORY SUPERVISOR FOR SPECIFIC ROOM ASSIGNMENTS.

That memo was dated four weeks ago. Twenty-eight days ago... six hundred and seventy-two hours ago...

Except that down here there's no day, no night, no sense of time passing. And everyone is living this way, now that the aboveground facilities are completely deserted.

I don't think I've seen the sun, except on guard detail, for almost a month. But at least I can get out once in awhile. Not like the docs, the technicians.

For the last fifteen days, double duty had become the norm, with all researchers working double shifts, technicians a sixty-five-hour week. Tension was running high, and Cutler's security teams had to break up two fights in the cafeteria in just the last five days.

And yesterday that shrink MacKenzie warned me that sleep disorders were becoming more common because of sun deprivation.

Cutler wondered how much longer the lockdown could continue until there was a breakdown of discipline—or an open revolt.

His gloomy thoughts ended when he heard the intercom.

"Cutler. It's Deavers. My office. Ten minutes."

"Roger tha—" The line was already dead.

He dressed, locked his quarters, and headed to the elevator. On the way, he noted that the recessed lighting on much of his level had failed—the third time in a month. It should have been fixed, but the maintenance staff was overtaxed, so they claimed.

Or maybe they're on an unofficial strike since that incident at the beginning of the week. Either way, I'm going to have to kick some butt to get this place in shape.

Cutler entered the elevator and rode up to Level One with Carol Hines. She held her straight brown hair back with one hand while holding a PDA in the other. Her face was pinched in a frown of concentration that consumed her, and she never looked up from the illuminated dial for the entire ascent. When the doors opened, she bolted for the diagnostic lab.

He headed in the opposite direction, to Major Deavers's office.

Cutler entered without knocking. Deavers gave him a lemon-sucking look.

"The eggheads want the wolves this morning. I've alerted the handlers and they're ready. Now I've alerted you."

"What do they want us for?"

"You're in charge of Subject X. Two-man team, with a third for backup. Tranquilizers only. No live ammo."

"I'll go myself, and take Franks. He's learned the ropes, he knows how to obey orders, and he can keep a cool head, usually. I'll bring Lynch for backup."

"What about Anderson? Erdman?"

"Erdman's off duty, and has earned the rest. Anderson's been real sloppy lately. Almost got himself cut to pieces by a perimeter laser he 'forgot' to deactivate before he headed outside for guard duty."

Deavers frowned. "Anderson was sharp enough to stop that escape attempt on Monday. The Director would've had our heads if there'd been a breach of security."

"Anderson got lucky. Or maybe he was just pissed off because he didn't get a cut of the bribe."

"How stupid do those guys in maintenance think we are?" Deavers asked. "Trying to buy their way aboard the supply chopper. As if we wouldn't notice…"

"They weren't thinking straight. Cabin fever. This lockdown has been tough on everyone. I'm surprised there hasn't been more trouble."

"Especially since we're short of experienced security personnel. We've got fifty-five armed guards in this facility—you'd think more than eight of them would learn how to handle the subject."

"For the record, we're down to seven who can do that. Hill's gone, remember?" said Cutler. "Let's face facts, sir. The rest of the guards, they just don't want to learn. Logan—Subject X—has them all spooked."

"Can you blame them?" said Deavers. "He gives me the creeps. With those wires and machines coming out of his head. That thing over his eye, the battery around his neck. He looks like the walking dead, like some kind of a robot zombie…"

LOGAN thought he was dead when the BTR smacked into him. The G36 flew out of his hand and clattered away, to be crushed under the tractor-sized front wheel. As eight tons lifted him off the ground, Logan was hurled through the cracked windshield by the momentum. Then the vehicle swerved off the road.

Torn and bloody from a dozen lacerations, Logan rolled inside the vehicle, to land in the lap of a headless man—the driver, his brains decorating the compartment. Vaguely, as if from a great distance, Logan heard cries of panic, then felt fresh air pimple his skin as someone opened a hatch.

Soon after, the heavy armored vehicle struck the lake. The jolt threw Logan against the dash just as a blast of water surged through the window. The torrent buffeted him as the compartment instantly flooded, but the frigid water stung Logan back to consciousness.

Battered by the mini-tsunami, Logan opened his mouth for a deep breath and gagged on water. He nearly passed out again—wanted to pass out, into the comforting warmth of oblivion—but he fought against the suicidal urge. He forced his eyes open and tried to orient himself. He got a little help from the vehicle's interior lighting, which had not yet shorted out. Though hindered by water that still gushed into the passenger bay of the fast-submerging vehicle, Logan knew he would get out.

While the BTR sank front-first, a booted foot connected with Logan's shoulder and he grabbed it. His captive carried him upward, and all the way out of the driver's compartment—into the rear of the armored carrier.

Suddenly, Logan's head broke the surface and he sucked air. Right next to him in the fast-flooding compartment, a Korean officer sputtered and choked as he treaded water. Logan recognized the other man's rank by the bugle draped over his right shoulder—the North Koreans still used bugles to issue commands in battle. When the man saw Logan, he shouted something incomprehensible and fumbled for the pistol on his belt.

I'll have to shut him up quick or he'll tell his pals that I'm still alive. Can't let him get away.

Logan grabbed the man by the throat and pushed him under. Already the water level inside the compartment had risen to the edge of the rear hatch. Soon Logan would have to get out or be sucked under with the BTR.

Outside, searchlights already played on the water, and Logan could hear the men on the road calling for their stricken comrades. Making a clean break was not going to be easy.

Meanwhile, the man struggled against Logan's grip. Still forcing the officer's head under the surface, he reached down with his right hand and yanked the Model 1 fighting knife from his belt. Logan stabbed out once, twice. After the third thrust, the Korean went limp in his grasp and Logan released the man.

The water bubbled up to his chin. Logan took a deep breath just as the tail end of the fighting vehicle slipped beneath the liquid darkness. He held on to the hatch, waiting until he was two or three meters under, then he kicked outward in an attempt to swim as far away as he could get from the sinking hulk before the undertow dragged him to his doom. Ultimately, Logan was able to clear the wreck and swim away.

He kept on swimming, just under the surface of the black water, until he could no longer withstand the lack of oxygen. As spots blotted his vision, Logan cut the surface and gulped air. A hundred meters away, he watched North Koreans scurry down to the shoreline to rescue their comrades.

Exhausted and relishing the air, Logan deduced that there was a current, because he was being carried slowly toward the dam. He lay on his back, floating, until the chattering voices faded, the glare of the searchlights dimmed, and even the beating of the helicopter blades was muted. Then he swam to the shore, crawled out of the water, and scrambled up the incline. Unnoticed by the soldiers, he crossed the road and ducked into the trees, then ran deeper into the woods until he reached the foothills. Finally, when he was sure he was not being pursued, Logan slumped down behind a tree to rest.

Gasping, he checked his condition. His second battle suit, like the flesh on his back, his thighs, and his torso, was in tatters. He'd probably left a trail of blood all the way up the hill, but hoped the North Koreans were too sloppy to notice. As he tore a chunk of material from his camouflage suit, Logan cursed.

That's the second set of duds I lost tonight. At this rate, I'll be butt naked by morning.

Suddenly, he felt like laughing.

Hell, at least I didn't get shot.

He checked his watch. Barely thirty minutes had passed since he parted company with Miko. He now had ninety minutes to circle around the mess on the road and climb the hill to meet her.

Groaning, seeping blood, and shivering from the wet and the cold, Logan stumbled to his feet and pressed on.

○————————○

FIFTEEN minutes after his meeting with Deavers, Cutler took Franks and Lynch to the surface, where they walked the ground that was going to be used for the morning "experiment."

The sun had just risen, a dull yellow ball over the mountains. And though it was cold and getting colder, Franks was as eager to get outside as Cutler. Lynch did nothing but complain because he'd been on duty all night and now he had another eight-hour shift because of the scheduled experiment.

The ground in question was a parcel of rolling, snow-covered land within the compound. A bevy of two- and three-year-old saplings and a few reedy pines dotted the topography. The entire area was encircled by double four-meter walls of chain-link fencing that would be electrified for the actual experiment. Already the technicians and sound men had set up remote cameras and microphones on steel posts planted deep into the frozen ground, high up in the trees, and on top of fence posts.

The trio circled the perimeter, double-checking to make sure there were no gaps in the fence where a wolf—or Subject X—could slip through and escape. Halfway around, they came to a tall, barred gate with multiple layers of steel fence beyond. From somewhere inside that prisonlike maze, they heard howls and angry snarls of a pack of timber wolves.

"What's got 'em so stirred up?" asked Lynch.

"We're downwind," Cutler replied. "They can smell our scent. It's driving them nuts."

"Geez," said Franks. "Why are they acting so aggressive? It's like they want to kill us or something. That pack sounds as if they're ready to rip us apart."

"They're starving," Cutler replied. "Maddened with hunger. Once they're out of those cages, they will drag down anything that moves, regardless of size."

"What the hell do those eggheads need starving wolves for?" Franks asked, shivering against the cold.

"They're going to put Subject X inside this fence, then let out the wolves and film the whole thing."

Franks whistled. "What's the point?"

Cutler shrugged. "Your guess is as good as mine," he said with disgust.

○————————○

MIKO burst from cover when she saw Logan struggling up the slope. She raced to him and took his arm.

"Lean on me," she whispered, and he willingly slumped against her slight but strong frame.

They stumbled up the hill and into a crude shelter Miko fashioned from pine branches. Inside, she snapped a chemical glow stick and laid Logan down on a bed of moss and leaves.

Her face was full of concern in the dim light. "I feared you would never return," she said as she stripped off his clothing and cleansed his wounds for the second time that night.

"Told you… I could take it," he wheezed, choking back a dry cough. Her cool hands felt soothing, but soon Logan began to shiver.

"Here, drink this," she said, thrusting a warm flask into his hand. He gulped the hot tea gratefully.

"Nifty device," he said, admiring the flask's battery-operated heating element. "You're just a bundle of tricks."

She smiled. "Unfortunately, the tea is instant."

"Never tasted better in my life."

After a few minutes, Logan felt revived. He propped himself on his elbows. Miko lurked at the entrance to the makeshift hut, NV binoculars to her eyes.

"What do you see?"

"Nothing. No one suspects that we are here. The soldiers are convinced that you died in the lake. They pulled several of their comrades out of the water—dead and alive. From what I could understand, some of their men are still missing."

"Lost my Heckler & Koch."

"Yes. One of the soldiers found the remains of your weapon on the road. He took it with him when they left."

"And Langram? Did you see anything or anyone on the other side of the lake?"

Miko lowered the binoculars and faced him. "They captured your friend. Soldiers brought him down from the hill. His arms were bound and they... mistreated him. He was placed inside an armored car and driven in the direction of the dam. I am sorry."

Logan was quiet a long time, his face grim. Finally, he spoke. "Maybe we can rescue him. We have a chance. They think I'm dead and they don't even know about you."

Miko's face was tense. "But even if we could find him in that complex and manage to free him, where can we go?"

"We evacuate with your team. Where are they picking you up? Is there a specific time, or do you have to summon an extraction?"

"I... I have no way out," she confessed. "I had planned to get out with you, after my own goal was accomplished."

"What are you, a kamikaze? Did your government send you on a suicide mission?"

"My government... my superiors... don't even know I am here. I took on this mission by myself. For personal reasons."

To her surprise, Logan threw back his head and laughed until he was wracked by a coughing spell.

"Are you all right?" Miko asked, springing to his side.

"Swallowed a little too much of that lake," he said, feeling a pleasing warmth creep through him as she stroked his head. As drowsiness began to claim him, Logan chuckled softly.

"A renegade, just like me, huh? Shoulda guessed."

Miko smiled down at him through a tumble of hair. "Mr. Logan, you do not know the half of it."

"If I felt better, I'd make you tell me the whole story... but right now... I'm too damn tired."

"Then sleep, Logan-*san*. You need rest. You are only human."

As Logan's eyes closed, he whispered a reply. "Only human? I wish, Miko... I wish."

○────────────○

THOUGH the sun had risen, the surface temperature had dropped precipitously since their trip outside at dawn. Despite clear skies, a frigid

Arctic wind howled down from the north. Right now it was a few notches below zero degrees Celsius, and dropping steadily.

Swathed in several layers of undergarments, his uniform, and a cocoon of Kevlar body armor, Cutler still shivered against the cold. Blasts of chilly air blew under his helmet so that his breath turned to vapor. And even though it offered no protection from the cold, Cutler didn't dare remove his helmet. The danger was too great.

With a long electronic staff, forked on one end and attached to a battery pack on the other, Cutler carefully directed Subject X across the snow-covered expanse to the middle of the fenced-off perimeter. The electroprod—dubbed a "pitchfork" by the handlers—deadened Logan's senses yet allowed him to be led about on his own two feet. "Like walking the dog on a leash," Lynch quipped as they prepped for the experiment.

Cutler wasn't sure what the docs had done to Logan in the past six weeks or so. He didn't look brainwashed—more like brain-dead. He figured Logan's senses must be numb or the cold would be getting to him, because the "subject" was stark naked in the snow, covered only with Teflon "sensor ports" embedded in his chest, neck, arms, and torso, where surgical probes had been inserted.

As Cutler led Logan to the designated area, Lynch and Franks followed a few steps behind, ready to take the subject down with tranquilizer guns at the first sign of rebellion. But Logan remained docile, his bare feet shuffling zombielike through the snow, dragging dozens of wires and tubes in his wake like shackles on a felon.

"Right here," said Lynch, digging his booted foot into a mound of snow stained with blue dye.

"Where are the goddamn techs?" Cutler demanded. "Logan still has to be hooked up."

"Here they come," said Franks.

Two technicians, bundled in ill-fitting Kevlar body suits and dragging too much equipment, set to work as soon as they arrived. They began by hooking the loose wires to a computer terminal buried in the snow at Logan's feet.

"What's that?" asked Franks.

The man kneeling at Logan's feet looked up. "This box is a wireless link to the computers in the lab, including the REM device. These feeder cables will keep our boy docile until the docs decide it's time to turn him loose."

"Yeah, when these wires get unplugged—watch out," warned the other technician.

"Seen him in action yet?" Cutler asked.

"Just heard rumors," the tech on the ground replied as he tested a circuit.

"I've seen him in action," said Franks. "And I plan to be long gone when they unleash him."

"Hey, Dooley," said the man in the snow. "This wrangler's seen Subject X in action."

Franks turned red. The man called Dooley turned and thrust a pocket-sized computer into the agent's hand.

"What's this?"

"The feeder cable release control. When Doc Cornelius gives you the word, you press this button and the monster is loose."

"Man, why me?" Franks asked.

"You're a wrangler, ain't you?"

Meanwhile, the technician activated the wireless box at Logan's feet, then entered a code into the keypad on top.

"Okay, Agent Cutler," he said, rising. "Remove the electroprod, then move back to the shelter."

With trepidation, Cutler deactivated the staff and detached the twin prongs from the magnetic locks embedded in Logan's temples. To his relief, Logan acted the same as he had throughout the entire process. From the moment they came above ground to the time they hooked him up to the box, Subject X didn't even blink, just stared straight ahead, eyes unseeing.

The security team backed away from Subject X, tranquilizer guns held ready. At sixty meters they turned and bolted for the concrete surface shelter near the wolf cages. They would wait in that compact bunker cluttered with communications equipment until their services were required again.

The technicians joined them a few minutes later—after all the connections had been tested, the cameras and sound systems activated, and Logan subjected to a final stage of "preparation." The techs stripped off their gear and took their places at the communications console. Cutler and Franks grabbed some coffee from a flask and peered at Subject X through a narrow slit. Franks held the feeder cable control like it was a bomb he'd prefer to get rid of. Lynch, uninterested, curled up on a bench and took a nap.

Outside, the subject stood stock-still, legs braced, up to his calves in thirty centimeters of powdery snow. A brisk wind stirred Logan's hair, and carried the scent of warm blood to the wolf cages.

Almost immediately, the animals howled in anticipation as they moved around in a frenzy, hollow-eyed with feral hunger.

○————————○

"AMAZING work, Dr. Hendry!" exclaimed Dr. Cornelius. "Subject X has increased his muscle mass by a third and lost more than a third of his body fat in just under six weeks. Your chemical treatments are nothing short of miraculous."

Dr. Hendry waved Cornelius's compliment aside and grinned. "It was a thorny problem, but all it took was a fresh approach to figure out a solution."

They stood in the main lab, near a buffet table laden with a continental-style breakfast. Two dozen doctors, researchers, and technicians had worked through the night to prepare for this day's critical experiment. It was Dr. MacKenzie who took it upon himself to arrange for breakfast to be delivered by the cafeteria at dawn.

Carol Hines sat near the two doctors, a cup of tea cooling at her side. She paid no attention to their conversation as she ran down the complex programming checklist in her lap.

"I'm surprised you didn't use steroids," Cornelius said between bites of cheese Danish.

"No, no. Steroids are quite unsuitable. The results of steroid use are temporary, and there are far too many harmful side effects."

"So how did you solve the problem?"

"Once the researchers at Johns Hopkins University determined that the protein myostatin limits muscle growth in humans, it was fairly simple for me to devise a specific enzyme to block that protein, allowing Subject X to bulk up in record time."

Cornelius looked forlornly at his own belly, which protruded over his belt. "Man, you've got to let me try that stuff, Doctor."

"Good morning," the Professor announced as he entered the crowded lab. Dr. Cornelius turned, a Styrofoam cup of hot coffee in one hand.

Hines looked up from her chart as the Professor crossed to their side.

The Professor directed his first query to Ms. Hines. "So this may be the big day, eh?"

"We're hoping so, sir," she replied.

"Good, good…" He turned. "Dr. Cornelius. Do you have anything for me to review?"

Cornelius gulped down the last of his Danish. "Well, we believe we've overcome the supraendocrine gland problem."

The Professor was impressed. "How so?"

"A simple trabeculae matrix," Dr. Hendry interrupted. "It was staring us in the face the whole time."

"But you've got it now," said the Professor.

"We believe so, sir," Cornelius replied. Not an endocrinologist, he was taking his cue from Dr. Hendry.

"Excellent work," said the Professor. "Have you released all of Logan's feeder cables?"

"Not yet, sir."

"Then do it now, Dr. Cornelius. Let the experiment begin."

Cornelius nodded, then faced the rest of the staff. "Everyone to your places," he commanded. "Experiment two of six to commence in two minutes."

Hines took her seat at the REM workstation and unlocked the controls of the device. Her face was placid as she faced them. "I'm ready."

"Biomonitors ready," said Dr. Hendry.

"CAT scan ready!" called Dr. MacKenzie, his red hair wild and uncombed.

"Cameras ready… audio ready," crackled voices speaking from the communications bunker on the surface.

Cornelius leaned over his terminal and keyed his mike. "Wranglers, release all cables and reel them in."

"Copy, sir," Franks replied.

On the wall-sized HDTV screen appeared the image of Logan, immovable in the center of the snowy expanse as the feeder cables dropped from his chiseled body.

The Professor, eyes locked on the screen, sat down behind the central terminal and licked his lips.

"Now, Dr. Cornelius. Show me what Weapon X can do."

12

PREDATOR

"**THREE...** two... one. Set. This is Experiment Two of Six. Defense."

Dr. Cornelius paused to scan the lab. "Everything check? Cameras? Monitors?"

"Fine," said Hendry. Other voices muttered affirmatives.

"Dr. Cornelius."

"Yes, Professor."

"Mr. Logan—"

"Subject X," Dr. MacKenzie corrected. "He no longer has a name."

"Subject X seems to be covered in ichor."

"Sheep's blood, sir," Cornelius explained. "Quicker scent. We want the wolves to act aggressively."

"I see." The Professor's eyebrows rose. "Ingenious. Lovely."

For many minutes, the figure stood like a monolith in the vast frozen expanse. Carol Hines found herself listening to the sound of the wind transmitted by the speakers, drawn to the image of Subject X on the screen. More minutes passed, filled with the sounds of ticking monitors, hushed voices. The howl of the wind was joined by the howl of the wolves.

While technicians calibrated their instruments, Cornelius helped himself to a third cup of coffee. Time seemed suspended as more checks and rechecks were carried out.

Finally, Carol Hines spoke. "He's been out there in subzero weather for more than twenty minutes. Can't we get on with this?"

Cornelius lowered his cup without tasting it. "We are following procedures, Ms. Hines."

Over the speaker, the cries of the hungry wolves intensified.

"Readings, Dr. Hendry?"

"Heartbeat, pressure, all okay."

"Maybe we should have him do some stretches, loosen up. Cold muscles can get pretty stiff," the physical therapist suggested.

"Not his muscles," Hendry replied. "They are conditioned to perform at the optimum level despite cold or long periods of immobility."

Over the blaring speakers, wet snarls mixed with angry barks. The animals were getting impatient, lashing out at one another in their zeal for fresh kill.

"He can hear them?" asked Cornelius.

"Yes, sir. I'm sure of it," said the audio technician, speaking from the bunker outside. The voice link was crystal clear. "We can hear the wolves behind a half foot of concrete without the sound system. If Subject X can't hear them, he's deaf."

"Yet there is no adrenal rise... odd," muttered Cornelius.

"Not odd at all," declared the Professor, eyes bright with anticipation. "It means that your reprogramming has worked, Dr. Cornelius. Weapon X feels no fear."

Cornelius gazed at his screen. "Prepare to release the gate."

"Roger," said the voice of an animal handler positioned inside the animal control compound on the surface.

"When did the animals last eat?" the Professor asked.

Cornelius shrugged. "Don't know. Handlers?"

"Copy," the animal handler replied. "Chart says about six days ago, sir."

"Well, gee, they can have my Danish."

The voice came from the status tech station, followed by some laughter. The Professor turned in his chair and glared at the offender.

"Release the gate," said Cornelius.

The visuals were split between two cameras. On the big screen, the laboratory staff simultaneously watched the wolves bursting through the open gate and Logan standing rigid in the snow.

"He's not reacting."

"Give him a chance, Cornelius."

"I mean there's no blood pressure rise, no increase in heart rate."

The timber wolves scrambled across the snowy field, paws churning up great gouts of snow. The alpha male leaped ahead of the pack, a one-hundred-seventy-pound, red-brown brute with a long, foam-flecked snout and a lolling tongue. Scrawny from lack of food, the wolf's wiry muscles rippled under its ruddy fur.

"God, he's not moving," whispered one of the techs.

"Is he alive?" the Professor demanded.

"Yes, of course!" Cornelius cried.

"But he's not moving."

"Good God..." Carol Hines averted her eyes.

As the wolves surged ahead, the camera switched back to single screen—the animals were so close to the subject that they were both in the same shot.

The Professor's face was grim. He focused his harsh glare on Dr. Cornelius. "Do you have data for me?"

Cornelius, eyes on the screen, shook his head in bafflement. "He's just... not reacting."

"Blast!" The Professor jumped up from his chair and approached the screen. "Is it a physical disability?" he asked. "The claws, perhaps?"

"No, I doubt that." Cornelius faced Dr. Hendry for validation, but the other seemed to be too busy to notice.

"If his claws function, then why doesn't he use them, Doctor?" asked the Professor.

The wrangler cried out, "They'll rip him to pieces!"

At last, Hendry looked up, to meet Cornelius's desperate eyes. "He won't be able to heal if he's torn to bloody chunks," said Hendry.

Cornelius spun around to see Carol Hines's face turned away from the monitor. "Hines, do your job!" She turned back to the monitor, fingers poised over the keyboard, her face red.

"Up the response column now!" Cornelius commanded.

Carol Hines programmed the new data into the transmitter, hit the send key, then watched the screen.

Somewhere in Logan's deadened brain, a switch dropped—a chemical rush that kick-started a slumbering portion of his mind. A burst of electrochemical activity in the left prefrontal cortex stimulated Logan's aggression, and a glimmer of awareness flickered behind his unblinking stare. The spark lasted a split second—long enough for Subject X to hear, see, smell, and comprehend the danger.

But the wolves were already on him. The alpha leaped off the snow and slammed into the mutant and the others surrounded him. Jaws clamped on legs, on arms, dragging Logan to the ground...

───○────────────────○───

SLAVERING, *snapping jaws. Hot, foul breath. Teeth digging, tearing, ripping. Vicious.*

Logan swam through a sea of nightmarish images and woke up fighting—arms waving blindly as he fended off phantom predators. With a cry he sat up in a bed of leaves and moss. He opened his eyes to blinding sunlight, until the appearance of a silhouette dimmed the bright glare.

"Who—"

Two fingers gently covered his lips. "Hush, Logan. You are safe," a quiet voice soothed.

"Miko?"

"*Hai.*"

Logan blinked. "Must have been dreaming," he muttered, the terrible images fading like wisps of morning fog.

She stared at him, her expression curious.

"Do I look that bad in the morning?" he growled, looking away.

"Not at all. You look perfectly fine. And there is the mystery."

"Yeah, well…"

"You fell into a deep sleep. I thought you had gone into shock. Then I thought you were dead," she said, her tone muted. "But as I watched you in the morning light, I observed that gaping wound on your chest."

With the tip of her index finger, Miko gently touched a spot between his pectorals. "Open and bleeding last night. Healed by morning. Now not even a scar."

He stared straight ahead; she settled on the ground next to him. "Anyone else would be dead."

"I'm not like anyone else."

She waited, silent. Finally, he spoke. "Have you ever heard of mutants, Miko?"

"*Hai.* But to be truthful, I never thought mutants were real. Just a superstition, like moving things with your mind, or EPS—"

"You mean ESP. Extrasensory perception."

She nodded.

"Well, mutants are real. I know because I'm a mutant. I found out—

never mind how—just a couple of years ago. Knowing changed me, but not for the better."

"Yet your abilities? Surely you've had them for a long time?"

He faced her. "I always knew I was different, even as a kid. People treated me differently, too. Like they knew there was something unnatural about me."

"Alienation. Everyone feels that way when they are young."

"But I'm not young, Miko. If I told you how old I am, you wouldn't believe me. Don't you see? There was something different about me. I never got sick like other people, wounds healed quickly. But it wasn't until I went to war that I found out how different I really was…"

"You are immune to disease and do not age at all. How is this a problem?"

"It's a problem. Watching someone you love grow old and suffer and die while you remain forever young… Yeah, that's a problem—"

She winced at the comparison. "I see. Like watching a parent die?" she whispered.

"Yes. Like a parent. Only it's your lovers, too. And even your children, if you had any…"

He pressed his fists to his temples and closed his eyes. "And I don't even know why I'm different. I was trouble for everyone around me since the day I was born. I don't deserve this 'gift.' Why me?"

"When there is no answer to a question, why ask?" Miko replied. "But now I understand."

"Do you? Can you?" he shot back. "I've lived in Japan. I am familiar with your language, your society, your ways. The Japanese stake a lot on conformity. In your world, I would be even more of a misfit. Someone like you could never understand that."

Miko shook her head. "Do not be so sure, Logan-*san*. I also know what it is like to be an outsider."

"What, you flunked third grade?"

"Have you ever heard of comfort women?" she asked.

"Like prostitutes?"

"Not prostitutes, Logan. Slaves to their Japanese masters. In World War Two, soldiers took thousands of women from their homes and used them. My grandmother was a comfort woman, taken from her farm in Korea by a high-ranking officer, brought to Tokyo to be his mistress. My mother was their child."

As Miko spoke, she played with a ring on her middle finger. "After the war, the Koreans did not want these women back because they were considered defiled. Many had borne half-Japanese children. Such children are shunned in both countries, as are their descendants, even today, in these enlightened times."

The sound of a passing jet fighter high overhead made them pause. The aircraft vanished as quickly as it appeared.

"You say you know Japanese society, Logan-*san*," Miko continued. "Do you know that mixed-race children are excluded from the best schools, no matter how talented or intelligent we may be? Did you know that we are relegated to the lowest positions in Japanese corporations—salaryman or secretary—never to rise higher?"

"So you ended up in civil service?" Logan asked

"Yes. The SAT accepted me because I was useful. I had skills they needed—I spoke Korean like a native, could pass for a Korean if necessary. Something I have done in past assignments."

"But you're not on assignment now?"

"No, Mr. Logan. I am here on my own, on personal business."

"And that personal business is inside that complex at the base of the dam?"

"*Hai.*"

"It's a sure bet Langram is there, too."

"Last night you said you were going to rescue your friend."

"I intend to go after Langram. It's such a stupid, suicidal move, the Koreans might just fall for it. You can come with me and finish your personal business as long as it doesn't interfere with mine. Or you can try to get out of North Korea on your own."

"I will come with you, Logan. When do we go?"

"Tonight, after it gets dark. It'll take us an hour to get past the dam, another two to get down the hill and inside."

"Until then?"

"We eat, Miko. Then we rest. It's gonna be a long night."

"You have an appetite?" Miko asked.

"Yeah. After one of those healing comas, I wake up hungry as a damn wolf."

"THEY'RE eating him alive!"

"I'm getting no response," cried Cornelius. He pushed Carol Hines out of the way and started banging on her console. "He should have been triggered. We've lost it."

On the screen, the wolves were a snarling, squirming mass swarming over the struggling mutant. Subject X fought back weakly as ripping claws and gnashing jaws closed on his unprotected belly and slashed at his throat.

Suddenly, Cornelius looked up from the REM console. "It's coming through. The epinephrine is rising…"

The Professor appeared at his shoulder. "Eighty-six… ninety percent… ninety-five…" The man clapped his hand on Cornelius's shoulder. "He's fighting back!"

A moan of agony blared from the speakers. On the screen, Logan's right forearm emerged from the sniveling, slavering pack. The groan became a frightful roar of rage and defiance. Suddenly, the wolves reared back, yelping, their muzzles flecked with blood, as three adamantium claws sprung from Logan's ravaged flesh.

"Listen to that feral roar. Gentlemen, we have succeeded!"

"I don't think that sound is bloodlust, Professor," Dr. Cornelius said. "I think it's pain."

A welter of blood poured from the claw extraction points, rolling down Logan's outstretched arms as he stumbled to his feet.

"Splendid." The Professor nodded his head, adjusted his square glasses. "It will make him all the more savage."

Over Logan's roar, the scientists heard a snarling whelp that made them wince. Logan burst from the middle of the barking curs. The alpha leaped at his throat. With an uppercut that impaled the animal and lifted it over his head, Logan slashed the wolf in half at the torso—severing its spine in a chopping gesture that neatly divided the howling creature.

Hot, steaming blood rained down on Logan, saturating his face, neck, torso. He ducked a leaping female and thrust his right arm back to pierce the skull of another male.

Carol Hines averted her eyes as Logan disemboweled a yelping she-wolf, then slammed its broken, writhing body against another. Though she avoided the image, Hines could not block out the gruesome sounds—barks, howls, grunts, whelps, and whimpers of animals suffering, dying…

"Readings, Cornelius," the Professor commanded.

"Heart rate just shot off the scale, Professor. And you don't want to know the high levels of adrenaline, epinephrine, serotonin. Phenomenal stress level. He could burn out."

"Is that likely?" the Professor asked, alarmed.

"I don't know," Cornelius answered truthfully. "The metabolics alone... it's beyond human. And the wounds he's already received..."

"Those wounds haven't slowed Logan yet," noted MacKenzie.

A half-dozen dead wolves sprawled on the ground. Others gasped their last frost-steamed breath. A few struggled in the slippery muck, dragging broken limbs, their entrails staining the snow yellow-brown-red.

Then a sustained howl pierced the air as Logan pinned the alpha female to the ground with the claws of his left hand while using his right to cut the flopping bitch to pieces. Blood and gouts of fur and flesh flew with each brutal swing, yet no mortal blow was struck. Logan was deliberately prolonging the creature's agony.

"He's far more bestial than those he's slaughtering," Cornelius observed.

The Professor was all smiles. "What a perfect choice Logan was," he declared with smug satisfaction. *And how foolish of me to doubt the Director.*

Carol Hines appeared behind them, her eyes fixed on the screen. "Professor, can't we stop it now? Save the animals that remain? It's just senseless slaughter."

The Professor was shocked by her suggestion. "I think not, madam. I am enjoying this far too much. Let the animals save themselves. Survival of the fiercest. It's nature's violent way."

"Professor, I've got a fluorescent analysis now, and a CAT scan," called Dr. Hendry. "Would you like to see them?"

"Just give me your results on the scan."

"Activity in the left prefrontal cortex—" began Dr. MacKenzie.

"Ah, I see—the part of the brain that seeks vengeance," the Professor interjected.

"You are correct, Professor," MacKenzie replied. "It's also the part of the brain that is active when people prepare to satisfy hunger, a craving. Hunger and the lust for revenge are hardwired—and appear to be related."

"And the fluorescent analysis?"

"On-screen," said Hendry.

A square section of the violent images on the screen froze, broke away, then filled the entire monitor—Logan's raised right arm, claws extended.

"Yes. Can you hold on that?" the Professor asked.

The screen went blank, then the same picture reappeared—but as an X-ray image. Logan's claws and adamantium bones silver-white; vessels, tendons, muscles a medley of muted grays.

"We need more detail," the Professor complained. "Give me a re-emission on the osteograph."

"One second," said Hendry's assistant.

The image morphed, then melted into a blur. "Bring it in to either hand," instructed the Professor.

Suddenly, the image of Logan's clawed right hand filled the screen, bones still silver-white, but nerves, veins, tendons all shaded a multitude of hues. The image was three-dimensional, and as they watched, Dr. Hendry shifted the perspective so they could view the anatomy in action from every conceivable angle.

"Look at that," the Professor cried. "The perfect synthesis of human trabeculae and adamantium. Bone, bonded to the hardest metal in the world, inside the body of a berserker."

The Professor stepped up to the screen as if he were about to embrace the image. "Logan. Weapon X. The perfect fighting machine. The perfect killing machine."

Dr. Hendry interrupted the Professor's revelry. "There is some excessive distortion in the metacarpals. That could be the cause of the subject's pain upon extrusion, as Dr. Cornelius suggested."

"How so?" It was Carol Hines who asked.

"The adamantium appendages seem to cause him discomfort as they activate," Hendry told her. "Some of it is undoubtedly due to the damage the adamantium prostheses cause to his own skin as the claws rip through, but he may also be experiencing a general ache, similar to a child who is teething."

The Professor faced Hendry. "You'll look into that?"

"Yes, Professor."

"Good. Then take us back to the battlefield."

With a beep the image vanished, to be replaced by the prerecorded scene in the bloody snow. The sound returned as well, though the howls and cries of the wolves had been silenced forever.

Logan stood, legs wide, in the center of the bloody tableau, arms outstretched and dripping hot gore.

"Program complete," Cornelius announced. "We seem to have gone through all our wolves."

Carol Hines turned away from the screen.

"A total massacre. Splendid. This exercise couldn't have gone better," said the Professor. "And look at Logan! I think he wants more. Do we have more?"

"No," said Ms. Hines.

"Pity…"

Then a long, continuous canine howl echoed throughout the lab; an alarming sound that sent shivers of superstitious dread down the spines of civilized, educated scientists and researchers. The cry was feral, animalistic—yet somehow ominously human.

Cornelius spun to face the Professor. "Good God. He's roaring like an animal."

"Ah! And you thought it was just pain that made him cry out, Cornelius— but no." The Professor stood, fist clenched in front of his face as he stared at Logan's image on the screen, listening to the sustained bestial bellow.

"The wolves would kill for food, or territory, perhaps," said the Professor, his voice rising in intensity. "But this mutant… this living weapon… his passion is the *fear* of his prey. He finds relish in the odor of blood. Fear is the key. Fear is his motivating factor."

The Professor's rant ended as did the mad howl. Instantly, the laboratory grew quiet.

The Professor turned to address them all.

"Despite his original protestations, his struggles against us, I know we've done Logan a great favor," the Professor declared. "His most bestial needs are about to exceed his most primitive dreams… In our service, of course."

He faced Cornelius. "You can turn him off now, Doctor."

Cornelius returned to his console as Carol Hines resumed her position behind the REM keyboard. They both prepped their systems for powering down.

On the screen, Logan dropped to his knees, where he swayed as the claws slid back into their sheaths. Then, without a sound, he toppled face-first into the bloody snow like a puppet whose strings had been severed.

Legs jerked like the spasms of the dead, and Logan flopped in the wolf guts and settled on his back.

"Wranglers?" Cornelius radioed.

"Copy," Cutler replied, his voice tense—an effect of the scene he'd just witnessed from the bunker.

"Bring Logan in."

Suddenly, the Professor stepped forward. "Please cancel that order, Cornelius."

Cornelius wondered why he had just been overridden. But he knew better than to question the Professor's command. *Better to take a diplomatic approach.* "Cancel…"

Then Cornelius turned. "I'm sorry, Professor," he began. "I thought we were done for the day."

"We are."

"Then?"

The Professor turned his back on the screen and walked to the exit. "Leave Logan out for the night," he called over his shoulder. "I like the idea of him resting in his own gore. He needs to become one with the guts of his glory."

"But it's fifteen degrees below Fahrenheit out there," Cornelius protested. The winter day was so short, the sun was already beginning to set behind the mountains.

"All the better. Toughen him up, eh?" The Professor paused at the door, then turned to face Cornelius again. "You can monitor his vital signs from here, can you not?"

"Yes, of course," Cornelius replied.

"Splendid. Then we've accomplished much this day. Good evening to you all."

○———————○

"YOU are now guests of the provisional military government. Though you are Western oppressors…"

The Professor heard the harsh voice. Authoritarian. Insistent. A barking horn of spartan bravado.

Don't bother me now. Too much to do to be sidetracked by ancient history.

He'd worked through the night, then all the next day. As night fell again, he'd returned to his technological lair to review unending loops of data. Sleep was an illusion, a distant oasis that provided no rest, no peace. Instead, he sat erect in his command chair, as he had for endless days.

"Once the interrogation is complete, you will both be released. Nothing will happen to you or your child as long as you... cooperate fully."

Annoyed, the Professor tossed his glasses onto the console. A road map of thin, red lines marked the whites of his eyes. He rubbed them with long-fingered hands.

I know I'm right...

Fear is the key.

Control Logan's fear and you control his aggression. Control his aggression and you control him. And then you have the perfect killing machine. The perfect defense...

"Do not fear for your boy... He will survive as long as you please us. I hear he is quite intelligent, your son. It would be a shame if something happened to him... to you both..."

Go away.

"Not until I've gotten what I want from your mother, boy. Not until she pleases me..."

The faces were around him again, circling like the wolves stalking Logan. Cruel. Feral. Savage. Mocking. And one face above all...

Colonel Otumo.

At eight, the Professor was small and wiry for his age. His father was a renowned epidemiologist, his mother the heiress of a Vancouver business empire. They'd journeyed to Africa to do good works, to help the impoverished, cure the sick.

Noble sentiments wasted on savages...

Father was somewhere in the jungle, inoculating tribesmen's children in remote tribal villages. He and his mother had remained in the capital city, a rude former colonial town built on the shore of a muddy African river. While his father was gone, a military coup had cast the West African nation into bloody chaos.

Pale, terrified, he hugged his mother's skirt that night. Trembling behind oversized glasses, watching tanks roll through dusty streets, soldiers beating back unarmed men and women. He heard shots, saw panic, smelled burning tires and the stench of fly-specked, bloated bodies rotting in the tropical heat.

When daylight came, so did martial law. Police and bureaucrats from the overthrown regime were captured and herded off to a sports stadium. Firing squads worked all day and through the next night.

That second night, the hotel's thin door bulged. The tromp of heavy boots on wooden floors, locks kicked through, servants and hotel workers beaten and shot. He'd run to his mother's room for safety. Colonel Otumo had already arrived with his officers.

Tall. Beige uniform. Crisp and pressed. A soldier.

Father had told him soldiers were like policemen—men to be trusted. Respected. Here to serve and protect.

"Where is your husband, the Western doctor?... That answer is not sufficient... What is your reason for coming to our country?... No, that is a lie. You represent the criminal interests of the North American colonial powers, no use denying it..."

At first, the men acted somewhat civil—Otumo most of all—Oxford-educated, well-spoken, he could discuss William Blake's poetry, British history, Marxist economics, or methods of torture with equal eloquence. But all too soon the polite conversation turned completely brutal.

An eight-year-old could barely understand the events unfolding. He knew the soldiers were cruel and loud, his mother sobbing and afraid.

As day turned to evening once again, the soldiers took his mother away. She kissed him and told him to be brave... that she would be back with him soon, and forever. He tried to follow, crying, screaming, but the other soldiers laughed and beat him down with their rifle butts.

After that, he lay on the floor, listening as, from another part of the hotel, his mother's sobs, her pleas, finally her screams, broke through the black night. Meanwhile, the soldiers... did things to him. Things he did not understand. They did things to his body that hurt so much he retreated into his mind until he was far away. In a vast desert, alone. What was happening to him couldn't be happening, and so he watched as if through a glass, or a camera, or another person's eyes.

Morning brought a blast of wind and beating blades. The helicopters descended from the high clouds in the African sky. Men in black-skinned suits carrying big guns blasted their way through the hotel. The guard sitting over him rose to flee but was shot through the eye. Then, for the second time in twenty-four hours, men burst into the room. A man picked him up off the floor.

"You're safe now, boy. Understand? Safe," he said in a thick British accent. The man pulled off his hood. "I'm a soldier, son. Here to rescue your mother and father. Do you know where they are?"

Dumbly, he pointed down the hall. The men moved through the building, shooting and knocking down doors.

"Oh God," someone choked. "She's in here."

"Mother!" he'd cried, hurling himself down the hall.

"Don't let him see her!"

But he was too determined—a small animal squeezing between giraffe legs—and he did see her, sprawled on the bed, before they picked him up and carried him away.

In the helicopter, he sat mute, listening to the British soldiers speaking over the command net.

"Why did they do that to her?" a soldier whispered when they thought he couldn't hear. "Why'd they cut off her—"

"Quiet! The boy," hissed the officer.

"But why, sir?"

"Colonel Otumo calls it tribal justice. When his troops attack a rival clan, they… mutilate the women that way. So they can never suckle their young or bear more children…"

"What's going to happen to the boy?"

"Found his father in the jungle. Be here later today. They're going back to Canada, I'd reckon… no point in staying here."

When he saw his father that day, he said nothing. When they flew back to Canada, he didn't speak. When he turned nine, his father sought help.

"Despite his terrible trauma, your son exhibits a phenomenal intellect. He's a perfect candidate for our school. He's brilliant, IQ among the top one percent, and he's at just the right age to absorb knowledge without effort."

"I only want the best for my son… he's been through so much."

"At our academy, your son will be surrounded by peers. Boys of a gentle, academic nature who'll understand his… intensity. The trauma he experienced."

So his father shipped him off to a boarding school, then married his nurse.

In school, he missed his mother, he drew pictures of soldiers, hung them by his bed like talismans to ward off evil, taped them to the ceiling above his head. He lay awake, telling himself that one day he would have his own soldier to protect him from all the bad things.

As he matured, his reserve increased. He stuttered. He felt afraid of everything. He exhibited violent tendencies.

His father found another boarding school, where he arrived at fourteen. But the new school was far less… accommodating.

"Big brain, stutter for us. Ca… ca… can you do th… th… that?"

My tormentors. The mocking Greek chorus that was my peers.

Finally, one of the older boys found him in an empty classroom and just touched him.

"My God. The police at Bedford Science Academy. Disgraceful," said Dean Stanton to his father.

"That poor boy. What did my son do to him?"

What did I do? I took the scalpel I was using to dissect a formaldehyde-drenched frog and hacked at his face, again and again. And when I was done, under all that blood, I saw what I'd done… what I wanted to do to Colonel Otumo's face.

"You understand, Doctor, that we have to cover this up. The school's reputation must not suffer."

"But the victim—"

"His father will understand. A graduate. School tradition and all. But we'll have to send your son away, perhaps to a school in Switzerland. In any case, he can never return to Bedford. We cannot let this incident mar our reputation."

"But what about the victim?"

"The family, of course, will demand a financial settlement. But I'm sure your wife's fortune—"

"My late wife's fortune."

"Indeed. Your fortune will surely cover the expense."

My education continued, unmolested. I had discovered the secret… the key to controlling humans.

Fear was the key.

With Weapon X, the ultimate soldier, the key is in my hands.

"I didn't like spending the whole goddamn night in this freezing bunker, that's for sure," Lynch said for about the hundredth time.

"Come on, Lynch, you're giving me a headache," said Franks, who was already suited up.

But Lynch wouldn't shut up. He just kept talking and scratching his growling stomach. "Figure it out, Cutler—triple duty—that's double-time-and-a-half for the last eight-hour shift. Can't wait to see Deavers's face when I put in that overtime requisition."

Cutler had done his best to ignore Lynch since dawn, but he was only human. "Don't spend it yet. We might be in here all day, and all night tonight, too. That means no breakfast and no lunch—and you without a bag of chips."

"Don't even say that. Don't even, Cutler." His voice went up an octave. Cutler had suspected that Lynch was suffering from cabin fever before they'd got trapped in the bunker. Now he was sure Lynch was losing it.

Can't blame him. Stuck in this bunker for twenty hours now, waiting for the eggheads to decide what to do.

"Don't get your underwear in a bunch over your beloved junk food, Lynch," said Cutler. "If you've got the munchies, you can always take your chances outside. Go on, walk right past him to the fence. Hell, Logan might not wake up."

Lynch slumped on the bench where he'd spent most of the night. "I may be hungry, but I ain't crazy, Cutler. That's your vocation."

Cutler turned his back on Lynch to stare through the narrow view slits. Logan had spent the night laying in the now frozen gore, wolf carcasses stiffening around him. For all he knew, Subject X was dead.

A blessing, after what I saw…

Cutler was still processing the senseless scene he'd witnessed the day before. He couldn't figure out how that butchery could have anything to do with research, with knowledge—with creating the perfect weapon.

It wasn't an experiment. It was more like an atrocity, a massacre. Blood sport, not science.

Franks looked up at Cutler, his youthful face curious. "Was he like that when you brought him in?"

"Who?"

Franks gestured with his chin. "Logan. Weapon X. Word is you and Erdman and another guy brought him in. That he was a wanted criminal or something—wasn't a volunteer at all."

Cutler saw no point in lying. "He was tough. Gave me this—" he pointed to the scar that cut his eyebrow in half and divided his forehead. "Guess I had it coming, though, seeing what they have done to him so far."

The intercom buzzed, and the communications console came to life. One of the technicians rose from the corner where he'd been curled up and kicked his friend. Yawning, they both crawled into their seats and flipped a few switches.

Lynch poked Franks. "This is it, kid. We're going home."

The intercom crackled to life. "Wranglers?"

"Cutler here."

"This is Cornelius. Bring him in."

Lynch slapped his knees and started to suit up. Franks and Cutler strapped on their helmets. Before they went out, Cutler tested the power on the electropod.

"Ready?" said Cutler at the hatch. Franks nodded, face grim. Lynch cradled the tranquilizer gun. "Let's go," he barked.

Cutler threw the latch and stepped outside. The cold hit him like a fist and the wind howled loudly—he hadn't noticed it was blowing from inside.

Franks came out next, and Lynch brought up the rear after he'd secured the hatch behind him. The technicians inside the bunker hardly seemed to notice they'd gone.

"Stay back about fifteen paces, Lynch. Franks and I will come up on either side."

"Roger that, sir."

The morning was overcast, the mountains shrouded in haze. As they crossed the snowy expanse, the hoarfrost crunched under their heavy boots.

"God, look at that," whispered Franks. He stared down at something red and bloody in the snow. Cutler refused to look. The wolves were all dead, their carcasses frozen solid. Solidified blood smooth as wine-colored glass and slippery under their feet. Franks slipped and Cutler shot him a look. "No sudden moves," he yelled.

But Cutler himself nearly jumped backward when he saw Logan's open eyes. They stared at the sky as if he were watching clouds. Franks and Cutler moved to surround him.

Cutler positioned the control prongs over the magnetic clamps in Logan's temples. Then he flicked the button. The magnets locked with a click loud enough to be heard above the howling wind.

With a gentle tug, like pulling the reins of a horse, Logan sat up, then rolled to his knees. Cutler brought the pole up and over his head stepping around the subject, per protocol.

When Logan finally stumbled to his feet, Franks moved in with the leash and clamped it around the mutant's throat. Logan didn't even blink. Still, as a precaution, Lynch aimed the tranquilizer gun at the small of his back.

Cutler gave Logan a push, which caused the mutant to lurch forward, shuffling stiffly toward the pen and the underground elevator beyond.

13

GOLEM

"DR. Cornelius, sir? Sorry to disturb you—"

The astonished technician stood with a stack of files in his hands, staring in muted shock at the patchwork man sprawled on a steel operating table.

"Huh? I can't hear you." Cornelius shook his head and tapped the mask-and-visor combination that muffled his hearing. The tech had found the doctor surrounded by several assistants, stooped over Logan, Cornelius's face inches from the subject's.

"I said I'm sorry to disturb you," the tech repeated, speaking loudly. "Dr. Hendry wants you to have the results of yesterday's brain angiography, along with the figures on the blood gas test from the diagnostic lab."

Cornelius paused, scalpel in hand, though he barely glanced up from his task. "Great. Um, just put them on the pile," he mumbled.

"Sir, ah, Dr. Hendry wanted me to tell you—"

"Just give me one second," said Cornelius.

The tech watched as the doctor pierced the corner of Logan's right eye, then slid the scalpel down all the way to the base of the man's nose. Cornelius jumped back as a spurt of black blood narrowly missed splattering his visor. The gash he made was deep enough to expose bone.

As blood bubbled up from the wound and pooled on the yellow stain-resistant surface of the operating table, an assistant in a gore-spattered lab coat placed a small diamond drill in Cornelius's hand.

Using a laser dot projected from a ceiling-mounted surgical scope as his guide, Cornelius activated the power tool and drilled a small hole into the subject's exposed skull, right below the eye socket. Bits of bone flecked Cornelius's visor. As the shrill, dentist-chair whine filled the room, a pink-tinged tear rolled down Logan's cheek. An assistant quickly wiped it away with a cotton swab.

"Careful, Dr. Cornelius," warned Carol Hines, seated at the CAT scan monitor a few feet away. "No more than two centimeters into the brain pan or you risk damage to the nerve cluster."

"Done." Cornelius pulled back and cut the power. He set the drill aside and faced the tech. "You had a question?"

The technician nodded. "Dr. Hendry would like you to suspend the blood anomaly test until after this phase of the experiment is complete. He says since the lockdown his resources are limited, and the hematologist has been tied up for three days—"

"I know how long he's been tied up," Cornelius snapped. "I'm tired of waiting for results from that 'expert' as well. So what's Hendry's point?"

"He... Dr. Hendry said he needs the hematologist for his own work. Said if you told the specialist what you are looking for, the work might go faster."

As he spoke, the young tech's eyes never strayed from Subject X on the table.

"If I knew what I was looking for I'd have found it myself!" Cornelius replied.

"Sir? Is that what you want me to tell Dr. Hendry?"

"No. Tell Dr. Hendry that he and his staff are not here to question my requests, only to fulfill them. Tell him to remember who is in charge."

As the technician backed out of the lab, Cornelius angrily returned to his work. He snatched a long copper probe from his assistant's hand. Then he looked up at Carol Hines. "Ready?"

"Ready," she replied as she adjusted the angle of the real-time brain scan.

"That's fine, Ms. Hines. Freeze that image." Cornelius watched a monitor embedded in the wall. "I can see the nerve cluster quite clearly."

Stooping over Logan again, Cornelius slid the long needlelike probe through the fresh-drilled hole and into Subject X's brain with a single smooth thrust.

Cornelius stepped back as the assistant moved in with Teflon thread to seal the flesh around the protruding probe. With the procedure completed, Cornelius tore the hot mask from his face. Unlike his two assistants, who were clad head to toe in laboratory whites, Cornelius wore only a gore-streaked surgical apron over his shirt, vest, and tie. It made him feel like he'd just stepped out of a Victorian novel—a harried London physician, perhaps, or an East End slaughter-man...

"Stitch him up," Cornelius tossed over his shoulder. "I'm back in fifteen."

As he went, Cornelius snatched new files from the top of the teetering stack, leaving a bloody thumbprint on the cover sheet. He wiped his sticky hands on his apron, then strode into an adjacent lab, where he tossed the files onto an empty desk and doused his hands at the sink.

Somewhere in the back of his mind, Abraham B. Cornelius, M.D., was disgusted by the sloppy surgery he'd just performed—operating without anesthetic, without sterile implements or sterilized conditions. He doubted he'd even remembered to wash his hands after breakfast and before he'd begun working hours earlier.

My techniques these days are positively medieval, he thought, *but in the end, it really doesn't matter. Sepsis has no more effect on Logan than a mosquito bite.*

In the past weeks, as the Professor pressured Cornelius and Hines for faster results, Cornelius was forced to take shortcuts. One of the first protocols he'd dispensed with was sterile lab conditions.

Too damn many operations happening for such safeguards. Two this week, three last—and that doesn't even count minor procedures like the one I've just performed.

Retraining and reprogramming Weapon X wasn't Cornelius's only goal, either. He'd decided to launch his own private quest to unlock the secret healing potential of Logan's blood.

But as he leafed through the latest report, he discovered that the hematologist was no closer to explaining the "unusual structures" or the "curious proteins" found in Logan's blood than he'd been eight days ago.

The electron microscope might help, but Hendry has booked that facility solid. He's keeping me away from his precious toy out of spite, I'm sure of it.

Cornelius slammed the cover on the files and pushed them aside. With conditioning trials about to begin, he knew he would have even less time to devote to the study of Logan's phenomenal immune system. Performing tasks assigned to him by the Professor ate up virtually all of his waking hours.

Perhaps when this preposterous Weapon X program is back on track— when the Professor has made Subject X his walking, stalking, killer-on-a-string—then I can catch a break, do the real work with Subject X. The work Logan was born for...

Over the speaker, a soft-spoken command interrupted his desperate thoughts. "Dr. Cornelius, please report to Lab Seven at once…"

○────────────○

"HEY, Rice! Where're you going?"

Communications Tech Rice spun around to find a man approaching him from the opposite end of a darkened corridor.

"Is that you, Cut?"

Cutler emerged from the shadows a moment later. Rice recognized him and visibly relaxed.

"You looked spooked, Rice. What're you up to? Feeling guilty?"

Rice shook his head. "Thought you might be the Professor, that's all. He's been riding our butts for a week now. I don't think that guy ever sleeps. And with this big remote guidance test tomorrow, the whole communications department is working double time to get the technology up and running. The job stinks, man."

"Yeah, we miss your sunny disposition down in security," Cutler replied. As he spoke, Cutler located a precise point on the steel wall and slammed it with his fist. The lights in the corridor sprang to life, bright enough to cause both men to blink.

"A two-billion-dollar complex, and the lights don't work," said Rice. "This place is falling apart."

"You seen Anderson?"

"Yeah, this morning, with Subject X."

"That's what I thought," Cutler said. "I go in to prep Subject X for the 0800 experiment and find his cell empty."

"Doc Cornelius called for him at 0430. Anderson was on duty and brought Logan down to the lab himself."

"Without adequate backup. And Anderson never entered the transfer on the docket or wrote it up in the roster. That's three security protocol violations. And to make it worse, until I ran into you I didn't have a clue where Logan was. How good a security chief does that make me?"

Rice chuckled. "About as good as the last one, I reckon."

"Don't ever let Deavers hear you say that. I'm his second choice."

"Hell, Cut, I wouldn't have chosen you at all."

○————————○

THE Professor entered the lab at 0759. He wore a crisp, white lab coat over his tailored suit, a clipboard tucked under his arm. With relaxed confidence, he stepped up to the operating table.

"How are we proceeding, Dr. Cornelius?"

"Spinal codes are in," Cornelius reported. "It's just a matter of final sensor grafts now."

The Professor stared down at the unconscious Subject X. Logan lay flat on his back on the adjustable operating table. The probes Cornelius had placed in the subject's brain now had huge feeder boxes connected to them. The devices dangled from Logan's cheeks, under eyes that had been sewn closed with surgical thread. Bundles of fiberoptic wires threaded their way in and out of the subject's flesh through punctures at each of Logan's critical nerve clusters.

His forearms were raised and locked into restraints, hands open. Each finger had a long electromedical probe embedded at its base that stuck in the air like an antenna. Thin fiber-optic cables ran between his fingers like delicate webbing, and thicker bundles of Teflon-coated wires snaked in and out of the muscles in his forearms like artificial veins.

More wires were being added to Logan's feet, ankles, and behind his knees by a group of technicians supervised by several of Dr. Hendry's staff physicians. Electricians and communications specialists primed a thirty-pound battery and hooked it up to a steel cybernetic helmet married by wireless connection to Carol Hines's Reifying Encephalographic Monitor.

The Professor tapped the microwave-receiving box dangling from a thick wire bundle attached to the base of Logan's spine.

"And the distribution of the signal? What is our range?" he asked.

"About a three-mile radius, sir," Cornelius replied.

The Professor frowned. "But that is so very limited, Doctor. Is that all you can give me?"

"Professor, if you want a puppet, you have to have strings." It was clear from the doctor's tone that Cornelius saw the remote control phase of the experiment as a waste of time and effort.

The Professor's frown increased. "Yes… indeed… I do want a puppet, as you put it. But my design specifically called for a radius of at least ten miles."

Cornelius nodded impatiently. "I know that. But the batteries are just too heavy. I don't know why we couldn't have stayed with the on/off system, anyway. Weight wasn't a factor, because we didn't need batteries for that."

The Professor focused his cold eyes on his colleague. "I will have my way on this, Cornelius. A ten-mile radius."

Cornelius met the Professor's gaze for a moment, then relented. "Okay. Load him down. See if I care. You can turn him into a traveling radio station if you like."

Hearing the short-tempered exchange, Carol Hines looked up from her terminal, then quickly averted her eyes.

"Your dissent is noted, Dr. Cornelius. But let's not be testy, hmm?" The Professor's tone dripped with condescension.

Cornelius's attention was focused elsewhere. "Those braces can only keep the incisions open for so long, you know," he barked at a member of the surgical team.

The tech, face covered with a surgical mask, nodded. "Yes, Doctor. I can see that clearly. The flesh is actually forming around the clamps here."

"Then work faster, man."

"Any problems, Ms. Hines?" asked the Professor.

"Computer indicates leakage of semen and marrow into the intracellular fluids."

One of the surgeons cursed. "You heard the computer," he said to the technicians. "We're losing goop here. Keep those holes plugged and move with more expedience."

One of the surgeons freed Logan's hand and laid it flat on the table. "Give me a right stem, short fiber," he called.

"Short fiber right stem is on ninth," his assistant replied.

Suddenly, Logan moaned.

"Good God, he's coming around!" cried the Professor.

"Don't get jumpy, Professor," Cornelius said. "We have to keep him floating so that we can trace the relay flux in his nervous system. If he were out, some critical synapses wouldn't be firing."

The Professor visibly paled. "Do you mean he's conscious?"

Logan groaned again, his head rolling to one side.

"Yes, partly," Cornelius explained. "Maybe a little too conscious. Add two millimeters of Pheno-B."

"Yes, Doctor," a surgeon replied. A moment later, the man slipped a hypodermic needle into Logan's carotid artery.

The Professor's interest seemed suddenly piqued. "So Logan can feel what we're doing to him, eh?"

Cornelius nodded, face grim. "Most of it, yeah. I don't like it, but it can't be helped. Of course, Ms. Hines will soon wipe any and all memory of this… procedure from Logan's mind. But right now… well, the poor guy's in a lot of pain."

As if to emphasize Cornelius's words, Logan moaned twice, the last a keen of agony.

"Pain is a principal of life, Dr. Cornelius," the Professor declared. "Not that I subscribe entirely to the dictum."

"Of course," Cornelius muttered, trying to turn his mind away from this aspect of his work. But Logan would not let Cornelius forget his torment. The subject's head moved from side to side as the groans continued.

"Four more millimeters of Pheno-B," Cornelius commanded. "And try to keep him from shaking or he'll damage some of the delicate connections."

Subject X began struggling weakly against his restraints. His head lolled to the side and his mouth opened. Logan gagged, then ejected the contents of his stomach. A green bile, followed by a spray of saliva and blood, spattered the table.

"Readings, Hines?" Cornelius called.

"Sensory cortex monitor is overloaded, Doctor. There are no readings."

"Good God… off-the-charts pain." Cornelius leaned close to Logan's head, muttering. "Poor son of a bitch is unconscious at last. I hope he finds some peace in his dreams."

o———————o

SON of a bitch… Some peace in his dreams.

Logan heard the voice as if it were next to his ear. He opened his eyes, but the only person who could have spoken was curled up beside him on the pine branches, fast asleep. Could be the North Koreans on the hunt? Better check.

He rose slowly, trying not to disturb Miko, crawled to the hut's entrance, and gazed outside. The sky was clear and cloudless, the late-afternoon sun stabbed down through the thick pines in yellow and orange columns of light. A few birds sang in the tree; an errant breeze stirred the branches. Otherwise there was only silence in the approaching twilight.

Must be crackin' up... hearing voices this whole mission...

Then, as Logan strained his ears, he heard another sound—engines in the distance, muffled by the trees. He ducked back into the shelter and gently shook Miko awake.

"There's activity down on the road. I'm going for a quick look," he whispered.

"What kind of activity? Men? Vehicles? How do you know?" she asked, instantly awake.

Logan popped a garment can, worked the material until it expanded, then stripped off his rags and slipped into his last battle suit. Like the others, it was formfitting, with a splinter camouflage pattern ideal for blending into the surrounding forest.

"We should stay together," Miko said.

"No," he told her. "I can travel better alone. Rest up, we're taking off in a couple of hours. I'll be back in thirty minutes or less."

He took Miko's binoculars and handed her his remaining firearm, a lightweight M9 Beretta. Perfect for a HAWK jump because of its compactness, the M9 didn't have enough stopping power to satisfy Logan, who preferred bladed weapons, anyway.

Logan tucked the Randall Mark 1 fighting knife into his boot and from Miko's belt took a second, long-bladed weapon, which he wielded like a sword. Without a backward glance, he slipped through the opening and was gone. She watched as he darted down the slope and melted into the long shadows of the fading day.

Among the trees, the sounds went dead, but Logan could make out engine noises in the distance, and soon he heard human voices calling across the water. He emerged in a clearing that gave him a view of the road and lake beyond. An armored personnel carrier and two Chinese-built trucks were parked below. He counted three men around the vehicles; twelve more by the lakeshore, including an officer. A small boat was trolling back and forth close to land. Three soldiers aboard tossed hooked ropes into the water.

On closer examination, Logan spied skid marks on the tarred road and wheel tracks in the dirt—this was the spot where he'd ridden the BTR-60 to its watery grave. The Koreans were dragging the lake for their missing troops. This wouldn't have bothered Logan except for one thing—if they dredged up the dead officer, the Koreans would realize the man had been stabbed, not drowned. They might deduce that Logan had survived the plunge, or they might just figure he died in the fight and his body was still at the bottom of the lake. Of course, the soldiers would keep looking. And when they didn't find Logan's corpse, all hell would break loose.

Either way, time was running out. He and Miko would have to move now, before the Koreans realized they were here. But as Logan turned to ascend the slope, he heard more voices—these coming from the woods on either side of him.

Then he heard a noise that galvanized him into instant action—the sound of barking dogs…

∘────────────────∘

THEY sat Subject X in a chair. Spine straight, head erect, breath shallow, he was naked except for hundreds of multicolored wires that dangled from his body like feathers. Eyes stitched shut, nose pinned, mouth plugged, the cobra-hooded mane of wild black hair his crown, Logan resembled the mummy of a savage warrior king prepared for a ceremonial funeral.

A thirty-pound battery, which powered the adamantium-plated cybernetic helmet that sat at the subject's feet, hung from his neck like an unwieldy medallion. When hooked to the electrodes in his temples and the relays below his eyes, it would filter everything Logan saw, smelled, or tasted through the virtual-reality processor inside the helmet.

The Professor stood close to Subject X, examining the inputs and the raw, puffy flesh around them. "So, have the sutures healed?"

"Not all of them, Professor. But enough for the purpose." Cornelius glanced at his watch. "Or we could wait a few more minutes, if you prefer."

The Professor, hands folded behind his back, shook his bald head. "No, no. Let's get on with it, Cornelius."

Cornelius rubbed his chin. "Okay, the cables are a problem. They are clumsy and bulky, but can be reduced eventually. The power source—that unwieldy battery—is temporary, of course."

He crossed the lab to stand near the surgical team assembled behind the remote control transmission terminal. The actual manipulation of Logan became the responsibility of one of the communications specialists—a technician named Rice, who sat behind a large control panel.

"In the coming weeks, we'll try to compact the boxes, but I can't guarantee that." Cornelius tapped a key and a perimeter map appeared on one of the overhead monitors. Overlaid on that map was a red circle.

"We're looking at the range of these devices displayed over the test field," Cornelius explained. "For anything over a hundred and fifty yards, we'll need to use the helmet device to pull in the signal. The cybernetic circuitry inside that steel dome dramatically increases the range."

The scarlet overlay expanded until it almost filled the screen. Then the monitor went black, and Cornelius faced the Professor. "Other than that, we're in business."

"And what is the range, Cornelius?"

"A little over nine miles, sir." Cornelius could feel the Professor's displeasure. But he was too tired, and too disgusted with the work to really care.

The Professor snorted, then faced Rice at his terminal. "And the control console here. It isn't based on my original design."

Cornelius nodded. *A joystick*, he thought ruefully. *The Professor wants a goddamn joystick, as if Logan were some kind of video game character.*

"You wanted the extra power, Professor," he replied. "We had to modify the control surfaces to achieve it."

Cornelius tapped Rice. "Staff, show the Professor the layout of your top board."

"Sure, okay," Rice replied, rising. "It's easy, sir. These button codes are based on your data. You press them in sequence. Forward, back—"

"And the levers are controls. I understand," the Professor said tersely, annoyed that a mere tech should brief him on technology he had actually pioneered.

"Give us a brief demonstration, Rice," Cornelius directed.

"It isn't necessary," said the Professor. But to his chagrin, the impertinent technician pressed on.

"Watch," said Rice as he tinkered with the controls. Logan's arm twitched, then the flesh on top of his hand bulged from within.

"You got full articulation of the claws," prattled the staff tech. "Like this little piggy went to market—"

The first claw emerged.

"This little piggy stayed home—"

Two more steel claws emerged in a welter of blood.

The Professor shoved Rice aside. "I get the idea, and your entertainments are extremely out of place."

"I… s-sorry, Professor," Rice stammered.

"I hardly need instructions on how to operate my own device." The Professor touched the controls, then toggled the levers. "Yes… watch this…"

Logan jerked to his feet, then tottered unsteadily—two steps forward, one back. With each grotesque lurch, the dangling wires whipped and the battery clattered along the floor.

"You see, Cornelius, how the naturalistic movements imitate the human…"

"Yeah, yeah, I see that…"

"And how discreet adjustment creates the effect—"

Suddenly, Logan spun with such force that the heavy battery yanked him off balance. His legs became tangled in the cables and wires and he tumbled to the floor like a stumbling newborn.

The laughter of the staff caused Cornelius to wince. While he understood that the pressure on them had been mounting through weeks of lockdown and hours of difficult surgery, he thought the humor misplaced.

"*Shut up!*" the Professor shouted with more passion, more rage, than Cornelius had ever seen the man exhibit.

"Sir, I'm sorry—"

The Professor turned on him. "Cornelius, your staff are absolute fools. Ignoramuses."

Cornelius faced the medical staff. "Okay, boys, that's it. Get out of here."

"Yes, get out, buffoons!" the Professor barked. "This is a scientific endeavor and should be treated with the proper gravity. I… I've never been so insulted."

"Please, Professor," Cornelius said curtly, in spite of himself. "Dr. Hendry's medical staff did a good job and you got what you wanted."

Except for Logan, still sprawled on the floor, Cornelius and the Professor were alone. Cornelius poured a cup of coffee.

"Here, take this," he insisted, thrusting the cup into the Professor's hand. "And can we just call it a day? It looks to me like you haven't had a rest since the Weapon X project began."

"No!" the Professor shot back. "We've accomplished nothing today. The experiment is not over, Cornelius. I have to know for sure if it's safe."

Cornelius glanced at the man on the floor. Logan looked dead; even his chest barely heaved. If it wasn't for the continuous beep of the heart and respiration monitors, the doctor couldn't be sure there was any life left in that tortured frame.

"He's safe," Cornelius said softly. "He's wired and shut down. Let it go, Professor."

"You misunderstand. I meant if *I* am safe, you fool. Me! Subject X tried to choke me to death. Remember?"

"Look," Cornelius explained. "When the power is on, you've got him by the tail. When it's off—like now—he's just dead meat. You wanted it, you got it."

Then he turned his back on the Professor and walked to the exit. At the door, Cornelius paused. "But you have to be sure, right?" he said with a weary sigh. "So go, Professor. Spit in his eye. Then you can be sure."

He opened the hatch.

"Where are you going?" demanded the Professor.

"I've had enough of this circus for one day," Cornelius replied. "I'll send in the wranglers to clean up the mess. See you tomorrow."

When the hatch closed, the Professor looked down at Subject X. He watched Logan's chest rise and fall for a few moments. Then, tilting the coffee cup, the Professor poured the scalding contents over Logan's upturned face. Black liquid splashed and beaded, leaving red blisters that quickly faded to white, then pink, under the Professor's relentless glare.

With a final kick to the subject's rib cage, the Professor turned his back on Logan and strode out of the room, satisfied now that it was safe. Despite the pain and the humiliation he'd just administered to the once fierce and independent Logan, the mutant didn't even flinch.

Cornelius did it, the Professor thought triumphantly. *The reprogramming worked. Now I control Weapon X...*

14

THE HUNT

"CATCH," hissed Logan, tossing Miko the binoculars.

He'd almost arrived at the top of the hill, to find Miko already clad in her formfitting camouflage suit, waiting behind cover, Tac drawn. Logan had been about twenty paces from her when he'd heard the barking dogs and the sound of voices.

"My gun," Logan loudly whispered.

Miko drew his M9 from her belt and tossed it down to him. The clips followed.

"Go," said Logan, pointing to the woods behind her as he tucked the weapon into its holster. "Take off up and over the hill, circle around the soldiers and the dogs. I'll lead the hunters away from you for as long as I can, give you a head start."

"But—"

"Don't argue. The dogs have already got my scent. Move before they catch yours. Head for the complex, bust in. Do your business and then rescue Langram if possible. If they get me, I'll do what I can from inside."

The sound of beating blades cut through the dusky sky.

Logan cursed. Helicopters meant they must have found that dead officer...

Miko turned her eyes upward, then looked down at him. "Logan, fight. Do not surrender."

He glanced over his shoulder. The dogs closed in, their barks louder, more insistent. "I may not have a choice. Now take off!"

Without another word, Miko turned and raced up the slope, to vanish among the low-hanging pines. Logan hopped over the rotting trunk of a fallen tree and ran in the opposite direction. As he ran with leaps and bounds down the hill, he also moved away from the dam and the dogs and soldiers who pursued him. He knew that in the long run, flight was hopeless. He had few escape options—trapped in the middle of enemy territory. The North Koreans had the home ground advantage.

With helicopters and searchlights and dogs, with soldiers and armored cars, it was only a matter of time before the hunters caught up with him.

○———————○

AS the stalker's bare feet silently padded through the snow, a motion detector caught the movement, and a camera quietly focused its lens on the subject. Even in the dusk's deepening shadows, the camera effortlessly followed the hunter as he tracked down his prey.

"He's within one hundred meters of the target now—" Cornelius looked away from the HDTV screen to glance at his watch. "At three minutes, precisely."

The Professor watched the monitor, anxious to assess his creation's performance. "Rather impressive," he muttered, chin resting on his long-fingered hands.

"Camera five on subject," a video tech called.

"Switch to camera eight and bring him in close."

"Switching."

A frontal shot of Subject X appeared on-screen. Naked from the neck down but for the batteries and microwave receivers clustered around his waist, Logan's head was completely encased in a gleaming cybernetic helmet. Wires dangled from the headpiece to cocoon his torso. Most of the embedded feeder connections that sent signals directly to the subject's nerve clusters had been removed, to be replaced with a less cumbersome wireless system that allowed for freer movement.

"Ninety-seven yards at three minutes twenty-seven seconds," Cornelius announced.

"He's downwind," observed the Professor. "He has the scent."

Over the constant howl of the wind, the microphones picked up the *snikt* of the adamantium claws sliding from their sheaths.

"Claw extrusion, right hand. Some blood release is evident," noted the Professor.

"We need some kind of terminals there," said Cornelius. "Something to keep the flesh apart. Make a note, Ms. Hines."

The woman looked up from her REM monitor. The mind machine was running on automatic, at maximum output, sending a preprogrammed signal to Logan's brain. Carol Hines was receiving only limited feedback from the information the subject was processing, but it was enough to deduce his next move.

"Less than fifty yards now," Carol Hines said. "It appears the target is coming toward our subject, not moving away... his heart rate is elevated. Adrenal rise with carpal flux—"

"Left claw extrusion."

"Camera ten, please..."

"This is it," Cornelius declared. "Keep the brain monitors up and running. We won't get a second chance..."

Carol Hines began speaking into the voice log on her terminal. "Mister Logan. Set... I mean, Subject X, Set Twelve... Stimulus response quarry one, duration from zero four minutes and twenty-one seconds—"

THE grizzly bear emerged from behind a copse of leafless trees, lumbering forward on its short hind legs, forearms spread wide, claws bared, snarling.

With a string of hot drool dripping from its snapping jaws, the creature grunted a challenge, then roared angrily when the human stood his ground.

Without the benefit of a preprogrammed command, Subject X deftly avoided a swipe from one massive paw, crouching low to duck the blow, then slipping around the beast to administer a few stabbing jabs to the creature's torso.

Moving in front of the bear, Subject X thrust with his right hand, the adamantium blades sinking deep into the raging beast's rippling red-brown flanks.

The grizzly whirled, off balance. Logan saw the opening through the lenses of the virtual-reality visor—the signal dispatched to the brain by direct optic nerve inputs. Logan drew back his right arm for another thrust. The steel claws plunged through fur, hide, flab, and muscle, directly into the creature's heart.

Jaws gaping, lips flecked with gore, the bear's roar of defiance faded into a wet gurgle in its throat as it choked on its own blood.

Subject X brought up his left arm for a quick, slashing cut, and the bear's head literally leaped from its shoulders and spun away, to tumble into the bloody snow, eyes staring blindly.

A fountain of arterial blood gushed from the stump, steaming in the cold. The headless body of the bear wobbled and Logan drew back his right arm in a shower of gore. Without the indestructible claws to prop it up, the grizzly's carcass slumped to the ground at Logan's feet.

Subject X stepped forward, looming over his vanquished foe, ready to deliver the *coup de grace*. But except for its dying spasms, the decapitated bear did not move. Even the black blood ceased to flow as the damaged heart ceased to beat.

Programmed goal achieved, Logan stood stock-still, arms wide, legs braced, steel claws dripping gore, as if someone had turned him off. According to the readings Carol Hines was receiving, Subject X had lapsed into a kind of mind loop. His brain remained active yet not fully conscious.

○———————○

"SUPERB. Bravo!" the Professor cried. "An utterly impeccable killing. The time has come, Cornelius. The weapon is primed and perfect. He's ready for his first mission."

The statement shocked Cornelius. *No*, he thought in a panic. *You can't take Logan away from me now. My study of his immune system will be over before it's begun...*

Though his mind raged, outwardly Cornelius remained calm, arguing logic that the Professor could understand. "I'll agree that the demonstration was impressive, Professor. But the transmitters limit his effective range... and they're so cumbersome. And the helmet cuts his vision—"

"Thirty percent, both sides," offered Carol Hines.

"—and the transmission lag delays his responses for what could be a critical split second in a tight situation. Worse than anything are those bulky battery packs. They're nearly ten pounds apiece, and the microwave receiver weighs even more. Everything's so clunky and in the way."

Carol Hines glanced at the screen. "Shall I retract his claws, Doctor? Or wait?"

"Yes, go ahead, Ms. Hines."

"I agree that it's not optimum, and it's not what we planned," said the Professor. "But we do have the weapon in our control, correct, Doctor? Ms. Hines?"

Cornelius nodded.

"As long as Logan's brain is subject to the REM waves, he is under our control," said Carol Hines.

The Professor's eyebrow shot up. "A qualification, Ms. Hines?"

"Merely an observation, sir. The Reifying Encephalographic Monitor is an effective tool, but it must be utilized properly."

"Explain."

"Well, Professor… the REM sends out frequency-specific brain waves that interfere with the normal functions of the right and left frontal cortex of the brain."

"And that's what makes Logan docile? Controllable?"

"Not precisely, Professor. The REM device takes control of the subject in three stages. In its initial phase, the waves effectively deactivate the right and left frontal lobes of the brain—cutting the subject off from all memory, emotion, self-awareness, and the ability to distinguish between the real and vividly imagined experience. Though hearing is unaffected, the proximity of Broca's area—the part of the brain that controls speech—means that Logan's vocal abilities beyond the most rudimentary are also eradicated."

"We don't need him to speak, Ms. Hines. We need him to hunt, to kill," said the Professor.

"Yes, sir. During the second stage, the REM destroys or suppresses the subject's actual memories and replaces them with false memories and experiences we create ourselves. At NASA, the implanted memories were used as learning tools, a kind of virtual reality exercise to teach pilots of space shuttle emergency procedures. We went no further than that because of certain unforeseen side effects."

"No one told me about any side effects," grumbled Cornelius.

"We're well past that stage, Doctor, so the question is moot. Please continue, Ms. Hines."

"In the case of Weapon X, the implanted memories will be used to manipulate him, make him believe things that aren't or weren't true, in an effort to make his mind more… pliable. We can manipulate his fear, paranoia, activate feelings of vengeance, anger, rage…"

The Professor tapped his chin impatiently. "Yes, I understand, Ms. Hines. Get to your point."

"We are now in the middle of the third stage of the subject's retraining—the critical command-and-control phase—but psychological integration is not yet complete, which means that Logan is not yet completely under our control."

"But he obeys our commands. What am I missing?"

"Once the third phase is complete, Weapon X will be self-sufficient. He will not need the REM waves to keep him in thrall because his own brain will be programmed to obey without them. But right now, the subject still needs the microwave receivers and a power source. If the brain waves generated by the REM device cease to reach his brain or if the batteries fail or something breaks down, then we will lose control of the subject."

"He'll go wild? Attack?"

"Not likely, Professor. Probably he will simply shut down, or fall into a mind loop similar to the state he reverts to after a training session. There is danger only when a modicum of someone's personality, their individuality, survives the initial phase of REM integration. That can cause conflicts in the id, the subconscious, that can result in explosive bouts of violence."

"So he's safe?"

"Yes, Professor. In the case of Subject X, I'm positive we've utterly eradicated his personality. Nothing of the man called Logan remains in his mind."

While Carol Hines spoke, Cornelius buzzed the wrangler pen.

"Cutler here."

"Bring the subject."

Cornelius swiveled his chair to face the Professor. "You see our situation, sir. Logan is working—but not to optimum potential. Not yet. I think that with a little more psychological—"

The Professor cut him off. "No. No more psycho-anything. I want action now."

"Action? Chopping a grizzly into bloody pieces—that's not enough action for you?"

The Professor's eyes narrowed. "I didn't create this weapon to be some imbecilic game warden, Cornelius."

"So what are you saying here?"

The Professor shifted his gaze to the screen, where Logan waited docilely while the wranglers approached him.

"I am saying that our killer is ready."

"But it isn't all cut-and-thrust, Professor. A bit more time to eliminate some of the kinks in the system, that's all I'm asking."

"No. He is ready," the Professor repeated in the tone of a spoiled child.

"Ready for what?"

"The great test, Doctor." The Professor spun to face Cornelius. "What is the most dangerous game of all?"

Cornelius blinked. "Bengal tiger?"

"Man, of course."

Cornelius stared at the control console, face grim.

Pretending to work, Carol Hines and Technician Rice listened intently to the exchange.

"Well, we don't have any humans in stock right now," Cornelius said at last.

"Then we'll have to get some, won't we?"

Cornelius's eyes flashed in anger. "You're not serious, of course."

"On the contrary, Cornelius. I'm deadly serious."

"My God," the doctor protested, appalled. "If you think I'll sit at these controls and make Logan... that's complete madness. Do you know what you're saying?"

"I always know what I'm saying, Cornelius. So I'll brook no arguments." The Professor turned his back on the room and strode to the door.

"We're... we're not finished with this debate," Cornelius rasped.

But the Professor entered his own world. He stopped listening to Cornelius. His focus was on Weapon X and the grand experiment he was about to conduct.

"I will be in my control room," the Professor declared as the hatch closed behind him.

○———————○

LOGAN was fairly certain Miko had gotten away clean. That knowledge kept him going, even after he heard a second helicopter join the hunt.

Every step I take leads them a step farther away from Miko...

Twice Logan took time-consuming detours and double-backs to avoid large clearings where he could be seen from the air. He knew from experience it would be better after dark, when the choppers would have to use searchlights.

But all this running is for nothing if those helos are equipped with infrared or thermal imaging. They will find me easily once it gets dark...

For now, Logan ran as quietly as he could, until the only sound he could hear was his own breathing and the distant baying of dogs. No matter what happened, he was determined to go down fighting.

After all, why make it easy for them?

As the yellow sun sank low on the horizon, Logan broke out of a wall of pines as straight as telephone poles, their lower trunks mostly stripped of branches. Just ahead, a narrow stream of clear, icy water tumbled down the rocky slope to the lake far below. Without breaking stride, he plunged into the shallow pool, shivering as he slathered mud on his face, his hands, to hide what the splinter camouflage did not. He even rubbed the brown sludge into his hair in an effort to dull the sheen. Though he'd gotten a severe buzz cut before the mission, two days had passed and he now had a full head of long hair again.

Logan followed the stream for about a kilometer—an old but effective trick to throw the dogs off his scent. He knew that the bloodhounds would soon find his trail again, but he hoped the search would slow them down. Sometimes bloodhounds would be distracted by other animals, but these hills have been purged of all wildlife by the starving population in the area. Logan hadn't seen any creatures larger than a bird or insect since he'd arrived.

More and more, the landscape—brown grass, sloping hills climbing to jagged mountain peaks, forests of gaunt, tall pines—reminded Logan of the Canadian Rockies where he'd grown up. Logan found himself reaching back through a century of memories and experiences to conjure up every trick of woodcraft he'd learned from the Blackfoot Indian trackers he'd known in his youth.

When he reached a rocky area where he would leave scant footprints,

Logan exited the stream and sprinted through the forest. The foliage was denser here, so as he swept past, Logan was careful to bend branches rather than break them, crossing more hard ground than loose soil, more rocks than mud. For an instant, memory carried him back, until Logan felt like the boy he'd once been—a wild youth on an even wilder frontier.

In the gathering gloom, Logan glanced at the fluorescent glow of the chronometer-and-compass combination on his wrist. According to their original plan, Miko should be slipping past the dam about now and making her way down the valley to the top secret complex below—if she hadn't run into trouble, that is.

Suddenly, Logan paused to listen to an insistent beat of distant propellers. Down among the trees, the sound was muffled and he could not decide what direction the noise came from.

It was sheer instinct that threw Logan to the ground a moment later. It was training that made him press himself into the dirt as a helicopter passed directly over his head at an altitude of less than fifty meters.

Son of a bitch! Didn't even see it coming.

The thick trees hid Logan well, but he knew they also obscured and distorted sound, which aided his pursuers.

He lay on the ground for a few minutes, heart racing from the close call. Finally, Logan heard the dogs yelping in confusion behind him. They had lost his trail, for now at least.

Logan rolled to his feet and began to move swiftly between the trees again, this time keeping one eye skyward to scan the breaks between the branches for any sign of pursuit. But soon the sun set behind the mountains and the valley became shrouded in deep shadows.

Just when Logan thought things would get easier, he burst through the tree line into a vast clearing. At the same time he heard the roar of an engine and the beat of blades. He ducked back into the trees and peered cautiously through pine needles. Within a minute, an MD-500 arrived overhead, its searchlight cutting an arc through the twilight. Illuminated by the glare were hundreds of ragged stumps that used to be trees. About a hundred meters away, a steel tower bristling with cables punctuated the clearing. The power lines ran up the slope to another tower, then over the hill.

Across the wide, desolate swath—perhaps three, maybe four hundred meters away—more forest, more cover. Behind him, Logan heard the dogs again. They had picked up his trail and were closing in.

The bastards have been herding me all along… pushing me to this clearing where their helicopter gunners can pick me off. All those guys in the chopper have to do is wait for me to make a break for it.

Too bad for them I'm not that stupid.

Patiently, Logan watched the single chopper cruise up and down the clearing, its searchlight effectively covering every inch of ground. He used their light to scope out the landscape, but the results were not promising. There were no ditches, no dips or rolls in the ground to hide behind, and absolutely no vegetation beyond some ankle-deep brown grass and hundreds of tree stumps sticking out of the earth like grave markers.

From somewhere in the night, Logan could hear the echoing beat of the second helicopter.

Sounds like it's covering the road. Which means it will take a couple of minutes to get here if there's trouble.

Logan knew time was running out. He would have to act now or risk capture. Longing for the stopping power of his familiar Colt, Logan drew his Beretta, checked the clip, and flicked off the safety. Then he hunkered down in a bed of pine needles and ignored the sound of the approaching dogs as he waited for the helicopter to make another low-level pass.

Logan's patience was rewarded a few moments later. The MD-500, moonlight glinting off its bubble canopy, swept overhead. A column of light stabbed down through the trees, and Logan had to slip deeper into the brush to avoid its glare. As the helicopter passed over his hiding place, Logan discovered there were two men onboard—the pilot and a soldier armed with a sniper rifle. The gunner's door was open, and the man's foot hung out of the cabin, to rest on the landing skid.

They're not looking for a prisoner, Logan realized. *They're planning to gun me down from the air.*

The dogs were close now. He had perhaps ten minutes, no more than fifteen, to make a move before the hounds sniffed him out. As the helicopter circled the top of the hill for another pass, Logan took several deliberately slow and calming breaths.

Then, when the helicopter was almost on him, its searchlight beam rippling along the uneven ground, Logan burst from cover and ran right into the middle of the clearing.

○────────────○

CUTLER didn't like the way Subject X was behaving.

Something about the bear hunt had gotten under Logan's skin. Though he looked like a walking dead man, he sure wasn't acting like a zombie tonight.

When the wranglers found Subject X, he loomed over the dead grizzly, muscles twitching. Lynch said that he was shivering from the cold. Of course, he had a point. Logan was naked, and it was more than ten below zero. But the cold had never bothered Subject X before, so Cutler couldn't understand why it would affect him now.

To Cutler, Logan's sudden jerks and ticks more resembled the actions of his boyhood pet, a dog who flopped and twitched when he was in the throes of a dream. At one point, as Cutler was about to connect his electroprod into his helmet port, Logan shook his head like a horse wildly flapping its mane.

The prod locked into place on Cutler's second try and he carefully steered Logan toward the pens and the elevator. But they hadn't walked more than ten meters before Logan paused, seemingly reluctant to move forward. His helmeted head lifted, as if scanning the darkening sky.

Cutler pushed, and Logan shambled ahead. But his steps were hesitant, and instead of dropping his shoulders under the weight of the heavy cybernetic hardware, Logan jerked it from side to side as if he were alert and watching.

"Cuff him," Cutler commanded.

"Come on, Cut. He's a freakin' zombie, wh—"

"I said cuff him, Lynch. Don't make me give a command twice."

"Cripes, okay." Lynch pulled the plastic flex-cuffs from his belt and fit the bracelet over one forearm, then brought it back and snapped it to the other wrist. Logan didn't resist, but Cutler still would've liked to look Logan in the eyes, which were totally obscured by the heavy adamantium helmet.

The handcuffs seemed to have done the trick, however, for Logan remained docile on the ride down the elevator. At the door to Lab Two, Cutler was greeted by Anderson, who was waiting for him and dressed in full body armor.

"What are you dressed for, the winter ball?"

"Major's orders, Cut. Deavers wants you in his office, pronto."

"Can't the boss wait until I get Logan locked down for the night?"

"Sorry, Cut. Major says now, and hop to it. The Professor just laid some big experiment in our laps. Deavers says it'll take all night to get things prepped for tomorrow."

Cutler cursed and thrust the electroprod into Anderson's hand. "Watch him closely. Logan is acting funny tonight."

"You mean funny like in the lab the day they made him walk? Rice showed me the tape—hilarious."

"Just watch him, Anderson. And don't get sloppy."

As he headed for the elevator, Cutler ripped off his helmet and ran his hand through his sweaty hair. Without shedding his armor, he rode the elevator to Level One, lost in thought.

Another goddamn experiment. I wonder what that crazy egghead Professor has in store for Logan—and for us now.

○————————○

THE men in the chopper saw Logan as soon as he broke from cover. The aircraft immediately swerved to intercept the exposed figure that raced across the clearing.

Logan zigzagged to avoid the shot he had learned would come, his spine tingling in anticipation. He had learned from hard experience that you never hear the shot that gets you, so when the supersonic blast shocked his ear, he knew before the tree stump exploded in front of him that the sniper had missed.

As the chopper rolled over him, Logan tumbled across the ground and slammed into the shattered stump. At the speed the helicopter was traveling, he knew the sniper would only get one shot on the first pass. But Logan also knew that the pilot would not make that mistake again. His second run would be low and slow, giving his partner time to aim.

While the chopper made a circle in the sky and came back at him, Logan extended the M9 with both hands and waited for the approach. His breath came in ragged gasps as he fought back panic, especially at the moment when he had to close his eyes against the searchlight's glare or risk losing his night vision.

As the MD-500 leveled off, the searchlight dipped, and Logan opened his eyes to see the sniper lean out of the canopy. He quickly calculated the range, then adjusted the handgun and fired three shots in quick succession—all of them directed at the pilot.

A spark erupted as the first shot glanced off the bulletproof canopy; then another flash followed as the glass cracked. The third shot dinged off one of the blades as the pilot swerved to avoid Logan's fusillade. His maneuver was so abrupt and unexpected that it jolted the sniper out of his seat.

As the helicopter spun away, Logan watched the sniper air-swim all the way to the ground. He heard a loud crack, like a branch breaking under ice, as the sniper shattered his spine on a tree stump. The rifle landed next to its owner, and Logan took off across the clearing to retrieve it.

The helicopter pilot must have summoned help, for Logan heard the sound of another engine approaching the area—still out of sight, but coming on fast. Meanwhile, the pilot of the first helicopter regained control of his aircraft and was scanning the ground with the searchlight, looking for his fallen comrade. As Logan watched the copter's approach, his foot caught something and he went down.

He spit dirt and stared into the face of the dying sniper, now draped like a broken doll over the stump. The man's eyes moved from side to side. He made a gurgling sound, but with a shattered spine he wasn't getting up. So Logan didn't waste time finishing him off. Instead, he fumbled on the ground until he found what he'd tripped over—the sniper rifle, its scope shattered, the barrel bent. Logan cursed and tossed the useless weapon aside.

He ducked behind the dying man as the helicopter flew overhead. But this time, the searchlight played across the tree line at the edge of the forest—the pilot had obviously lost track of him. After the chopper raced by, Logan went through the sniper's belt. He found a Chinese-made pistol and a high-explosive grenade.

Logan tucked his M9 into its holster and leveled the more powerful Chinese handgun at the returning helicopter. The chopper bore down on him. Its searchlight reached out to pin Logan in its dazzling brilliance. The beacon made a nice target, even with his eyes half-closed, and Logan aimed for the light. He emptied the magazine with quick, successive shots. In an eruption of sparks and broken glass, the light went dim.

The helicopter still approached, moving under forty kilometers per hour and less than fifteen meters off the ground. Logan discarded the empty handgun and pulled the pin on the grenade. As the helicopter roared over his hiding place, Logan tossed the explosive through the sniper's open hatch.

The pilot saw the lobbed weapon bounce into his cabin. Losing control of his aircraft, he struggled to find the explosive before it detonated. The aircraft veered wildly as the man seized the bomb and tossed it out. The grenade blew up just inches from the landing skid, its explosion jolting the aircraft.

Unfortunately for the pilot, the helicopter's wild trajectory had carried him into the path of the power lines. The whirling blades cut through the electrical cables and the fuselage slammed directly into the tower.

In a magnesium white flash of crackling power, the MD-500 disintegrated, showering burning debris down onto the barren field. The explosion washed over Logan, heat scorching his flesh and setting his hair afire. He rolled to extinguish the flames, then jumped to his feet as a second helicopter dived low over the trees and raced toward him.

The familiar chatter of an AK-47 greeted Logan. Bullets rained on him from above. He would not be able to avoid automatic weapon fire for long. As the chopper rushed to cut him off, Logan ran back into the forest, even though the sound of the dogs was nearly as loud as the helicopter overhead.

At the trees, Logan was suddenly pinpointed by a huge column of light—a third helicopter had arrived. Logan zigzagged out of the brilliance even as he heard the crack of a rifle. He threw himself to the ground as the searchlight beam passed over him, illuminating two infantrymen with rifles aimed in his direction. Logan drew his Beretta and squeezed off two quick shots. Both men went down in sprays of blood.

Logan jumped to his feet and literally dived into the woods. As he hit the ground between two thick tree trunks, the butt of a rifle slammed against his head and the tip of a bayonet pierced his guts. He howled as the man holding the bayonet stepped out of hiding to drive the blade deeper into his belly. With the knife pinning him to the ground, more soldiers, like a wave, rushed to his side and pummeled Logan with their rifles.

Someone barked an angry command and the soldiers drew back. An officer leaned close to Logan's face, screaming threats in Korean. Feigning unconsciousness, Logan reached down with a bloody hand and slipped his fighting knife from its sheath.

One more kill and I won't go to hell alone...

Logan lashed out, and rammed the four-and-a-half-inch blade into the man's throat. The knife just stuck in his Adam's apple. A quick slash and the officer's arteries parted. Hot blood spattered all over Logan as the Korean fell away.

The pummeling resumed, more savage than before, until Logan mercifully slipped into darkness.

o————————o

"COME on, Anderson, let's get the Professor's zombie strapped down. The cafeteria closes in ten minutes and I want a hot meal. They're serving steak and fries tonight."

Using the prod, Anderson guided Logan into the diagnostic chair. Without bothering to restrain the subject's arms, as required by security protocol, Anderson started to detach the cybernetic helmet. Lynch watched him curiously.

"Prof says to remove the dome but keep him wired on the points," said Anderson.

"So we should leave the batteries on, then?"

"Yeah, I guess so," Anderson replied as he detached the visor and reached for the helmet. "And set the in-line alarm, right?"

"Guess so," said Lynch. "Okay, alarm set."

As the helmet was lifted, there was an explosion of awareness inside of Logan's benumbed brain. One thought flickered through his semiconscious mind.

One more kill and I won't go to hell alone...

o————————o

"I don't know about this, Ms. Hines."

Cornelius stood in the center of the lab, shoulders hunched. "First I'm told we're creating a kind of supersoldier with Experiment X. Then it turns out he's some sort of mutant animal thing, so the adamantium bonding and the agony he endured in the process sends him cuckoo..."

Working beside Carol Hines at the REM terminal, a brain specialist from Dr. MacKenzie's staff paused to listen.

Cornelius, oblivious, continued his diatribe.

"Now the Professor's talking about the 'perfect killing machine' and all that most dangerous game crap, as if this poor guy is some kind of assassin or something. It's like, what is this weapon going to protect us from, the Commies?"

Cornelius frowned. "I never intended to build weapons. I got virtually blackmailed into this whole affair, you know. No... I guess you don't."

Carol Hines turned to the specialist. "Why don't you take your coffee break now, John?"

"But I'm on duty until—"

"Take a break, John."

The man nodded, then departed in a rush. When he was gone, Carol Hines swiveled in her chair to face Cornelius.

"I'm not too big on soul-searching," he told her. "But I've got some responsibility to humanity... and I don't have murder inside me, Ms. Hines... No matter what you may have heard. I'm not a killer. I'm not like the Professor."

Carol Hines remained silent for a long time. When at last she spoke, her voice was soft but determined.

"If you need me, Doctor, I will support you. In anything you decide to do."

Cornelius opened his mouth to reply but was interrupted by a shrill and sudden wail.

"The alarm!" he cried. "On source, Ms. Hines."

The woman swung around and hit the source button. On the gigantic monitor, the interior of Lab Two—Subject X's cell appeared. Logan was standing, helmet gone, claws extended. His left arm was poised to strike, and from the steel claws on his upraised right arm a dead wrangler dangled limply, leaking gore like a fresh side of beef on a meat hook.

15

WEAPON X

"THE alarm is coming from Lab Two. It's Mr. Logan. He's loose."

Carol Hines had managed to keep the fear out of her voice but not her eyes. She gawked at the security monitor, watching as Logan drove his left fist into a second guard—impaling the body, his gleaming claw points springing through the victim's back, rendering the man as inert as a rag doll thrown on a pitchfork.

Cornelius lunged for the intercom, punched the button. "Professor! Professor!"

"What is it, Cornelius?" The Professor's tone was saturated with the annoyance of a superior unexpectedly disturbed by an inferior.

"You maniac!" Cornelius roared. "The 'most dangerous game,' you said. Now you're using our own security personnel as guinea pigs? How could you? You're insane."

"What?" The Professor turned to face his own monitor. On the screen, Logan was pummeling the exit door. "This is not my doing, Cornelius. I am not in control!"

The alarm became a blaring Klaxon, filling the complex with its shrill, urgent wail.

Cornelius adjusted the intercom, sent his voice over every channel, shouted the warning to every level. "All security to Zone Two. Weapon X has escaped."

Cutler was just approaching the door to Deavers's office when the storm began. He turned and tore back to the armory, expecting to meet at least fifty guards on site—SOP for a call like this one.

"Professor," said Cornelius over the direct link. "My emergency shutdown is not functioning. Use your command center monitor controls to shut off the power."

"I'm trying, Cornelius. The cutoff is not working. I think Logan's batteries are still engaged."

"What happened to your fail-safe, Professor?"

"It isn't working, I tell you. Logan's helmet is off, but some fool left the power packs in place. He's moving at will, out of control, and he's not receiving our signals."

On the Professor's monitor, Logan tore up the security door with the ease of a jaguar shredding human flesh, his adamantium claws passing through stout steel. Stepping through the debris and into the corridor, he confronted a young technician moving equipment from one lab to another. A single elegant slash and the man went down in a widening crimson pool.

Two guards armed with tranquilizer guns rushed through the corridor. Their radios crackled. "We got three men down and two active. Request permission to shoot."

"Of course, man, shoot!" The Professor's superior tone had disappeared, replaced with a voice near panic.

A ceiling-mounted security camera relayed the action that played on-screen for Cornelius, Carol Hines, and the Professor. Two guards in the foreground fired continuous bursts of sedative darts into Subject X. Logan treated them like school yard spitballs. He brushed away the bothersome projectiles and continued traveling.

All of the guards backed away, slowly at first, then faster. "Security… We need live ammo down here. Repeat. We need—"

In one fluid movement Logan speared the first guard, the unbreakable claws penetrating Kevlar, fabric, tendon, and bone. Effortlessly, he tossed the pierced carcass over his shoulder. The second guard's gun he knocked aside as claws slit open the man's heart and lungs. Over the loudspeakers, gurgling screams horrified listeners throughout the research complex.

In the main lab, where Cornelius foolishly assured himself that the darts were enough to stop the subject, scientific bewilderment supplanted near-hysteria.

"Sir, how could this have happened?" he asked the Professor, his voice relaxing into a respectful, dispassionate tone. "Logan was harnessed up, how could he—"

"It's not over," Carol Hines interrupted. "The tranquilizers appear to be noneffective."

She glanced up from the REM console. Cornelius met her eyes: Fear had seeped back into them, along with something else—something resembling excitement.

Hines had discovered that although Subject X could not be controlled by the scientists, he could still be monitored by them. Constant data streamed into Hines's REM machine, giving her a clear readout of Logan's actions and his present capabilities. One thing was more than apparent to her—his brain activity, which was supposed to be suppressed, began running at full throttle. Logan became sentient. Fully aware, his mind morphed into a smart bomb fully engaged.

Cornelius slammed his console. "This is crazy, Professor. Can't you do something?"

"My system is down. I've no control over Weapon X whatsoever," repeated the Professor.

"Then who does?" Cornelius demanded.

"Yes…" the Professor murmured. "Who does, indeed?"

Behind the Professor's frightened gaze came a mysterious realization. Whatever it was, he didn't voice it to Cornelius.

"This is an emergency," Major Deavers interrupted over the intercom, his voice anxious, reaching. "I'm losing men in Zone Two. I need an advisory on this—"

IN the armory, thirty-three guards had assembled. Cutler found them not suiting up, but gaping at the security monitor.

Friggin' amateurs.

"Who's down?" he barked.

"Anderson and Lynch in Lab Two," said Erdman. His face was a pale round surface cratered with worry lines. "Pollock and Gage in the corridor."

Cutler watched the playback. "Who's the other corpse?"

"Some technician. Poor son of a bitch got in the way of that psycho lab rat," Erdman told him.

Cutler turned to the rest. "Gear up. I'll break out the live ammo—"

"Deavers is still waiting for the Professor's authorization on that," said Erdman.

Cutler sneered. "Screw that shit! I'm authorizing live ammo—I'm taking no chances."

As the men strapped on Kevlar body armor, Cutler punched in a multi-number code on the wall-mounted keypad and yanked open the door to the weapons bay. The guards clustered around him while he passed out the serious muscle—Heckler & Koch UMP .45 caliber submachine guns with 25-round magazines.

o———————o

ON his monitor, Cornelius watched Logan cleave through an airtight hatch in less than a minute. The door was made of two-inch carbonized steel. It failed to matter.

"Professor," called Cornelius through the intercom, "can you seal the corridor from your remote location?"

"Seal?"

On the smaller monitor, Cornelius saw the pinched face of the Professor blanch a pale, pasty color.

"Yes. Contain Logan inside of Zone Two?"

The Professor sputtered. "I… I… Nothing is functioning here. And you… you saw what he did to that hatch…"

"Please," Major Deavers bawled over the intercom. "Will one of you give me a directive here? Professor? Dr. Cornelius? Dr. Hendry? We got a world of trouble coming down. Over."

"Can you close any part of Zone Two from your command center, Professor?" Cornelius repeated, trying to break through the Professor's stunned paralysis.

"Sir," Carol Hines interrupted. "Logan is moving away from Lab Two. Approaching Zone Three and D-Block."

Cornelius and Hines shared a look and the very same thought—
Dr. Hendry and his staff are in D-Block.

"Security! Move to D and Zone Three," Cornelius cried into the intercom.

"He's entering the service tunnels," Carol Hines warned next.

Cornelius began to sweat. "If he gets in there, he could go anywhere. Even to the surface."

"Doc!" It was Major Deavers. "I got five men down. We're gonna need more than tranquilizers to handle this situation."

Cornelius didn't answer. For a moment, his attention was wholly diverted by the puzzling sight on his small monitor. The Professor was having an animated conversation over a secure frequency. Cornelius listened intently. The conversation might be one-sided for his ears, but he had to hear it—

"... Are you aware of what's happening at this time?" the Professor was asking.

"Dr. Cornelius? This is Deavers. Do you copy?"

Cornelius cursed. "Yes," he told Deavers. "I... uh, I copy."

"We can't take him without artillery. Do you understand?"

"Yes... yes," said Cornelius, still trying to listen in on the Professor's private communication.

"... That is correct," the Professor was saying on his end, "Experiment X is out of my control. Running amok, you might say..."

"Ms. Hines," Cornelius snapped, pointing at the Professor on the small monitor. "Who is he talking to?"

"Computer shows exterior unit, sir. Satellite transmission can't be traced. He's obviously forgotten to turn off his intercom, doesn't know we can hear him."

"... Precisely..." continued the Professor. "Killing everyone in sight... But you see, Logan is fully harnessed. Yet my control panels are inactive..."

"Doc! Professor!" yelled Deavers. "For crying out loud! You gotta authorize weaponry. I got men down there—two of them. Trapped in Level Three by the sealed hatches. Logan's blocking the security ladder and they have to get past him to get out. They're armed with tranquilizer guns—goddamn peashooters. They haven't got a chance in hell."

Cornelius shifted his gaze to the monitor tracking Logan. The pair of security guards moved cautiously through a dim access tunnel. They looked like sewer rats to the scientist, foraging rodents, and Cornelius suddenly realized that's exactly what they were. Crawling without forethought, without higher intelligence, without any better awareness than the hapless vision provided by the weak, battery-powered beams of their flashlights dancing on the walls and ceiling. Before Cornelius could cry out, a stab of light pinned Logan, who was crouching against the wall like the higher form he was, like all higher forms who need do nothing more than wait for their traps to spring.

The moment the guards saw Logan, they nervously raised their tranquilizer guns.

"Don't fire! Don't fire!" Cornelius screamed. "Deavers, get your men out of there. Now!"

Too late. The sound of the firing darts, like toy popguns, reverberated off the tunnel's close walls. Screams came next, echoing down the metal-lined underground tube in shrill, earsplitting waves, as Logan charged.

"Security Zone Three!" Deavers screamed. "Get out of the tunnels—"

Logan struck the first guard in the abdomen. His adamantium claws plunged through Kevlar and flesh with equal ease. When the claws were withdrawn, they left a cavity so large the man's intestines flowed onto the floor in a steaming pink-and-yellow mass.

As the second guard turned to flee, a slashing cut severed his left shoulder from his torso. The appendage slid sideways to the floor; still twitching as it hit the ground. Barely alive, gushing black blood, the hysterical guard crawled out of camera range.

Logan did not pursue.

"Oh God," rasped Deavers "That was Conran and Chase."

In the armory, the security men reacted to the butchery with revulsion and rage.

In his command center, the Professor continued to drone on, still oblivious to the fact that Hines and Cornelius were listening in. His conversation became background music to the mayhem.

"… We are losing our security guards somewhat precipitately…" the Professor shared with his satellite uplink.

"Professor," called Cornelius, finally breaking in, "I need your clearance to issue the men firepower. Do you read me, Professor?"

"… Given this… I'd like to ask… do you have a hand in these occurrences?"

Cornelius turned to Hines. "He's not listening to me. I think he's lost his mind."

Carol Hines did not respond.

"Ms. Hines?"

She appeared to be hypnotically focused on the data streaming into her Reifying Encephalographic Monitor.

"Carol!"

Carol Hines looked up, her face hopeful. "Sir, I think I've found something important."

○————————○

CUTLER had organized the men into what he hoped was a formidable enough force to counter Weapon X.

Because of the tight quarters they would be forced to fight in, Cutler had only issued fifteen UMPs to those he judged to be his best men—personnel with years of military experience, or those who kept their heads despite the chaos going on around them. Among that group was Agent Franks.

"Stick close to me as we go into action," Cutler said to Franks as he thrust the weapon into the agent's hands.

The rest of the guards were outfitted with short-barreled M14s, semiautomatics that had a much slower rate of fire than the machine guns. Right now, Cutler judged his men too jumpy to work effectively without close supervision, so he figured that the less bullets flying, the less chance of friendly-fire injuries.

And how many bullets is it gonna take to stop Logan, anyway? Cutler speculated. *He's only human—well, sorta...*

Now, armored up and armed, Cutler led his men into the service tunnel above Zone Three. Once inside, he formed them into a phalanx—a wedge-shaped formation with the highest concentration of firepower at the apex.

"I'll take point," Cutler said, hefting his UMP.

"No, I'll take point," said Erdman, stepping into position.

"What's the problem, Erd? Don't trust me?"

"I do trust you, Cutler. That's the reason I want to take point," Erdman replied. "Major Deavers is vacillating, trying to convince the eggheads we should be armed. But you took charge, made sure we were armed despite what the mad scientists want. That makes you the only leader we got."

Then Erdman grinned behind his visor. "Anyway, I want another shot at that bastard."

Cutler relented and moved to the right flank.

"Okay. Move out."

o————o

"MR. Logan has breached three zones and is now within two hundred and twenty yards of the Professor's command center on Three and C-Block," said Carol Hines.

"Jesus." Cornelius rubbed the back of his neck. Sweat was trickling from every pore of his body, his brown beard felt like it was crawling with insects.

"And it is not a coincidence, sir," continued Hines. "I've traced his movements from the holding bay at Lab Two. He has made a definite path to the Professor's quarters."

"I don't know, Ms. Hines. Doesn't seem logical. How could Logan know where the Professor is?"

"You'll recall that he just hunted down a bear in less than four minutes, Dr. Cornelius. Our Mr. Logan has shown uncanny tracking abilities."

"But that was a controlled situation, Ms. Hines."

Carol Hines glanced at the small monitor, where the Professor continued his strange conversation. "And who says this isn't a controlled situation, sir?"

"… I see, I see," said the Professor. "Sort of biting the hand that feeds, eh?… A clean sweep, as it were… get rid of the deadwood, eh?"

Cornelius activated the intercom. "Security? Major Deavers? Break out the big guns. Shoot to kill."

"Did the Professor okay it, then, Doctor?" Deavers asked.

"No," Cornelius said as he watched Logan's swift progress toward the Professor's sanctum. "But he won't mind, believe me. And make that on the double, okay? Over."

Deavers signed off, leaving only two pronounced sounds over the general hum of the equipment in the lab: the ticking of Hines's monitor and the droning voice of the Professor.

"… There is just one thing… let me ask… should I leave now, or should I take refuge here while—as you put it—Weapon X clears the deadwood…"

Cornelius stared at the madman on the screen, having a polite conversation while chaos swept through the entire complex. As he watched, the Professor's chair exploded upward. A clawed forearm ripped through the steel plates from the floor below.

Screeching, the Professor fell as Logan moved through steel and concrete, slashing his way up, reaching for purchase and the chance to find his hated prey.

Cornelius took a startled step back from the monitor. "Good Lord. We've got to do something."

Ms. Hines stood, hugging herself, face tense. "The security force is almost there, sir. They should be able to handle it."

"But we should help him, too… shouldn't we?"

Carol Hines could not reply. She began to sob with terror as she listened to the Professor's shrieks. Cornelius stepped closer to her, but when he reached out to put his arm around her shoulders, she shrank from him.

"Don't touch me! Don't ever, ever touch me!" she shouted, trembling uncontrollably.

○———————○

THE guards exited the service tunnel on Level Three. The elevators were shut down and the stairwells sealed, per emergency security procedures. Fortunately, there were no innocent civilians wandering the corridors. If anyone was here, they were probably quivering behind sealed hatches.

The alarms still blared, however, and the din was becoming a distraction. "Why doesn't somebody cut that damn thing off?" Altman complained.

"Can't," said Cutler. "Only our pal Deavers can turn it off, from the security command center."

A voice crackled in their helmet receivers. "This is Deavers to all security units. Assemble immediately in the armory, where heavy weapons will be issued."

"Speak of the devil," whispered Altman.

Erdman tapped the headset in his helmet like he couldn't believe his ears, then turned to the men behind him and slightly lifted his Heckler & Koch UMP .45 caliber submachine gun. "That's our major. On top of the situation, as usual."

Laughter followed from a few of the men, but most were too nervous to respond. They had all seen what happened to Anderson and Lynch, to Chase and Conran. They were filled with dread but weren't about to admit it, least of all to their comrades.

On the right flank, Cutler played lieutenant to Erdman's tough sergeant, letting Erd shoot the orders and prop up the men's spirits while he focused on the overall strategy—what there was of it. He decided now was a good time to report to "management."

"Cutler to Deavers. Come in…"

The major reacted as if he'd heard the voice of God. "Cutler! Are you in the armory?"

"Just finished issuing heavy weapons. Sir? Could you cut that damn alarm?"

"Alarm? Yeah, sure, the alarm." A moment later, silence descended like a forest snowfall.

"Where are you, Cutler?" Deavers asked, some of the old authority returning to his voice.

"We're moving toward Level Three, Zone Three now."

"How far are you from C-Block?"

Cutler raised his hand to Erdman, who halted them all. "Major," Cutler replied with a whisper. "We're right outside of C-Block now. What's the situation?"

"Weapon X is—"

Deavers's reply was cut off as they heard a scream, followed by the Professor's panic-stricken pleas. "Help me! Help…"

"—coming for the Professor," Deavers said. "He's—"

Cutler cut the major off, then used his master communications code to cut off Deavers's transmission from the rest of his crew, too. He looked up, to see Erdman staring at him with curious eyes.

"Deavers isn't down here, so he's not in charge anymore," said Cutler. "I'm calling the shots."

Erdman nodded approvingly, then turned to face the others. "Let's move it."

The hatch to the Professor's command center was closed but not locked. On the opposite end of the corridor, the second entrance was ajar, according to the real-time images coming through to Cutler's helmet screen.

"This is it," said Cutler. "We're going through both doors at the same time. Erdman, take ten men and circle to the other entrance. You got fifteen seconds to get into position. Now go!"

As they hustled around the corner, Cutler faced the rest. "You," he called to Franks. "Take these men and block the exit to this level. If Weapon X gets through us, it's up to you to take him out."

"But Cut—"

"Now!"

Franks turned and led nine relieved security men to the elevator shaft on the opposite end of the long corridor.

Cutler faced the dozen men still with him. "Five seconds," he whispered as he silently unlatched the hatch and popped it open a crack. "Three… two… one… Go! Go! Go!"

Cutler slammed his shoulder against the heavy steel hatch, and it swung open. He leaped over the threshold, UMP raised.

The Professor was on the floor, pinned helplessly under the weight of his ergonomic command chair, which had been uprooted from its mounts in the floor. A giant hole yawned where Logan had burst through. Wires dangled and sparked in the opening.

Agent Abbot came in right behind Cutler. "Where's the bastard?" he cried. "Where's Weapon X?"

With a feral roar, Weapon X leaped to the floor directly in front of them—he'd been lying in wait among the heating and air ducts over their heads.

"Look out, Cut!" Abbot shouted, shoving him aside and raising his UMP.

But Logan was faster. With a slashing backhand, he knocked the machine gun out of Abbot's grasp. Then he brought down his right, claws extended. The adamantium steel cut through helmet, skull, and brain, dividing the agent's head into four neat slices, like a ripe watermelon on a cutting board.

Abbot's legs kicked out and he slammed onto the deck with a clang. Cutler rolled away from his comrade's twitching corpse as Weapon X lunged for him, claws striking sparks from the metal floor.

Then Erdman burst through the other hatch, UMP blazing. At least three shots danced across Logan's naked torso, each followed by an explosion of gore. But Weapon X didn't even flinch as he spun to face his newest foes. With a single quick stroke, Logan decapitated Erdman. The head bounced off the wall, the body took one final step forward before it toppled. Dying spasms pumped off three more shots, which blew out monitors and shattered computer consoles.

Behind Erdman, another guard pumped three shots into Weapon X at point blank range, forcing him back.

"Get the Professor outta here!" Cutler screamed as he struggled to his feet. Two men raced past him, then a third and fourth. One dropped to the Professor's side while the other three struggled to lift the heavy chair and drag the shrieking man out from under it.

"It's okay, Professor," a guard said in a voice loud enough to be heard over the chaos. "We've got you now. You're going to be all right..."

More shots, ripping into Logan, tearing the command center up in a shower of sparks.

"He... he tried to kill me," the Professor cried. A bullet bounced off the wall and sent debris spilling onto the Professor's upturned face. He howled as his glasses were knocked away. "My glasses... can't see."

"I got them, sir," said the guard leaning over him, his voice echoing behind his visor.

The Professor slipped his rectangular-rimmed glasses on, but suddenly, he heard a hollow, meaty sound. The man looming over him stiffened and his eyes rolled up in his head. He opened his mouth and blood burst from it, to coat the inside of his visor. The guard slumped over him, the weight of his dead body and the Kevlar armor he wore crushed the Professor.

With a strength born of desperation, the Professor pushed the corpse aside. He reached up his hand to grip the edge of his command-and-control console.

A silver slash. For a long, agonizing moment, the Professor's world was defined by pain—sudden, excruciating, all-consuming. Reflex made him yank his arm back. Through tearing eyes, he saw the stump gushing gore, cleanly severed at the wrist.

"My hand!" howled the Professor. Then, as his own blood splashed his face, rage replaced anguish.

"Kill him! Kill!" shouted the Professor. "Destroy Weapon X now!"

Strong arms grabbed his torso as two guards dragged the Professor out of the command center, into a side corridor.

Meanwhile, Cutler watched as the guards, firing and moving forward with precision, forced Logan to give ground until his back was against the wall. But as they aimed their machine guns to finish him off, Weapon X surged forward unexpectedly, disemboweling a guard who was foolish enough not to retreat.

Cutler, seeing his men die one by one, threw himself into the fray, only to be knocked aside again. He tried to get a clear shot at Logan, but the fighting was too close. Weapon X seemed to be completely covered by a mass of squirming, fighting guards struggling vainly to bring him down.

"Did you get the Professor out?" Cutler cried. "Did you get the Professor out? Come in. Answer me, somebody. What's going on?"

"Professor secured," came the reply. "He's okay."

Cutler heard other voices as well. Shouted commands, screams of pain and surprise.

"Target's all over the place... No clear shots... Get back... Too late... Losing men... Goddamn monster..."

Cutler watched as Altman was lifted off his feet by claws embedded in his torso. Logan slammed the man's head against the ceiling with so much force, his Kevlar helmet shattered. When Altman hit the ground, his broken face stared up at Cutler, nose twisted, eyes askew, like the face on a Picasso painting.

Over a dozen body shots, no effect. It's a stupid, senseless massacre. Fuck!

Cutler keyed his communicator. "Fall back, everybody. Fall back... into the corridor..."

———o————————o———

TO Agent Franks's surprise, the elevator doors on Level Three opened. Dr. Cornelius and Carol Hines hurried out, intent on reaching the Professor's command center.

"Whoa!" Franks cried, stopping them. "You can't go that way. You're heading for a firefight." As if to punctuate his words, Cornelius and Hines heard multiple shots, shouts, and screams.

"Damn it," Cornelius said in frustration. "Aren't you going to do something?"

"I have my orders," Franks told him, face grim as he listened to the frenzied voices over the communications network.

"Get back in here... Losing men... monster... Bloody massacre..."

Then a security guard stumbled around the corner, one hand clutching his side where blood flowed freely from a deep gash that bared the bones of his rib cage. His other arm barely propped up the pallid Professor.

First Carol Hines, then Dr. Cornelius pushed past Agent Franks and hurried to aid the injured men. Franks and two guards reluctantly followed. The rest stayed behind as the last line of defense.

The Professor groaned and stumbled, glasses askew, curled into a tight ball as he limped along, his stump tucked into his belly to slow the bleeding.

"Try to stay still, Professor. And stay calm," said the guard, laboring under his own wound.

"I'm bleeding to death," squawked the Professor, eyes bright with pain. Back inside the Professor's sanctum, the battle still raged with screams and shouts and shots fired.

"Command, we need a stretcher down here, fast!" said Franks.

Deavers's excited voice replied. "What the hell is going on down there? Someone shut me out of the net! How can I give commands if—"

"Sir, we need a stretcher," Franks interrupted.

"On the way," came the bitter response.

Agent Franks reached out to catch the Professor, allowing the man who'd brought him out to lean against the wall, then slump to the floor as his legs failed.

"A stretcher is coming, sir," Franks told the Professor. But when he tried to help the man, the Professor pushed him away.

"I don't need a stretcher, you fool. It's my hand that's missing, not my leg."

"Oh, no… oh, goodness," Carol Hines whimpered when she saw the blood, the stump.

The Professor took a few lurching steps, then spied his colleagues. "Cornelius," he rasped. "Help me. Get me out of here."

Cornelius saw the gruesome limb, too. "Goddamn… we're gonna have to stop the bleeding."

"We need a tourniquet," said Ms. Hines, taking hold of the injured arm. "Dr. Cornelius, give me your tie."

Cornelius whipped the silk off his neck and Hines used it to bind the crimson stump. Franks hunched over the man who'd brought the Professor out, then stood, shaking his head. "He's dead."

Suddenly, more shots erupted in a blaze, followed by a frenzied call over the communications net. "We need backup! We're—" The voice was cut off in a choking scream.

"Who was that?" asked one of the guards.

Franks just shrugged. "Wasn't Cutler… maybe he's down, too."

"So what do we do, Franks?"

Franks looked at the dead guard on the floor. Then he raised his UMP and faced the others. "We have orders to stop Weapon X if the others don't, so let's go!"

"Hold tight, Professor," said Hines, indicating the knotted tie. "Try to keep your han—your arm raised. That should hold it for the time being."

"We must get you to the infirmary right away. Can you walk?" Cornelius asked.

"I can run, Cornelius," the Professor said in a voice that was surprisingly strong. "Just get me away from here. But not to the infirmary."

"Sir," Carol Hines protested, "you must be seen to."

"We must get to the adamantium reactor hold." The Professor pushed past them and hurried toward the elevator.

"What? Why, Professor?" Cornelius called.

"Because it's the only safe place from Weapon X."

"But security will take care of Logan, Professor."

"Don't be stupid, Cornelius. They don't stand a chance."

○————————○

MAJOR Deavers was a broken man. A bureaucrat without authority, an officer without a command.

From the security center, he'd watched the monitors helplessly as his men were butchered by Weapon X. He'd screamed into the microphone, knowing that his troops couldn't hear him—that the treasonous Cutler or maybe Erdman had deliberately blocked his transmissions. He'd pounded the console as his men died one by one, then en masse.

But for all the shouting and pounding, Deavers failed to do the one thing that might have helped. He could have gone down to the armory, put on a suit of armor, and joined his men on the front line. But he wouldn't.

A manager just doesn't do that sort of thing.

That's what Deavers told himself, anyway.

Now he wasn't sure who was alive—only that most of his men were dead. Some lay in the corridor, others near Lab Two. They were heaped to the ceiling in the Professor's own command center.

It's not my fault... it was a rebellion... a mutiny.

Deavers suspected his men had listened in on his conversation with Dr. Cornelius.

Maybe they thought I was indecisive... but I argued from the start that the heavy weapons should be issued. I can't help it if the bosses see things differently...

Deavers blamed circumstances for those first deaths—Anderson or Lynch violated protocol, got sloppy. But he also suspected his own men believed that Conran and Chase died because he—as their commander—was too slow to react. The major also suspected his troops were angry that he didn't issue the heavy weapons on his own authority.

Deavers thought that judgment unfair.

Men like Erdman, Franks, and especially Cutler... they don't understand there's a chain of command. That it's important for someone else to take the heat for the hard calls.

Deavers knew that Weapon X had cost someone big money. The way he saw the situation, it wasn't up to him to decide whether the experimental subject should be gunned down or not. That kind of decision had to come from the top, from someone above his pay grade.

One thing I learned in all my years—never stick your neck out. Not in combat, and not in management. Let men like Cutler and Erdman strap on the guns and go into the trenches.

Yeah, the peaceniks got it right. The best soldiers are the ones who never have to fight. I learned that lesson, all right, but Cutler never did. That's why Cutler never rose to the top.

Deavers's desperate rationalizing was interrupted when Specialist Rice burst into the command center.

"Rice, glad you're here," said Deavers. "I need someone to go down and reconnoiter Level Three. Most of—"

"Sorry, Deavers, I don't take orders from you anymore."

Rice reached out and snatched the command card off the clip on Deavers's overalls.

"Hey—"

"I need this card to access the main supercomputer for a critical download."

"Why?"

"Look around, Major. The crap's hit the fan. Too much critical data will be lost if the whole complex goes up in smoke. I'm going to retrieve it, copy it."

"You got orders? From who? The Professor?"

Rice snorted. "Orders. That's all you care about, isn't it, Deavers? Okay, let's say I got orders, from someone more important than you, more important than Cornelius, or even the Professor..."

"The... the Director?"

"I have orders, Deavers. That's all you need to know."

While Deavers watched, seemingly paralyzed, Rice opened the weapon case and drew out an automatic. Then he headed for the door.

"Rice!" cried Deavers. "Are you and the Director going to try and fix this mess?"

Rice shook his head. "There's no fixing this, Major."

Then Specialist Rice took off, leaving Deavers alone to ponder the ashes of his spiraling career.

o———o

"SECURITY, Zone Three, respond," Franks called. He and eight other men waited outside the hatch to the command center, hoping for a response from inside.

"Security, Zone Three—"

A voice wracked with pain cut through Franks's transmission.

"Sir... we're... we're..."

Then dead air.

Franks glanced over his shoulder at the others. "Lock and load. No fancy stuff. No encirclement. Just shoot and scoot. And toughen up, too. Ignore everything you see in there except Logan... you shoot that bastard to pieces."

Franks slapped a 25-round magazine into his UMP. "On three..."

Three seconds later they burst into the command center, coming through the hatch firing, then fanning out to either side. Franks heard gasps and muffled groans over his headset. He had to stifle an exclamation of his own.

In the middle of the room, Weapon X spun to face them, arms flung wide, claws extended. The creature was bent low in a feral crouch, ready to pounce. Logan was covered with gore from head to toe—and this time it wasn't sheep's blood.

He stood on a mound of bodies piled two and three deep, packing the command center like a carpet of human remains. A few of the guards twitched or groaned, but most were dead and the rest dying. The walls were repainted in red, dripping darkly. Loose entrails, shredded organs, and severed limbs made the metal floor slippery.

Logan's eyes burned as he saw the guards enter. With a silent snarl, he took a step forward.

"Fire! Fire! Fire!"

One of the men cut loose. Computer panels exploded under the hail of bullets. The room filled with sparks and the deafening thunder of firearms discharging nonstop. A moment later, the fire control system activated, drenching the cloud of gun smoke with a fog of blasting halon.

"Can't see!" someone cried.

"He's moving past me, Logan's co—*ack*!" The call ended when the agent's helmet microphone was severed along with his throat.

"Look out, I—"

A muscle-bound, two-hundred-fifty-pound guard flew out of the fog, slamming against the far wall with no more effort than it took an angry little boy to toss aside a toy soldier.

"Pull back! Pull back!" Franks cried as he fired blindly into the soup. He heard a scream and someone stumbled out of the mist—Agent Jenkins, his torso stitched with bullets. Eyes wide, hand reaching out for help, the man went down.

Behind him, Weapon X hurled forward. Franks fired, but the shot went wide. Then a cutting sideswipe knocked him to the ground and he landed hard, stunned.

As Logan swept past him, Franks tried to rise but found his legs oddly tangled. He wondered if his foot was caught. When he looked down, he saw his legs flopping on the ground a few feet away, both severed at the hip. He slumped uncontrollably to one side as a torrent of blood spilled out of stumps that were once thighs.

Dimly, Franks heard someone call his name. On the other side of the command center, propped against a shattered console, Cutler leaned, gasping. His chest gaped, lungs and a slowing heart visible behind dripping gore.

Cutler's mouth was moving, but his rasping voice barely registered over the communications net. Finally, as he fought for consciousness, Franks could make out Cutler's words, which he kept repeating until he died.

"I recognize him now... Logan. I know who he is..."

With his last breath, Franks keyed the microphone and reported to Deavers, who'd been demanding to know their status for the last five minutes.

"Nothing left, sir," Franks wheezed. Then he sensed a movement nearby. With his last bit of strength, Franks lifted his head to see Weapon X looming over him. He closed his eyes and started to whisper his epitaph.

"Sir... he's coming... for me."

16

APOCALYPSE

"THIS is it, Cornelius. Break the seal. We will be safe here."

Cornelius shrugged. "Yes, if you don't count the radiation burns."

The Professor brought Cornelius and Carol Hines to a massive set of double, steel-plated, lead-lined blast doors. The elevator had carried them to the deepest level of the facility, where neither Hines nor Cornelius had ever been despite the many weeks they'd spent inside the secret complex.

The atmosphere was close and stale, the corridors warm from the ambient heat of the adamantium smelter on the level above. Recessed lighting in the steel-lined corridors seemed hardly adequate to dispel the gloom. Ozone and industrial smells suffused the subterraneous chamber, which constantly boomed and echoed as a result of thousands of automatic mechanisms still operating.

The doors themselves were branded with a black-and-yellow radiation symbol. Bold red letters spelled DANGER. Still clutching the blood-soaked tourniquet, the Professor gestured with his chin to a glass case embedded in the wall. "Ms. Hines, get that gun."

While Cornelius punched the Professor's code into the keypad and swung the huge doors open, Hines broke the glass and pulled the single M14 off the rack. Two fully loaded magazines were also inside the case. She grabbed them, too.

"Load it, please."

Carol Hines snapped the magazine in place and presented the weapon to the Professor.

"Not to me, you idiot. What can I do with a gun? Give it to Cornelius."

Hines thrust the weapon into the doctor's hands, happy to be rid of it. Cornelius held the weapon at arm's length, as if it were contaminated.

"What's going on here, Professor? Just what do you think I'm going to do with this rifle?"

"Fire it, Doctor. At the first opportunity…"

The Professor led them inside the reactor room and commanded Cornelius to seal the hatch. The place was fully automated, with banks of computers, terminals, and switching and rerouting stations lining the walls. Digital readouts continually flashed the core's internal temperature, pressure per cubic foot, and other critical information as the machines went about their preprogrammed tasks, oblivious to the apocalypse unfolding in the complex above.

As Hines approached the central terminal, built-in motion detectors activated the computer keyboard, the monitor, the communications equipment. She set to work, and in a few seconds views from the security monitors on the upper levels appeared on the screen.

Safe behind the sealed hatch, Cornelius turned to the Professor. "So you want me to fire this rifle, eh?"

"You may not be able to kill Logan, but if you could shoot away the power packs on his belt harness. That should stop him."

Cornelius was no sharpshooter, hadn't fired a weapon since high school. And even if he had been, the entire premise of the Professor's theory was based on his fallacious assumption of control.

"This is ridiculous," Cornelius countered. "Even if Logan is still alive, the systems are down, he can't—"

"The system is not down," the Professor declared. "It is in the hands of another."

"Who?" Cornelius asked. *The bastard you were chatting up while the guards were being butchered?*

"It is not your place to know that, Cornelius."

"You've got a lot of gall, Professor. Asking me to shoot a man, but you won't tell me why—"

"Don't wave your morals in front of me, Cornelius. I would think that a man who murdered his wife and child would be a little more cold-blooded."

An audible gasp could be heard from Carol Hines. Cornelius faced her, but she'd already turned her attention back to the central terminal's keyboard, refusing to meet his gaze.

"And in case you've forgotten," the Professor continued, pressing his case, "not very long ago, you ordered the guards to kill Logan."

Cornelius nodded, face grim. "That's right, Professor. I wanted Logan dead, but I wasn't willing to get my hands dirty doing it myself. The fact is, I'm not a killer. I don't have murder in my heart."

"Well, you'd better find it somewhere or—" With a moan, the Professor dropped to one knee. Cornelius slung the weapon over his arm and helped the man into a chair.

"Look at you. You're bleeding buckets here. I have to bandage you up."

The Professor coughed. His face was milky from loss of blood, but his eyes were bright, their expression bitter. "I am considered deadwood, Cornelius. To be cleared away. Just deadwood…"

"Dead meat, more like it," said Cornelius as he removed the tourniquet. Blood trickled from the clotted stump, but Cornelius quickly covered the injury with cloth torn from his shirtsleeves. "You're delirious, Professor. All this stuff, your wound. You're going into shock."

"You are ever the fool, aren't you, Cornelius? If that door doesn't keep Logan back, you will soon discover what shock is…"

Cornelius refused to be baited by a dying man. "Yeah, well, I think the quicker we can get you to the—"

"Hines!" shouted the Professor. "Will you stop that infernal tapping! I can't think!"

She raised her hands from the keyboard. "Yes, sir. Sorry, sir. The computer shows Mr. Logan to be fully active—"

"I knew that, blast it!"

"His battery packs are more than eighty percent drained, soon they'll give out."

"Not soon enough, Ms. Hines…"

"No, sir. Actually, Logan is quite close. He's in Tunnel Two. Moving in this direction."

The Professor pushed Cornelius aside and stumbled to the terminal. "Get away, woman! Let me get in there."

The Professor stared at the screen. Cornelius didn't think it was possible after all the blood he'd lost, but the man managed to pale another shade whiter.

"Is this terminal connected to the main supercomputers?" the Professor asked.

"It is the main computer, sir."

The Professor realized they were standing directly above the buried computer mainframe. "Yes, of course," he said in sharp annoyance as he began to type.

Carol Hines tried to assist. "Pardon, sir… that's not the proper code—"

Cornelius called to her. "Hines? Let it go. It's out of our hands. I don't think we're a part of this game anymore."

Finally, a communicator chirped and the Professor spoke, his voice a rasp. "This is the Professor. Please answer… you must come in, please. Talk to me…"

Silence greeted his plea.

"Are you surprised that Logan didn't kill me? Why are you doing this to me? I am not part of the rabble. You must know that. Answer me, please… don't let me die here!"

"We don't have to die, Professor," argued Cornelius. "None of us. This gun. I can use it, to protect us—"

But the Professor ignored Cornelius, listening intently for a voice that never came.

"I can shoot off the power packs, like you said, Professor. Give you and Ms. Hines a chance to get away. I can—"

The shrill scrape of metal on metal interrupted them. Then a booming crash echoed off the chamber's walls as something heavy struck the floor.

"What's that noise?" cried Cornelius.

Ms. Hines covered her heart. "I think Mr. Logan has finally found us, sir."

The sound of footsteps followed, reverberating through the massive chamber. Suddenly, the lights flickered, the consoles grew dim. Then everything went black for a seemingly endless moment, before the battery-powered emergency lights automatically activated.

"The power's down!"

"Those sounds. Outside," hissed Cornelius. "Logan is in the walls. He's coming through."

"Help me! Help me, please!" screamed the Professor into the inactive communicator. He slammed the console with his remaining fist. "Blast you… blast you for this!"

Cornelius looked at Carol Hines. "I don't know who he thinks he's talking to, and I don't care." Then he noticed she was trembling uncontrollably. "Are you scared?"

"Yes, sir. Very. Are you?"

Cornelius nodded. "Part of me, to death… But another part… I think I'm ready to see my wife again."

Hines stood close, looked up at him. "What… what the Professor said, about your wife—"

"It's not true. That's what the police think, and that's fine with me. The truth is more pathetic. I'm sure you don't want to know."

"No, I do… tell me."

"My child was born—defective. I searched and searched for a cure for the disease, but I failed—me, an immunologist, and I couldn't even save my son."

"He died?"

Cornelius looked away. "Paul was dying… slowly. A piece at a time. I worked every day and half the night in the medical laboratory searching for a cure while my wife lived daily with our boy's pain… saw it every hour, listened to the cries. It finally broke her.

"One night, I came home from the lab, found them both dead. My wife had poisoned our son with some of my medical supplies and then killed herself."

"And the police blamed you?"

"I let them blame me. Madeline was a Roman Catholic. Her faith, her family were important to her… suicide is a mortal sin, so is murder. It was better all around if I got the blame. I had nothing to live for without her, anyway…"

A crash interrupted his recollections. From somewhere behind steel walls, machinery tumbled.

Cornelius's fingers tightened around the cold metal barrel of the automatic rifle. "Logan's inside now. He's got to be."

Carol Hines's slight body still trembled.

"Listen to me," Cornelius said. "When Logan comes through here, I'll deal with him. Finish him off, distract him—whatever I can do. You get out. Run as fast as you can. Forget about the Professor—he's gone already—and forget about me."

"But—"

"Listen. I've had enough of this life and I'm ready to die. Probably deserve to, for what I helped the Professor do... turn a man into a monster—"

Another crash, and the emergency lights flickered. They heard a long squeal as the turbines on the level above ground to a halt.

"The power's really gone now," said Carol Hines. "The turbines for the adamantium reactor have shut down."

"That's the last of our worries, Ms. Hines."

"The turbines maintain the adamantium coolant, Doctor. Without power, it will reduce to the charged compound. We must purge the core or this whole complex could blow up within the hour."

The Professor, still hunched over the console, looked up when he heard her words. "All deadwood... all burned up... blow it all and we all die," he muttered. "Yes... that's what I should do. Blow it all up..."

From above, an oily substance dripped onto the Professor's bald head. Warm and wet, he thought it to be hydraulic fluid—until it trickled down his cheek and splashed onto the deactivated consoles. Even in the dim light, the Professor knew blood when he saw it.

He looked up just as Weapon X burst out of the ventilation shaft over their heads. A bellowing roar and Logan landed in a crouch, adamantium claws gleaming in the scarlet glow, to confront the astonished Professor. The man whimpered and stumbled back, transfixed by the sight of the thing he had toiled so long and hard to create and mold.

Chemically enhanced muscles ripping, mane wild, flanks quivering like those of a hunting lion about to launch, Logan bared gore-flecked teeth. The virtual-reality inputs had been ripped from his face and only loose, sparking wires remained. His eyes flowed scarlet tears. His naked hide ran with ribbons of blood. The battery packs still dangled from his waist. With every heavy step he left a crimson footprint.

"Shoot him! Shoot! Shoot!" shrieked the Professor. "Kill him while you still can!"

But when Cornelius looked into Logan's eyes, he saw pain, weakness, confusion—and humanity. Weapon X should have struck them all down, yet Logan appeared paralyzed, wavering, seemingly reluctant to lash out, as if his bloodlust had been spent.

Cornelius lowered the rifle. "Look, Professor. He's faltering. I think he's had it. He's too weak to attack, he's lost a lot of blood."

"That blood is what's left of our security guards, you fool! He's controlled and programmed to kill all of us. Use the gun now, while we still have a chance!"

Cornelius switched off the safety and raised the muzzle of the rifle, aiming from his hip. But Weapon X now seemed more human than monster, and he could not bring himself to pull the trigger.

"He isn't moving, Professor. He's finished."

"Do as I command, Cornelius!"

With his good hand, the Professor punched the doctor in the jaw. Cornelius flinched from the blow, his trigger finger twitched, and the M14 fired. With the weapon set to full automatic, a third of the magazine—eight shots—burst from the muzzle in less than two seconds, spraying the control room.

Some of the bullets bounced off the floor, some struck the computer banks behind Weapon X in an explosion of silicon, plastic, and glass. But three lucky shots struck Logan in the chest, stitching across his pectorals and making him dance like a marionette until he spun into the smoldering debris behind him.

Logan dropped. Cornelius blinked, the rifle held limply in his grip. "I... I got him. I got him. He's—"

With a low, throaty growl, Logan began to stir.

The Professor screamed. "The power packs, Cornelius! Get the power packs, shoot away the receivers. Shut down his brain!"

Still sprawled on the floor among the shattered computers, Logan lifted his chin, then shook his head to clear it. His bloody lips curled into an angry snarl when he saw the weapon in Cornelius's hand.

"He... he's still alive. Th-that's incredible," Cornelius stammered, his limbs paralyzed.

"Shoot, you fool. Shoot before it's too late."

Cornelius's eyes met Logan's. Hines screamed.

"You blasted idiot!" bellowed the Professor.

With a single thrust, Logan ran Cornelius through, the adamantium claws ripping into his belly, severing his spine, and bursting through the back of his shirt. With a wheeze, Cornelius folded around Logan's arm. His round glasses slipped from his nose, shattering on the floor, as his killer lifted him off his feet, then slammed his broken body onto the main computer console.

A moment of awareness was left in Cornelius, no more than a final, flickering breath. Enough time to see the demon's raging face blur into an angel's; enough time to watch a monster's wiry mane become a lustrous head of perfumed hair; enough time to hear his wife's delighted laughter for the rest of eternity.

"Idiot! Idiot!" the Professor screamed as he ran to the exit. Carol Hines followed, sobbing. At the double doors, she caught up with the Professor, tugged his good arm.

"Stop, sir. Stop. We must go back—"

The Professor pushed her aside. "Get away from me!"

"But we can't just leave him. We have to help Cornelius."

The Professor glanced back over his shoulder, half-expecting to be transmuted into a tall pillar of salt. Logan had pinned Cornelius to the computer terminal, and was slicing the doctor's tormented corpse the way he'd ripped into the she-wolf, piece by gory piece.

"There's no helping him, you stupid woman. Can't you see he's dead? I couldn't help him even if I wanted to. Neither could you."

The Professor stumbled through the now open hatch.

"Where are we going?" Hines cried.

"I must get to the reactor, so stop sniveling and pull yourself together. I need your help now."

Hines wiped away tears. After a final glance over her own shoulder, she raced to catch up to the Professor.

"Yes… yes, I'm with you, sir."

○————————○

THE two batteries failed almost simultaneously.

The larger power pack directed energy through the somatosensory cortex to the central fissure of Logan's brain, then along the top of the frontal cortex, which controls basic and skilled movements. As its reserves were spent, Logan collapsed like a balloon that had lost its air. All voluntary and most involuntary muscles were shut down at the same moment.

The transition was so abrupt, it was as if an on/off switch had been thrown. If it wasn't for the continued functions of the man's brain stem—thalamus, hypothalamus, midbrain and pituitary—Logan's lungs and heart would have stopped functioning, too, and he would have died instantly.

The second battery powered the microwave receiver wired into Logan's right and left frontal cortex via the direct inputs through his eye sockets. Drained of energy, the cortex-suppressing waves broadcast by the Reifying Encephalographic Monitor were no longer being fed into the area of Logan's mind that contained his emotions, his memory, and his self-awareness.

Suddenly freed of the machine's hypnotic thrall, Logan's mind exploded in a psychedelic tsunami of wildly conflicting images; chaotic, divergent thoughts, and profound and intense emotions. He lay in a hallucinogenic fugue for mere seconds, but with his hyperactive brain, the passage of real time meant nothing. Bombarded by images, assaulted by sounds, he twitched and moaned, unable to absorb or comprehend the kaleidoscopic panorama. Soon the confused delusions coalesced into a piercing point of light, bright as burning magnesium, that expanded in his mind as his awareness grew.

Logan's consciousness reemerged from the dark depths of his unconscious on a glowing column of spiking brilliance that morphed into a spinning ladder—a pathway that spiraled down to the deepest core of his being. On each step of that ladder, a face, a name, an identity—yet all of them one and the same individual, the same soul that now inhabited the paralyzed, pain-wracked body that sprawled and spewed bile and blood on the reactor room floor.

As he lay, awaiting death—hungry for extinction as a release from the bone-searing agony of the past months—his mind was flooded with spectacular visions of violence, of pageantry, of martial glory, and of a gleaming figure at the very center. He knew that death would not come, for that was his burden.

He saw all the shapes he was and all the lives that he'd led, all the guises and masks which had been, which are, and which shall always be but corporeal manifestations of the "I" that was Logan. Mere physical forms shedded like snakeskin at the end of each existence, as the spirit moves on to occupy a new form, a new shape, a new individual. And for this brief moment, Logan knew and experienced them all.

So began the melding of his past with the world's history…

I am...

Swathed in fur hides and uncured leather, flesh mottled with red clay and war paint. I beat back the onslaught of the Others—those who walk on two legs, who use clubs and spears, but are not men.

The rude stone ax heavy in my hairy hands, I smash skulls like eggs and, ravenous after the battle, I feast on my enemies' hearts and wash in their blood.

Called the Hand of God, I wield a sword made of bronze. My shield is leather and beaten lead. I fought and I died in the desert sands of Jerusalem, struck down by the demon Ba'al in a holy war long forgotten by mankind, though it echoes through eternity.

Here I die with my king, arrow-pierced Leonidas, as the Persian chariots burst through the Spartan defenses at the mountain pass called Thermopylae.

At Carrhae, I retreat with Cassius's legions, cut to pieces by the Parthians who tricked the Legionnaires into breaking formation, then massacred the Roman troops with cavalry.

In burnished steel armor, astride a stirrupless saddle, I beat back the Huns who seek to destroy Roman civilization and thrust the world into the ignorance and superstition of the Dark Ages.

I ride a Mongol pony into Samarkand with Genghis Khan. We leave mounds of sun-bleached skulls and utter desolation in our wake. Harvesters of death.

My chain mail encrusted with rust and sweat-salt, I hack my way over prostrate Jerusalem's walls with the Knights Templars. I put the Infidel to the sword and liberate the Holy Lands in the name of my most holy Pontiff, Urban the Second.

At Bosworth, I wear a white rose and die in the marsh during Lord Stanley's bloody advance.

I am captain of the mercenaries, I besiege Magdeburg with the Roman Catholic armies of Gustavus Adolphus. No one could stop us. Overwhelm the Hessian defenders and butcher thirty thousand Protestant men, women, and children.

Both sides fight for the glory of God. I fight for plunder.

Wind chimes tinkle in the chill night air. The garden sparkles with crystalline ice. I wear a sky blue silk kimono; my skin is yellow. I dance in the falling flakes, silver blade flashing, dark ninja blood staining the virgin snow as black-clad forms fall dead at my feet.

Perfectly dealt, my strokes slash out a haiku of death, each cut a decapitation, each lunge a disembowelment.

I fight for the emperor and my shogun master.

I trek across the deserts of Egypt and the steppes of Russia with Napoleon. Our triumphs, our cruelty are legendary, our retreat through a freezing hell our penance.

At Veracruz, we remembered the Alamo by invading Mexico via the sea and defeating the Mexican Army in their own streets.

I die in a dusty ditch next to a wheat field in a place called Antietam, then spring to life.

On the walls of old Peking, I stand side by side with heroes, to beat back a horde of Chinese hatchet men who seek the deaths of all foreign devils.

For fifty-five days we hold, a hundred United States Marines who defeat a two-thousand-year-old empire.

I feel the wood and fabric of my SPAD shudder under the chattering machine guns. I watch a Fokker DVII crumple in the air, its wings burning as it plunges, spinning, to the Western Front far, far below.

I love a Blackfoot Indian girl named Silver Fox.

I meet Hemingway in Spain.

I fight in the trenches, breathe poison gas.

I parachute into Normandy on D-day.

I wage war in Malaysia, Vietnam, Korea, Laos, Cambodia, France, Belgium, Austria, Germany, Japan, Afghanistan, Algeria, Istanbul, and Peking.

In Jerusalem, in Actium, Rome, Paris, Fort Pitt, Yorktown, Moscow, Osaka, Cambrai, Flanders, Belleau Wood, Guernica, the Sahara, Caen, Berlin, Dien Bien Phu, and Hanoi.

All of them were me. Me. The Eternal Warrior. The Hand of God, the Master of War. An immortal spirit with no beginning and perhaps no end, only an eternity of suffering and strife and the tide of battle. No peace, no rest. No love, no family, no home. The sword my only mistress, the battle-rent banner my testament.

With stone and wood, with bronze and iron, with steel and adamantium as my tools, my weapons, I live the warrior's life, die the warrior's death a thousand times over. My lives line up behind me on parade, and I can see them all, like dim silhouettes marching over Golgotha.

I've suffered the spear's tip and the headsman's ax, the slashing sword, the arrow's pierce, the crossbow's bolt. I've drowned. Been burned. Crucified. Blown asunder. Felt the hangman's noose.

And in the end, all that pain ever led to was a finality that is never truly a climax, only another beginning in the endless, eternal cycle of blood and conflict, as inevitable as the rising sun, the phases of the moon, the passing of stars, the falling rain.

o———————o

LOGAN awoke as if from a long dream.

An endless parade of death… yet no release. Not for me…

Like smoke the wisps of memory scattered; the soul-shattering insights, the revelation of Logan's peculiar genesis and unique destiny forgotten, buried in his subconscious for a day, a century—or perhaps forever.

With blood-caked hands, Logan reached up to clutch the edge of the computer console. He opened his eyes, but even the dim emergency lights seemed too bright, too blinding, and he blinked against the glare. Pulling himself to his feet, Logan rose on unsteady legs and found himself standing over a corpse.

The man was middle-aged, with a reddish-brown beard, round glasses fallen from a ruined face, eyes closed as if in repose, lips frozen strangely in a half smile.

"I know this man. In a memory… from a dream… a dream of dying…" Logan's voice, hoarse from disuse, cracked into a wracking cough. Trembling on his unstable legs, he reached up to find sparking wires dangling from his ruined cheeks. Without ceremony, he ripped them loose, wrenching the probes out of his brain in a gush of semiclotted gore.

He howled in anguish, and the pain served as a reminder of more recent agonies. In a rush, memory returned. Faces and forms and familiar voices filled his mind—inseparably these features were linked to his torment, their voices a barbed lash that stripped away his soul and seared him bone-deep. They did things to him, these people, things he still did not understand. They kidnapped him, drugged him, ripped him to pieces, and glued him back together again. And this series of unbearable events kept repeating itself in an endless loop.

And for that, they will all pay…

But, dominating his mind, there was one face above all. A predatory face, lean and hungry, on a frame tall and thin. Patrician features, hairless scalp, rectangular glasses through which stared the eyes of a savage raptor.

A memory of pain...

Logan knew it was the face of his creator and his tormentor. His god and his devil. The creature who robbed him of his humanity to forge him into a living weapon.

It was only fitting, then, that the Professor should become the next victim of Weapon X.

17

THE STORM

CAROL Hines punched in the Professor's code and opened the security door. The Professor led the way through a hot, narrow, winding maze of corridors and ventilation shafts to a steel access ramp. They climbed the incline to the adamantium smelting facility's control center. She soon realized their location. "Professor, if we could purge the core, we could at least save the complex."

"Of course, Ms. Hines. My plan exactly. After all, what could be more important than the data we've collected, the memory of Experiment X?"

Bypassing the enclosed control room, they exited the corridor on one of the open platforms above the reactor's fission gate—a circular, multileveled, bowl-like structure of gleaming metal more than a hundred meters across. In the center of the mammoth machine, the lead-lined, adamantium-encased exhaust pit descended fifty meters down and was covered by a steel grate. Walkways surrounded the entire configuration, and the Professor and Carol Hines now stood on one of the highest.

Fifty meters over their heads, the pipelined ceiling glowed amber in patches as flashes of fire and debris burst through straining metal seams, splattering metal magma through the grate to the exhaust pit below.

"The containment is cracking already, Professor. We must release the fission gate before the entire facility melts down."

"Yes, Ms. Hines, but it's a matter of getting Logan into the exhaust pit first."

"But sir, there's not much time left!"

The Professor's eyes were bright with feral cunning. "I need a lure of some kind, you see. Someone to trick Logan into the pit. Don't you understand? He would be incinerated in seconds."

Carol Hines looked at the Professor, trying to comprehend what he was saying. "I'm sorry, sir?"

The Professor loomed over her. "Yes, that is too true, Ms. Hines. I am sorry. Truly sorry. Let us take a moment to consider our options. It is clear what you must do…"

Carol Hines ducked as a shower of sparks burst through the metal plates above their heads. A loud crash followed as sections of melted pipes plunged into the exhaust port in a red-orange molten ball.

"Ms. Hines. I know you have worked long and hard for our Experiment X…"

"Yes, sir. Thank you, sir…"

"You have been a real boon to the good Dr. Cornelius, too."

"Oh, poor Dr. Cornelius." Tears pooled in the woman's eyes.

"Yes. He gave his life for the project… why, I dare say you would do the same, would you not, Ms. Hines?"

"Sir?"

"Give your life."

At last, Carol recognized the intentions burning behind the Professor's eyes and she understood what her role was to be in this, the final act. This time, however, she refused to be a tractable and compliant volunteer in her own destruction.

"No. No, sir. I would not want to die." Her voice, even to her own ears, was surprisingly strong.

The Professor fixed his gaze on her. It was hateful—an angry, disapproving, parental sneer. Though frightened, Carol Hines stood her ground, met his stare with her own.

"Bait, Ms. Hines. I need bait."

"Why… why would you want to hurt me, Professor?"

"Because, my dear lady—"

The Professor lunged, surprising her. Before she could regain her balance, Carol Hines tumbled over the rail.

"—there is no other way."

She screamed all the way down, until her body struck the hot metal grate mounted just above the exhaust port.

"Don't break your neck on the way down, Ms. Hines," the Professor called, "because I want you to scream and yell and draw that mindless beast into the pit."

While he ranted, the Professor climbed a staircase to the control booth. Before he entered the glass-enclosed, soundproof structure, he turned and shouted his farewell to the woman he'd consigned to the pit.

"Come on, Hines, scream, will you? Think of the horror of it all. Use your imagination."

At the bottom of the exhaust port, Carol Hines raised herself onto her elbows and shook her head to clear it. She tried to rise, but her leg was bent at an odd angle and would not support her weight. When she looked up, she saw the Professor through the glass panels. His mouth moved, but she could not hear his words. Then Carol Hines lifted her eyes to the high ceiling, where molten metal was beginning to drip in glowing orange icicles. She screamed.

The Professor saw her mouth gape and laughed. "There you have it, Ms. Hines. Bravo!"

An electronic voice cut through the man's rants.

"Computer control operating."

"Computer, activate a satellite link to Director X... Code 324 Omega 99 plus."

"Activated."

"Now give me the current thermal breakdown."

"Two hundred thirty thousand at seventy thousand cubic meters."

"Advise on those numbers."

"Open fission gate immediately."

"Begin purge sequence and open manual control to me." As he spoke, the Professor reached out with his remaining hand and gripped the manual control lever overhead.

"Control open. Purge begin—"

The Professor turned to face the microphone. "I want you to listen to this," he said. "I want you to hear the end of your dreams, and mine."

On the level directly above the fission gate came an explosion as a door blew outward. In the center of the blast's corona stood Logan, framed by the glow. Seemingly untouched by the fire that swirled around him, Logan advanced through flames until he spied the cowering woman. With a throaty growl, he hopped onto a railing to stare down at her.

"Come, come, creature. Into the pit with you," yelled the Professor, his cries muted by the glass walls. "I'll crisp you like bacon, like the mutant meat you are."

Logan sniffed the air as if sensing a trap. Carol Hines whimpered and tried to rise, her movements drawing his attention. Grunting, he leaped off the rail to land in a crouch on the steel grate directly in front of her. Slowly, Logan paced forward, stalking her, all six claws extended.

Limping as she tried to back away, Carol Hines's voice broke, her words divided by sobs. "Mr. Logan... I don't know if you can understand me... I don't... don't want to die."

Logan's eyes were wide and alert, but there was no indication he comprehended her words.

"It's... it's the pain, Mr. Logan... I can't stand pain. I was burned once—chemicals—and I never forgot the pain..."

In the booth, the Professor sighed in disgust.

"Good God, Ms. Hines, don't beg. You are living the last few moments of your pointless existence. Don't waste them pleading to a mindless animal. How grotesque. How undignified."

Carol Hines stumbled and collapsed onto the grate. Instead of trying to rise, she averted her eyes and covered her head with her hands. "I know you want to kill me," she sobbed. "But please, kill me quickly... please, I beg you."

An animalistic rumble began in Logan's throat but emerged as rasping words. "I... I understand. I understand you..."

Hopefully, Carol Hines looked up.

"You don't matter... to me," muttered Logan.

His head slowly turned, until Logan faced the man inside the booth. "I want him—"

The Professor pulled the lever, and the blinking digital display switched from STANDBY to PURGE.

Over their heads, the glowing steel ceiling opened like a clamshell. Carol Hines looked up to see a dozen white-hot nozzles, like the exhaust port of a rocket. As one, the nozzles opened, too.

"Oh God!" she cried. "He did it. He opened the fission gate!"

She staggered to her feet, but her shattered leg prevented her from running. As molten metal and waves of invisible radiation poured down on them, Carol used her final seconds on earth not to cower, but to warn the man she'd willingly tortured to save himself.

"Run, Mr. Logan… Run!"

Then molten metal, seething, superheated chemicals, and waves of radiation washed over Carol Hines until she vanished in a writhing burst of fire.

From somewhere, the electronic voice of the computer boomed through the facility.

"Discharge: two hundred and forty thousand megatherms at seventy thousand cubic meters. Current rate: seven hundred FPS. Velocity: two thousand. Acknowledge."

In the booth, the Professor's pain-ravaged face was alight with savage glee. "Acknowledged," he told the computer.

Then he faced the microphone. "This is the Professor," he said into the satellite communicator. "Experiment X is destroyed, and I, I am his destroyer. Do you hear me? I beat you, you treacherous son of a—"

"Purge proceeding," said the computer, "six hundred FPS…"

"I served your every demand! Yet you turned against me…"

"System override… four hundred… three hundred… two hundred. Thermal rate noncritical. Purge sequence canceled."

"What?" the Professor roared. "You… you are controlling the fission gate, aren't you?"

"Purge shutdown complete… Fission gate clear of radiation. Temperature four hundred and seven degrees… Three-fifty… two hundred…"

"My God," the Professor moaned. "Is… Is there nothing you cannot do?"

○————————○

AS Carol Hines screamed her final warning, thousands of roentgens of ionized radiation washed over Logan, scorching his flesh, boiling his blood. Vaguely, as if from a great distance, Logan heard the woman's dying cries amid the clamor of the fission gate's exhaust ports, saw her faint silhouette disappear as wave after wave of unimaginably destructive energy was released, until his own eyeballs began to burn, his eardrums seared and turned to ash.

Then, with an agonized scream of his own, Logan dropped to his hands and knees as more radiation, along with splashes of molten metal and gouts of dripping adamantium, poured down from the leaking containment vat overhead. His cries ceased as his lungs singed and his vocal cords burned. His breath came in violent, choking gasps.

Logan was literally flayed alive by fire as layers of flesh, muscle, and tendon cooked away in a split second. But as each cell, each nerve ending was incinerated, more nerve tissue, more cells were generated by his phenomenal biology to replace them. The phoenix-like process accelerated as more and more roentgens of raw radiation blasted him. Logan's flesh and muscle seemed to flicker in and out of existence and he became a walking metal skeleton, burned to ashes and restored, only to be incinerated once again.

Radiation has an affinity for bone tissue, and even a single dose of radiation as small as twenty-five roentgens produces a detectable drop of circulation lymphocytes—white blood cells. Continued exposure will quickly initiate cancer in even the most healthy individual, which meant that the elevated amount of radiation drenching Logan not only should have killed him ten times over but also caused acute, fatal radiation syndrome if he had by some miracle survived.

However, adamantium now sheathed his skeleton, effectively shielding Logan's blood-producing bone marrow from radiation damage, keeping enough cells alive and functioning inside of Logan's ravaged body to continue his extraordinary cycle of healing and renewal after each new wound, each new torment.

As raw agony coursed through every nerve ending in his body, Logan stumbled defiantly to his feet. With muscles stiff and scorched, with tendons crisped by fire, he shambled toward the distant control booth. Through eyes milky white and blurred by heat, Logan could see the Professor inside the glass-enclosed cage, pounding his remaining hand and ranting into a microphone. Though each step cost him enormous effort, though each movement was excruciating, a more powerful torture spurred Logan on.

As his fingers curled and shrank to bony knuckles under the stream of devastating energy, Logan used his adamantium claws to half-climb, half-drag himself up the metal staircase. At the window, he saw his own reflection—a glowing, living effigy smoldering with each vengeful step.

On the other side of the glass, the Professor felt Logan's eyes on his back. He turned to see Weapon X, still alive, still advancing on him like a relentless pit bull, wounded but determined to strike at the one who abused him.

"Good God in heaven," the Professor cried. "You are still transmitting to him. Controlling a corpse… a walking dead man."

With an awful crash, the pane exploded inward in a shower of crystalline shards. The Professor reared back, raising his bloody stump to ward off the razor-sharp splinters that rained upon him.

The Professor hit the floor as Logan landed, legs braced, to tower over him. Claws extended, Logan grabbed the man by the collar with black, blistered hands and lifted him until his ravaged, smoking face was mere inches from the Professor's own.

"Am I dead?" Logan gasped. "Is that what you… did to me?"

He stared into the Professor's eyes. He saw fear there, and madness, too.

"Dead!" Logan groaned like a tormented ghost. "A walking dead man, am I?"

The Professor's eyes widened as he stared with hatred at the furious, burning thing. He spit his defiance in Logan's face, then flailed his arms to break free. "I'll tell you what you are. You are an animal…"

The Professor's words detonated in Logan's mind. He screamed, "I am Logan. Logan! Do you hear me… I am a man—"

Logan jerked him over his head.

"—And you… you are an animal! You are my monster!"

With a crash and the crunch of splintered bone, the Professor slammed down, to sprawl across a console. Whimpering, he turned away from Logan to punch the intercom. "Security! Security! Help me," he cried. "For God's sake—"

Logan slashed down, parting the Professor's remaining hand from its wrist. As his claws retracted, a feeble gush of the Professor's blood spilled onto the console. The crimson gore made hardly a splash, as if there wasn't enough of it left in the man for a real spurt.

With the radioactivity fading, Logan's skin began to reform over pink, stringy muscle. His features began to reappear, though the flesh was pitted and blistered, his hair and ears gone. With both sinewy, fleshless fists he grabbed the Professor by the throat and yanked him to his feet again. The man moaned and tried to break away. The effort was a limp jerk in Logan's adamantium grip.

The Professor's eyes glazed over and he moaned again. Logan shook him back to reality. When the scientist looked into his monster's eyes, Logan's regenerated lips curled and he laughed.

"Now we both got our paddles bollixed, eh?" growled Logan. "But do you really think that makes us... even?"

The Professor turned away from Logan's stare, muttered an unintelligible reply.

"Well, I don't."

Three bright silver points sprang out of Logan's arm. The Professor watched in horror as the claws slowly slid from their thick muscled sheaths. As Logan's grin morphed into a mask of rage and retribution, the Professor kicked and squirmed, helplessly, uselessly. Then the Professor began to howl, a long, mournful wail of dread, anguish, even regret.

Supporting the struggling man with his left hand, Logan plunged his claws into the Professor's groin. The man's eyes went wide and he bellowed like a gutted pig. Slowly, Logan slid his claws out of the man's body, then thrust again, this time piercing the Professor's quivering belly. The Professor's head lolled, his eyes rolled up in his head, he coughed crimson bile.

Logan thrust again, then again, and again—to pierce heart, lungs, throat. Finally, Logan raised his arm, touched the Professor's pallid forehead with the tips of his claws, and then—slowly and deliberately— he thrust the blades through the skull and into the brain. The Professor twitched once, and Logan lowered his corpse to the floor.

"Now we're square... got that, you bastard? Now we're even..."

Rage not yet spent, Logan bent low and lifted the limp body off the ground. With the Professor's dead arms flung wide, his glasses askew, Logan tossed him through the broken window and down into the seething pit far below. The Professor's carcass struck the superheated fission gate, and with a steaming sizzle, disintegrated.

Uttering a grotesque sound something between a snarl and a laugh, Logan turned his back to the shattered window and took a single step forward. Suddenly, the entire room seemed to shift on its axis. Hit by a wave of nausea and a jolt of lancing pain inside his skull, he clutched his head with both hands. Then, without a sound, Logan collapsed to the ground.

○———————————○

HIS first awareness was of pain. Cautiously, Logan opened his lids, to squint with tearing eyes against harsh white glare.

"Easy, mate. Take it easy," said a gruff voice close by. A rough hand touched his forehead. "It's me—"

"Langram?"

A silhouette loomed over him, its shadow blocking out the overhead light. "Didn't think you cared, Logan."

Logan tried to smile, but it hurt too much. "Actually, I was coming to rescue you—"

Langram put his finger to his mouth, gestured to the light fixture with his head. "They're very enlightened around here," he cautioned.

Obviously, the cell was bugged, maybe rigged with surveillance cameras, too, up in the light fixture.

"We're in jail?"

"We're prisoners, if that's what you mean."

"How have they been treating you?" Logan asked, still on his back.

"Better than you, from the look of ya. Here, let's get you up."

Logan propped himself on his elbows and blinked against the fluorescent glare. "Don't they believe in 'lights out' around here?"

Langram glanced upward at the bank of lights over their heads. "I think it's supposed to be psychological torture or something. Reminds me of my last desk job. Pretty scary stuff."

The spartan room consisted of bare concrete floor, sickly yellow walls, high ceiling, one door, no bedding, a tin pot in the corner for a toilet.

Logan checked himself out, feeling his aching legs and bruised torso. No broken bones. Maybe a cracked rib or two. He felt woozy and nauseated, so he probably had a concussion. All in all, nothing to write home about.

His splinter camouflage suit was torn and bloody, his utility belt, knife, and wrist chronometer-compass were gone, and his pockets were empty.

Logan finally sat up and leaned back on his arms.

"Watch your right hand, there. I think it's fractured. The bones around your wrist seem out of whack."

"My arm feels okay, considering how the rest of me aches."

"Well, Logan, you're lucky we don't have any mirrors, or you'd feel even worse."

As he spoke, Langram casually brushed his bruised chin, then used his thumb to point left. Logan let his eyes drift as he spoke, and saw what Langram was pointing to. The cell was nothing more than a glorified steel closet. The door was metal, with a small wired window inset near the top.

"Comfy digs. How long have I been here?"

"A couple of hours ago, two Korean soldiers brought you in and threw you on the floor. I thought you were dead, but you seemed to have made a remarkable recovery."

As Langram spoke, he sent Logan a series of prearranged signals through seemingly innocent hand and body gestures, a trick known to most special forces troopers throughout the world. As he told Logan how he was tossed unconscious into the cell, Langram also walked his fingers backward along his own leg—signaling that, for the time being, they were stuck in that cell.

Next, Langram made a cutting gesture across his own throat, and Logan nearly grinned.

Mission accomplished... Langram had discovered exactly what the Koreans were up to.

Finally, Langram yawned and stretched, then flapped both of his arms once.

So the Koreans don't know our real escape plan, only the one that was in our mission profile. We're halfway home already—once we get out of this cell...

Logan wanted to tell his partner about Miko Katana of the SAT, about how she might already be somewhere inside the complex, working to free them. But trading that kind of information was impossible while the enemy was watching and recording their every word, every gesture.

Logan also wanted to ask Langram what he'd found—what the North Koreans were really doing in this facility.

Have to wait for the after-action report, I guess...

"Anybody else stuck in this dump?"

Langram flicked imaginary lint from his nose with his right index finger. "Nobody special."

One prisoner... and someone important to the Koreans. Must be that Japanese researcher Miko's looking for.

"When do they serve grub around here?"

"Here—" Langram tossed him a small wooden bucket. "I saved you some."

Logan reeled at the powerful smell of *kimchi*—aged, pickled cabbage—mingled with hot spices and the sickly sweet odor of rotting meat.

"Thanks," said Logan without a trace of irony. Ravenously, he shoveled the putrid mess into his mouth with both hands.

An hour later, they heard a sound on the other side of the door. Then the lock clicked.

"Uh-oh, visitors," whispered Langram.

He quickly sat up and slid across the bare floor, his back to the far wall. Logan followed his lead.

It seemed to take a long time for the metal door to swing open, but when it finally did, both men were taken by surprise.

Logan tensed. "Miko?"

"Huh?" grunted Langram.

Tac drawn, the Japanese agent stood in the doorway. Just as she opened her mouth to speak, alarms went off throughout the building.

"The surveillance team saw her," Logan cried. "Let's get the hell out of here."

"You know this chick?"

"No time for introductions now," Logan cried. "Let's move!"

Outside the cell was a hallway constructed of insulated concrete, with several doors on either side. Over the Klaxon blare, Logan heard pounding footsteps. A Korean officer rounded the corner and Miko shot him through the eye. His body jerked and slammed against the wall. Before the soldier sunk to the floor, Logan ripped the man's pistol from its holster.

"What happened?" Miko cried over the din.

"I think the North Koreans spotted you on the surveillance camera in our cell," Logan replied.

"Sorry, Logan-*san*."

"Don't be. I was getting tired of that place any—"

He paused to fire the pistol. At the opposite end of the hall, a Korean private dropped his AK-47 and sunk to the floor. As the weapon clattered to the concrete, Langram dived, slid across the floor, and snatched it up. A spray of automatic weapon fire spattered the walls behind him.

Langram rolled on his back and fired around the corner. Logan and Miko heard a grunt, and another soldier dropped while two more scrambled backward. Logan's partner fired again and the siren abruptly ceased.

"Damn, I hate alarms," said Langram. Then he rolled to his feet and kicked the dead man's machine gun across the smooth floor to Logan.

Langram joined them a moment later, and they moved swiftly along the narrow corridor, then around a bend.

"Look out!" Miko warned.

Logan turned as a man lunged at him from an open door, clutching a bayonet.

"Not again," growled Logan. He knocked the weapon aside, shoved the barrel of his own machine gun into the man's surprised face, and pulled the trigger. An explosion of bright red gore and gray brain matter decorated the wall, and the man flew backward.

"We must hurry," Miko called.

"Miko…"

The voice was faint, weak, but it stopped the woman in her tracks. She yelled something in Japanese, and the voice replied in the same language.

"What the hell is going on?" Langram asked Logan, his eyes riveted to the corridor behind them. "Why are we stopping?"

"Miko's an agent of the Japanese Special Assault Team. She's on a mission, too."

Langram's eyebrow went up. "Crowded around here, ain't it?"

"Miko…" The strange voice behind the cell door was louder.

"I'm here," the woman cried. She fished in her pocket and drew out a lock pick. Logan and Langram took position on either side of her. In less than five seconds she had unlocked the cell. When the door swung open, a horrible stench clawed at their nostrils.

On the ground, a middle-aged Japanese man lay in a pool of his own offal. The cell was similar to Langram's, but filthy. Dried food and excrement encrusted the floor, the smell of urine permeated the walls, and the smell of decay clung to every remaining corner. Logan saw the reason for the unwholesome conditions. The man's arms and legs had been broken, and the bones still protruded from his calves. His skin was purple and black around the wounds, and gangrene was eating away at his vitals.

Despite the horrendous sight and smell, Miko hurried into the room. "Father!" she sobbed as she rushed to the man's side.

Logan watched the tragic reunion, his face grim. "You know who he is?"

"Yeah," Langram replied. "His name is Inoshiro Katana. Expert in chemical compression. I heard the officers discussing him when they thought I'd blacked out during interrogation."

Logan nodded. "You might as well tell me what's going on in this place, 'cause we're not getting out of here alive."

As Langram spoke, he stared down the hall, where he was sure the enemy was gathering to rush them. "The North Koreans are making the nerve agent sarin. I've seen tanks of trichloride, sodium fluoride, phenylacetonitrile—"

"What's the point of hiding it?" Logan asked. "Kanggye Chemical Factory churns out tons of the stuff for the North Korean military. Everybody knows that."

"They're working on a binary delivery system here. Two neutral agents stored in a small container. Both substances are harmless, but combine to form sarin at the moment of use. They're trying to pack enough poison into a dispenser the size of a can of soup—which is why Dr. Katana is so important to them."

Pounding footsteps thundered from the opposite end of the long corridor. The noise was followed by barking voices. The clatter of weapons and the click of thrown bolts echoed down to them.

"They're coming," Langram warned. "We've got to go if we want to at least make the effort to escape…"

Logan watched Miko stroke her father's hair. "What about him?"

Langram looked at the broken man inside the cell. "What do you think? We can't carry him, and we can't leave him here."

"Miko," Logan called. "They're coming."

"My father, I can't—"

"No, Miko. You must," rasped her father.

"But I can't leave you here."

Suddenly, the man's pain-etched face became stern. His words were a reprimand, as if he were addressing a truculent adolescent. "No, you cannot leave me here, Miko. You know what you must do."

"No, I—"

"You must. For my honor. For the family's honor."

"Here they come!" yelled Langram as he opened up. The booming chatter of the AK-47 was deafening in the tight quarters. At the end of the hall, several tan uniforms appeared, only to drop, stitched with bloody holes.

"Grenade!" Langram yelled.

The egg clattered to the ground at Logan's feet and he kicked the explosive back to its owner. Someone screamed, then the blast washed over them, filling the narrow corridor with choking smoke.

Ears ringing, Logan stuck his head around the corner. "They've retreated. This is our chance," he cried.

"To go where?" asked Langram.

Logan pointed to the corridor they'd just passed through. The explosion had blown one of the doors off its hinges. Instead of another cell, there was a flight of steps.

"Where's it go?"

"Who cares!" Logan kicked Langram's butt to start him off, and the man sprinted across the open corridor as bullets zinged off the walls, the floor. He dived through the doorway as Logan returned fire. Langram stuck his head out the door a moment later. "It's an exit!"

Logan faced the interior of the cell. "Miko, we've got to—"

The words stuck in his throat as Miko aimed her Tac at her father's head. The man looked into the muzzle of the weapon, eyes unwavering. Her hand trembled, just a little. Before she squeezed the trigger, the woman steadied her arm, then averted her eyes. The shot, though expected, made Logan wince. Dr. Katana twitched, then lay still.

Miko's sorrowful mission accomplished, she turned away from the corpse on the floor and squeezed past Logan into the corridor. Her face was grim, and she refused to meet his stare.

"Where are we going?" she asked.

"Through that door and up," Logan replied.

In a burst of covering fire, he and Miko darted across the corridor and up the stairs.

18

BREAKING POINT

"GOT a problem here," yelled Langram.

Logan heard a steel door clang at the top of the stairs. With Miko guarding his back, Logan took the steps two at a time and charged through the hatch, to the outside. The night was cool and overcast, the lake's moisture heavy in the air. Logan had emerged from one of the circular "fuel storage" tanks in the middle of a field. Twenty or more identical tanks stood all around. None held fuel, however. Many were hollow shells, others hid smokestacks and ventilation shafts that fed air to the underground tunnels.

Intelligence was right for once, Logan realized. *The tank farm's just camouflage to hide the poison gas factory.*

Miko emerged from the stairwell, quietly closing the steel hatch behind her. "The soldiers ran right past me, down the corridor. I don't think they know we are outside."

"They'll know soon enough."

Logan heard a cry and spied Langram a few meters away, grappling in the shadows with a soldier. Both men had a grip on a single AK-47, each trying to yank the automatic rifle from the other. Another Korean lay limp on the ground. Before Logan could react, Langram kicked out, and bone snapped. The North Korean regular went down, knee shattered. Langram yanked the automatic rifle free and aimed.

Logan rushed forward. Soon the soldier tried to rise, but Logan smashed the man's larynx with his elbow. The Korean kicked booted feet as he slowly choked to death. His lips barely moved, but no sound beyond a gurgle dribbled out. Langram held the soldier down with his foot until the man died, silently and wide-eyed. It took a long ninety seconds.

"Glad you could make it," said Langram, winded.

"Did you shoot him?" Logan asked, gesturing to the second dead man on the ground.

"I was out of ammo. Shoved the barrel of my rifle into his eye."

Logan saw the AK-47 on the ground, its barrel bloody.

"Good," he whispered. "Nobody heard us yet..."

Miko stepped around the two men, Tac in hand. She carefully scanned the area with her night-vision binoculars. "Clear."

Langram and Logan tossed the corpses.

"An AK-47, two magazines."

"A 47 for me," said Langram. "One magazine. This is gonna go hand-to-hand real quick."

"I need a blade," grunted Logan.

Langram tossed him a web belt with a Korean-made bayonet and sheath. The blade was as long as Logan's forearm, thin and sharp. Logan strapped the belt around his hips, drew the knife, and twirled it in his hand. "It'll do."

"Logan, over there," Miko said softly.

Logan took her NVGs and immediately spied a Korean armored personnel carrier, large enough to carry ten men. The vehicle sat on an access road less than a hundred meters away, only partially obscured by a storage tank. The APC's rear hatch was open, the driver on the pavement, leaning against one of the six oversized tires, smoking a cigarette. In the glow of the interior lights, the cabin appeared to be unoccupied. Over the sounds of the night, Logan could hear the poorly tuned engine idling and smell its exhaust.

Between them and the road stood several storage tanks, each the size of a small house.

Best to get by them without too much noise.

"That's our ticket out," Logan said, showing Langram the vehicle. Then, to Miko, "Got the time?"

Miko checked her chronometer. "Oh-two-forty."

Langram and Logan synchronized the old-style windup watches they'd taken from the dead soldiers, then strapped them on.

"We've got one hour, nineteen minutes to get to our extraction point, four klicks away," Logan told Miko.

She seemed unconcerned. "Are we going to take that vehicle?"

"We'd better or we'll never make the rendezvous unless we run.

There's a Pave Hawk coming for us, and if we're not at the extraction zone, we lose our ride."

She nodded, face neutral.

"Miko," said Logan, stepping closer to her. "I want you to know I'm sorry—"

She cut him off. "Do not speak of it again. I did what I must, and I will do as I must for the duration of this affair—"

"You're going to get out of here," Logan said. "With us. You're going to make it and so are we."

"*Hai.*"

Miko would not meet his stare, but Logan saw death in her eyes. He'd seen it in the faces of other Japanese warriors he'd known, back when they were fighting each other, the Russians, the Koreans—pretty much everyone in sight.

Though there were modern Japanese making cars and video equipment, Logan knew that for nationalists like Miko, the samurai code of Bushido still lived, still exerted a powerful influence over their lives. *Miko believed in honor, duty—and she proved it by her risky actions, tonight.*

Langram lowered the NVGs and handed them back to the half-Japanese woman.

"That soldier is definitely alone out there," he said. "Maybe these stiffs are his pals and he's waiting for them to make their rounds. I say we flank him before he wakes up and notices his buddies are missing."

Logan nodded. "So what's your plan?"

"You two go left, I'll cut around that tank over there and circle him. We hit the driver in—" Langram glanced at his watch. "Four minutes. Unless I get there first."

"What if he drives away?" asked Miko.

"We wave bye-bye," said Langram. Then he took off.

Miko and Logan cautiously circled a "storage tank"—really just a wooden shell—and reached the armored personnel carrier on cue. Langram was there, waiting. He had already taken care of things.

"Where's the driver?" asked Logan.

"In a graveyard. Very dead." Langram replied. "I planted him over in the bushes."

Langram climbed into the personnel carrier and through to the driver's compartment while Logan went through the weapons bin, where he found the driver's machine gun, another on the rack, and a leather bag of ammunition dangling from a seat. In the cab, Langram threw a flashlight and a bag of rice cakes on the torn seat, then whipped a plastic-encased map out of a metal box and shook it open. "Better than Triple A, mate."

While the men studied the map, Miko quietly curled up in the corner, hugging her legs, her handgun dangling from one hand.

"We're less than four kilometers away," said Logan. "Get on this road, follow it along the river valley, past this fishing village to the hills beyond."

"That chopper better be waiting for us," said Langram as he jumped into the driver's seat. He shifted the vehicle into gear, and the APC lurched forward on its six massive wheels. Langram quickly made a U-turn and went in the opposite direction.

Logan climbed into the seat next to him and lay the machine gun across his lap. Miko had another AK-47 strapped to her back, the leather case of ammo on her shoulder. She rose up on her haunches, gazing placidly through the bulletproof glass at the road ahead.

"There's the highway, but there's no gate on this end of the complex," said Logan, rechecking the map. "You'll have to make one."

"Right through the fence," said Langram.

"You know that'll alert the Koreans."

"Don't look now, but I think they're already alert!" Langram yelled, grinding the gears and stepping on the gas.

From a false storage tank directly ahead of them, a dozen soldiers burst through a steel door. Leading them was an officer clutching a pistol and gesturing wildly at the oncoming vehicle.

"Maybe we can bluff them," said Langram.

A shot bounced off the armored car, then came a sustained crackling as all the soldiers opened fire at once. Bullets glanced off the thick-skinned personnel carrier like acorns bouncing off a car, filling the cramped compartment with noise.

"Guess that didn't work," cried Langram. "Hold on!"

He swerved enough to clip the first soldier who reached the roadway. The broken man flew backward into the arms of the men behind him. As his troopers were bowled over, the officer blew a whistle and fired a pistol at the APC. The bullet bounced harmlessly off the shatterproof glass next to Logan's head.

Then came a crash as the APC flattened a chain-link fence and rolled over the twisted debris. Another jolt, accompanied by blinding sparks and crackling volts, shook the vehicle as it ripped through the electrified fence. Langram jerked the steering wheel, and the six tires skidded along damp grass before lurching onto the tarred road with a bump. The heavy armored personnel carrier lumbered away, Langram put on the gas and got them moving at the vehicle's top speed of forty kilometers per hour. Logan watched the soldiers recede in the rearview mirror. From somewhere behind them, the angry wail of another alarm faded in the distance.

"We lost 'em," said Langram.

Logan gripped his machine gun. "The hell we did. They're gonna be up our ass in no time."

Langram looked at his partner, only half-surprised to see a grin on Logan's face.

"A bloody, broken heap on the cell floor a couple of hours ago, and now you're itching for action. I guess all the rumors I heard about you are true, Logan."

Logan ignored his partner. "Coming up on the village," he said. On the horizon, dark silhouettes were framed against the moonlight.

Minutes later, they rumbled through a ghost town. Headlights illuminated dark wooden shacks, every one abandoned. Doors hung from hinges, grass grew wildly around the ramshackle structures. The stone gate at the entrance to the village had tumbled to the ground. In the black water, boats were moored, some of them half sunk. Sundered fishing nets blew idle in the wind.

Farther along, a large cannery facility loomed in the night, completely desolate and tumbling into the river, piece by piece.

"The pollution from that poison gas factory upstream has been real bad for the local economy," said Logan.

Langram swerved to avoid a two-wheeled cart abandoned in the roadway. "At least there are no goddamn civilians to get in the way."

"No one lives in this place. It is a land of ghosts," said Miko, staring straight ahead. "Their leaders make poison while the people starve to death."

Logan frowned as he squinted into the horizon. Miko turned away from the window, lost in her own tortured thoughts.

The APC skidded around a corner, and Langram shifted gears as they began to climb up a low hill. They were still paralleling the river. To their right the forest had become dense once again, the land rising to low hills on either side of them.

"Almost home now," said Langram. "Less than a kilometer, then we can ditch this piece of junk and take to the woods."

As they crested the hill, the engine sputtered and Langram worked the clutch. "Don't die on me now you piece of—" A string of curses followed.

"I can't believe it's this easy," said Logan. "Why haven't they chased u—"

His question was interrupted by a loud crack as the personnel carrier was rocked by a sonic boom from the antitank projectile that zoomed over their heads.

"Look out!" Miko cried.

Bridging the road fifty meters ahead was the boxy silhouette of a North Korean tank, surrounded by dozens of soldiers. Behind the tank, several large trucks were parked to the side of the road, disgorging troops.

"Hold on!" bellowed Langram.

With a lurch, they were thrown to one side as the APC left the road and bumped across rough, rocky ground to the dense forest ahead of them.

"We can lose that tank in the woods," Langram cried. His words were nearly drowned by the sounds of cracking tree limbs as their vehicle struck down a sapling and tore the branches off several low hanging pines.

Logan clutched the roof with one hand, his AK-47 with the other. As the APC rumbled up a steep slope, its wheels spinning through loose dirt, Logan saw fire burst from the muzzle of the tank still parked on the road. He heard the report of the cannon a split second later—just as the large shell ripped through the trunk of a tree in their path.

Wood splinters filled the air, and Langram hit the gas. Miko was thrown to the steel floor as the personnel carrier lurched forward. It hopped a ditch, skidding on wet, smooth rock. The APC leaned to one side. Langram fought the wheel, trying not to roll over.

"Got it," he cried as the vehicle stabilized.

Inside the cab, as Langram concentrated on driving, Logan and Miko hung on. None of them heard the tank's third shot or saw the muzzle's blast. But they only felt the spine-cracking impact as the sabot round tore through the carrier's steel armor like a rock through a plate glass window.

The personnel carrier shuddered, then blew into halves. Both ends tumbled down the hillside, spewing fuel, tires spinning.

○────────────────○

SOMETHING lurched inside his brain. Logan found himself spinning through a void.

No, it's not me... I'm just lying here. It's the whole world that's rolling over.

He heard a mechanical *tick*. Then a *whir*, like the sound of a tape rewinding. The noise seemed somehow comforting and he lay, eyes closed, listening to the constant drone until it faded from his consciousness. Finally, another *click* snapped him awake. Logan heard a *beep*, and a woman's voice spoke his name.

"Mr. Logan... I don't know if you can understand me..."

He opened his eyes to stare at a metal ceiling, its recessed lighting dim. On the floor, bits of silicon and shards of glass sparkled around him. Looking up, he saw the observation window had been broken, spears of glass still in the frame, some spattered with black drops. Computers were smashed, their monitor screens shattered.

"... Use your imagination, Ms. Hines," a voice boomed. "Think of the horror of it all..."

I can't think... must've been some party, and someone ruined it.

Logan rose, wobbling on unsteady legs. *My clothes are gone*, he realized. *The soldiers... they must have taken them...*

Then his memory faded like vapor, and Logan wondered vaguely who "they" were. Woozy, he leaned against a computer console, staring at hands stained with clotted blood.

My own... or someone else's?

"... He's lost a lot of blood..." said the voice.

"Yeah," growled Logan. "I'd like to see the other guy."

The voices came from all around him—the walls, the ceiling, the consoles. They spoke in a crazy loop. Logan heard snatches of busy conversations that did not seem to connect in any rational way.

"... Deadwood... Please respond... Logan is alive..."

Despite his pain and bafflement, Logan smirked. "You bet I am..."

"... But security took care of Logan, Professor... I'm bleeding to death... Bloody massacre..."

"There will be, pal, when I find you..." Logan wheezed. *Especially if you don't shut up and let me get my bearings...*

Logan slumped in a chair. Eyes closed, head drooped over a computer terminal, he tried to recall where he was, how he got here.

"... Mr. Logan has shown uncanny tracking abilities..."

"Yeah, and I'm butt naked, too."

"... Killing everyone in sight. Running amok, you might say..."

Logan opened his eyes—and saw a severed hand lying on the console in front of him. He jumped backward, out of the seat.

"... Are you aware of what is happening at this time? I'm losing men in Zone Two..."

Logan warily scanned the room, slowly backing into a corner. "Who's pulling this stunt? Answer me!"

Near his ear, the voice boomed from a speaker—

"... Deadwood. I'm deadwood, Cornelius..."

—and Logan knew.

It's a recording... Some kind of random playback. Nobody's controlling this. I'm alone here.

Panic gripped him. *Got to get out...*

"... Weapon X has escaped... I am not in control..."

He bolted for the door. Took the metal staircase to a platform below. He looked down into a deep metal well, smoke curling up from the bottom. Logan soon turned away from the pit and found a hatch, blown open, its lock twisted on the floor. The yawning tunnel behind the door led to another corridor. At the end of that corridor, a long hall fanned out in either direction. Logan paused, wondering which way to turn.

Smoke... the smell of ozone... machinery humming. This place is industrial... maybe military... don't like the army and they don't like me. Better get out of here before I get drafted...

He crossed the threshold, past the broken hatch, and followed the long, blood-spattered corridor, then turned right.

Place is a maze—or a tomb.

He wandered through the dimly lit steel cave until he reached an elevator.

There was no power and the doors refused to open, but Logan soon found the stairwell. He climbed the steps until he saw the radiation warnings.

Must be a reactor… gotta be people there. Nobody leaves a reactor running when they're not at home…

But the reactor's control room was deserted, the core running on automatic. The entranceway seemed undisturbed except for a section along the wall that was a shattered, smoldering wreckage. He detected a whiff of cordite.

Shooting… what went on in this place?

He saw a weapon lying on the ground, a Heckler & Koch UMP, barrel bent.

Why the gun? This can't be a military installation, too sharp. These computers are Buck Rogers… the army doesn't have state-of-the-art facilities like this… could be S.H.I.E.L.D.… maybe. But why would Fury's bunch mess with me?

Logan sniffed the air again, and this time he smelled blood. Finally, he spied the body of a portly, middle-aged man sprawled across the main console. Mesmerized, he approached the grim scene, gazed down at the dead man's features.

He wore a lab smock, stained crimson. His ribs protruded from a ruined chest. The man had been gutted, brutalized. Yet his face seemed composed… almost resigned, which made the violence done to him all the more horrendous to Logan.

He's been cut—real bad—three in the gut, then eviscerated. Brutal… senseless. Unless there's some kind of sick vendetta.

He stared down at the man's features, at the glasses shattered on the floor, and started to remember.

I… I know this man. In a memory, a dream. A dream of dying.

Logan reached into his mind for an identity, an emotion—some connection to this man. He came up with nothing. Whoever he was, Logan bore him no animosity. He left the reactor room, moved on.

He found a dead man several levels higher. The man lay face down near a cart of equipment that had been overturned. He'd also been slashed, his carotid artery laid bare by a bladed weapon.

Not the only victim, either. He knew there would be more.

Death. This place reeks of it. Hanging in the air like heat… but who did the killing?

Afraid of the answer, Logan held up his hands, stained by congealed blood.

All over me, but no wounds... my blood? Must be... or did I knife this guy? What'd he do to me? This corpse... the one in the reactor room. And that hand back there. That severed hand...

A memory flickered and died. Logan's limbs began to quiver and his back slammed against the wall.

Did I finally flip out? Lose my mind and kill everyone in here, and now I don't remember it?

He moaned and clutched his head.

Wouldn't be surprised... my old partner Langram warned me that this would happen, sooner or later. "In times of peace, a man of war sets upon himself." That's what he told me once. Said I was a man of war... or was it a born warrior? Anyway, why am I thinking of Langram? Is he here somewhere? Did I kill him, too? I need a fucking drink.

The recorded conversations, which sounded like technobabble for so long that they'd faded into the background, suddenly invaded Logan's consciousness when a frightened voice repeatedly cried out his name.

"... Mr. Logan... Mr. Logan, sir." A woman.

"... Come, creature. Into the pit..." a man's voice screamed, choked with emotion.

Suddenly, Logan's forearms ached. He rubbed them, felt muscles bulging under the skin. An uncontrollable spasm made them roil unnaturally. Pain permeated his arms.

"... I don't know if you can understand me, sir." The woman again. Pleading.

A sharp pain lanced through his wrists, and he flexed his hands.

"... I can't stand pain," the woman sobbed. She was barely comprehensible. "Physical pain. Burned with chemicals... Please, I beg you. Kill me quickly..."

Is it Miko? No. This doesn't make any sense.

Logan's fingers curled into a tight fist as agony gripped them. He stared down at hands frozen into clutching claws. Soon something warm and crimson. Three bloody wounds like stigmata on the tops of each hand. Then steel claws emerged from their sheaths, ripping through tortured flesh, extending their full length. He threw back his head and howled.

"... Run, Mr. Logan, run!" the woman cried. A moment later, a scream, and Logan knew she was dead, too.

"... Am I dead?"

This time, he recognized the voice. His own.

"... Dead? Am I a walking dead man?"

"... You are an animal!" screamed a voice tinged with insanity—and suddenly, a face to match that cry exploded into Logan's mind. Bald. Patrician. High cheekbones, rectangular glasses. Arrogance melting into an expression etched with fear.

My tormentor. He must die! Or is he already dead?

"... I am Logan," his own voice boomed from hidden speakers. "Logan! I am a man..."

He stared down at the blood-dewed silver claws in disbelief. His mind broke as waves of memory drowned all reason. The violence continued to build in Logan's mind.

Animal? Yes, I am an animal, a beast and a machine. A thing they made me.

Logan held his arms extended, silver claws protruding from his wrists. He tried to rip one of the blades out, gashed his hand to the bone—and in the wound, under the gore, the silver adamantium steel gleamed.

They found me. Found me out. Learned my secret. Brought me here. Cut me. Got into my body.

"... Animal!... You are the animal..."

Tortured me. Tore up my mind. Got to get away, away from here... now.

Logan ran. Blindly. His own recorded voice shouting in his ears, battering his brain with images of merciless and deliberate torment. Endless. Soul-searing.

I'm running. Running in a dream.

Moving full bore, he slammed into walls, burst through partitions, leaped over savaged corpses. The floor sprouted spikes that pierced his feet and still he ran. Time stretched and the atmosphere thickened. His legs and arms felt weighted, his progress slowed. Behind him came the sound of snapping fangs, like claws scraping on chalky tombstones.

Something on my heels, moving with me like a living shadow. Tracking me by the smell of my blood.

Logan ran faster, afraid that if he stopped or even slowed, the shadow thing would catch up, overwhelm him, suffocate him. Drag him down into the darkness forever.

And I won't be able to scream, or fight it off, because it'll be inside me… under my skin… inside my bones.

Using the abhorrent steel claws to slash through a bolted door, Logan raced up a flight of stairs—felt like hundreds. Each stair sprouted a ragged spike, each step became piercing agony.

Running like a truck. Barreling uphill with a full load… trying not to flip, to fall. Can't keep up this pace. I'm losing ground, and that thing… It's gaining…

He felt a force tugging on him, drawing him back even as he tried to surge forward.

It's grabbing at me. Snatching at me with veins like ropes, pulling me back. Tendons like chains, like wires—like strings and a puppet.

Then the field of spikes he'd been running through crawled along the floor, along his body. Suddenly, Logan was sprouting spikes, just like the floor, the walls. Long. Sharp. Gleaming metal. They burst, bloodless, from his shoulders, torso, hips, thighs.

Long, thin fingers curling around my ribs… Muscles stretching, spine bending back… It's tearing at me, dragging me back into its hungry darkness.

As he ran, Logan left a gory trail—crimson footprints.

It's on my trail… At my shoulder. Cutting me with spikes. Breaking into me. Hot breath, searing pain. Flesh burning, bones turned to magma. The putrid stench of death in my nose, my mouth.

The claws that reached into his body began to tear at his mind. Logan's senses dimmed. An electronic hum dominated his hearing. A blue pall fell over his eyes. He struggled against the almost hypnotic influence, but the blue fog turned ebony black, and the weight of the void fell heavy on his consciousness.

Can't get away… Must get away. Must run forever… fight forever. Never give in to the darkness. Never surrender to the beast. A man. Can't forget…

But out of the blackness, the shadow rose, suffocating him, dulling his mind, crushing his will. Logan moved his lips, but discovered he'd lost the ability to speak.

He felt an icy rage squeeze his brain. A rage that was not his own. A hatred for all men that he'd never felt before.

It's got me… and it wants revenge. It's turning me inside out. Darkness unending. Behind me, around me. It's everywhere. The shadow's everywhere. I'm everywhere…

As the void washed over him and consciousness winked out like a thrown switch, Logan heard a tiny voice from somewhere deep inside of his abyss.

"Don't give up," it said.

Can't go on… bones dense like lead. Like iron. Knees giving in…

"Don't give up…"

Shot through like steel in the heart caving in—

"Don't give up."

—under the weight. The weight of the beast.

19

ENDGAME

"IT'S extraordinary, is it not, Cornelius?"

The Professor stared up at the monitor, hands locked behind his back. "Amazing that Weapon X, a creature of such power, is shaken by his own shadow. Driven by fear of himself to something akin to a nervous breakdown."

Dr. Cornelius, at Carol Hines's shoulder, glanced at the readouts on the woman's REM terminal. Slowly, the device's waves were being reduced, releasing Logan's brain from its murderous dream thrall.

"It is impressive, Professor. More impressive still is the way he's pulling through. Fighting back. Despite it all, there's a core element to Logan's personality that battles on, even when the odds seem hopeless. Exterior camera, Ms. Hines."

"Switching…"

The image on the HDTV monitor morphed. The frozen picture of Logan's bleak dream-scape—a nightmare in purple and scarlet, with a desolate black void for sky and bony white spikes protruding from the virtual ground—was replaced by a chilly exterior shot of the complex.

Pale moonlight glistened off freshly fallen snow. A frigid wind howled down from the nearby mountains, shaking diamond-dust ice crystals from the white-blanketed branches. The bitter-cold night unmarked by clouds. A spray of stars and a bright hunter's moon cut the sky's silky blackness.

"So you think he has pulled through, beaten back his fear and self-loathing, eh?" the Professor asked, his lips a challenging sneer. "We shall see what we shall see."

"Yes, I guess we will, Professor. Logan's still standing, isn't he?" Cornelius gestured to the image on the screen. Logan, silhouetted by the brilliant moon, legs braced in the snow, arms at his side, claws like icicles hanging from his wrists.

The Professor leaned toward the monitor, savoring the raw power of the thing he'd created and now controlled. On-screen, Logan's naked flesh gleamed palely in the moonlight, crowned by a shock of raven black hair. Slabs of bulky muscle, rigid as concrete, plastered his chest, and thick, corded bands crisscrossed his arms, loins, thighs. Legs spread, crouched— he was a juggernaut ready to explode, Logan's flanks quivered like an excited animal, his hot breath came in moist, steaming clouds.

The mutant faced a white-striped Siberian tiger—starved, of course, as per the Professor's instructions. Man and beast stood frozen in place, eyes locked. The cat curled its lips to bare merciless fangs.

"Logan didn't buckle," said Cornelius. "He didn't give in. He didn't even retract his claws when we gave him the power to do so."

The Professor placed his index finger in front of his lips. "Hush, Cornelius. He has found the snow leopard."

"Siberian tiger, sir."

"Yes, thank you, Ms. Hines."

Cornelius cleared his throat. "We could have set this up better, you know."

The Professor faced him. "How do you mean, Doctor?"

"If Logan actually had to hunt the cat down, confront it, to kill it of his own volition, instead of the tiger just being there, threatening him… this experiment would have been a little more telling if Logan's will were somehow engaged, I think."

"Yes," the Professor replied thoughtfully. "I suppose you're right. But still, this is an acceptable scenario for one possessing the subject's simplistic perceptions."

On the screen, the tiger opened its jaws. The snarling sound crackled through the speakers after a split-second delay. Its ferocity grew with each passing second.

"Please synchronize the sound system, Ms. Hines."

The snarl became a gurgling roar. Though the tiger was hungry—very hungry—it seemed cautious of its adversary. The tiger's flanks rippled, its tail flashed from side to side; the creature backed up and crouched, ears flat. Even then, it would not spring.

In the end, it was Logan who lunged first, attacking the big cat a split second before it leaped at him. The antagonists slammed into each other, Logan's arms rising and falling as he repeatedly stabbed the roaring feline.

"Look at that!" Cornelius cried. "Logan's right in there. He's just as wild and savage as before."

But the Professor shook his head. "He may seem so, Doctor, but in the past few days, Weapon X has been altered irrevocably. His savagery is now tempered by ego and ratiocination. It is not savagery we see, but cunning."

On-screen, Logan and the creature grappled in fury, neither gaining the upper hand.

"Look how he fights, Cornelius. Any hesitation, a moment of fear, trepidation, or merely caution—and he will be undone."

"Yes, literally," said Cornelius. On the monitor, Logan and the tiger rolled across the snowy expanse. The tiger's claws raked at the man's soft belly while he slashed at the creature's exposed throat. Blood drops decorated the combatants.

The Professor sighed. "It has, of course, been necessary that Logan not know of his indestructible skeleton…"

"Which won't help him if he gets disemboweled, anyway."

"No, Dr. Cornelius. In that case, he would learn the truth the hard way—and with much pain."

"Camera four, Ms. Hines."

"Yes, Doctor. Switching…"

The scene changed, and so did the contest. Now Logan was up, his knee thrust into the tiger's chest. The butchering began. Black blood stained the snow, and gore flew in great gouts at every blow from Logan's long claws.

"He's gaining the advantage, Professor."

"Yet not so long ago, Weapon X beheaded a grizzly bear without hesitation. Without so much as a tussle," the Professor said regretfully. "That is what I call gaining the advantage."

The tiger's quick movements were less frenzied. The beast was weakening from exhaustion and lack of blood. Logan continued to rip the creature, his own grunts of exertion mingled with the cat's growls of pain and rage.

"You have to have faith, Professor," Cornelius said. "Look, I'll lay you a hundred on Logan. What do you think of that?"

The Professor made a sour face. "This is not a game, Cornelius…"

"Give me a full close-up on camera number six, Ms. Hines!" cried Cornelius. "And wake up, or we'll miss half the action. I don't think I've seen Logan's reflexes faster than they are now."

"Switching…"

With renewed strength, the tiger reared up and lashed out with a vicious blow from one of its front paws. Logan pulled back just in time, the claw tearing a ragged canal across the muscles of his chest.

Cornelius faced the Professor. "You're telling me this is no game? If that blow would have connected, it could have gutted Logan and I'd be out a C-note."

The Professor chuckled. "You don't see it, do you, Cornelius? That was a feint. You are correct about his reflexes. They are more nimble. And so is the mind of our subject. Weapon X was drawing the creature out for the kill. Watch and learn."

"Pull in closer, Ms. Hines," said Cornelius.

The tiger drew back its front paw to strike again, leaving an opening for Logan to exploit. With a deadly lunge, he sunk his steel claws into the beast's soft throat until his fist met the animal's gore-streaked fur, and the tips of the blades protruded from the dead beast's wedge-shaped skull.

"A magnificent blow!" cried the Professor.

Over the speakers, the snarls ended abruptly. As Logan struck a second time, plunging his claws into the tiger's heart, his own raking breath could be heard over the loudspeakers.

"God! Another blow—straight to the heart. Son-of-a-bitch Logan is more brutal than ever." Cornelius faced the woman. "Give me readings, Ms. Hines… heart rate, respiration, adrenal levels."

Carol Hines checked her monitor, then blinked in surprise. "No readings, sir. Mr. Logan is off-line for this. He's performing without the influence of the REM device."

"Excellent," said the Professor. "Weapon X has executed his mission without benefit of our direct commands. Only our influence, his conditioning, and the reprogramming techniques we applied, are controlling him at this point."

"Fantastic!" said Cornelius, grinning. "Then I guess it's mission accomplished. Logan is functioning autonomously, per your original specifications, Professor. What do you say to that?"

"It is remarkable, indeed, Dr. Cornelius. His instincts and reflexes, though perhaps more pragmatic, more careful, seem quite undiminished. More important, his ferocity is still unparalleled."

Cornelius chuckled. "Pity I couldn't get you to take that bet, eh, Professor? It would have been easy money."

Peevishly, the Professor crossed his arms. "I will not sully the nature of our scientific endeavor with wagers, Doctor."

Cornelius refused to be cowed. After months inside this facility, after weeks of lockdown, he finally saw the end of this odious experiment just over the horizon, and his mood was high.

I have all the samples of Logan's blood and tissue that I will ever need for my immunology experiments to continue, long after I leave this place, mused Cornelius. *The Professor's right about one thing, though. The existence of Weapon X will alter the course of history. Not as a destroyer, however, as the Professor envisions, but as a healer and a boon to all mankind...*

On the HDTV monitor, Logan rose, bloodied but undefeated, the tiger broken and lifeless in snow turned crimson. The subject stared straight ahead into a fathomless distance.

Cornelius sank into a chair. "I believe you have underestimated your prize, Professor," he began. "In that little virtual-reality scenario of yours, Logan was set up. We gave him a chance to escape. Yet he didn't run. Instead, he turned around and savagely assassinated the lot of us. Then we jammed his psyche with his fear of his own mutant nature, and even that didn't faze him."

The Professor's eyebrow rose. "Meaning?"

"I'd say he came through your final test with an A, wouldn't you?" Cornelius replied.

"Yes, yes, he was aggressive enough," the Professor replied. "And yet he failed to kill Ms. Hines. An act of mercy that leaves doubt still lingering in my mind."

"We discussed this with Dr. MacKenzie in the postexperiment briefing," Cornelius replied. "He spared Hines because she was never a threat to him. It's as we conjectured—Logan will only kill if threatened with harm, or... well..."

"Out of hunger?" posited Carol Hines.

"Yes, or out of hunger. And why would he want to eat Ms. Hines, anyway?" Cornelius joked.

"Yes, all right, Cornelius," said the Professor. "I suppose we should consider this experiment a successful one—flawed though it may be."

Carol Hines looked up from her own terminal. "If I may say, Doctor, I think Mr. Logan only killed you in the VR scenario because of that accidental shooting. I don't think he would have attacked you if the circumstances were different."

Cornelius thought about it for a moment. "You may be right, Ms. Hines—"

"Hmph," grunted the Professor.

"In any case," Cornelius continued, "Weapon X... Logan... made a rational decision within the parameters of the situation he experienced, and relied on a modicum of rational judgment rather than reacting with naked aggression. Which makes him a smart weapon, indeed."

"I shall have to consider a new round of tests, turn Logan over to MacKenzie for the next phase of operations," muttered the Professor.

"Have the wranglers pick up Logan, Ms. Hines."

"Yes, Dr. Cornelius."

She tapped the intercom and a voice crackled in reply. "Cutler here..."

"Please bring the subject inside, Agent Cutler. Subject X should be taken to D-Block this time."

o———————————o

"YES. D-Block. I know, Ms. Hines... over."

Cutler keyed off the intercom and rubbed his tired eyes. The hatch to the armory opened and Agent Anderson entered.

"What the hell are you doing here, Anderson? Franks is the name on this morning's duty roster."

Anderson paused, but would not face his boss. "I guess you just got out of bed, eh, Cut?"

"Yeah, ten minutes ago. You'd sleep for three whole hours, too, if the Professor didn't have you on duty for the nuttiest experiment on record. Logan was running around on the grounds outside, lost in some kind of delusion or something. I thought he'd run away, but the eggheads got him under their thumbs. Shut Logan down until a little while ago..."

Anderson would not meet the other soldier's gaze. Cutler noticed. "What the hell is wrong with you?"

"You... you didn't hear about Franks, then?"

Cutler stared. "What about Franks?"

"Two hours ago. The handlers were moving that Siberian from the cage to the compound. Tiger got him—"

"What?"

"Franks was prodding the thing out of its cage so Logan could hunt it down. The tiger turned, ripped Franks."

"How bad?"

"Took his arm off. Franks bled to death before Dr. Hendry could get to him. Lynch wanted to shoot the tiger as soon as he attacked Franks, but Major Deavers stopped him. Said the Professor would be pissed if Weapon X didn't have something to hunt..."

Cutler slumped onto a bench without knowing it. He stared at the far wall. "That bastard Deavers... that son-of-a-bitchin' suck-up."

"You can't blame it on the Major," Anderson replied. "Really, I saw the tape, Cut. There was nothing anyone could do for Franks."

Cutler nodded. Then he stood and quietly began to suit up. As he donned his Kevlar armor, he began to speak—more to himself than to Anderson.

"Franks was okay," he said. "You could count on him. He took this job seriously, tried to do his best. Now he's just another goddamn ghost haunting this place."

"Come on, Cut, don't take it so hard."

"Don't take it so hard? That's a laugh. I'm not taking it at all. I feel nothing. Numb. Like I'm half-dead myself. Like I'm just a ghost, and so is everybody else in here. This... place. The desolation. This lockdown. This sick, twisted experiment..."

Anderson glanced at the overhead security monitor. "Hey, Cut... the walls have ears, y'know."

"I'm not the only one, either. MacKenzie told me people are freaking out, especially in the last week or so. The Professor's been on duty, like, twenty-four seven, running that damn dream machine they have down there." Cutler locked eyes with Anderson. "You been having dreams?"

"Huh?"

"Dreams, Anderson? Or nightmares?"

Anderson seemed guarded. "Who wouldn't… in a place like this?"

"Well, I've been dreaming. A lot. Different stuff. Last night, I dreamed about something that happened a long time ago. When I was active duty… a corporal in the Special Forces… in another country…"

"Jesus, Cut. Don't get spiritual on me, and don't wig out. I can't take it. You're security chief. The rock, man. If you crack up, what chance do the rest of us have?"

Cutler tried to shake off the ill mood, but found it completely impossible. He blamed it on the news about Franks. The truth was that he woke up with a feeling of oppression, as if something bad were about to happen.

Or already had.

Maybe it was a premonition. Maybe he was thinking about Franks and didn't even know it.

Another ghost to haunt this place…

"Forget about it, Anderson," Cutler said at last. "I'm just pissed about what happened to Franks, that's all."

Cutler laughed—a bitter, mirthless sound—then lifted his helmet. "Suit up, and let's get this over with."

As they stepped out into the cold and tested their electroprods, Cutler remembered the night he'd caught up with Logan, outside the rundown gin mill in that crappy part of town. He'd wondered at the time who the guy really was, knowing only that Logan had some kind of connection to the military or military intelligence—as Cutler himself did, then and now.

At that time, Logan was considered an expendable "package"—a piece of discarded military hardware that was being recycled into something new with predictable military efficiency. But suddenly, things had changed. Now Logan was the valuable commodity and the people around him were the disposable ones—guys like Hill and Franks, Anderson and Lynch.

And me.

Cutler could not help thinking that maybe he deserved what was happening. Maybe the way he'd treated Logan was coming back to him. In spades.

As they moved across the snow to the scene of carnage, Cutler felt trapped, like he was stuck in an endless loop of twisted cruelty. The frozen black blood on the snow—glass-smooth; the slashed animal on the ground; the smell of spilled blood. All of it gave him a shiver of déjà vu, a sense that he'd been here before and would experience these things again, perhaps endlessly.

Just like one of the ghosts that haunts this place...

◦————————————◦

CORNELIUS thrust his hands into his pockets and rocked on the balls of his feet. "So what have we got here, Professor? Logan thinks he's killed everyone inside this complex, all to get to you—the focus of his vengeance."

The Professor paced uncomfortably. "Yes, go on."

"Now, thanks to the REM machine's induced dreams, Logan knows he isn't human. Not only is he a mutant, but he now possesses a near-indestructible skeleton, a piece of technology that further alienates him— further separates him from his own humanity. And with all of that, he also knows it was you who harnessed his dark secret, who used that hated part of himself—the mutant part—and turned him into Weapon X."

"Indeed," replied the Professor, staring at the monitor. "So Logan had no choice but to destroy me, did he not? As we are compelled to destroy our old gods to make way for new ones. In the act of killing his creator, Logan's once inculpable savagery is transformed into the cunning of a ruthless killer—an inspired bit of 'psychological transference,' as Dr. MacKenzie called it." Finally, the Professor faced the doctor. "I savor these events, Cornelius."

Cornelius nodded before he twisted the knife. "Of course, you did hedge your bets a little, Professor."

"What? How do you mean?"

"Making up all that stuff about how you were actually working for somebody else... some great power or something... as if you were a stooge or a flunky instead of the genius behind Experiment X."

The Professor met Cornelius's gaze and knew the man was suspicious. "A mere psychological ruse..." murmured the Professor.

"It was a good one. Setting yourself up for your own murder, but then playing at being betrayed by the real creator of Weapon X at the climax. Were you trying for a little ambiguity—a way to cast a shadow of a doubt in Logan's mind? Or were you working for sympathy? Testing your subject to see if he'd reason that you weren't the real threat, that he'd spare you the way he spared Ms. Hines? Either way, it's clever. Really tricky."

The Professor offered an enigmatic half smile. "Indeed, Dr. Cornelius. All just a dramatic ploy that… proved a great deal about the nature of the beast, hmm?"

"Well, all in all, it's been a good day, right, Ms. Hines?"

But the woman did not reply. Lost in thought, she frowned up at the monitor. On the screen, the wranglers were approaching the motionless man crouched in the snow.

"Are you okay, Ms. Hines?" Cornelius asked. "You seem tense."

"Yes, Hines. You don't seem to be sharing the doctor's celebratory mood…"

"Something is bothering me, it's true," Carol Hines replied. "But I don't know if I'm free to speak of it, Professor. The information is classified. And I signed an agreement not to speak of the matter, even after I left NASA's employ."

"If your secret involves our work here, then surely you are compelled to speak," sputtered the Professor.

Carol Hines nodded. "Yes, sir. I suppose you are right…"

20

REDEMPTION

LOGAN felt something touch his head, someone tug at his clothes. He opened his eyes and stared up at a seat swinging precipitously from a single bolt. His eardrums still reverberated from a terrible noise he could not recall from memory.

"Logan..."

He twisted his neck and spied Miko on the ground beside him. Her face was bruised, and a long piece of shrapnel—probably a chunk of the shattered APC—was lodged in her shoulder. The flesh around the metal was puckered and seeping blood.

He rolled over, checked her out. "Where's Langram?"

"Still in his seat."

Logan looked up and saw his partner dangling limply from the driver's seat. His leg hung on the steering wheel. Obviously, the cab had overturned, but Logan could not recall the exact circumstances of the accident.

He quickly rolled to his feet and checked his partner's pulse. "Langram's alive!"

Logan hauled his partner down, and saw blood oozing from a head wound. Langram's leg was also broken.

He's lucky. Clean break, not a compound fracture, but Langram isn't going to be jogging anytime soon. Guess I'll be hauling him up to the extraction point.

Miko crawled to Logan's side, struggling to stand up. "Take this," grunted Logan, yanking the AK-47 off his shoulder and handing it over to her. "Can you walk?"

"*Hai.*" She turned away; he stopped her. Before she could protest, Logan yanked the shrapnel out of her arm.

She paled, bit her lip, but made no sound.

"You are samurai," he reminded her in Japanese, prompting Miko to smile despite her discomfort. Logan found the first-aid kit, dumped a tube of disinfectant into the bloody hole, then stuffed it with gauze, which he taped in place.

"Let's go."

Rising, Logan hefted his unconscious partner over his wide shoulders, then helped Miko off the ground. Outside the shattered armored personnel carrier, the dark forest was alive with sounds. Voices shouted from the woods below, mingling with the clank of tank treads. Searchlights pierced the night, shining between trees—but nowhere near Logan and company's actual position. They had lost the North Koreans for a little while at least.

"Which direction should we go?"

Logan scanned the area but could not see beyond a few dozen meters in any direction because of the dense foliage. *Is any part of this mission not a pain in the ass?*

"I need your compass."

Miko held the device under his nose.

"Northeast." Logan pointed. "Through that line of pine trees. There's supposed to be a flat plateau at the top of this ridge. We should be real close."

Logan glanced at his watch. The face was shattered, but it was still ticking. *Almost twenty minutes before the chopper's ETA. Hope we're not too early, or the soldiers might catch up to us before the helicopter does.*

They heard voices, much closer. Then the sound of men moving through the forest floated to their position.

"Up here," whispered Logan. He stumbled along on a low rise, and caught a log to haul himself the rest of the way. Miko scrambled on the slope next to him, moving quickly despite her wound.

A searchlight beam stabbed through the trees, pinning them in its light as they crawled over the edge of the low cliff. Voices erupted, soon followed by the incongruous sound of a bugle.

"Here comes the cavalry," huffed Logan, sprinting between trees. Miko stumbled to the ground underneath a tall tree. Logan paused, waiting for her to catch up.

"I will hold them back, give you cover," she called.

"No! Come on."

"Do not worry. I will follow."

"There's too many of them. The soldiers will overwhelm you."

But Miko turned her back on Logan and aimed the AK-47 toward the distorted silhouettes dancing in the wavering glow of search beacons. Her weapon barked, sending tracers burning through the night-shrouded woods. Frenzied cries, then sporadic and ineffectual gunfire replied. Bullets whizzed through the trees and snapped against branches. Miko fired again and kept on firing. Logan heard screams and the slap of bullets against flesh.

Logan turned. Legs pumping, he continued the difficult ascent to higher ground. Behind him, he heard more shots—first rifles, then the steady chatter of Miko's machine gun. Muffled by the trees, the sounds of shattering glass and a dying man's cry made their way to his ears. Then a searchlight winked out of existence.

"Good girl," he grunted. Breath ragged, muscles weakening, Logan relentlessly pushed on. Over the sound of his breathing, he listened for noise of a firefight, but the forest was suddenly quiet. He risked peering over his shoulder, and saw the searchlights scanning the forest far below his vantage point.

Maybe Miko's on the way… maybe she'll catch up to me soon.

Struggling under his partner's weight, Logan placed his foot on a loose rock and it broke from the ground, pitching him forward. He landed on his face, Langram falling limply off his shoulders. When Logan looked up, spitting dirt, he found himself at the top of the slope, a small plateau spread out before him.

The landing zone… this is it!

Logan rolled onto his back, sucking in the cool night air. Heart racing, he lifted a shaky arm and glanced at the phosphorescent hands on the Korean watch.

Nine minutes to go… nine minutes to find Miko, get her back here… then we can all go home.

Logan moved away from Langram and got to his knees. But as he tried to rise, a shape loomed out of the darkness, and a booted foot smashed into his face.

Logan blinked back the explosion of light inside his head. Harsh voices barked at him. When Logan's eyes focused again, he saw khaki uniforms all around him. *North Korean regulars.*

Must've been waiting for us. Figures. This mission was FUBAR from zero hour...

More orders shouted in Korean. Warily, the soldiers hemmed Logan in, though none seemed willing to get within reach of him.

"Know me by reputation, eh?" he muttered, aware that the bayonet was still in its sheath on his belt.

"Get up now, get up," the officer cried, no doubt exhausting his entire English vocabulary.

"Yeah, yeah, you got me." Logan staggered to his feet, hands above his head. A soldier moved within arm's length to grab Langram, but Logan chased him back with a lunge and a sneer.

"No move, no move!" the officer screamed, waving his pistol.

Logan weighed his options, wondering if he should strike now or wait for a better chance—which might disappear altogether if the Koreans noticed he was still armed. Then excited voices emerged from the darkness beyond the circle of soldiers.

The ranks parted, and two soldiers tossed a beaten and bloody Miko to the ground next to Langram.

Logan wanted to go to her, but knew better. He noticed Miko stir, and her eyes fluttered, to focus finally on him. Weakly, she tried to smile, but gagged on blood instead. Logan saw that the woman's front teeth were missing.

"You dirty bastards." Logan's knuckles whitened as he tightened his fist, glared at the officer with a look that said he wanted to put his fingers into the screaming man's eye sockets.

The Korean officer seemed empowered by Logan's anger. Still out of reach, he displayed his pistol and aimed it at Miko's head.

"No." Logan's voice was a warning. Unemotional, stark. "You've got us. That's enough."

"Now she die!" the officer cried.

The shot cut through the night like a nuclear explosion. Miko's body jerked once as the top of her head was blown off. The sound of the single shot, and its terrible consequence, caused even the hardened North Korean soldiers to wince and avert their eyes.

Logan struck.

In a flash, the bayonet was out of its sheath and in his hand. Logan knocked the officer's pistol aside and the weapon discharged again, striking one of the surrounding soldiers in the groin.

Logan spun the blade and plunged it into the Korean's chin, up through the skull and into the brain. The officer went limp, cross-eyed. Logan yanked the blade free and threw the dead man into his soldiers' arms.

A half-dozen rifles crackled, splitting branches and chipping bark off trees. They missed Logan, who was already behind them, slashing one throat after another before the bayonet tip snapped in two, lodged in a Korean's thick skull. Weaponless now, Logan ran.

Fortunately for him, the Koreans had been using searchlights. To a man, they lacked night vision. Though Logan could see them clearly. Khaki uniforms standing out against the night.

Logan raced for the forest, bowling over a soldier and smashing his larynx with his boot. More shots whizzed around his head. Then a bullet caught Logan's shoulder and spun him around. He stumbled up a small rise and plunged into the bush.

Bleeding, Logan crawled behind a tree. He heard voices all around him. It sounded like a hundred men were searching the area. Logan knew it was only a matter of time before they hit the jackpot.

He thought of Langram helpless and Miko dead, and panic suffocated him. The bullet wound and the pumping adrenaline made his limbs quiver uncontrollably, especially his forearms, which were suddenly suffused with lancing agony. As he stumbled to his feet, the burning pain continued, more intense than the shoulder wound.

Logan traced his left wrist in the darkness. Under tortured flesh and muscle, something stirred.

The men who hunted him forgotten with the arrival of this strange new agony, Logan watched as the flesh on top of his wrists burst in a squirt of crimson. A moan escaped his lips as six claws made of pristine, ivory-colored bone emerged from sheaths hidden undetected under Logan's flesh. Curved, honed, the claws extended one foot from their base to their razor-sharp tips.

Nearby, a Korean soldier heard Logan's cries. He fired a shot into the trees. The shell struck the trunk next to Logan's head, sending wood chips and bullet fragments into his skull. Logan reeled as if punched, lights exploded in his mind. He stumbled and slid back down to the ground.

The soldier saw Logan's legs sticking out from behind the tree and alerted his sergeant. Cautiously, thirty infantrymen converged on the area, weapons aimed…

○────────○

THE Logan who emerged from behind that tree was not the same wounded, fearful man who cowered behind it moments before. That man was gone, smothered by a berserker rage that consumed him, scourged him, burned his personality away—transforming Logan into a vengeful killing machine, a raging bundle of superfast reflexes and instinctive fighting ability honed as sharp as his claws over centuries of constant strife. Logan was now a warrior born, connected by psychic strings to a range of martial skills gathered throughout a thousand lives lived in endless warfare.

Pale white claws gleaming in the moonlight, Logan dropped into a crouch and leaped from cover. The first to see him: the man who fired the shot. The North Korean saw the claws, too—before they plunged into his eyes.

Down without a whimper, the gun fell from the Korean's limp hand. Logan ignored the weapon. The feral savagery that possessed him now would not be sated without the satisfying feel of the blade ripping flesh and splintering bone.

A dozen soldiers turned as Logan burst from cover, their movements in slow motion to Logan's superaccelerated senses. He tore through their ranks, severing limbs, slashing throats, ducking and stabbing as the stunned soldiers vainly tried to defend themselves against the lethal living weapon that slaughtered them.

Rifles cracked. Machine guns chattered. Logan could sense, almost see the bullets' glow in the gloom, hear the wavering shock waves, and deftly avoided each shot. He stabbed and thrust, slashed and ripped his way through ten, twenty men as more soldiers emerged with a collective howl from the forest.

Logan waded into them, a murderous juggernaut. Grasping, desperate hands tried to drag him down. Logan shook them off like pygmies. Tenaciously, a three-hundred-pound giant in khaki locked his hands around Logan's neck. A double uppercut lifted the man—impaled—over Logan's head and his innards spilled to the blood-soaked ground.

One officer tried to rally the soldiers into an execution squad. Logan discerned the tactic and charged the troops before they had a chance to assemble.

Another stepped forward and shoved a bayoneted rifle into Logan's belly. With a roar he decapitated the man, tore the rifle out of his guts and hurled it like a spear. The bayonet struck a different soldier in the chest, slamming him against a tree.

A demolition man tossed a satchel charge in Logan's direction. The high-explosives landed in a dead soldier's lap. Logan scooped up the package, shoved it into another man's arms, and tossed the howling trooper to his comrades. The explosion sent gouts of gore and bone-shrapnel ripping through the enemy ranks.

More soldiers began firing from the forest. Logan sneered, bared blood-flecked teeth, and dived once more into the bush. In the dark shadows of the forest, he circled the soldiers, stalked them, then butchered them, one by one.

○———————○

THE MH-60 Pave Hawk flew above the brown landscape, hovering only a few dozen meters over the ground—"nape of the earth," the military pilots called it, a most dangerous maneuver. Racing through the night, over the hilly North Korean terrain, at a constant, computer-controlled altitude of thirty-five meters off the ground, made for a bumpy ride. Each hill, each tall tree, had to be navigated. With the hatches open, and two of the eight soldiers aboard hanging by their safety lines out the door, the harrowing flight resembled the most sadistic roller-coaster ride ever invented.

The Pave Hawk, a Canadian variation of the United States Air Force Search and Rescue aircraft, was basically a Blackhawk helicopter filled with an array of specialized avionics that made a night flight over enemy territory at two hundred and fifty kilometers an hour possible. The low altitude was necessary to avoid North Korean radar, which was effective above a height of seventy-five meters. Avoiding radar was necessary when the aircraft in question was violating thirty-seven international laws and seven treaties by its very presence in North Korean airspace, never mind its mission.

Inside the soldiers' helmets, the pilot's voice announced their location. "LZ in thirty seconds…"

"Watch the night-vision scope," cautioned the copilot. "There are power lines strung all over these hills."

One of the soldiers hanging out the door activated night-vision goggles and scanned the river and the road that paralleled it.

"Colonel Breen, tank on the road."

The officer appeared at his shoulder.

"Over there, sir. Some trucks, too."

Breen stared at the tank, then saw the trucks, and more soldiers rushing into the woods at the base of the plateau.

"Colonel... the men down there are expendable. We're not supposed to land, not even to pick up the package, if the NKs are in sight," the pilot warned.

Breen frowned, and his eyes narrowed in concentration. Finally, the tall man spoke, "Lock and load. We're going down."

The Pave Hawk circled the plateau and came around for a second approach.

"I see firing down there, sir. And lots of bodies..." said the man in the doorway. As the chopper dipped, the observer dangled more than halfway out the door, one hand on his safety strap, the other on the NVGs attached to his helmet.

Breen squeezed his shoulder. "Keep your eyes open, Corporal Cutler. And be ready to take over that machine gun when we hit the ground..."

A graceful arc put the Pave low over the landing zone. Cutler let loose with a burst of automatic gunfire when the chopper made a first pass. To his surprise, the Koreans melted into the woods without returning fire.

"Descend, descend!" barked Colonel Breen, signaling the pilot to power down. Before the Pave Hawk settled on the ground, Corporal Cutler stepped out, into a field of death.

The plateau was carpeted with corpses. The pilot managed not to land on them only with deft maneuvering of his controls.

Through Cutler's night-vision goggles, the entire scene was a green-tinged nightmare of mass murder. Corpses were sprawled everywhere, and though they appeared to be the victims of a firefight, none had been shot. There was little evidence of explosives, either—no stench of cordite, no shattered ground or splintered trees, no bullet-riddled bodies. Yet virtually every dead soldier had been dismembered, disemboweled, beheaded, their insides and outsides ravaged beyond belief.

As the others fanned out around Cutler to secure the perimeter, Sergeant Mason cried out, "Got someone on the ground here! He's not Korean."

Breen raced to the sergeant and peered down at the man. Unconscious, he wore tattered splinter camouflage and had sandy hair in a buzz cut.

"That's one of them," said Breen.

The medic arrived a moment later, checked the man's pulse, shone a flashlight into his eyes. Suddenly, the man woke up, pushed away the light. "Who..."

"Easy soldier," said Breen. "We're getting you out—"

"Colonel!" another soldier cried. "Found a woman over here. Dead. Somebody blew her head off. Think she may be Korean."

"Leave her," said Sergeant Mason.

But Langram lifted his head. "She's Japanese," he cried, his voice hoarse. "Bring her out, too."

Breen looked into Langram's eyes. "Where is your partner? Where's—"

"Colonel. Found the package," Mason called.

Cutler turned at the cry. He was close and curious, so he crossed the corpse-littered ground to his sergeant's side.

Mason stood over a kneeling figure, long hair, splinter camo in shreds. The man's face was downcast, staring at the ground. Cutler couldn't tell if he was alive or dead.

"Need a medic over here," called Mason.

"Only got one doctor," said Cutler. "And he's still working on the other guy."

The sergeant looked around at the decimation. "What the hell happened here?" he whispered, face pale under war paint.

The kneeling man was covered in gore—his own and the blood of others. His arms were particularly ravaged, flesh seeping liquid crimson from deep gashes above the wrists. Mason reached out cautiously and touched the man, who did not react. Mason checked his pulse.

"He's fine. Calm... I don't get it. This guy's a mess, but he might as well be sleeping, based on his heart rate."

In the gloom, Mason used his flashlight to search for injuries. "Got it in the head. Look, wood splinters are still sticking out of the wound. Hold the flashlight..."

Mason thrust the flashlight into Cutler's hand, then felt the man's legs, then his arms. "His wrists feel weird, like they might be fractured. He's probably in shock. Stick with him, Cutler. I'll fetch the medic."

Cutler stood anxiously over the silent man, gazed at the dead laying in heaps around him. The stench of spilled blood was choking, and Cutler raised his kerchief to cover his nose and mouth.

The move seemed to startle the man on the ground. He winced, then slowly lifted his head.

"You okay?" Cutler asked softly. The kneeling man did not speak. When he opened his eyes and locked stares with the soldier looming over him, Cutler reeled back in horror.

Sergeant Mason arrived a moment later, the medic in tow.

"Cutler? What the hell's wrong with you?"

"That guy… the look in his eyes. Savage. Like he could kill me with just a stare. Like he wanted to."

Meanwhile, the medic had gotten the man off his knees and stumbling on his own power to the helicopter.

"Let's go, Cutler. We've overstayed our welcome. The Koreans are gonna come back any minute now."

But Cutler just stared at the man as the medic helped him into the helicopter.

"Jesus, Sarge. Who the hell is he?"

"Our package, son. He's on a classified mission and so are we. That's all you or I need to know."

That was answer enough for Cutler. Truth to tell, he didn't want to know the identity of the man. He would rather forget—forget this mission and the massacre. The look of soulless, bestial savagery reflected in that nameless man's eyes scarred Cutler. It would not fade from his mind.

21

INTERLUDE AND ESCAPE

"PLEASE, Ms. Hines, tell us your secret," said Dr. Cornelius, grinning.

The Professor frowned impatiently. "Yes, yes. Get on with it."

Carol Hines glanced up at the monitor, where a pair of wranglers in protective suits were about to collar Logan with their electroprods. Then she lowered her eyes and swung her chair around to face them both. "As I said, this happened when I was at NASA, working with the REM machine for several months—"

"Astronaut training simulations, as I recall," the Professor said.

Carol nodded. "That's how the work began. But after a few months of REM training, Dr. Powell of the Space Administration's psychology department devised a new experiment… one that would test the astronaut's reaction to fear."

"Indeed." The Professor listened more intently.

"The test was to be a routine simulation of a space shuttle reentry, but a specific set of circumstances would go wrong as the ship hit the atmosphere, building to the shuttle's destruction. There was nothing the astronauts could do to stop the accident from happening. That was the point of the exercise."

"And the subjects… they thought the experience was real?" Cornelius asked.

"Of course. From the moment of interface until the REM was switched off, the subjects believed what was happening was real.

"Dr. Reddy, the mission control chief, became furious when he found out the test had been conducted, angry that he was not informed. He also feared there would be adverse psychological effects, some of them lingering. But Dr. Powell brought him evidence to the contrary. According to Powell the astronauts seemed absolutely empowered, almost emboldened by their virtual near-death experience."

"Of course," said Cornelius. "They faced personal extinction but survived—the very same feeling we get after a particularly scary amusement park ride, but multiplied exponentially."

"Three astronauts experienced the simulation," Hines continued. "Two men, one woman, all of them experienced space shuttle pilots. In the weeks after the simulation, they each reported vivid, recurring dreams. A month later, one of the men died in a traffic accident—"

"I read about that," said Cornelius. "Head-on crash in Florida. A punk with a hot rod smashed into him or something."

"In truth, it was the astronaut who was flirting with death. He was playing chicken with a youth on a deserted stretch of highway. Neither of them swerved, so I suspect it was ruled a tie."

The Professor raised an eyebrow. "Humor, Ms. Hines? How uncharacteristic. Is this a tall tale?"

"Not at all, sir. As I said, the astronaut transformed into a thrill-seeker. NASA's public relations machine concealed the truth."

"And the others?"

"The other man was slated for the next shuttle mission—as its pilot, in fact. He was tested periodically in the ensuing weeks and deemed fit."

"And the woman?"

"Six weeks after the simulation, she disappeared without a trace. Left her husband and small child. The FBI suspected foul play, but NASA managed to hush it up, blaming her disappearance on marital woes. They found her, though, about three weeks later."

"And?"

"She was arrested in Nevada. The woman had joined a motorcycle gang. She started running drugs through Mexico, shooting heroin, working nights at a Reno brothel… in the end she got arrested by the local police for stabbing a young woman to death in a barroom brawl."

"Living on the edge… flirting with disaster," Cornelius said thoughtfully. "And the other pilot?"

"That's the strangest part," Carol replied. "It was Major Wylling—"

Cornelius sat up. "The pilot on the shuttle that crashed?"

"Yes. When the black box was recovered, the events that caused the disaster were re-created in simulation—and they precisely mirrored the false accident in Dr. Powell's psychological simulation. A leak in the coolant system led to a corrosive substance that came in contact with the superheating fuel cell, which then ruptured, causing the final, fatal explosion."

"A coincidence, surely," scoffed the Professor.

"A trillion-to-one coincidence, according to NASA's computers," Hines replied. "Dr. Reddy insisted the simulation was to blame, which the other scientists said was absurd on its face. At first, Dr. Reddy suggested Astronaut Wylling somehow sabotaged the system himself—a self-fulfilling prophecy. But Dr. Able, the chief engineer, objected to that theory. Said some of the key components involved in the crash were impossible to get to, and had been sealed for months before the fear experiment ever took place."

"Sounds like an academic food fight," said Cornelius.

"A bureaucratic war did break out between Dr. Powell's psych department and Dr. Reddy and his supporters in mission control."

"Who won?"

"To bolster his case, Dr. Reddy brought in other experts," Carol Hines replied. "Physicists. Theorists working in quantum mechanics. Dream psychologists. Brain specialists. Even a parapsychologist. They discussed the problem behind closed doors. I testified, because I ran the REM program during the experiment."

Cornelius rubbed his brown beard. "What did they conclude?"

"They spoke of Werner Heisenberg's Uncertainty Principle, Carl Jung's Collective Consciousness, and the simple power of suggestion. A psychiatrist lectured the panel on the potential of the subconscious mind and the possibility of a self-fulfilling prophecy without physical intervention. In the end, the majority concluded that the REM machine probably induced a prophetic trance in the participants of the fear experiment—a hypothesis, if you will. Some process similar to what the Oracle of Delphi or the Old Testament prophets experienced."

○———————○

CUTLER cautiously approached Weapon X, electroprod extended.

Something about this poor sap didn't feel quite right tonight. The way Logan stood over the dead tiger, maybe how his eyes were only half-closed, or how his head was cocked. It was as if he were listening. The fact that Logan had not yet retracted his claws troubled Cutler.

"Watch him, Anderson," Cutler warned as they approached.

The sound of Cutler's voice triggered something in Logan—a ghost of a memory, perhaps. Suddenly, he lifted his head, opened his eyes, and locked stares with Cutler, who reeled back in recognition.

All the other times he'd dealt with Subject X, the man was a zombie—eyes glazed, shuffling like a sleepwalker—but this time Logan was no limp victim, no trained animal to be "handled."

His eyes. Seen them before… I know who this man is.

Faster than Cutler or Anderson could react, faster than merely human reflexes could respond, Logan brought up his bloodstained claws and lashed out.

o━━━━━━o

"MY God, madam! What are you suggesting?" the Professor cried. "This is not science, it's magic, sorcery. Or perhaps divination."

"I am suggesting nothing, Professor," said Carol Hines. "I did not formulate the theory. I am only telling you what panel members—a group of highly esteemed scientists and researchers—concluded."

"What happened after that?" Cornelius asked.

"Of course, the truth was hidden from the public, even though Dr. Reddy insisted that the results of the simulation at least should be shared with other scientists. Reddy even gave the theory a name—the Nostradamus Effect, after the fifteenth-century prophet."

"Preposterous," the Professor snorted.

"You are not alone in thinking that, Professor. Dr. Powell and some of the others, including NASA's chief engineer, Dr. Able, used Reddy's intransigence in the matter against him. In the end, the blame for the shuttle disaster dropped squarely in Dr. Reddy's lap and he was forced out in disgrace."

"Understandably so, Ms. Hines," said the Professor. "What a ridiculous theorem. That man was a fool."

"And yet enough evidence exists to support the prophetic effect of the REM device, at least to one body of scientists," Hines replied. "Despite general skepticism about the Nostradamus Effect, NASA never again utilized the REM device, and its operation was phased out of training completely within a year."

Cornelius chuckled. "That's a great campfire story, Carol. Cute. Real cute. Next you'll be telling us that Logan will be coming for us in the dark of night."

The doctor glanced up at the HDTV monitor and blinked in surprise. "Where is Logan? And where are the wranglers?"

Hines spun in her chair. "Off camera, sir."

"I can see that, Ms. Hines. Put them back *on* camera, please."

"Switching, sir."

The next camera in sequence was positioned near the elevator doors. It revealed nothing. And the security cam inside the car showed it to be empty, too.

Carol Hines keyed the intercom. "Security, where's Mr. Logan?"

"Wranglers have him, Ms. Hines."

"Wranglers, come in," she called. "Wranglers? Do you copy?" There was no reply.

"Switch to camera five, back in the field," Cornelius said.

Hines gasped when she saw the new image on screen. In the foreground, two wranglers lay dead, hacked to pieces, their body parts mingled with the slaughtered tiger's. In the background, Logan strode through a sundered chain link fence toward the elevator and the underground complex.

Suddenly, the Klaxon blare of the alarm echoed in the complex's steel corridors.

"Security!" the Professor cried. "What is wrong? What is the siren for?"

"Not sure," Major Deavers replied from the command center.

"This could be serious," said Cornelius. "Shut down Logan's transponder, Ms. Hines. That should send Logan into a mind loop and settle him down for good."

Carol Hines tapped her keyboard, then slammed her fist down. "No response," she said, her usual monotone shaded with panic. "The transponder is in override... from an outside source. There's nothing I can do."

"Security! I ask again: What is wrong?" the Professor screamed.

"Sorry, sir," a voice replied. "This is the guard outside of your lab. Someone is breaching the security perimeter, in the elevator, on his way down here. The level is in lockdown. We're armed an—"

His words died in a terrible scream. Over the loudspeakers, Cornelius, Carol Hines, and the Professor heard shots, shouts, screams... chaos.

The Professor was visibly trembling. "Don't worry," he whispered. "We're safe behind these walls. Logan doesn't know we're here, he—"

A grating sound interrupted him. Three diamond-sharp claws began tearing through solid steel. The door to the laboratory shook, then fell from its hinges.

Logan loomed in the doorway, snarling.

Desperately, Carol Hines tried to regain control of Weapon X through the REM device. As he burst into the lab, control of the subject eluded her, though she did manage to interface with Logan's brain sufficiently enough to project his thoughts.

On the HDTV monitor, Carol saw an image of herself in Logan's mind. Malignant and small—almost diminutive compared to the giant that he was. She watched in horror as her virtual doppelganger was beheaded with a backhand swipe of Logan's claws, only a split second before she felt the actual slash of death. Her own head leaped from its shoulders in a fountain of blood.

While her brain died from lack of oxygen, Carol Hines considered a final irony. *I was right... never should have stuck my neck out... sure to get it chopped off...*

Logan came at Cornelius next. As he lunged, the doctor saw his virtual twin on the monitor, in the guise of a grim, medieval torturer, with a surgical mask for a hood and angels of death—wearing the faces of MacKenzie, Hendry, Chang, and many others—hovering in the background.

"That's not right," moaned Cornelius in the moment of his long and brutal murder. "I'm a doctor... a healer... I help people..."

Finally, Logan turned on the Professor.

The scientist backed up. He begged, pleaded, whined, and finally howled as Logan severed one hand, then the other. Kneeling, then crawling, imploring Logan to spare his life, the Professor looked up at the monitor right before death cast its pall over him.

On the screen, he saw no genius. No architect of the flesh. Certainly not a god. Not even a man, really... just a frightened, sobbing little boy crying for his mother, pleading for mercy—utterly powerless in the face of a cruel, arbitrary, uncaring fate.

EPILOGUE

THE slaughter continued all night. By morning, as the rising sun broke over the mountains, Logan had killed them all. Carol Hines. Dr. Abraham B. Cornelius. The Professor. Dr. Hendry and his cadre of physicians. Dr. MacKenzie and all of his psychiatric specialists. The guards. The wranglers. Even the technicians, maintenance workers, and kitchen staff.

At some point during the massacre, a communications specialist named Rice tried to download the Experiment X files and had triggered the recordings made during the experimental procedures. Those recordings continued to play over the loudspeakers in a random, disorganized loop for the rest of the night.

When the butchery ended, after the top secret experimental medical complex had been transformed into an abattoir, the recording of a long conversation continued to broadcast over the facility's audio network.

As Logan moved toward the exit of the underground facility, climbed the endless flights of stairs that led out of that hell to the bright morning and the snowy surface, the recording played on.

"… Good morning, Ms. Hines…" Dr. Cornelius. Voice tinny.

"… I was wondering, sir," Carol Hines. "May I speak with you?…"

"… Sure…"

"… I keep thinking about Mr. Logan…"

"… Don't we all?…"

"… and what we're doing… before I came here… was Mr. Logan here?…"

"… I don't know what you mean, Ms. Hines…"

"… Did Mr. Logan volunteer for this?…"

"… Uh… No…"

"… Was he abducted, then?…"

"… I'm not too proud of this, but yes, I believe he was…"

"… We're doing something bad, aren't we, Dr. Cornelius?… Mr. Logan was forced into this…"

"… I don't know about forced, Ms. Hines… see, if you listen to the Professor, then this whole situation is all preordained. It's like Logan's destiny…"

"… But how could the Professor know Mr. Logan's destiny, Doctor?…"

"… To be honest, Ms. Hines, I don't know…"

"… All I see is him suffering… the Professor seems to enjoy inflicting pain on Logan… it's like torture, sir, not science…"

"… Well, you know, some men… they have the worst destinies… I should know…"

"… Oh God…"

"Hey, don't cry, Ms. Hines… I'm sorry. That crack about destiny… it was a lousy thing to say…"

"… I'm—I'm sorry about the tears… feel so silly…"

"… Look… this poor slob doesn't have much of a life, anyway… he's a mutant… Logan isn't even human…"

"… But he is human, Dr. Cornelius… you can't tell me that you don't see it… in his eyes… you can see… he's a man… a man who's being turned into a monster…"

"… I don't know what to tell you, Ms. Hines… I'm going on what the Professor said… Maybe anything other than that is out of my league…"

"… I think the Professor is a liar, sir…"

"… Maybe…"

"… I wish I had never become involved in this experiment, Dr. Cornelius…"

"… Yeah… me, too… now come on, cheer up, Ms. Hines… It'll be over soon…"

AS Logan emerged into the daylight, he struck down his final victim, a communications specialist. Dying, the technician scattered computer discs into the snow. Logan left one bloody footprint, then trod on.

For Logan, this final killing was nothing more than an afterthought. His bloodlust was spent. Weary, he shuffled forward into the dawn. Within minutes, snow began to fall, and a massive blizzard surrounded him. Then, for a moment, through the white, windblown haze, Logan spied a figure standing on a rocky peak, framed by the rising sun.

Legs braced, strong and proud, the figure of a samurai, sword drawn, shimmered like a ghost—or a memory.

That vision is me, he realized.

Not the debased, fallen man he had been before he'd been abducted and dragged here. Not the mind-ravaged weapon he was intended to be. But the man he'd been long ago, during his never-ending lifetime, but in another century.

I fought for honor, found peace in the sound of wind chimes and the rustle of snow…

That snow covered him now, clinging to his blood-spattered form, icing his hair, swathing crimson flesh in virgin white. *Reborn…*

Logan searched his memory for more traces of his past, but so much was lost. He clung to that single pristine vision of a time when he had honor. Bushido.

A noise intruded. Beating blades. Rhythmic, mechanical. A helicopter approached the facility. Logan swiftly and instinctively moved away from it, into the woods, deeper into the winter storm.

He had lost his way a long time ago. Fought for so long. In the end, he misplaced the reason and battled only himself—

No. I will not be a tool… nobody's puppet… and never again a mindless weapon… I'm a warrior. A warrior born.

Throbbing overhead, the beating blades became louder, roaring unseen above, then fading until the sound lost its way in the wind.

They carried me into this hellish torture chamber, dead to the world… they carried me in, but I'm walking out… upright… on my own two feet.

The storm intensified, the frigid wind whipped his flesh, but Logan was impervious to the elements. The undefiled brutality of the wild called to him. In his mind, he answered…

I am Logan… I am a man… heading into the wilderness.

ABOUT THE AUTHOR

MARC CERASINI lives in New York City and is the author of thirty books, including the *New York Times* nonfiction bestseller *O. J. Simpson: American Hero, American Tragedy; Heroes: U.S. Marine Corps Medal of Honor Winners; The Future of War: The Face of 21st-Century Warfare*; and *The Complete Idiot's Guide to U.S. Special Ops.*

He is the author of the *USA Today* bestseller *AVP: Alien vs. Predator*, based on the motion picture; and two original *24: Declassified* novels, based on the Emmy Award–winning television series *24—Operation Hell Gate* and *Trojan Horse.*

With Alice Alfonsi, Marc is the coauthor of the nationally bestselling mystery novels *On What Grounds, Through the Grinder, Latte Trouble, The Ghost and Mrs. McClure* and *The Ghost and the Dead Deb*. With Alice, he is also the coauthor of *24: The House Special Subcommittee Investigation of CTU*, a fictionalized guide to the show's first season.

He cocreated the *Tom Clancy's Power Plays* series and wrote an essay analyzing Mr. Clancy's fiction for *The Tom Clancy Companion*. Marc's techno-thrillers include *Tom Clancy's Net Force: The Ultimate Escape*, and five action/adventure novels based on Toho Studios' classic Godzilla, among them *Godzilla Returns, Godzilla 2000*, and *Godzilla at World's End.*

Marc is also the coauthor of a nonfiction look at the Godzilla film series, *The Official Godzilla Compendium*, with J. D. Lees. With Charles Hoffman, Marc is the coauthor of forthcoming *Robert E. Howard, A Critical Study.*

ACKNOWLEDGMENTS

FIRST off, kudos to Barry Windsor-Smith, who conceived *Wolverine: Weapon X* as a graphic story over a decade ago. His fantastic artwork inspired many of the quirky details of this novel, and his epic story was large enough to invite further exploration.

To Stan Lee, who gave us the X-Men.

To my editor, Ruwan Jayatilleke, who brought lots of great ideas to the table, then stood back and let me digest them, and to Ed Schlesinger, who shepherded this novel from limited release to mass market.

To Dr. Grace Alfonsi, M.D., for helping to make Logan's transformation medically plausible.

To my brother Vance and my niece, Tia.

To my pals Chuck, Bob, CJ, Paul, and Criticus.

Finally and most importantly, to my muse, Alice Alfonsi, who worked as hard and as long on this project as I have.

And to mutants everywhere.

Book Two
ROAD OF BONES

by David Alan Mack

For Kara, who makes my own road
a better one on which to walk.

"[History is] a record of unjustified suffering,
irreparable loss, tragedy without catharsis.
It's a gorgon: stare at it too long
and it turns you to stone."
—Barry Gewen, *The New York Times,* June 4, 2005

1

A single leap and Miyoko Takagi was over the electrified fence. She landed, silent as a flake of snow falling on water, behind a patrolling security guard who had just turned his back.

Her gloved hand covered his mouth as her *kusarigama* found his heart. He twitched in her lethal embrace for a moment, then his body went limp. She pulled her blade from his chest, wiped it clean on his leg, and lowered his corpse into the shadows.

Ahead of her, two more of her fellow ninjas neutralized two more perimeter guards—one with a poison blow dart, the other with a throwing star. Both guards fell without a sound in the darkness, out of view of the security cameras that ringed the exterior of Tanaka Biotechnology's world headquarters.

Miyoko plucked three *shaken* from inside her black uniform and hurled them all with a single flick of her wrist. The throwing stars sailed apart on precise but subtle angles. Each one severed the data line of a different security camera. The path to the rear loading dock was now clear for the second team to move up. The loss of video signal would be certain to provoke an alert inside the building's security center, but if all was proceeding as planned, two of her ninjas were already there.

She traversed the underside of the loading dock's overhang in an inverted climb and stopped above the door to the building's main shipping office. Through the slats of the door's top ventilation grating, she saw inside the main freight-handling area. Its workers and managers lay unconscious on the floor. *Good*, she thought. *Sumotomo released the gas already. That should take care of all but the secured floors upstairs.*

Two more security guards turned the far corner and walked toward her. Pressed against the ceiling overhang, Miyoko remained absolutely still. Another trio of *shaken* was ready in the fingers of her right hand. This part of the dock was well lit and monitored by the cameras; she would have to wait until the security cameras deactivated before neutralizing the two men below. Killing them now could compromise the entire mission.

All this effort for the benefit of fools. Miyoko resented the daimyo for burdening her with two gaijin on this mission. *My ninjas could have acquired the daimyo's prize without help from these amateurs. Maybe not tonight, but eventually.*

Unfortunately, for some reason, the daimyo was not willing to be patient this time. She blamed Alexei Pritikin, the Russian to whom the daimyo had given her as a consort. Though the daimyo had told her that her assignment was to defend Pritikin, she'd understood that her presence had been requested by the Russian for a purpose entirely different from protection.

The fact that Pritikin was undeniably in love with her only slightly ameliorated her contempt at having been offered up like a geisha. Quiet fury coiled her muscles as the guards walked closer. If they glanced up even for a moment, she would be revealed. Like so many full-time security personnel, however, they had grown bored and performed their tasks by rote.

Above the main door to the freight area, the security cameras' red power indicators dimmed. Her ninjas inside the skyscraper had prevailed; its security system was offline.

Miyoko unleashed two of her *shaken* at the guards, struck each in the carotid artery. They fell dead before they had time to know that they'd been killed. Then she flung her third throwing star toward the main gate along the rear alley, cutting its lock in a flash of sparks.

Now we get to see what the gaijin can do, she mused darkly.

○────────────○

SURGE and Slake—a.k.a. Gregor and Oskar Golovanov—waited in the shadows near the T-shaped intersection of two narrow alleys.

"*Chort vozmi*, juice me up," Gregor said. "I can fry the grid and frag the fence, and we can walk in."

"No," said his twin brother, a fellow mutant. "The daimyo said to let the ninjas clear the way."

"Whatever," Gregor said, shaking his head in disgust. He could unleash enough different types of energy to burn, disrupt, disintegrate, stun, or kill just about anything on earth—but only if his brother first drained the power from something else and transferred it to him. A "symbiotic link"— that's what it had been called by the Soviet researchers who had poked and prodded and measured and tested the brothers since they were old enough to remember... and until they became old enough—and powerful enough—to escape.

He looked at Oskar and brooded. *Same blond hair, same blue eyes, same cleft chin—and not a damned thing in common.* "This is ridiculous, Oskar," he said in an irritated whisper. "We could be inside by now. Charge me!"

"From what, Gregor? The electric fence?" Oskar rolled his eyes. "There's not enough amperage to get us inside, never mind take out the security grid... Just wait for the signal."

Several dozen meters beyond the electric fence, past a perimeter patrolled by armed guards and ferocious dogs, the imposing glass-and-steel façade of the Tanaka Biotechnology Corporation's world headquarters loomed high and mighty into the night, a new fixture on the skyline of Osaka, Japan. Somewhere inside this tightly defended fortress of science was the prize that the brothers had been sent to acquire and deliver.

They were near the building's rear loading docks, which were secured by a fifteen-foot-tall electric fence topped with barbed wire. Every fourth fence post was topped by a slowly swiveling video camera, of a kind that Gregor knew had been made to detect everything from infrared radiation to tachyon interactions, a feature that revealed most "invisible" interlopers. Whoever had designed this building's security systems had done so with mutants in mind. Gregor wasn't sure he wanted to know what was waiting for them inside the building, but he knew that if it relied on energy to work, then it would be no match for his brother's power-siphoning touch.

He looked at his watch. "We've been standing here for over an hour," he grumbled.

Oskar arched one eyebrow, an expression of his contempt for Gregor's impatience. "What, are you in a hurry? Got a hot date?"

"Maybe I do," Gregor said, trying not to sound defensive.

"No, you don't," Oskar said, just a touch too confident in his tone for Gregor's liking.

"And how would you know?"

"We won't be here long enough," Oskar said, his eyes fixed on the building across the alley. "And Miyoko would kill you."

"Mm-hm," Gregor mumbled dismissively. "I can handle her."

"Sure you can," Oskar said.

"Give me enough juice, I can fry anybody."

"You have to see them to fry them, Gregor. She's a fucking ninja. You'd be dead before you knew what hit you."

Gregor looked at his watch again and sighed.

"What'd she say the signal would be?"

"That we'll know it when we see it."

No sooner had he said it when, on the other side of the electric fence, two security guards stopped in the middle of their rounds and collapsed silently to the ground. At the same moment, the cameras on the fence posts halted in mid-swivel, and their red indicator lights dimmed and went dark. An evanescent flurry of sparks spat from the gate's lock as it was bifurcated by a *shaken* moving faster than the human eye could see. With a long, whining creak of dry hinges, the rear gates of the Tanaka Biotechnology Corporation's headquarters lolled open.

"I guess that's our signal," Gregor said.

Oskar grimaced with disdain. "You think?"

The brothers moved quickly across the dark alley, toward the loading docks. They passed two unconscious dogs and approached a door that was sandwiched between two of the platform's tall metal-slat gates. Before they were halfway there, the door opened, spilling dim light onto the dock outside.

Gregor still found it odd to observe the effects of the ninjas' actions without ever seeing the hooded assassins themselves. Oskar moved ahead of him and preceded him up a short but steep flight of stairs and then through the door.

Half a dozen TBC workers in gray coveralls lay sprawled on the concrete floor. Inside a nearby office, their balding, slightly overweight night-shift supervisor was splayed across his own desk, facedown on a pile of papers. There was no blood in sight anywhere, just the faintly medicinal odor of expired chloroform gas. True to form, the ninjas had chosen the path of least resistance and least effort; the workers had been unarmed and had posed no threat, so it had been deemed sufficient simply to knock them unconscious. Gregor knew that the guards waiting upstairs would not receive such mercy. *At least, not from me,* he promised himself, unable to suppress a sadistic smirk of anticipation.

On the left was a door that led to a fireproofed stairwell; on the right was an open freight elevator.

The brothers faced each other and shook hands.

"Good luck," Gregor said to his twin.

"Good hunting," Oskar replied. He jogged away from Gregor and opened the door to the stairwell, then bounded down the steps toward the subbasement.

Gregor walked briskly into the freight elevator and shut its safety cage, which closed from the top and bottom, like a set of metal-mesh jaws. Seemingly of its own volition, the elevator jerked and lurched into motion, then rattled upward on steel cables that vibrated with an almost musical resonance.

If their accomplices had done their jobs properly, Gregor knew, Oskar would have an unimpeded path to the building's primary power center. From there, he could drain the building's dedicated generators and tap into an almost limitless supply of raw power from its connection to the municipal electrical grid. With all the unbridled electromagnetic forces that Oskar's efforts would unleash in the subbasement, there had been no point in equipping him with any kind of radio-frequency transmitter; the signal would be garbled by all the EM interference, and it likely would be unable to penetrate the steel and concrete shell of the skyscraper's foundation.

Not that Gregor needed any such link to Oskar to know when it would be time to attack. When his brother tapped into the juice, Gregor would know. He'd feel the tingling in his fingers, the heat on the back of his neck, the trembling adrenaline rush.

Soon enough, he'd have more raw power than he'd know what to do with—but he was certain he'd think of something.

○─────────○

IT had been a quiet evening on the sixty-eighth floor until the wall behind the elevator bank exploded.

Private security guard Yoshi Tamura dived to the floor behind the soda machine and covered his face. A hundred thousand needlelike splinters of wood were airborne, dancing on a plume of fire. Then the lights went out. Dust settled in the darkness. Yoshi's ears throbbed, his hearing dulled by the blast.

From the far end of the corridor, narrow flashlight beams cut through the stygian haze. As they sliced past one another, he barely glimpsed blurs of movement along the walls, floor, and ceiling, like dark phantoms or shadows unchained from substance. *Ninjas*, Yoshi realized. Most of his own training had been in a more noble vein of the martial arts, but he'd learned enough of the ways of *ninjutsu* to recognize it in action.

A lone figure emerged from the elevator shaft and swung on a rope into the corridor. The guards who were aiming the flashlights from the other end of the hallway fixed their beams on the intruder. He lifted his arm in their direction and showed them his empty palm.

"Freeze!" shouted one of the guards. "Get down on the—"

A blinding flash and a thunder crack. The flashlight beams went dark, and the charnel odor of burnt meat filled the passageway. The intruders walked away from Yoshi's position.

He activated his two-way radio to call for help. Static, loud and constant, dominated every channel in his earpiece. *Scrambled*, he realized. *So much for backup.*

Moving with well-rehearsed grace, Yoshi stripped off his uniform shirt, revealing his long-sleeved black turtleneck… and the dark scabbard that was strapped diagonally across his back. He pushed off his shoes, under which he wore black-canvas *tabi*—one of the few practices he had adopted from *ninjutsu*. After taking a moment to reassure himself that he was alone and undetected, he donned a black balaclava to maximize his harmony with the shadows. Steady in his hand, his *wakizashi* glided free of its scabbard without making a sound. Brandishing the short sword, he set out in pursuit of the intruder he had seen—while remaining mindful of all the others that he couldn't see but nonetheless knew were there.

Darkness suited him. It was familiar, comfortable. He put on a pair of snug-fitting night-vision spectacles and skulked to the corner, stealthily navigating the obstacle course of broken concrete, pulverized brick and drywall, and fractured wooden debris. The air was thick with the cordite stench of overheated metal and broken stone. From the ragged gap in the wall behind him, he heard the snap and crackle of severed electrical wires.

Beyond the corner, there was only more darkness, dim even with the benefit of his UV glasses. Distant voices, panicked and plaintive, could have been only more security guards. One by one their voices were silenced—a whisper of steel through the air, the heavy *thump* of bodies falling to the dusty floor. Yoshi prowled forward, following the faint trail of sound.

A vibration in the air was all the warning he had. It was enough. He dodged, and the ninja's blade lunged past him. One cut across the ninja's throat ended the battle. Yoshi caught the man's corpse and lowered it quietly to the floor, wary of alerting any of the other assassins lurking about.

The intruders were moving quickly. He had assumed that they would be after the stockpiles of rare pathogens that were used at TBC for top-secret research. As he passed the storage areas, however, he saw that they were untouched. The ninjas and their human cannon were after something else.

Yoshi stepped onto the syrupy slickness of spilled blood. To his left lay another guard. *No sign of respiration*, Yoshi noted. *No point checking his pulse, he's gone.* He moved toward the next intersection, which led into a heavily barricaded central corridor. Then the darkness turned to golden sunrise: a fiery blast erupted beyond the next corner, momentarily overwhelming his UV glasses. Squinting against the glare, he saw four ninjas perched along the corner or dangling in the nook between the wall and the drop-tile ceiling. They were silhouetted in the red-orange light. As surely as the blast had revealed their presence to him, it had announced his own to them. Subtlety immediately lost its value.

The explosive glow faded like dying hope, and the ninjas rushed toward Yoshi, as if they were one with the encroaching shadows. Still half blind, he felt their approach, read the patter of footfalls and the hushing song of arcing steel.

A block, a parry, and an uppercut. One of the ninjas fell.

Yoshi ducked and turned, swung his blade to make another block, closer than before. He feinted right, lunged left, drew the closest ninja forward into a careless thrust. Yoshi's *wakizashi* pierced the other man's throat, through muscle and cartilage, then flicked out, severing the carotid artery.

Weighted chains snared his ankles before he could dance free. A hard upward tug landed him on his back. Rather than struggle to escape, he pulled forward on the chains by tucking his knees to his chest. As the ninja holding the chains was pulled forward and down, Yoshi's *wakizashi* jabbed up and twisted, impaling the man as he landed against Yoshi's feet. Then Yoshi pushed back and launched the man at his last remaining comrade.

The fourth ninja ducked clear. Though it was a risk, Yoshi expended half a second to untangle his feet from the chain of the *kusari-gama*. Then he sprang back to his feet—and realized that the last ninja had either fled or hidden himself beyond discovery.

Another explosion rumbled, again from the hallway that led to the top-secret laboratory. Forced to choose between seeking out the vanished ninja and going after the cannon, Yoshi decided that the man with the firepower seemed to be the one for whom the ninjas were running interference. That made him the higher-priority target.

Yoshi turned the corner and halted. A fiery tunnel of demolished metal and reinforced concrete stretched out ahead of him. He had expected to find the cannon man working his way through the multiple reinforced barricades; the blast that had cleared this path, however, had been singular and focused. As a further testament to the control of its creator, the devastation stopped shy of the final wall, which would have rent a smoking scar in the façade of the building, drawing all kinds of attention from the outside world. That wall was pristine, its paint unblistered and its "No Smoking" sign respectfully unburned, despite being illuminated by the firelight of all that had been laid waste in the dozen or so meters between there and the intersection where Yoshi stood.

Footsteps crunched across crumbled cement and broken glass at the far end of the hallway. Then a short, unimposing man was prodded forward, toward the smoldering impromptu passage. The man was one of the scientists Yoshi had often seen there, working late into the night, for the past several months. Fair-haired and bespectacled, he was in his late forties, and he wore a classic white lab coat over his wrinkled and coffee-stained dress shirt and rumpled trousers. Clutched in his folded arms was a metallic case. Behind him was the walking cannon.

Yoshi ducked behind the corner before either of the men saw him. *Hostage situation.* He abandoned all the strategies he had considered up until that moment and sheathed his sword. *Changes all the rules. Can't risk getting our guy killed.*

Using equipment left in place by the now-dead ninjas, Yoshi pulled himself above the drop-tile ceiling, then reeled in the rope and softly lowered the displaced tile back onto its square in the aluminum grid. Moments later, he heard the cannon say to the scientist in Russian-accented English, "Turn left."

The two men passed directly beneath Yoshi... then their footsteps stopped. Yoshi lifted the corner of the drop tile to see what was going on. Below, the cannon inspected the bodies of the three dead ninjas. He looked at the scientist. "Take a few steps back," he said. The scientist did so, and then the cannon pointed at the ninjas—and disintegrated them, one by one.

"Keep moving," the cannon said as he gave his hostage a shove, and the two of them continued their quick-step march back toward the breach in the elevator shaft's wall.

Yoshi dropped back down, landed gently, and went into a crouch. *Have to follow them*, he decided, stealing forward in a hunched run. *Trail them, get past this interference, and call for backup. Maybe slow their getaway.* He was careful to remain far enough back to avoid being detected but close enough not to lose sight of the intruder and his hostage.

In less than a minute the pair was back at the breach in the wall. The cannon man took the briefcase from the scientist, then he knotted a rope harness around the smaller man's torso and pushed him into the elevator shaft. Reaching in, he grabbed a second, more professional-looking harness, stepped into it, and passed through the breach into the elevator shaft.

Rushing forward to the breach, Yoshi peeked upward first, to see if the intruders were heading toward the roof for extraction by helicopter. There was no sign of activity up there, except for the turning of the elevator's winches and the trembling of its cables. He edged forward and looked down to gauge the intruder's descent toward his escape.

A four-pointed *shaken* bit into Yoshi's throat.

Reflexively, his hand reached toward the wound, but he knew already that it was too late. The *hira shuriken* had severed his carotid artery and his larynx. Death would be swift and silent. He pitched forward and plunged headfirst into the elevator shaft. Falling was heavenly, like freedom. Then he was snared in a tangle of metal cables, jerked to a hard and sudden stop, trapped in a suddenly constricting noose of steel.

Yoshi Tamura, honored *bushi* of the Tanaka clan, offered a final heartfelt prayer to his ancestors, then surrendered as darkness took him into its silken embrace.

○━━━━━━━━━━○

ALONE in the subbasement, Oskar felt Gregor's appetite for power subside. When Gregor's need was at its greatest level, Oskar felt it like a hunger, a gulf of desperate emptiness in his gut. He had learned early in his career with Gregor that he couldn't store much energy; his body wasn't designed to act as a battery. He was more like a capacitor, a circuit through which vast reservoirs of raw power could be channeled to his brother.

One thing that Oskar could not do was take power from living things: plants, animals, people, fire—all were immune to the effects of his energy-siphoning talent. Any nonliving power source would do, though: a live wire, a microwave beam, even sunlight, though it was too diffuse to be of any practical value to Gregor. The more concentrated the energy supply, the better. Car engines could pack a quick punch; a city's electrical grid was more reliable. Lately, Oskar had begun to wonder if he could absorb the normally lethal radiation of a nuclear reactor while siphoning its power. It was an experiment that so far he'd lacked the courage to attempt.

He withdrew his hands from the electrical junction. Immediately, he missed the rush of connection, the warm glow of conductance that accompanied his transmissions of power to Gregor. His symbiotic connection faded slightly as the bond of energy diminished and returned to its normal level.

Steam hissed and ventilator systems throbbed in the sparsely lit, drab gray sublevel. Oskar stepped quickly, slipped through narrow passages between tall banks of machinery and generators and phone-switching clusters. In less than a minute, he was springing back up the stairs, climbing the three switchback flights to the loading bay.

The timing was perfect. He walked through the door just as the safety cage of the freight elevator parted to reveal Gregor and the man they'd come to get. "Dr. Falco," Oskar said to the pallid, trembling scientist. "So good of you to join us." Falco glanced suspiciously at Oskar and said nothing in reply.

Gregor grabbed the slim, bookish man by the cuff of his lab coat and pulled him toward the exit. "Keep moving, Herr Doktor," he said. "We're on a schedule." It had always troubled Oskar to see how his brother's personality changed immediately after one of their missions. Flush from the infusion of raw power, Gregor became edgy, aggressive, hostile. It brought out a cruel streak in him, one that had grown darker and more pronounced during the years that they had worked together as mercenaries.

Oskar followed his brother through the door to the loading platform, down the short, steep stairs, and back out the open gate toward the alley. From the darkness, a black van pulled up in front of the gate and skidded to a halt. Its side door slid open as the brothers and Dr. Falco approached. Gregor pushed the scientist forward; the man banged his shin roughly against the edge of the van's doorway and yelped in pain.

"Nice manners, Gregor," Oskar scolded, while helping the hobbled Dr. Falco into the van.

Shrugging his shoulders, Gregor defensively shot back, "What do I look like? His valet?"

"You don't dress well enough to be a valet."

A female voice from inside the van rebuked them sharply: "Both of you, shut up and get in." They did as they were told.

Gregor waited for Oskar to get in, then pulled the door closed behind them. The van accelerated smoothly and quietly as it hurtled headlong into the urban nightscape of Osaka.

"That place was wide open," Gregor boasted. He cracked his knuckles. "I shoulda got in some target practice, fried a few more walls just for fun. Coulda burned the whole place down."

"With us inside it," Oskar chided him. "Brilliant."

"I told you two to shut up," said the woman driving the van. The threat in her tone was as implicit as her instruction.

You'll get us both killed one of these days, Oskar brooded, unwilling to look at his brother while silently cursing him. *Never thinking, never planning ahead. Foolish. Careless. Reckless*. But that had always been the way with the two of them. Oskar had always been the thinker, the planner, the strategist; he'd had to be. Gregor had always been able, by instinct, to wield the power given to him by Oskar. But it had always been Oskar's responsibility to guarantee that there would be enough energy to get a job done and that he could get to it without putting himself in jeopardy.

Unlike Gregor's talent, Oskar's skills hadn't come naturally. Caution, foresight, contingency planning—these were all vital contributions that

Gregor mocked, but Oskar's penchant for overpreparation had saved them both on numerous occasions.

One of these days, he knew, *it won't be enough.*

With Gregor, nothing was *ever* enough. All his appetites were equally insatiable: gourmet food, luxury sports cars, vintage wines and liquors, designer clothes, five-star hotels, exclusive call girls... Gregor's philosophy was that with his great power had also come great entitlement.

Eventually, of course, all of Gregor's desires came to ruin. He would eat and drink himself sick, then vomit half the night and wake up the next day too hoarse to speak. Priceless bottles of wine often became targets for his demented variety of pulse-blast skeet shooting. All his cars ended up wrapped around trees or telephone poles, or smashed into other cars, or submerged beyond recovery in a lake or a river. Every suit he wore was reduced to tatters inside of a week. Hotel rooms were transmogrified, seemingly overnight, into boxes of rubble. And Oskar had yet to see one of Gregor's achingly beautiful, thousand-dollar-an-hour prostitutes depart his company without a black eye or a bloody, broken nose to remember him by.

The only commodity that Gregor coveted more than all those others put together, of course, was power itself.

It did not, in Oskar's opinion, bode well for their future.

2

LOGAN kneeled on the white stone slab, rested his empty palms on his thighs, and bowed his head. A breeze, sweet with the promise of rain and the scent of new cherry blossoms, rustled the leaves of drooping boughs overhead, dappling the graveyard with pale dawn light. Around him, generations of the dead lay in close company beneath ancient trees, honored by legions of leaning stones whose surfaces were thick with deep green lichen. Decades of acid rain had washed the markers white as albinos and worn down their inscriptions until they were all but illegible, beyond understanding, like a conversation cut short.

A million blades of grass trembled in silent unison. From somewhere close by came a sparrow's lonely song.

Mariko Yashida's gravestone towered in front of Logan, backlit by the rising sun. Its smooth, pale marble was as hard as his own heart, which still sank into despair when reminded of Mariko's absence. He had brought her a single red rose as a tribute; it rested at his feet—one perfect bloom for the one true love of his life, gone now all these years.

Her portrait was set into the face of the stone monument and protected by a transparent plate of Plexiglas. It hurt to look upon her as she had been. His guilt pursued him like an inquisitor; it reminded him of the pain and terror he had seen in her eyes when the blowfish toxin began to wreak its hideous effects on her nervous system. In the theater of his memory he relived her fateful request, the moment when she'd asked him to give her a merciful death. To let her die by his hand.

Honoring her request had been the right thing to do. That hadn't made it any less horrific. To see her impaled on his claws, on those shining blades of adamantium, had sickened him. He'd felt the fluttering tremors of her dying heart as death took her. When at last he'd pulled his claws free and realized that they were slicked with her blood, he'd had to fight a momentary temptation to use them to commit seppuku.

Killing her had cost him a part of his soul, the part that had known how to trust. How to hope. How to forgive. It lay buried now beside the memory of the one woman who had been able to look past his feral countenance and believe in the man he had struggled—and was still struggling—to be.

Some of his wiser friends had suggested that he focus on better memories during his visit today. *As if I could ever forget*, Logan told himself. This already grim anniversary was one that, with good reason, Logan had learned to dread. His foes had made a habit of visiting chaos and tragedy upon him, and on those close to him, at this time of year. Once, he'd nearly lost his foster daughter, Amiko, to Sabretooth and his accomplices, who had decided that the anniversary of Mariko's death should mark the opening day of Wolverine Hunting Season. Logan had become increasingly wary of this date ever since.

He reached up and rested one hand on the cold stone. *I miss you, darlin'. Every single day.*

The sun rose higher, spilling golden light and endless shadows across the countryside. Another billow of cool air snaked under Logan's loose, bomber-style leather jacket and rust-colored canvas shirt. He was traveling incognito, without his costume, whose insulation he had grown accustomed to. He didn't mind the cold, really; it simply had been a while since he'd last noticed it.

He considered reaching back to his weathered brown rucksack and digging out a scarf that Rogue had badgered him into packing before he'd left the Xavier Institute… How long had it been since they'd parted company? He couldn't remember offhand. Months, at least. He hadn't kept track of the days. Hadn't needed to. Hadn't wanted to.

All he'd really wanted was to get away for a while—from everyone, from everything. But no matter where he went, his troubles always seemed a step ahead of him. In every town, on every lonely stretch of road, in every sprawl of ostensibly untamed wilderness, it was *something*. An old friend in need of help. An old adversary with a score to settle. An innocent person in danger, who would live or die by the grace of Logan's intervention, or lack thereof.

He'd heard the footsteps from nearly a hundred meters away. Whoever it was moved decisively, without any attempt at silence; the footfalls were marked by the distinctive *click* of high heels on stone. The brief intervals between steps suggested a person of medium height. A subtle, delicately floral essence of perfume was borne ahead of the visitor on a hush of morning air.

This better be a dame, Logan thought, *or this is gonna be weird*. Withdrawing his hand from Mariko's grave monument, he stood and turned to face the only other person in the graveyard.

She was Chinese; he saw that on first glance. Slender and innocently beautiful, she moved with a balletic grace, and her pace didn't falter as he gave her his full attention. Her long black hair was wind-tossed. It moved as though it were dancing in time with the tempo of her ivory-hued, spike-heeled pumps clacking against the paving stones. She looked young, barely out of her teens, but she carried herself with elegance and poise.

Her sense of fashion was distinctly Western and modern; she wore a white business suit, cut by a professional to flatter her figure. Its jacket was of the two-button variety and slightly longer than a man's suit jacket would have been. Beneath the long, narrow V of its notched lapels, a shimmering band of white silk was all that showed of her chemise. As she moved closer, Logan noticed a subtle, off-white, narrow-vertical-stripe pattern in her jacket and her trousers.

She clearly wasn't armed, but she also moved with the confidence of someone who didn't need to put her trust in weapons.

Several meters away from Logan, she stopped. "Mr. Logan," she said with a slight bow of her head. "My apologies for disturbing you here."

"You can't be that sorry," he said. "After all, you're here." After a few seconds, when it became clear to Logan that the young woman wasn't going to be baited into an argument, he added, "So, you know my name… What's yours, kid?"

"Tse Wai Ying," she said. "And I would prefer that you not address me as 'kid.'"

"Suit yourself, doll," Logan said, intentionally defying the spirit of her request. He fished a box-cut Punch Rare Corojo from an inside pocket of his jacket, extended a single claw from between the first and second knuckles of his right hand, and expertly sliced off the tip of the cigar. He retracted the claw back into his forearm with a twinge of pain and a barely audible *snikt*. Fishing in another pocket for his Zippo, he asked, "What can I do for you?"

"My employer humbly requests the honor of your visit this morning. She is in need of your aid."

He clutched the cigar between his teeth as he opened and lit his Zippo with a snap of his fingers. The Corojo lit easily and evenly. He savored a mouthful of its smooth, rich smoke, then expelled it with a gentle puff. "And your boss would be—?"

"Lady Setsuko Tanaka," Wai Ying said.

Logan's jaw slackened. He almost dropped his cigar. "What's happened? Is she all right?"

"She is unharmed, Mr. Logan," Wai Ying said. "But a terrible crime has been committed against her, and she asks for your assistance—and your… *discretion*."

Setsuko was the daughter of Masao Tanaka, a man who had befriended Logan in the 1950s during his years of training in isolation at Jasmine Falls, in the high mountains of Japan. Logan had been forced to leave Jasmine Falls after accidentally cutting his sparring partner, Miyagi, while training with swords beneath the falls. Later, when Logan had sought permission to return and resume his studies, the sensei had initially been of a mind to turn him away. Tanaka, however, had spoken on Logan's behalf, vouchsafing his own word of honor that Logan could be trusted. It was one of the most selfless things that anyone had ever done for Logan up to that point; he'd pledged an honor debt to Tanaka and his kin that day.

Now, decades later, that debt had finally come due.

He curled an index finger around the cigar and took it from his mouth. "I'm guessing you have a car?"

"It's waiting for us at the cemetery gate, yes."

Logan nodded. "Fine." He stuck the cigar between his teeth and turned back toward Mariko's grave marker. Once more he pressed his palm against the glass-smooth, icy stone surface. *Duty calls, darlin'. Like always.* He leaned down, picked up his rucksack, and slung it casually over his shoulder. It didn't weigh much; he hadn't planned on staying long, and he always traveled light anyway. He took a few steps toward Wai Ying and gestured to the gate. "Let's go."

○———————○

THE moment Logan saw the "car" that was waiting for them at the cemetery gate, he realized that Wai Ying possessed a peculiar gift for understatement. The vehicle that had sat idling while she'd gone in to collect him was a black stretch Mercedes limousine, its entire elongated body cleaned and buffed to a perfect mirror brilliance.

The driver, a gray-haired Japanese man, opened the rear passenger-side door and dipped the visor of his hat politely in Logan's direction. "Excuse me, sir," he said with a mild accent, then pointed at the lit cigar in Logan's left hand. A moment later, the chauffeur recoiled from Logan's withering glare.

"*Daijyoubu-desu*, Hattoro," Wai Ying said. The driver nodded curtly and stepped aside. Logan tossed his rucksack through the open door, then climbed in and settled into the limo's luxurious leather rear seat. The interior of the car smelled brand new.

"Back to the tower," Wai Ying said as she climbed in and sat down next to Logan. The chauffeur closed the door behind her, then walked back to the front of the car. Wai Ying gestured toward the bar, which was recessed into the walls of the rear passenger compartment. "Would you care for a drink?"

"It's six-fifteen in the morning," Logan replied.

"We have espresso," she said.

"Maybe later." Up front, the chauffeur settled into his seat. Gravel crunched under the tires as the limousine pulled away from the gate and accelerated quickly downhill, back to the main road. The rural countryside blurred past outside the dark-tinted windows. Logan noted, from Wai Ying's spectral reflection on the car window, that she was watching him. Her expression was one of intense curiosity.

"Go ahead," he said. "Ask."

She accepted his invitation without embarrassment. "You're the one they call Wolverine, aren't you?"

Smirking slightly, he puffed once on his cigar and exhaled a small cloud of smoke. "I been called lots of things."

"Which name do you prefer?"

"Logan'll do just fine."

She leaned forward and took a thermos and a small porcelain sipping cup from the bar. As soon as she twisted open the thermos's lid, Logan's acute sense of smell was flooded with the rich, sweet aroma of freshly brewed espresso. A second whiff convinced him that the brand was Perla Nera. Wai Ying poured a double shot into her cup. Catching his stare out of the corner of her eye, she offered him the cup. "Care for some?"

"Why not?" He accepted the drink. She reached forward and poured another double for herself. She set it down in a drink nook on the door and put away the thermos. Then she lifted her espresso and turned back toward Logan. "*Salute*," she said.

"Bottoms up," Logan replied. They downed their espressos in unison. He let out a satisfied breath as he savored its lingering flavor. "Thick as mud and strong as the devil," he said. "Just the way I like it."

The limo made the turn toward the highway and continued to pick up speed. Wai Ying and Logan rode together in silence for what felt to him like a long while. Watching the signs, he noted that they were headed toward Osaka.

"So," he said, breaking the silence, "how long have you worked for Setsuko?"

"The details of my employment are confidential," she said.

"Of course they are."

"I'm sure you understand," she added.

"Not really."

Wai Ying appeared to consider her response carefully—or perhaps she was pondering whether she should respond at all. After several seconds, she said, "The Japanese government has not been as *openly* hostile as those of many Western countries, but it remains… *suspicious*. Secrecy is a virtue here."

Logan nodded his understanding: she was a mutant. So far, Japan had been spared a lot of the political strife that folks like Senator Kelley and his ilk had stirred up in the United States, but the Japanese government was undoubtedly wary of the potential threat to its authority that mutants represented. *New and different* was always something to be feared, no matter the time or place; experience had taught Logan that bitter lesson many times. He asked, "Do you have an alias that you go by?"

"I've never seen the need for one," she said. "And I don't wear a costume."

"Good choice." He exhaled another puff of smoke. "Truth is, they all start to look alike after a while."

"You wear a costume, though, don't you?"

He looked out the window and frowned at his own haggard reflection.

"Not at the moment," he said. "Not for a while now."

"Why? Did something happen?"

Logan stifled a grim chuckle until all that was left was a muffled grunt of disillusionment. "Somethin' always does, doll," he said. "Somethin' always does."

o——————o

THE last time Logan had seen Setsuko Tanaka, she had been only a child, wide-eyed and vivacious. As the cherrywood double doors of her corner office swung open ahead of him, he beheld her as she was today: a trim and striking woman in her late forties, attired in a charcoal-gray blazer, plum-colored blouse, black skirt, sheer stockings, and spike-heeled black Manolo Blahniks. Where once her eyes had radiated trust and optimism, she now wore the steely gaze of a seasoned corporate chief executive.

She strode forward to greet Logan. Several paces apart they halted; he bowed to her, and she reciprocated the gesture. He was careful to hold his bow just a fraction of a second longer than hers. With that formality out of the way, she stepped forward, closing the distance between them, and reached out to shake his hand. "Thank you for coming, Logan-san."

Shaking her hand, he nodded politely. "It's my honor to be of service, Tanaka-sama."

She motioned with a wave of her arm toward a pair of chairs in front of her enormous mahogany desk. "Please, have a seat."

"I'd rather stand," he said as he followed her toward her desk. "It was a long ride in."

"Whichever you prefer," Setsuko said, moving behind her desk. Wai Ying followed Logan into the office and shut the double doors behind her. Taking a moment to look around, Logan noted that, like the rest of the building's interior spaces he had seen so far, it seemed to have been deliberately stripped of personality.

Setsuko waited until Logan joined her at the desk before she spoke. "I'll get straight to business," she said. "A few hours ago, this building was invaded and burglarized by a combined force of ninjas and mutants. They absconded with three things: our only sample of an experimental new drug that we've nicknamed Panacea, a set of flash memory cards containing all our research on how to synthesize the drug, and our chief Panacea researcher, Dr. Nikolai Falco."

Logan sighed. "This is gonna get complicated, isn't it?"

"I'm afraid so," Setsuko replied.

"In that case, I guess I'll sit down."

He sagged into the chair behind him, and the two women settled into their own seats. Setsuko folded her hands in front of her on the desk and continued. "Panacea is a drug derived from a plant that our researchers discovered in Brazil more than a decade ago. Since then, the original plant has been rendered extinct by clear-cut logging in the Amazon basin. We've been trying to synthesize it artificially for years, and we were on the verge of a breakthrough when this happened."

"All right," Logan said. "I'll bite. What's the big deal about your new drug?"

"It can cure anything," Setsuko said.

"What do you mean, 'anything'?"

"Exactly that, Logan-san," she said. "*Anything. Everything*. Illness, infection, injury… cancer, tuberculosis, the common cold—it can cure them all, and any other affliction you'd care to name. Viral, bacterial, congenital, it doesn't matter. We call it Panacea for a reason."

"The perfect drug," Logan muttered.

"Well," Setsuko demurred, "I wouldn't call it perfect. It does have one serious, unfortunate flaw."

He leaned forward. "And that would be—?"

"From the first dose," Setsuko said, "it obliterates the patient's immune system forever. Unfortunately, while the damage it does to the patient is permanent, its curative properties are temporary. The patient's health—and life—depend from that point forward on frequent booster injections."

"How frequent?"

"A person who receives it once will have to be dosed again every twenty-four hours for the rest of his life."

The more Logan heard, the more he hated what he was being told. "And if the patient doesn't get his dose?"

"Patients who stop taking Panacea die within seventy-two hours of their last injection. *Every time*."

"Jesus Christ," Logan whispered, horrified. "And you wanted to mass-produce this stuff?"

Anger hardened Setsuko's expression. "Of course not," she said, her offense at his implication sharp in her voice. "For years I've forbidden my people even to discuss it outside the lab. We've all been aware since the beginning of how this drug could be abused if it fell into the wrong hands. Our goal has been to separate its healing properties from its toxic ones. I vowed from the start that we would never reveal this drug to the world until we'd made it safe."

Logan bowed his head with shame. "My apologies, Tanaka-sama. Please forgive my presumption."

"It's already forgotten," she said, then she picked up where she'd left off. "Dr. Falco was preparing to synthesize a safe version of the drug when he was kidnapped and the sample was stolen." She got up from her chair and paced toward the south-facing panoramic window to Logan's left. "The drug, its synthesis formula, and the one man who knows more about it than anyone else on earth are now all in the hands of some unknown third party, whose intentions for it are at best unknown."

"Let me guess," Logan said, his inner cynic rising to the fore. "You want me to save your scientist and steal back your missing wonder drug, right?"

"And we'd like you to do it without alerting the public—or attracting any... *official* attention."

"I get it," he grumbled. "Confiscation with prejudice."

Perhaps sensing his distaste for the nature of her request, Setsuko said, "This isn't some petty theft I'm asking of you. A man's life is at stake—and possibly the fate of all humanity."

Logan folded his arms across his chest. "If you ask me, you oughtta destroy it, not bring it back. As long as you have it, it'll be a target." Then he added ominously, "*You'll* be a target."

"I'm sure your pessimism is well founded, Logan-san," Setsuko said. "But I've devoted the past decade of my life, the future of my company, and my entire fortune to the perfection of Panacea. I can't—*won't*—give up on it now, not when it's so close to becoming a reality."

"And when you're so close to becoming Japan's newest billionaire," Logan added.

"Funny thing about philanthropy," Setsuko replied. "You have to *have* money before you can give it away."

It was probably a white lie, Logan figured. At the very least a distortion. He'd heard of more than a few wealthy people who liked to write thousand-dollar checks and call themselves philanthropists. As much as he wanted to believe that Setsuko wasn't just exaggerating her charitable intentions, she had too sharp an edge to her demeanor for him to believe that she was just a saint in sinner's clothing.

Before he could call her bluff, she added, "At the very least, please help rescue Dr. Falco."

With a heavy sigh, he unfolded his arms and nodded. "All right, you have my word: I'll do my best to save him." Reacting to Setsuko's inquisitively raised eyebrow, he continued, "And I'll see if I can get your wonder drug back."

Setsuko lowered her head in a courteous nod. "Thank you, Logan-san. You honor us." She picked up a slim, brown cardboard file folder and handed it to Logan. He flipped idly through the few pages inside—a biographical one-sheet about the missing Dr. Falco and a few digital photos of the metal carrying case used to transport the Panacea sample. "I'll be making available all my best resources to assist you," she said. "A TBC private jet, an unlimited expense account, our communications and security intelligence network, and the aid of my personal bodyguard."

Personal bodyguard? "You ain't gonna tell me it's—"

"I'm sure you and Ms. Tse will make an excellent team."

"No offense," Logan protested, "but I work better alone."

"It's not negotiable," Setsuko insisted. "She'll be your pilot, your gal Friday—and your sole link to our resources."

Wai Ying lowered her chin and fixed Logan with a sly smirk. "Don't worry," she teased. "You're in good hands. I won't let anything bad happen to you."

Logan had no words that adequately conveyed his contempt for this turn of events, so he rolled his eyes and frowned instead. "Let's get this show on the road," he said, rising from his chair. "Take me down to the break-in."

○———————○

A rush of alarming odors overwhelmed Logan's senses the moment he, Setsuko, and Wai Ying got off the elevator at the sixty-eighth floor. The hallway that they stepped into looked untouched, but the smells alone told him to expect to find a killing field around the next corner: charred wood and bitter ash, cooked flesh, fresh blood.

It wouldn't have taken his enhanced hearing to note the dozen or so voices talking about one piece of evidence or another. The camera flashes reflecting off the walls ahead were also a dead giveaway that a forensic team was hard at work.

He strode quickly ahead of his two companions and turned the corner. A squad of men and women all wearing identical dark blue windbreakers lined the hallway. Most of them were working inside the segment near the end, where a scorch-edged tunnel had been blasted through multiple redundant security barricades. Some of the technicians kneeled beside the bodies of slain security guards. Others busied themselves collecting bits of debris or snapping photographs or measuring things. Regardless of the job each person was doing, Logan noted that all their equipment was brand-new and state of the art.

Passing several of the investigators as he stepped through the violently crafted breaches, Logan noted a curious absence of insignia anywhere on any of the technicians' matching garments. His knack for suspicion asserted itself.

"These aren't the cops," he said over his shoulder to Setsuko. "These are *your* people."

"Yes," she replied.

"You haven't called the authorities?" He was appalled. "These people are dead. How're you gonna spin *that*?"

"Carefully." Off his accusatory glance, she added, "We don't want to alarm the public."

"Or risk losing your happy little monopoly," he said. Then he turned the corner and saw the lab that the barricades had been meant to protect. Outside of the Xavier Institute and a few other cutting-edge facilities, he had never seen anything like it. Equipment and computers were piled high in the dimly lit space, reaching toward a distant ceiling and encircled with an endless serpent of power cables and data lines. Forks of electrical power snaked between arcane-looking components, and bright blue flames danced inside chromatographic analyzers. Banks of plasma screens scrolled with sequences of genetic code, flickered with electron microscope images, or rearranged themselves in a never-ending digital simulation of a complex-looking molecule that Logan could only presume was the reason for all this carnage: Panacea.

He turned back toward Setsuko. "I'm betting the folks over at S.H.I.E.L.D. don't know you've got a copy of their genetic sequencer," he said, jabbing backward over his shoulder with his thumb. "And I don't think the NSA planned on sharing its new parallel mainframe design, either."

"Angels don't succeed in the tech sector, Mr. Logan," Setsuko said. "Innovation is the key to advantage."

"Gee, that's catchy," Logan said. "Too bad I forgot my notebook, I'd jot that one down." Walking back past her and Wai Ying, he said in a low, irritated tone, "Try to keep up."

They followed him as he stepped carefully back through the blasted tunnel. He pointed at bodies or bits of evidence along the way while he narrated, a tour guide of the morbid and grotesque. "Uniform dimensions and stress patterns on all the breached barricades," he said, running a fingertip along the scorched edge. "This was all done with one shot." Pointing down at one of the dead guards, he observed, "Minimal blood spray on the floors, walls, or victims. Each of your guards was killed with a single strike that severed the carotid artery, larynx, and spinal cord. Narrow blade, probably a *ninja-to*." He kept walking while he pointed straight up. "The ninjas moved freely by staying above the drop-tile ceiling. Whoever installed that here oughtta be shot."

His boot scuffed a thin layer of dust on the linoleum. He kneeled down and dragged his fingertips through it, feeling its grit. As he lifted his fingers to his nose, the telltale odor of a crematorium was unmistakable. "Are all your people accounted for? Living and dead?"

Setsuko sounded surprised at the question. "Yes."

Logan stayed in a low crouch for half a minute, surveying the distribution of fine powder on the floor. "Then someone killed three of the ninjas, right here. Looks like the same guy who opened a hole in your lab dusted his accomplices on the way out." Pointing past the corner ahead, he asked, "That leads behind the elevator bank?"

Wai Ying nodded and answered for her boss. "That's right."

He stood and continued following the trail of destruction. Setsuko and Wai Ying remained close behind him. Stepping over two gruesomely charred bodies that had fallen one on top of the other, he remarked, "They were the first ones to die." Pointing ahead, toward the haphazard gap in the concrete wall on the right, he said, "Your friendly neighborhood fireballer came in through there. Probably gained access to your freight elevator." Once again, Wai Ying nodded to confirm his deduction. "Textbook entry," he said.

Peering through the gap and down into the abyssal darkness of the elevator shaft, he saw the beams of helmet lamps and a cluster of bright orange safety lines. Several rescue workers and a pair of elevator engineers freed a twisted, bloody corpse from a tangle of steel cables. They began hoisting it back up toward the breach, where a black body bag waited on the floor.

He looked sidelong at Setsuko. "Whose body is that?"

"Yoshi Tamura, our *bushi*," she said. "If you're right, and someone killed three of the ninjas, it was probably him. He was the ace up the sleeve of our security division."

Logan scowled. "An ace up your sleeve don't mean much when the other guy's got a royal flush."

He looked back down at the broken body of Yoshi Tamura. The rescue team lifted the *bushi*'s corpse level with the breach. As the cadaver swung over the edge, Logan saw the glint of something metallic in Tamura's savaged neck. He guided the body softly to rest on the floor, on top of the black bag. Fishing through the mangled meat of the dead man's neck and throat, he grasped the metal object embedded between the corpse's cervical vertebrae. It came free with a wet noise and pulled a ragged tail of muscle and tissue behind it. Logan shook bits of bone from the ninja *shaken* and wiped the four-pointed throwing star mostly clean on Tamura's torn clothing. Engraved on the center of the *shaken* was a peculiar emblem that Logan had never seen before:

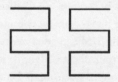

He tried rotating it ninety degrees. It didn't become any more familiar. He showed it to the two women behind him.

"Recognize it?" They shook their heads no. He tucked the *shaken* into his jacket pocket. "Neither do I," he said. "But I know a clue when I see one."

MIYOKO steered the van off the road, through an ungated entrance into the dockyard. The sprawling expanse of weed-cracked asphalt and rusted, abandoned cargo machinery was like a forgotten piece of Osaka's industrial past, tucked behind some ramshackle buildings on the far western edge of the city's bay. She guided the van through the slalom of derelict equipment and empty shipping containers, then hooked a hard right around the corner of one of the dock houses and stepped on the brake. The vehicle came to an abrupt, gravel-crunching halt.

The smell of the sea greeted Miyoko as she opened her door and got out of the idling van. She stepped toward the vehicle's rear, then pulled open its broad side door. It glided open with a low, smooth echo of weighty metal. Inside the rear compartment of the van, Oskar and Gregor sat on either side of the comically overrestrained Dr. Falco, who lay on the floor between them. Miyoko pointed at the identical mutants. "You two. Out."

The brothers traded quizzical expressions, then did as she had instructed. She stepped back and gave them room to climb out. They stood side by side in front of her, openly suspicious of her intentions.

She reached inside the folds of her black uniform jacket and pulled out a pair of travel-agency envelopes. She handed one to each of them, then waited while they opened them and inspected their contents. Oskar made sense of the situation first, and he looked and sounded annoyed. "Airline tickets?"

"There are two cars inside the dock-house garage," Miyoko said. "Leave separately, ten minutes apart. One of you departs from Yao Airport, the other from Osaka International. New passports are inside the envelopes."

"This wasn't the plan," Gregor said, mirroring his brother's irritated state. "We were supposed to deliver the scientist to the daimyo himself."

"That will be my responsibility now," she said. "Yours is to leave the country without attracting any more attention than you already have."

Oskar held up his boarding pass. "But separate flights? Separate *airports*? Was that really necessary?"

"Bad enough the daimyo sent me gaijin for this mission," she said, narrowing her eyes with contempt, "but he sent me *twins*." She pulled the van's side door shut. "Wait until I'm gone, then get out of here. And try to be forgettable."

She got back in the van, shifted it into gear, and accelerated away before the blasting brothers realized that, in addition to flying separately, they both would be flying coach.

o———————o

CONTENT to bide his time in silence and not provoke his captor, Dr. Nikolai Falco had made himself moderately comfortable after the twin brothers were evicted from the vehicle. He'd sat up and stretched his legs out in front of him. Roughly an hour after the van had departed the dockyard, the driver had pulled over and removed his bonds. She hadn't said anything, not an apology or a warning. One moment his hands had been bound behind him and his mouth gagged; the next he was free of constraints. He'd considered saying thank you, but under the circumstances it seemed inappropriate.

Hours had passed since then. The van's journey had continued uninterrupted. Peeking out the windshield, Falco saw that the sky was dimming with the advent of dusk. He was uncertain what direction they had been traveling. If the woman had driven south, they could be near the tip of Kyushu by now. If her path had been northward, they might be somewhere near Yamagata. Or they might be simply driving in circles around Osaka; Falco had absolutely no way of knowing for certain.

If the woman up front found his sangfroid unusual, she did not remark on it. Falco wasn't particularly worried about what would happen to him. Unlike several of his peers, he had no spouse or children to concern himself over. Most of his friends had fallen away over the years, as he had submerged ever more deeply into his research. As he'd gotten older and begun to see the true potential of his work, his isolation had become less of a burden. He was happy to live for his work; his destiny was greater than anything he had sacrificed in its name.

Of course, his captors likely had their own plans for his research and his inventions, so for the moment his life was in their hands. If his scientific vision was to have any hope of being fulfilled, he would have to comply with their orders.

For now.

○━━━━━━━━○

THERE was nothing Logan liked better than a good workout.

He hurled a burly bald thug who was twice his size and had a face like a boiled ham. Baldy had already proved that he could take a punch. Now Logan wanted to see how the guy took a fall.

Not so well. The guy dropped onto a bar table like a sack of wet cement, splintered it on impact. Then he slid across the beer-slicked concrete floor and collided noggin-first with the wall.

Two of baldy's buddies tried to grab Logan from behind—one with an arm around Logan's throat, the other seizing the slack in his leather jacket. A simple hip throw landed Logan's would-be strangler on the floor at his feet. A back kick sent the second man stumbling backward; he landed on his ass in the corner and started dry-heaving. Meanwhile, his friend on the floor did the sensible thing: he covered his face.

Logan picked up the guy who was choosing to see no evil and unceremoniously heaved him through the bar's grimy front window, into the rain-slicked and neon-lit Tokyo gutter.

Clapping his hands clean, Logan walked back to the bar and sat down next to Wai Ying, who sipped her vodka straight up with an air of droll boredom. He nodded to the bartender. "Sorry 'bout the mess," he said. "Tack on a Sapporo, will ya?" Angling a thumb in Wai Ying's direction, he added, "She'll pay for it."

She nodded her weary assent to the bartender, then glanced sidelong at Logan. "Did they know anything?"

"About what?"

"The symbol on the *shaken*," she said. "That is why we're here, right?"

"Yeah, but not to talk to those clowns."

"Then what was that about?"

He shrugged. "About thirty seconds of exercise."

"If you want exercise, we have a gym at the Osaka office."

"Show me a gym that lets you throw people through windows." The bartender delivered Logan's beer with a less than perfectly clean pilsner glass, which he set aside. Logan downed a healthy swig straight from the bottle, then allowed himself a moment to appraise Wai Ying's charms. "Of course, there are other kinds of exercise."

"I'm sure you'd find it most demanding," she replied with mocking faux sweetness. "But I doubt I'd break a sweat."

"Cold," he said, then swallowed another mouthful of beer.

She took a sip of her vodka, then set down the glass, dead center on her square napkin. "What are we hoping to learn here, Mr. Logan?" The bartender started to refill her half-empty glass, then paused as the phone behind the bar rang. He turned away to answer it as Wai Ying continued, "So far, this excursion seems to have been a waste of our—"

"Phone for you, Mr. Logan," the bartender said, handing him the cordless receiver.

Lifting it to his ear, Logan deadpanned, "I thought I told you never to call me here."

"And I thought the *yakuza* told you not to go in there anymore," replied National Police Agency organized-crime inspector Raiken Watanabe.

Logan took a quick sip of his Sapporo. "Since when do I listen to them?"

"Since when do you listen to anybody?" It was late, and Watanabe sounded tired. "I put that symbol through the computer. No links to any groups or people we know of."

"'Course not," Logan said. "That'd be too easy. Can you tell me *anything* about it?"

"It's ancient, a Chinese symbol called Fu."

"What is it? Occult? A tong sign? What's it for?"

"A bunch of different things. Depends who you ask."

"Boil it down for me."

Watanabe yawned. "The more benign reading is that it stands for collaboration or partnership. But in some circles it stands for authority, divine power, and the right to judge."

"Knowing my luck, the second one sounds about right."

"Maybe they're both right, and you're outnumbered."

"And on that happy note," Logan said, "I owe you a beer."

"Are you kidding? You owe me a whole bar by now."

"Go back to bed." Logan turned off the cordless receiver and put it back down on the bar. Then he picked up his bottle of Sapporo and drank with his head tilted back, emptying it in a steady stream down his throat.

Wai Ying watched him drink. "Who was that on the phone?"

He put the empty bottle down on the bar. "No one."

"What's happened?" She followed him as he got up from his stool and walked toward the door. "What are we doing?"

"'We'?" He was already out the door onto the teeming sidewalks of Yamanote, one of the sleazier neighborhoods of Tokyo. Block after block was lined with sex shops, nightclubs blaring music geared toward drunken foreigners, and dive bars whose attempts to seem "edgy" were, in Logan's opinion, undermined by their proclivity for featuring karaoke machines. "*We* aren't doing anything. Go home."

He ignored the blaring of horns and a slew of Japanese epithets as he jaywalked through a street choked with some of the weirdest cars he'd ever seen, all jockeying for position. Tiny shoeboxes with wheels cutting off hulking SUVs. Crafted-plastic show-off cars adorned with black-light neon trim and photorealistic murals. The one thing they all had in common was the hideous, homogenized technopop music that thumped inside their fragile shells.

Pushing his way through the sidewalk pedestrian traffic on the opposite side of the street, he glanced left and saw Wai Ying weaving with him through the obstacle course of moving bodies. "You're not ditching me," she said without looking at him. "I can help you."

"What are you gonna do? Tuck me in? I'm calling it a night." He bounded up the stairs to the elevated train platform, hoping to catch the Yamanote line back to his hotel. She remained behind, at the bottom of the stairs. "Get some sleep, ace," he shouted to her over the street noise. "Today's a bust. Tomorrow we start over."

4

SWATHED in a web of mosquito netting, trapped in a blanket of her own sweat, Nishan awoke in fear. It was routine now; it happened several times a night. Even in the deep hours of darkness, the African heat and humidity pressed down on her chest. The air reeked of stale sweat and infected flesh.

She rolled over and felt her way through the netting. Her eight-year-old son, Nadif, lay sleeping beside her, his arms wrapped protectively around his younger sister, Kanika. Despite the sweltering weather, both were shivering. Nishan pressed her palm against Nadif's emaciated chest, felt the heaving of his protruding ribs as he struggled for every breath. In his arms, Kanika trembled as well. Both had been ill on and off for a few weeks now. They had seemed to recover the day before yesterday, but now their symptoms had returned, worse than before.

Nishan shook the children awake. Their eyes opened, glazed and heavy-lidded. Neither moved or made a sound. She looked into her son's eyes. "Nadif? Can you hear me?" His chin dipped slightly, indicating that he did. "You're shaking," she said to him. "So is your sister. You have fevers. You both need the doctor. Can you carry her?"

His head lolled toward the floor, all the response he could give. He wouldn't be able to carry Kanika. Nishan was too weak from hunger and prolonged illness to carry both her children, or to make two trips to bring them both to the clinic. Her only hope would be to bring the clinic to them. Crawling, she fumbled through the layers of diaphanous mosquito nets and dragged herself out from under them. She found one of the support beams that held up the roof and pulled herself to her feet. Then she padded out of the communal hut and ventured alone into the night.

The rest of the village was deathly quiet beneath the ghostly light of a waxing half-moon. Inky darkness was washed with dark shadows; there were no lights at night. Partly it was to preserve the fuel in the clinic's two small diesel generators; it also helped avoid drawing the attention of nocturnal, roving squads of Tanjawar militia, who were always, it seemed, on the prowl for supplies or for blood sport.

Nishan's bare feet faltered upon sharp rocks that littered the village's central dirt road. The dust underfoot was still warm, gritty, and damp; the rains had been heavy for several weeks, spawning vast clouds of hungry mosquitoes. Even after three days of clear weather, the ground still did not feel dry.

Most of the huts along the road were empty now, burned by the Tanjawar during one of their countless raids. They were charcoal shells, collapsed in upon their own ashes, funeral pyres for the hopes and dreams of people who once had called this place home. The government had pledged to stop the Tanjawar's rampages and then had done nothing. The United Nations had sent a few dozen unarmed "peacekeepers" to quell the violence; very soon, they, too, had done nothing.

The only people who had ever kept their promises in Zibara were the doctors; they had come with more than just good intentions. They had brought medicine, machines, and full suitcases, which had implied that they planned to stay. The hand-painted sign they had hung from a stake in front of the village's largest enclosed building—now the clinic—bore three simple letters: MSF, which stood for *Médecins sans Frontières*. The healers had come from parts of the world that Nishan could only imagine: rich Western countries, newly stabilized Asian nations, other parts of Africa and the Middle East. They spoke numerous languages, though the ones that most of them had in common were French and English. During the past two years, Nishan had learned a fair amount of both tongues from a teacher who traveled with one of the doctors. In turn, the doctors had made an effort to learn to speak the local Zibarese dialect.

Nishan climbed the wide but rickety steps to the doctors' dormitory. She slipped through the drapery of mosquito netting that blocked the door, then found herself inside. Stepping softly on her thickly callused feet, she moved down the row of cots, which were cocooned in more netting, in groups of three and four. It was like trespassing in a spider's web.

She found the pediatrician, Dr. Rachanee Charoenying, fast asleep. Taking care not to snag any of the delicate netting around the doctor's cot,

Nishan navigated through its overlapping folds.

Dr. Charoenying was a Thai woman in her late twenties. According to the male doctors who worked with her, she was quite beautiful; they admired her golden skin and lustrous black hair. None of them had ever won her affections, however; she was the kind of woman who held herself tantalizingly out of reach. With her patients, though, she was as warm and compassionate as she was meticulous and thorough. And when it came to procuring needed medicine or supplies from the distant patrons on the other end of the doctors' shortwave radio, Charoenying was by far the most passionate; she never took no for an answer.

Nishan gently rested her hand on Charoenying's shoulder.

Groggy and disoriented, Charoenying blinked open her eyes. "Nishan? *Quel…?*"

She spoke to the doctor in French, the language they best had in common. "Doctor? Please wake up. My children are sick."

"Where are they?"

"They were too weak to move, and I can't carry them."

Charoenying rubbed her eyes with the back of her hand. "What are their symptoms?"

"The same as before, but worse."

The doctor nodded. She extended her foot and shook the cot next to hers. The older, white-haired man sleeping on it, an Irish doctor named Dannell Maguire, woke up and rolled over, looking very annoyed at Charoenying. "What?"

"Get up and bring your bag," Charoenying snapped as she got off her cot. She was already mostly dressed, in lightweight clothes suited to the sub-Saharan locale. Only her feet were bare; she slipped them into a pair of rubber sandals. Then she reached under her cot and grabbed a heavily scuffed, black leather medical bag with a broad, padded shoulder strap.

Beside her, Maguire forced himself to a sitting position. He slipped on his mud-caked loafers, then found his own satchel at the foot of his cot. When he stood, he looked like an angry pile of unwashed laundry.

Charoenying said to Nishan, "Take us to them."

Nishan led the two doctors out of their dormitory and down the main road, back to her own hut. Weaving adroitly through the netting, they soon were all kneeling beside Nishan's children. The doctors listened with their stethoscopes, took temperatures, drew blood with slender syringes, shone tiny lights into the children's eyes and ears and throats.

Speaking softly, Charoenying asked Nadif, in Zibarese, "Does it hurt?" The boy nodded. "Tell me where."

"My stomach," he said. "And my head."

"You have a headache?" Nadif nodded. "How does your stomach hurt? Sharp, like a knife? Or sick?"

"Sick," Nadif whispered. "Dizzy-sick." He coughed.

Behind Nadif and Charoenying, Maguire had been coaching Kanika through the same series of questions, with all but identical results. The two doctors turned their backs and conducted their whispered conference in English. In the stillness of the hour, Nishan heard every word, but, though she spoke English, half of what they said made no sense to her.

"Looks like falciparum," Maguire said.

"I know, but there might still be time," Charoenying said.

"If it's cerebral—"

"We don't know that," Charoenying interrupted.

"We don't know anything until the blood work comes back."

"But if it is," he continued, "they need mefloquine."

"We haven't had any for weeks. All we have left is doxycycline."

"But we can't give that to—"

"Children under eight, I know." She glanced over her shoulder at Nishan, as if to say, *Please give us room.* Looking back at Maguire, she said, "Maybe we can get an airdrop from—"

"Unless it's an epidemic, we're not getting an airdrop," Maguire said.

"Please," Charoenying replied bitterly. "The whole damn continent's an epidemic. Christ, it's practically a *pandemic*. We are one viral change away from—"

"Preaching to the choir won't get you any mefloquine."

"No, but yelling at those clods in Cairo until they get off their asses just might." She blinked away her frustration, then looked back at Maguire. "Are there any free beds in the clinic?"

"Not yet," Maguire said. "But the mamba-bite victims won't last much longer. We'll have beds by tomorrow."

"I want them marked for these two," Charoenying said. "Don't let that *connard* Yang poach them like he did last time."

Maguire nodded. "I'll take care of it." He pushed aside the netting and slipped free, then walked away, stepping gingerly over the sleeping bodies that littered the slatted floors.

Charoenying removed the stethoscope that was draped over her shoulders and around her neck and put it back in her bag. "There's not much we can do right now," she told Nishan, once again in French. "We don't have the right medicine for your children, and there aren't any open beds in the clinic."

Helplessness made Nishan feel paralyzed even as panic made her want to do anything, even a million things at once, to help her children. "What am I supposed to do?"

"Make them drink a lot of water. Use a damp cloth to cool their heads and keep the fevers down. If they have new symptoms, especially vomiting or diarrhea, find me or Dr. Maguire immediately." Nishan nodded, numb with fear. Charoenying gently clasped Nishan's shoulder. "I'll be right back with some water and clean rags. Wait here."

Nishan watched Dr. Charoenying slip away into the night. Despite her certainty that the pediatrician would return, she began to cry without making a sound, not a sob or a whimper, for fear of waking her hut mates or frightening her children. *No medicine? No beds? Wet rags is the best we can do for my babies?*

She tried to tell herself to be thankful that her children were still fighting for life. Across Zibara, millions of other mothers wept tonight for children who were forever lost—to disease, to the genocidal rampages of the Tanjawar, to thirst or starvation. In a land of savage horrors, her children still drew breath, and it was her motherly duty to cling to hope, for their sake if not for her own.

But she knew, in her heart, that there was no point in hoping anymore. Death, that insatiable beast, had come in force to Zibara—and by fire, famine, or sword, it would devour them all.

5

LOGAN waited until he heard the blade swinging down toward his face before extending one set of his claws to block it. The *katana* never made impact; as he had expected, its wielder had checked her swing, halting it millimeters shy of contact. He extended his second trio of claws from beneath the crisp white bedsheets and twisted, trapping the sword flat against his bed. Then the pointed tip of a *wakizashi* tickled the underside of his densely whiskered chin.

"Hello, Yukio," he said. He had heard her slip into his hotel room more than a minute earlier. She was skilled, but not enough to elude his preternatural senses. Air disturbed by her passing had fluttered the curtains ever so slightly, and her scent was as familiar to him as that of his foster daughter, Amiko, whom he had left in Yukio's care many years ago.

Yukio crouched above him, perched nimbly on his queen-sized bed. She smiled. "*Konnichiwa*, Logan-san." He retracted his claws. She sheathed her swords across her back, then stepped off his bed and threw open the curtains, revealing a broad view of the Tokyo cityscape far below. The distant lights were reflected on her spiky black hair. "Not your usual hovel," she said.

"Not my idea," he replied, pushing aside his sheets. "What are you doing here?"

"I could ask you the same thing," she said, pacing around the foot of the bed. "Quite a ruckus you kicked up. How many *yakuza* dens did you toss tonight? Five? Six?"

"Something like that." He sat up and scratched the back of his neck. "What's it to you?"

"Starting a war?" She smirked and added, "Without me?"

"No," he said. He plodded across the room in his boxer shorts and

DAVID ALAN MACK

retrieved his robe from the chair near the window. "Just looking for a few honest men."

Watching him intensely, she asked, "To tell you what?"

He lifted an empty beer bottle from the end table next to the chair and picked up the *shaken*, which he had been using as a coaster. With a flick of his wrist, he tossed the throwing star in a slow arc to Yukio, who snatched it from the air with her thumb and forefinger. As she eyed it up close, Logan said, "To tell me where that came from."

"Then you were wasting your time," she said. "The *kobun* won't know about this."

"You've seen it before?"

"A few times, lately. Mostly as it's flying past my head."

"So it is a *yakuza* sign?"

"Not exactly," she said, tumbling the *shaken* over the backs of her knuckles. "It represents an alliance with the *yakuza*, but it's never them throwing it."

"An alliance," Logan repeated. "With who? The tongs? The triads?" Yukio simply stared at him while he worked it out for himself. *Who else uses ninjas?* He frowned. "The Hand," he said.

She tossed the *shaken* on his pillow. "And they're in bed with the *yakuza*. In other words, a nightmare waiting to happen."

He broke the seal on his minibar and fished out a fistful of tiny Jack Daniel's bottles. "I'm having a drink," he said while he unscrewed one of the caps. "Want one?"

"No, thank you." He felt her watching him as he emptied five shots of sour-mash whiskey into a tumbler and cut it with a splash of seltzer. He was using the tip of one of his claws to stir his drink when Yukio said, "She's fine, by the way."

There was no need for her to elaborate. He knew that she was talking about Amiko. "You saw her? Recently?"

"Yes," Yukio said. "She's learning fast. Mana says she's impressed with Amiko's progress."

Logan swelled momentarily with pride. *That's my girl.* Then he remembered that the burden young Amiko had chosen to take on might one day put her on the front line against horrors unlike any found in this dimension. *She knew what she was doing. We all take risks. Have to respect that.* "That's good," he said.

"I know she'd love to see you," Yukio said, trying not to push or pry but failing miserably.

Logan tilted his head back and drank his whiskey and soda in a few large gulps. The sour bite of the whiskey in his throat sharpened his focus on the moment. "I wish I could," he said, putting down the empty glass and picking up his blue jeans from the floor. "But if the Hand's part of this, I have to move fast—because they always do."

"By the way," Yukio said, "there are a couple dozen *yakuza* ninjas downstairs, waiting for you."

"Pathetic," Logan said, stepping into his jeans. "In the old days, they'd have come upstairs and attacked me in my sleep."

Yukio pointed into the living-room area of his spacious suite. Only now did he notice a few pairs of *tabi*-shod feet protruding from behind the sofa. "Thank me later," Yukio said with a playful smile, and she tossed him his shirt.

"You're getting better," he admitted. "Normally, I'd say let's team up and shred the ones downstairs—"

"But you're traveling with baggage," she said. "I saw her. She's pretty, but a little bit corporate for you, isn't she?"

"It's not like that," he said, putting his shirt on.

"Mm-hm," Yukio said, then grinned. "Yet."

"We just need a quiet exit from the lobby, and then we're gone," he said. "Can you keep the boys in black off my back?"

"Maybe," Yukio said. "Think you can make it to the airport without pissing anybody else off?"

He sat down and started pulling on his boots. "I ain't making any promises."

"Of course not," she said. "You never do."

She stalked swiftly across the living room toward an open window. As she planted her hands to propel herself through it and out into the night fifty stories above ground, Logan spoke.

"Tell her I said hello?"

"Of course," Yukio said. "I always do."

And in a dark blur of muscles and motion, she was gone.

Keenly aware of time slipping away, Logan moved around the bedroom, packed his bag, and got ready to make another fly-by-night departure from the Land of the Rising Sun.

———o———————o———

WAI Ying was barely out of the elevator before Logan grabbed her arm and started pulling her at a quick step through the lobby of the Park Hyatt Tokyo toward the main entrance. His rucksack was strapped across his back; a lit cigar dangled from his jaw. He looked grimly focused.

Her laptop computer, slung in its soft case behind her back, bounced on her hip as she hurried with him past the front desk. She was grateful that she had laid out khaki casual wear and broad-heeled hiking shoes before going to bed a few short hours ago. It had made transitioning from a dead sleep to a dead run that much easier when he had rung her room at quarter to five in the morning.

"Shake a leg, lady," Logan said, as their limousine emerged from behind the center island of the traffic circle outside.

She pulled free of his grasp. "What's the rush?"

In a flash, he regained hold of her arm and kept going.

From somewhere off to her right, in the deeply shadowed recesses of the closed and darkened hotel restaurant, Wai Ying heard the clang of steel on steel, followed by a soft thump.

"A friend's got our back," Logan said, quickening his pace, "but we have to go. Now." The doorman tipped his hat at them as they walked past.

Something moved with a hiss in the air between her and the doorman. Logan's claws swept past her head, alarmingly close, and she heard the small *plinks* of tiny projectiles deflecting off his claws. Then a rustle of polyester and the meaty *thunk* of metal piercing flesh, and she saw the doorman impaled on the claws of Logan's other hand. Where the blades sank into the man's chest, Wai Ying caught sight of a dull black garment beneath his bright red uniform overcoat.

Logan pulled his claws free and retracted them. He reached the limousine ahead of her and pulled open the rear door. With a move that was half push, half throw, he propelled her into the back of the stretch Mercedes and followed her in. Through the open partition, Hattoro the chauffeur looked back for instructions. "Airport," Logan barked. "Punch it."

The car lurched into motion.

"Wait!" she cried. "My bags are—"

"Anything you can't live without?"

She clutched at her laptop case and remembered that she kept her cell phone and a limited makeup kit in there, as a precaution against luggage-handling errors when she flew on commercial airlines. Abandoning her wardrobe was an annoyance, but nothing that couldn't be corrected in whatever city they stopped in next. She settled back into her seat and massaged her temples. "Can you tell me now what's going on?"

He exhaled a puff of sharply pungent smoke. "The welcoming committee back there was courtesy of the Hand," he said, as if that was supposed to mean something to her.

"I'll need a little more to work with here," she said.

"They're an organization of mystical ninjas," he explained. "Part supernatural, part martial arts, and a hundred percent trouble. Their motive is simple: power for its own sake."

"Delightful," she said. "And they're the ones who stole the Panacea sample? And kidnapped Dr. Falco?"

"Looks that way," Logan said. He opened the minibar in front of the door and began poking through the liquor.

"I thought you didn't drink this early in the morning," she said, gently chiding him.

"Sun ain't up yet," he said. "Far as I'm concerned, it's still last night." He settled on a previously unopened bottle of Yukon Jack and cut away its plastic seal with the tip of one barely extended claw. After filling a shot glass, he hesitated; then he offered it to Wai Ying. "Ladies first."

At a loss for words, she satisfied herself with a scornfully lifted eyebrow. He shrugged, then knocked back the pale golden spirits in one throw.

"So," Wai Ying said, steering the conversation back on track, "if the Hand was responsible for the burglary in Osaka, what would they do with the Panacea formula?"

"Jesus," Logan said, shaking his head and pouring another shot. "What wouldn't they do with it? Blackmail, extortion, terrorism. There's no telling how they'd deploy it; they could spike the water, cut it into street drugs." He knocked back his second measure of whiskey, clenched his jaw, and exhaled through his teeth. "Hell, they could aerosolize it, take entire cities hostage." He put away the bottle and the shot glass. "Tell me something," he said. "Is this drug ready to go? How much time do you think we have on the shot clock?"

"That depends on the Hand's technological resources," Wai Ying said.

"Because of the drug's unique molecular and atomic properties, we weren't able to start decoding its structure until we invented the multiphase electron chromatograph cellular analyzer."

"Don't tell me—let me guess," Logan said, rolling his eyes in her direction. "You call it MECCA for short."

"Made the grant proposals easier to write," she replied. "To the best of our knowledge, the electron chromatograph is unique. The only other piece of hardware that's even similar is owned by the Fantastic Four."

"Hrm," Logan grunted. "This ain't their MO."

She was about to take the bait and say something dumb when she realized that he was joking. "Anyway," she said, "the good news is, without MECCA, it'll be impossible for the Hand to finish Falco's work—or mass-produce the drug."

The limousine merged onto the freeway, headed toward the airport. Even at this ungodly hour, traffic was already beginning to thicken within the Tokyo city limits. Hattoro did a masterful job of weaving the long vehicle back and forth through seemingly impassable gaps in the other lanes of cars. For several minutes, Logan sat quietly next to Wai Ying. He stared out the window at the blur of the thinning cityscape and puffed idly on his cigar. Finally, he asked, "What if someone built their own electron chromatograph?"

"Impossible," she said. "The schematics are top-secret."

"So was Panacea," Logan said. "But someone found out about that, didn't they?" He turned his head and looked at her, resolute in his convictions. "Someone inside your company is a mole who told the Hand about Panacea, and it's a good bet they smuggled out the design for MECCA while they were at it."

She shook her head; the urge to refute his hypothesis was irresistible. "It wouldn't be enough," she insisted. "Even if they have the plans, some of the components are impossible to buy or fabricate—they're classified hardware that we designed for the American military. Burglarizing an Osaka office tower is one thing; robbing hardened U.S. military installations—"

"Isn't their style," Logan interrupted. "Taking on the U.S. government would get messy, fast. That's the kind of attention they don't need or want right now."

She nodded, following his reasoning. "So, if they can't build it, buy it, or steal it—"

"Who says they can't buy it?"

It took her a second to catch up to him once again.

"The black market," she said. "That's where they'll get the parts."

"Exactly," Logan said. "They'll let money do their dirty work." He grinned and puffed his cigar again. "And if it's Yankee hardware they're looking for, I got a good hunch I know where they'll be shopping."

6

SIXTEEN hours after going wheels-up from Tokyo, Logan was sick of looking at the inside of TBC's corporate jet, which he had at first mistaken for a Cessna Citation X. "Right make," Wai Ying had corrected him, "wrong model." It was, she had explained, a Citation Thunderstar, the next generation of Cessna aircraft, capable of supersonic travel and boasting an operational range of more than 3,600 nautical miles. Its interior was comfortably appointed, with leather-upholstered seats, a well-stocked galley, and a host of high-tech satellite communications equipment. It even had a lavatory large enough not to induce bouts of claustrophobia.

But after more than thirteen hours in the air and three refueling stops of just under an hour each—in Calcutta, India; Addis Ababa, Ethiopia; and Dakar, Senegal—he'd had enough of being hurtled through the air in a metal tube. The only part of the trip he'd found bearable had been the time he'd spent flying the aircraft, taking over for Wai Ying while she'd used the jet's communications suite to buy a new wardrobe, which would be ready and waiting for her when they arrived in Foz do Iguaçu, Brazil.

"We just got our landing clearance," she said from the cockpit. "We should be on the ground in about twenty minutes."

"Great," he deadpanned. "I'll try to return myself to an upright position by then."

He tried to figure the local time in his head, but between changing time zones and the fact that he had never got the hang of the International Date Line, he gave up. Checking the local weather with the computer, he watched a Doppler radar image take shape on the wide-screen plasma monitor mounted on the forward wall behind the cockpit. It was just before seven A.M. in eastern Brazil, and already the day was shaping up hot and muggy.

He shrugged off his leather jacket and pulled off his long-sleeved pullover. His patience thinned while he dug inside his rucksack, looking for the blue Mayan-print tropical short-sleeve shirt that he was certain he remembered packing. *Dammit, where is it?* Its fabric felt familiar as his fingertips brushed it, and he pulled it free of his jumble of wrinkled clothes.

Outside the window, past the sharp sweep of the wing, the green chaos of the South American junglescape began to thin. A few minutes later, the snaking lines of dirt roads mutated swiftly into the deliberate grid of paved streets, and they passed over Ciudad del Este, Paraguay, just across the Río Paraná from Foz do Iguaçu. The jet made a gentle, banking turn above Lago de Itaipu and then passed over the packed crescent of high-rise buildings that constituted the heart of Foz do Iguaçu. Everything came into sharper focus as the Cessna descended and cut through the pollution haze that lay like a shroud over the city. As they neared Cataratas International Airport, he saw the awesome spectacle of the Cataratas do Iguaçu—a 2.7-kilometer-long region of the Rio Iguaçu that contained nearly three hundred majestic waterfalls, with heights of up to seventy meters. From the air, Logan was able to distinguish plumes of mist rising from the Garganta del Diablo—the Devil's Throat—a U-shaped waterfall nearly 150 meters wide and 700 meters long. Then the hard black line of the tarmac appeared beneath them, and Wai Ying guided the plane to a soft and perfect landing.

It took a few minutes for her to taxi the plane to its assigned hangar. As the aircraft rolled to a stop, Logan noted two cars pulling up outside. One was a nondescript, midnight-blue town car with dark-tinted windows. The other looked as if it had started life as a Jeep but had fallen victim to a mechanic with a lot of orange automotive paint and an adolescent fixation on flame decals. The driving bass and heavy beat of American hip-hop blared from the Jeep's oversized rear woofers.

There was no sign of who was in the town car, but riding in the open-top Jeep from Hell was a mismatched trio: a tanned, blond, beach-bum type; a brown-skinned man who looked to be a mix of Hispanic and local Indian; and a shaved-headed black man, who was driving. The three things that they all had in common were exaggerated muscles; abominable, *Miami Vice*–style vintage clothes; and broad, jungle-clearing machetes in leather sheaths strapped across their backs.

Logan snicked the end off a fresh Corojo and walked forward to the main exit hatch. He leaned into the cockpit. "Finish the postflight and get our customs clearance," he said. "I'll be right back."

Wai Ying was looking suspiciously out at the two cars that had stopped beside the Cessna. "Friends of yours?"

"Not exactly," he said as he unlocked the hatch.

She turned back to face him. "What are you going to do?"

He couldn't help but grin. "What I do best."

○————————○

THE flame of Logan's Zippo touched his cigar as his boot touched the tarmac.

All three of the Jeep boys were already in motion, moving to intercept him. The bald black man took the lead. Pointing his machete at Logan's head, he declared, "You're not welcome here."

The front half of the man's machete spun away into the air and clattered to the pavement a few meters away. Logan doubted that the man had even seen him make the cut. For a moment, he almost felt bad for the three morons standing in front of him. These weren't professionals, just conspicuous muscle better suited to working as bar bouncers than as bodyguards or hit men.

In a rare moment of charity, Logan decided not to kill them. While the leader was still staring at the stump of his machete blade, Logan gut-punched him. The man doubled over, and Logan elbowed him at the base of his skull, knocking him unconscious, facedown on the ground.

Blondie and the Indian attacked together, hacking clumsily with their machetes. Extending both sets of claws, Logan let their blades fall between his middle and outer talons, then he turned his wrists one hundred eighty degrees and disarmed each man. Retracting his claws, he lunged forward with a roar and tackled them. One punch was enough to break the blond's jaw. Before Logan could finish off the Indian, the man had sprung back to his feet and was making a classroom-perfect kick at Logan's head. *Too bad for you this ain't a classroom.* Logan caught the man's foot at its point of greatest extension and twisted it until the ankle gave a sharp, meaty snap. He kicked the Indian in the groin, then dropped him in a groaning, whimpering heap next to his pals.

Through it all, Logan's cigar had stayed securely between his teeth; its burn remained even and its flavor was smooth.

The rear passenger-side window of the town car lowered with a mechanical hum, revealing a gaunt, smartly dressed man sitting inside. At the end of his slender cigarette holder smoldered a pungent, dark brown Gauloise.

The passenger's name was Bouchard. He was a black-market arms dealer from the south of France. Logan had crossed his path once a number of years back, in the course of recovering some stolen Soviet nuclear warheads that Bouchard had been trying to sell to a well-funded doomsday cult.

Despite having watched Logan thrash his underlings half to death, he didn't seem intimidated as Logan sidled up to his car.

"Well done," Bouchard said, his accent as thick as ever. "I was warned you'd be coming. You might want to cut your visit short, though. I think you'll find that Foz do Iguaçu can be rather… *inhospitable* to people like you."

"People like me?" He blew a plume of smoke at the Frenchman. "You mean mutants?"

"No, Mr. Logan," he replied. "Heroes."

Logan chuckled. "Me? A hero? I don't think so, bub."

"What would you call yourself, then?"

"I'm just a guy doing a job," Logan said. "Besides, if I was a hero, I wouldn't be stealing your boys' hotrod."

Bouchard glanced at his incapacitated enforcers and *tsk-tsk*ed. "They aren't going to like that," he said.

"Too bad," Logan replied. "Tell your neighbors, Bouchard: I ain't here to bust heads. This is a friendly visit. And as long as nobody makes me feel unwelcome, that's how it'll stay."

"And if my neighbors don't feel friendly?"

"Well," Logan said, "then you and your pals better start stocking up on bandages." He tapped the ash from the tip of his cigar into Bouchard's lap. "Have a nice day."

The car window climbed slowly. Bouchard met Logan's stare with his own unblinking gaze, until the window was closed and all Logan had to look at was his own reflection. As the town car pulled away, Logan ambled over to the Jeep and grinned as he noted that the keys were still in the ignition. He vaulted over the welded-shut door into the driver's seat.

Behind him, Wai Ying descended the steps from the plane and

signaled the ground crew to go ahead and tow it into the hangar. She joined Logan at the Jeep. He turned the key. The vehicle's engine growled to life and purred richly.

Wai Ying eyed the Jeep skeptically, then climbed over the passenger-side door into the seat next to Logan's. She cast a glance back at the three hoodlums huddled in agonized curls on the ground a few meters away, then looked sidelong at Logan.

"Fancy," she said.

"I have moments," he said, then he stepped on the gas and sped off the tarmac, turning up the music as he accelerated.

○———————————○

WAI Ying's hair whipped behind her as the Jeep flew down the highway. The wind noise was almost enough to drown out the grinding, relentless sonic assault of the stereo.

Foz do Iguaçu seemed to her like a city of contrasts. As they cruised away from the airport toward the city proper, on the Avenidos des Cataratas, the land on either side of the road had the naked look of a jungle beaten into submission. Then, past a minute's worth of blurred exurban squalor, the city rose up ahead of them, a dense cluster of ultramodern glass and steel towers. From a distance, it had the architectural profile of a major city, yet its streets looked all but unpopulated, even on a weekday morning. Traffic was light in the center of town, and few pedestrians were anywhere in sight.

"There are lots of black markets in the world," she said over the music and the wind roar. "What makes you so sure the Hand came here?"

"Two things," Logan replied as he swerved through some slow-moving traffic. "First, thanks to the 'war on drugs,' there's a lot more high-tech here than other places. Some of it was used for barter by the CIA when they were setting up their own drug cartel back home. Second, Foz do Iguaçu has one thing a lot of other black-market towns don't: nearly sixty international banks competing for the world's money-laundering business. The kind of stuff the Hand needs to buy costs more money than you can fit in a suitcase, which means they need a seller who can handle wire transfers. This town washes at least twelve billion dollars a year in black-market cash."

She shook her head in disbelief. "If this place is so notorious, why don't the authorities do something about it?"

"What? And give up their piece of the profits? Dream on." He was completely serious. Rather than contemplate the scope of the world's corruption, Wai Ying let herself admire the various storefronts that passed by in a blur as Logan sped up again.

Just as she was starting to feel at home among the broad avenues lined with posh boutiques and international banks, the city transformed itself in the turn of a corner. Heading northwest on a gravel road beside the Río Paraná, she and Logan cruised through a series of shantytown slums. Lean-to shelters were propped against run-down buildings that looked as if they had been imported from another era.

The Jeep lurched to a halt in a cloud of dust.

When the beige cloud dissipated, Wai Ying squinted against the low-angle glare of early morning sunlight. Logan had driven them to a bar. Above the bar's door was a neon sign that looked as though it probably hadn't worked in close to a decade; it read, "*A Terceira Axila*." She had seen a lot of dive bars. This one looked ready to be condemned.

Masking her distaste with an air of boredom, she drummed her fingertips on the outside of the car door as she looked at Logan. "And we're here because...?"

"Because this is the first place I always look for Nando," he replied, then turned off the engine.

"Nando?... Don't tell me—the local microbrew?"

"The local fixer," Logan said as he climbed out of the Jeep and walked around the front to the passenger door. "I know some of the players around here, but Nando knows all of them." He offered Wai Ying a helping hand out of the Jeep, and she accepted it. "If anyone's gonna know who the Hand would've gone to for spare parts, it'll be him." As Logan assisted her, she felt a slight surge of excitement at how strong he was; in his hands she felt light as a feather. Once her feet touched the ground, he let go and walked ahead of her toward the front door of the bar. "And if I know him, this is where he'll be."

"At seven-thirty in the morning?" she asked, checking her watch. "Kind of early to start drinking, isn't it?"

"Or kind of late for last call," Logan replied, pushing open the door. She followed him inside.

There were too many types of stink for her to count them all. Old cigarette smoke mingled with the stale ammonia smell of urine; the half-rotten wooden floorboards were dark with spilled beer, with vomit and bloodstains, with burn marks and bullet holes. Every one of the few liquor bottles lined up on the shelf behind the bar was of a cheap brand that she had never heard of. Booths steeped in shadow lined the wall opposite the bar counter. A half dozen tables occupied the floor space between the two; every table was unoccupied and littered with filthy, dreg-bottomed glasses, overflowing ashtrays, and dozens of beer bottles all bearing the same nondescript local label. In the back of the room there was a neon-lit jukebox that looked as if it had been stolen from a strip club.

Most of the bar stools were empty, except for the ones occupied by the snoozing bouncer at the end near the entrance and the decrepit, smoke-swaddled whore perched in front of the door to the lone toilet. The bartender, a paunchy and balding man in his forties, stood behind the bar and counted cash; a long-barreled .45-caliber Colt revolver lay on the bartop in front of him. He looked up at the new arrivals, squinted into the morning light, then nodded to Logan. "*A quanto tempo não o vejo,*" he said.

"*Sim,*" Logan replied. "*Onde está Nando?*"

The bartender lifted his chin toward the booths. Wai Ying followed his gesture, and then she saw a pair of trousered legs splayed horizontally across one booth seat, knees folded over the corner, feet touching the floor. Logan walked over to the booth and sat down in the empty seat. She followed him to the booth but remained standing at his side. From the other side of the booth came the soft, regular rasp of a snore.

Logan spent a minute enjoying his cigar, puffing steadily until a thick head of ash formed on its tip. He blew a few smoke rings. Then he reached across the table and tapped off his ash in the far corner of the other seat.

A snort led to a gagging cough, then a mumbled curse was followed by the wooden thump of someone sitting up quickly and knocking his head into the underside of the table. After a few more grumbled epithets, a slim, fair-skinned man in his thirties sat up across from Logan and Wai Ying. His dark hair was slightly tousled, and his white silk designer shirt was mildly wrinkled. Dark circles under his eyes branded him as the kind of man who routinely pushed himself too far—perhaps for work, or for play, or for both. After he blinked away his confusion and recognized

Logan, he flashed a smile of perfect teeth. "Hey, buddy," he said, extending a hand across the table. "Great to see you."

"Likewise," Logan said, grinning warmly as he shook Nando's hand. Gesturing in Wai Ying's direction, he made the introductions. "Nando, this is Tse Wai Ying; we work together. Wai Ying, meet Nando Velasquez, an old buddy of mine."

She and Nando traded half-smiles and nodded politely at each other. Then he had to go and ruin the moment. "*Enchanté*," he said with an atrocious French accent that made her wince.

"The pleasure's all yours," she said.

Half a second later he got the message and turned back toward Logan. "What're you doing back in town, man? Last time I saw you, you were off to help some freedom fighter up in… what was it? El Salvador?"

"Nicaragua," Logan said.

Nando nodded. "Right, right. What was his name?"

"De la Rocha," Logan said.

"Yeah. De la Rocha." He shook his head slowly. "I don't know what got into you, man. You had to know that was a lost cause. Why'd you get involved?"

Logan shrugged. "What can I say? I got a soft spot for underdogs. Speaking of which, how's life treating you?"

"Can't complain," Nando said. "I get around, I get over, I get by. It's a living." Smiling at Wai Ying, he added, "Of course, my coworkers aren't quite so beautiful as yours."

"You're too kind," she said sweetly, then turned her tone sour. "Comb your hair."

The handsome young Latino's flirtatious grin faltered. Logan cleared his throat and regained his friend's attention.

"I need you to make some inquiries for me," Logan said. "See who might be able to scare up a few hard-to-find items."

Nando subtly checked the room for eavesdroppers. Eyeing Logan with caution, he prompted him: "Such as…?"

Logan reached into his jeans pocket and took out a folded slip of paper. He pushed it across the table to Nando, who lifted it like the hole card in a game of seven-card stud. His expression was perfectly neutral as he read it and pushed it back to Logan. "Hardcore," he said. "You here to buy?"

"No," Logan said. "I want to know who already has."

"Not sure I can get you that," Nando said. "Best I can do is tell you who might've been in a position to sell."

"That'll do."

Nando nodded. "Okay. I'll need a few hours."

"Fine," Logan said, then gestured with his thumb over his shoulder at Wai Ying. "America's next top model here has to go pick up a new wardrobe, and I could use a nap."

"Do you have a place to stay yet?" Nando asked. "If you don't, you can crash at my place. It's not much, but I have a spare room and a clean couch." He glanced back and forth between them, trying to determine if he'd just committed a *faux pas*. "I mean, assuming the two of you aren't... *y'know*..."

"No," Wai Ying said, maybe a little too emphatically. "We're definitely *not*—"

"The couch'll be fine for me," Logan cut in.

"All right, then," Nando said. "*Meu repouso é seu repouso*."

7

LOGAN'S sensitive hearing made the incessant hum of the high-voltage power lines above Nando's house difficult to block out. After an hour tossing and turning on the couch, he'd learned to think of it as white noise, but there was no such easy remedy to help mask the chain-saw growl of Nando's snoring. From two rooms away, and through two closed doors, it had shaken the walls like a force of nature. If not for the fact that Logan needed a favor from Nando, he might have strangled him in his sleep.

Wai Ying had returned to the house around noon and promptly begun complaining about how far Nando lived from the center of town, before segueing into her criticisms of his neighborhood, a low-income housing development off Brazil Highway 277. Logan, without bothering to open his eyes—since that would only have encouraged her to continue talking—had extended one set of claws, which pierced the floor. To his relief, she had taken his meaning clearly and retired to bed.

Now it was dark out, and he was rising to face the night. Nando was long since up and out of the house; Logan had heard him leave around three or four in the afternoon. Until the fixer returned, Logan and Wai Ying would have to wait for him in his slovenly sanctum.

Logan went looking for something to eat. It proved more difficult than he had expected. The kitchen was a shrine to dirty dishes, which were stacked in an unstable pyramid, filling and obstructing the sink. Logan considered throwing them away so he could make coffee, but he couldn't be certain Nando owned a coffeepot. He opened the fridge and grabbed a beer instead.

He walked back into the living room as Wai Ying emerged from the spare room, dressed in simple, dark casual clothes. She carefully plucked a sweatshirt off a chair and sat down. "I love what he's done with the place," she said.

"It's easy to do," Logan said. "Just drop all your stuff out of a helicopter. It'll look like this."

She chuckled slightly. He liked the sound of her laugh.

"So what's the story with you and Nando?" she asked. "It's hard to believe you two ever moved in the same circles."

He tilted his head and gave a wan smirk. "You'd be surprised some of the circles I move in," he said. "As for Nando and me, we met in Rio about twelve years ago during Carnaval. I staggered into a bar looking for a fresh bottle of beer, and I found him getting his ass kicked by four guys built like gorillas. Turns out the lead gorilla had a wife who Nando'd had the pleasure of knowing biblically, and the other three apes were the guy's brothers. Since I hadn't been in a fight for the last few hours, I stepped in and settled their hash. Then Nando and I went bar crawling the rest of the night, and we've been buds ever since."

"Touching story," Wai Ying said. "Toss in a trip to a brothel and you can sell the movie rights to Cinemax."

"Too late," Logan said. "Fox already optioned it."

From down the hall came the sound of the front door opening, then footsteps, and the closing of the door. Nando walked into the living room and waved at his guests. "Good, you're both up," he said. "I think I've got the lead you're looking for. Ready to go?"

"We could use something to eat first," Logan said.

Motioning for them to follow, Nando replied, "I figured you'd be hungry. There's burritos in the Jeep. Let's go." Nando was two steps down the hall before he realized that neither Logan nor Wai Ying was following him. He turned back, eyes wide with impatience. "Come on," he insisted.

"All right," Logan said, forcing himself off the sofa. "But these better be damned good burritos."

<hr>

AN hour's drive and two damned good burritos later, the trio arrived at a darkened intersection just a few short blocks from the Ponte da Amizade—a.k.a. the Bridge of Friendship, the principal crossing point for smugglers moving between Brazil and Paraguay.

The Jeep rolled to a quiet stop in the darkness beneath the drooping branches of a tree on the corner. Diagonally across the street was a dilapidated warehouse surrounded by a parking lot of fissured, uneven pavement. Logan stubbed out his cigar on the outside of the passenger door as Nando turned off the headlights and the ignition. Pointing at the warehouse, Nando said, "That's the base of operations for a guy the locals call Cavalo. He's the only smuggler in town with enough juice to get the kind of stuff you had on your list."

Logan studied the exterior of the warehouse, looking for fire escapes, ladders to the roof, skylights, or other potential covert points of entry, as well as for vantage points from which lookouts or snipers might be guarding the building. "How do I get in to see him?"

"I could call him," Nando joked. "Ask for an appointment."

"Do it," Logan said.

"I don't think that's a good idea," Nando said, running his fingers anxiously through his hair. "I mean, he's not gonna want to answer the kind of questions I think you'll be asking, and trying to push him around on his own turf... let's just say I don't think he'll go for it."

"It's not up to him," Logan said, still surveying the warehouse. There seemed to be a rear entrance, but it was likely to be defended by alarms, surveillance cameras, and maybe even booby traps. That left the front door.

Nando sounded worried. "Look, man, I know you're a badass and all, but he's got a lotta guys on his payroll. Pros—not jagoffs like those guys you whupped at the airport. Cavalo's the kind of guy you absolutely *do not* cross. *Compreenda?*"

"I know what I'm doing," Logan said. "Make the call."

With obvious reluctance, Nando fished his cell phone from his jacket pocket. He covered its keypad with his cupped hand while he dialed with the other.

While Nando carried on his whispered phone conversation, Logan looked back at Wai Ying, who was barely able to conceal her annoyance with the entire situation. When she met Logan's stare, he asked, "Problem?"

"You shouldn't go in there alone," she said.

"It's safer this way," Logan said. "Trust me."

"Don't be a fool," she said. "I can help you."

"No offense, doll, but I don't think you can scare these guys with your stunning fashion sense and your no-limit charge card. Just leave this to me."

"God, you're an idiot," she said, then sat back and looked away, ending the discussion.

Nando folded his phone closed and looked at Logan. "Cavalo's agreed to meet you," he said. "Didn't even ask why."

Logan nodded. "When?"

"Now," Nando said. "I think it might be a trap."

"Of course it's a trap," Logan said. He climbed out of the Jeep and started walking toward the warehouse.

"What're you gonna do, man? Walk in the front door? You'll be surrounded before you get three steps inside."

"That's what I'm counting on," Logan said with a grin. "If I'm not back in an hour... I don't know, blow the place up or something."

o——————o

THE warehouse doors slid apart as Logan approached them. They were tall enough to permit entry by a large cargo trailer and were pulled open by what sounded like a simple chain motor. Inside the warehouse, areas of shadow dominated the few pools of dim, yellow incandescent light. Four large and street-toughened men greeted Logan at the doorway. Each man carried a Heckler and Koch MP5K submachine gun and wore Kevlar body armor.

The one in charge, an ugly brute with a face that looked to Logan as if it had been lit on fire and put out with sandpaper, held up his hand, signaling Logan to halt. "Raise your hands and turn around," he commanded in Portuguese. Logan did as he was told. Sandpaper-face said, "Search him."

One of the other men patted Logan down, then reported, "He's clean. No weapons."

"Turn around," Sandpaper-face said. "Two steps forward."

Logan did an about-face and walked inside the warehouse. Sandpaper-face and one of his buddies moved aside to Logan's left. The other two who had met him stepped to the right.

Dead ahead of him, two more men, armed with submachine guns, stood in the middle of the rectangular building's open middle area. Behind them, lurking between a forklift and three barrels marked with red rings at the top and bottom, was another thug, carrying an Uzi machine pistol. Another gunman stood on top of a small mountain of wooden packing crates.

The view to Logan's left was blocked by a parked forklift, a row of four huge beer vats, and a one-row stack of fifty-five-gallon drum containers. On his right, at floor level, three more shooters crouched behind large wooden boxes. Above them, on top of another mound of wooden boxes, were two more guys with guns.

In the rear right corner, an electrified-fence cage surrounded the stairs to the balcony, which ringed the left, right, and rear walls of the warehouse's interior. Nine more men with MP5Ks looked down from there—three on the left, five on the right, and one at the back, next to the only person in the place, other than Logan, who wasn't sporting a weapon.

"You must be Senhor Logan," said the man with no gun.

Before Logan could reply, Cavalo walked back into his office, and a flurry of bullets slammed into Logan's chest.

Nine-millimeter rounds ripped into his body, ricocheted off his adamantium-coated skeleton, tore though his internal organs. The angry stutter of automatic gunfire at point-blank range was deafening, but it couldn't drown out his howls of pain.

Just as quickly as the barrage had begun, it ceased. Blood sheeted down Logan's torso, arms, and legs. His legs buckled. He dropped to his knees and doubled over. The four guards closest to him pressed in, weapons still aimed and ready. As he stared at the pool of his own blood that surrounded him, his second wave of agony began. His mutant healing factor began mending him, knitting together shredded muscles, closing severed arteries, rebuilding liquefied organs—all of it happening sub rosa, beneath his blood-soaked, bullet-torn clothing.

Then his rage kicked in. And his claws came out.

He sliced through the knees of the two men closest to him. They fell forward, blood fountaining from their severed limbs. Logan finished each man with an upward thrust into the heart, then retracted his claws and grabbed a submachine gun.

He head-shot Sandpaper-face and the other advance man.

The other gunmen to his left resumed shooting at him.

Dodging left toward the nearby forklift, he fired at the two men directly ahead of him, in the middle of the warehouse.

As they fell, he strafed his shots left, across the red-ringed barrels behind them. As Logan had hoped, the barrels exploded, sending orange flames and metal debris in all directions—and eliminating the shooter behind the far forklift and the one on top of the crates behind him.

Firearms weren't Logan's preferred weapon, but he'd fought in enough wars to know when and how to use them.

Gunshots *zing*ed off the forklift chassis as he ducked behind it. Despite the acrid bite of gunpowder that filled the air, he caught the cologne-heavy scent of someone else ahead of him, concealed behind a ten-foot-tall stack of bulky metal containers. At a full run he shoulder-checked the stack, which collapsed backward onto the man who'd been using it for cover. A short buzz of gunfire—probably a reflexive squeeze of the trigger, Logan guessed—was muffled by the falling cargo.

Logan saw no one else at floor level on the left side of the building. The beer vats and pyramid of oil drums would give him decent cover, but not for long. He heard the men shouting conflicting orders at one another. As soon as they got organized, this was going to get a lot harder. He had to move before the gunmen came at him from both sides.

He extended one set of claws and slashed through the first support beam holding up the left-side balcony. Then he sprinted the length of the building, staying low and in the shadows, cutting through all the other support beams, one after another. By the time he reached the back of the building, the creaking of wood under stress turned into a groan, and then into a roar as the left-side balcony collapsed and fell flat against the wall, dropping the three men from up above to the concrete floor.

While the three fallen men were still sorting out what had happened, Logan used his claws to cut the steel bands holding the oil-drum pyramid together, then gave the stack a swift kick. Black barrels rolled like wheels and pummeled the three hired thugs. A quick burst from Logan's weapon punctured the first barrel, which erupted in a fiery blast, then belched out a dense wall of greasy black smoke.

A burst of gunfire raked Logan's back from above. He ducked under the rear balcony and cursed himself for getting careless and forgetting about the man at the back of the warehouse.

Gritting his teeth against the searing pain of his healing factor kicking into overdrive, he literally stumbled over an open box of fragmentation grenades. He reached down, picked one up, clutched the safety lever, and removed the pull pin. Leaning half a step out from under the balcony, he lobbed the grenade up and over in a shallow arc, then dodged to his left as he heard it *thunk* onto the balcony above.

Two seconds later, an explosion turned the left third of the rear balcony into smoldering toothpicks.

Wooden debris rained down around Logan, and the gunman who had just shot him landed hard on the floor, dazed but still clutching his assault rifle.

Logan's first slash cut the weapon in half.

His second strike gutted his would-be assassin.

Multiple footfalls thumped across the balcony on the right side of the building and snapped across the concrete floor, on the other side of the stacked boxes that he had set on fire when he'd detonated the barrels twenty seconds earlier.

Screw this, Logan decided. He kneeled next to the box of grenades. One by one, he began pulling pins and hurling them. The first few he tossed over the burning boxes, to slow down the gunmen trying to flank him. The next four he hurled long, across the length of the right-side balcony, which quickly was torn apart, killing two of its five shooters and bringing the other three down to his level.

He was out of grenades. By his count, and judging from the voices and footsteps that he heard, there were still seven men taking concealed positions and making flanking maneuvers. A disturbing thought nagged at him: *There's got to be another box of grenades in here… and they know exactly where it is.*

Not willing to risk one of these guys scoring a lucky shot that would enable them to peg him with a grenade, Logan decided it was time to rearrange the battlefield to his advantage.

With a dozen short, pinpoint bursts, he destroyed every lightbulb in the warehouse. Shattered glass and fading sparks rained down to the floor. The only light came from isolated, crackling patches of burning crude oil and the smoldering debris that now littered the floor. It had exactly the desired effect: every one of his opponents came to a halt.

He put down his now-empty submachine gun. Moving with speed and feral grace, he skulked around the box mountain and ambushed one of the gunmen, covering the man's mouth with one hand while impaling him on the claws of the other.

Six little Indians, Logan counted.

He stepped over the body of a man he'd killed with one of his grenades and reached the second stack of boxes. Scaling it was easy; they had been stacked in a step pattern, probably to make it easier to recover goods from the upper sections.

Crawling to its rear edge, he found two more gunmen, one at each corner, their backs to each other. Lowering himself over the edge, he touched down silently. Snuck up on the one facing the rear of the building. Grabbed him in a choke hold and broke his neck. The snap was loud and wet. Logan spun around with the dead man in his grip, using him as a shield. His compatriot at the other end of the stack spun and fired, riddling his ally's corpse with bullets. Logan drew the dead man's sidearm and snapped off a shot, hitting the other man in the throat.

Four little Indians.

Logan dropped the dead man and tucked the pistol in his waistband. Then he heard the patter of running footsteps, moving away from him. Climbing back atop the stack of boxes, he spied the last four henchmen scrambling out the front door of the warehouse and sprinting for their lives into the night.

Guess they aren't as stupid as they look.

He jumped down to the floor and walked back to the forklift near the front entrance. It powered up with a rumble and a foul belch of diesel smoke. Logan stepped on its accelerator and steered it through the maze of wreckage he'd left in his wake, toward the electrified fence that surrounded the stairs to the upper level, where Cavalo's office was located. He pushed the forklift to its maximum speed, waited until it was a couple of meters from the fence, then jumped out. The lifter plowed through the fence in a shower of sparks and crashed into the rear wall.

Walking up the stairs, Logan considered the possibility that Cavalo might have already fled his office through the back door. *If he's still there, he could be waiting for me with anything,* Logan knew. *A Gatling minigun; a flamethrower; hell, a rocket launcher, for all I know.*

Logan reached the top of the stairs and stepped into the doorway of Cavalo's office. The black marketeer sat at his desk, facing the door.

In front of him was something Logan definitely had not expected: a bottle of twenty-one-year-old Balvenie single-malt scotch, with two shot glasses.

"Come in, Senhor Logan," Cavalo said. "You've done me a great service. Now let's talk about what I can do for you."

"Mighty civilized of you," Logan said. He walked slowly toward the chair in front of Cavalo's desk. "But if we're such good buds all of a sudden, what was with all the fireworks?"

"A calculated risk," Cavalo said. "My apologies, but it was necessary. I had to let them provoke you so that I could be reasonably sure you'd kill them."

"You *wanted* me to kill them?"

"Oh, absolutely," Cavalo said. "Half of them had already made deals with my competitors, and the other half were trying to. It was only a matter of time before they turned on me." He picked up the bottle and poured two shots of scotch into the glasses. "Your arrival happened to come at a fortuitous moment, so I took advantage of it. I hope you're not too offended."

"That'll depend on whether I get what I came for, bub."

"And that would be?" Cavalo offered one of the shot glasses to Logan, who picked it up and knocked it back in one swallow.

The scotch was smooth and complex, faintly sweet with a hint of port. Logan set the empty glass back on the desk, then retrieved his list of high-tech parts from his pocket.

He handed the list to Cavalo. "Did you recently acquire any of the items on this list for one of your clients?"

Cavalo studied the list for a moment, then said simply, "Yes. All of them."

"Who was the client?"

"No idea," Cavalo replied. "I don't meet most of my clients face-to-face. Most of the time I deal with cutouts, middlemen. The only thing I know about the client is the number of their Cayman Islands bank account, from which they transferred their payment to my Luxembourg account."

"That'll do," Logan said. "Give me their account number, and we'll call this deal done."

Cavalo nodded and pulled a small handheld communications device from his jacket's inside pocket. He tapped a few buttons, then jotted down the bank name and account number on a piece of scrap paper, which he handed to Logan.

"Thanks," Logan said. He got up from his chair to leave, then paused. "Good luck hiring a new goon squad."

"I don't think I'll need them where I'm going," Cavalo said, reclining in his chair. "Thanks to you, I can finally retire… *Adeus*, Senhor Logan."

"ALL I'm saying," Gregor complained, "is that it wouldn't have cost that much more to let us fly business class."

"You have to let this go," Oskar said, then he returned to the task at hand. The twin brothers stood with their backs to an alley wall. Their motorcycles were parked behind them. Oskar leaned around the corner and watched the warehouse through a pair of binoculars.

"It's just so damned petty," Gregor said. "It's not like they're hurting for cash, so why go cheap on us?"

"Security, remember?" Oskar lowered the binoculars and shot an evil look back at Gregor. "We stood out like crazy. Besides, you got a lot of nerve calling them petty when you're the one bitching because you had to pay for your own drinks."

"Easy for you to say, you had a direct flight. I had four connections, and they lost my fucking luggage."

"Shh," Oskar hissed as he watched Logan through the binoculars, leaving the warehouse. "He just came out the front." Logan got into the Jeep with his two associates. "He's back in the Jeep." Moments later, it pulled away from the curb, made a U-turn, and sped away. "And they're out of here."

"Shouldn't we follow them?" Gregor asked.

"No," Oskar said as he broke cover and walked toward the warehouse's rear entrance. "We know where to find them. Let's go check on Cavalo." Gregor followed him through a jagged gap in the chain-link fence that ran the length of the warehouse's parking lot. As they neared the stairs, Oskar held up a closed fist.

Gregor halted and waited while Oskar checked ahead of them for traps. He reached out with one hand and closed his eyes. Patterns and currents of energy flow tingled his mutant senses. Different colors and textures of energies began to distinguish themselves as his senses focused. The glassy perfection of infrared sensor beams; the violet waves of an active motion sensor; the hot-and-cold nodes of an open circuit waiting to be closed and either sound an alarm or set off a trap.

He looked back at Gregor. "We're going in the front."

They circled the building and strolled inside. The place looked as if it had been hit by a bomb. They knew Wolverine only by his reputation, but he seemed to be everything that they had heard, and no doubt more. Bodies and wreckage, fire and smoke; the inside of the warehouse was a killing field.

At the top of the stairs, they found the door to Cavalo's office wide open. His back was to them. A .44-caliber Desert Eagle semiautomatic pistol was holstered under his left arm. He was hunched over an open safe and busily stuffing shrink-wrapped bricks of cash into a black duffel.

On a table just inside the door stood a simple lamp. Oskar held it in place and yanked its power cord free of its base. The snap turned Cavalo about-face; he reached for his pistol, then froze as he recognized the twins.

Oskar twisted the ragged end of the exposed electrical wire around his index finger. Sweet power flooded through his body. "He's all yours," he said to Gregor, whose grin made it clear he, too, was savoring the sudden influx of fresh energy.

"We're very disappointed in you," Gregor said to Cavalo. "You went mano a mano with Logan…You had the chance to do the honorable thing, and you blew it."

Cavalo put down the duffel and stood tall. "Honorable?" His mien was defiant and his tenor scornful as he faced his executioners. "You know nothing of honor," he said.

"I know that we trusted you to respect our employer's privacy," Gregor said. "And I know that Logan's one of the least forgiving people in the world. So if he was here and let you live, it's because he got what he came for." Gregor stepped forward and raised his open palm toward Cavalo. "Because you told him what he wanted to know."

"*Foda-se,*" Cavalo cursed. "*Filho da puta.*"

A continuous ray of white-hot energy leaped from Gregor's hand and engulfed Cavalo in a crackling shroud. The gangster's screams were momentary, cut short as his body disintegrated. Gregor ceased fire. A ghost of atomized gray ash dissipated in a slow wafting breeze. Gregor folded his hand into a finger gun, lifted it to his face, and comically puffed across his index finger, like a child playing at being a gunslinger.

"Nice shot," Oskar said. "Let's get out of here."

"Sure thing," Gregor said, then he stepped forward and picked up Cavalo's duffel full of money. He zipped it shut. "This time we fly first class."

"Deal," Oskar said. "Once we frag Logan, we'll have earned it." He led Gregor out of the office, back onto the balcony outside. Looking down at the devastation that Logan had wrought, Oskar entertained a moment of caution. "Call me crazy," he said, "but I think we should call for backup."

○————————○

"DINNER is served," Nando called from the kitchen.

Logan pulled on a gray T-shirt and let it hang untucked above the waist of the second—and last—pair of blue jeans he had brought along for his visit to Japan. It occurred to him that he might want to add a few more pieces to his wardrobe soon if he was going to keep getting into fights in his street clothes.

He stepped out of the bedroom into the living room. Wai Ying sat on the couch with her satellite phone cradled against her ear. He gestured toward the kitchen, trying to indicate that she should end her call and join him and Nando, but she adamantly refused to pay attention to him.

"Read it back to me," she said, then nodded as she listened and compared what she was hearing to what was written on the slip of paper Logan had received from Cavalo. "Yes," she said. "That's the one. Find out who owns that bank account." She listened again, this time growing annoyed. "I know it's illegal, do it anyway. We've got hackers on the payroll for a reason, use them. I need that—hang on, I have another call."

Logan waved again. "Dinner's rea—"

She pressed a button on her phone. "Hello? Yes, I want the Citation Thunderstar fueled and ready to fly ASAP... I don't care, bill us... Just have the plane ready. Good-bye." Another tap on the phone. "I need that name, Hiro, and an address to go with it. Get it done. *Sayonara.*" She hung up with a petulant stab of her fingertip on the phone's keypad and threw a flustered glare at Logan. "What?"

"Dinner," he said.

"Fine," she said, then pushed herself up from the sofa.

They joined Nando in the kitchen and sat down. In the center of the table was a platter of piping-hot pancakes. A bright yellow stick of real butter and a jar of Canadian maple syrup stood next to it.

"They smell great," Logan said.

"Dig in," Nando said proudly.

Wai Ying surveyed the repast with a bemused grimace. "Pancakes? For dinner?"

"They're my specialty," Nando said.

"They're also the only thing he knows how to make from scratch," Logan said, spearing a short stack of four flapjacks with his fork and dropping them onto his plate. He cut off a slab of butter and spread it liberally across the pancakes, then doused them thoroughly with syrup. Nando and Wai Ying helped themselves and went through the same motions. Logan waited until they had buttered and slathered their own pancakes before taking a bite of his.

From the moment they hit his tongue, he knew something was seriously wrong with the pancakes. He noticed only then that they were much too thin. They had a rubbery resistance when he cut through them with his fork. It was like chewing on a Frisbee made of paste. Across the table, Wai Ying and Nando were experiencing much the same reaction.

"Not to be rude," Logan said, "but these pancakes suck."

Nando nodded his agreement. "Um… yeah."

Wai Ying quietly disposed of her half-masticated mouthful in her napkin. "Excuse me," she said.

Logan pushed his plate away. "What the hell happened, Nando? You used to have these things down to a science."

"I don't know, I can't explain it," he said. He got up from the table and walked over to the counter. Picking up the box of bake mix, he looked flummoxed. "I followed all the directions. Used all the right ingredients." He carried the box over to the table and put it down as he slumped back into his seat. "It just doesn't make sense."

"Maybe your skillet wasn't hot enough," Wai Ying said. "Or maybe the milk was sour."

"It's not sour," Logan said. "I can smell it from here. It's fine." He picked up the box and sniffed its powdery contents. Then he read the text on the box. "I think I've found your problem," he said, handing the box to Nando. "Have a look at the cookbook offer on the side panel."

Nando read the side panel and shook his head. "So? It's a cookbook offer. What about it?"

"Look at the entry deadline," Logan said. "It's *fifteen years ago*." He watched Nando wince as understanding dawned. "Nando, how long has that box of bake mix been sitting in your cupboard?"

With a sheepish look and an apologetic shrug, Nando replied, "I don't get many visitors, *amigo*."

"At least none who stay for breakfast," Wai Ying quipped.

The shot to Nando's pride was so brutal that Logan felt it. He gently chided Wai Ying, "Was that really necessary?" As she opened her mouth to respond, they all heard a muffled explosion from outside. "Get down!" Logan shouted as he hit the deck.

And the house exploded.

○————————————○

GREGOR'S first shot severed the electrical transmission line that ran above and behind the row of slum houses.

As soon as the HVDC—high-voltage, direct-current—line touched ground, Oskar removed his hand from the housing of his motorcycle's idling engine. He sprinted over to the fallen electrical wire and picked it up.

It was a 9.7-millimeter, seven-strand galvanized steel cable. Its six-hundred-kilovolt current, the most powerful of its kind in the world, originated from the Itaipu hydroelectric plant several miles west, at the head of the Río Paraná. Buzzing in the palm of his hand, it felt like a permission slip to play God. He let the raw power flood into and through him.

Gregor waited several dozen meters away, next to the SUV, in which he and Oskar had traveled with their Hand-provided backup. Oskar watched his brother's posture change, from an anxious hunching to a regal looming, as the wave of energy coursed into his hands.

Gregor pressed his wrists together and pointed his palms at one of the houses. A bright, golden corona formed instantly around him, a halo of excess electrical fury.

Then a flash of light and heat engulfed the house. The attack had moved at the speed of light, too fast to be observed. Fire and sparks erupted high into the hazy night, lighting up the sparsely built ghetto for half a kilometer around. Chunks of the building flew apart in a storm of splintered, burning wood. Then a geyser of fire swallowed the house into its foundation.

Despite the distance and the cacophony of destruction, Oskar heard his brother laughing, like a dark god triumphant.

The fires retreated into themselves as the initial blast faded away, and a tower of inky smoke climbed into the sky. Gregor pointed with a hand ringed in dancing lightning at the charred remains of the house. He looked back at the SUV and commanded its occupants, "Go find the bodies."

Instantly, the SUV's two rear doors and hatchback opened. Six ninjas tumbled out of the vehicle and dashed into the aftermath of Gregor's attack. Firelight glinted on the blades of their swords and, from Oskar's vantage point below the HVDC tower, turned them all into silhouettes.

Mopping up wasn't the exciting part of the job, but being a professional meant being thorough and remaining on-site until the mission was confirmed as done.

For several seconds the ninjas stabbed and poked their way through the jumbled wreckage. Then a pile of dusty debris heaved upward and obscured the smoldering pit in a dense, dusty cloud.

The sounds of metal clashing against metal and the screams of dying men made it clear to Oskar that this fight wasn't over—it was only just getting started.

o———————o

WAI Ying told herself repeatedly that the weight of the house was an illusion, that its burden was all in her mind.

It still felt like it weighed a ton.

She huddled beneath her dome-shaped force field with Logan and the surprisingly sanguine Nando. She'd followed Logan's directions to get down, but when the house erupted into fire and fury, her instincts had taken over. She'd crossed her arms, ducked her head, and projected an invisible shield around herself and the men.

Crimson flames and broken rock had swirled around them like an apocalyptic tornado. Splintered wood and household items, scouring blasts of superheated sand, clouds of shattered glass, billows of toxic smoke, all of it had buffeted her shield—and not one bit of it had passed through. Then the floor had collapsed and they had fallen into the basement, followed by the rest of the ranch-style house.

Now it was all piled on top of them; if her concentration slipped, this basement would become their shared grave. As the sounds of shifting earth and settling debris faded and stopped, Logan calmly took stock of the situation.

"Nice talent you got there," he whispered. "Wish I'd known about that before Cavalo's boys shot me full of holes."

Wai Ying muttered through a clenched jaw, "I offered."

"That's right," Nando said softly. "She did."

"We can play the blame game later," Logan said. "Wai Ying, you're doin' great. Can you expand that force field?"

She winced as she nodded. "I think so," she said, even though she wasn't certain it was true.

"How fast? Just a little at a time? Or all at once?"

Her sensei's words came back to her: *Effort is an illusion.*

"Any way you want it," she said, willing herself to believe that she could deliver on her promise. *There is no burden.*

"Then I'm gonna need one big push," Logan said. "Only when I tell you." He sounded worried about her. "You sure you're up to this?"

For a moment she almost felt as if the load had grown lighter. She met Logan's concerned stare. "Give the word."

He cast his eyes upward and listened, apparently detecting subtle vibrations that neither she nor Nando could pick up. All she could hear was her own labored breathing, but Logan appeared to be shifting his gaze from one spot to another, following targets that only he could sense. "Get ready," he whispered, then held up three fingers and started folding them down. *Three, two, one.* He pointed at her, and she took that as her cue.

All things are equal. In her mind's eye her force field swelled instantly, like a blowfish inflating itself against a predator. Above her, the layers of dirt and debris exploded away, ejecting a massive crater's worth of thick, sooty dust.

"Let it go!" Logan shouted as he sprang away, and Wai Ying terminated her force field. Her entire body sagged with relief—then she realized that the dark cloud of dust was raining back down on her and Nando. The pair covered their faces as the heaviest particles fell and coated them in ash and soil.

Then came the metallic ringing of blades clashing with adamantium claws and being broken in twain. Two heavy *thumps* followed right away, then two more. Several seconds later the dust started to settle, and Wai Ying saw the dim outlines of Logan and two ninjas, locked in combat. His opponents lunged at him from the front and rear simultaneously, blades swinging in lethal arcs—and yet, when the flurry of action was done, it was the ninjas who collapsed, in pieces, to the ground.

Logan prowled forward, out of the pit of what was once Nando's house. Wai Ying grabbed Nando's arm. "Come on." She yanked him up and pulled him along as she hurried after Logan. As they neared the top of the crater, she peeked over the edge and saw Logan advancing toward a fair-haired man who held fiery spheres of energy in both hands. She wanted to tell Logan to fall back, take cover—but then she reminded herself that he was a professional; he knew what he was doing.

Then he hollered a war cry and charged at the blond man.

Twin bolts of lightning leaped from the man's hands. They blasted Logan into the air and sent him flying clear over the crater. He left a grayish trail of smoke along his trajectory and crashed down hard on the rocky ground.

The blond man wound up to fire another blast.

Wai Ying lunged up and out of the pit as he fired. She projected a concave force field in front of him. His attack rebounded off it and blasted away part of the roof on a house across the street, then continued on the same angle and blasted apart a large insulator coil on one of the distant high-voltage electrical towers, dropping a cascade of sparks.

The blond man's fistful of power seemed to flicker for half a second, and he looked anxiously in a different direction. Tracking his line of sight, Wai Ying spotted another man—the fireballer's identical twin—standing beneath the closest electrical tower, hands clenched around a fallen power line.

That one must be the power plug, she realized, even as the one tossing the blasts recharged to maximum capacity and took aim squarely at her. *Have to do this right*. She didn't even want to think about what would happen if her force field didn't hold.

She didn't wait for the blast to come; when it did, her force field was already in place, curved and angled as precisely as she could in the fraction of a second she had been given to do it. Needles of heat stung her face as the attack rolled off her invisible shield. And at almost the exact same moment, the base of the nearby electrical tower disintegrated in a flash of fire and lightning.

The blast threw the second twin away from the tower, toward the houses. He tumbled through the air and landed hard, facedown in the dirt.

Wai Ying braced herself for another attack, but the blond blaster was already climbing into the seat of the idling SUV. Seconds later, it kicked up a dusty spew of gravel as it sped out to the fallen twin and stopped. The driver got out, picked up his brother, and put him in the back of the truck.

Then he climbed back behind the wheel, and the SUV disappeared down a backcountry trail into the night.

Nando climbed out of the crater and took a few halting steps into the street. He turned and looked back. Trudging around the perimeter of the hole was Logan, whose clothes were tattered and singed. Wisps of smoke rose from his charred but swiftly healing body.

He and Wai Ying joined Nando, flanking him as he stared into the pit. The trio stood together in silence for a moment.

"So," Nando muttered, half in shock, "*that* happened."

"Everybody all right?" Logan asked. Wai Ying and Nando both nodded. Logan grinned at Wai Ying. "I like your style." More thoughtfully, he added, "You saved my ass tonight. I owe you."

She gave a small, single nod of appreciation. "What about you? Are *you* all right?"

"I've been crispier," he said. "Nothing a few beers and a loofah won't fix." He slapped Nando's shoulder in what, between men, passed for a comforting gesture. "Sorry 'bout the house."

"What? This?" Nando dismissed the situation with a wag of his head and an ironic grimace. "Don't worry about it. I have a cleaning lady, it'll be fine."

"Come on, buddy," Logan said, as he and Wai Ying guided Nando away from the smoking rubble and toward the Jeep. "We'll give you a lift into town, and Miss Corporate Card'll get you a suite at the Bourbon Cataratas on our way to the airport."

"You're leaving?" Nando asked.

"No choice, *irmão*," Logan said, glancing at Wai Ying. "We have to follow the money."

8

GUNSHOTS cracked in the darkness, from the edge of the village.

Nishan awoke before the first echo faded. Then came the hoofbeats and distant, panicked screams. She sprang from the floor, between the beds in the clinic where her gravely ill children lay. Fear gave her strength; she lifted Nadif and Kanika, one in each arm, and carried them out of their shared tent of mosquito netting as quickly as she was able. They barely awoke as she hobbled toward the rear exit of the clinic. Around her, the other patients were either too ill or too disoriented to react, but they were not her concern.

She opened the door by colliding with it. It squawked on its rusty hinges, rattled as it rebounded off the outside of the building. Bearing the weight of both her children made her unsteady. She stumbled down the short stairs to the rocky ground. Ahead of her, past the few meters of clearing that ran behind the elevated structure, there was nothing but flatland.

Fleeing into the open would be pointless. She could barely survive alone out on the barren, difficult terrain. With her children in tow it would be impossible.

The hoofbeats and gunfire drew closer.

Men were shouting and women were screaming.

Nishan dropped to one knee and looked under the clinic building. It was a tight space, no more than half a meter off the ground, and it was thick with weeds, spiderwebs, and garbage. On all fours she backed herself into the crawl space, then dragged her children in after her—Nadif first, then Kanika.

She moved away from the edge. Too much chance of being seen there. She pushed with her heels while hanging on to her children's forearms. Rocks gouged into Nishan's back. Weeds tickled her limbs, and webs stuck to her face. A few inches at a time, she and her children moved toward the center of the clinic building, directly beneath the middle aisle. Faint lines of light broke through the gaps in the floorboards above. When she had reached the center of the building, she let go of her children and rolled onto her belly, the better to hide her eyes.

Then the hoofbeats and angry voices were in the street in front of the clinic. Automatic gunfire stuttered several times. Heavy stomping footfalls climbed the clinic steps and spread out inside the building. Nishan heard the men speaking above her, and she understood little of what they were saying—most of the Tanjawar militiamen were Arabic and spoke a different dialect from the one she and other black Zibarans used. It sounded as if they were stealing medical supplies, including patients' intravenous tubes and their mosquito netting.

There was some kind of argument. It ended with several long bursts of gunfire that sent bullets screaming through the floorboards on either side of the building, directly below where the patients' beds would have been. Where Nadif and Kanika and Nishan had been less than two minutes earlier.

Then the gunfire ceased, and Nishan wished that it hadn't. With the shouting and shooting past, there was nothing to drown out the anguished screams of women—and young girls, Nishan realized with horror as she recognized several of the voices. Pleas for mercy that became desperate begging for freedom, and then nothing but heartbreaking wails of terror and pain.

It was a sound Nishan had heard more times than she could count, and she was certain it was the same in any land and in every language: the sound of rape.

She pressed her hands to her face and buried her weeping in the ground, grateful only that her children were too deathly ill to cry out in fear and betray their hiding place. Desperate to block out the agonized screams of girls and women being brutalized, Nishan focused on anything else—the sweltering heat and suffocating humidity that drenched her with sweat; the creeping itch of bugs traveling across her skin; the taste of dust in her mouth and the sting of tears in her eyes.

But nothing could muffle that awful sound, and nothing could erase her own horrible memories.

It had been more than a year since her own rape, but every Tanjawar raid resurrected that night in her thoughts, as vivid and terrifying as it had been the first time. She still felt the men holding her wrists and ankles; the hot welts rising on her back, where the men had beaten her with leather belts because she had struggled; the pain and shame of being violated while the men laughed and drank whiskey and took turns. But none of that had been the worst part of their crime.

The Tanjawar thugs had made her children watch.

Now the thugs were out in the street, once more laughing like drunkards while they took turns with someone else's mother, someone else's sister, someone else's daughter. And there was nothing that Nishan could do except hide.

She lost track of time, and in the blink of an eye the light seemed to change. Dawn broke, and the Tanjawar, like roaches, scurried to vanish from sight. Hoofbeats and rallying cries resounded through the village, followed by more gunshots.

Then something made of glass shattered inside the clinic, followed by another, and another.

Nishan caught the odor of kerosene moments before a low rush of ignition rumbled over her head. The space beneath the clinic rapidly grew hotter, like an oven. Frozen by fear, Nishan knew that she had to get herself and her children away from the fire, but revealing herself while the Tanjawar were near was too dangerous. She couldn't risk it. To stay put was to die by fire, to run was to die by the sword.

Fear stretched the seconds as she listened to the hoofbeats rise to a gallop, then fade slowly into the distance. Taking hold of Nadif and Kanika once more by their forearms, she scrambled on her back as quickly as she could toward the edge of the building. Above her the floorboards were disintegrating, turning to red embers, stinging her face with dropping sparks, blinding her with hot ash.

A few meters away, a large chunk of the floor collapsed, hastening the implosion of the entire building. Nishan struggled not to lose speed as she neared the edge. Her face broke free first, into the musky but open air. Kicking her way free, she was half out when Kanika and Nadif's soot-smeared faces were clear of the building. She tugged them the last of the way out, then carried them again, one in each arm, as she limped from the blaze of the clinic, which at last crumbled into a massive funeral pyre. As soon as she had moved far enough away that its heat was no longer a threat, she let herself collapse, exhausted, to the ground next to her children.

Most of the village was on fire.

The streets were littered with the dead—all of them men and boys. Some were villagers; others were Médecins sans Frontières doctors or technicians. Among them was white-haired Dr. Maguire.

Crawling atop the carnage, in search of kith and kin, were scores of women and girls, all of them bloodied, bruised, and ravaged. One young girl, perhaps no more than ten years of age, lay alone in the middle of the street, her eyes wide and blank, her thin dark body trembling in a fetal curl, her arms wrapped around her blood-soaked legs. All around her, the other women and girls wore the same numb expression. No one cried any tears, because they would have been wasted—there was no one left who could offer comfort. This was a place without salvation.

Mountains of greasy smoke rose from the burning buildings, announcing the village's victimhood to every other town for miles around. Come tomorrow, Nishan knew, the smoke would rise from somewhere else, and people in every other place who could see it would pray that their homes and families would not be next. But sooner or later, everyone was next.

Nishan drifted up and down the main street, covering her nose and mouth with a damp cloth to block out the charnel odor of burnt flesh and the stench of dead bodies decomposing beneath the merciless African sun. She was desperate to find any of the MSF doctors alive, to find anyone who could help continue treating her children. Around every corner and in every shadow she searched for Dr. Charoenying, but there was no sign of the Thai physician. Just more bodies, more pits of smoking ashes, more examples of this place's endless privations and suffering.

Soon enough, the dead were accounted for, and names were attached to the bodies. One by one the corpses were added to the fire where the clinic building had stood, and it claimed each new cadaver like the devil's maw, ever hungry for souls. This place had become Hell on Earth, and the crackling flames rising from a pool of rendered human fat were the proof.

By midday three cars full of officials arrived from the capital, along with a truck carrying an unarmed platoon of UN peacekeepers. They all proved equally useless. When Nishan begged them for medicine for her children, they told her that they didn't have any, and that the Tanjawar had stolen the MSF's supplies and emptied the pharmacy.

All the doctors except for Dr. Charoenying had been murdered. Charoenying, witnesses said, had been taken by the Tanjawar, though whether it was because they'd demanded her medical services or because they had other plans for her, no one knew—and no one cared to speculate.

All that Nishan would ever know for certain about Dr. Charoenying was that she never saw her again.

9

DR. Nikolai Falco attached another bundle of data connections to the electron chromatograph scanners, then paused to verify his work against the detailed schematic on the floor at his feet. He had been provided with an extremely accurate set of plans for reconstructing the MECCA system, and all the necessary tools and equipment. Well, almost all of the equipment; several key components of the system remained unavailable to him, so he had worked around their absence as best as he had been able.

He had yet to see his captor's face. Miyoko, the woman who had driven him out of Osaka, had later drugged him unconscious. When he awoke several hours ago, feeling distinctly queasy, he was here. As for where "here" was, he couldn't really say.

There were no windows. The walls, floor, and ceiling were made of dull gray metal. He was being housed in a small anteroom next to the spacious lab whose systems he had been ordered to assemble. His "quarters" consisted of a cot, a bare electric lightbulb dangling on a frayed wire, and an industrial portable toilet wedged into the corner. A sliding panel near the floor was used to deliver food and take away refuse. A bottled-water dispenser stood beside his cot.

The doors were another curiosity. They were similar to the kind of airtight portals used in labs that worked with hazardous biotoxins, but these looked even more formidable, as if they had been armored to withstand a sizable explosion.

A constant thrumming pulsed under Falco's feet. He wondered if it was the rumble of generators, or perhaps the drone of a large-scale ventilation system. The air was warm but also noticeably well filtered in his quarters and in the new lab he was constructing. Based on the specs that he was working from, the lab would eventually have to be dust- and contaminant-free, just like the one he'd been taken from in Japan.

The work would normally have been slow and tedious for one person, but many of the larger components were being delivered preassembled, and entire bundles of cables had been set in place to provide power distribution, grounding, and data transfer even before he'd begun his assigned task. Now he was at the final step, which required the integration of several components that everyone working at Tanaka Biotechnology had been repeatedly assured were unique and impossible for a competitor to acquire. If what he had been told was true, this project for which he had been conscripted would be over right now.

But when the access panel on the wall beside the main portal lifted open, a wheeled pallet rolled through, bearing every single one of the items that were supposed to be impossible to get. The panel dropped closed once the items were safely inside. Falco walked over to the pallet and checked each of the high-tech items that rested on it. He knew right away that these hadn't been stolen from the TBC lab; all the original components had been marked with hidden serial numbers and booby-trapped so that their removal from MECCA would result in their immediate destruction. Yet here they were.

The main portal opened, unlocked from the other side. Backlit in the doorway was the silhouette of a tall, powerfully built man. He stood with his hands folded behind his back and spoke English with a Japanese accent. "Dr. Falco," he said. "I trust you have everything you'll need to finish?"

"Looks that way," the German scientist replied. His own accent was slight in comparison to that of his visitor. "You're quite resourceful."

"I command significant resources," said the silhouette. "It is not exactly the same thing." The visitor took a half-step forward. Light spilled across his trousers and the bottom edge of his matching suit jacket, both of which were silvery gray and smartly tailored. "Please answer my original question: Do you have everything you need to finish the lab?"

Looking around, Falco answered, "Yes."

"How long until it is operational? Be specific."

"I will need at least ten hours to complete assembly and run diagnostics from the mainframe," Falco said.

"Once your equipment is functioning, how long will it take you to refine your formula for mass production?"

"I cannot really say," Falco admitted. "I am close to isolating the drug's curative compounds, but its side effects—"

"The side effects do not concern me," the visitor said. "I want a formula for mass-producing the drug in its current form."

Falco hesitated to answer; he had no idea what this man intended to do with a mass-producible version of raw Panacea. *Whatever he's planning*, Falco reminded himself, *you're his prisoner, so you don't get any say. Just play along and don't provoke him.* Composing his face into a mask of calm, he replied, "I can finish the formula in approximately twelve hours."

"How much of that is labor, and how much is computer processing time?"

"About half and half," Falco said. "Once I finish my tests and put in the data, the mainframe will complete the formula."

"Excellent," the man in the suit said. "How portable will the drug be? Will it require strict temperature control? Limited illumination?"

"Refrigeration," Falco said. "It's a very durable compound, as long as it's kept cold."

"Understood," the visitor said. He turned as if to leave, then pivoted back. "Is there anything—within reason—that we can provide to make your stay more comfortable?"

Falco frowned. "Not unless you can teach your cook to make a proper bratwurst with sauerkraut, or get me a decent beer."

"I'll see what can be done," the silhouette said. "I will return tomorrow. Please have the formula ready for production."

This time the man walked away into the darkness, and the heavy portal swung closed. The pneumatic hiss of an airtight seal was followed by the dull, heavy thud of security dead bolts moving solidly into place.

Falco had not been harboring any illusions about his status, but there now could be no doubt that he was a prisoner. He surveyed the scope of the task ahead of him and realized that he felt severely fatigued. *Maybe I should rest before I continue*, he decided. The same dizzy, nauseated sensation that had assailed him when he'd first awoken returned as he plodded back toward his anteroom. He eased himself onto his cot and lay back slowly, until his weight was off his feet.

Many deep, calming breaths later, he felt more relaxed and more centered, but his low-grade vertigo continued. Then he noticed the lightbulb on its long, frayed wire. It was swaying. Only very slightly, and by small degrees, but it was swaying.

Falco realized where he was: *I'm on a ship.*

10

THE Russian customs officer eyed the passport that Logan had handed him, moved it aside to take another look at Logan himself, then went back to staring at the passport. "*Nyet*," the man grumbled, even though no one had said anything or asked any questions. He was exactly what Logan had long ago learned to expect of any career civil servant: literal-minded and stubborn.

Clearing customs at Pulkovo Airport in St. Petersburg, Russia, was proving a great deal more difficult than it had in Brazil. For one thing, the Russian customs officers actually had computers that worked, and showed that neither Logan nor Wai Ying had received a tourist invitation or a proper visa for entry. For another, Logan felt that the officers had been suspicious of him from the moment he'd stepped out of the Cessna jet—no doubt because he was still wearing the same charred and shredded clothing that he'd had on when he was getting barbecued by the twin mutants.

He'd meant to have some new clothes delivered to the plane during its second refueling stop, in Vienna, but all the garments that had been waiting at the hangar had proved to be the wrong size, and there had been no time to exchange them. So now he found himself looking as if he'd gone ten rounds with a flame-breathing wheat thresher. It wasn't exactly the best first impression he'd ever made, but it wasn't the worst, either.

Wai Ying paced back and forth along an imaginary straight line behind him, chattering rapid-fire Japanese into her cell phone. She was trying to find some way to leverage Setsuko Tanaka's connections to persuade the Japanese government to intervene and extricate herself and Logan from this mess before it escalated into an international incident.

The automatic sliding-glass doors behind them opened. Logan turned and nodded to his old friend and Cold War–era Soviet contact, Alexander

Zivojinovich—or Ziv, as Logan had always called him. It had been almost fifteen years since he'd last seen Ziv. He was pushing sixty now, he had put on weight, and his blond hair was thinning on top and starting to look more silvery gray.

Ziv's smile hadn't changed at all, though. He chortled as he surveyed Logan's shredded shirt and pants. Logan's only intact pieces of attire were his leather jacket, because he'd left it in the plane during the trip to Brazil, and a pair of snakeskin boots that had proved to be damned near indestructible, no matter what he'd done to them.

"Logan, *moi stariy droog*," Ziv said as he crushed him in a bear hug. "I see you're as sartorially challenged as ever."

"Good to see you, too, Ziv," Logan replied. He made gestures of introduction. "Wai Ying, this is an old buddy of mine: Alexander Zivojinovich. Ziv, for short."

"A pleasure," Ziv said with a courteous nod of his head. Wai Ying said nothing in reply; she just nodded at Ziv.

The customs officer shouted, "Who are you? These people—"

"These people are guests of the state," Ziv snapped. He marched to the counter, reached inside his trench coat, and produced a vinyl flip-fold, which opened to reveal a Russian government ID. "Issue their visas immediately and have them delivered to the Grand Hotel Europe on Nevsky Prospekt." Then Ziv plucked both their passports from the officer's hand, turned on his heel, and stalked swiftly back to Logan and Wai Ying.

Jaw agape with surprise, Wai Ying slowly folded her cell phone closed and tucked it back into her purse. She glared at Logan. Ziv walked past them and said, "My driver picked up your bags from the hangar. He's waiting for us outside." He passed through the sliding-glass doors and led them out of the office, then through the modern-looking terminal to the exit.

Logan followed his friend outside to the ground transport area. It was just after sunset. Instantly Logan's breath became visible in the frigid air, white plumes vanishing before him as he moved. Wai Ying walked beside Logan. They strolled toward a black limousine that idled several meters away. In an aggrieved whisper, she asked him, "You knew he was coming?"

"I called him from Dakar," he replied. "Figured we'd need the help."

"Any special reason you didn't tell me?"

He flashed a shit-eating grin in her direction. "'Cause I like the way you look when you get riled up."

Her eyes narrowed, her lips pursed with tension, and Logan was almost certain that he saw the tiniest hint of steam emerge from her ears. He blamed it on the weather.

They crouched and stepped into the back of the limousine with Ziv. As soon as the door closed, the car was in motion, racing away from the airport toward St. Petersburg city center. Logan reached inside his leather jacket and pulled out his last two Punch Rare Corojo cigars. He offered one to Ziv, who happily accepted it. While Logan snipped the end of his cigar with one of his claws, Ziv produced a sterling silver cigar cutter from his overcoat's side pocket and clipped his own. Logan snapped open his Zippo and lit his Corojo, then held the flame steady while Ziv puffed his cigar to life. Flipping the lighter closed, Logan settled back into his seat. He savored a few rich puffs while enjoying the discomfited look on Wai Ying's face as the off-white tendrils of smoke snaked around her.

"So, Ziv," Logan remarked, "I thought you retired from the KGB."

"The KGB doesn't exist anymore," Ziv said with a sly grin. "You know that."

"Fine, call it the FSB if it makes you happy," Logan said. "I still thought you were retired."

"Section chiefs don't retire," Ziv said. "They just become 'inactive.' Fortunately, it doesn't say that on my credentials." He closed his eyes and took another long pull on the Corojo. Exhaling, he said, "I know a place in town that can get you excellent Cubans, if you'd like."

"I would," Logan said.

Wai Ying cleared her throat a bit overdramatically. Logan felt his eyebrow arch with annoyance, by pure reflex.

Ziv's reaction was a far more dignified, urbane smirk. "To business, then," he said. "Your message was rather cryptic. What brings you here?"

"A few days ago, some classified materials were stolen from a private laboratory in Japan," Logan began.

"The specifics aren't important," Wai Ying interjected, apparently worried that Logan didn't know how to be discreet. "Let's just say that whoever took them could use them to commit genocide and engage in blackmail on a global scale."

"To do that," Logan said, continuing the briefing, "they needed some gear that they got on the black market in Brazil. We've linked the Cayman Islands account that paid for the gear to a Russian citizen, a man named Alexei Pritikin."

Ziv nodded. "Anbaric Petroleum," he said. "The oil mogul."

"That's our boy," Logan said.

"We already have reason to believe that the *yakuza* are involved, and possibly another organization, known as the Hand," Wai Ying said.

"*Svyataya Maria*," Ziv mumbled. Logan recalled that Ziv had helped thwart several attempts by operatives of the Hand to establish a foothold in the former Eastern Bloc nations. The Russians had expended so many resources combating groups like the Hand that they'd eventually bankrupted themselves, which had been a major factor in the Soviet Union's 1989 collapse.

Ziv's countenance was grim. "These materials they stole," he said to Logan, "are they as dangerous as Ms. Tse claims?"

"Worse," Logan said. "A lot worse."

"We need to investigate Pritikin, up close and personal," Wai Ying said. "I think he's using his company for more than just financing, but we'll have to data-mine his entire life before we can connect the dots."

"And we have to do it now," Logan added. "He and his pals have a head start, and they're moving fast; we have to be faster."

"First things first," Ziv said. He nodded to Logan.

"Before we can do anything, we need to get you some new clothes." Then, in a dark and deadly earnest tone, he said, "As for Mr. Pritikin... I know exactly how to proceed."

○━━━━━━○

DESPITE Wai Ying's insistence during the ride to the hotel that there was no time to delay in pursuing the Pritikin lead, Ziv had made it clear that the opportunity to act would have to wait until the following night. He didn't even want to divulge the details; Logan guessed that Ziv was probably concerned that Wai Ying would let her impatience get the best of her.

Logan had done his part by telling Wai Ying to trust Ziv's judgment; the man was a professional, and he'd brief them when he finished planning the op. It wasn't what Wai Ying had wanted to hear, but Logan had been relieved to have the night to recover his equilibrium; hopping back and forth through time zones had left him feeling dragged out. *Nearly getting blown up and then spending more than ten hours helping fly a jet nearly ten thousand miles will do that to a guy,* he'd reminded himself.

As usual, Wai Ying had spared no expense at the hotel. She'd booked herself into one of its terrace rooms and Logan into another. He had been too tired to appreciate its style when he'd first arrived; all his attention had been captured by the pleasantly strong water pressure in the stinging-hot shower and the fact that the bathroom's marble floor was electrically heated from below. After toweling himself dry, he'd crawled onto the king-sized bed, where he'd fallen asleep before he could finish untucking the corner of the duvet.

He awoke late in the morning to the glow of daylight, warm and diffused by the pastel orange draperies in front of the French doors to the terrace. Scratching a few wandering itches across his torso and ribs, he sat up and took in his surroundings. Most of the furniture appeared to be antique. Two slender padded armchairs faced the bed, which was flanked by two fragile-looking nightstands. A small end table sat between the armchairs; on top of the table was a crystal bowl filled with fruit. In the corner of the room was a small writing desk, above which hung a wide, gilded wall mirror. The overall décor of the room was evocative of the tsarist era.

Logan stepped over to the desk, picked up the phone receiver, and pressed the button for room service. The operator answered immediately. "*Gornichnaya,*" she said, and he figured that was Russian for "room service." He cobbled together what little Russian he remembered from his Cold War days working behind the Iron Curtain and made a halting attempt to order eggs Florentine, a rare steak, well-done potatoes, and a pot of black coffee. By the time he hung up, he wasn't sure what would be coming for breakfast; he just hoped that it would be hot and untainted by borscht.

Noticing in the mirror that he was naked, he grabbed one of the white terry-cloth bathrobes off the back of the bathroom door and tied it loosely shut at his waist. Then he picked up the phone again and this time dialed the concierge. He was greeted by another pleasant-sounding voice, male this time.

"Do you speak English?" Logan asked.

"Yes, sir," the concierge said. "What can we do for you?"

"I need a personal shopper to get me some new clothes."

"Very good," said the man on the phone. "Do you need anything in particular?"

"Nothing fancy," Logan said. "Just a basic wardrobe. T-shirts, underwear, shirts, some blue jeans—"

"American-style blue jeans are very expensive in Russia."

"Just charge it to my room." He decided that, as expenses went, this was one that Tanaka Biotechnology owed him right now. He gave the concierge his size information, then hung up the phone and flipped channels on the satellite television while waiting for his breakfast to arrive.

The meal that eventually was delivered (after an interminable, hour-long wait) consisted of a broccoli omelette, a bowl of potato soup, and a side of steak sauce. *Guess I'll have to work on my Russian*, Logan mused as he signed the room check. *At least these bozos got the coffee right.* He wheeled the rolling tray table out onto his terrace and wolfed down his meal while admiring the view of Arts Square, whose most notable structure was the Church of the Spilt Blood. *Sounds like my kind of church. If I went to church, that is.*

It was early afternoon when the personal shopper dropped off Logan's new clothes. He got dressed quickly, pulled on his boots and his jacket, and finally left his room to find Wai Ying. There was no answer at her door, and he didn't hear any activity from inside her room. *Probably out setting a world record for buying shoes*, he figured. Turning back toward his room, he toyed with the notion of stealing a nap and testing his Russian again; he was fairly certain he'd just remembered how to say "champagne," "caviar," and "Swedish massage."

Before he got more than three steps back to his room, however, the elevator doors opened down the hallway, and Wai Ying stepped out, followed closely by Ziv. She was carrying a pair of garment bags; he toted a polished-aluminum briefcase. Three more people, hefting large plastic toolboxes, exited the elevator behind them and appeared to be following them.

"Ah, good," Ziv exclaimed to Logan. "You're up. Come with us, there's a lot to do."

Logan eyed the approaching procession with mounting suspicion. "What's goin' on?"

"The plan," Wai Ying said. "Ziv and I worked out the details over breakfast."

"Hang on," Logan said. "There's a plan?" He watched Ziv with an accusing stare. "Ziv, you made the plan without me?"

Ziv shrugged. "Your own fault for sleeping all day and then stuffing your face out on your terrace." He tilted his head in Wai Ying's direction. "She was up at daybreak. Caught up to her running laps around Arts Square." With an extra touch of teasing sarcasm, he added, "If only you had her discipline, you might've made something of yourself by now."

Though Wai Ying wasn't looking in Logan's direction, he thought he noticed the slightest hint of a self-satisfied smirk on her face as she opened the door to her room. Ziv and his three-person entourage followed her in, and Logan entered last.

Wai Ying laid the garment bags flat on the bed. Taking a closer look, Logan noticed that both bags bore the logo of the Gostiniy Dvor department store, which was located directly across Nevsky Prospekt from the hotel.

Ziv sat down at the writing table and opened his briefcase. From it he removed a slender-profile laptop computer, which he opened and activated. Meanwhile, the anonymous trio had split up to different corners of the room and opened their bait-and-tackle-style toolboxes. One of them had a collection of sewing needles, threads, fabric swatches, cutting implements, and measuring tools. The other two were packing an impressive array of sprays, gels, dyes, combs, miniature hair dryers, and assorted hair-care and manicure products.

Logan didn't like where this was going at all.

"Somebody want to fill me in?" he asked.

"You're going undercover," Ziv said.

"Correction," Wai Ying interrupted. Looking at Logan, she continued, "*We're* going undercover."

"Undercover where?"

Ziv answered while typing rapidly at his computer. "The mansion of Alexei Pritikin, owner and president of Anbaric Petroleum." He swiveled the laptop around so that Logan could see the floor plan now displayed on its screen. "He's got a lakeside estate in Vaskelovo, about forty minutes from here."

Eyeing the tailor, hairdresser, and manicurist, Logan inquired, "And that has what to do with them?"

"They're here to make you presentable," Wai Ying said.

"For...?"

"Pritikin's hosting a fund-raising dinner tonight, filling his war chest so he can challenge Oleg Shumeyko for his seat in the Duma. The FSB bought tickets for the party, with guest names to be declared later. Two of them are now yours."

"Gee," Logan said, "I'm honored."

"You should be," Ziv said. "But we have a lot to do before tonight. I have to create new passports for you two and send your aliases on to the event planner for the guest list. But before we get to that, there's a much more serious issue to contend with."

Logan become keenly aware that everyone in the room was looking at him. "And that issue would be...?"

In as serious a tone as Logan had ever heard him use, Ziv replied simply, "Your hair."

○————————————○

SIX miserable, odor-filled hours later, Logan's wild coif continued to defy all attempts to tame it. The stylists had tried mousse to no effect. Hairspray had only made it stiffer and more difficult to work with. Straightening chemicals and relaxers had produced only short-term gains, because his mutant healing factor seemed programmed to rebel against even the most basic cosmetic alterations. Now they had moved on to a mixture of maximum-hold gels, which bought them enough obedience from his dark, feral mane to set it in place. Spying his reflection in the wall mirror, he had to admit he looked almost respectable.

By comparison, his manicure had gone off without a hitch. Logan had never known until this afternoon that he had "exquisite cuticles" or that a man's fingernails could be described with the term "scrumptious." He still had his doubts on the second point. For a moment, he'd considered extending his claws and seeing whether the manicure included a buff-and-polish, but Ziv—ostensibly having intuited Logan's intentions from his grin—had simply shaken his head no and left his warning at that.

There was a knock at the door. Ziv answered it, accepted a padded envelope from someone on the other side, then shut the door. He walked over to Logan, opened the envelope, and handed him a new Canadian passport. Logan flipped it open and grimaced at the photo, which he'd always hated. The name next to it read "James Howlett III." Nodding, he looked up at Ziv. "Nice work."

"Glad you like it," he said. "In case Pritikin checks up on you, we've set up a cover background for you, complete with dummy phones, business cards, a website, the works."

"I almost dread to ask," Logan said. "Who am I?"

"A high-end wine-and-spirits importer," Ziv said. "Specializing in rare European wines and fine liquors."

"You just want to see me squirm in there, don't ya?"

"Don't worry, you'll have all the help you need." He handed Logan a translucent plastic device that resembled a small kidney bean. "Put this in your ear. It's a subaural transceiver."

"Who's gonna be listening in?"

"I will," Ziv said. "While you and Ms. Tse are inside, I'll be running the op from a surveillance van a few kilometers away." He held up a maple-leaf-shaped lapel pin with what looked like a ruby set in its center. "Mini-camera. I'll see what you see. Try not to get it wet."

"Yes, Dad," Logan said, rolling his eyes. "What's our objective once we get in?"

"Break into Pritikin's private home office," Ziv said. He pointed to the floor plan of the mansion, which he had printed out on several sheets of letter-sized paper and taped together on the wall for Logan to study while the stylists fought with his hair. "It'll be on the top floor, in the north wing. The reception is being held in the south wing."

"That's a lot of open space in there," Logan observed. "How much do we know about Pritikin's internal security?"

"Not much," Ziv said. "He has armed guards inside and outside the house. And his office is probably wired."

"Count on it," Logan said. "After I'm in the office, what then?"

"Power up the computer," Ziv said. "It has a secure hard-line connection to Anbaric Petroleum's internal network." Ziv reached in his pants pocket and took out a tiny, flat piece of plastic that had a slender connection interface at one end. "This is a flash memory stick," he explained. "On Pritikin's computer, you'll find a port on the side of his keyboard. Once you've started the machine, attach this. It'll run a program that'll help me hack into his machine from the van. Once I'm in, I'll clone his drives and any encrypted files I can find on the network. When I'm done, you pull the flash stick, shut down the machine, and go back to the party."

"Sounds too easy," Logan said.

"For you, sure," Ziv said. "I'm doing all the hard work."

"Just keep tellin' yourself that, bub," Logan said. He hooked a thumb toward the lounge, where Wai Ying was changing her clothes. "If my job's so easy, why's she taggin' along?"

"She'll be posing as your wife. When you excuse yourself from the reception, she'll cover for you till you get back."

"My *wife*? That's rich. Who's gonna believe that?"

Another knock at the door pulled Ziv away. When he returned, the tailor followed him inside, holding two more garment bags and a shoebox from the posh department store across the street. "Your disguise," Ziv said, as the tailor laid the bags down on the bed and unzipped them. Logan followed Ziv's curling-finger summons and stepped over to the bed to examine the clothes.

It was a classic black-tie ensemble: a two-button Ralph Lauren black tuxedo jacket and pants, a white formal shirt with an off-white herringbone pattern and French cuffs, a charcoal-colored vest, and a black bow tie, of the variety that actually had to be knotted by hand. Secured in a small plastic bag were the accessories: gold cuff links and studs and an ivory-hued silk square for the jacket's breast pocket. Inside the shoebox were a fresh pair of black wool socks and a pair of Gucci shoes that had been polished to perfection.

"Sharp threads," Logan said.

"We started with the best and made some improvements," Ziv said. He reached under the jacket's collar and detached a black flap that had been secured with Velcro tabs. It was wide enough to cover the space between the two lapels of his suitcoat. "For those moments when you'd prefer to be incognito," Ziv said.

"Very thoughtful," Logan said. "Anything else? Magnets in the shoes? Lasers in the cuff links?"

"If we'd had a few more days to prepare, maybe. But no."

"Too bad."

Ziv handed Logan a platinum wedding band. "Put this on and go get dressed. The valet has your car ready downstairs."

Logan was heading toward the bathroom when the door to the suite's lounge opened and Wai Ying stepped into the bedroom. She had her hair up, revealing the soft-ruffled straps of her red scoop-neck Valentino dress, which had been matched perfectly to her crimson Manolo Blahnik spike heels. On her left hand she wore a sapphire-and-diamond engagement ring and a diamond-crusted wedding band. An Arctic white fox stole was draped over her shoulders, giving a decidedly Russian flair to her ensemble.

She scowled and snapped at Logan, "Aren't you dressed yet?"

Logan tossed a sullen look Ziv's way. "I take it back," he said. "She sounds *exactly* like a wife."

11

NO other car in the world that Logan had ever heard sounded quite so perfect as a 1985 Ferrari 308GTS Quattrovalvole.

The one he was driving tonight was red, as mint as the day it had rolled off the assembly line, and blessed with enhanced carburetor performance. Idling, it purred; in motion, it roared. He'd protested at first that it was too flashy for his cover story, but Ziv had merely waved away Logan's concerns. "It'll be fine," he'd said. "Trust me."

Bringing the Italian sports car to a stop in the cul-de-sac in front of Pritikin's mansion, Logan realized that Ziv had been correct: the car didn't stand out at all. He and Wai Ying were surrounded by other guests exiting rare and exotic vehicles of every kind. An emerald-green Lamborghini Countach was stopped directly in front of Logan's Ferrari. Behind him a Jaguar XJ220 went from a silver blur to a halt less than a foot from his rear bumper. A clean-cut valet drove past in a white Mercedes-Benz SLR, followed a moment later by another uniformed young man driving a gleaming black Aston Martin Vanquish. Pritikin's benefactors, it seemed, were both rich and inclined toward conspicuous displays of wealth.

Logan turned off the engine and left the keys in the ignition. He got out of the car, walked around the front to the passenger side, and opened the door for Wai Ying. She accepted his outstretched hand, and he helped her out of the car. A fair-haired young man in a valet's uniform caught Logan's eye as he and Wai Ying climbed the wide, white marble stairs to the mansion's main entrance. Logan nodded to the valet, who hurried into the Ferrari and accelerated away to a distant parking area.

The night was damp and cold, and the air smelled heavy to Logan; there was a snowstorm moving in. Ahead of and behind him and Wai

Ying, men in tuxedos and trench coats guided women in evening gowns and furs up the stairs. Most of the guests entered the party as couples, but a few small clusters of friends or business associates had formed where the crowd grew denser, near the mansion's broad, wide-open double doors.

A small flock of coat-check girls weaved through the arriving guests, handing out claim tickets while spiriting away countless fur coats, wraps, and stoles to a spacious wardrobe somewhere just off the main foyer. One of the women relieved Wai Ying of her fox stole and handed the claim ticket to Logan, who tucked it in his jacket's front pocket. He jutted out his elbow slightly toward Wai Ying, and she daintily slipped her own arm through it. Moving along with a small knot of other guests, they drifted upstairs into the palatial estate.

Marble and mahogany were the materials of choice. Arched doorways led to long hallways lined with rooms. Most of the passages were blocked by velvet ropes on brass stands. Man-sized white marble statues lined the main hallway. Logan didn't know if any of them were famous, or even if they were authentic. Most looked Asian, but a few were clearly of Central American origin. Behind them, the walls were decorated with broad tapestries and enormous oil paintings. Overhead, suspended at regular intervals from the high, vaulted ceiling, were cut-crystal chandeliers.

The rhythmic melody of a waltz resounded from the ballroom directly ahead. Several men and women stood in front of the doors, checking guests' invitations. Logan and Wai Ying stepped into a line of guests. When they reached the front of the line, he handed a man an envelope containing his and Wai Ying's invitation. The usher checked the intricately milled and embossed document by scanning it with a dim red laser beam from a small device in his hand. An indicator light on the back of the device turned green. "Welcome, Mr. Howlett," he said as he handed the invitation back to Logan.

"Thank you," Logan said, tucking the card back into his pocket. He led Wai Ying past the ushers, into the main ballroom. Couples twirled and turned in perfect form on the parquet dance floor. A legion of serving staff dodged through the room, dispensing wine and champagne and collecting empty glasses. Logan plucked two flutes of Dom Perignon from a passing server's tray and handed one to Wai Ying. They clinked their glasses and sipped slowly while walking a slow circuit of the room. He quickly lost count of the number of different perfumes and colognes his mutant senses picked up.

As Logan had expected, the music was provided by a few dozen live musicians. Behind the music, a low murmur of conversation and clinking glasses filled the room like white noise. When he focused, he was able to eavesdrop on any of several conversations near him. To his chagrin, they were all in Russian, so most of the nuances were lost to him. He caught enough, however, to realize who most of Pritikin's guests were.

"This room is full of Russian mobsters," he muttered, as much to Wai Ying as to Ziv. He knew that both of them heard him, because Wai Ying also had been given a transceiver, and they all shared the same continuous, digitally encrypted signal.

"Of course it is," Ziv said via the earpiece. "There isn't a business or a politician in Russia today that isn't in bed with the mob. Call it the price of capitalism."

A waitress offered them their choice from a selection of phyllo pastry shells stuffed with pesto and brie. Wai Ying took two of the appetizers and handed one to Logan, who popped it whole into his maw. Only after he'd swallowed it did he notice Wai Ying's icy stare and realize that a less enthusiastic response to the food might be in order.

Wai Ying studied the room and said, "No sign of Pritikin."

"He's the kind who likes to make an impression," Ziv said. "Look for him to enter the ballroom by walking down the east staircase, right behind you."

Logan turned and looked up the mountainous, curving stone staircase. He admired its intricately carved marble railings, banisters, and balusters. Heavy scarlet curtains blocked the view of the hall beyond the archway at the top. There was a slight flutter in the curtains, caused by some motion behind it. "I think he's about to make his big entrance," Logan observed.

"Move away from the staircase," Ziv said. "Try to blend in with the crowd."

"Screw that," Logan said. "I want to get a good look at the sonofabitch."

"Logan, don't be a fool. You're supposed to be undercover. Just lay low and stick to the plan."

"He's a player, Ziv," Logan said. "It's time to size him up. Now stop yakkin', you're distracting me."

Ziv's muttered Russian curses buzzed inside Logan's ear as the scarlet curtains parted. A trim, tall Russian man in his late forties emerged. Walking arm-in-arm with him was a striking Japanese woman in a modern kimono, one that Logan could see had been styled to afford her a greater freedom of movement. From an overhead speaker, a man's voice announced, first in Russian, then in English, "Ladies and gentlemen, please welcome your host, Alexei Pritikin, and Ms. Miyoko Takagi." The announcement was repeated in several more languages as the couple gracefully descended the staircase to thunderous applause. Pritikin waved graciously to his supporters and flashed a politician's calculating smile.

With every step that Miyoko took, her preternatural grace and poise made Logan more suspicious. Everything about her was precise and controlled; her economy of movement was superbly disciplined. It was rare to find such a quality of focus in even the most gifted martial-arts masters. Whoever she was, Miyoko was a factor that Logan knew not to underestimate.

She and Pritikin reached the bottom of the stairs and began working their way through the crowd. Pritikin did the talking. He shook hands and doled out promises and nicknames as he went. Miyoko remained silent, but Logan noted the way she eyed every person within several meters of Pritikin. She was trained for combat, for assassination.

"Okay, Logan," Ziv said, unable to hide his agitation. "You got your close-up look, now back off."

Ignoring the tinny voice in his ear, Logan sidestepped through a gap in the crowd and put himself directly in Pritikin's path. Wai Ying stayed with him, staring down a man who tried to block her from reaching the front of Pritikin's receiving line. Logan mustered his least frightening smile as Pritikin stepped forward and extended his hand. The smooth, practiced manner he had displayed with his other guests faltered as he came face-to-face with Logan, but only for a moment. He shook Logan's hand firmly as he stole a glance at the maple-leaf pin on Logan's lapel. "Thank you for coming," he said in flawless, uninflected English. "So glad you could make it."

Playing along, Logan maintained eye contact with Pritikin while nodding sideways in Wai Ying's direction. "I'm sure you remember my wife, Wai Ying."

"Of course," Pritikin said, lying with aplomb. "Wonderful to see you again."

Just as Logan had expected, Wai Ying took the wind out of Pritikin's sails. "We've never met, Mr. Pritikin," she said. "Nor has my husband made your acquaintance before today."

Another half-breath of hesitation. Then Pritikin heaved a sigh and smiled broadly. "Yes, you've caught me. I'm relieved, actually. I thought my memory had failed me." He reached out and shook Logan's hand again. "Alexei Pritikin."

"James Howlett the Third," Logan replied. Then he turned to Miyoko and scrutinized the details of her kimono. "Ms. Takagi," he continued. "It's an honor to meet someone who has such exquisite taste in kimonos."

Her expression was unreadable. "You admire it?"

"Very much," Logan said. "Correct me if I'm wrong, but I'd say it's hand-painted, in the traditional *yuzen* style—by master Kunihiko Moriguchi himself, if I'm not mistaken."

"You have a trained eye," she said, her tone neutral.

"Just an eye for beauty," Logan said, pulling Wai Ying gently to his side.

Miyoko whispered something in Pritikin's ear. His smile didn't falter as he listened, but his eyes darted quickly, his gaze falling on everything except Logan and Wai Ying. Then his face brightened and he looked at Logan. "It's rare to meet someone of such refined tastes," he said. "Miyoko and I would be honored if you'd both dine with us at our table this evening."

"We'd be delighted," Logan said, nodding his assent.

"Excellent," Pritikin said. "I have a few more guests to greet, Mr. Howlett, but we'll look forward to seeing you in the banquet room shortly."

"Absolutely," Logan said. Then Pritikin and Miyoko moved away, continuing to press the flesh with his campaign contributors and would-be allies and benefactors.

Once they were out of earshot, Wai Ying glared at Logan. "Are you out of your mind?"

Ziv immediately joined in over the transceiver: "What the hell are you doing, Logan?"

"I needed a closer look at her kimono to be sure," Logan said. "It's subtle; if you don't look closely, you'll miss it."

Wai Ying was beyond flustered now. "Miss *what?*"

"The repeated pattern in its design," Logan said, pulling a Cuban cigar from inside his jacket. "It's the same Fu symbol that's on the *shaken* we found in Osaka. She's a member of the Hand. Which means they're either using Pritikin, or they're in business with him." Using the silver clipper he'd borrowed from Ziv, he trimmed the end of his cigar while he let his report sink in with his partners. He lit the cigar with his Zippo.

"All right," Ziv said. "That's a good lead. But you nearly blew your cover getting it."

"Almost," Logan said, exhaling a puff of smoke. "Didn't."

"Regardless," Ziv said. "No more stunts, Logan. This is a recon, not a showdown."

Escorting Wai Ying toward the banquet room for dinner, Logan replied, "You do it your way, Ziv. I'll do it mine."

○———————○

"IDIOT, *eto ne moya zhena,"* boomed Russian oil minister Yassev Soltsin, the fat man sitting two seats to Logan's left. *"Eto sobaka!"*

Six of the eight people at Alexei Pritikin's table guffawed heartily—everyone, in other words, except for Logan and Wai Ying, neither of whom possessed a sufficient grasp of Russian to get the joke. Soltsin's wife, Mariska, sat beside Logan and tried unsuccessfully to mask her embarrassment; her husband had been cracking jokes ever since they all had been seated for dinner. On the opposite side of the circular table from Logan sat Pritikin. Miyoko sat to Pritikin's right, opposite Wai Ying. The other couple at the table, Logan had learned during the curt preprandial introductions, were Ukrainian-born media baron Darius Mikalunas and his Croatian wife, Angelika Digorizia.

Logan feigned interest in the small talk but kept his attention on Miyoko. The ravishing Hand assassin had whispered in Pritikin's ear repeatedly. Every time she'd done so, Pritikin had glanced at Logan and Wai Ying. Logan tried to discern what she was telling the oil mogul now, but he found it difficult to hear her over the jabbering that filled the room.

Wai Ying pointed at Logan's plate with her fork. "Have you tried the escargots?"

Half grimacing, half smiling, he said, "I'm waiting for dessert." They were up to the fourth course of dinner, and Logan couldn't name half the foods that were on the table. The soup was a thin broth clouded with miso and tangled with filament-thin green tendrils. As delicate and sculptural as the appetizer had been, Logan had deemed it fundamentally inedible. Now he was staring at an entree whose overabundance of butter made him fairly certain that the chef had been trained in France.

To the best of his ability to tell, the only part of his meal that had so far met with his satisfaction had been the draft Guinness, which had been poured from a keg imported directly from Dublin. It was like a tower of creamy black velvet in a glass. As a result, the four glasses of wine that had been poured so far for each guest—a different varietal with each course of the meal—sat untouched in front of him while he sipped his beer.

The tenor of the conversation among Pritikin and his guests was not what Logan expected. Instead of Pritikin playing the part of a supplicant looking for funding, Yassev and Mikalunas seemed to be courting his favor, heaping praise and making vague promises all through dinner. Wai Ying leaned over to Logan and whispered, "The way they talk, you'd think he'd already won the election."

Talking softly, Logan replied, "Knowing the way voting machines work these days, he probably already has."

Mikalunas was waxing ecstatic about the entree, then he detoured into a halting appreciation of the wine. "They're all quite remarkable, Alexei," he said. "Especially the red with the entree. Truly first-rate. What did you say the label was?"

Before Pritikin could answer, Miyoko cut him off and gestured in Logan's direction. "Perhaps you should ask Mr. Howlett," she said. "I'm made to understand that rare wines and liquors are his area of special expertise." She lifted her own glass of red wine in a toasting gesture toward Logan. "Mr. Howlett, would you honor us with your thoughts about the red?"

Silence fell over the table as everyone looked at Logan with varying degrees of interest and expectation. Wai Ying's demeanor betrayed nothing, but Logan could almost hear the increase in her heart rate.

Ziv sounded a bit flummoxed, too. "Hang on," he said over a rapid flurry of tapping and clicking noises. "I'm checking the feed from your lapel cam, maybe I can see the label on the bottle from when it was poured."

Wai Ying made an admirable attempt at running interference. "I'm certain my husband wouldn't want to bore you all with his—"

"It'd be my pleasure," Logan said, offering a polite smile to Miyoko and Pritikin. "Just let me cleanse my palate first." He took a swig of water, swished it liberally, then swallowed.

Pulling his glass of red wine to a patch of open space on the white linen tablecloth, he rested his fingertips on the base and jogged it gently in a tiny circle, creating a steady, high swirl inside the half-filled glass. "Lovely color," he remarked. "Almost purple… Remarkable body." He stopped swirling the wine, satisfied that it was sufficiently aerated, and picked up the glass by its stem. "Long legs," he observed. "And smooth." Tilting it forward, he closed his eyes, leaned his nose fully inside the voluminous Bordeaux glass, inhaled deeply. The aroma was like lying on his back in a field of Alpine strawberries.

Scents mingled in his memory, triggering visions of years gone by, of mountainside villas and simpler times, of the Second World War and friends long dead and buried. Recollections of tastes and textures and long Mediterranean afternoons…

"The Gros Vien grape," he said finally. "High-altitude varietal, very rare." He imbibed a large mouthful, held it, and savored it for many seconds before he swallowed it. "The fruit has tremendous character," he said. "Youthful, richly acidic." He leaned into the glass and breathed in its perfume once more, just to be certain. "I had no idea you were so decadent, Mr. Pritikin. So few bottles of the '61 Chambave Rouge left in the world, and you're serving one to people who don't even recognize it." Rising from his chair, he continued, "To be honest, I'm appalled that your sommelier would allow it to be served with this kind of entree, instead of the rustic northern Italian cuisine it was meant to accompany."

Logan took a cigar from his pocket and snipped its end, then put away the clipper and picked up his glass of Chambave Rouge. "Now—with your leave, Mr. Pritikin—I'd like to find some place I can enjoy the rest of my wine with a good cigar." Nodding to the other couples, he added, "Gentlemen; ladies."

Leaving the table of stunned faces, he walked quickly toward the banquet room's exit. As he left the room and began searching for a way out to one of the terraces or balconies, he heard Ziv's amused chuckle in the earpiece. "Sounds like you've learned a few things since the eighties."

"I've been at school," Logan retorted.

○———————○

THE Chambave Rouge proved more compatible with Logan's cigar than he'd expected. It was a pleasant surprise.

He'd found a quiet place to smoke: a balcony at the rear of the building, facing the mansion's sprawling grounds. A light snowfall had begun during dinner. Flakes wafted down into the estate's halo of light and alighted upon the expanse below and everything in it. The scene glowed bluish-gray beneath dozens of pale lamps mounted on nineteenth-century antique posts. Topiary sculptures stood silent vigils amid the property's slumbering fountains and icicle-draped benches. Several hundred meters away to either side, obscured by the slow-moving curtain of snow, solid walls of pine trees flanked the estate like dark battlements. Directly ahead, past the manicured gardens, was a frozen lake. Its far side appeared undeveloped, an unspoiled stretch of virgin coastline backed by more of the same dense pine forest. *Put a glass dome over it and label it "Welcome to Russia," and you can sell it in a gift shop*, Logan thought as he watched the snow fall.

Below him, at ground level, a man in a dark suit walked silently along the perimeter of the house; his overcoat bulged under the arm, exactly where a shoulder holster would be. Logan waited for the guard to pass by; when the man rounded the corner, Logan decided it was time to go to work. Abandoning a fine Cuban cigar only half smoked went against his nature, but, with regret, he snuffed the robusto in a few centimeters of freshly fallen snow heaped on the wide stone railing in front of him.

Logan turned his back on the winterscape. One quick tug freed the black flap hidden beneath his lapel from its Velcro tabs. He secured it in place beneath the other lapel, concealing his shirt. Then he began climbing.

Handholds were easy to come by, thanks to the building's intricate trellises and window frames. In a few easy moves, Logan pulled himself onto the part of the roof that overhung the balcony. He was one level away from the topmost section of the roof, which reached the entirety of both wings of the mansion. The ice on this level was thick, and the new snow made the curved roofing tiles especially slippery.

Moving with caution, he sidestepped to a corner and took hold of a drainpipe. Testing it to make certain its fittings were solid, he scaled it. His hands slipped once, then again; the pipe was also slick with ice, which melted beneath his hands. He sought out the roughest patches of its surface and fixed his grip.

A few awkward moments later, he was on top of the mansion, surrounded by the aimless drift of snowflakes weaving drunken paths to the ground. Immediately he dropped to a low crouch, to improve his balance on the frozen, flurry-dusted surface. Keeping one foot on either side of the roof's peak, he swiftly traversed the length of the mansion. In less than a minute, he'd passed an enormous skylight that dominated the center of the roof and reached the north wing.

Edging down the slope, he was uncertain whether he was on target for Pritikin's office window ledge.

"Ziv, position check."

"Close," Ziv answered. "One meter to your left."

"You're sure?"

"Your GPS is reading five-by-five," Ziv said. "Once you're over the edge, it'll be a three-meter drop to the ledge below." Now it was Ziv's turn to sound uncertain. "You're positive you can stick that landing?"

"What are you, a gymnastics coach? I'll be fine." Logan descended the roof in half-steps, using the tips of his claws like climbing spikes in the roof tiles. At the edge he dug in one claw a bit deeper, pivoted around it, then sank his other claws in for additional support. He lowered himself over the edge and dangled for a moment. It was only three meters from the soles of his shoes to the ledge outside Pritikin's office window, but that ledge was icy and coated with fresh, powdery snow. If Logan missed it, or if he lost his footing, it would be a sixty-foot drop to a concrete walkway at the rear of the house. Not enough to kill him, but it would hurt like hell and be a damned inconvenience. *Better nail the landing, then, canucklehead.*

He retracted his claws and let gravity take him.

His feet hit the ledge and slipped. He reflexively stabbed his claws into the sandstone façade of the mansion, arresting his fall. A second or two later he steadied himself and wedged his toes into the corners, against the window frame. He pulled his right claws free of the wall and retracted them; the left set he kept in place, as a precaution.

"Okay, I'm at the window."

"What kind of security does he have on it?"

"I'm checking," Logan said, as he peered past his reflection to study the inside of the window frame. He paid special attention to the middle, where the top and bottom halves of the window met. "I don't see any magnetic contacts. He might be using a glass-break sensor."

"Cutting through the glass without tripping the circuit will be tricky," Ziv said. "If we'd thought to prepare for—"

Logan opened the bottom half of the window. "It ain't locked, Ziv." Hanging on to the window, he retracted his left claws and crouched to look inside the room. "Checkin' the corners. No passive infrared, that's good." Closing his eyes, he listened for a few moments. "I could be wrong, but I can almost pick up a tone inside the room."

"Ultrasonic?"

"Probably," Logan said. "Looks like he's runnin' a motion sensor in there. Ain't in the corners; betcha it's disguised."

"If it's tied in to the mansion's primary security grid, it might look like an electrical outlet."

Another long look at the room, including a slow, careful peek over the edge at the wall below the window, didn't help. "All the exposed outlets are in use. Gotta be something else." In front of the window was Pritikin's desk and high-backed leather chair. The desktop was mostly bare, except for a wide flat-screen monitor on a sleek pedestal, a phone, and a Tiffany lamp with an octagonal shade. The desk faced the door to the office. On the left wall hung a flat-screen plasma television; the wall to the right was dominated by a tall bookshelf crowded with leather-bound volumes. One orderly row stood above another, the uniformity only rarely interrupted by small objets d'art.

Then Logan found what he was looking for: a single book that didn't look as if it belonged. It was three times thicker than any other tome in the room, and its spine had two matching circles—one at the top, one at the bottom. Most suspicious of all, it bore no title or author's name.

"Got it," Logan said as he climbed through the window and walked directly toward the faux book.

Ziv sounded apoplectic. "Are you insane?"

"Trust me," Logan said calmly. He was banking on the fifteen-to-twenty-second delay built into most motion-sensor alarms—a feature intended to allow an owner to enter a room and deactivate the sensor manually before the alert sounded.

"Abort, abort, abort!"

"Don't get yer panties in a bunch," Logan said. He lifted the "book" from the shelf; it was made of lightweight plastic. The back of it, opposite the spine, was recessed. Inside the nook was a numeric keypad and a few other controls, none of which was adjustable while the device was active. Below the keypad was a simple red toggle switch—confirming that this motion sensor was exactly the kind of cheap-knockoff, eastern European piece of crap that he'd thought it was. Logan flipped it from on to off, then put the book back on the shelf. "Five-by-five, Ziv. You can breathe again if you want."

"Too kind," Ziv grumbled.

Logan sat down at Pritikin's desk, pulled out the keyboard shelf, and powered up the computer. As expected, there was a port on the side of the black keyboard for the flash memory stick Ziv had given him. He retrieved it from inside his wallet and inserted it into the slot. "Stick's in," he muttered.

"I'm on it," Ziv replied. "And... we're in. I'm cloning his drive now and patching in to the Anbaric Petroleum server."

On the computer monitor, nothing seemed to be happening. At the moment, Logan felt slightly... superfluous. "Mind if I poke around his office?"

"Do as you like. Just don't touch the computer."

As offices went, Pritikin's was tidy and free of anything that even remotely resembled a sentimental touch. There were no photographs. All the small decorative pieces seemed to have been chosen for their aesthetic qualities; nothing had the quirky or idiosyncratic feel of a memento or keepsake. The books were mostly in Russian, including several by Tolstoy and Dostoyevsky. Taken in its entirety, it presented the appearance of a man who took life—and himself—all too seriously.

"I'm done," said Ziv, interrupting Logan's appraisal of the room's contents. "Wrap up and get back to the party."

"On it," Logan said, crossing to the desk. He removed the flash stick from the keyboard and shut down the machine. Tucking the slender digital device back inside his wallet, he returned to the fake book on the shelf and rearmed its sensors. Aware of the short time delay, he hurried to the window. The snow was falling more quickly now, and it pelted against him as he climbed out onto the ledge and pulled the window shut behind him. Using his claws, he scaled the stone wall of the mansion, then found his handholds on the roof's edge. With one muscular pull, he vaulted himself back up onto the roof.

Standing there, waiting for him with a *ninja-to* in one hand and three *shuriken* between the fingers of the other, was Miyoko.

"Lies do not become you, Logan-san," she said. "Or should I call you Wolverine?"

"Call me whatever you want," he said. "Your funeral."

Snowflakes, ethereal and silent, dipped and swirled and stalled in their descents around and between Logan and Miyoko, each regarding the other with an unblinking stare—a battle of wills, a test of nerve. She had him at a disadvantage; not only did she hold the high ground, near the roof's peak, but her *ninja-to* could strike from a greater range than his claws could reach. He would have to breach her defensive circle or else face a slow battle of attrition, a death by a thousand cuts.

Then her three *shuriken* cut through the curtain of snow, gleams of black and silver blurring through the flakes. By the time Logan's reflexes impelled him to motion, the metal stars had already struck him—one in his throat, another in his cheek, the third deep in the meat of his left shoulder. The bite of impact lasted for a fraction of a second, but by the time Logan regained his focus, Miyoko was lunging at him with her sword.

Her first slice he deflected with his claws.

He charged at her, his battle roar more of a blood-frothed gurgle. As he'd hoped, she sidestepped his attack, enabling him to move farther up the roof, away from the edge.

Her blade severed the Achilles tendon above his right heel. A second blade—shorter, probably a dagger—plunged between his unbreakable ribs and shredded part of his right lung. He stumbled forward and broke his fall with his elbows, since his claws made it hard to land on his palms.

Logan plucked the throwing stars from his throat and face; they were identical to the one that he had found in Osaka. He scrambled back to his feet. Miyoko was circling him, taunting him with feints. A breeze snapped the billowing fabric of her kimono, which Logan remembered had been tailored in a unique manner, to afford her total freedom of movement—an attribute that his tuxedo didn't share.

Logan felt his slashed tendon repair itself even as he pivoted on the icy tiles, tracking Miyoko. Her flowing black hair danced and twisted in the teasing wind, a dark halo framing her emotionless face. He swung his claws in a wide slash at her, but he found only empty air, falling snow, and darkness.

Then came another brutal cut, gouging deep into his back.

Miyoko was supernaturally fast, more agile and dexterous than even a ninja's training could account for. The Hand had been known to use magic to enhance the abilities of its most senior members. He surmised that Miyoko was one of those whom the organization had gifted with its most potent charms.

He turned toward the attack, squared his stance, and raised his arms, one in front of the other, to defend his throat and head. Her sword sliced across his left forearm, adding another trail of blood speckles to the thin sheet of snow on the roof.

As she brought the blade around for another slash in the opposite direction, Logan stepped into the hit, blocking it with his left claws. He punched forward with his right toward Miyoko's center of mass. She turned her torso clear of his lunging attack and with her free hand grabbed his wrist. Her right foot shot up, struck his groin, then bent quickly back from the knee, lifted, and snap-kicked him in the face.

A torquing pull spun Logan through the air, pointed his feet toward the sky, rotated his whole body around his shoulder. He landed hard on his back.

Miyoko's knife swung fast, in a tight arc toward the underside of his jaw, looking to pierce the soft flesh behind his chin and drive up into his brain for a quick death blow.

He rolled to his left and pushed himself back to his feet.

Explosions of pain flared across his body—a burning slash through his left ear, a deep gash in his right flank, a *shuriken* suddenly wedged between his shoulder blades. Miyoko was moving so quickly that Logan could barely see her.

Then he heard her laugh. *She's toying with me*, he realized. *She thinks this is funny.*

He backpedaled toward the middle of the mansion, weathering Miyoko's harrying blows. His healing factor struggled to keep up as the ninja shredded his clothes and his flesh, one vicious slice at a time. As he reached a broad, flat section of the roof near the central skylight, he had begun to sense a pattern to her assaults, a rhythm. *Like a ballet*, he told himself. *You just have to learn your part of the dance.*

Little was left of his tuxedo except for loose, blood-soaked tatters. His hair was wet and heavy with melting snow. Miyoko dealt out cuts faster than his body could heal. Sheets of his blood soaked his chest and back, his arms and legs. Another *shuriken* slammed into his temple, in front of his right ear.

Here it comes, he thought, imagining the next step in Miyoko's invisible dance of steel and darkness. Then, even though he couldn't see more than a blur of her in the corner of his eye, he pivoted and thrust his claws into the night—

—and they found flesh and bone, blood and sinew, a body pliant and warm and fragile.

Miyoko dropped her sword. She writhed and struggled, impaled on the claws of Logan's right hand. Then her training reasserted itself and she attacked once again with her knife, thrusting up at Logan's chin. He caught her left hand by the wrist, but she pressed upward. Her strength was superhuman. She added her right hand to her efforts, forcing the blade up until it broke the flesh under Logan's jaw. Misting gales from her ragged breaths teased his face.

Thrown off-balance by the burden of her weight and the ferocity of her struggle, he stumbled backward. Miyoko growled like an animal as she fought to push her blade just a few more inches, into his head. Logan felt his feet slip. He didn't want to let Miyoko get him onto his back. The additional leverage of being on top of him while they fell would likely be all she needed to finish him.

He twisted his right hand, ground Miyoko's internal organs into paste, ruptured her thoracic aorta… but something—maybe rage, maybe magic—wouldn't let her die.

Logan's foot landed on something angled upward behind him. Before he could adjust his footing, the surface he'd stepped on gave way under his and Miyoko's combined weight.

They were falling. For the first half-second, it seemed to happen in slow motion: the delicate crunch of breaking glass, followed by the musical screech of a windowpane fracturing.

As they dropped backward through the skylight, his claws finally pierced Miyoko's heart, which trembled and then seized. His memory flashed on the final moments of his beloved Mariko, expiring on his claws… then he clutched the ninja's dead body as they plummeted like stones inside a storm of shattered glass, ten meters down, into the mansion's natatorium. Undulating ribbons of dark blue light danced on the surface of the water below. He retracted his claws and let go of Miyoko's body a moment before they splashed into the heated indoor swimming pool.

The water embraced Logan, then it smothered him. His feet touched the bottom, and he pushed himself upward. Breaking the surface with a grateful gasp of air, he checked to make certain that Miyoko was really dead. Her lifeless eyes stared into the pool as a deep scarlet cloud of her own blood spread around her.

Ziv's voice crackled over the earpiece. "Guys, we are now officially screwed. Get out of there, both of you."

Wai Ying's voice followed. "How do we get back to the car?"

"We don't," Logan said, wading toward the edge. "Leave through the kitchen and meet me out back, near the cottages."

"All right," Wai Ying replied. "See you there."

He was climbing out of the pool as he heard the approach of running footsteps and the clacking of automatic weapons being primed for action. There were men coming from every entrance.

The rear wall of the natatorium was an enormous, floor-to-ceiling grid of windows. It looked out on the gardens behind the mansion and the lakeshore down below. Logan decided that since his clothes had already been turned to confetti and his body was still fighting to heal the wounds that Miyoko had dealt him, he had nothing to lose by taking the easy way out.

He sprinted toward the glass wall, shielded his face and throat with his arms, and hurled himself through it, out into the garden and the cover of darkness.

And, just as he expected, it hurt like a sonofabitch.

○———————○

KEEPING a straight face hadn't been easy.

Wai Ying had remained seated at the dinner table with Pritikin and his VIP guests while Logan had left on his covert mission to tap the computer in Pritikin's office. She'd been listening to the exchanges between Ziv and Logan as Miyoko rose from the table and left the banquet room. She'd considered warning them that Miyoko was no longer at dinner, but that would have required her to excuse herself from the table, and Pritikin had chosen exactly that moment to engage her in small talk.

"I've cut your channel to Logan," Ziv had whispered in her ear while Pritikin rambled. "I don't want him distracted."

Nodding absently at Pritikin, she masked her response by grinning at some upbeat remark of his and then muttering, "Delightful."

Then had come the fighting words between Logan and Miyoko, followed by the alarming sounds of cold steel whistling through thick winter air and striking fabric and flesh. She'd responded by plastering an insincere grin on her face and taking another sip of the rich, fruity Chambave Rouge. Even as she'd been forced to listen to Logan's grunts and roars of pain, she'd picked halfheartedly at her dessert, a towering chocolate concoction whose curving, swooshing architecture looked more ambitious than Frank Gehry's museum in Bilbao.

Shattering glass, a splash of water, and a sputter of static rasped in her ear. She winced and reflexively reached a hand toward the side of her head before she caught herself.

Pritikin abandoned his anecdote and leaned forward, looking concerned. "Are you all right?"

"Yes," Wai Ying said. "Fine. Just a headache."

"Nothing too serious, I hope," he said.

"I do sometimes get migraines," she lied.

He nodded, then motioned to someone across the room. "Let me have one of my people bring you something for the pain."

As she glanced over her shoulder, she noticed men in dark suits moving discreetly toward all the guest exits from the banquet room. Two more men were crossing the room from behind her, taking long strides as they detoured around tables. This wasn't a first-aid call. She got up from her chair.

Ziv's voice squawked again in her ear and told her what she'd already figured out for herself. "Guys, we are now officially screwed. Get out of there, both of you."

Her cover was blown. Subtlety was no longer necessary.

A sweep of her hand sent a wave of repulsor force surging away from her, overturning tables and flinging people like rag dolls to the floor. "How do we get back to the car?" she asked, hurling another half-dozen tables and nearly fifty people into the air. Behind her, Pritikin and his VIPs were already running for cover.

"We don't," Logan replied over the transceiver. "Leave through the kitchen and meet me out back, near the cottages."

"All right," she said, kicking off her shoes and jogging backward inside a protective hemispherical force field toward the kitchen doors. "See you there." Bullets ricocheted off her invisible shell and tore dusty divots from the banquet room's marble pillars. She reshaped her defensive screen as she neared the door, reducing it to a curved wall in front of her as she backed through the swinging portal into the hustle and bustle of the kitchen.

A shout like a bulldog's bark rattled her nerves. "*Stoy! Ruki vverkh!*"

She turned her head and saw a beefy, sandy-haired man in his thirties. He was pointing an assault rifle at her. Smiling sweetly, she turned slowly to face him. "Sorry," she said, "I don't speak Russian."

"Put up your hands," he said with a heavy Russian accent. He braced his rifle against his shoulder and aimed at her. Calming her nerves, she focused her concentration on the narrow space inside the muzzle of his weapon.

"I lied," she said. "I do speak Russian. And I know you won't shoot, because you're too much of a *pider* to kill a woman." Then she flashed an evil grin and walked right at him.

He pulled his trigger, and the barrel of his rifle exploded as multiple rounds struck the force field she had projected inside the weapon's muzzle. The flash of ignited gunpowder was blinding, and the sharp crack of detonation drowned out his instantly silenced howl of pain. He collapsed to the floor, his face burned, bloody, and studded with metallic debris.

The kitchen doors slammed open behind her. She ducked to cover behind a stainless-steel counter, projecting a clumsy shield around herself as she dropped to the floor. Above her, two large and nearly full soup terrines simmered over gas flames. With a thought, she launched the terrines at the guards pursuing her. Heavy thuds of impact mingled with shrieks of agony.

Back on her feet again, she dashed sideways out of the kitchen, hurling a storm of cooking utensils and pans of hot grease at anyone who tried to walk through the door from the banquet room. It was only a few more meters to the back door. The heavier outer door had been propped open, to allow cool air to ventilate the steamy kitchen. Wai Ying pushed through the closed screen door, out into the night, to freedom—

Directly into one of Pritikin's guards. The man's hand clamped around her throat and started crushing her windpipe. Suddenly, her ability to focus kinetic fields betrayed her. The panic flooding her mind was too great, too immediate. All she could think of was her desperate need for air denied, the vertiginous spin of swirling snow flurries cocooning her. Her hands flailed futilely against the man's viselike grip.

Any second now her cervical vertebrae would snap, she knew it—

Logan's adamantium claws erupted out of the man's chest. His grip slackened and released. The claws vanished back inside him, and he buckled and fell straight down like a marionette severed from its master. Wai Ying was still swooning from asphyxia as Logan clutched her shoulders and steadied her. "Ace! You all right? Say something."

Giving him a blurry-eyed once-over, she said, "You look terrible."

"You're all right." Logan pulled her away from the mansion, toward a set of what looked like guest cottages along the lakeshore. Wai Ying felt light-headed as she stumble-sprinted away from the mansion with Logan. The snow numbed her feet.

"Logan?" Ziv sounded nervous. "Where are you going?"

"The sat-recon you showed me—it was recent?"

"Taken yesterday."

"Then get the van runnin', bub. We're comin' in hot."

They rounded the corner of the nearest cottage, and suddenly Logan's exit strategy made sense to her. Parked behind the cottages were several snowmobiles. He jumped on the nearest one, jabbed one claw into its ignition, and twisted. It growled to life. "Get on," he said, "in front of me."

"You'd like that," she said.

"The bullets will be coming from behind us," he said.

She mounted the snowmobile and hunched down in front of him. Just as he'd predicted, the gunshots started seconds later, as he accelerated away from the mansion, out onto the frozen lake. She shouted over the wind roar and engine noise, "You sure the lake is solid?"

"Nope," he shouted back, twisting the throttle to maximum.

Riding on a snowmobile, in Wai Ying's opinion, was a lot like riding on a motorcycle. A really fat motorcycle. With skis. On ice. Actually, about all they had in common were the handgrip controls for the brake and throttle and the bitter sting of cold air in one's face.

She hunkered down behind the windshield and guarded her face from the screaming wind with her arms. Glancing backward, beneath Logan's arm, she saw three snowmobiles, each manned by two of Pritikin's guards, pursuing them into the snowy night.

Bullets *zing*ed past her and Logan and *ping*ed off the ice. Several more shots slammed hard into Logan's back, jerking him forward with each impact. Wai Ying could barely hear the shots above the buzzing drone of the snowmobile engine. A fresh hail of gunfire strafed the ice to either side of their snowmobile, then a single shot struck home into its engine with a deep metallic *thunk*. Immediately, they began losing speed, and the engine belched grimy black smoke. *At least it'll make it harder for them to see what they're shooting at,* she figured.

Logan quickly zigzagged his course, no doubt to muddy his pursuers' aim just a little more. "Nice smoke screen," Wai Ying shouted over the now-grinding engine. "That'll buy us about ten seconds."

Cocking one eyebrow at her, he said, "You got a plan?"

"Actually, yes." She rested her palms on the center of the handlebars and lifted herself off the saddle. Gracefully, she twisted at her hips, steadied herself by placing her hands on Logan's shoulders, and turned herself to face him. Then she straddled him on the seat, gripped his torso with her left arm, and leaned over his left shoulder. "Punch it."

She kept her eyes on the drifting curtain of oil smoke they'd left behind them, and she gathered her strength and focus. Extending her hand toward the black cloud, her breath caught in her throat, which clenched in anticipation.

The pursuing snowmobiles emerged from the inky darkness, and Wai Ying unleashed a single, massive cone of force at the ice in front of them. The invisible wave struck with a deafening boom. One of the pursuing snowmobiles veered wide to safety as an enormous swath of the lake's ice sheet disintegrated into froth and swallowed the other two vehicles.

Logan steered their own snowmobile off the lake and up into the forest on the far side, dodging at unsafe speeds between thick-trunked pine trees, lurching and slaloming over the uneven ground. About fifteen meters away through the trees, the last pursuing snowmobile was closing the gap, having found a less challenging path through the woods. "Get closer to them," Wai Ying said. "Before they cut us off."

Logan didn't debate her, he just did as she'd asked. Weaving and scraping past stumps and rotting logs from dead trees, he blazed a diagonal trail back toward the clear path to their right. They tore past a drooping bough, scattering pine needles and twigs, and emerged ahead of their pursuers.

The timing would have to be just right, because the element of surprise was everything. Pointing her palms outward and slightly behind her—which was in front of her and Logan's snowmobile—she unleashed two wide but flat planes of pure kinetic force. Splintering cracks gave way to the shriek and groan of green wood bending, and then the rifle-shot snap of that same wood breaking. By the time gravity finished what she had started, she and Logan were safely away. Their pursuers at least had the good sense to abandon their speeding snowmobile and take a rough tumble into the snow, rather than ride their machine into the sudden collapse of a dozen massive pine trees.

Less than a minute later, Logan and Wai Ying were clear of the woods and cruising downhill toward Ziv's waiting van.

She noticed that Logan was grinning and chuckling to himself. "What's so funny?" she asked.

He smiled. "I knew there was a reason I married you."

○————————○

A pale, narrow ladder of snowflakes reached down through the shattered skylight and dissolved on contact with the surface of the heated swimming pool. Alexei Pritikin sat at the pool's edge, numb. Floating in the water was the body of his lover, surrounded by a slowly roiling cloud of her own blood. Shock, horror, and disbelief smothered his thoughts. He was furious and paralyzed, raging at his own helplessness to defy fate.

Footsteps echoed as they approached. He looked up at Mikhail, who was in charge of the mansion's security detail. The aquiline-featured bodyguard wore an expression of a kind that Pritikin had never before seen on his face: contrition.

"They escaped," Mikhail said. "On a snowmobile, across the lake. We have six dead and three seriously wounded."

"Have Piotr talk to Mikalunas—not a word of this gets in tomorrow's papers. Then take your things and leave."

Mikhail started to nod in confirmation, then he wrinkled his brow in confusion. "Sir?"

"You're fired," Pritikin explained. "Get out."

By necessity, Pritikin had been ruthless in his ascent to power. Subordinates who'd failed him had been dispatched without pity. Competitors had been crushed without mercy or hesitation. When the law had stood in his way, he'd bent it, broken it, or defied it; when there'd been no other way, he'd simply had the laws changed to suit his needs. His business was oil. What he provided everyone needed—and if the only way for him to give it to them was for the government to rewrite the law, then so be it. A criminal, some had called him; a gangster. He hadn't argued. They were probably right. Hell, he knew they were right. But what did it matter? So he'd profited from wars; someone was going to, it might as well be him. He'd lied, blackmailed people in positions of power, even had a few politicians killed.

Nothing he'd done made him a monster. Opportunity had conspired with desire to send him down those paths. Anyone in his position, knowing the stakes as he did, would have done the same. What was the alternative? Allow the world's oil supply to dwindle? Give free rein to chaos when the Western world was finally made to understand what "peak oil" really meant? Unthinkable. The world needed time to plan its transition to a new form of energy; in the interim, barring any kind of socialistic governmental interference, someone was going to make a profit. Pritikin had decided decades ago that the someone in that equation would be him.

He knew that he was a criminal; he'd never denied it. But he was also a man, and he'd loved Miyoko, more than any other woman he'd ever known. It hadn't mattered to him that she did not love him in return, or that she likely never would. Her beauty had been without equal, and his heart had been lost to her from the moment he'd seen her. Now she floated facedown in the water, disemboweled, her viscera dangling loosely below her. The bloodstained fabric of her kimono undulated around her, tendrils reaching out in a futile effort to anchor her to the physical world, though her spirit was obviously long departed.

Vengeance was in order. "I'll kill him," Pritikin muttered to no one. Having dismissed Mikhail, he thought himself alone now with Miyoko's body. "I'll eat his heart," he grumbled, quaking with anger. "If it takes my entire fortune, if it takes the rest of my life. I'll kill him for this."

The man behind Pritikin sounded smug and condescending. "Take care when making curses against Wolverine," he said. "I've yet to meet anyone who didn't come to regret it."

Pritikin took a deep breath and slowly counted to ten. He stood, straightened his jacket, and composed his face into a mask of sophisticated disinterest. Then he turned to face his unexpected visitor, Keniuchio Harada.

Harada looked exactly as he had every other time Pritikin had met with him: trim, focused, and attired in a silvery gray business suit. His shirt was an off-white with silvery pinstripes. The only splash of color in his ensemble was a silver-hued silk necktie emblazoned with a bold red Japanese rising sun design. On the index finger of his left hand, an ornately engraved silver band gleamed as it caught the light.

"You know I hate when you drop in with that teleportation ring of yours," Pritikin said. "It's damned rude."

"Exigent circumstances," Harada said, nodding toward Miyoko's body. "I told her not to face Wolverine alone, but you know how she was: stubborn."

Recoiling with indignation, Pritikin said, "You knew who he was? And you let him walk into my house without warning me?"

"I warned *her*," Harada said, nodding at Miyoko. "Defending you was her responsibility."

"And avenging her will be mine," Pritikin said.

Harada shook his head. "That would be unwise." The Japanese *yakuza* overlord walked to the edge of the pool and gazed forlornly upon his fallen assassin. "Wolverine is not just any mutant; he's one of the oldest, and one of the toughest. Your resources are formidable, Alexei, but they aren't equal to the task you've set for yourself. I would suggest you leave Miyoko's retribution to more capable hands."

Pacing behind Harada, Pritikin retorted, "I don't give a damn what you'd *suggest*. I'm not *yakuza*, and I'm not part of the Hand. I'm your *partner* in this operation, not your flunky."

"You aren't thinking clearly," Harada replied, shaking his head. "I admit, Miyoko's death is a terrible loss; she was a great assassin. And I know that you cared for her deeply. But our venture is at a critical stage; you mustn't let your emotions trump your judgment. This is a time not for rash action, but for a calculated response."

Pritikin stepped up and put himself face-to-face with Harada, who towered over him. "*Calculated response?* Such as?"

"When the operation is irrevocably engaged," Harada said, "then we can satisfy our debt of honor against Wolverine."

"Not good enough," Pritikin replied. "He had enough time to reach my office. If he accessed my computer, he might know about the *Pandora*."

Harada said calmly, "I've already assumed that he does. Steps have been taken."

"I'm sure," Pritikin said with a frown. He turned his back on Harada and walked toward the natatorium's closest exit.

"Where are you going?" Harada asked.

"To do us both a favor," Pritikin said.

He was halfway to the doors when Harada's offhand comment brought him to a halt. "Ah, yes—your vaunted Red Star team." As Pritikin turned slowly back toward Harada, the *yakuza oyabun* added, "I was wondering when you'd deploy them."

Paranoia colored Pritikin's tone as he walked slowly back to face Harada. "How do you know about them?"

"Some secrets are harder to keep than others," Harada said with a grin. "Three suits of powered battle armor, each one manned by a former Spetsnaz trooper. Impressive, really. Though I'd expected you to save them for something of a… *less precise* nature than fighting Wolverine."

Naturally, Harada was right. Pritikin's research team had developed the three suits of mechanized battle armor as prototypes for an eventual battalion of powered-armor soldiers. The long-term purpose for such a force was to be ready to secure his claims to oil fields in the Caspian Sea region, as well as in the deserts of Zibara. It was a necessary precaution; if and when the reality of the globe's rapidly diminishing supply of crude oil became commonly understood, riots and then war would follow in rapid succession. Nations would aim to follow America's lead in Iraq and start seizing petroleum and natural-gas resources while there were still some to be exploited. The only private entities that would be able to retain control of their assets would be those, such as Halliburton, that had made themselves indispensable to their government, or those like Pritikin's company, Anbaric Petroleum, that had armed themselves and were prepared to hold on to their property by force.

"I will employ my resources as I see fit," Pritikin said. "And I don't give a damn what your code of honor says about it."

Harada loomed over Pritikin and said in a grave tone, "I will tolerate your wrathful behavior only so long as it does not put our operation at risk. We are each other's means to an end, Mr. Pritikin—but I have already obtained what I need from our arrangement. Only my word of honor compels me to repay my debt to you." Harada's beatific expression became a murderous glare. "I suggest you remember that."

12

ZIV drove like a maniac. The van lurched from side to side as he veered around what few other cars were out on the snow-swept, forest-lined highway. Every tight turn hurled Wai Ying and Logan back and forth in the van's cramped rear compartment, which was packed with high-tech equipment. Wai Ying stayed near the front, while Logan huddled near the back doors, glancing occasionally out the windows into the speed-blurred nightscape.

They were already an hour away from Pritikin's mansion and clear of the snowstorm, but Ziv hadn't slowed down, not once. Wai Ying clutched a padded seat mounted on a glide track in front of the computers and monitors and glanced forward to see where they were going. They were skirting the St. Petersburg city limits, taking a less traveled route to Pulkovo Airport. Unable to hide her surprise, she said to Ziv, "Aren't we going back to the hotel?"

"*Nyet,*" Ziv snapped. "Too dangerous."

"But our clothes," she protested. "Our passports—"

"Already on the plane," Ziv said, swerving around a slow-moving, boxy-looking economy car.

Wai Ying leaned into the van's rocking motion, then turned her accusatory glower on Logan. "Your idea?"

Logan shrugged. "Didn't want to wear out our welcome. Figured no matter how it went, we'd better get on the road."

"Good point," she said. "Ziv, whatever intel you downloaded, I'll need to copy it to my laptop before we leave."

"Already done," he said. "Your computer's back in its case, near the rear door. Once we get to the airport, we'll frag the van and analyze the data in the air."

It took Wai Ying a second to parse that. "We?"

"That's right," Ziv said. "I can't stay here after this fiasco. This was supposed to be a low-profile recon. I guess I ought to be grateful you didn't torch the place."

From the back, Logan quipped, "If I'd had more time—"

"Shut up," Ziv said. "I called in favors to get you into that party. Now my contacts are as good as burned—and my pension along with them."

"I'd almost feel sorry for ya if I didn't know you had four tons of gold bullion stashed in Zurich."

Ziv laughed. "It's not worth much to me if I'm not alive to spend it, comrade. So wherever the wind takes you next, it takes me as well."

"The more the merrier," Logan said. "Speaking of which, we're being followed."

Checking the rearview, Ziv replied, "I don't see anyone."

"Neither do I," Wai Ying said, looking past Logan out the rear windows. "There's no one behind us."

"I didn't say it was a car," Logan replied. "There's a tunnel up ahead. Stop in there and kill the lights."

The van passed into a dark, two-lane tunnel carved through a jutting mound of gray mountainside. In the middle of the tunnel, Ziv brought the van to a halt and turned off its lights, as Logan had instructed. Logan picked up Wai Ying's laptop case and handed it to Ziv. "Get clear of the van and take cover past the far end of the tunnel, just in case."

"What are you going to do?" he asked.

"What I do best," Logan said. He took Wai Ying by the hand, opened the van's rear doors, and led her into the darkness. "With a little help from my friend."

○————————○

TWO hundred meters above the ground, Vadim Ilyanov guided his battlesuit in a tight circle above the lonely stretch of rural highway where he and his two compatriots had last seen the van, less than two minutes earlier. "Still no sign of it," Roman, his second-in-command, reported over the secure comm.

Kiril, the third man in the team, added, "They must have stopped inside the tunnel."

"Of course they did," Vadim said. "Cut the chatter and pick up your infrared." He turned off the night-vision settings and activated the infrared filter on his own holographic head-up display. The HUD rerendered the wooded hillside below in washes of cool green and pale blue, superimposed over a topographical wireframe of the surrounding terrain.

His suit's vertical takeoff and landing thrusters gave off a high-pitched hum but little other sound. From the ground, he and the other members of Red Star were essentially inaudible. Even more important, they were nearly invisible, thanks to their battlesuits' combination of stealth features, ranging from radar-dampening composites to active-mode optical cloaking.

"I've got something," Kiril said. "One bogey, exiting the north end of the tunnel." A tiny but bright red figure appeared on Vadim's HUD as well. Over the comm, Roman confirmed the sighting. "Roger that. Orders, sir?"

Vadim primed his suit's arm-mounted .50-millimeter cannons. "Weapons hot," he declared. "Kiril, flush him out and drive him uphill, it'll slow him down. Roman, drop in behind him, don't let him retreat. I'll go for high ground, and we'll box him in." Both men acknowledged their orders and initiated a swift descent to engage the target on the ground.

Less than a hundred meters up the mountainside was a clearing wide enough for Vadim to set down without disturbing the surrounding trees. He accelerated to it, then hovered while the suit reoriented itself into a standing position. From his vantage point in the cockpit it was fluid and not at all disorienting, thanks to the battle armor's gyroscopically stabilized cockpit. His HUD confirmed that he was solidly on the ground and set to advance "on foot" to engage his target. Through the thick forest, there was no sign of the target's infrared signature. Soon enough, however, all Vadim would have to do would be to target any explosions he detected in the forest and fire at will.

Sending three battlesuits after one unarmed man seemed wasteful to Vadim, but orders were orders. Mr. Pritikin had provided the satellite intelligence identifying the van that had fled from an attack at his estate, and he had made it clear that he wanted Vadim and his men to find that van, destroy it, and kill its occupants. *If only all my assignments were so easy*, Vadim mused ruefully.

As if on cue, that's when the explosions started.

The glare filters on his HUD engaged as incendiary plumes lit up the night and stripped bare broad swaths of the forest. "*Got him!*" Kiril crowed over the comm. "He's toast!" Vadim patched in the tactical display from Kiril's system and replayed the last several seconds from his battle camera. Kiril had locked his targeting crosshairs on the running humanoid figure they'd flushed out of the tunnel, then fired a volley of RPG-7 high-explosive rockets from his suit's shoulder-mounted launchers. The recording indicated a direct hit.

"Nice work, Kiril," Vadim said, switching back to a real-time link with Kiril's tactical monitor.

"*Da*, Kiril," Roman added. "Good shot."

"Thanks," Kiril said. "Should we—" He paused abruptly, and Vadim saw why in the sudden jumble of data from Kiril's onboard computer. Hydraulic pressure was dropping quickly in the legs of the younger man's suit.

"Kiril," Vadim cut in, "did you get hit by shrapnel from your own ordnance? Your hydraulics are damaged."

"They—they were fine a second ago," Kiril stammered. "I don't... I don't understand. I just lost my left hip actuator." His voice grew more alarmed as he continued. "Right hip actuator offline. Guys, I'm stuck."

"Dammit, Kiril, lift off," Vadim said, propelling his battlesuit through the forest at a run. Using the cybernetic link between his arms and those of the gigantic armored exoskeleton, he swatted trees out of his path. Inside the suit he couldn't hear them snap, but he felt their feeble resistance as they broke apart and fell away with each sweep of his arms. His running steps shook the entire battlesuit, and he remembered the thunderous impacts and ground-shaking tremors these massive war machines caused when accelerated to a full sprint.

"Wing mechanism's jammed," Kiril said. "Guys, I'm FUBAR over here, and I'm starting—" His transmission stopped there.

"Roman," Vadim shouted, "converge on Kiril's position! He's under attack! Kiril, activate your IC!" It was only another twenty meters to Kiril's position. A few more seconds running. Roman's transponder was closing from the opposite direction. Vadim didn't know what kind of mutant fiend Kiril had met on the battlefield, but if the battlesuit's infantry countermeasures could slow its attack for a few more moments...

After catapulting forward through the last thick tree trunks, Vadim's battlesuit landed squarely, weapons armed. In front of him was Kiril's battlesuit; its exterior was scratched and gouged, and it smoldered from the recent activation of its fiery antipersonnel self-defense system. The left side of its cockpit canopy had been shattered and torn apart.

Roman's battlesuit broke through the trees behind Kiril's crippled unit. As he had been trained to do, he dropped to a more stable defensive posture and waited for new orders.

Through the gray veils of smoke, Vadim saw Kiril's silhouette waving to him from inside the damaged battlesuit's exposed cockpit. Then Kiril pointed down, below his machine. Vadim checked his ventral scanners and noted the scorched humanoid form on the ground. "Kiril, are you all right?"

From the other battlesuit's cockpit came Kiril's "out of action" hand signal, followed by a tapping against the side of his helmet.

"Roman, his comm's out," Vadim said. "Go frag the van. I'll evac Kiril and get a recovery team for his suit."

"Yes, sir," Roman replied, then he guided his battlesuit back to its upright position, turned it back downhill, and proceeded toward the south end of the tunnel.

Vadim guided his own armored titan in slow steps until it was nose-to-nose with Kiril's. He released his canopy lock; it detached from the armored chassis with a hydraulic hiss. As he reached under his seat and retrieved his first-aid kit, a blast of cool, pine-scented winter air surged into the temperature-controlled cockpit. Then he stood up to see a rocket-propelled grenade scream into his cockpit and turn his world to fire.

○————————○

LOGAN rolled out of his long fall to the ground. Above, the RPG warhead ripped through the exposed cockpit of the second battlesuit he'd destroyed in as many minutes. Burning fuel and twisted black hunks of machinery slammed to the ground as Logan sprinted clear, in pursuit of the third and final walking tank, which was now going after Ziv and Wai Ying.

Wrecking the first machine had been easy for Logan. Wai Ying had provided him with an invisible, undetectable force field for cover from its missile attack. Jumping through the fire cloud that had lingered after the blast had hurt a lot, but only for a minute, and the pain had spurred his climb up the metal marauder's legs to its torso. He'd cut through every servo, wire, tube, and circuit board on his way to the top. By the time he'd scaled its back to sever its transmission antenna, the steel walker had been all but paralyzed. Cutting into its cockpit had been like ripping open a present; the pilot had even been kind enough to arm an exterior antipersonnel system that Logan was able to use to dispose of the man's body.

Following the third giant exoskeleton through the forest was easy; keeping up with it wasn't. Despite its size, it was fast and agile. In addition, it also didn't have to navigate the obstacle course of fallen pine trees that it left in its tracks.

Tremors rocked the cold, hard ground. Booming thundersteps echoed in the night. Leaping from one fallen tree trunk to another, Logan raced to catch up with the last armored cybersuit, his gusts of breath voluminous and white in the frigid air. Then he stopped, perched in a low crouch atop a sheared-off stump. Listening, he realized that he didn't have to chase the titanic war machine anymore. It was coming back, directly at him.

Logan turned downhill and ran like hell.

Rockets lit up the night. Flashes of light and thunder rained cordite brimstone into the forest. An infernal chain-saw roar of .50-caliber guns droned beneath the blasts. The barrage sheared off treetops and turned them to sawdust before they hit the ground. Sharp reports from a dozen grenades were barely pops in the nightmarish din that swelled around Logan.

A blast hurled him forward, a leaf in a firestorm. Heavy bullets raked his back as he fell, ripping away large chunks of his flesh. Another explosion scoured him with burning shrapnel. He struck the ground in agony, his body torn and seared, his skin flayed. Screams of rage lay trapped inside his chest, unable to escape his bloody, shredded throat. His fingers clawed the carpet of dried pine needles, dug at the cold black dirt underneath. Instinct told him to get up, keep moving, but his leg muscles were still knitting themselves back together, magnifying his suffering.

The hum of engines and servos counterpointed a regular cadence of deafening booms, the thunderous herald of several tons of metal striding at a quickstep. Determined not to meet death with his back turned, Logan fought against his ravaged body, forced himself to roll over onto his back. The metal colossus came to a halt towering above him, an iron god gazing with contempt at a mere insect.

Logan gathered the phlegm from his throat and spat it at the weathered, gray foot of the beast. "Go on, you bastard," he said in a voice like a cougar's growl. "Bring it."

A ruby-red flash of laser light danced over Logan's eyes. The machine's targeting system was locked.

Its autocannons blazed—sending a stream of crimson tracers arcing away into the trees, deflected as if by providence.

The last two rockets in its shoulder-mounted launchers leaped forward with a deep *whoosh*—then detonated, nova bright, less than three meters from the battlesuit.

Rocked by the point-blank explosions, the metallic behemoth stumbled backward, its torso spun off-center. When the smoke and fire dissipated seconds later, it had righted itself, but Logan could see that its cockpit canopy had been badly fractured, and the armor on its chassis had been cracked open. For a moment, it didn't move at all, suggesting that its pilot had been stunned.

Logan tilted his head backward. At the edge of the glade, huddled under a fallen tree, was Wai Ying. Her open palm and unblinking stare were trained steadily on the giant machine. The operator of the walking tank swiveled the machine's torso to aim its autocannons at her. A moment later, the gun barrels cracked and ballooned out, then exploded into pieces as misfires touched off conflagrations in their ordnance packages. *Plugged up the barrel*, Logan realized. *Damn, she's good.*

His muscles had repaired themselves enough that he could move again. Scrambling onto all fours, he crawled for cover beneath a stack of overlapping toppled trees.

Behind him, the iron goliath charged forward, on a straight path for Wai Ying. Instead of running, Wai Ying moved into the open, kneeled, and raised her open palms above her head.

Logan grinned with admiration. *Meeting it head-on. Good for her*. He picked himself up. Rolled a painful crick out of his neck. Extended his claws. Grinned. *Can't keep a lady waiting.*

He charged into battle with a roar. The thirty-foot-tall battlesuit was stomping down at Wai Ying, but every crushing blow of its enormous steel foot glanced off her unseen defensive force field. Building up speed, Logan sprinted the final steps, pushed off his right foot, and leaped at the monstrosity's back.

The machine's torso pivoted in a blur and swatted Logan with its mangled right autocannon, which was still effective as a blunt-force weapon. On impact, Logan's vision became faint and spotty. A sensation of weightlessness lasted until a tree halted his lateral flight. None of his bones broke—thanks to the adamantium, they were unbreakable—but he could have sworn they compressed and collapsed into a new and wholly unnatural shape. He bounced off the tree and fell in a dazed heap to the ground.

Swinging its disabled left-side autocannon like a golf club at Wai Ying, it launched her into the air. In midair she adjusted her pose, spreading her arms and legs into an X shape. She ricocheted off trees without seeming to hit them and then cartwheeled away downhill, safe inside her unseen sphere of protection.

This time, Logan chose stealth rather than a head-on assault. He kept low to the ground, dodged beneath and between precariously piled trees, then darted out toward the hulking walker's left flank. Its left foot lifted up, then crashed back down with such speed that Logan was barely able to roll clear and avoid getting turned into salsa. Rather than wait for it to take another stomp at him, he sprang forward onto its foot.

His first blow sank his left claws deep inside the foot's main structural support. Slashing with his right at its principal pivot point, he reveled in the fountain of viscous hydrocarbon lubricant that sprayed outward.

He ducked behind the ankle assembly as the machine's left autocannon swung down to swat him away. As he'd hoped, the machines had not been designed to be able to hit themselves. *Now I just have to get to the cockpit before—*

A fine mist of burning fumes stung his eyes. He scrambled blind up the machine's leg and was less than halfway over its knee when its antipersonnel system doused its left leg in caustic acid. His already tattered clothes now smoldered where a few drops made contact, and the soles of his shoes slagged as he pushed off an acid-smeared edge for leverage.

Ignoring his half-melted footwear, Logan pulled himself up as quickly as possible. He'd barely reached the hip actuator when blue-white arcs of electricity skipped across the battlesuit's exterior. All he could do was grit his teeth and hang on as every muscle in his body convulsed. White-hot bolts of artificial lightning scorched his back and singed his hair.

The electrical assault ended. Smoke snaked off him in long, wispy coils. He could barely breathe. Reddish haze clouded his vision. His entire body quaked; he couldn't unclench his white-knuckle grasp on the machine's hull. Two deep breaths gave him strength. Nothing was left in him now but battle rage, the primal drive of the animal that owned his soul.

Hand over hand, he climbed and clawed his way up the machine's back. Stabbing at the rounded surfaces, he was rewarded with the pungent fumes of high-octane fuel. One hard swipe of his claws made a hash of the shielded communications bundle behind the cockpit.

Clicking noises came from either side of him. Survival instinct propelled him from a crouch to a superhuman vertical leap, high above the walking tank's head. Twin flamethrowers mounted on its shoulders bathed the back of the machine's chassis in napalm. Streams of burning jellied gasoline drizzled off the steel behemoth, setting fire to the ground below.

The flames were still spewing like the breath of Hell when Logan made a solid landing on the cockpit canopy and tore it apart with three easy hits. Metal and glass scattered like confetti, stinging his exposed chest. Then there was nothing between Logan and the battlesuit operator except the man's nine-millimeter sidearm. Flashes of fire pulsed from its muzzle.

Bullets slammed into Logan's gut and chest. They only hurt. After the fourth shot, Logan tore the weapon from the man's grasp, chucked it into the air, and cut it to pieces with his claws. Metal fragments and gunpowder dusted the inside of the cockpit. Logan retracted his claws and pummeled the battlesuit pilot. Ribs cracked like toothpicks, a collarbone snapped with a wet popping noise, bloody sputum flew in long streams with each sledgehammer hit. The man's nose flattened from a single jab and dumped bright red blood down the front of his jumpsuit.

He'd stopped fighting back and lifted his open hands instead. "*Perestan!*" he cried through broken teeth. "*Ya sdayus!*... I surrender!" Logan ceased his attack and backed off.

The rational part of Logan's mind came slowly back into focus between heaving breaths. The adrenaline rush subsided, leaving only enervation and trembling limbs. Making eye contact with the battered Russian, he asked, "You work for Pritikin, right?" The man nodded weakly. "I figured. I'm gonna let you live so you can give him a message." He leaned into the cockpit and poked the man's chest as he spoke. "What happened at the mansion was business. But this"—he gestured at the battlesuit—"this makes it personal." Yanking the man by his collar until he was halfway out of his seat, Logan snarled and lowered his voice to a menacing whisper. "You tell that sonofabitch I know who he is—and now I'm *pissed off*."

He head-butted the man unconscious, dropped him back into his seat, then used his claws to destroy what was left of the cockpit. The machine's internal power plant shut down with a pathetic, falling whine.

The walk back to the van was long, cold, and painful. By the time Logan rejoined Wai Ying and Ziv, the van was idling at the south end of the tunnel, ready to resume its journey to Pulkovo Airport. He climbed in through the open back doors and shut them behind him. Then he sagged to the floor, exhausted.

"Are you all right?" Wai Ying asked.

Logan sighed. "Just tell me there's beer on the plane."

COOL and slick with condensation, the unopened bottle of Molson Golden pressed against Logan's temple was the perfect remedy to the pounding headache that lingered in his skull.

As soon as he, Wai Ying, and Ziv had reached the plane, he had grabbed the beer from the fridge and collapsed onto one of the luxurious padded seats in the passenger cabin. He'd sunk into the deep embrace of the broad seat and savored the frosty relief of the beer bottle on his brow. After a minute, he'd twisted off the cap and guzzled the brew, then asked Ziv to fetch him another. The two old friends had repeated that scenario several times in the past hour, to the point that Logan had lost count of how many beers he'd had, not that it really mattered, since his mutant healing factor made it impossible for him to get drunk—much to his chagrin.

Logan put down the beer bottle and opened his eyes. Ziv sat on the other side of the fold-out table between their facing seats, which were near the front of the cabin. The Russian tapped and clicked at Wai Ying's laptop computer. His brow was creased with fervent concentration. Yawning, Logan rubbed the fatigue from his eyes, then he opened the beer. "Where are we?" he asked, and took a long swig.

"Making our descent into Vienna," Ziv said without looking up from the computer screen.

"Whadda we got? Anything interesting?"

"Perhaps," Ziv said. "Pritikin's security was really quite good—kind of a new twist on visual matrix encryption—"

"Can we skip the gee-whiz crap and get to what I need to know?" Logan's headache was still bothering him, and he was in no mood to sit through one of Ziv's jargon rants.

Ziv, clearly annoyed, grunted and turned the laptop toward Logan. "Aside from the garden-variety money laundering that goes with paying off politicians, most of Pritikin's business and personal finances are fairly ordinary."

One of Ziv's bad habits that had worsened with age, in Logan's opinion, was his tendency to withhold information for dramatic effect until someone asked for it. Since the only other person in the cabin with Ziv was Logan, that task had unavoidably fallen to him. "Most are ordinary? Which ones ain't?"

Reaching over the top of the screen, Ziv pointed at a highlighted line on a complicated-looking spreadsheet. "This one. Six months ago, Anbaric Petroleum bought a six-thousand-TEU container ship, the *Pandora*, Liberian registry."

The numbers were nothing but a jumble to Logan. He shrugged. "What's so odd about that?"

"His company operates nearly four hundred oil tankers, but until six months ago they'd never owned a freighter."

"Maybe he's expanding his business," Logan said.

Leaning across the table, Ziv tapped a couple of keys on the laptop. Two new windows crammed with data opened on the already crowded screen. "In the six months since the ship has belonged to Anbaric Petroleum, it hasn't delivered even one piece of cargo, anywhere. It's made three refueling stops, but until a few days ago it'd never taken aboard even one piece of freight. Yet a satellite photo shows its deck fully loaded."

"Okay," Logan said. He pointed at the screen.

"What else?"

"The *Pandora*'s last port of call was Pôrto Alegre, Brazil—easy trucking distance from the site of your little dust-up in Foz do Iguaçu. She made port the day after your Osaka robbery, received a sealed, forty-foot 'hicube' shipping container, and weighed anchor as soon as it was aboard."

"And where was it heading?"

"Next port of call," Ziv said, "Cape Town, South Africa."

Shaking his head in disbelief, Logan said, "You came up with all this in just an hour?"

"What can I say?" Ziv replied with a faux-humble shrug. "I'm a professional. I also checked on your playmates from Brazil." He tapped a key on the laptop. Pictures of the fair-haired twins who'd attacked Nando's house appeared on the screen. "Oskar and Gregor Golovanov, a.k.a. Slake and Surge. Part of the Soviet mutant-research program in the late eighties." It was hard for Logan to tell, but he felt as if his headache was getting worse the longer Ziv kept talking. "Oskar's a power siphon, has a gift for absorbing electrical current. Gregor's the blaster, releases energy as heat, magnetic pulses, lightning, you name it." Another key tap called up old KGB dossiers about the brothers. "They're symbiotically linked," Ziv continued. "Without Oskar, Gregor's got no power. And if the KGB's tests are right, without Gregor, Oskar is a walking time bomb." He closed the laptop. "They escaped Soviet custody a couple decades ago, went rogue."

Giving free rein to his rotten mood, Logan replied, "Is this gonna be on the test? 'Cause I forgot to take notes."

"Have another beer," Ziv shot back, rolling his eyes.

Outside, the nighttime lights of Vienna rose to meet the Cessna jet. With a mechanical whining and grinding, the landing gear unfolded from the aircraft's nose and belly.

Wai Ying called back through the open cockpit door, "Buckle up, boys, we're about to land."

While Ziv put away the laptop, Logan shifted his half-empty bottle of beer to the drink holder on the narrow maple-wood shelf beside their seats. The high, melodic hum of wing flaps adjusting to a landing configuration sent sympathetic vibrations through the deck. Ziv opened the wall panel, folded down the hinged tabletop into the bulkhead, and secured the panel in its closed position. Then both men fastened their seat belts and settled back to await wheels-down in Austria's capital.

"So what do you think?" asked Ziv.

Logan downed another swallow of beer. "I think we have to find that ship."

13

NISHAN carried her barely conscious daughter along a dirt road choked with charred debris, festering excrement, rotting bodies, and a horrifying array of living human wreckage.

Entire families lay collapsed together from exhaustion and dehydration. Peering through the honeyed light of a drifting dust cloud, Nishan tried to find the end of the line for food and water; a Red Cross truck had arrived just minutes earlier with fresh supplies. As the dust curtain passed, her already meager hopes diminished again. The bedraggled parade of the sick and the dying that had packed this road *was* the line.

"Hang on, my angel," she whispered to Kanika, whose fragile body sagged limply in her arms. The girl's eyes were dull and unfocused, as if staring into another world—or perhaps into the next world, the land beyond life's border. Breaths came slowly to her now, and her chest barely rose with each feeble gasp.

Wary of anyone and everyone, Nishan looked back and made certain that no one had disturbed the threadbare lean-to shelter she had built for the children. It had taken her most of the day yesterday to scrounge unburned wood and mosquito netting from the lost buildings. Nadif, who was faring as poorly as his sister, lay there now, alone and awaiting Nishan's return, which seemed much longer delayed than she had expected. The choice to carry Kanika had been motivated by practicality as much as by precaution; even though both children were frighteningly emaciated, Nadif was still taller and heavier than Kanika. And since Nadif was a boy, Nishan did not have to fear that he might be raped while she left him to fetch water and food.

"Maybe they'll have medicine," Nishan whispered to her daughter, even though experience had taught her the folly of hope. Kanika continued staring at nothing; she no longer responded to the sound of Nishan's voice, and her skin felt radiantly overheated all the time now, even in the deep watches of the night. Dr. Charoenying's grim diagnosis had haunted Nishan for several days. Now she knew the truth, felt it in her soul: her children were going to die. It was no longer a question of if, but of when and how painfully.

Up ahead, nearly fifty meters away, the crowd surrounded the Red Cross truck like ants swarming on a fallen morsel. Fear and desperation twisted through everyone, binding them like a chain, shackling them with misery. It had been less than five minutes since the volunteers on the truck had begun dispensing clean water and bags of grain, but already the crowd susurrated with fearful whispers: *What if there's not enough food for everyone? What if they run out of water? I need medicine—do they have medicine? Shouldn't the old people go first? Shouldn't the children go first? Why can't pregnant women go first?*

From the sky overhead came the steady *whup-whup-whup* of a circling black helicopter with American markings. Its thumping rotor noise was like a demon's drumbeat. Inside the helicopter, men who looked well fed and bored slouched against their mounted machine guns. Once, many months ago, Nishan had asked Dr. Maguire if there was a risk that the helicopter men might fire on the villagers. The white-haired Irishman had responded with a mirthless laugh and ruthless honesty: "The Americans don't think you're worth the cost of a bullet."

The crowd's murmured worries turned suddenly into an electric current of panic. Women grabbed up their infants and struggled to push free of the clutch of pressed bodies. Children on the fringe of the mob scattered. The men nearly trampled them all in their haste to save themselves. Everyone fled from the Red Cross truck. Then a new sound drew closer, and Nishan was finally able to discern it from the helicopter's incessant, thundering tempo: hoofbeats.

All around Nishan people were frantic, looking for anyplace to hide. Some crawled beneath the maggot-ridden corpses in the road and pretended to be dead. Others ran out toward the plains, hoping to take cover in the parched brown stands of tall grass. Nishan stood her ground in the middle of the road. There was no place she could run to while carrying Kanika, so she decided not to waste the effort.

Dozens of dust-covered men on camelback rode past Nishan, all of them firing short bursts from their assault rifles and whooping in some Arabic dialect. Quickly they surrounded the Red Cross truck. Angry words flew back and forth between the men on the truck and the Tanjawar militiamen. The argument came to a quick end when the unarmed Red Cross volunteers found themselves looking into the muzzles of a dozen Kalashnikov rifles. Seconds later, with strict military efficiency, the Tanjawar commander directed the off-loading of all the truck's supplies, which were packed into the militiamen's mostly empty saddlebags and backpacks.

It was a routine that Nishan had seen before. First the Tanjawar would devastate a village and make certain that word of the pillaging reached the government in Kaltoum. Then the government—which made only the most superficial effort to pretend that it didn't, in fact, endorse and sometimes direct the Tanjawar's rampages—would dispatch a fresh shipment of aid supplies, under the watchful gaze of one Western peacekeeping force or another. Then the Tanjawar, always in need of fresh supplies for their troops, would steal the aid shipment. The peacekeepers, Nishan had been told, were not allowed to intervene unless the Tanjawar fired upon them directly. If some civilians were killed, or if some homes were reduced to cinders, the peacekeepers dismissed it as an "internal Zibarese matter." In other words, they did absolutely nothing.

The militiamen finished loading the truck's cargo onto their camels. A rallying cry from the leader sparked wild stutters of gunfire and a chorus of prideful yells. Then they galloped their camels away toward the nearby hills.

The angry chatter of their battle rifles lingered in Nishan's memory like the sulfurous bite of gunpowder in the air. She stood in the middle of the road, staring at an empty truck and a future that held nothing but broken promises.

Part of her was grateful; the Tanjawar had been so intent on raiding the supplies that they had paid no mind to her or Kanika. Then she looked down at her dying child's face—and cursed the Tanjawar for not being more generous than the Americans with their bullets and sparing her and her children from the dark promise of slow death that now circled them.

Nishan turned and walked slowly back toward the shelter where Nadif lay, silent and expiring by degrees. The fresh supplies were gone. There was nothing left to do now but conserve the few drops of water that they had left and try to make it through another night. For a moment, she considered praying for a miracle.

Then she remembered: *This is Africa. There are no miracles here.*

14

EXITS ticked by while Logan stared out the window at the blur of the landscape, happy just to be back on the ground after a long night in the air. He'd flown the Cessna jet from Vienna to Addis Ababa, Ethiopia, and then on to Cape Town, while Wai Ying had slept. They'd touched down just before dawn, local time, at Cape Town International Airport and had cleared customs just after seven o'clock. At Ziv's suggestion, Wai Ying had agreed to keep a low profile as they left the airport; she'd hired a privately operated minivan to take them to a hotel.

Tinny pop music warbled from the minivan's dashboard speakers as it raced up the N2 highway, past seemingly endless clusters of shantytown shacks. The sprawling squalor grew sparse, then surrendered to the rising gleam of the city, which glittered in the long morning light. Summer was in full force in the southern hemisphere, and the air was humid and strangely alive with the promise of a scorching afternoon to come.

From a distance, the city looked like a clumsy patchwork, a hastily assembled grid with random patches of forest breaking up the brown slopes of sun-parched hillsides. It reminded Logan of the fur of a dog afflicted with mange.

Twenty minutes after leaving the airport, they had switched from the N2 to the N1, which skirted the waterfront near Duncan Dock. A few minutes later the driver followed Wai Ying's directions and got off the highway at the Coen Steytler exit, which he followed out toward the Victoria & Alfred Waterfront hotels. To the right of the minivan, the turquoise waters of Table Bay rippled and shimmered beneath a pale sky. Brightly colored sails unfurled as a handful of private boats navigated gracefully out of Victoria Basin into the bay, toward Robben Island and the open sea.

The minivan followed the edge of the waterfront and began heading northeast on Breakwater Boulevard. The eastern view was dominated by the rough-hewn slopes of Table Mountain, which, along with Signal Hill, gave the city an almost mythical quality.

Soon the driver turned the minivan onto East Pier Road, then slowed and came to a halt at one of the largest and most opulent accommodations in all of Cape Town: the Table Bay Hotel.

Wai Ying thanked the driver in Afrikaans and paid him in a fistful of South African rands that Logan hadn't even realized she'd been carrying. By the time he and Ziv exited the minivan, she was already directing the hotel's porters to unload their luggage and summoning the concierge to expedite her check-in, which she'd reserved the night before from Vienna.

Ziv and Logan stood together, hands in pockets, staring up at the magnificent white palace of a hotel that towered before them. Finally, Ziv just shook his head. "She has to be kidding."

"I'll give her this much," Logan said as he took two Cuban cigars from his pocket. "She knows how to pamper herself." He handed one of the cigars to Ziv. "Can I borrow your cutter? I'd rather not make a scene with the claws."

Nodding, Ziv found his cutter, trimmed the edge from his own robusto, then handed the miniature guillotine to Logan. "It's extravagant," Ziv said, gesturing at the hotel. "But it makes sense. As long as we get rooms facing east, we'll have an unobstructed view of both Duncan and Schoeman docks."

Logan clipped the end of his own cigar. "We could've had that from the Holiday Inn," he said, handing back the cutter. Fishing out his lighter, he added, "Instead, we're running our stakeout from a five-star hotel with a sailboat marina." He flicked open his Zippo and ignited his cigar, then held the flame steady for Ziv while he lit his.

After savoring a few puffs, Ziv exhaled a mouthful of sweet smoke. "And the problem with that would be what, exactly?"

"Never said it was a problem," Logan replied. "I'm just worried, that's all."

Concern colored Ziv's expression. "Worried? Why?"

Logan grinned. "Because I'm startin' to get used to it."

○———————○

JUST as Logan had expected, Wai Ying had set herself up in the best accommodations the hotel had been able to offer and declared her luxury suite to be their new base of operations.

He wasn't complaining, by any means. Throughout the many decades of his life, he had stayed in some miserable places: a roach-infested cold-water flat in Madripoor, a hostel in East Germany whose cots all had been rife with lice, a thatched-roof hut in Sri Lanka that had only served to slow down the rain rather than keep it out. He wasn't even counting the numerous hard nights he'd spent in the wilderness, whether it had been the frigid, knifing cold of a Canadian winter in the Rockies or even just the banal misery of huddling among the homeless beneath a highway underpass during an Arizona summer.

Now, courtesy of Wai Ying's seemingly unfettered expense account, he and Ziv had been booked into their own luxury rooms. Rarely had he ever lived so lavishly. Even at the Xavier Institute, his accommodations had been modest; he'd stayed in a private dorm room like most of the other adults. Now he found himself in a bright, airy, expansive space. With a king bed. And a big-screen, high-definition, satellite-signal television, unlimited access to a minibar, and round-the-clock services of every kind, from food and laundry to anything else he could ask of the concierge. All he could think of was to request more cigars.

Though he considered his room extravagant, it was nothing compared to the accommodations Wai Ying had arranged for herself. She was comfortably ensconced in the Lion's Head presidential suite. It boasted an entrance hall, a lounge, a fully equipped kitchen, a dining room, a dressing room, and a spa bath with scenic views, all in addition to a bedroom that, by itself, was more than twice the size of Logan's room.

More important to their mission, however, its balcony offered a commanding view of the Victoria & Alfred Waterfront, including the entirety of the commercial docks to the east. Beyond the orderly gridwork of the city jutted Table Mountain, the defining feature of Cape Town's landscape.

Logan and Ziv stood on the balcony, observing the activity below. At the moment, it was Ziv's turn to look through the binoculars that had been purchased for them by the concierge, at Wai Ying's request. Logan asked, "Anything coming in?"

"*Nyet,*" Ziv said as he scanned the horizon.

Logan didn't need binoculars to examine the container ships that were currently in port being serviced by the row of cranes. Even from several kilometers away, he could discern the names painted on the ships' hulls. None of them was the *Pandora*.

"I'm getting hungry," Logan said. "Are you hungry yet?"

Ziv lowered the binoculars. "It's only been an hour since breakfast."

"Boredom gives me an appetite," Logan said.

Inside the suite's lounge, Wai Ying's cell phone rang. Ziv and Logan both looked back at it. Wai Ying strode in from the bedroom, attired in a new, dark burgundy variation of the same suit she'd been wearing when Logan had first met her, several days ago in the cemetery. She picked up the ringing phone and answered it, then paced away toward the dining room.

"Slave to fashion, that one," Ziv remarked.

With a shrug, Logan replied, "I've seen worse."

"Let me guess," Ziv shot back with a grin. "That girl in Prague?"

"For one," Logan said, remembering the alluring female spy from the Eastern Bloc who had tried to seduce him on Ziv's orders, back when they were still competitors in the Cold War. "I was thinking more of that Hungarian girl you strung along by promising to help her become a supermodel."

Ziv feigned indignation. "I thought she had potential."

"You thought a five-foot-three twenty-six-year-old with a chipped front tooth was gonna be a supermodel? Gimme a break."

"What can I say? I'm an optimist." He lifted the binoculars and made another slow pan of the horizon. "You're right, I'm bored and hungry. Are they still serving breakfast?"

Logan checked his watch. "No."

"Damn," Ziv said. "I could've gone for more eggs Benedict."

"Yeah, what a shame," Logan said. "Your life is so hard."

An updraft carried the scent of chlorine from the hotel's Jacuzzi and the brine of the harbor. Seagulls floated on the noonday air, wings glowing with reflected sunlight. From the marina and boardwalk came the sounds of music and laughter, people talking, the ringing of a dock bell. Aromas from several varieties of food teased Logan's hyperattenuated olfactory sense. Yet, with such a rich spectrum of sensory delights to hold his interest, he found himself focused on the sound of Wai Ying's hushed voice from two rooms away. He couldn't hear what she was saying, but he could sense the extremely agitated way that she was saying it. As she returned to the lounge, she shot a look of exasperation toward Logan, who nudged Ziv.

Walking toward the two men, she flung away her cell phone onto the couch. "You can stop watching the harbor," she said.

"What happened?" Logan asked.

She rolled her eyes. "The official story? Twenty-four hours ago, a freak storm sank the *Pandora* in the South Atlantic."

Ziv groaned. "Where did she go down?"

"No one knows," Wai Ying said. "Lost without a trace, no survivors. Just gone."

"Hang on," Ziv said. "What about its GPS system?"

Wai Ying shook her head. "They lost the signal from its transponder about an hour before they lost radio contact."

"Convenient," Logan interjected. "The most reliable part of the entire navigation system failed, but the radio still worked so they could tell us about it—for the record."

"Exactly," Ziv said, nodding. "It's still out there."

Wai Ying shook her head. "Not likely. Setsuko called in a favor with a friend at the NRO. They came up with nothing."

"Doesn't make sense," said Logan, whose years of work for the intelligence community had acquainted him with the abilities of the U.S. National Reconnaissance Office. "I don't care where that ship is—on the water or under it—they can find it."

"The Classic Wizard network?" Ziv asked.

"Exactly," Logan said. "They could find a rowboat in the middle of the Pacific if they wanted to. No way they'd miss a container ship."

"Not if someone found a way to hide it from them," Ziv said. "You saw that optical-cloaking tech Pritikin's walking tanks were using. What if he figured out how to put it on a ship? It might be invisible to radar, sonar, and satellites."

"Well, get ready for bad piece of news number two," Wai Ying said. "Pritikin himself vanished yesterday. We had four satellites tracking his every move; there's no record of him leaving Russia, but the next thing we knew he was gone."

"First his ship sinks, then he goes missing," Ziv said. "Forgive me if I don't send lilies to his memorial just yet."

"After everything he and the Hand went through to get their hands on Panacea," Logan said, "no way they're gonna let it get lost at sea. Betcha ten to one Pritikin's on that ship."

Wai Ying folded her arms and looked back and forth between Ziv and Logan. "Gentlemen, we have to find that ship. *Now*."

"Then what are we waiting for?" Ziv asked sarcastically. "Let's get to work. I'll take the Atlantic. Logan, you take the Pacific. Miss Tse, be a dear and check the Indian Ocean. After all, it's just an invisible ship, floating somewhere on the continuous body of water that covers three-quarters of the planet's surface. How hard could it be?" Wai Ying's eyes narrowed as she fumed silently in Ziv's direction.

Logan walked away. "I'll be in the bar."

○———————————○

A neon-orange X marked the spot. Despite the bulky headphones that protected Alexei Pritikin's ears, the rotor noise drowned out every other sound as the sleek EC-135 passenger helicopter descended toward the landing pad on the container ship's aft deck. The struts touched down with a wobbling bump, then the helicopter settled to rest. Ground crewmen crouched as they jogged to Pritikin's door and opened it for him. He unfastened his safety harness, removed his headphones, and climbed out of the chopper into the painfully loud clamor and swirling winds of the rotors' downwash.

Although the vessel was at anchor in a secluded harbor, the horizon still rocked in a manner that made him queasy. Pritikin had never liked the sea; he'd bought a yacht strictly for entertaining clients, but he had yet to unmoor it from its slip in Odesa; feeling a tide of nausea churn in his stomach and vertigo spinning in his head, he doubted he ever would. It took a great effort to hide his seasickness as he crouched and hurried away from the chopper and down a few short flights of stairs to a lower deck, where Keniuchio Harada waited for him, attired as ever in his impeccable silver-gray business suit.

Harada nodded to greet Pritikin and yelled over the rotor noise, "You made good time."

"What the hell am I doing here?" Pritikin shouted back, skipping the pleasantries and cutting to business.

With a tilt of his head, Harada invited Pritikin to follow him. He guided him away from the landing pad toward a starboard hatch that led to an interior passageway. Once the heavy metal hatch closed behind them, the noise from the helicopter was gone, replaced by the low hum of the ship's internal ventilation and plumbing systems. The passage was claustrophobically close; its low overhead was packed with thick pipes and steam-hissing valves.

"Sorry to tear you away from your business in Russia," Harada said. "It's just a precaution."

"A precaution?" Pritikin had been unhappy at being summoned by Harada. If it turned out to be for nothing, or for something trivial, he was going to be furious. "Against what?"

They turned left and descended a steep, narrow stair-ladder toward the main deck, several flights down. Their shoes clanked loudly on the gray steel steps. "Wolverine learned more than we thought during his visit to your home," Harada said. "He and his friends are in Cape Town right now."

"So what?" Pritikin said, following Harada as he circled back to another ladder nestled directly behind the one they'd just descended. "The *Pandora*'s not going to Cape Town."

"And by now Wolverine knows that," Harada said, gracefully gliding down the ladder to the next deck and landing with perfect poise. "The problem, of course, is that he's looking for this ship at all. Clearly, he already knows too much."

Clambering down the ladder to rejoin Harada, Pritikin felt slow and clumsy—an unusual sensation for him, since he'd always enjoyed both excellent health and good coordination. Compared to Harada, however, he was a weakling, a doddering fool. The fact that Harada was more than two meters tall made the Japanese crime lord intimidating enough, but the clearly phenomenal strength and grace that he possessed made it obvious to Pritikin that Harada was something more than human.

Catching his breath, Pritikin said, "Let him look. No one's going to find this ship unless we want them to."

A wan smile conveyed Harada's derision. "Your cloaking system might fool the eye, Mr. Pritikin; it might even fool machines. But there are greater forces at work in this world. And against those, I fear it will be of little help."

Harada opened another hatch and stepped through onto the main deck. Noise from the helicopter and the ocean washed over them once more. An unbroken wall of multicolored steel shipping containers, stacked four high, stretched across the width of the ship. Ushered by Harada, Pritikin stepped through the hatch, then waited while Harada sealed it behind them. The deck had been freshly mopped; it was still streaked with rapidly evaporating, ammonia-scented liquid.

They walked toward the far left corner of the container mountain. "You still haven't explained why I need to be out here in the middle of nowhere," Pritikin said, hoping that bravado would mask his unease at being seasick.

"You are here, Mr. Pritikin, because you are currently the weak link in our security." Harada stopped at the padlocked doors of one of the bottom containers. The lock had a digital keypad rather than a numbered wheel or keyhole. Harada tapped in a lengthy sequence of numbers as he continued. "Though Wolverine knows the Hand is involved, his ability to identify our members is extremely limited. My role in our operation remains unknown to him. You, on the other hand, are an exposed asset." The lock's bolt released with a sharp *click*, and Harada removed it. "Wolverine and his allies could use you to compromise the security of the *Pandora*—if they knew where to find you." He opened the container doors, revealing a dimly lit corridor that stretched far longer than any one container's length and was intersected by other corridors. "The only place I can be certain they don't know how to find you... is here."

"I can't stay here forever," Pritikin said as he trailed behind Harada, who led him into the secret passages. "I have to be in Kaltoum tomorrow to meet with the Zibarese oil minister."

"And you will," Harada said. "As soon as my people handle the Wolverine problem."

"And when will that be?"

"Soon," Harada said.

They turned a corner into an intersecting corridor and arrived at a pressure lock. Harada opened the hatch, stepped through, and motioned for Pritikin to follow him. "This is the first decontamination phase," he said. "In the next compartment, we'll put on protective gear over our clothes." As soon as Harada sealed the hatch behind Pritikin, the lights changed to a ruddy crimson, then an electric blue. A hiss of rushing gas preceded a painful popping sensation in Pritikin's ears.

The next hatch opened automatically. They stepped through into a room with several baggy biohazard outfits hanging in open lockers. The hatch at the far end of the compartment was marked in several languages, warning that the area on the other side was a sterile environment. Pritikin put on one of the hazmat suits, helped Harada secure his own gear, then remained still while Harada returned the favor. Once their suits registered secure, Harada led him through into a small pressure lock. All the air was removed from the chamber, then the final hatch rolled open to reveal a masterpiece in chrome and steel.

Bathed in flat white light, two dozen stainless-steel fermenters stood in three rows of eight. The high-pressure, airtight bioreactors were linked by a complex series of pipes, valves, and wiring surrounded by temperature and pressure gauges and complex chemical analyzers. Each one was more than three meters tall and just as wide.

"It's all working properly?" Pritikin asked.

"Perfectly," Harada said. "Dr. Falco has done an admirable job under less than ideal conditions." He rested his right hand on the surface of one of the fermenters, as if stroking a beloved pet. "Every one of these is brewing five million doses of Panacea right now."

"How soon until they're ready?"

"The test batch will be ready for your meeting with the oil minister," Harada said. "The first full batch will be ready later that day. As soon as we can crate it, we'll send it on to the mainland."

"Excellent," Pritikin said. Nodding with his chin toward a window of one-way glass that looked in on Dr. Falco and his laboratory at the far end of the production plant, he asked, "When are we done with him?"

"As soon as the process is automated," Harada said. "Then we can shift production to the plant in Yangon."

"Good, good," Pritikin said. He started walking back toward the pressure lock. Harada followed him without complaint.

They didn't talk again until after they had navigated the complex process of removing the suits and decontaminating. Harada led Pritikin back out to the main deck. By now, Pritikin's seasickness had abated slightly, and he was able to appreciate the briny smell of the sea—for about five seconds, until he got a good whiff of diesel exhaust and felt a surge of bile climbing up his throat.

Harada looked amused. "Are you all right, Mr. Pritikin?"

"Fine," he lied. It took a moment before he could continue. "I'm glad your operation is running so smoothly. Now that I've completed my part of our agreement, when can I expect you to fulfill yours?"

Motioning for Pritikin to keep pace with him as they walked aft and back inside the superstructure that housed the ship's command center, Harada replied, "Steps are already being taken."

"Such as?"

"The foreign minister in Aschabad who blocked your pipeline request is being persuaded to change his mind," Harada said. "The mullah in Afghanistan who took your money and then reneged on the deal is being... replaced." He opened a door for Pritikin, then followed him through, pointing ahead and to the right, toward the officers' mess. "As for your former partner in Karachi, who cut his own deal with the Americans—we'll deal with him by tonight." They entered the officers' mess and were greeted by the mingled aromas of beef stew and fresh-baked rolls. "You needn't worry that I've forgotten our agreement. Your long-delayed Caspian pipeline will be approved within the week, and the funding for it will be in place as soon as Panacea makes its global debut."

Pritikin's face was warm with embarrassment. "I shouldn't have doubted you, Mr. Harada." He bowed his head. "I apologize."

"Not necessary," Harada said. "I should have kept you better apprised of our efforts."

With a wave, he summoned over a steward, then motioned to Pritikin to sit down with him. As soon as he and Harada were seated, the steward stood at attention beside their table. "What can I get for you, Mr. Harada?"

"Two bowls of stew," Harada said, "two Tsing Taos, a basket of rolls, and some steamed vegetables." He glanced at Pritikin, then added, "And a glass of water for my guest."

The steward nodded and walked briskly toward the galley. Pritikin looked askance at Harada. "A glass of water?"

"To wash these down," Harada said, handing him a pair of motion-sickness pills. "No offense, Alexei, but if you vomit on my suit, I will kill you."

That'd be funny, Pritikin realized, *if he wasn't completely serious.* "Hurry up with that water," he yelled to the steward.

○——————○

OSKAR Golovanov climbed the dark gray concrete stairs two at a time. He was in a hurry to reach his brother's room, which was on the ninth floor of the seediest dive hotel in São Paulo.

Walking up the back emergency-exit stairwell hadn't been Oskar's first choice; he had planned to take the lift. When it had finally arrived, however, after a delay of several minutes, its doors had opened to reveal an indigent man lying half-conscious and doubled over on its floor. A reek of body odor, wine-scented breath, and stale urine had wafted out of the lift car into the lobby. The stench was then further compounded by the man's sudden loss of bowel control.

And so, Oskar was climbing eight flights of stairs.

For the sake of keeping a low profile—and also for Oskar's peace of mind—he and Gregor had checked into separate hotels, under aliases. As always, Oskar had remained the principal contact for their orders from Mr. Harada. Less than twenty minutes ago, his cell phone had rung, and he had answered it promptly, to receive Mr. Harada's latest instructions.

Now his task was to relay those orders to Gregor, get him packed, and extricate him from whatever squalid catastrophe he'd wrought this time. True to form, of course, Gregor hadn't answered his cell phone or his hotel-room line when Oskar called to rouse him. Having no other choice, Oskar had accepted that he would have to collect Gregor in person, but he resented it all the same. He feared that his twin brother would likely be in no better condition than the man in the elevator.

Ever since their forced retreat from the fight in Foz do Iguaçu, Gregor had been even more sullen and violent than usual. Before Foz he had been grouchy, but now his temper had turned volcanic, and the liter bottles of alcohol that seemed never to leave his hand proved unable to drown his black moods.

At the eighth floor, Oskar pulled open the already ajar fire door and stepped into the corridor. Cigarette burns freckled the stain-blotched carpeting, and the bitter smell of old tobacco smoke seemed to cling to the tacky, yellowing wallpaper. He noted the ripped upholstery on an armchair that had been evicted from one of the rooms. Sickly greenish light oozed from the bare fluorescent fixtures overhead. Loose-cornered wooden frames hung just shy of right angles around art prints so boring that their selection had to have been the work of a committee.

As Oskar neared the end of the hallway, he heard the shattering of something fragile, followed by a feminine-sounding whimper of either fear or pain. *Business as usual for Gregor, then,* he brooded as he arrived at the door to his brother's room. Reluctantly, he knocked, then waited. Several seconds dragged by and became half a minute. Then came his brother's inebriated drawl from the other side of the door.

"Who ish it? Whaddayawant?"

"It's me, Gregor. It's Oskar."

He heard coughing through the door. "Go away, I'm fine."

"Open the door, Gregor. We have new orders, we have to go."

A groan turned into a growl behind the door, then came the *clack* and *thunk* and scrape of bolts and chains being unlocked.

The door swung open. Gregor hung off it like a monkey with no bones. He looked up with droop-lidded, bloodshot eyes and slurred, "Wherewegoing?"

"Cape Town," Oskar said. "Let me in. You have to pack."

Oskar gently pushed past his brother into the hotel room. Even by Gregor's standards, the level of damage was impressive. Enormous cavities had been punched or kicked or otherwise smashed through the drywall; every piece of furniture was broken to one degree or another. Broken glass sparkled on the floor, bathed in the hazy afternoon light that slanted steeply in through the shattered fragments of the window.

Oskar took a few cautious steps farther inside, mindful of what was crunching under his shoes. Amid the fragmented ruins of countless cocktail glasses, he found the pulverized remains of Gregor's cell phone. The room's phone and its television, he noticed, were both conspicuously absent.

Looking to the left, he eyed the bathroom. Water drizzled from the broken toilet bowl and cascaded over lethal-looking shards from the savaged mirror. Jagged-edged halves of bottles lay jumbled together in one far corner of the bathroom; in the other huddled a trembling, half-naked, bloodied woman.

Studying her face, Oskar felt pity for her. In all likelihood, she had been quite beautiful before she'd stepped inside this hotel room; she never would be again. Her face had been battered, her teeth broken, her lip slashed or possibly even bitten. Oskar couldn't tell, and he didn't want to know.

He sensed his brother lurking behind him, looking over his shoulder, eyeing his handiwork with false contrition. A sick glee that Gregor could barely suppress tainted his words with insincerity. "I got carried away," he mumbled.

"Go pack your things," Oskar said, burying his disgust in the cold baritone of professionalism.

Gregor shambled away and awkwardly retrieved various articles of clothing from the debris of his room. In the bathroom, Oskar tried to comfort Gregor's traumatized whore. "It's over," he said in a soothing, low voice. "Whatever he did to you, it's done. He's not going to kill you. I won't let him."

The prostitute said nothing, she just hugged her legs and tucked most of her face behind her knees, until all that he could see were her two eyes, wide and dark and frightened. She was so slight, so fragile-looking… against his better judgment, he let himself really look at her. She wasn't a woman; she was just a girl, probably not much more than fifteen years old. *Another of Gregor's appetites I wish I knew nothing about*, he realized. Revulsion churned hot bile into his throat, and he finally turned away, surrendering to the utter hopelessness of the situation. The best he could hope to do now would be to get Gregor out of this room as quickly as possible, before the local authorities caught wind of what Gregor had done.

A few minutes later, Gregor stood off-kilter in the middle of the room and clutched a lumpy, dark green canvas duffel. "I'm ready to go," he said, his breath rank with tequila fumes.

Oskar kept a grip on the back of Gregor's shirt, partly to propel his brother out the door and partly to keep him upright. Gregor weaved sloppily down the hallway.

When it came time to descend the stairs to the ground floor, it became obvious to Oskar that Gregor was not up to the challenge. To save time, he dropped Gregor's duffel of clothes down the meter-wide gap between the two sides of the switchback staircase. The canvas bag bounced its way down and struck the concrete floor far below with a heavy slap.

Then Oskar hefted his brother over his shoulder in a fireman's carry and portered him down the stairs, out the hotel's rear entrance, and across the street, where he dumped him unceremoniously into the backseat of their rented car—to which Oskar had wisely kept the keys. With Gregor safely in the car, Oskar returned to the hotel, retrieved Gregor's duffel, and brought it back to the car, where he tossed it into the trunk beside his own bags.

All the way to Guarulhos International Airport, Gregor mumbled in a drunken stupor. As they neared the rental-car return lot, Gregor sat up in the backseat, possessed of a sudden clarity. "Where the hell are we going?"

"I told you this at the hotel," Oskar said patiently. "We have new orders from Mr. Harada. We're going to Cape Town, South Africa, to kill Wolverine."

"Yeah!" Gregor roared, as if he'd just won the lottery. He interlaced his fingers and cracked his knuckles. "Payback time."

For the next three hours, until they boarded their flight to Cape Town, Gregor was a bundle of energy and nerves, like a boxer before a prizefight. Oskar knew that what he was seeing in Gregor was a classic bipolar mood swing. *He probably doesn't even remember what he did to that poor kid back at the hotel*, Oskar realized. *Probably doesn't remember she even exists… He's coming unglued.*

The prospect of Gregor going mad terrified Oskar, and not just because they were brothers. Even when Oskar wasn't trying to absorb energy, he did. There was almost no place on earth he could go without being exposed to some kind of directed energy; microwaves had become ubiquitous. It was a low-grade effect, enough that his presence could dim a lightbulb or garble a cell-phone call, but the gain was cumulative. Sooner or later, he would build up too much charge to hold on to.

If Gregor went insane, there was no predicting what kind of damage he might do with a full charge from Oskar. But an even more troubling scenario now kept Oskar awake at night: *What if he dies? What'll happen if I can't release the energy I absorb?*

Oskar didn't know the answer to that question.

He didn't want to know.

15

LOGAN took a breath, fixed his eyes on the TV above the bar, and counted to ten as Ziv waved a cell phone in front of him.

"Just make the call, Logan," Ziv said. He slammed the phone down next to Logan's plate, rippling the cocoa-dark surface of his pint of Castle stout. "The *Pandora*'s not coming to us, and we're out of leads. He's the only one who can help us."

Logan didn't know how Ziv and Wai Ying had tracked him to this local pub, nearly a mile from the hotel. It had taken him half a day to find a place that had decent food, good beer, Johnny Cash in the jukebox, and a bartender who was always ready with a light for his cigar. But in they'd walked, before he'd had more than two bites of his swordfish steak.

A sip of the stout and a puff of his Cuban, and Logan collected himself enough to look at Ziv and say, "I ain't talkin' to him, and you damn well know why."

Wai Ying leaned in from the other side and met Logan's glare with her own unrelenting gaze. "I don't. Tell me."

He took another swig of his beer. "No."

Even thinking about Xavier's betrayal made Logan angry, and he wasn't going to discuss it.

Ziv sighed and signaled Eddie, the bartender, to bring two more pints of stout. Looking past Logan at Wai Ying, he said, "Logan's the kind of man who holds a grudge."

"I never would have guessed," Wai Ying said flatly.

"This is none of her business," Logan cut in.

Ignoring him, Ziv continued, "A few years back, a mutant named Magneto tore out all of Logan's super-duper adamantium, nearly killed him."

"Grudge-worthy," Wai Ying admitted with a half-nod.

"Ziv, I'm warning you," Logan said, low and hostile.

"Skip ahead a few years," Ziv went on. "Everyone thought Logan'd hacked off Magneto's head. Xavier took Magneto's body back to Genosha for burial. Smiley here objected."

"He didn't deserve to be buried," Logan said, unable to hold the reins of his bitterness. "Shoulda left him rotting in the street, where dogs could piss on him."

In the mirror behind the bar, Logan noticed Wai Ying's urbanely arched eyebrow. Eddie set down the two pints of stout. Ziv picked his up, took a long sip, then continued his narrative. "So, bad enough that Xavier goes to show Magneto the respect of a funeral, but here's the funny part: it wasn't really Magneto that Logan iced. Some impostor or something. Anyway, make a long story short—"

"Too late," Logan grumbled.

"—Xavier and Magneto are working together, rebuilding the parts of Genosha that got leveled by the Sentinels."

An awkward silence fell over the trio. Everyone sipped their beer, and Logan savored a few rich mouthfuls of his robusto. The blue-gray smoke curled away in serpentine coils toward the slow-turning ceiling fan.

Logan's thoughts turned inward, to a part of himself that he didn't like to face. For years he had looked up to Professor Charles Xavier, had almost thought of him as a mentor. At a time when Logan had been convinced that he was coming to the end of himself, Xavier had offered him a chance to be something more than a living weapon, more than an animal prowling the fringe of the world: he had offered Logan a chance to live like a man. Then Charles had befriended the man who'd tortured Logan in ways more terrible than any he had ever known. Thinking of Xavier calling that monster a friend felt like the metal being rent from his bones all over again.

Wai Ying set down her beer and leaned her back against the bar so she could face Logan. "I've never met these people, but if what Ziv said is true, I think you're right to hate them," she said. "But I'm not asking you to invite them to dinner. This isn't a social call. We're talking about the lives and freedom of millions of people. Maybe billions."

He knew she was right. Servicing his grudge at the expense of innocent lives was an evil he couldn't live with. Glowering at his reflection in the mirror, he picked up the cell phone.

"This might take a few minutes," he said. "I don't exactly have him on speed dial."

He dialed the mansion in Salem Center, New York, identified himself to the switchboard operator, and asked to be connected to Xavier. Then he walked away to the most secluded corner of the bar, behind the jukebox, while the operator put him on hold.

About five minutes later, there was a click on the line, followed by Xavier's hesitant, cautious salutation: "Logan?"

Hearing the older man's voice provoked deeply conflicted feelings inside Logan. In many ways, Xavier had filled a paternal role in Logan's life; he had been all the things that Logan's father never was: patient, wise, and encouraging. But there was no forgetting where Xavier was, or why he was there.

That's not what this is about. Suck it up and do this.

"Yes, Charles, it's me." Acid crept up Logan's esophagus as he fought to keep his tone civil.

"The switchboard said this is an emergency," Xavier said.

"Sit down and get comfortable," Logan said. "It's kind of a long story." As quickly as he was able, he told Xavier about Panacea, the black-market deal and its link to Alexei Pritikin, and the missing ship and oil mogul. "So we need to find Pritikin," he finished, "before he and his pals start dolin' out Panacea around the globe."

"I'm not really sure I can find him, Logan," Xavier said. "You're asking me to seek out one mind among billions—a mind that I've never met before."

"C'mon," Logan said, incredulous. "I've seen you pull off harder tricks than this."

"Back when I had Cerebro, certainly," Xavier said. "But I don't have anything even remotely comparable here. I would have to reach out and try to isolate one unfamiliar voice from the noise of all the other human psyches on earth."

Logan hated when people avoided coming to the point. "Are you saying you can't do it?"

"I'm saying I can't make any promises," Xavier said.

"You don't have to. You're the best there is, Charles. And right now, you're the only chance we've got."

From the other end of the phone line came Xavier's tired sigh. "I'll do everything I can."

"Good enough," Logan said. He was about to say good-bye when Xavier cut him off.

"Logan… I know you resent my decision to stay in—"

"Don't apologize," Logan shot back. "You did what you did. Let's leave it at that."

"I wasn't apologizing."

Logan closed his eyes for a few seconds while he raged in silence. "The switchboard has my number," he said. "Call me when you know where Pritikin is."

"And if I can't find him?"

"Then a few billion people are gonna become slaves."

○————————————○

ALEXANDER Zivojinovich paced in front of his hotel-room window. Outside, sunrise had turned to early morning, and the long rays reaching through the streets of Cape Town felt new, as yet unspoiled by the disappointments of a day squandered. He hadn't slept well the night before. After goading Logan into calling Charles Xavier for help, Zivojinovich and Wai Ying had joined Logan for dinner at the pub before returning to the hotel. At that point, there hadn't been much else to do, and everyone had said a muted good night.

Bad dreams had fueled his restlessness, but now he knew that the real source of his anxiety was simply a lack of forward motion. *We've been at this hotel too long*, he chastened himself. *The ship's not coming, we know that. Staying in a place this flashy just draws attention. We should have moved to a less visible hotel yesterday.*

In the distance outside his window, Table Bay glittered, an azure canvas dotted with the colorful triangles of sails, which captured the warm breezes and propelled sleek boats through the gently rolling waves. Duncan Dock and Schoeman Dock both teemed with activity: forklifts and cranes shifted cargo; stevedores loaded and unloaded pallets; shipping containers were hooked to trailer trucks and hauled away.

It's another perfect summer morning in Cape Town, and I'm pacing my room like an inmate.

A glance at the clock confirmed what he already knew: it was slightly after half-past seven. *Time for breakfast*, he decided. *Then maybe I'll catch up to Wai Ying at the spa.* He slipped on a pair of shoes and a clean shirt, then left his room and took the elevator downstairs to the lobby.

As he'd hoped, the Atlantic Restaurant was open and not too crowded. On the way to a nearby open table, he stopped a waiter and ordered some coffee. For a moment he considered ordering the eggs Benedict again from the à la carte menu, but then a twinge of psychosomatic pain tugged inside his chest and he steered himself toward the buffet. Eyeing his options, he helped himself to a plate of fresh fruit, a bran muffin, and a pair of hard-boiled eggs. Temptation called to him again in the form of a chef's offer to prepare a fresh Belgian waffle with Canadian maple syrup, but a peek down at his own burgeoning waistline gave Zivojinovich the fortitude to refuse. Minutes later, however, the idea of "the waffle that might have been" made his low-fat, low-carb breakfast seem less than satisfying.

He finished his meal shortly before eight o'clock and charged it to his room. Upstairs, the health spa was moderately busy with guests exercising, getting massages, or swimming in the heated saltwater pool. Though Wai Ying had gone directly to the spa after checking in the morning before, and had made a point of boasting how she almost never missed her morning workout, she was nowhere in sight. Neither was she in the pool, or in the steam rooms or the Jacuzzi.

It's a wonder she doesn't already have me running errands, he mused with a grin. Wai Ying had made quite an impression on him in St. Petersburg; clearly the woman was a personality to be reckoned with and not inclined to leave things to chance. That trait was what he liked best about her, even if he found her personal style to be extravagant to the point of imprudence.

A short while later he stepped off the elevator and walked toward the Lion's Head suite. The door was propped open by a housekeeper's cart. He slipped inside past the cart and nodded to the maid cleaning the bathroom. The rest of the suite was quiet. "Wai Ying?" he called, and was answered only by the faint echo of his own voice. Walking quickly, he made a quick survey of the suite; her things were still there, but she wasn't. He took his cell phone from his pocket and dialed her number. The call dumped directly to voice mail; her phone was either off, out of signal range… or no longer functional.

More than forty years of service in the spy business had made Zivojinovich paranoid, and that paranoia had saved his life many times over. He flipped his cell phone closed, picked up the receiver of a phone in the suite's foyer, and pressed O. The front desk operator answered, and at his request connected him to Logan's room.

The phone rang four times, then it, too, went to voice mail.

His next stop was his own room, where he retrieved his SIG-Sauer P226 pistol and shoulder holster from the room's safe. He covered the weapon by donning a black sports blazer, so as not to draw attention in public. Then he proceeded directly to Logan's room, taking the stairs rather than the elevator. He emerged from the stairwell, one hand resting on the grip of his sidearm. There was no one in the hallway, no sign of trouble. He unholstered his pistol and stepped briskly down the hall to Logan's door. Fixing both his hands on his weapon, he held it in front of him and pressed his ear to the door. All seemed quiet.

He stepped to the hinge side of the door and put his back to the wall. With his foot, he tapped three times on the door.

Inside the room, a shuffling sound was followed by a grunt. Soft footfalls drew closer, and the bright pinpoint of light through the peephole was eclipsed. Then he heard Logan's voice through the door: "Ziv? Is that you?"

"Yes," he replied. "Let me in."

Metal *clacks* accompanied the release of the door's multiple bolts and latches, then it cracked open to reveal Logan's bleary stare and hairy bare chest. "Ziv, it's too damn early for—"

"Wai Ying's missing," Zivojinovich said. Logan didn't respond right away, so the Russian continued, "I checked her room. All her things are there, but she's not. She doesn't answer her phone, and it dumps right to voice mail. Considering the kind of people we've been pissing off lately, I think we—"

The bathroom door inside Logan's room opened, and Wai Ying padded out, sleepy-eyed and barefoot and attired only in one of the hotel's complimentary white terry-cloth bathrobes.

Suddenly, Zivojinovich felt monumentally stupid. He looked at Logan and struggled to find some way to backtrack or otherwise extricate himself from the situation with even a modicum of grace. Logan, for his part, said nothing, but his stare was enough to keep Zivojinovich silent as

Logan let go of the door, which closed with a frame-rattling thud.

Zivojinovich holstered his weapon, straightened his jacket, and grimaced with embarrassment as he walked to the elevator. "Well," he said to himself, "at least that wasn't awkward."

○————————————○

LUNCH later that day was exceptionally awkward.

Logan sat between Wai Ying and Ziv, who both kept their attention on the plates of food they'd barely touched. Not more than half a dozen sentences had passed between them since they met in front of the restaurant. Skipping breakfast had given Logan an appetite, however, and he was devouring a rare filet mignon and washing it down with neat whiskey.

Wai Ying sipped her water.

Ziv took a small bite of his lunch. "Good conch fritters," he muttered. Logan and Wai Ying both nodded mutely.

If I'd known everyone was gonna be this weird, Logan brooded, *I never woulda slept with her.*

Resting in the center of the table was Wai Ying's cell phone. A few times each minute, Wai Ying stared at it. Just as often, Ziv also eyed the phone. They were fixated on the small flip-top device, as if they could simply will it to ring.

Logan swallowed a large bite of meat, sipped his Maker's Mark, and set down the glass forcefully enough to get their attention. "Knock it off, will ya? You're makin' me edgy."

Wai Ying abashedly averted her eyes from the phone.

"Sorry," Ziv said.

It was a start. Logan returned to sawing off another chunk of his steak.

"We might want to switch hotels," Ziv said offhandedly. When he noticed Wai Ying's surprised glare, he added, "We don't need to watch the docks anymore, and this is a bit too high-profile to be safe."

Shaking her head, Wai Ying speared a forkful of salad. "We won't be here much longer. As soon as Xavier calls, we're gone."

"If he calls," Ziv grumbled.

"He'll call," Logan cut in, surprised at how quick he'd just been to defend Xavier, considering all that had happened.

Silence fell back over their table. Wai Ying picked through her salad, extracting the black olives and setting them aside. Ziv pushed a few pieces of his conch fritter to one side of his plate, then nudged them back to the other side. And they both kept trying to sneak glances at the cell phone.

"For Pete's sake," Logan said. "You look like you're waiting for someone to ask you to the prom. Just eat your damn lunch." He picked up the phone and stretched in his seat so he could tuck it into his pocket. "When it's gonna ring, it'll—"

The phone rang.

He scowled at it then glanced at his companions as he flipped it open. "Hello?"

Xavier sounded weak, out of breath. "Pritikin's in Zibara," he said. "In Kaltoum, the capital."

Logan couldn't hide his concern. "Charles, are you okay?"

"It wasn't easy finding him, Logan. Keeping track of him now is difficult. Someone or something is trying to hide him."

The Hand, Logan surmised. Their magical abilities sometimes extended to shielding their thoughts. They were probably helping Pritikin remain incognito while he aided them in whatever plan they'd set in motion for Panacea.

Logan asked, "Where is he now, specifically?"

"In motion," Xavier said. "He just got off a private jet, at Kaltoum Airport. He'll be leaving Zibara later today."

"And going where?"

"I don't know," Xavier said. "His mind is masked." His voice faltered as he added, "I can't track him much longer."

"You don't have to," Logan said. "We'll take it from here." His next words were not as difficult to say as he'd expected them to be. "Thanks, Charles. I owe you."

"Good luck, Logan," Xavier said, then he hung up.

Logan closed the phone and lobbed it across the table to Wai Ying, who caught it in one hand. "Call your people in Osaka," Logan said. "We need tracking satellites pointed at Kaltoum Airport. We're looking for a private jet that arrived in the last hour. The professor says it'll be leaving later today."

"When? Going where?" she asked, as she flipped open the phone and pressed the speed dial.

"No idea," Logan said. "But once the satellites have a lock, we can run this op from upstairs."

Ziv looked as if he felt left out. "Can I do anything?"

"Sure," Logan said, as he pushed away his plate and stood up. "Get the check."

○————————○

BACK in the Lion's Head presidential suite, Logan watched over Ziv's shoulder as the older man clicked through scads of satellite data, which had been routed from the NRO to Wai Ying's laptop in less than an hour. On the one hand, Logan marveled at the amount of pull that she and Tanaka Biotechnology seemed to wield in the global intelligence community; on the other, he wondered just how many U.S. federal laws had been violated acquiring this intel.

"I've got Pritikin's plane," Ziv announced. With a click, he magnified the image on the screen. It was a sleek, gleaming white twin-turbofan jet. "Looks like they're refueling."

"Let's get the Cessna ready to go wheels-up ASAP," Logan said. "We're not losing this guy again."

"He's not getting away," Ziv said. "We've got a tracking network in place now. Wherever that plane goes, we'll see it."

"Not good enough," Logan said. "I want to be right behind that sonofabitch wherever he lands next."

Ziv looked over his shoulder at Logan. "What for? We can track him in the air and on the ground. We can let him lead us to the *Pandora*. Even if it's cloaked, we'll be able to see where he goes dark and pinpoint the coordinates."

Shaking his head, Logan replied, "Waiting's too risky. If we try to reach it after Pritikin's aboard, they'll see us coming long before we see them. Besides, there's no guarantee the ship won't move before we get there. If I'm gonna take it out, I have to strike as soon as we find it."

With a dubious expression, Ziv folded his arms and swiveled his chair in Logan's direction. "And how will you get aboard the ship? Hide in Pritikin's luggage? FedEx yourself? Trojan fish?"

"Trojan fish," Logan repeated. "That's a good one. I'll add it to my list of possibilities."

"In other words, you don't actually have a plan."

"Sure I do." He snicked off the end of a cigar with one claw. "Same plan as always."

"You mean you're making it up as you go," Ziv said.

Logan flipped open his Zippo and lit his cigar. "Exactly."

Wai Ying stepped out of the bedroom and set down her last two suitcases against the wall. "I just talked to the bell captain," she said. "The hotel staff is packing your bags for you. They'll be downstairs when we're ready to go." She walked over and joined them at the laptop. "Where's Pritikin now?"

"Somewhere in the Zibaran capital," Ziv said. "We couldn't get a fix on his ground transport, so we have to wait for him to come back to his plane before we pick up his trail."

Logan waited for Wai Ying to respond, but after several seconds of silence, he noticed that she was staring intently at the screen, her mien pensive. Finally, she looked at him and said, "It can't be a coincidence that he's in Zibara. Not now."

Logan didn't know what she was driving at. "How so?"

"He's an oil man," she said. "Geologists have been saying for years that they think there's an untapped reservoir of crude under Zibara, but no one's been able to find it. Meanwhile, Zibara has epidemic infection rates for both AIDS and malaria."

Now Logan understood. "And what better way to seal a deal for Zibara's oil than to take its people hostage with Panacea?" He frowned. "Ziv, set up a signal intercept on the land lines from the control tower at Kaltoum Airport. Pritikin's plane has to file a flight plan before it lifts off. As soon as we know where it's going, I want to be wheels-up inside the hour."

"You got it," Ziv said. He turned to the laptop and went immediately to work on the wiretaps. Logan gave him a fraternal pat on the shoulder, then turned and made for the door.

"Where are you going?" Wai Ying said.

"Down to the gift shop," Logan said with a dour look at Ziv. "I want to see if they have any Trojan fish."

16

KHALEED al-Rashad was not an unreasonable man. A lifelong civil servant, he had built his entire career in government on the art of compromise, and on knowing which battles were worth fighting. It had been three months since Prime Minister Qamran el-Fatah had named him to Zibara's newest cabinet position, minister of petroleum resources. At the time, al-Rashad had thought it to be the most fortunate promotion he had ever received. Today, however, he was having the distinct misfortune of making the acquaintance of Alexei Pritikin, a Russian thug in an Armani suit.

"Bullshit," Pritikin said with a sneer as he flung the folder of economic projections back across the negotiating table. "I'm not spending billions to build your pipeline. First you want to tax me to death for *finding* your oil, now you want me to subsidize your national infrastructure, too?"

"With all respect, Mr. Pritikin," al-Rashad replied, "as Zibara's sole oil contractor, you would be reaping the greatest profit from that pipeline. It's only fair that—"

"Screw you," Pritikin interrupted. "I'm not paying for your pipeline. You are. And while you're at it, you can cut the export tariff in half. I'm running a business, not a charity."

Pritikin was the owner and chief executive of Anbaric Petroleum, which had pinpointed the locations of Zibara's once elusive reservoirs of easily recoverable, high-grade crude oil. If Anbaric Petroleum was accurate in its estimate of the reserves' volume—just over 109 billion barrels' worth—Zibara was the third-most oil-rich nation on earth, behind only Saudi Arabia and Iraq.

Apparently, Pritikin believed that his geologists' fateful discovery somehow afforded him immunity from Zibara's laws. Minister al-Rashad was finding it extremely difficult to disabuse Pritikin of this flawed assumption.

"Mr. Pritikin," al-Rashad began in a carefully practiced, diplomatically neutral tone of voice. "I am aware that your oil-exploration contract with Zibara grants you unique privileges with regard to drilling rights, as well as substantial financial incentives. But I am also certain that it does not exempt you from taxation, nor does it restrict our authority to levy new taxes. In addition, it obligates you to absorb up to fifteen percent of costs related to—"

"I've read the damned contract," Pritikin said. "Hell, I wrote half of it. But that was then. The situation has changed, and our deal is changing with it."

Civility was becoming increasingly difficult for al-Rashad. "Perhaps this is how one conducts business in Russia, Mr. Pritikin, but in Zibara, men are decapitated for lesser offenses than the breaking of a national contract."

"Save your threats for someone who's afraid of you," Pritikin said as he rose from his chair. His retinue of lawyers and junior executives did likewise. "You're reducing the export tariff by half, and you'll finance the pipeline without my money." He closed his brushed-aluminum briefcase. "Furthermore, Anbaric Petroleum will be deducting its exploratory costs from its revenues until our investment is recouped." Pritikin marched out the door, trailed by his entourage.

Determined not to let the arrogant Russian have the last word, al-Rashad followed him. As he elbowed his way forward through the crowd of young men in dark gray suits, al-Rashad became fatigued; his forty-eight-year-old body felt older than its years. By the time he caught up to Pritikin, they were outside in the afternoon swelter, descending the broad stairs of the Interior Ministry toward Pritikin's waiting black limousine and its SUV escorts. Prismatic flares of sunlight reflected off all the vehicles' immaculately buffed exteriors.

"You arrogant bastard!" al-Rashad shouted at Pritikin's retreating back. "By tomorrow, your competitors will be making us rich! Can you outbid ExxonMobil? Or ChevronTexaco? How much do you think BP will pay for exclusive drilling rights? You'll never take one drop of oil from my country! That's a promise!"

Pritikin stopped at the back door of his limo and turned to face al-Rashad. Squinting into the glare of the sunlight, Pritikin smirked. "Spare me your threats," he said. "You're going to agree to every one of my demands."

Al-Rashad pushed himself nose-to-nose with the smug Russian. "And why would I do that?"

The oil mogul almost chuckled as he opened the car door. Out of the car leaped al-Rashad's ten-year-old son, Mustaf. "Father!" the boy cried with joy as he pushed past Pritikin and hugged al-Rashad around his legs. The youth's eyes were bright with hope, his embrace strong, his footing rock-solid.

Al-Rashad rested his hand on his son's head and tried to conceal his horror that Mustaf was walking at all.

Sixteen months ago the boy had been diagnosed with osteosarcoma—bone cancer, the doctor had explained to al-Rashad and his weeping wife, Parveen—in both femurs. Every protocol had failed to halt the progression of the disease, which had metastasized into the blood vessels and surrounding tissues of Mustaf's legs. Radiation therapy was not helping. Last night the doctors had suggested to al-Rashad that they consider amputating both legs while there was still a chance to save Mustaf's life.

Breaking the news to Parveen had been heartrending. "Allah have mercy, Khaleed," she'd cried. "Allah have mercy on our son!" Now al-Rashad was staring at his healthy, smiling boy.

He looked accusingly at Pritikin. "Explain."

"It's called Panacea," Pritikin said. "It cures anything, as long as you keep taking it every day for the rest of your life. Fortunately, I have access to an unlimited supply." Pritikin motioned to his entourage to begin getting into their vehicles. Engines roared to life, and the humid summer air grew heavy with exhaust fumes. "Your son is now in perfect health," he continued, lowering his voice. "But if you don't meet my every demand before my plane leaves the ground in ninety minutes, the boy will never get another dose—and he'll be dead in less than seventy-two hours." He patted al-Rashad's cheek. "That's a *promise*."

Pritikin tousled Mustaf's black hair, then got into his limousine. As soon as the door slammed shut, the car lurched from the curb and accelerated away in a dusty nimbus, followed by its gleaming black convoy of SUVs.

Watching the procession of vehicles race away, al-Rashad clutched his son and wept in silence. He knew that he had no choice; he would have to endorse all of Pritikin's insane demands and convince the prime minister to accept them.

He knew that he ought to thank Allah for his son's life, but he couldn't… because that which had made Mustaf whole had also made him into a slave.

17

EDDIE the bartender set down Logan's braised lamb shank and crispy *pommes frites*, handed him a set of utensils wrapped in a napkin, then whisked away Logan's empty pint glass to refill it. With a flick of his wrist, Logan unfurled the napkin and caught the utensils with his free hand. Eddie had just brought back the refilled glass, and Logan had just begun cutting through a hunk of succulently tender meat, when Ziv barreled through the front door and halted at the threshold.

"We're rolling," he said.

Logan dropped his fork and knife on top of the bar as he stood up. He pulled a few hundred South African rands from his pocket and slapped it down. "Keep the change, Eddie."

Eddie waved farewell to Logan, who followed Ziv out the door.

Ziv made a beeline to an idling, black-sapphire BMW Z4 convertible and vaulted over the door into the driver's seat. Not feeling quite so dramatic, Logan circled around to the passenger side and opened the door to get in. Before he finished closing the door, the two-seat sports car shot like a rocket down the busy city street.

"So I'm guessing we're in a hurry," Logan said over the growl of the engine and the roar of the wind.

"*Da*," Ziv said.

The leather interior of the car smelled brand-new. A glance at the odometer confirmed that the car had less than six thousand kilometers on it. "Nice ride," Logan said. "Please don't tell me she put this on the corporate card."

"*Nyet*," Ziv said. "Borrowed it from the hotel parking lot." Ziv yanked the wheel hard and whipped the roadster through a wild turn onto Eastern

Boulevard, cutting off at least four other cars. Unlike most people Logan had ever met, Ziv tended to accelerate through turns instead of slowing down.

Logan pushed in the dashboard lighter and fished a robusto from his jacket's inside pocket. "What's going on?"

"Wai Ying's already at the airport," Ziv said as he swerved through a slow-moving knot of traffic. "Pritikin's plane filed a flight plan—they're en route to Murtala Airport in Lagos." A cacophony of car horns blared behind the Z4 as Ziv blew through a red light. "Customs'll clear our passports at the gate."

"Good to know," Logan said. The lighter popped out from the dash. He lit his cigar. "Can we catch up to Pritikin?"

Ziv whipped through a U-turn and cut off a line of cars on the N2 highway on-ramp. "*Nyet*. We can make Lagos in one hop, but we'll be about an hour behind him."

With the melodious precision of an opera singer, the Z4's engine changed its tune, rising and falling and climbing again, as Ziv pushed the car to its maximum speed on the highway. The risks that came with moving at that velocity didn't bother Logan, but he was irked that the gusting wind was rapidly devouring his cigar. He tapped a few centimeters of gray ash from its end and watched it scatter into the car's airstream.

Although the day had started out sunny, the sky was now growing overcast. The soot-dark bellies of storm clouds hung low overhead, promising a downpour. Logan exhaled a puff from his cigar. "Great flying weather," he said.

"This?" Ziv flashed a broad grin. "Try landing a Piper Comanche at José Martí International in the middle of a Category Four, while drunk on Two Fingers tequila." He waved dismissively at the leaden sky. "This is *nothing*."

Logan shook his head and almost laughed. "Whatever you say, Ziv. Whatever you say."

○——————○

OSKAR watched through his binoculars as the ground crew prepared the Tanaka corporate jet for takeoff at the East Hangar of Cape Town International. The fuel lines had been disconnected and put away, the wheel chocks were being removed, and the Asian woman who had thwarted them in Brazil was pacing beside the jet, talking on her phone, and checking her watch every ten seconds.

He and Gregor were concealed in an ancillary hangar that was part of the Aviation Center, across a taxiway from the East Hangar. While Oskar stood in the narrow gap between the towering hangar doors, peeking out through the field glasses, Gregor sat behind him on a Ducati motorcycle, slumped forward onto the handlebars, moaning through his hangover.

Though Oskar had pleaded with the flight attendants on the flight from São Paulo not to serve Gregor alcohol, his request had been ignored. Gregor had waited until Oskar went to the lavatory; during that brief interval Gregor had bribed the attendants into selling him more than twenty shots of vodka, which he'd promptly imbibed, knocking himself unconscious. Oskar had smelled the cheap spirits on Gregor's breath when he'd returned to his seat. Hours later, Gregor had awoken violently ill and vomiting into his own lap when the plane touched down in Cape Town. Oskar had not shown him the least degree of pity.

Gregor sat up, belched, and spit a thick wad of milky saliva onto the hangar's concrete floor. His voice was hoarse from vomiting. "Let's just frag the plane now," he said.

"No," Oskar said. "We wait for Wolverine to get on the plane. Take it out during liftoff."

"That's the dumbest thing I've ever heard," Gregor said. "I can barely see it standing still, and you want me to hit it when it's going over three hundred kilometers an hour? *Tvoyu mat.*"

"Takeoff is when they'll be most vulnerable," Oskar said.

Gregor fished one last tiny bottle of airplane vodka from his pants pocket and twisted off the cap. "Doesn't matter how vulnerable they are if I can't hit them." He downed the shot. "As soon as Wolverine shows up, I'm frying them."

Oskar frowned at his disheveled mess of a brother. "Are you sure you can hit them from here?"

"Give me enough juice and I'll just have to be close."

"That's not encouraging," Oskar groused.

Another glob of spit hit the floor behind Oskar's feet. "So much for my career in motivational speaking," Gregor said.

The sound of a sports-car engine echoed off the clustered buildings of the Aviation Center. A black BMW Z4 roadster turned off Beechcraft Road and veered toward the East Hangar. It screeched to a halt in front of the Cessna Thunderstar. Two men clambered out and walked toward the Asian woman. One of the men was Wolverine; the other Oskar had never seen before.

Lowering the binoculars, Oskar looked back at his twin. "They're here," he said. He stepped over to the circuit-breaker station. As soon as the wire cutters were in place to put him in touch with the electrical main, he nodded to Gregor, who turned the ignition key of the Ducati. It purred to life; then, with a twist of its throttle, it roared like a steel tiger.

Gregor put on his helmet and flashed an evil grin. "Juice me up, Oskar. It's showtime."

———o——————————o———

LOGAN was out of the BMW the moment it came to a halt. Ziv followed a half-second behind him, and together they walked quickly toward Wai Ying. She flipped her cell phone closed and raised her voice above the whine of the Cessna's engines. "That was Setsuko," she said. "They've identified the mole: a senior chemist named Jiro Kazaki."

Ziv asked, "Will he talk?"

"Not likely," Wai Ying said. "They found him in his apartment with his head cut off."

Logan frowned. "That's the Hand's idea of a retirement program." He nodded with his chin toward the Cessna. "Ready to fly?"

"We will be," Wai Ying said, "as soon as Ziv moves his midlife-crisis-mobile out of the way." She turned and started climbing the jet's fold-down stairs.

With a long-suffering shake of his head and a roll of his eyes, Ziv turned around and jogged back toward the Z4. Logan glanced in Ziv's direction as he moved to follow Wai Ying into the jet—then he saw a man on a motorcycle on the far side of the taxiway. The motorcyclist's hand was pointed in their direction and surrounded by a crackling halo of electricity.

Ziv's pistol was clearing its holster as Logan shouted to Wai Ying, "Shield!"

The BMW exploded in a yellowish-white fireball. Ziv's body disintegrated in the flash. Burning gasoline and glowing-hot debris slammed into Logan. His shirt shriveled and turned to ash. Airborne from the force of the blast, he tumbled wildly, then slammed facedown and slid hard across the tarmac. Fire cooked his skin and vaporized his hair, leaving behind only a sickening, acrid stench.

Nothing was left of his world but shadows and agony.

Waves of noise pounded in his head, like the crash of the ocean inside his skull. From somewhere far beyond the wall of sound came the crackle of flames and the shrill timbre of a panicked voice shouting his name. He tried to turn his head and get his bearings, only to discover that his eyelids had been cooked shut. His fingers curled in on his palms like dead spiders. A million blistering needles stabbed across his body, belatedly delivering the news that he had been burned alive. His face was pulled taut in a death's mask rictus of pain.

There was only rage now. Fury and darkness. The animal urge to survive, to pull free of a trap, to retaliate.

Brittle skin cracked and flaked and bled as he forced himself to crawl. The odor of his own flesh was sickly sweet in his nostrils. His mutant healing factor was sluggish, overtaxed.

All he wanted was to scream, to howl, to roar. Instead, hot air hissed in his throat—dry and soundless, wordless, empty and hollow, as primal and as inchoate as his suffering.

High-pitched and louder now, the voice of panic was bright in his mind, but words were too much, too difficult. His skin was on fire; his muscles twitched with violent spasms as he pulled himself over the unyielding ground.

Thunderclaps and flashes of lightning. The wrath of the gods was close now, so close.

As he dragged his charred body across the tarmac, he felt bloody pieces of himself being left behind, chunks of flesh cooked off his bones.

His left eye cracked open, and he forced it wide. Through a milky-red haze he recognized the familiar shape of the plane above him and, inside it, the watery outline of a woman beckoning frantically for him to come to her.

She was the one shouting. She was afraid.

Blinding light, like the sun pulled down from the heavens, surrounded the plane with a terrible booming. Heat washed over Logan's body, renewing the torture of his broiled flesh. The clarity of pain resurrected his voice in disjointed grunts and splutters as he clawed his way up the short staircase into the jet. A groan became a snarl and then a howl, and then swelled into a battle roar.

His right eye pulled open, just as watery and bloody as the left one had been half a minute ago. Coherence forced its way back into his thoughts, self-awareness reasserted itself.

Christ, I'm growing new eyes.

Wai Ying's voice was both strident and fearful. "Logan, do you understand what I'm saying? Answer me!"

He coughed out a mouthful of blood and phlegm.

"I... hear you."

A nerve-rattling blast rocked the plane, and Wai Ying's composure with it. She stood with her arms out to her sides, palms open and facing out, obviously fighting to shield the plane from the energy assault. "You have to fly the plane," she said, then gasped in pain and exhaustion. "I can't shield it and fly at the same time."

Lying on the deck of the passenger cabin, skin scorched into charcoal, his face and head and body all burned clean of hair, his clothes reduced to sooty rags... Logan almost laughed. "You've gotta be—"

"On your feet, soldier!" she snapped at him. "Get off the deck and close that goddamn hatch! *Now!*"

Hearing the order was like having a switch flipped inside his brain. Suddenly he was back in boot camp, all those decades ago, being conditioned by a Canadian Army drill sergeant, being infused with military discipline. An order was an order.

Red pulses of agony darkened his vision as he pushed himself onto his knees and then pulled himself to his feet. He found the automatic closing mechanism for the hatch and pressed it. With a hydraulic whine, it lifted shut.

"Get this bird in the air, soldier! Do it!"

Stumbling and weaving like a drunk, he caromed off the thickly padded seats, leaving dark blood smears as he went. He lumbered forward into the cockpit, where he fell backward into the pilot seat and landed heavily and off-center. His hands found the yoke by instinct, but he couldn't read the bright screens of instrument data. Doesn't matter, he decided. He shoved the throttle forward. The jet rolled toward the taxiway.

Another explosion of light and heat rebounded from the unseen barrier in front of the plane. Logan shielded his eyes with his forearm, which he now saw was still smoldering.

The jet reached the taxiway. Logan steered it to the right, toward the approach to the airport's main runway. Outside, the man on the motorcycle was accelerating forward in pursuit. Logan turned and looked back at Wai Ying. "Behind us."

She nodded feebly. Logan's vision had cleared enough that he could see she was weakened and bleeding from her nose. Each energy blast took a gruesome toll on her. Their only hope was to lift off and get above the cloud cover, where they could evade the fireballer's line-of-sight attacks.

The deafening percussion of multiple impacts followed the plane down the long taxiway. The safe taxi speed was posted at twelve knots; Logan pushed the Cessna to twenty knots and hoped no one pulled out in front of him. He crossed three taxiway intersections at full speed without incident and guided the jet through a slight right turn—against posted directions for aircraft movement—toward the main runway.

The Cessna jerked forward, jolted by the increasingly powerful blasts from their attacker. Logan closed his leathery, cracked, bleeding hand on the throttle. He increased the aircraft's ground speed to forty knots as he steered it left onto the main runway, then he pushed its turbofans to full thrust as he aligned the nose of the jet with the runway's center line for takeoff.

Fifty knots. Sixty. Seventy. The center line became a blur.

A jarring impact hammered the plane from behind. Logan fought to keep from losing control. His skin and muscles were knitting back together even now, and it felt as if his body were squirming with barbed fishing hooks. He winced against the pain.

When he opened his eyes again a second later, his vision was clear—and so was his view of the Boeing 767 cargo aircraft descending toward the runway ahead of him.

The Cessna hit a hundred and twenty knots. It was too late to stop. Logan's only hope was to increase his speed and try to slip under the 767 before it touched down, and pray that its pilots were able to see him and pull up.

A hundred and thirty knots: thirty-five more for the Cessna to reach takeoff velocity. He pushed the jet to its limit.

The hulking mass of the 767 loomed large outside the windshield. Tracking its descent against his acceleration, Logan realized that he wasn't going to make it. The Cessna was at a hundred and sixty knots;

he suddenly regretted all the times he'd said he'd rather be cremated than buried, because it looked as if he was about to get his wish.

Then the massive cargo aircraft's nose lifted. Wavy curtains of heat distortion shimmered behind it as its pilots struggled to climb over the Cessna Thunderstar.

Logan was about to call himself the luckiest canucklehead on earth when a massive red pulse of energy sliced over the Cessna and obliterated the 767.

A mountain of blazing wreckage and tons of decimated cargo dropped onto the runway in front of him. He pulled back hard on the yoke. The nose of the Cessna lifted, and the sleek business jet lanced through the bloom of orange flames and roiling black smoke. Its twin turbofans sputtered and whined in the heart of the fire cloud, then surged back to life as the jet broke through into open air. Its airspeed climbed rapidly—two hundred knots, then two hundred fifty. Numbers ticked swiftly higher on the digital altimeter. A few more blasts trembled the aircraft as it neared the low-lying clouds. As soon as the gray vapors embraced the plane, Logan banked left while continuing to climb. After a minute without more hits from below, he leveled their flight.

"We're clear," he said to Wai Ying, whose arms fell slack at her sides. She slumped forward and collapsed to the deck, drained of every last bit of strength and willpower.

Clutching the Cessna's yoke like a life preserver, Logan knew exactly how she felt.

○————————○

OSKAR sat on his idling motorcycle and waited for his brother.

Crooked pillars of smoke drifted and twisted away from the Aviation Center, toward the runway. Across the taxiway, small gasoline fires burned amid the car debris and black, carbonized soot. The humid air was heavy with fumes.

Sirens wailed, bleated, shrilled in the distance, grew louder. People were evacuating the Aviation Center and the East Hangar. Fire alarms rang steadily inside both buildings.

To the west, a couple of kilometers away, a gargantuan black mushroom cloud bled upward and spread across the dreary gray canvas of the sky. Oskar had felt his brother unleash a massive burst of energy a moment before the explosion that had spawned that terrifying plume of darkness.

The soft buzz of Gregor's motorcycle echoed ahead of him, off the walls of the hangar buildings, before he emerged from behind a corner and rejoined Oskar on the taxiway near the East Hangar. Gregor slowed quickly and rolled to a stop beside him.

Oskar noted his brother's scowl and knew the news wasn't going to be good. "They got away?"

"Lost them in the clouds," Gregor muttered as the shrieks of police sirens closed in.

"Then that explosion—"

"Cargo plane," Gregor said. "Tried to block the runway."

So much for making it look like an accident, Oskar brooded. "All the exits are closed," he said. "First responders are moving in."

Gregor was openly sarcastic. "Really? I was wondering what all those sirens were for. Thanks for the tip."

"The police are looking for us," Oskar said, waving his pocket-sized police radio scanner at Gregor. "Apparently, a few thousand people inside the airport saw a man on a motorcycle shooting at the planes." He tucked the radio back in his pocket. "The helicopters will arrive shortly, followed by every antiterrorist commando in Cape Town."

"What the hell was I supposed to do, Oskar? The girl with the force shields is tougher than I thought." His fists balled with frustration. "If I'd just had one more shot—"

"It's too late," Oskar said. "We're burned in Cape Town. I've called the daimyo for an extraction."

That brought Gregor up short. "You did *what*? Are you out of your goddamn mind? He'll kill us."

"Probably," Oskar replied, knowing that it was true. He revved the throttle of his Ducati and moved it into gear. "We're meeting him inside the auxiliary hangar in two minutes. Let's go." With a twist of his hand, he accelerated away. A moment later he heard the drone of Gregor's motorcycle following him.

They slipped through the narrowly open doors of the auxiliary hangar and veered left to a stop in the shadows. Both cycles' engines went quiet in a breath as they disengaged the ignitions. Oskar got off his bike and abandoned his helmet on the concrete hangar floor. He sat down on a crate and checked his watch; roughly thirty seconds remained until Mr. Harada would appear courtesy of his teleportation ring and pluck the twin mutants out of harm's way.

Looking back, he saw Gregor casting his eyes around the cavernous space, as if seeking something.

"What are you looking for?" Oskar inquired.

"A power source," Gregor said. "You'd better juice me up in case the boss is in a bad mood."

Oskar checked his watch: ten seconds to extraction. "If the boss is in a bad mood," he said, "it won't make any difference."

○————————○

WITHIN an hour after leaving Cape Town, Logan's body had repaired and rebuilt enough of his flesh for him to be in constant, torturous pain. Dry, desiccated hunks of skin sloughed off his forearms as rapidly regenerating dermis displaced it from below. The hair on his chest and arms grew so quickly that he could watch it get longer. And he knew that his facial and cranial hair was reëmerging because of the persistent, maddening itch that crawled over his scalp and the nape of his neck.

Reaching back to scratch, his hand separated from the plane's controls with a wet sucking noise. The handles of the Cessna's yoke were sticky with his dried blood and partially liquefied fatty tissue. A charnel odor hung thick and disgusting inside the confines of the jet. *Cleaning this up will be fun.*

The pain that burned across the entire surface of his body, though it was scathing and omnipresent, was almost manageable now. It added fire to his rage, and venom to his vow of revenge on the men who'd killed Ziv. He hadn't seen the second twin on the ground at the airport, but he remembered how Wai Ying had said they'd worked together in Foz do Iguaçu. The second man had been there somewhere. Logan was certain of it.

Ahead of the Cessna, puffy banks of clouds were stacked miles high, like organic sculptures of dirty cotton. The sapphire dome of the sky darkened to indigo high overhead. Forty thousand feet below, fleetingly glimpsed through mist-smeared gaps in the white skyscape, were the greenish-brown smudges of central Africa, creeping slowly under the Cessna's nose.

Wai Ying entered the cockpit in halting, unsteady steps. Resting her hand on the back of the copilot's seat for balance, she eased herself into it with the gingerly caution of the recently injured. Her nose had stopped bleeding. A patina of dried blood covered her upper lip and chin—dark brown, caked, and cracking like a thirsty riverbed. With bloodshot eyes she checked the instrument dashboard, then, apparently satisfied, slumped back into her seat. "You look messed up," she said.

"You've looked better, too."

She half smiled, then lowered her eyes as sadness dimmed her countenance. "I'm sorry about Ziv."

"Don't be," Logan said. "He lived like a soldier, and he died like one—on his feet."

She brushed a few stray locks of her tousled black hair from her face. "It just seems like a horrible way to die."

"Worse than some," Logan said. "Better than others. It was fast." He felt his own jaw tighten with anger. "What pisses me off is that he got iced by a couple of scumbags. Ambushed, like a punk in the street."

Conversation was scarce for a little while. Silence suited Logan just fine. Wai Ying busied herself checking their position and plugging numbers into the onboard computer. Logan focused on keeping the jet steady and true to its course. Finally, she sighed, with what sounded like both exhaustion and frustration. "We're losing time," she said. "Pritikin'll be on the ground at Murtala almost two hours ahead of us."

"I was afraid of that," Logan said. He looked up and around at the cockpit. "We've been feeling a bit weak on thrust ever since boom boy lit us up in Cape Town."

Wai Ying nodded. "That's part of it. I also usually project a conical force field ahead of the plane to reduce wind resistance and improve our fuel efficiency." Wiping some of the dried blood from her lip, she added, "I really don't feel up to it right now, though."

"We can't risk losing him in Lagos," Logan said. "If he pulls another vanishing act before I pick up his scent—"

She cut in, "I know, Logan. With the parts they acquired in Brazil, and the time they've had since then, there's no telling how much Panacea they've manufactured by now." After a momentary hesitation, she asked, "When you said 'pick up his scent,' you were speaking figuratively, right?"

"Take it any way you like," Logan replied. "But we have to catch up to Pritikin on the ground."

A devilish gleam enlivened her eyes. "Then we'll just have to make sure we know where to find him when we get there." She reached forward and picked up the copilot's headset from the second yoke. As she put it on, she was punching numbers into the radio communications interface.

He started to ask, "What are you—"

She silenced him with a show of her palm. A moment later, she was speaking into her headset mic, to someone on the ground.

"Operator? Patch me through to the NDLEA in Lagos, please." After a short delay, she continued. "Hello? I'd like to report a shipment of sixty-one kilos of Afghan heroin that will be trafficked through Murtala Airport in approximately ninety minutes… Yes, I'll hold. Thank you."

Logan cocked a half-regenerated eyebrow at her. "Heroin?"

She shrugged. "'Go with what works,' my dad always said." Looking away, she switched back to her conversation with the authorities on the ground. "Yes, that's right… It's a Gulfstream G550, registry Roger Alpha 4573 Kilo… The heroin is hidden in the passenger compartment… There's also forty-six million dollars in laundered U.S. currency notes in the hold." The person on the other end peppered her with questions, to which she rolled her eyes, then replied simply, "They're not planning on staying in Murtala for more than an hour. I suggest you get moving." Then she cut the channel.

"You do realize that Nigeria's one of the most corrupt countries on earth," Logan said. "They don't give a damn about drug smuggling."

Wai Ying took off her headset. "I know." She rested the headset back on the yoke in front of her. "But they *will* give a damn if a rich white foreigner—who *hasn't* paid them a bribe—lands in their country with sixty keys of smack and a brick of cash big enough to build a boat."

"You fight dirty," Logan said. "I approve."

"It's an art." Reclining her seat, she added, "That'll keep him busy in Lagos long enough for you to 'pick up his scent.'"

Logan smirked with appreciation. "You keep this up, I might just marry you all over again."

"Promises, promises," she said, and drifted off to sleep.

18

THOUGH the Nigerian officers sounded to Pritikin as if they were speaking English, they didn't seem capable of understanding a single word that came out of his mouth. "How many times do I have to tell you? There are no drugs on my plane!"

His jet had been allowed to land without incident or warning, and a towing car had arrived promptly to guide it into the refueling area near the short-term hangars. The moment his pilot had powered down the Gulfstream's turbofans, however, a wall of blinding halogen floodlamps had snapped on, bathing the jet in white light so intense that it seemed to have physical substance. Then fists had begun pounding on the outside of the hatch, and angry voices repeated the same phrase, over and over: "Federal police! Open up!"

Pritikin's first assumption was that this was all just a misunderstanding, or a case of mistaken identity. He had kept on thinking that until the officer in charge, a man by the name of Colonel Mfume, addressed him by name. "Alexei Pritikin!" Mfume had bellowed. "You are under arrest!" Pritikin had been forced to his knees with his hands on his head, and from there he'd been pushed facedown on the deck of his own private jet by a boot on his neck and the muzzle of a submachine gun at his head.

He and his entourage—pilots, bodyguards, prostitutes—had then been escorted off the plane one at a time and "processed"—a polite way of saying they'd been photographed and fingerprinted. Separated from the others, each passenger on the plane had his or her very own interrogator. Pritikin wondered if the other investigators were as dense as the one he was stuck talking to.

"Why don't you just tell us where the drugs are?" Mfume asked him, as though this was the most reasonable thing in the world. "The sooner we find what we're looking for, the easier this will be for you."

"There are no drugs on my damn plane," Pritikin said, unable to hold his temper in check. "No laundered cash, no drugs. Get it?" He'd been repeating this for nearly two hours. He clung to the slim hope that Mfume might begin to grasp what he was telling him any moment now.

Mfume, still doing a very good impersonation of a calm and reasonable man, nodded at Pritikin's statement, then summoned over one of his subordinates. "Start opening up the fuselage," he instructed the younger man.

Pritikin just couldn't stand it any longer. "Have you lost your mind?" He bolted up from his chair and was swiftly confronted by a line of large, brutish-looking Nigerian federal policemen. "You can't just rip holes in my plane!"

"Of course we can," Mfume explained. "We're the police."

He heard the sound of people descending the stairs of his jet. Hoping that the search might be over, he looked back—and saw that the uniformed men leaving his jet were carrying cardboard boxes that they'd loaded with every bit of loose personal property inside the plane. Jackets, dishware, electronic devices like phones and cameras, even the booze and mixers from his wet bar.

"You *yebani v rot*," Pritikin muttered. "You don't know who you're pissing off here. When I get done with you, you'll—"

"Threatening a police officer?" Mfume looked amused. "I didn't give you enough credit. You're braver than I thought."

A stunning blow hit Pritikin square in the center of his upper back, between his shoulder blades. The wind was knocked out of his lungs, and his legs abandoned him to gravity. In a hazy swish-pan of motion he was on the ground. Handcuffs closed with an icy click around his wrists and bit into his skin.

From a few meters away, he heard bottles smash. It was all so Kafkaesque that he began to laugh. He couldn't help it.

Mfume looked curious. "Is something funny, Mr. Pritikin?"

"Yes," Pritikin replied between huffs of laughter. "I'm going to have you killed, you ignorant *skotolozhets*."

The Nigerians probably didn't understand what he'd called them, but one of them kicked him in the back of the head anyway. Pritikin was almost grateful to be relieved of consciousness.

○———————○

EVEN from the air, Pritikin's jet had been easy for Logan to spot amid the sprawl of Murtala Airport. It was the one surrounded by a few dozen uniformed Nigerian federal police, a squad of drug-sniffing German shepherds, and a phalanx of floodlights. The entire scene was as bright as high noon in the Sahara, a white-hot beacon demanding attention in the otherwise unbroken curtain of night that had descended, humid and oppressive, upon Lagos.

Logan and Wai Ying observed the chaos around Pritikin's plane as their Cessna Thunderstar was towed slowly into a short-term hangar. Through their cockpit windshield they could still see Pritikin himself for a few more moments; he was on the tarmac and shouting, red-faced, at the Nigerian officer in charge. Pritikin seemed to pay no heed to the officers facing him in a skirmish line, hands resting on their submachine guns.

"He looks unhappy," Logan quipped.

"Very," agreed Wai Ying.

As their plane entered its hangar, they left the cockpit and moved back into the passenger cabin. They sat down across from each other and watched the fracas through the windows.

A procession of Nigerian police exited Pritikin's Gulfstream. Each officer carried a box of assorted loose items from inside the plane. Since none of it was likely to be the fictitious heroin that Wai Ying had reported, Logan could only assume that they were using the search as an excuse to loot the plane of anything that wasn't bolted to the fuselage. Not surprisingly, Pritikin seemed rather irate about their behavior. One of the uniformed officers responded by using his nightstick to club Pritikin on the back, between his shoulder blades.

Wai Ying winced in sympathy. "That had to hurt."

"Not nearly as much as it should've," Logan said.

Pritikin dropped to his knees, then pitched forward onto his hands. The officer who had struck him down handcuffed him.

"Well, that's a shame," Wai Ying deadpanned.

The last officer leaving Pritikin's plane tripped and dropped a box filled with bottles of scotch, which shattered on the tarmac. "No," Logan corrected her, "*that* was a shame."

One of the Nigerians kicked Pritikin in the head, knocking him unconscious. "Looks like he's out of action for a while," Wai Ying said.

Logan shook his head and got up. "Don't count on it. If I know the Hand, they already know he's running late. I bet he'll be free in less than fifteen minutes."

She followed him to the hatch. "A rescue op?"

"No, a legal one," Logan said. "Like most criminals, the Hand has a lot of lawyers on the payroll."

The hatch opened with a soft hiss and lowered with a hydraulic whine. "What's our next move?" Wai Ying asked.

"Get our plane refueled," Logan said. "Depending on how I do tailing Pritikin to the *Pandora*, we might need to move again in a hurry."

"Hold on," she said. "How *you* do?"

"No offense, ace," Logan said. "You're good in a stand-and-fight, but this is a different ball game. I have to go alone."

He braced himself for her counterargument, which he figured would be particularly vitriolic. Instead, she handed him a cell phone. "It's my spare," she said. "Speed-dial five to call me."

Logan closed his hand around the phone and nodded to her. "I will." He tried to tuck the phone in his pants pocket, then he realized he was wearing a tattered, fire-shriveled set of rags. He motioned toward the outside. "I'll grab some new clothes on my way out." Eager to avoid excess sentiment, he descended the stairs into the dimly lit hangar.

He ducked under the wing to the baggage compartment hatch and opened it. After shuffling aside a few bags, he found his duffel, opened it, and retrieved a pair of jeans and a pullover sweater, both black. He dressed quickly, choosing to forgo shoes. Stepping back as he closed the baggage hatch, his foot landed on a slick patch. From the odor, Logan knew that it was old motor oil. *That'll do*, he decided. He reached down and ran his fingers through it, then smeared the black greasy liquid over the tops of his feet; he finished with a broad, four-finger diagonal pull across his face, which he knew would make for a fine, organic-looking camouflage pattern. The excess he rubbed over his hands. As for the smell… where he was going, it would likely fit right in. *Time to go to work.*

On his way out he passed the Cessna's open hatch, where Wai Ying still stood, watching him. "Be careful," she said.

Logan turned back and permitted himself a wan half-smile in her direction. "Not really my style."

○────────────○

MOTION was a blessing for Logan, a sacrament under cover of darkness. Set free from the measured caution of human behavior, he trod silently on the borderline between the human and the animal, summoning the darker aspect of his soul, the core of his being that owed its allegiance to the primeval hunter within.

He kept his claws hidden. Stealth was the order of the moment. Concealed behind the stacks of cheap wooden crates, he was on the hunt. His blood rose with the moon as he circled closer to his prey. As he'd expected, lawyers—sent by either the Hand or the *yakuza*—had extricated Pritikin from the Nigerian federal police with stunning alacrity. Whatever threats had been made had been sufficient to scare the cops into giving Pritikin a wide berth as he walked tall out of their custody.

Trailing him back to the hangars was invigorating. Pritikin's scent was fresh and lingering, a blend of musk cologne and sweat laced with the perfume of metabolized scotch, Italian wool and leather, a hint of blood on his breath from the beating he'd taken a short time ago.

It was so very raw. So tangible.

He followed Pritikin into the cargo warehouse. While his prey walked right up the broad central aisle, Logan slipped into the stacks and scaled one to watch from the shadows above.

Inside the cargo facility Pritikin moved purposefully, trailed by his retinue and attended by men who wore coveralls and carried clipboards. The Russian strode quickly from crate to crate, tapping those he desired, and squads of cargo workers rushed to haul them onto a pallet or mark them with ink for future pickup.

His instructions to the foreman were quick and curt.

"A hundred more liters of this.

"Get five more of these.

"Pack this last.

"Cover those markings.

"Put this in storage.

"Destroy that manifest when you're done. No copies."

Through it all, the foreman nodded, his expression serious and his mouth pressed resolutely shut, as if he feared letting even a stray sound escape. Pritikin waved him away and beckoned over a pilot, who dutifully jogged to him. "Yes, sir?"

"As soon as the Chinook's loaded, we're going," Pritikin said. "Get the EC ready." The pilot nodded and jogged away.

Logan shifted his position so he could better reconnoiter the scene. From his new vantage point, he espied a Chinook CH-47F cargo helicopter hovering outside the warehouse, beyond the stack of crates opposite his position. The enormous chopper appeared to be a military-surplus bird modified for civilian use. Its rotors were already turning at near full speed, primed to depart at any moment. A small forklift was loading pine crates onto a pallet inside a slack cargo net beneath the Chinook.

A few dozen meters away from the Chinook's net was another helicopter; it was smaller, a passenger chopper. Based on the design of the airframe around the tail rotor, Logan surmised that it was a Eurocopter EC-135. The pilot to whom Pritikin had spoken returned to this bird, clambered into the pilot's seat, and started throwing switches. Seconds later its rotors turned sluggishly, then gradually gained speed as the Eurocopter's engine warmed up. Apparently, Pritikin planned to leave soon.

Taking a moment to think, Logan became painfully aware of his body still adjusting itself to his demands. Regenerating this much muscle tissue always left him feeling stiff. Growing back all his hair at once meant enduring a pervasive, relentless itching, especially on his scalp and face, and in his groin. Rather than ignore it, he made every effort to funnel the constant irritation into his growing reservoir of rage.

Options looked to be scarce at the moment. He couldn't really hope to blend in with the Nigerian ground crew, which ruled out walking up to the helicopters to stow away. Getting too close would get him noticed by Pritikin, who certainly knew Logan's face by now. Head-on was definitely the wrong approach.

As soon as Pritikin left the warehouse, the mood became palpably less tense. Lurking atop one of the stacks, Logan noticed that three of the cargo handlers immediately abandoned their duties and slipped away to a secluded nook in the mountain of boxes. The tallest one produced a pair of dice from one of his pockets and a fistful of cash from the other. His two compatriots also fished rolls of cash from their coveralls and flanked the man with the dice as he gave a puff of breath on the ivories and prepared to make his throw. Logan climbed down behind them.

A flick of the wrist sent the cubes tumbling across the pitted gray concrete floor. They bounced off Logan's oil-blackened foot and came to rest, a pair of lonely dots faceup. "Snake eyes," Logan said with a grin. "Tough luck."

If any one of the three saw the hits that knocked them unconscious, they gave no sign of it. Logan scooped up their cash and climbed back atop the crates, liberated to the shadows.

Surveying the warehouse, Logan saw just what he'd expected: the one guy who hadn't been invited to the craps game, doing all the work, moving crates to the Chinook. The skinny young man—he couldn't have been much older than nineteen, Logan guessed—drove the forklift clumsily, like someone who was teaching himself by trial and error. The man set down the pallet, already heavy with four crates, near one of the last two boxes to be shipped. Struggling with a crowbar to lift it enough to kick a wedge underneath, he grunted and groaned in frustration and pain.

At last he got the wedge under the crate, propping up its edge so that he could get the forks under it to put it on the pallet. He heaved a tired breath, rested the crowbar on his shoulder, and stepped backward—and halted as Logan's claws pressed against his back. "Please don't kill me," the kid whispered. "Natubo sent you, right? You came for the Semtex? It's in the janitor's closet, under—"

Logan shushed him. With terrifying slowness, he extended another lone claw in front of the man's bare, dark throat. He kept his voice low and menacing. "What's your name, kid?"

Shaking with fear, the man said, "Wathiongo."

"Pay attention, Wathiongo. You can get paid, or you can get killed. Your call. Choose."

One fear-shaken breath later, Wathiongo replied, "Paid."

"Smart choice." Logan removed his claw from the man's throat. "Here's what's gonna happen. You're gonna put me in this box, then you're gonna put this box in the Chinook's net. Follow me so far, kid?" The man nodded. "As soon as you do that, I'll cut myself an air hole and pass you this wad of cash." He reached over Wathiongo's shoulder and showed him the massive roll of money he'd taken from the gamblers. Then he put it back in his pocket. "Rat me out—" He plucked the crowbar from Wathiongo's grasp and tossed it straight up. As it fell, he lashed out with his free set of claws and sliced the iron tool into four pieces—two long and two short. The metal pieces clanged brightly across the cement floor. "And I'll cut your head off. Get the picture?"

Wathiongo nodded quickly.

"All right," Logan said. He retracted his claws and slapped Wathiongo fraternally on the back. "Let's get to work."

○————————○

THE inside of the pine shipping crate was cramped and left Logan almost no room to move, not even to shift his weight. Every bump and wobble of the imbalanced and overloaded forklift felt like a tectonic shift inside the box, which bobbled on the forks as it was moved out to the Chinook's cargo net.

Barely audible over the Chinook's rotor noise, the forklift's hydraulic motor whined as it deposited the crate with the rest of the shipment. A jarring bump heralded the crate's touchdown on the pallet. Voices overlapped outside, and he heard someone say, "What are you doing?"

Wathiongo answered, "Securing the crates."

"All right, make it fast," the first voice said.

Chains clanked over and around the box, followed quickly by the dull *thwap* of elastic cargo netting being pulled taut around the stack of cargo. Then came a soft knocking on the outside of the box—two short taps, a pause, then two more. It was Wathiongo signaling the all-clear.

Logan partially extended one claw, pressed it against the center pine board on one side, and rotated his wrist back and forth until, seconds later, he'd drilled through. Without a word, he pushed the roll of cash through the hole and felt it plucked away. Then receding footsteps, and the rumble of the forklift motor growing quieter with distance.

The Chinook's rotors increased speed; the pounding noise was deafening. Logan peeked through the hole he'd drilled. He had a clear view, facing in the direction of flight. Ahead of them, the Eurocopter made its steady vertical ascent. The horizon dipped and wavered as the Chinook hefted its load into the air, then steadied itself. Moments later, the Chinook fell in directly behind the Eurocopter, which was all but invisible in the darkness, nothing more than a set of flashing lights against the curtain of night.

Away we go, Logan mused, trying not to dwell on the thought that delivering himself to his enemies in a pine box might prove to be a bad omen.

19

SALT air. Briny and primal, the scent had reached Logan within minutes of the Chinook's departure from Murtala Airport. By his best estimate, the Chinook and the Eurocopter that it was following were roughly two hundred miles out of Lagos, hugging the Nigerian coastline. They were flying extremely close to the water—low enough to evade radar. The weather was clear; the moon was full and so bright that its features were washed out. Looking down, Logan saw the pale shimmer of moonlight on the crests of slow-rolling waves and the dappled forest canopy.

Ahead of the cargo helicopter, the EC-135's flickering lights beckoned like sprites in the darkness, luring the bigger, tandem-rotor aircraft on its secret journey.

Then the blinking lights of the Eurocopter went dark—vanished without a trace.

The Chinook slowed, hovered a moment, then continued slowly forward, steady and level. Moments later, a bizarre visual distortion rippled over the chopper and its cargo, twisting and warping the starlight and the dancing points of light on the water. Like a wall of heat radiation it swept through the inside of the crate. It tingled Logan's skin as it pushed over and through him. Hairs on the nape of his neck stood at attention, roused by a sensation of electric potential in the air.

When the effect retreated behind him, his vision cleared—and through his hastily drilled aperture he saw a massive container ship at anchor in a small harbor. Mounted on the forward deck was a small loading crane. On its aft deck was a small helipad, where the EC-135 had already touched down.

Inside the perimeter of the cloaking field, the stars and moonlight were distorted. The Chinook hovered above the stack of multicolored shipping containers and began lowering its net of cargo. Peeking through a sliver of space between the boards at his feet, he realized that the tops of several shipping containers were retracting, rolling back to reveal a spacious compartment hidden within. *Camouflage*, he realized. *Those aren't shipping containers—it's a structure disguised as shipping containers.*

The net full of crates descended slowly into the broad, poorly lit space, lowered by the Chinook's winch into the custody of a half dozen cargo workers, two of whom were operating forklifts. Working quickly, they pulled away the now-slackened netting and began unloading the crates from the pallet. Logan heard the deep thunder of the Chinook's rotors continuing overhead. His surveillance of the activity inside the hidden storage area was interrupted as a forklift moved his crate off the pallet and into the stacks.

Logan's crate fortuitously was deposited in a shadowy corner. Prying open the narrow crack between two boards with one of his claws, he watched as the ground crew removed the empty pallet from the netting. The Chinook retracted its net. As soon as it was clear, the ground team maneuvered a massive, rectangular shipping container mounted on a rolling dolly platform onto the same spot. Seconds later, the Chinook lowered a set of heavy-duty steel cables that clanked onto the deck. The ground crew set to work attaching the cables to the corners of the slingable metal box, which, to Logan's eye, looked like an ordinary, twenty-foot refrigerated shipping container—exactly what one would need for delivering perishable medicine to a remote location.

The steel cables snapped taut, then the refrigerated container was hoisted off the dolly and out of the storage area. Seconds later, it cleared the edge of the camouflaged roof, which began to creep shut with a resonant, mechanical hum. Before it closed fully, Logan saw the Chinook pivot one hundred eighty degrees and begin its journey back to Lagos.

Have to catch up to it later, he decided. *Job one is free Dr. Falco. Job two is sink this boat.*

He slipped one claw sideways in the gap between the pine crate's lid and its sides. Slowly, he sliced through the nails holding the lid in place. In less than a minute, he eased the lid up and away, then put it gently off to one side. He climbed out of the box and snuck deeper into the shadows, until his back was pressed against a bulkhead. He began moving aft.

As soon as the overhead doors had closed, four of the six cargo workers exited aft through a broad loading and unloading passageway. Thick steel doors pushed inward and barricaded the opening behind them. The last two workers moved lethargically amid the stacks, checking inventory.

Unlike many industrial ships Logan had traveled on, this one smelled almost antiseptically clean, as if it had been sanitized every day. As he passed by a ventilation duct, the cool air gently flowing from it smelled of ammonia mingled with the medicinal odors of alcohol and iodine. Even here, in a cargo area, the decks were immaculate.

Logan slipped behind a very neat and symmetrical stack of refrigerated containers like the one that had just been flown away. None of these seemed to be active; their compressors were off, and all their gauges were zeroed. The sheer number of them, however—forty in this stack alone, and two more stacks like it elsewhere in the compartment—alluded to the scope of the Hand's plans for Panacea.

In the corner he found an unsecured door. He cracked it open and listened. There were no voices, no footsteps, not even the soft tides of breathing. Just the low hum of air in the vents and the hiss of water and vapor in the pipes. He slipped through the door into a flatly lit passageway. Its bulkheads were of the same widely ribbed metal as the shipping containers that its exterior had been made to resemble. He checked the corners. No surveillance cameras. The deck looked uniform, nothing to suggest pressure pads or motion sensors. Featureless walls left no place for the installation of infrared sensor beams. His bare feet made almost no sound as he stole quickly through the passageway toward its less well-illuminated far end.

The throb and thrum of the ship's engine room was louder here, deeper. Around the corner was a shorter passage. Three doors were spaced at regular intervals along its aft bulkhead. Still no sign of surveillance. Logan moved swiftly and checked all three doors: in order, they were marked "Exit," "Ladder," and "Lab." The last door was the only one that was secured, with a numeric keypad and magnetic dead bolts. He considered just slicing through the bolts, but he knew from lessons learned the hard way that doing so would probably trigger an alert. If he was going to keep his promise to Setsuko and make every effort to save Dr. Falco, discretion would have to be the order of the day.

He checked the ventilation gratings along the top of the bulkhead and confirmed that they were all too short and too narrow for anyone larger than a toddler to move through. Cutting through the bulkhead itself was problematic; if he hit a major electrical bundle, he might fry himself to death.

After weighing his options, he listened at the door to the ladder. There was no sound of movement or human presence from the other side, and the door was unlocked. He inched it open and sniffed the air. More of the same disinfectant-tinged, purified air, cool and dry, no human or animal scents. Through the door. Up the steep metal steps, fast and light-footed. Another door, one level up, unlocked. All quiet again. A peek through confirmed a dark passageway with hints of blue light to one side and reflected white light from the other. Closing the door, he reached up over his head and unscrewed the blistering-hot bulb dangling from a black wire above the ladder landing. Cloaked in shadow, he reopened the door, crouched, and stole through.

The blue light was a caged bulb above a watertight door to his right. White light poured through an angled observation window that began five meters to his left and continued for twenty meters, taking up most of the passage's far wall. Skulking forward on all fours, Logan approached the corner and peeked down into the space below.

Arranged in three long rows were enormous stainless-steel machines, bulbous in shape, gleaming brightly under the flat, omnipresent flood of white light from scores of hanging fixtures high overhead. A seemingly endless labyrinth of pipes and tubes and wires connected the machines to huge vats and compressors. Entire bulkheads were covered with gauges and digital flat-screen displays. Four freestanding banks of computers were situated in the corners, each one inside its own Plexiglas safety barrier. Along the bulkhead to Logan's right was a pressure door.

Directly below Logan was the end of what appeared to be a fully automated production line. Robotic arms worked in tandem with precisely calibrated nozzles and a timed conveyer belt to fill sixty bottles at a time with a golden fluid that Logan could only assume was Panacea. He counted the seconds as the small glass bottles filled and the case in which they were packed was moved on to the next stage. Six seconds. Six hundred bottles per minute, with as many as ten doses per bottle. Three hundred sixty thousand doses an hour. Then he considered the size of the cases and quickly estimated that more than a thousand could have been loaded inside the refrigerated shipping container. More than half a million doses of instant slavery were already airborne and on their way to Africa.

At the far end of the production facility he caught sight of motion. Through a dark-tinted window, he saw a lone man walking across a lab, lit only by the pale blue glow of his computer screens. Even from this distance he recognized him from his Tanaka dossier photo as Dr. Nikolai Falco. He was relieved that the man wasn't dead yet.

Logan crawled below the edge of the observation window, to the door at the far end. Beyond it was another untrafficked set of steps. He descended the ladder quickly, found the door to the next level, and checked it before continuing on through another dull gray passage, toward what he hoped might be another entrance to Falco's laboratory.

At the end of the corridor was a watertight door. He looked through its circular view port; on the right, at the head of a T-shaped intersection, was another door marked "Lab." Unlike the other lab entrance, this one had no security keypad next to it.

A spin of the door's wheel released its bolts. The heavy metal portal swung open. An overpowering blast of ammonia and diesel fumes flooded Logan's senses. It was stronger than any routine shipboard operation could account for; in Logan's experience, whenever he encountered an odor so profound, it was because someone was expecting him and was using a powerful stench to mask their scent.

He extended his claws. Stepped through the door, ready and looking for a fight. Turned the corner at the intersection and met his foes head-on. Four people stood looking back at him.

Pritikin was safely at the back of the group. His hatred for Logan was obvious and fiery. The honesty of it was the only thing about Pritikin that Logan found even remotely admirable.

Standing in front of the Russian were the fireball twins.

At the head of their diamond formation was the man who clearly was in charge. Majestically tall, his powerful frame was expertly attired in a silvery gray business suit and a chrome-colored necktie. His shoes matched his suit and were polished to such perfection that they reflected the tip of his *katana*, which he had drawn and held casually in front of him. The weapon's scabbard was slung diagonally across his back, crisscrossed with the scabbard for a shorter sword, a matching *wakizashi*.

Logan eyed the *katana* carefully: in this man's hands, it was one of the few things on earth that his own adamantium claws couldn't cut through. He nodded at Silver Samurai.

"*Konnichiwa*, Keniuchio."

"*Konnichiwa*, Logan-san," Harada replied.

One of the twins had his hand against a junction box. The other had small sparks dancing off his fingertips.

"So," Logan said, "you've signed up with the Hand, eh?"

"Signed up?" Harada smirked. "No. I've taken command of a joint effort, adding their power to that of the *yakuza*."

"So it's true," Logan said, disappointed. Though Harada had started out years ago as Logan's rival in Japan, Logan had come to think of him almost as a friend. Shaking his head, he added, "Blindspot really did a number on you, didn't he?"

"Don't delude yourself, Logan," Harada said. "I've simply awoken to the truth, embraced what I really am. I put aside the childish fantasy of a hero I never was."

The twin with the crackling fingers took a step forward. "Let me frag him, boss." He lifted his hand. "I could fry his—"

Harada's sword slapped flat and hard against the energy thrower's chest. "No," Harada said. "If Logan dies, it will be at my hand, in honorable combat."

"Like hell it will," Logan said.

Now the hotheaded twin strained against Harada's blade. "Come on, let me finish this! I already made a crispy critter out of him once at—" His mouth snapped shut as the flat of Harada's sword slammed into the underside of his jaw, with its razor edge a hair's breadth from cutting his throat.

Cold and unforgiving was Harada's tone. "You will speak to Logan as your better, youngling. He is my fellow *ronin*, a warrior without a master. Even in defeat, he deserves respect."

"Can't say the same for you," Logan interjected. Seeing that he had Harada's full attention, he continued. "Using a drug with the world's worst side effect to enslave billions of people? That's the most gutless thing I ever heard of. And until right now, I'd never have believed you could do something so sick."

With a quizzical look, Harada asked, "What, exactly, do you think my ultimate objective is, Logan? Do you think I would undertake such a massive change in the global status quo for a mere blackmail scheme? Or some simple power grab?"

"Let me guess," Logan shot back. "You're doing it for world peace."

"Exactly," Harada said with a sly grin.

It wasn't the answer that Logan had expected. "Want to run that by me again?"

"What I am accomplishing here, Logan, is nothing less than everything that the combined wealth and effort of the entire Western world has failed to do in more than three decades of trying: I am going to bring peace, health, prosperity, and stability to the Third World—starting with Africa."

"For a price," Logan replied, keeping an eye on the twitching blasting finger of the anxious twin behind Harada.

Harada nodded. He made a sweeping arc with his sword as he spoke. "Nothing is free, Logan. You know that." The tip of the blade cut through the air between them in a figure eight. "The difference is that I'm prepared to offer something of value in exchange for the fealty of those I help—an end to poverty, to hunger, to pandemic disease. I shall set them free from need and want and suffering."

"Your generosity is touching," Logan said. "Hell, I bet you didn't even think about all the uranium and other mineral resources you'd score on this deal. And I'm sure Africa's gold, diamonds, and oil had nothing to do with your decision to enslave its people."

A disappointed sigh, then Harada replied, "What an ugly way of thinking about such a boon to humanity."

"Half a billion people working for their daily dose? Dissent becoming a death sentence? That don't sound like a boon to me. Sounds more like I shoulda killed your ass in Tokyo when I had the chance."

Logan lurched half a step forward, then halted as the fireballer's fingertips turned white-hot with energy.

"I can take him out right here, daimyo," the twin said.

The other twin shouted, "Don't be stupid, Gregor!"

"Shut up, Oskar." Fire-fingers looked to Harada for his orders. "Give the word."

"Your brother's right," Harada said. "A blast strong enough to kill Logan would sink the ship."

A sick smirk darkened Gregor's face. "I'll go easy on him."

Forks of lightning jumped from the man's fingers and snared Logan. Spasms racked Logan's body; his jaw clenched painfully and against his will. Stabbing bolts of hot pain skewered him from every direction. Writhing and growling, he felt himself slip away amid a blinding ring of fire. Then the circle of light and heat raced away as his mind plummeted into the darkness.

o———————————o

CONSCIOUSNESS returned with a shudder. It was pitch dark.

Logan's entire body twitched and jerked. A nervous flutter in his eyelid was followed by a yanking muscle spasm in his cheek. He felt like a fish with a hook in its mouth.

Ringing in his ears rose and fell like a Doppler effect. He felt groggy, disoriented. Despite the perfect darkness, multihued spots danced in his vision.

Under his palms and bare feet was cold, naked metal. Smooth and icy, it had the same perfectly sanitized odor as the cargo hold of the *Pandora*. He shifted his balance. Stood up, staggered to one side. His steps echoed in the empty space around him. "Echo," he said, to test the acoustics. His own voice came back to him, close and resonant.

Vertigo, another stumble to his left. He became aware that he was in motion, rocking in a shallow arc, like a slow-swinging pendulum. Muffled by the metal walls around him, he could barely hear the hum and grind of motors, the buzz and clatter of coiling cables. He pressed his ear against the wall.

The machine noise was louder, clearer. Outside were voices, shouting, overlapping. *Easy. More to starboard.*

Focusing, he picked out distinct voices.

Pritikin. "Get it over with."

Harada. "Be patient, Alexei. It's almost done."

Gregor the fireballer: "Back a little, over the edge. A little higher... Keep it steady, dammit! Dump the chum."

Over the edge? Logan dropped and flattened his ear to the floor, like an Indian in an old western. Below him he heard the scrape of steel, then the slap of waves lapping against the hull of the ship. In a flash, he realized that he was in one of the shipping containers, and that Gregor was about to use him for target practice. Then Gregor's last instruction repeated itself in Logan's thoughts: *Dump the chum.*

Sharks, Logan realized. *Sonofabitch.*

Extending his claws, he moved to the side of the box that was facing away from the man with hands of fire. He punched forward, through the steel wall, to start cutting his way out.

Everything exploded.

The blast at the airport had been nothing. Like a welder's flame, a massive pulse of white heat disintegrated the shipping container into a swirling fire cloud of shrapnel. Flames and chunks of steel ripped flesh from Logan's bones. He felt himself screaming, but there was no sound other than the consuming roar of the blast. He was the soft target in a volcanic blender filled with brimstone and razor blades.

Born again of fire, he fell from the burning womb into darkness—numb, stunned, blind.

Impact came hard, like landing on a bed of frozen nails.

Seawater paralyzed him with its icy bite, pulled him down like quicksand, surrounded him like a shroud. He gasped and it poured into his throat and lungs. Mixed with the water was the coppery tang of blood. Some of it was from the remains of bait fish; some of it was his own.

Watery darkness drew him down like iron to a magnet. Burned and torn, he was dead weight in its irresistible embrace.

Then came the first strike. A viselike pressure around his lower left leg. His sense of motion through the water increased. Another attack, seizing on his right arm, halted his movement. In less than a second he was caught in a tug of war between two sharks, their sawtooth jaws clamped through his flesh down to his unbreakable bones.

Crushing pressure bore down on him. He was sinking fast. Then another hit, a bump against the left side of his lower back, and a fresh cloud of his own blood stained the water.

Nausea and asphyxia fogged his thoughts with panic.

In a flash the pain hit, and pure rage took over.

He struck with his left hand at the shark tugging on his right arm. His claws tore into the beast's head with no effort. Instantly it released its fierce grip on him. Bending at the knee, he pulled his upper body to his trapped left foot, then slashed savagely at the first shark that had assaulted him.

He felt chunks of the aquatic predator rip loose, then he was floating free. Behind him, a near-silent rush of displaced water. Twisting like a corkscrew, he struck as he turned, and severed the front of the third shark's snout.

Logan was still all but blind in the lightless night-time sea, and his lungs were screaming for air. Red jolts of pain surged through him, made it hard to think, but instinct was not enough now. He was floating, deprived of any reference point, and his adamantium-laced skeleton made him too heavy to float to the surface. *Don't panic*, he commanded himself. *Think*.

There was less than half a breath still held in his lungs, and his only chance of surviving hinged on letting it go. He retracted his claws, cupped his hand a few centimeters above his mouth, and exhaled slowly, then felt which way the bubbles moved. They crept backward over his face, and he turned himself so that they rose directly from his mouth and over his fingers. *That's up,* he told himself. *Swim, canucklehead.*

His strength was fading, and he had only one arm and one leg able to kick and pull and fight against the leaden weight of the water above. There was no light, no sense of where the surface might be. The ocean yawned around him, its watery voice deeper and more ancient than life itself. Seawater burned inside his windpipe. As fast as his arm and leg fought against the sea, he felt as if he wasn't moving, as if he were fighting merely to keep from being pulled back into the depths.

At any moment more sharks could appear, and he'd have no air, no strength left to fight, no hope of breaking free.

A rippling gray shadow. Hallucination or salvation?

His hand found no resistance. It reached into the nether realm above. Then his head broke the surface, and the crash of air against his waterlogged eardrums was like a hurricane wind. The ocean pitched and rolled, and he bobbed passively on its surface, gulping down air and coughing out filthy brine. He lifted his right hand from the water and was satisfied to see that it was already well on its way to being mended. With effort, he rotated his left foot from the ankle. The rends in his flesh were almost healed; if he could get away quickly, he might avoid further attention from sharks.

Pivoting in slow, careful turns, he scanned the harbor, which shimmered beneath the full moon. No matter what direction he looked, he didn't see the *Pandora*. He closed his eyes, and he heard it—the voices of men working on its deck, the creak of its anchor chain, the slap of waves against its hull. A sniff of the night air brought diesel fumes from close by. For a moment, Logan was surprised not only that the ship was close enough for him to swim to but that it wasn't moving at all. Then he recalled that when he'd first seen it from his hiding place in the crate, it had been lying at anchor.

It made sense, he realized. With its cloak up, the only way for the *Pandora* to be an effective base of operations was for it to remain anchored at a precise set of coordinates. Logan, however, was just glad that he wasn't facing a several-kilometer swim to shore with the sharks.

He took slow, easy strokes as he swam toward the diesel fumes. It was important not to draw attention from the deckhands. The sound of waves lapping the hull was intimately close when he encountered the distorting effect of the cloaking field. He took a deep breath, submerged, and swam underwater until he reached the ship's hull.

Surfacing against the side of the massive container ship, he was able to get his bearings. He was at the starboard bow of the vessel. Above him, two massive anchor chains descended from the hull into the ocean. Both chains were pulled taut on long angles away from the ship.

A deep breath, and he slipped back beneath the dark water. With a powerful breaststroke, he propelled himself under the water toward the anchor cable. Half a minute later, his hand closed on the rough steel. He cautiously surfaced and glanced up at the ship's main deck. No one was looking in his direction.

Gripping the cable with both hands, he locked his ankles around it further down, then began pulling himself upward. Hand over hand, foot over foot, he climbed with smooth, easy motions toward the top of the cable. He worried that the water dripping from his sodden, shredded trousers would give him away, but between the wind and the waves and the hubbub on deck, a few drops of water that far overboard were inaudible.

At the top of the cable, he clambered through the circular aperture into the anchor winch compartment. Everything smelled like machine oil. The space was dark and unoccupied. He checked the door; it was unsecured. The passageway on the other side was empty. Using some oily rags that he found next to the winch, he wiped away most of the water from his body, replacing it with smeared black instant camouflage. He took off his pants long enough to wring them dry, then put them back on. He checked the passageway again. Still clear.

His list of objectives was growing. He counted five now.

Rescue the scientist.

Recover a sample of Panacea for Setsuko Tanaka.

Destroy the ship.

Stop the Chinook.

And kill Pritikin, Harada, and the twin mutant thugs.

Not necessarily in that order, he decided as he opened the door to continue his mission.

20

MURTALA Airport was a grimy, frightening place by daylight. At night, it was among the most intimidating locales Wai Ying had ever seen. Sequestered inside the locked confines of the Cessna, she huddled under a blanket in the passenger cabin, curled into the plush embrace of the jet's luxurious seats.

She had been drifting in and out of sleep, pursued by bad dreams, nightmares of falling, of running to stand still. In a few she'd watched Ziv vanish again, consumed by fire. Too edgy now to sleep, too exhausted to stay awake, part of her anxiety was a fear of being alone in this dangerous, sinister place.

Even more poignant was her admission to herself that she missed Logan. They'd known each other for less than a week, but already he'd become important to her, in a way that few men had since her father died nearly a decade earlier. Certainly, Logan could be brusque, sarcastic, and uncommunicative. The rawness of his anger and pain, which he wore outwardly like a badge of honor, made her nervous, scared her a little. But from the first moment she had seen him in the cemetery, she'd known he was more than he appeared—soulful, conflicted, complicated. And the rose he'd brought to Mariko's grave had spoken of a romantic's soul.

She wasn't going to kid herself. Men like Logan weren't good candidates for long-term relationships. They didn't like to stick around. Always off to the next crisis, another adventure, the wide horizon, the lure of the unknown. It was a testament to what a remarkable woman Mariko must have been that she had inspired such lasting devotion in a wanderer like Wolverine. *Her death must have been a defining moment for him*, she concluded. *What would it take for a man to risk falling in love again after losing someone who meant so much?* It seemed like the kind of loss that would make a loner of anyone.

Then, like a taunt from her subconscious, she remembered a line from Oscar Wilde's *Picture of Dorian Gray*: "When a man marries again it is because he adored his first wife." Wai Ying shook her head and laughed at her own irrepressible optimism. *Hope springs eternal.*

Tucking her head onto the pillow she'd propped against the wall, she closed her eyes and tried to relax herself enough to drift off once more to sleep. Like the blanket, the pillow smelled freshly laundered—cool and crisp and laced with the vaguely floral scent of detergent. Then a low murmur, like a weak heartbeat, vibrated up through the body of the plane, through her seat, shook her awake. Minute by minute it grew stronger, deeper, more distinct. Soon she recognized it—the pounding *fwup-fwup-fwup* of a Chinook helicopter's tandem rotors.

She tossed aside the blanket. Stepping quickly to the cockpit, she found the binoculars and scanned the airfield for signs of ground crew activity. A cluster of men, including one with lighted signal batons, surrounded a low, flatbed dolly.

Rapid and powerful enough to shiver her teeth, the noise of the Chinook passed directly overhead. The baton man waved and coached the Chinook into position. Roiling plumes of dust kicked up from the rotor wash as the massive aircraft hovered above the flatbed. Wai Ying craned her neck and saw a twenty-foot-long metallic shipping container slowly descending from the Chinook, whose markings matched the one that had departed a little more than two hours ago. With help from the ground crew, the container was planted squarely on the wide, low dolly.

Four men climbed on top of the container and detached the sling cables, which were hoisted back into the air. The rotor noise faded as the Chinook departed. A small towing car drove up and hitched itself to the dolly. After a few lurching false starts, the car pulled its payload to a slow crawl across the tarmac, out of Wai Ying's sight.

Cursing softly, she lowered the jet's hatch ladder and snuck out, alone into the night. She slipped under the plane and stayed in the shadows as she jogged to catch up with the towed container. Dodging between low, dilapidated buildings and scampering across wide avenues of cracked asphalt whose fractures were packed with cigarette butts smoked down to their crumpled filters, she managed to get ahead of it.

She pressed herself flat against a wall. The towing car and the container crept past, traveling a floodlit path.

They turned onto a wide taxiway that led directly to the main runway. Waiting there was an enormous C-130 Hercules cargo aircraft. Its four engines were warming up, the propellers filling the air with a chainsaw-like buzz. The towing car halted at the massive aircraft's lowered rear ramp. The metal container was unhitched from the towing car, which drove away. Four men, attired in the black uniforms of ninjas, exited the plane and attached cables to the container, which was then hoisted slowly inside the C-130. Three teams of men removed the chocks from beneath the C-130's broad wheels. Another signalman directed the plane's pilots to bring their engines to full power.

Wai Ying ducked back behind the corner and considered her next move. Letting the plane get away with what she suspected was a massive shipment of Panacea was unacceptable, but she wasn't in a position to halt its departure by herself. When Logan returned, he would be the better person to handle this.

If he returns, warned her inner pessimist.

Shaking off her fears for Logan's safety, she pondered trying to follow the C-130, then realized that doing so not only wouldn't help her, it would also effectively strand Logan in Nigeria. Another peek at the gargantuan plane brought her to her senses. *It's a propeller plane,* she told herself. *You can give it a head start, as long as you know where it's going.* Carefully, she navigated the shadows and dark corners back to the Cessna Thunderstar.

Safely back inside the jet, she made an encrypted call to TBC headquarters in Osaka. The switchboard operator answered. "Tanaka Biotechnology."

"This is Wai Ying," she said. "Put me through to extension five-five-six-eight."

A click on the line, then a single, deep, buzzing ring. A man's voice answered the extension. "Satellite Recon."

"Hiro, Wai Ying. I need a redirect on the tracking bird."

As always, Hiro Kagehara was a consummate professional, never asking why but simply following orders. "Go ahead."

"Pick up a C-130 Hercules on the main runway at Murtala," she said. "Markings two-alpha-seven. Maintain visual, track its chatter. And Hiro? Do not lose them."

WOLVERINE: ROAD OF BONES

"Roger that," Hiro said. "Tracking bird has the ball."

"Thanks, Hiro, you're a prince." She hung up and reclined in the pilot's seat with a heavy sigh. There was nothing more to do but await Logan's return. Staring at her worried reflection in the windshield, she braced for a long, lonely night.

○————————○

HARADA led the Golovanov twins and Alexei Pritikin through a narrow passageway aboard the *Pandora*, toward a ladder that would bring them back to the aft helipad.

"I still don't see why we have to go with him," Gregor complained. "Logan's toast, and you're in the clear."

"Mr. Pritikin still has enemies and rivals," Harada said. "And there are other potential threats to our operation. Just because you've dealt with Logan, don't make the mistake of thinking success is guaranteed." Looking back over his shoulder at Gregor's anger-knitted brow, he added, "Besides, you're all Russian. You should have lots to talk about."

They passed through a heavy door and ascended a switchback ladder inside the aft superstructure. Their steps clanked and echoed sharply off the blue-gray bulkheads. Slightly winded, Pritikin spoke between heaving breaths as they climbed. "Can I go back to my mansion yet?"

"Soon," Harada said. "My people are making some much-needed improvements to its security. For now you should plan on staying in Istanbul while we lock down the pipeline deal."

Pritikin nodded. "Fair enough." The foursome reached the top landing, and Harada pushed open the outer door to the main deck. A low whistle of wind poured through the open portal, warm and briny and tainted with the odor of aviation fuel. The EC-135 sat idle on the helipad, its pilot apparently still belowdecks.

Harada was the first person through the door onto the narrow walkway, and Pritikin followed close behind him. As Gregor stepped through the door, Harada saw the blur of motion half a moment too late to act. An impact bashed the door shut, slamming Gregor between it and the bulkhead.

Pritikin bolted away from the door—only to collide with Harada, who pushed the cowardly Russian aside and over the railing. Flailing and yelping in distress, Pritikin tumbled several meters to the next deck and landed hard.

That left no one between Harada and Wolverine, who was crouched low, in a battle stance, claws extended and reflecting the moonlight. Harada reached over his shoulder and drew his *katana* from its scabbard. "You're making a mistake, Logan."

"Done talkin'," Logan replied, and he lunged forward.

Harada charged into the first wild swing of Logan's arms. Projecting his mutant power into his blade, he deflected the first swipe, parried an upthrust, then counterattacked, slashing a deep cut across Logan's chest. Undeterred, Logan pressed his assault. Every slash of his claws came faster than the one before, every blow landed with greater power.

Dodging left, Harada took a killing shot at Logan's neck. The *katana* wedged into the muscle behind Logan's right shoulder, then halted as it struck his scapula. In the blink of time it took to pull the sword free, Logan slashed him brutally across the midriff. It felt like razors of fire. A warm stain of blood bloomed instantly across Harada's shredded shirt. Logan jabbed with his right hand. Harada barely twisted clear in time.

I need more room, Harada realized. A single leap and he was over Logan and behind him. He catapulted himself off the narrow catwalk of the superstructure, turned and tumbled in the air, reversing his facing, and landed on the wide-open metal surface of the fake shipping containers.

Logan slammed down in front of him, arriving on the hollow steel battlefield with a boom like a cannonball.

They circled each other for a moment, then Logan barreled straight at him, roaring with fury. Harada feinted right, ducked left, and spun to strike Logan in the throat. Inches shy of contact his blade was blocked—and snared between two of Logan's unbreakable claws. Logan's counterstrike was a blur. Arching his back like a limbo dancer, Harada felt the tips of the claws cut through the air a millimeter from his face.

He used Logan's grip on his sword as an anchor and kicked him under his jaw. Logan stumbled backward, and Harada's sword slipped free.

An explosion, bright and furnace-hot, erupted between them. Concussed by displaced air, Harada tumbled backward, then rolled back to his feet. A smoldering hole had been blasted in the fake shipping containers. On the other side of the charred cavity, Logan was scrambling back up from all fours, shaking off the burns and the gashes from metal debris. Harada looked back up at the superstructure and saw Gregor leaning against the railing, fighting to remain on his feet, the right side of his face lacerated and bruised.

An energy thrower with a concussion, Harada fumed. *He'll destroy everything!* He knew that turning his back on Wolverine would be suicidal, but if he didn't halt Gregor's barrage, the consequences might be far more disastrous. Harada sprinted across the container tops, racing to intercept Gregor before he fired another blast.

Logan chased Harada, closing the distance quickly. He was about to overtake Harada when Gregor unleashed another firebolt.

The blast struck Logan square in the chest, and the report flattened Harada against the steel underfoot. Charred and wrapped in a fetal curl, Logan tumbled wildly across the multicolored steel surface and fell into the gap opened by Gregor's first attack. Smoke, thick and brownish-black, coiled up from inside the ragged hole in the steel.

Moments later came sounds of metal hacking through metal. Logan bounded up from the crater and flung three freshly cut steel wedges through the air. The metal chunks embedded in Gregor's gut, throat, and right eye. The fair-haired young Russian howled in agony and staggered. Then, just as Harada had feared, Gregor started firing wildly. Clutching one hand over his eye even as blood poured from his slashed throat, he hurled one thunderbolt after another, missing Logan and Harada but blasting massive holes through the ship, all the way down into the sea.

Less than two seconds after the insane barrage had started, Harada had scaled the superstructure, back to the catwalk. One stroke of his *katana* removed Gregor's head, which sailed into the open air, over the side, and into the water. His body crumpled to the catwalk, its firestorm quelled, its lifeblood cascading across the rough-textured steel walkway and streaking down the gray bulkhead below.

Logan climbed over the railing in pursuit of Harada, who backpedaled clear of the blood-slicked section of the catwalk. Feral and snarling, Logan was not going to bargain, not even going to waste breath on words. Killing Logan when he was like this would be exceedingly difficult, but not impossible.

Harada drew his *wakizashi* and readied himself for Logan's charge. In a blur it came, raw force and rage, unstoppable, unavoidable. Harada fell backward and let Logan run roughshod over him, risking a split-second of vulnerability for a chance to deliver one perfect, instantly fatal stroke.

Logan pinned him on the catwalk.

Lifted his claws to take Harada's head.

Then Harada struck, driving his *wakizashi* into Logan's gut, behind his sternum, through his heart.

A twitch, then a violent convulsion as Logan rolled off Harada. The *ronin* once known as Silver Samurai snapped back onto his feet and pivoted to jab his *katana* under Logan's chin, up into the brain pan. He lunged for the coup de grace—

And once again his blade was snared in Logan's claws.

With his left hand Logan held Harada's blade hostage, while his right pulled the *wakizashi* free of his torso. All but gutted, Logan looked up at Harada… and flashed the bloody grin of a predator.

The *wakizashi* stabbed upward. Its tip sank into Harada's abdomen for a split-second before he thought to let go of his *katana* rather than let himself be run through with his own blade. Now he was unarmed, wounded, and bleeding badly. Logan rose slowly back to his feet, his wild eyes never blinking as they probed Harada for weakness and fear.

Nowhere to fall back to, Harada knew. No time to regroup. In a single twist of his teleportation ring, Harada removed himself to a safer location—and abandoned the *Pandora* and its precious cargo as collateral damage. Regret gnawed at him, but then he put that feeling aside. *It doesn't matter*, he consoled himself. *We already have what we need. This battle is lost—but the war is about to be won.*

○———————○

FEAR spun Oskar's thoughts into a flurry.

He'd felt Gregor's death in the form of a massive wave of feedback. Instinct had driven him to try to shut it out, to block it, but it was too raw, too powerful. Never in Oskar's life had he feared electricity until this moment, as his body quaked and collapsed from the onslaught of his brother's expired life force.

Maybe I've gained his powers, he thought optimistically. He extended his hand and tried to release a bolt of energy. Nothing happened. Instead, he felt the familiar flow of ambient energy entering his body, which siphoned it all without trying. Oskar could never stop charging; with Gregor gone, he knew it would be only a matter of time before he overloaded.

The door to the outside catwalk opened, revealing the burned, bloody, half-naked, and still-smoldering form of Logan. His claws were extended, his eyes wide with bloodlust. The pugnacious mutant strode through the door and reached to grab Oskar, who scrambled away toward the ladder and plummeted headfirst to the next deck.

Oskar's only impulse was to flee. He caromed off bulkheads as he ran. His thoughts were bright with panic; they spun inside his mind, whirling faster by the moment, like moths trapped between a burning bulb and a lamp shade, wings banging and burning in a futile struggle for freedom. He ran without having a destination, focused only on escape, on survival. The door ahead of him was ajar. He paused only for a moment to yank it open. Then Wolverine's powerful hand gripped the back of Oskar's neck and slammed his face against the bulkhead.

Darkness fell like a cut circuit.

When he awoke, Oskar felt like a spectator to the slow return of his own consciousness. He watched the passageway's overhead drift through his field of vision for a few moments, until he became coherent enough to know that he was being dragged. Too groggy to struggle, he tried to move his hands and his feet, but they were held fast. His wrists had been secured behind his back, and his feet were bound at the ankles.

Logan was taking him deep into the lower decks of the *Pandora*. Here the diesel fumes and the clattering din of engine noise were overwhelming. As Logan pulled him through a flooded intersection, Oskar saw through an open door that a fire was raging in one of the adjacent compartments. No one seemed to be there to put it out. He wondered if the crew had already abandoned ship.

The floor-level tour of the engineering deck halted at a door marked "Engine Room." Logan opened it. The machines inside were deafening and high-pitched. He reached down and snagged Oskar by his collar again, and pulled him into the compartment.

Oskar felt the raw current that coursed through this area. When he looked at it with his mutant senses, he saw how bright its machines were, how radiant, how robust. All the Pandora's onboard electricity was generated here, including the power for its energy-hungry cloaking field.

Just being within a few meters of these systems was flooding his body with power that he couldn't release—at least, not in any way that would be safe. The proximity of such dynamos had him squirming in terror of the inevitable.

Logan picked up Oskar from the floor, gut-punched him harder than he'd ever been hit before in his entire life, and draped him backward over the ship's primary alternator. Raw power flooded into Oskar's body; the overhead lights flickered and dimmed for a moment. The rush of electricity racing through him was like a drug, heady and intoxicating. A sharp tug on his wrists snapped him back into the here-and-now, and he realized that Logan was tying his bound wrists to his ankles with a length of wire stretched beneath the alternator housing.

"Stop!" Oskar blurted. "You don't know what you're doing!"

"Wrong," Logan said, giving the twisted wire lashing one final pull for good measure. "I know exactly what I'm doing."

Then Logan turned and walked away, closing the door behind him. In just a few short minutes, Oskar's body became hot as it flooded with current siphoned from the ship's alternator. Sweat rolled from his brow and soaked his back. His pulse raced and his breaths grew shallow. There wasn't much time left, maybe a few minutes before he'd reach the limit of his ability to hold the charge. Mere minutes until he came to the end of himself.

Just a few minutes till I see you again, Gregor.

In life his twin had been a burden, an embarrassment, the albatross around his neck. Oskar had spent all his free time cleaning up Gregor's disasters, masking his mistakes, providing him alibis. *But at the one moment when he really needed me, I let him die.* Sorrowful and furious at the same time, he cursed himself for not having had the strength to deny Gregor's demand for power. *If I'd held back,* he castigated himself, *forced him to run, he'd still be alive, we'd finally be free...*

Oskar's jaw clenched as his muscles coiled with unspent power. The end was close now, so close. There was barely time left for one last, lonely act of contrition. *I'm sorry, Gregor,* he prayed, hoping that his slain brother could hear his apology and see his guilty tears. *I'm sorry.*

His tears ran dry... and then it was over.

LOGAN hurtled forward through passageways choked with smoke from the fires belowdecks. With Harada gone, Surge dead, and Slake on a short fuse to a big finish, there was no longer any reason to worry about setting off alarms. The ship's captain had ordered the crew to abandon ship, and no one had hesitated. *Pritikin was probably the first one off,* Logan figured.

As far as he knew, the last two people left aboard the *Pandora* were himself and Dr. Falco, whom he had seen moments ago through the observation window, struggling against his laboratory's locked door. The man was bloodied and burned, leading Logan to suspect that one of Surge's wayward blasts had been responsible for the scientist's injuries.

Coughing as he ducked under the blanket of sooty vapor hugging the overhead, Logan scrambled down the ladder and into the T-shaped intersection where he'd been intercepted by Harada. Three hard punches with his claws shredded the lab door's lock mechanism, and a battering push with his shoulder forced the portal open. He let his momentum carry him inside.

Falco was lying on the deck, barely conscious. Toppled equipment trays and shattered computers littered the floor. Several dozen ampoules of amber fluid had spilled from the pocket of Falco's lab coat. Logan knelt beside him. "I'm here to help you. Can you walk?"

The scientist shook his head. "Too late," he gasped through a pink froth of blood. "Toxic gas. Lungs…"

Logan picked up one of the ampoules. "Is this Panacea?"

Nodding, Falco spit to clear his mouth of blood, then he weakly grasped Logan's forearm. "Please… stop…"

"I know," Logan said. "The chopper left with a shipment. I'll catch up to it."

Falco tightened his grip, shook his head. "No," he said, more forcefully than before. "*You…* Stop… interfering."

Is this guy nuts? He pulled free of Falco's grip. "What the hell're you talkin' about, bub?"

"Let… the Hand finish… its work."

An explosion from below shook the ship, which groaned like a drowning elephant. Lifting the man by his shirt collar, Logan growled, "Don't you know what that stuff does to people?"

A demented smirk twisted Falco's features. "Better than anyone," he burbled, sputum overflowing the corner of his mouth.

"It'll turn people into slaves!"

The smirk became a grin. "Not for long," Falco said. "Not when my changes take effect."

Logan cocked his fist and twisted Falco's collar into a noose. "What changes?"

"Go on," Falco said. "Kill me… I can't… feel it anyway… Nerve damage." His snort of smug laughter made Logan coil with fury. "Too late for me… for Kazaki…"

"Kazaki?" Logan said, remembering where he'd heard the name. "Jiro Kazaki? The chemist who tipped off the Hand?"

Falco rolled his eyes in Logan's direction. "I did that," he said. "Set up Kazaki… to take the blame."

"The Hand murdered him," Logan said.

The dying scientist chuckled. "I figured."

Glaring, Logan demanded, "What have you done?"

"What I had to," Falco said. His voice faded swiftly. "What Tanaka… wouldn't let me do." He coughed. "No one knew… Changed the drug. Heals for a month… then it kills. Kills… everyone."

"You sonofabitch," Logan said. "Don't you know where the Hand's gonna use this stuff?"

After a slow nod, Falco's words came out long and dreamlike. "I know."

The crackle of spreading flames drew closer, moving between the bulkheads, raising the temperature rapidly. Logan shook Falco back to half-consciousness and shouted, "Why, goddammit?"

Falco shrugged his eyebrows. "Numbers," he said. "Too many people… not enough food… not enough oil." A wracking cough spewed dark blood over his lower lip and down his grimy shirt. Through a bloodstained smile, he boasted, "If we're lucky… my drug will kill two billion." He gagged on mouthful of blood, sputtered, then continued. "Maybe four."

Numb with shock, Logan mumbled, "Four billion."

A spasm traveled through Falco's body as death began to lay claim to him. It galled Logan that he had been sent to save this fiend's life. He let Falco lie flat on the deck, then reached down and scooped up a handful of the ampoules filled with Panacea. He removed the rubber caps, pulled open Falco's jaw, and poured in the drug. With a push on the man's chin, his mouth closed and his head tilted back. The swallowing reflex did the rest. Logan counted off the seconds while he listened to more eruptions stutter through the ship beneath him.

All at once, Falco shuddered awake, eyes bright and lucid. His surprise was betrayed by his sharp intake of breath. He looked with terror at the empty ampoules on the deck, then at Logan. "The drug? But—why?"

Logan regarded him with all the contempt he could pack into one scowl. "I just wanted to make sure you could feel this."

He punched his claws through Falco's chest, skewering his heart and staking him to the steel deck. He kept Falco pinned and stared into his eyes just long enough to be absolutely certain that he'd suffered, and that he was dead.

○————————○

ALEXEI Pritikin stood next to the EC-135 helicopter as its rotors warmed up and filled the air with thumping noise. After being pushed over the catwalk railing by Harada, he'd barely regained consciousness in time to find a submachine gun and shanghai the helicopter pilot off the lifeboat, to take him off the sinking ship by air. "There ain't enough time to do the warm-up," the pilot had protested, but a spray of bullets at his feet had persuaded him to make the effort anyway.

All the lifeboats were away now, bobbing atop the gentle crests of the bay, borne silently away into the night, toward the nearby shore. If the pilot turned out to be right, and the *Pandora* sank before the helicopter was ready to lift off, they would have no other means of escape but to attempt a long swim to shore through shark-infested waters.

An orange fireball erupted from inside the fake mountain of shipping containers, hurling shrapnel and spewing toxic clouds into the night sky. Flames raged across the foredeck. The *Pandora* listed sharply to port. The hull groaned, its death cry deep and mournful, as if the ship itself were aware that it had begun its descent to a watery grave.

When the spiraling plume of smoke drifted starboard with the wind, Pritikin saw a silhouette against the vermilion curtain of fire that was consuming the ship. A single man, leaping from one island of safe footing to another, crossing the inferno, then scaling the ship's superstructure. The long, fearsome claws extending from each of the man's hands left no doubt who it was.

Pritikin leveled his MP5K and opened fire.

Bullets *ping*ed off the deck and bulkheads. A few struck Logan, whose stride flagged but never halted. The weapon clicked empty, and Pritikin removed the spent magazine, tossed it aside, and slammed in the first of his two replacements.

Logan was closer now and moving faster, low to the ground, like a tiger on the attack. Firing on full automatic, Pritikin's weapon chattered angrily beneath the pounding drone of the EC-135's rotors, which were almost at liftoff speed. He raked Logan with a prolonged burst, and the mutant's stride faltered again—but he kept coming, until Pritikin's second clip ran dry.

Pritikin climbed inside the chopper but left the door open. "Go!" he yelled to the pilot. "Let's go! Now!"

The pilot struggled with the controls. Waves lapped over the port half of the *Pandora*'s main deck, which was slipping into the sea. As the helicopter began to slide left across the helipad, the pilot coaxed the aircraft up and off the aft deck of the ship. Then a heavy impact on the helicopter's right strut wobbled them enough that their rotors nicked the tilted deck of the ship, showering both with sparks.

Leaning out the door, Pritikin saw Logan clutching the landing strut. He fired a few short bursts at him, but the quaking of the chopper made it almost impossible to aim. "Shake him loose!" he shouted toward the cockpit. "Get him off of us!"

Then he saw Logan's hand grip the edge of doorway.

Pritikin held his weapon with both hands, steadied his aim. Waited for a clean shot at Logan's chest and head. Seconds later he had it, and he fired.

The bullets shredded Logan's chest, ripped into his face, sprayed blood across the inside of the chopper's passenger cabin. Logan almost fell backward, but he arrested his fall by driving the claws of his left hand through the cabin's deck, anchoring himself in place. And he just hung on and took it as Pritikin continued to fire, pumping every last bullet he had into him, until the weapon ended its barrage with an impotent *click*.

Then the bloody, shredded man in the doorway smiled—and climbed inside. He retracted his claws and advanced with predatory grace, then locked a single hand around Pritikin's throat. "Burning's too good for ya," he said in deep rasp. "Drowning's too good for ya… Sharks're too good for ya." Then he pulled Pritikin away from the wall and held him in front of the open side door. "But all three sound about right."

With one push, Pritikin was plummeting, dropping away from the helicopter. Free fall was both exhilarating and horrifying—then he made impact. His back twisted and his legs snapped under him. Jagged bones gouged through soft flesh. He bounced off the twisted bulkheads and tumbled across the deck of the *Pandora*. Flames licked at his face and crisped his hair. Burning oil and fuel stuck to his clothes. The agony of the fire was like the devil's breath. Then came the shock of immersion as he plunged into the sea and choked on the briny water.

When the first shark bumped against his shattered, bloody leg, he knew that it wouldn't be long before the last part of Logan's death sentence came true as well.

○————————○

LOGAN sat down in the copilot's seat, relieved to be off his feet and able to rest for a moment. Next to him, the pilot sat quietly, not moving and clearly watching Logan out of the corner of his eye. Glancing at the pilot, Logan extended a single claw and gestured at the man. "We gonna have a problem?"

"No," said the pilot, and he obviously meant it.

"Good," Logan said. "Take me back to Lagos." Detecting a familiar, pleasant aroma from the inside pocket of the pilot's jacket, he added, "And give me one of your cigars."

○————————○

JUST less than two hours later, the EC-135 set down at Murtala Airport. Its struts settled onto the tarmac with nary a bump, as if the helicopter were as light as air. The pilot powered down the engine, and the pitch of the rotor noise began to fall. "Nice landing," Logan said to him, then he punched him across the jaw, knocking him unconscious.

Out of the helicopter, Logan abandoned stealth and sprinted beside the taxiways, back to the hangar where he'd left Wai Ying and the Cessna Thunderstar several hours ago. It was a few hours before sunrise. Most of the airport was dark and empty as a ghost town. He hoped that Wai Ying had been able to get the jet refueled in the hour since he'd contacted her from the EC-135, en route from the sinking of the *Pandora*.

He remained at a full run until he dashed into the hangar. The jet was there, closed up tight. He knocked on the door and waited. After a few seconds' delay, Wai Ying peered through the door's circular window, then opened it and lowered the ladder.

"Are you all right?" she said.

"Fine," he said, climbing the ladder. "Lost your phone, though. Sorry."

When he got to the top, she embraced him with relief and affection. It caught him off-guard, so he just stood there for a second before he hugged her back. Feeling the silken texture of her hair, the softness of her skin—it brought back memories that he'd fought for years to put behind him. *God, how I've missed this*, he realized. *Like coming home*. His appreciation for the moment was bittersweet, tainted by the specter of a love long lost but never forgotten. He cleared his mind of thoughts and let himself be in the moment for just a few breaths longer… then it was time to return to the task at hand.

He broke free of Wai Ying's embrace. "Where's the C-130?"

"On its way to Kaiduguri Airfield in Zibara," she said. "TBC's tracking it now."

"Zibara? That's where we picked up Pritikin's trail yesterday."

Wai Ying nodded. "We're hearing chatter in Kaltoum that a private charity has made a deal with the Zibarese government to take over its relief programs. Care to guess this charity's name?"

Logan held up his open hand and pointed at it. Wai Ying nodded in confirmation. He frowned. "Ready to fly?"

"Ready," she said.

He moved forward into the cockpit and powered up the flight-planning computer. "How big is their head start?"

"About three hours," she said. "But the C-130's a propeller aircraft—maximum speed about three hundred eighty miles per hour. If we go wheels up in the next ten minutes, there's a slim chance we can beat them to Kaiduguri."

"They're never gonna reach Kaiduguri," Logan said. "'Cause we're gonna take 'em out before they get there." He switched off the computer and left the cockpit. Wai Ying followed him.

"Where are you going?" she asked.

Recalling the panicked young cargo handler's accidental confession about a load of Semtex hidden in a janitor's closet, Logan smirked and replied cryptically, "To get some cleaning supplies."

21

KNEELING beneath the lean-to shelter and between her children, Nishan dipped her ragged cloth in the bowl of cloudy water and wrung it half dry. It was Kanika's turn to have the cloth on her forehead. Nishan had been careful to keep track of whose turn it was as she alternated between Kanika and Nadif. Both children lay deathly still, their breathing too shallow to measure. All night, Nishan had kept watch over them, determined to stay awake and maintain her vigil against death's angel. *I won't let their souls be taken while I sleep*, she'd promised herself. *I will be with them every moment. Every moment.*

Dark violet streaks began to stand out in the eastern sky. Insects' nocturnal songs faded, and the birds awoke to fill the predawn hush with chirping melodies as pale sunlight washed slowly over the horizon.

Nishan no longer knew what to do, where to go, or whom to turn to. Not to God; prayer had failed her. Not to the government; it was in league with the men who had sired this evil. She couldn't even take comfort in curses. All the same cruelties had claimed her ancestors for as long as anyone could remember. If they had been powerless against this evil in life, how could she expect them to be of aid from the world beyond? Many of those who'd shared her fate had blamed God, had called him cruel, vicious, merciless. Nishan did not believe such talk, not even now, because the truth was even more painful. All the misery and evils that she had seen done had been the work of men, and all of it had gone unspoken and unavenged. This was not the product of a malicious deity; a cruel God would at least take an interest in human life, if only to inflict misery upon it. Life in Zibara was proof that God was indifferent—blind and uncaring, as distant as the stars and as cold as the grave.

An engine rumbled in the distance and drew closer. Rattling metal shook and banged as the vehicle navigated the uneven land outside the village. As the sound of tires crackling across a dirt road became clear, the vehicle's horn honked.

Though she was reluctant to turn away from Nadif and Kanika even for a moment, lest the angel of death take her children in those fleeting seconds, curiosity compelled her to crawl out from under the lean-to and see what the ruckus was about. When she tried to stand, she faltered. She had been kneeling for so long that her legs had grown weak and cramped. By the time she steadied herself, an open-top truck had come to a halt in the middle of the village—or, at least, amid some cinder piles where the village's center had once been. Its driver and passenger were both Asian men. The passenger stood up on his seat and called out to the villagers. "Come closer!" he cried. "We have important news! Please, gather 'round and listen, everyone." Following the shambling horde, Nishan drifted closer to the truck, wondering if they were being evacuated to one of the refugee camps. She had seen one of those places as a child; it was just as miserable as life anywhere else in Zibara, with the additional indignity of being imprisoned "for your own safety." If that's what these men were here to announce, Nishan had already decided to take her chances and flee toward Ethiopia.

"All right," the Asian passenger said, speaking loudly and slowly. "Listen now. We are from a new international relief organization called the Hand. We're going to be bringing you food, water, and a new medicine that can cure any illness."

No one believed what they had just heard. A shrill woman shouted back, "Any illness?"

"Yes," the Asian man said. "Malaria, AIDS, Ebola, cancer, anything. It can heal wounds, repair organs. It can—"

"Lies!" shrieked a scar-faced young woman clutching an infant to her emaciated breast. Her accusation was followed by more angry, disbelieving shouts from the crowd.

"How can we believe you?"

"Their medicine's a poison! They're out to murder us!"

"You're putting us in the camps, aren't you?"

"The Tanjawar will take it all, like they always do!"

Waving his arms for silence, the Asian man replied, "No, the medicine is not a poison! You're not going to the camps, and the Tanjawar will not harm you again—their pact with the government in Kaltoum is over. We will protect you from them."

Now the crowd's cynicism reached a fever pitch. "Like the Americans protected us? Or the British? Or the United Nations?"

Voices overlapped, growing more stridently bitter each moment. No one believed such promises anymore. Too many times had such relief revealed itself as a mirage, as a lure for the unwary or the too-trusting.

"Hear me now!" bellowed the Asian man, in a mighty baritone that silenced the crowd. "If the Tanjawar try to take your food, your water, or your medicine from the Hand, they will be killed. We are not the United Nations. We do not make promises we can't keep. If the Tanjawar interfere with our mission, we will not negotiate with them. I promise you again: we will *kill them*. We will kill them *all*."

Never in her life had Nishan heard someone make a promise so clearly or so forcefully. Whomever these men worked for, they were not the impotent diplomats of the West, or the noble but ultimately powerless doctors and nurses of Médecins sans Frontières, or idealistic but helpless clergymen and nuns. The Hand, whatever it turned out to be, was something different. Could that be reason enough to give hope one last reprieve?

"You talk big," a gnarled old woman croaked at the Asian man. "But *when* will you help us? When do we *eat*?"

This was it, Nishan knew. Always at this stage the promises became vague, the timetables of relief unclear. When it came time for specifics, this was always the moment when all the generous, hopeful pledges were exposed as good ideas bereft of substance, and the villagers' hopes again were dashed.

This time, the Asian man looked the old crone in the eye and answered, "In a few hours. The medicine is being flown in from Lagos now. As soon as it arrives, we're bringing it here."

Excitement passed like a virus from person to person. *Today? Food and water and medicine are coming in a few hours?* It was almost enough to make Nishan believe that she had been wrong about the value of prayer, wrong about the power of her ancestors, wrong about God.

Elation swept through her fellow villagers. Some held each other and wept with joy, praised God, or thanked Allah; some just cried and forgot words altogether.

Then Nishan caught herself. She would not weep or give thanks—not yet. Darkness still lay over the land; sunrise was still in the distance. There was no food yet on her plate, no water in her cup, no medicine in her children's mouths. Until there was, she would not celebrate. In a land of broken promises, only a fool believed in anything he wasn't holding in his hand.

She returned to the lean-to and crawled back beneath it, between her two children. Their chests barely moved now, the spans between their breaths growing longer. Nishan lifted the rag from Kanika's forehead and pushed it gently into the dirty water. Another half-twist, then she unfurled it, folded it half over itself, and laid it tenderly on Nadif's feverish brow.

Nishan wanted to believe that the Hand was telling the truth, that an end to the horror and suffering was at hand. She wanted to believe that a cure was coming in time to save her son and daughter. But she couldn't dare to hope, not now; if the Hand's promises turned out to be a lie, she would soon have nothing left… not even the dark comfort of sorrow.

22

LOGAN grew anxious. He strained to pierce the pale glow of predawn light rising from beyond the distant curve of the horizon. Dense, sculpted mountains of peach-tinted clouds surrounded the Cessna Thunderstar. Somewhere beyond this, or inside it, or below it, the C-130 Hercules was making its initial approach to the landing strip in Zibara. "Come on," Logan muttered to his unseen prey. "Where are you?"

Wai Ying nudged the Cessna into a shallow dive, picking up speed, pushing them well past Mach 1. "We're close," she said, obviously trying to reassure him. "You should get ready."

Like an arrow into cotton, the Cessna plunged through the cloud bank. The world outside vanished into a watery mist. Wai Ying kept her eyes on her instruments, ignoring the hypnotic, featureless gray void outside the cockpit window. Logan got out of his seat and started back toward the passenger cabin. He paused in the cockpit doorway. "You're sure you can do this?"

"No problem," she said. "I've got the easy job. You're the one jumping out of the plane."

"Just get in as close as you can," he said. "And don't try anything fancy."

The Cessna's engines whined as it dived. Logan climbed the slope of its center aisle, fighting against gravity, until he reached his rucksack, which was tucked under one of the seats. From the rucksack he retrieved several long, narrow bricks of Semtex-H plastic explosive and set them on one of the seats. At the bottom of the sack was a detonator and a roll of black gaffer's tape. Using the tape, Logan quickly secured all the bricks together into a single unit, then implanted the detonator leads, taking care to embed them deep and tape them into place. A quick test confirmed that the detonator was ready. He stuffed the entire bundle back inside his rucksack and slung its brown leather straps over his shoulders.

He returned to the cockpit just as the plane burst free of its obscuring veil of mist, revealing the long rays of sunrise reaching swiftly across the dusty landscape. Nearly three hundred meters below them and several kilometers ahead was the C-130 Hercules, barely staying above the gnarled, deadwood treetops as it hurtled toward Kaiduguri Airfield.

"They're only a couple minutes from landing," Logan said. "Get us in there now. And lock the cockpit door—I'm opening the side hatch."

Wai Ying looked over at him, eyed the rucksack, and raised one eyebrow to express her incredulity. "No parachute?"

"It'd just slow me down," Logan said.

She smiled. "Good luck."

"See you on the ground," he said, then closed the door behind him as he left the cockpit.

He stood at the side hatch and waited for the plane to level out of its descent. The engine noise grew louder and deeper as the Cessna reduced speed to match the C-130's velocity. Over the onboard PA, Wai Ying alerted him, "Ten seconds to intercept."

Logan overrode the safety locks and opened the side hatch.

Wind noise and jet roar—louder than a freight train, like an explosion that wouldn't end. Air blasted into his face, watered his eyes, stung his skin. His clothes snapped and fluttered around him like the filthy flags of destitute nations. The Cessna was low enough that explosive decompression hadn't been a problem when opening the hatch, but there was still a definite suction effect near the doorway, and he braced himself with both hands while awaiting his moment to fly.

Under his feet, the African savannah blurred by, a dark wash of sunburned beige and sparse splotches of green. *Only one chance at this*, he knew. *That's a long way down.*

The tail of the C-130 drifted into view. Wai Ying was guiding the Cessna on a diagonal intercept path toward the C-130's right wing. *They've got to see us on radar*, Logan thought. *Why aren't they going evasive?* Only two answers came to him: either the C-130 was on a schedule that it couldn't risk breaking, or someone was already aboard the plane and waiting to greet Logan when he arrived. *Please let it be ninjas*, he thought with a bloodthirsty grin. *Please.*

Seconds later the doorway of the Cessna was aligned with the nose of the C-130, about ten meters above. *That's as good a shot as I'm gonna get*, Logan figured, and he launched himself out the doorway, claws extended and ready. Free fall and wind resistance shot him backward, under the Cessna's wing as he fell. Reaching out with his adamantium talons, he skewered the top of the C-130's rear fuselage as he made impact. Like anchors finding purchase in a soft seabed, his claws brought him to a halt. Keeping his left claws in place, he pulled his right claws free to cut his way inside the plane. On the edge of his vision, he saw that Wai Ying had already guided the Cessna away and accelerated ahead, determined to land at Kaiduguri ahead of the C-130 in case Logan failed.

Time to drop in and say hello. He reached behind himself, plunged his right claws into the metal skin of the cargo plane, and made a broad, arcing cut, using his own position as the center of a circle, which then fell away beneath him, into the plane. He landed on top of it, pulling his left claws free, and came up in a low crouch, ready to meet his welcoming committee.

The Hand didn't disappoint him.

Two dozen ninjas swarmed from every direction. They tumbled, rolled, slashed, hurled projectiles. The first several hits cut the straps of his rucksack, which fell away into the shadows. *Shuriken* buried themselves into Logan's chest and thighs, blades slashed across his back, his shoulders, his arms.

Some of the blades were poisoned, and the toxins burned in his fresh, bloody wounds.

He pulled into himself, tightened his defensive circle. The ninjas, predictably aggressive, pressed their apparent advantage and moved in for the kill. And then Logan went berserk.

No effort, no thought, no conscience, just the primal drive to strike, to kill. Unleashed and uncontrolled, the animal predator in him struck at anything and everyone, reveled in the orgy of violence, the baptismal glory of warm sprays of blood against his face and chest. There were no friends or allies here, only enemies and prey. A target-rich environment. He remained fixed in place, beneath the shaft of daylight pouring in through the hole in the fuselage overhead, eviscerating all who dared to emerge from the shadows to challenge him. Severed heads and limbs piled up around him, and the scents of burlap and aviation fuel that he'd noticed when he first dropped through the fuselage had now been overpowered by a coppery stench normally not found outside an abattoir.

Then the rush of blades and fists ceased, leaving only the drone of the C-130's massive propellers and the howl of wind flooding in through the hole overhead. Logan stood alone in the massive, open space inside the cargo plane, peering into the darkness toward the front of the aircraft, where he saw the square outline of the shipping container from the *Pandora*—and the ghostly outline of an enormous, armored figure standing in front of it, posed like a statue and watching him.

"Always we return to the old ways, eh, Logan-san?" The words passed through Logan, around him, over him. Harada kept talking. "All you see is the fight, the bloodshed. Someone turns you loose and you go on a killing spree… but you never ask why." Silver Samurai took a few slow steps forward. He was fully appointed in his trademark titanium-white battle armor with a red rising sun on the chest, apparently not satisfied this time to trust his reflexes as his sole defense. "The Hand is bringing order to people who live in chaos, life to those who were cursed to die. With Panacea, we can end the genocides, remove the warlords, put an end to centuries of pointless war. We can bring these people peace, Logan." He stopped and smirked. "But I suppose you've never had much use for peace, have you?"

Forcing his thoughts to line up and push through the surging heat of his primitive rage, Logan answered slowly, "You're… making a mistake."

"No, I'm correcting one," Harada replied. "I'm fixing the weak, futile policies of the West. Putting an end to hunger, to war, to disease. Decades of promises have yielded nothing here, Logan. Every year, Africans die in greater numbers and America does nothing. Europe does nothing. Japan does nothing."

He was almost within striking distance now. Logan's mutant healing factor stitched his body back together as he watched Harada circle him, just out of arm's reach. "Hate to tell ya this, bub, but yer army of grateful slaves has an expiration date. And a pretty short one, to boot."

That provoked a wrinkled look of concern on Harada's face. "What are you saying, Logan?"

"Falco double-crossed you," he said. "Turned your miracle drug into a slow poison. Works for a month, then it turns toxic. Spread that stuff around and next month the planet's gonna be a lot less crowded."

For a moment, the truth seemed to register with Harada, but then he shook his head, choosing the easier path of denial. "I don't believe you," he said. "You're just trying to buy time, trying to postpone the inevitable so you can rally your X-Men or call in the Avengers. I can't allow that, Logan."

"I'm tellin' you the truth," Logan said. "Listen to me: Panacea needs to be destroyed. All of it."

"No," Harada said.

Logan rolled out a crick in his neck. He kept one eye on Harada at all times. Steeling himself for battle, he gave his foe one more chance. "I'm fraggin' the drugs, Keni. We can do it the easy way or the hard way. You don't want it the hard way."

Harada raised his blade. "I'll be the judge of that."

He lunged, thrusting his sword in and up. Logan deflected the blow and counterattacked. His claws ripped through Harada's layers of chest armor but only grazed the flesh beneath.

Both fighters' next flurries of lightning-quick strikes missed their targets and hacked long gouges in the metal skin of the plane, permitting long slashes of light to penetrate the C-130's dark interior. They attacked again.

A low block by Harada thwarted Logan's combination strike and left Logan open. Harada's *katana* slashed over Logan's forearms, then his knee cracked into Logan's jaw, knocking him backward. Logan fell hard on his back but rebounded to his feet almost instantly. He saw now that Harada had drawn his *wakizashi* and was employing a two-weapon fighting style. The deck was treacherously slick with blood.

Logan charged, hoping that momentum would carry his attack past Harada's defenses. His attack fell on empty air. He hit the left bulkhead; his shoulder collided with a large red switch that started a hydraulic motor in the rear of the plane. Then he felt the burning slice of steel through his Achilles tendons, and another slash severed his hamstrings. *Biomechanical cutting*, Logan realized. *Smart move.*

Claws retracted, Logan pushed up and away from the wall and tumbled backward through the air. Upside-down, his claws sprang back out in time to catch and trap both of Harada's swords with turns of his wrists. He slammed into Silver Samurai, and the two of them rolled across the deck, against the right bulkhead. Punching and gouging, Logan ripped apart the deck as Harada writhed and struggled to free his blades and himself. Keeping Keniuchio pinned for a few more moments was all that Logan needed for his healing factor to repair his torn ligaments and restore his mobility.

At the rear of the cargo compartment, the C-130's loading ramp was lowering with a groan of hydraulics and a shrieking blast of wind. Outside was a bright blur, the landscape blasted white by the blinding light of a freshly broken dawn.

Harada let go of his blades and used his superhuman strength to flip and throw Logan, who inflicted two horrendous gouges on either side of Harada's torso. Logan landed on the ramp and rolled to his feet just shy of going over the edge. Behind him was a high-velocity fall to an uncertain fate. Ahead of him, Harada recovered his swords and charged. Logan raced to meet him, determined to get some room between himself and the edge of the ramp.

All of Logan's rage and reflexes weren't enough to keep up with Harada, whose already formidable powers had been lethally enhanced with super speed by the Hand. For every three blows that Logan was able to block, two more hit home.

A stabbing thrust skewered Logan's liver. In a flash of silver, a razor edge slammed into his face and severed his upper lip and part of his nose, spewing blood into his mouth and down in sheets over his chest. His left bicep was cleaved in twain. Every hit came from an oblique angle, a blind spot, the one point from which he couldn't defend himself for a split-second. A snap kick in his shredded, bloody face knocked Logan backward, off-balance, and a sweep behind his knees put him on the deck, kneeling and twisted, his right clavicle exposed.

Feel the blade in the air, counseled his old sensei's voice, speaking to him now through the waves of blinding agony. *Hear its point pierce the silence. Know its moment.*

The blade was falling, its point seeking Logan's heart.

Its moment was near, and then it arrived.

Logan's right hand shot up and back, then turned. The blade of Harada's *katana* was snared, and its samurai wielder stood at Logan's right side, premature in his pose of triumph. With the captured blade, Logan yanked Harada down, doubled him over—then thrust his left claws up and deep through Silver Samurai's armor, through his all-too-human ribs of bone, into the spongy bronchi of his lungs.

Logan gave his embedded claws a half-turn. Harada gurgled, then dark blood frothed inside his mouth even as it ran down Logan's claws and soaked the outside of Harada's armor. Harada lost hold of his *katana*. Logan flung the weapon away, onto the ramp, where it clattered to a stop against the edge.

Then Harada's *wakizashi* gouged into Logan's throat. Logan knocked the weapon from Harada's hand, then retracted his claws as he fell to the deck and applied pressure to his savaged, erupting carotid artery. Harada, meanwhile, staggered forward, one hand covering his eviscerated right side, then fell to his knees and began to crawl toward his *katana*.

Logan turned and fought against vertigo to stand upright. His barely healed tendons screamed in protest, almost too stiff to move. Blood continued to gush from his face and throat. All that he knew was pain. He decided to let his wounds bleed; he wanted both his hands free for what had to come next.

Tattered and baptized in vivid crimson, Logan hobbled after Harada, who stopped crawling at the edge of the ramp as a jolt of turbulence knocked his sword over the edge, out of the plane, out of reach. As Logan inched up on him, Harada looked back, his eyes dulled with pain, dimmed from blood loss. His *wakizashi* lay on the deck, back where Logan had dealt Harada's mortal wound.

As Logan staggered forward, close enough almost to grab hold of him, Harada draped one leg over the edge of the ramp. He looked up at Logan with a doleful expression. "I could've given these people peace," he rasped through a mouthful of bloody foam. "The Hand could've given them a future."

"As slaves," Logan said. "And when the poison kicked in, you'd have killed them all. The biggest slaughter in history." Another half-step forward, and now Harada had his right leg and his right shoulder over the edge. *No way I can reach him before he lets go*, Logan realized. He raised his claws as a warning. "Don't make this harder than it has to be, Keni. Don't make me come looking for you."

"You won't have to," Harada said. "When it's time... I'll find you." Then he pushed himself off the ramp, into free fall, several hundred feet above a dusty plain.

Logan watched Harada plummet, even knowing what he would see. Several seconds later, Harada vanished in mid-fall—just a flash of light and color, then empty air. *Damn teleportation ring*, Logan groused. *Have to cut that off him first next time. Better yet, maybe I'll take the whole damn hand.*

He turned away from the ramp and limped with great effort back toward the front of the plane, leaving the ramp open behind him. There was little clearance around the sides of the shipping container, but it was enough to let him reach the pilot's side ladder to the cockpit. He used his arms to pull himself up, since his legs still weren't cooperating with his desires.

The pilot was sluggish on the draw as Logan entered the cockpit. By the time he had his sidearm drawn and aimed, Logan had already cut its barrel and slide into pieces with one slice of his claws. Bits of metal and a few grains of gunpowder pattered on the deck beside the pilot's seat. Belatedly, the copilot reached for his own holster, but stopped as Logan said, "Don't even try it." Climbing all the way inside the cockpit, he added, "You've both got parachutes. Use 'em."

The two pilots traded fearful glances, then scrambled down the copilot's ladder out of the cockpit and made a run for it. Logan settled into the pilot's seat and kept watch out the side window. Moments later, he saw two white parachutes blossom open and catch the sunlight as they drifted away behind the C-130.

He made a quick review of the gauges and was satisfied that the C-130 had enough fuel left to ensure Panacea's immolation. A gentle nudge of the yoke veered the plane away from Kaiduguri Airfield, out into a desolate stretch of land to the northwest. He opened the throttle and increased the plane's speed. The drone of the engines grew louder and higher-pitched.

Narrow columns of smoke rose along the horizon, just a few kilometers ahead. He aimed the C-130 at them. Then he leveled out the plane's flight at an altitude of just over two hundred feet and set the autopilot.

Logan limped down and out of the cockpit, past the tight clearance of the shipping container. Then he found his rucksack, tucked into a corner behind the protrusion for the left-side wheel well. He opened the sack. All the Semtex was still inside, secured together, the detonator wires in place. He armed the detonator and set the timer for thirty seconds. With a touch, the countdown began.

In halting steps he left the rucksack behind, on the deck next to the shipping container. He paused at the edge of the ramp. Counting the seconds in his head, he knew he didn't have time to think this over, and that was probably for the best.

He stepped off the ramp and pressed his arms to his sides. Tucking his chin to his chest, he fell headfirst toward the ground. For several moments stretched by adrenaline, he heard only the low roar of air and felt nothing but the regularly increasing pull of gravity. It was freedom, tranquility, just himself and open air, without burdens, in the light of sunrise.

Then the C-130 exploded above him, closer than he would have expected, but far enough away not to pose any threat. The fireball was a deep reddish orange, like a marigold of flames in bloom amid a cloud-streaked sea of blue. Heavy grayish-black smoke billowed, no doubt thick with incinerated aviation fuel. Burning, smoky debris fell from the cloud, like dark angels cast out of a fiery heaven. Chunks of fuselage and fragments of wing spiraled to earth, leaving corkscrew smoke trails to drift in the humid African breeze. One intact propeller spun as it dropped into gravity's merciless embrace.

Logan turned his eyes from the plane to face his own moment of reckoning. Larger than life and faster than he could have imagined, the ground was rising to meet him, dark and rocky and unforgiving. The landscape was uncommonly, almost unsettlingly beige, and unrelieved by the graces of nature or the touch of human arts. There were no broad-limbed trees to break his fall, no conveniently placed ponds or lakes, not even a deep but slow river toward which he might struggle to direct his fall. Just the ground, simple and brutal and waiting like a reaper with mile-wide arms to greet him on impact.

He used his last few seconds of free fall to do a couple of midair somersaults, just for the heck of it. Then he flattened out and faced the sky as he fell, arms and legs wide. *Bring it.*

Then the sky turned black.

<hr>

LOGAN'S eyes fluttered open slowly. Pain hammered inside his skull with diabolical ferocity, turning like a drill that bore holes through all his thoughts.

He didn't remember making impact, but obviously he had. He was sprawled on his back, on a muddy patch of ground. His vision was hazy and tinted red, and no matter how he tried he couldn't move, not even his fingers or toes. An odor of blood was heavy in the air, and he realized that it was his own. The mud in which he lay had been moistened by his pulverized soft tissue. *Musta mashed goddamn near everything*, he reasoned.

His head was lolled to one side, just enough that he could, with effort, look down the length of his body. *Everything still looks like it's attached*, he noted. *So far, so good.* Above him, a cast of vultures circled, slow and patient. He heard a few more on the ground nearby as they stepped cautiously around him, trying to determine whether it was safe yet to eat him.

The sun was low on the horizon; it was still early morning. *Can't have been here long*, he figured. Looking out across the blighted plains, he saw dark smoke rising from the strewn wreckage of the C-130. Between the initial explosion and the incendiary effect of the plane's fuel, he was certain that he'd accomplished his mission: Panacea had been destroyed.

A good day's work, he told himself.

Exhaustion and injury caught up to him at last, and a dark wave of fatigue swept over him. Despite the excruciating throbbing in his skull and the million-twisting-maggots sensation of his flesh slowly reweaving itself from the inside out, one thought nagged at him as he let go and drifted into the comforting shelter of unconsciousness.

Man, I wish I had a cigar right now.

23

KHALEED al-Rashad hung up the phone and looked out the window of his den. His son, Mustaf, splashed joyfully in the swimming pool. All traces of Mustaf's osteosarcoma had been erased, leaving only the bright, curious young boy whom Khaleed had treasured as a gift from Allah every day since he was born.

Also vanished now was any hope for prolonging Mustaf's life. Coastal patrols had just investigated an explosion in a harbor near the border between Nigeria and Cameroon. A freighter registered to Anbaric Petroleum had been found scuttled in a burning slick of fuel. Most of the crew had escaped, but among the unfortunate few whose bodies had been recovered from sharks swarming the wreckage had been Alexei Pritikin.

The first call al-Rashad had made after getting the news was to Kaiduguri Airfield, to see if Pritikin's cargo plane had arrived with its shipment of miracle drugs. *Maybe there's still time to divert it here*, he'd thought. *Time to stockpile the drug for Mustaf.* But then Kaiduguri's tower supervisor reported that the plane had veered off-course just after 0621 hours. Minutes later it had vanished from radar and was believed to have crashed in Tanjawar territory, to the northwest.

There was nothing left to do now but await the inevitable.

Khaleed left his den and walked outside, across the perfectly maintained greensward behind his home, then onto the broad walkway of Spanish tile that surrounded his pool. Parveen, his wife, sat poolside, her eyes brimming with tears as she watched their miraculously healed son submerging and crashing back up through the pool's sparkling azure surface. She swept a thick lock of her black hair from her cheek and squinted against the blazing morning sun as she smiled up at Khaleed, who buried his torment and smiled back at her.

How do I tell her these are his last days? That his future died with Pritikin?

Rationalizing the situation didn't help. He told himself over and over again that even this brief reprieve was a blessing, despite the swift end that was going to follow in less than three days' time. But it felt like a cruel joke, to dangle health and freedom and a future in front of a boy doomed to die, a boy who had never harmed anyone, whose only sin had been to have Khaleed for his father.

Mustaf climbed out of the pool. Dripping wet and giggling, he ran to Parveen and hugged her. She kissed his wet head and clutched him to her. Then the boy pulled away from her and jogged clumsily to Khaleed, who kneeled to greet him. He caught the boy in a bear hug and all but crushed him to his chest, committing to memory the sound of his son's voice, the smell of chlorine in his hair, the solidity of his presence. All too soon he would be gone, and memories of these things, recollections pale and insubstantial, would be all that remained.

He held his son but could not hold back his own tears, which rolled in fast cascades down his face. Parveen watched him and read the truth in his eyes. She could see into his soul with a glance, she always had been able to, so he knew that she could see that his tears were shed not in joy but in mourning.

Pushing away from Khaleed, Mustaf asked, "Father? Why are you crying?"

"I'm just thanking Allah that you're well, Mustaf." He pressed his palm against his son's cheek. "Now that you don't need the medicine anymore, you can eat anything you want," Khaleed said. "Whatever you want, for lunch, for dinner, just ask. And I think we should invite all your friends right away to come celebrate with you."

Excitement filled the boy with energy. "You mean it?"

"Yes, Mustaf, invite them all. We'll make a party of it."

Mustaf embraced him again. "Thank you, Father!" Then he let go and ran inside the house to call everyone he knew.

As soon as Mustaf closed the sliding-glass door behind him, Parveen wiped away a fresh sheen of tears from her own face.

"How long does he have, Khaleed?"

Khaleed hung his head in grief. "Less than three days."

For a long moment, Parveen hid her face in her hands and fought for breath while resisting the desire to collapse into wracking sobs. Khaleed knew exactly how she felt—stunned, helpless, undone. She couldn't look at him or at the house, so she turned away and gazed into the rippled depths of the pool. "Will he suffer?"

"I don't know," Khaleed said, and it was the truth.

He felt cut off, shut out, as if Parveen was blaming him for this tragedy. Keeping silent, he knew that he wasn't to blame, that if Panacea hadn't claimed Mustaf's life three days from now, the metastasized cancer likely would have within a few more months. It was just the insult of an apparent cure that made the reality of the matter so powerfully bitter.

Parveen sighed so deeply that he wondered if there could be even half a breath left within her. "Why has Allah done this to us, Khaleed? Why?"

"He didn't," Khaleed said. "Evil men did this. For oil, for money, for power. This is what man does —not Allah."

Rage swelled in her voice. "Then why does He permit it?"

"Imam Yosef says that Allah made us all free to do as we will, for good or for evil. If He made it impossible for us to do evil, we would be nothing but slaves. We must choose." He walked slowly, cautiously, to her side and took her hand. "I choose to make these last few days with Mustaf ones of joy. If he must be taken from us, let us love him while we can." Parveen squeezed her eyes shut, and Khaleed pulled her to him and cradled her head on his shoulder. "Let him tell Allah how we loved him. Let us love him enough to make Allah proud."

LOGAN awoke to the blinding flare of the noonday sun. Its blistering heat was a hammer, the earth its anvil, and his body the raw mass trapped between them. He squinted hard and turned his head away from the glare. Several meters to his left, someone sat watching him.

Raising his arm to shield his eyes, he saw that the watcher was an emaciated black woman. The landscape of her face was etched with deep lines of tragedy, but her eyes looked lifeless. Flies congregated on her skin and buzzed around her as though she were already dead. She made no effort to shoo them away.

He sat up and took stock of himself. Filthy from top to bottom, attired in nothing except a tattered pair of pants and some bloodstained rags that used to be a shirt. His wounds from the battle in the C-130 and the fall had healed. All his muscles were stiff and his joints almost literally creaked as he turned to face his visitor and rub the back of his neck.

"Hey there," he said to the woman. "What's your name?" She didn't respond; she just stared at him. Affectless. Numb.

Slowly he got to his feet and bent himself backward until he heard a satisfying crack and felt a knot of pressure unwind in his middle back. The air was hot and dry, laced with the earthy fragrances of baked dirt and drought-withered plants.

His eyes swept over the harsh country that surrounded him. Barren plains of parched dust reached away in all directions and only in the distance gave way to raw rocky hills. In the middle of one empty expanse sat an animal's sun-bleached skeleton, picked clean by predators and scavengers and scoured smooth by wind-driven sand. Forlorn and stripped of flesh, it spoke to the ancient beast in Logan's soul, cried out the bloody truth of the world's endless, eternal violence.

Then his eyes fell upon an off-white cloud of dust kicking up in the distance, drawing closer. He stood and waited, having nowhere to go and nothing to do when he got there. Several minutes later, the Jeep inside the dust cloud became visible as it bounced over the uneven terrain. There were two people in the vehicle. The passenger pointed in Logan's direction.

Meanwhile, the gaunt woman sat nearby, her eyes fixed on Logan. He assumed she had to be aware of the Jeep as it closed to within fifty meters, but she paid it no regard.

The Jeep slowed and then stopped in front of Logan. He nodded to its occupants, both dusted the color of chalk. Wai Ying sat in the passenger seat. "Are you all right?" she said.

Logan shrugged. "You?"

She nodded, then introduced her driver. "This is Gary Lee," she said. "He's a park ranger here in Zibara." Lee nodded to Logan. Wai Ying continued, "He said he can take us as far as Kaltoum. From there, we're on our own."

Suspicion creased Logan's brow. "What about the Cessna?"

Wai Ying averted her eyes, clearly embarrassed. "TBC took back the jet," she said. "We're stranded."

"Because I destroyed the Panacea, right?"

She nodded. "That… and they got my expense report." Unable to suppress a smile, she confessed, "I think I set a company record. And I'm pretty sure I've been fired."

He chortled for a moment. "Good for you. Don't worry about getting home. I'll have some cash wired over when we reach Kaltoum. We'll be fine." Logan was about to climb inside the Jeep when he remembered the Zibarese woman sitting on the ground watching him. He turned and took a few steps toward her. Wary of spooking her, he asked softly, "Miss? You need a ride?"

The woman met his inquiry with a suddenly fiery gaze. "It was you," she said in French-accented English. "I saw you fall from the plane… You destroyed it."

Held by the force of her hatred, Logan nodded. "Yes."

"The miracle drug was on that plane?" she asked.

He wondered how much she knew about Panacea. "Yes," he replied.

"Why?" Grief radiated from her even though she didn't shed a tear or make a sound. Behind her, Logan only now noticed the two short mounds of recently excavated and refilled soil, and the short entrenching tool that lay between the narrow piles of dirt, which was still dark from being freshly turned over.

The mounds were too short to be for adults, he realized. *The graves of children. Her children.*

"I had no choice," he said, immediately regretting that he'd resorted to so trite a verbal defense.

"My children needed that drug," she said, more desperate than angry. She stepped closer, until she was right in front of him. "I needed it. And you destroyed it."

"I had to," he said. "It was a poison."

"The men from the Hand said—"

"They lied," Logan interrupted. "It would have seemed like a cure, but in a month it would've killed you all, and billions of other people."

The woman spit in Logan's face. "I don't care about other people!" She pointed in turn to the two graves. "I cared about Nadif! About Kanika!" Her fists clenched with sorrow and rage. "Some cure is better than no cure."

Logan shook his head. "Not this one," he said. "Even if it could've been fixed, you and your kids would've had to take it for the rest or your lives, or else you would've died. You'd have been slaves of the Hand."

Shock and disbelief contorted her face. "So? So what? We're already slaves—to the warlords and the Tanjawar, to the foreigners who ration our food and water, to the doctors who decide what cures we can have! We live like cattle waiting for slaughter. Is that not slavery? At least we would have been free of disease, free of hunger, safe from the warlords and the rapists... Who were you to choose our fate for us?"

Logan stood before her, stunned and silent, unable to fathom the abyssal depths of her suffering. Despite more than a century of walking the earth and witnessing its evils, he still couldn't wrap his mind around the scope of the tragedy that defined this country and its impoverished, abused people. He wanted to tell her that he understood her sorrow, that he could share in some measure of her pain, but he knew that was a lie. There was no way he could empathize with the millions of people around the world, most of them in Africa, who were destined to die from diseases to which his mutation had made him immune. And there was nothing he could do that would help any of them. Violence was his sole vocation, his only talent. Brute force was of no value here. This was not a battle for men such as himself. Something told Logan that a man like Charles Xavier could do a lot of good in a place like this. He hoped he was right.

Nothing more to do, nothing left to say, Logan turned away from the Zibarese woman and climbed into the back of the Jeep. He gave a small nod to Wai Ying, who signaled the driver to head back to Kaltoum. As the Jeep made a U-turn, Logan watched the grieving mother settle slowly on her knees between the graves of her children, her eyes still piercing his soul with her bitter accusation. He could see the fatigue that plagued her, the sorrow and the hunger and the disease that all had taken their toll and had left her spent and broken, too beaten even to weep for her children. Beneath the white-hot orb of the sun and the pale vault of the sky, her silence was her mourning shroud.

Riding back to Kaltoum, every time Logan closed his eyes, he saw her, flanked by those tiny graves... and he knew that her specter would stalk his dreams, reminding him of his impotence in the face of true evil, for as long as he lived.

24

ALONE at last, Keniuchio Harada lay in bed, swathed in bandages and tucked under crisp white-linen sheets. He was surrounded by medical machines, all beeping or thrumming. A slow drip filled his arm with painkillers, saline, and nutrients, while a catheter drained his bladder in a slow, near-constant trickle. The naso-gastrointestinal tube that wound through his sinus and down his esophagus into his stomach was monitored every few hours for signs of internal bleeding. The morphine was doing its part to dull his pain, but the massive, rude gouges in his side throbbed with a deep, relentless ache.

It was fortunate for him that the modern-day *yakuza* tended so well to its own. Surgeons and pharmacists were kept on retainer, and private hospital facilities such as this one provided a crucial haven for highly placed *kumicho* during emergencies. When, without warning, Harada had appeared, bloody and all but incapacitated in the doctors' midst, they had snapped into action without hesitation, eager to serve their *oyabun* in his hour of distress.

His armor would be repaired, his swords replaced. With enough medicine, transplants, and money, his wounds would heal. Only his pride, cut down by Logan's claws like autumn wheat before a scythe, would carry a scar from this debacle.

All this work for nothing, he brooded, closing his hand around the one remaining vial of Panacea in the world. He had grabbed it during his first visit to the *Pandora*, without really thinking about it. Now its golden fluid was all that remained of his dreams of worldwide order and power.

The vial had contained ten doses; a team of scientists who worked for one of Japan's more discreet intelligence services had expended all but one running an exhaustive series of tests, trying to unravel its chemical mysteries. In the end, they confirmed what Wolverine had already told Harada on the plane: the miracle drug had been turned into a slow poison. Within a month, it would build up in the brain tissue of anyone who took it and induce fatal strokes, seizures, and aneurysms. Just as Logan had professed, Falco had deceived everyone—his employers at Tanaka Biotechnology, the *yakuza*, even the Hand. He had framed one of his coworkers as the mole, meaning that Harada had ordered the wrong person assassinated after the formula was acquired. And if Logan had not intervened, Harada's orderly world would have ended in the largest slaughter of human beings in history.

And yet... the drug still commanded his imagination with its possibilities. If its natural curative and addictive properties could be divorced from its artificially introduced toxic elements, there might still be hope for bringing an end to chaos, disease, famine, and war. But the tiny sample he held in his hand was not enough for research. It was little more than a single-shot, perfect-health death sentence.

So tired, he thought as a timed release of morphine spread warm relief through his body. Lolling his head toward the window, he watched the colorful pinpoints of light in Tokyo's nightscape slowly soften and fuse into a muddy wash of pastel hues. Everything became indistinct, uncertain, and Harada's thoughts drifted to ruminations on missed opportunities.

The alliance between the *yakuza* and the Hand had fallen apart with the loss of Panacea; all their joint plans had been predicated on the unique bargaining power that control of the drug would have given them. Oil resources; gold and silver and diamonds; uranium ore; cheap manual labor. It all had been within their grasp, and as it slipped away Harada was no longer of any use to the ninjas and their secret society. All their lines of communication had suddenly gone dark, vanished into the past like the ninjas themselves into the shadows. The Hand had never really understood Harada's desire for order, for peace. All they had been able to see was the promise of power for its own sake. Where he had espoused a vision, they'd had only an agenda. Now both sides had nothing.

Harada opened his eyes as the door to his room opened and four men entered. They were his *saiko-komon*, his senior advisers, and they all wore serious expressions. Kuhido, the eldest of the four *yakuza* brethren, carried a bottle of sake. His second, Kanashima, carried a porcelain cup. Shinoda and Kokusui followed close behind. All four *kobun* gathered at Harada's bedside.

With a polite nod, Kuhido said only, "Harada-san."

"*Konnichiwa*, Kaziyoshi," Harada rasped, forcing words past the tube in his throat.

Kanashima held the porcelain cup. Kuhido filled it with sake, then handed the bottle to Shinoda. Then Kanashima handed the cup to Kuhido, who drank first.

Kuhido passed the cup to Kanashima, who took a sip. In turn the cup passed to Shinoda and then to Kokusui, who then offered it to Harada. Harada accepted the offer of the cup with a nod. Kokusui tilted the bowl and let a single drop of sake fall on Harada's tongue. As soon as the ritual was done, the four men nodded to Harada; then Shinoda, Kanashima, and Kokusui all bowed to Kuhido. Kanashima collected the sake bottle and handed the cup to Shinoda, and the foursome left Harada's hospital room without speaking another word.

The fact that Kuhido had tasted the sake first had symbolized his ascendance to *oyabun*, the top position. Rank had followed in descending order with the passing of the cup. The fact that they had allowed Harada to drink at all meant that he was still considered a brother, though no longer fit to lead. He would not be killed while lying in bed, and if, when Harada was recovered, he chose not to challenge Kuhido, then the transfer of power would be bloodless and final.

It's for the best, Harada decided.

There would be other opportunities. Even before the Panacea fiasco, he had been contacted by old allies inside the Japanese government. Word on the street was that the new prime minister was looking to pay handsomely for professional protection. Being a bodyguard had seemed to Harada at the time like a retrograde career move; now, the idea of being the right hand to the leader of a growing national power on the world stage held slightly more appeal than it had yesterday.

Harada decided to look into it... tomorrow.

Tonight, he would dream of a world that might have been, a global empire of order and harmony, a worldwide hegemony under his authority, its people's fates and actions guided by his wise and beneficent leadership... and then he would dream in vivid colors of taking his revenge on Wolverine, for condemning the world to repeat all its worst mistakes for another generation.

If his chemists ever restored Panacea to its original form, he would use it to make his first dream come true. To make his second dream a reality, all he would need would be a sword.

25

TWILIGHT crept through the softly clashing boughs overhead, and Logan knew that it would soon be time to leave. His visits to Mariko's grave often were cut short; not today. He'd spent the afternoon in quiet meditation before the marble monolith devoted to her memory. The red rose that he had brought last week still lay on the base of the monument, though the flower was now blackened and shriveled from desiccation.

In years past, Logan's graveside ruminations had been about his life that might have been, the possibilities that all had slipped away with Mariko's last breath. Sometimes, he'd simply questioned fate. Why had she been taken from him? Why her? Such questions never found answers. The universe was not cruel, but it was arbitrary, and the truest answer to most questions of *Why?* was *Because it happened.*

A low wind hushed between the stones, then dwindled to a whimper. Logan breathed in the approaching night and found it sweet with the scent of freshly cut grass. He reached up and pressed his hand against the cold, glassy marble. *I used to think livin' without you would be the hardest thing I'd ever do*, he confessed to Mariko's unseen spirit. *Turns out I was right.* In a blink of memory, he reflected on all the people who'd ever hurt him, betrayed him, or broken their bond of trust. Despite all the grudges he still carried, none weighed as heavily on him as the one he bore against himself: *I didn't give her the poison, but I was the one who stabbed her in the heart.*

He looked down at his forearms and pictured the adamantium claws that lurked within them. *They can cut through damn near anything, but what good does it do?* Suddenly, his greatest weapons seemed useless. They hadn't been able to cut the poison from Mariko; they could help him destroy a flawed drug, but they were powerless to end the suffering of a billion people dying of hunger, thirst, and disease. He could slay a dozen ninjas, but he couldn't give a grieving mother back her children. His claws held no cures, no promise of a better future, just a faster way to destroy the present, one life at a time.

Lost causes, he brooded. *That's all I seem to fight for these days.* It made sense to him, though—what other battles were really worth fighting? Evil and greed always seemed to trump the better angels of man's nature; cruelty always gained the upper hand in its struggle against mercy. The rich always got their way at the expense of others, and deceived the poor and the weak, like that Zibarese mother, into accepting lives of injustice rather than rebelling against those who had taken advantage of them. Those the rich couldn't fool they bullied.

All over the world, for more than a century, Logan had seen nothing but endless variations on an eternal theme: *The strong prey on the weak*. It was the essence of nature and the primitive instinct that raged in his own heart; it was the animal in him, the feral spark that lived for the hunt, for the kill, pure and honest in its brutality. But it was also the part of him that most needed the civilizing discipline of his human soul—the conscience that could rein in the beast that lurked inside him, feasting and growing strong on his rage and sorrow.

Shadow settled over the graveyard. Logan looked up at the dark mass of marble before him, perhaps hoping for a moment of insight, a glimmer of meaning… but he found only the cold reproach of stone.

There's just one thing I'm really good at, he brooded, staring at his clenched fists. *And it doesn't do any good. If I kill a million bad men, a million more'll take their place, just 'cause they can. It never ends. There's always somebody takin' more than they deserve, and six billion morons who let 'em do it. How'm I supposed to fix that with my hands?*

Logan got up from his knees and zipped his leather jacket half closed. It was time to leave; Wai Ying would be waiting for him outside the gate with their motorcycle—which he had bought, since she was now unemployed and broke. They hadn't decided where to go. Maybe to Tokyo, maybe farther north to Sendai, or out of Japan completely. He also didn't know how long they would be together, but what couple ever really did?

What mattered now was simply that, for the first time in years, he was embarking upon a journey for its own sake, just to be on the road, in motion, away and free.

He walked away from Mariko's grave and didn't look back. As he neared the gate he saw Wai Ying. She waved. In her white riding leathers, she was like a pale ghost in the gathering gloom. Riding off with her into the night, their plan unwritten and destination unknown, would be an act of faith: in Wai Ying, in the future, in himself.

I know I can't change the world. Maybe I can't even change myself. But it's worth a try.

He joined Wai Ying at the motorcycle. They climbed on the bike, him in front, her in back, arms around his waist. He turned the key, kicked the starter, twisted the throttle. A buzz-saw growl coursed from its engine, a song of freedom. The bike lurched into motion.

The road of Logan's past was littered with fallen friends and enemies, soaked in the blood of the innocent and the guilty, built on the bones of the just and the unjust. He was leaving that path behind, in search of a better one. In the roar of an engine he was away, on the road to his future.

It was a journey long overdue.

ACKNOWLEDGMENTS

PEOPLE often think that being a writer sounds like hard, lonely work. Sometimes it is. But just as lonely—and far less lauded—is the lot of the writer's spouse. My lovely wife, Kara, deals with my reclusive moods, my nights spent brooding behind closed doors, my semi-permanent air of mental distraction as I work on my stories inside my head when I'm supposed to be focusing on other things—such as what our dinner guests are saying. For all your seemingly inexhaustible forbearance, my love, thank you.

Next up is my friend Glenn Hauman, who helped me come up with the first germ of an idea for this book. He was the one who suggested a plot based around a miracle drug that kills its users when they try to go cold turkey. Glenn also helped me acquire decades of past issues of *Wolverine* on CD-ROM, so that I could research this book properly. Thanks, my old friend; I could not have done this without your help. You rule.

Some of the story lines to which I made reference in the text of this novel include *Path of the Warlord*, written by Howard Mackie, and *Soultaker*, written by Akira Yoshida. Furthermore, my principal antagonist, Silver Samurai, was the brainchild of writer Steve Gerber, and the Hand would not exist but for the pen of comic-book legend Frank Miller. My thanks go out to all these gifted scribes.

Of course, as long as I'm thanking people for inspiring the story line, I should tip my hat to *New York Times* columnist Nicholas Kristof, whose columns about the genocidal crises in such places as Darfur and Chad helped to inspire this book's central plotline. Thank you, Mr. Kristof, for continuing to make people aware of a tragedy that all too many of us find far too easy to ignore.

My friend Steven Wexler took time to share his martial-arts expertise and suggested a number of sources that I used in my research of sword and knife combat. Thanks for the pointers, Steve. They helped.

Peppered throughout this book are snippets of dialogue in a number of foreign languages. Because I am pathetically monolingual, I needed to enlist the aid of a number of language consultants to pull this off and get it right. Tomoko Kanashima vetted my Japanese; Sonia Kuchuk and her parents translated the various bits of Russian; and Carlos Carranza and his "Brazilian mafia" provided the book's tidbits of Brazilian Portuguese. *Muchas gracias* to all of you, my *amigos*, for all your help.

Keeping watch over the English portions of the book was editor par excellence Marco Palmieri, for whose patient guidance I am always grateful. Thanks also are due to former Pocket Books associate publisher Scott Shannon, who first suggested to me that I should write a *Wolverine* novel. Luckily for me, Ruwan Jayatilleke of Marvel Comics agreed with Scott.

I also feel that I should thank my in-laws—Keith, Donna, and Diana—for being so supportive of all my work. You're probably the only members of my family who will actually pay for a copy of this book.

ABOUT THE AUTHOR

DAVID ALAN MACK is the author of numerous *Star Trek* novels, including the *USA Today* bestseller *A Time to Heal* and its companion volume, *A Time to Kill*. Mack's other novels include *Star Trek: Deep Space Nine—Warpath*; *Star Trek Vanguard: Harbinger*, the first volume in a series that he developed with editor Marco Palmieri; *Star Trek: S.C.E.—Wildfire*; and numerous eBooks and short stories.

Before writing books, Mack cowrote two episodes of *Star Trek: Deep Space Nine*. He cowrote the episode "Starship Down" with John J. Ordover. Mack and Ordover teamed up again to pen the story treatment for the episode "It's Only a Paper Moon," for which Ronald D. Moore wrote the teleplay.

He currently works as a consultant for *Star Trek: Lower Decks* and *Star Trek: Prodigy*.

Mack currently resides in New York City with his wife, Kara. Learn more about him and his work on his official website: http://www.davidmack.pro/.

Book Three
LIFEBLOOD

by Hugh Matthews

To Richard Pedersen, who clued me in.

OTTAWA, CANADA,

THE PRESENT

COLD.

Just as the gray day slid toward evening, the north wind brisked up, bringing rain so cold it turned to ice that stuck to whatever it touched. The bare branches of the trees along Elgin Street were sheathed in a glistening armor that dragged them down and froze them to the ground. The smallest twigs had snapped but the chill coating held them in place, would not let them fall.

The small man in the plaid wool jacket and black knitted cap walked into the wind, broad shoulders hunched, scarred hands deep in the pockets of his tattered jeans. But his face met the icy blast straight on, let the frozen crystals sting his skin and make the bones beneath the flesh ache, as if they were being scraped by knives.

Pain was good. Pain was real. It cut through the fog inside him, slashed through the roiling, colorless nothingness that stuffed his head. With pain came memory—or what passed for recollection in a mind that could not connect faces to names nor places to events, a mind that did not know if the pictures it conjured to fill its inner screen came from true recall or false, maybe just from dreams, or stories he'd heard. Or from the nightmares that chased him, screaming in rage and horror, back into wakefulness, back into the fog.

Heya, heya, heya. At first he thought the chant was coming from inside his head. Sometimes he heard voices, random scraps of speech, mostly in English, sometimes in other languages that he understood. *Heya, heya, heya* it came again, louder now as his steps took him past Confederation Park. Off to his right, unseen behind the white rain, someone was beating a drum, a simple double-beat rhythm to accompany the voice.

I've heard that before, the man thought. He stopped and let the sound pass through him, held his mind back when it tried to get a grip on the memory. He'd learned that grasping didn't work, would make the recollection disappear, like trying to grab smoke.

Heya, heya, heya with the drum beating underneath—*bom-bom, bom-bom, bom-bom*—like somebody had cut open the world to show its living heart, he thought. And that brought up an image: a man split from gullet to groin, lying on his back, looking up, his eyes clouding in death.

Who is that man? He couldn't help reaching for the memory, but even as he grasped for it, the picture faded, the dead eyes the last to go. Still, the drum and the chant continued. The small man turned toward them and went into the park, not following the concrete path that was slick with ice but walking through short winter grass that crackled and broke beneath his heavy boots.

Something big ahead, he thought. Through the rain he saw a block of gray surmounted by dark shapes—people, animals, a great bird with wings spread wide. Now he came close enough to see that it was a monument. On a massive granite base stood four figures, three men and a woman, cast in dark bronze. Around them were four animals—grizzly, wolf, bison, and caribou— and above their heads a giant eagle soared. On the front of the plinth, a plaque announced in English and French that the monument commemorated the sacrifices of the First Nations, Métis and Inuit men and women who had worn Canadian uniforms in wars and peacekeeping missions.

The drumming and chanting were coming from the far side, but the small man's eyes had dropped from the heroic figures to the two rows of flowered wreaths, standing on wire tripods, that were ranged along the steps leading up to the monument. He had a vague sense that the presence of the wreaths meant that it must be not long since the Remembrance Day observances of November 11. The date brought a flash of memory—a soundless image of men with weary faces and mud-spattered uniforms throwing helmets shaped like soup bowls into the air, some with mouths set in bitter smiles, some weeping openly—then the picture was gone.

One of the wreaths drew his gaze. It stood apart from the others, a small circle of dark red flowers woven through evergreen boughs. At its center, encased in plastic, was a framed photograph of a man with strongly aboriginal features, the cheeks flat-planed, the narrow eyes almost asiatic. He wore a beret with a parachute badge. Beneath the picture, a wide ribbon bore the legend SGT. THOMAS GEORGE PRINCE, 1915–1977.

The chant and drum grew louder, but the small man did not move. He stared at the black-and-white image and the man in the photo looked back at him with the confident half smile of the consummate warrior, a smile that said, *I know who I am and I know what I can do.*

But it wasn't the smile that held the man motionless in the freezing rain, staring at the image while the ice built on his shoulders and covered his wool cap like a helmet. He stared at the picture of the aboriginal sergeant in the old-fashioned, British-style Canadian Army uniform and more images came: bright sunlight on dry earth, small trees with dark leaves and clumps of green fruit—olive trees, said his own voice in his head—a dusty road and soldiers marching in puttees and canvas webbing, bolt-action rifles slung from their shoulders.

"I know you," he said, his voice a grating whisper. And as he spoke the drum ceased, the chant ended on one last *heya.* The small man stooped and reached for the photograph. It came free of the wreath. He pulled the ribbon loose and wrapped it tightly around the plastic-covered cardboard, then he opened his coat and stuffed both prizes inside, against the worn checked shirt that covered his hard-muscled torso.

He buttoned the coat back up. Now he stood in the falling sleet that whispered as it struck the ground, no longer noticing the bite of the wind that made the ice-covered trees rattle like dead men's bones. He put his hand to his chest, pressed the cardboard against the beat of his heart, and said again, "I know you."

When he stepped around the monument to find the drummer and chanter, no one was there.

THE EMPTY QUARTER, SAUDI ARABIA,

THE PRESENT

HEAT.

Outside the camouflaged hangar, disguised to look like a low-rise in the barren landscape, the air rippled with desert heat under a sun so fierce it seemed to turn the sky white. The lean man with close-cropped iron-gray hair stood within the open doors, the toes of his polished black boots just behind the line of light and darkness that separated the hidden building's shade from the searing blast of the sun. His ice-blue eyes followed the progress of the VTOL jet as it came in low and slow to hover in a cloud of grit a short distance beyond the open hangar. The plane, mottled with desert camouflage paint, settled onto its three wheels. Its whining thrusters throttled down, then turned aft to roll the jet slowly into the hangar.

Wolfgang Freiherr von Strucker turned on his heel with parade-ground precision and accompanied the aircraft into the darkness. Behind him, swarthy men in loose, long-sleeved robes of white cotton, their heads bound in flowing white scarves secured by a doubled black cord, rushed to roll the outer doors closed. The jet's engines cycled down and its double canopy levered up as the Arabs pushed a wheeled staircase into position. The pilot remained in his place, making notations in the airlog, while the man in the rear seat left the plane and descended to the hangar floor.

"*Salaam aleikum,*" said von Strucker, the traditional Arabic greeting accompanied by a curt dip of the head and a click of heels brought sharply together, which the baron had learned as a cadet in a Prussian military academy long, long ago.

"*Aleikum salaam,*" said the visitor, in the accents of Yemen, adding only the smallest gesture of one hand. He wore a Savile Row suit with an understated pinstripe, but his olive-skinned face had the stark grimness of a desert warrior and his liquid brown eyes were lit from within by a gleam of fanaticism that had made him the chief of operations for the shadowy Islamist cabal known as the Foundation.

"We will go below," the Prussian said, leading his visitor toward an elevator at the rear of the hangar. A moment later they were descending deep into the living rock of the desert, the elevator door opening on to a subterranean corridor walled, floored, and roofed in reinforced concrete. Boot heels clacking on the polished surface, von Strucker led the way to a heavy metal door guarded by an Arab man in combat fatigues, who snapped to attention as the two men approached.

Von Strucker acknowledged the salute with a fractional nod, then reached behind the guard to tap a code into a numbered keypad beside the door. The barrier slid silently into the wall, revealing an unlit room beyond. The two men advanced into the room, the door sliding closed behind them. The Prussian indicated a low square table, ten feet by ten, that dominated the center of the space. Its top held sixteen square blocks of a city in miniature: houses in the classic Arab style, with windowless outer walls enclosing courtyards and gardens. The models were faithful replicas, von Strucker knew, of a particular neighborhood in the city of Amman, capital of the Hashemite Kingdom of Jordan. The walls surrounding the table were covered with huge blown-up photographs of the city and large-scale, detailed maps, marked in places with broad red arrows and concentric black circles that represented lines of fire and calculated gradations of blast damage.

The Yemeni cast his eye over the table and the wall displays, his face impassive.

"The plan is complete," von Strucker said. "We have run simulations based on all likely scenarios and several that are barely possible. The outcome in each case is certain: neither the Jordanian foreign minister nor the American ambassador will survive their encounter with the Green Fist."

The visitor leaned over the table, reached into a representation of a street, and touched a manicured fingernail to the rear of a toy limousine whose fender bore a miniature Stars and Stripes. He flicked the little car, sending it careering down the avenue to strike the curb outside the model of the foreign minister's house. It flipped over, its tiny wheels spinning.

The Yemeni's dark eyes looked up at von Strucker. "The plan," he said, "is changed."

The Prussian stiffened. "The plan," he said, "is perfect."

The visitor picked up the overturned car and set it aright again. "Yes," he said, "this plan is. But a new opportunity has arisen. We are calling it Operation Severed Head."

The baron was used to sudden changes of strategy from the Foundation. "Who is the target?" he said. "And where will we strike?"

The Yemeni smiled a cruel smile. "The Green Zone," he said, "in Baghdad."

"And who is the target?"

The Yemeni's thin lips framed their heartless smile again as he savored the thought. Then he told the baron the name of the man who was marked for death.

OTTAWA, CANADA,

THE PRESENT

"I want to find out about this man."

The librarian hadn't heard the man's approach. She looked at the photo of an aboriginal soldier that had appeared on her desk, then at the hand that had placed it before her. There were strange scars between the knuckles, scars on top of scars, as if sharp knives had been thrust into the flesh more than once. She looked up and a cold shock went through her when her eyes met his. She'd seen plenty of crazies—the public library was where the street-dwelling insane passed some of their tortured days—but this one was different. She saw a hunger in his gaze, and behind that hunger she sensed a savagery that was barely contained. He was like something from a bygone age, a time when disputes were settled with spilled blood and torn flesh.

"I want to know who he was," the man said, the voice more like an animal's growl than human speech. And now he flung something else onto the woman's desk, a small bundle of wadded cloth. She pulled at an edge and it became a crumpled ribbon of black satin stitched with letters of gold. She read the name and the dates and a great wash of relief went through her. She could be rid of him.

"Come with me," she said, rising. Her desk was on the edge of the open area that welcomed visitors to the main branch of the Ottawa Public Library. She now set off across the foyer toward a free-standing set of six shelves that displayed several books beneath a computer-printed banner, decorated with stylized red poppies, that read LEST WE FORGET. On a middle shelf stood a small hardcover book, its title *Tommy Prince, Hero*. She took it and handed it to him and as his scarred hand closed on the small volume, she saw a light come into his eyes. It put her in mind of a scene she'd seen in a nature documentary, when the camera had caught a close-up of a timber wolf just as it came out of a stand of pines and saw a yearling moose calf stranded in deep snow.

She shivered, but the man didn't notice. He was already turning away, carrying the book toward a table and chairs. She watched him as he sat and spread its pages open before him, hunched over it as if he were starving and the book was food. Melting ice dripped from his knit cap onto the paper and he carefully wiped the droplet away with his sleeve, then took off the hat and set it down beside him.

The woman backed away, then turned and went swiftly back to her desk. She got her purse out of the bottom drawer and went quickly to an inner door, using a card slung from a lanyard around her neck to swipe open the security lock. The library would be closing in another hour and she had decided to spend that time downstairs in the quiet of the stacks. If the man needed any more help, let someone else provide it.

o———————o

HIS name was Logan. He was pretty sure of that much, because the envelopes with cash in them that were slipped under the door of his apartment once a month had that name printed on them, and nobody had ever showed up to say, "I'm Logan, where's my money?"

The apartment was a nondescript condo in a converted warehouse in Bytown, the oldest part of Ottawa, named for the colonel of Queen Victoria's Royal Engineers who had laid out the original town next to the fork where the Rideau and Ottawa rivers met. Logan was also sure he didn't own the space he lived in—he never got tax notices—and he figured that whoever was sending him the money was also taking care of the rent.

He'd tried waiting at his door, ready to yank it open the moment the envelope was slid under. But all he had achieved was that he got no money that day. Loitering in the hallway or keeping a watch on the building from across the street brought the same result. So when money day came, he went out and walked the streets, peering into faces that always found a reason to look away fast, wanting to see just one person he recognized— one body he could grab and hold immobile in front of him while he said, "I *know* you. Do you know me?"

And now, at last, he had found a face that rang his bell. Tommy Prince—the name meant nothing. But about the face he was sure. When he stared at the photograph, he could see that same face wearing other expressions, could see it from other angles.

Now, hunched over the book at the library, he wanted to tear through the pages, rip the information out of it, satisfy the craving. Instead, he carefully wiped away a drop of water that fell from his hair. He turned to the first page and began to read.

THE EMPTY QUARTER, SAUDI ARABIA,

THE PRESENT

"IT cannot be done," von Strucker said.

"It must be done," the Yemeni said, adding, "*Inshalla*." If God wills it.

The Prussian passed his hand over the stubble of his hair and said, "The security is too tight."

"There is always a way," said the visitor. "Find it."

"Why there? Why not somewhere else?"

The Arab's eyes shone. "Because it is Baghdad, the city of the Caliphs, the successors of the Prophet, blessings and peace be upon him." He paused, then said, "And the timing is most propitious."

"What is special about the timing?"

The Yemeni clasped his dry palms together and touched his crossed thumbs to his lips. "It is a time," he said, "when the enemy is at his most... sentimental."

OTTAWA, CANADA,
THE PRESENT

SERGEANT Tommy Prince was an Ojibway from the Brokenhead band on the Canadian prairies. A descendant of the great Salteaux chief Peguis, he grew up to be an expert hunter in the wild lands around southwest Lake Winnipeg. When World War II began, he volunteered for the Canadian Army, where his skills as a marksman and tracker made him a natural for the first combined special forces unit, the Devil's Brigade, that brought together the cream of Canadian and U.S. fighting men for behind-the-lines operations in the Italian and Normandy campaigns. He became the most highly decorated aboriginal soldier in Canadian history, receiving the Military Medal from King George VI and the Silver Star from President Franklin Delano Roosevelt of the United States. He later returned to uniform and fought in Korea, where he was wounded and was decorated again for valor, then came home to be treated as "just another Indian," in a time when it was illegal for Native Canadians to vote or buy a bottle of whiskey.

It took Logan less than an hour to go through the slim volume. He read about the time Prince had repaired a field telephone cable in full sight of German infantry by pretending to be a cantankerous Italian farmer stooping to tie his shoe. He read about the time Prince led his special forces comrades deep behind enemy lines to capture more than a thousand German soldiers who thought they were safely bivouacked far from the front. He read about how the aging veteran, forgotten and sunk into poverty, had to pawn his ten hard-won medals to buy groceries.

"They use you, then they throw you away," he said to himself, but his voice carried and people looking for books on nearby shelves decided that what they were searching for must be in some other part of the library. The Ojibway soldier's story rang echoes from the deeper cellars of Logan's mind. Some of the incidents itched at the edge of his consciousness, like the remnants of the dreams that clung to him when he awoke in the mornings, but always wisped away when he tried to examine them.

"But it can't be," he said to the sergeant looking out at him from the picture in the book, the same image he had torn from the commemorative wreath. "You were too long ago."

The Canadian Army's Italian campaign had been waged in 1943 and 1944, more than sixty years ago. Tommy Prince himself had grown old and died, had been dead now for thirty years. If Logan had known the man—and some part of his mind insisted he had—then Logan himself could not be much less than a hundred years old.

He looked at his hands. They were hard and scarred, but they were the hands of a man still in his prime. He ran one of those hands over his face, his fingertips rasping on the coarse black stubble that grew back almost as fast as he could shave it. His touch told him that his face was seamed with harsh lines around the mouth and at the corners of the eyes, but it was not an old man's face.

He realized that his other hand was gripping the book so tightly that he was bending its cardboard cover. He set the book down and ground his teeth in frustration, jaw muscles bunching under his thick sideburns. *A false lead*, he thought. *Somebody yanking my chain.*

There were times when he sensed that what had happened to his mind was no accident. He had no bumps or concave depressions on his skull that argued for a head injury. *Somebody messed with me. Somebody wants me like this.* He thought again about the words that had sprung out of him when he read about the Ojibway hero sliding into neglect and poverty: *They use you, then they throw you away.*

There was truth in that. He knew it, if he knew nothing else. But then a second thought hit him: *They haven't thrown me away. Like a valuable piece of equipment, they've scrubbed me clean and put me in storage—against the day they need me again.* Either way, somebody had done this to him, stolen his memories—stolen his *life*—and somebody was going to pay.

He looked again at the picture in the book. It was the first page in a section of black-and-white photographs. He'd already flipped through them once, the images of soldiers and shattered buildings tugging at things buried too deep in him to come out into the light. Then he noticed a detail: a roadside sign, black letters on white paint. It read "Ortona."

I've seen that sign. I know that word. The book didn't have much to say about what Ortona was. Maybe Tommy Prince hadn't spent much time there. Logan got up and went back to the display with the poppies and the banner whose words—"lest we forget"—were an unwitting mockery of his situation. Another volume on the top shelf caught his eye, this one a big, coffee-table book, full of pictures. Its title: *Canadians at War: The Italian Campaign.* He took it back to the table and spread it open, flipped through the pages—and fell into the past.

THE EMPTY QUARTER, SAUDI ARABIA,

THE PRESENT

THE VTOL jet had been refueled and rolled out onto the apron, the hawk-nosed Yemeni back in the jump seat. Von Strucker watched it lift off vertically, then rotate at fifty feet and move off across the uninhabited desert, an area as large as France, that covered southern Saudi Arabia and the coastal nations of Yemen and Oman. The aircraft would fly under radar height for most of the journey south, then appear on air traffic controllers' screens as a private jet owned by a minor sheik whose ancestral lands were in Yemen's rugged western mountains. No air traffic controller would question its identity—at least not twice.

The hangar doors rolled closed and the Prussian descended again, this time to a deeper level than the planning room where he had conferred with his visitor from the south. As he stepped from the elevator, he heard the voices of men raised in Muslim prayer—it was one of those five times of the day—and when he entered the training room, the sixteen mujahideen were kneeling on the prayer mats, their foreheads pressed to the floor. Then, as one, they sat back and each turned left and right, saying, "*As-salaamu aleikum wa rahmatullah*," to wish each other peace and the blessings of Allah.

Then they rose and rolled up their prayer mats and formed two lines facing each other, shaking out their arms and flexing their knees. The baron watched approvingly. This afternoon's training was in unarmed combat, and these men were not just as good as any special forces cadre in the world; they were better. They were the best. He had seen to that.

Their leader was a tall, sinewy Pashtun from Helmand province in Afghanistan. His parents had named him Batoor, but the men of the Green Fist had given him the Arabic nickname Al Borak—the Lightning. That had been the name of the Prophet Muhammad's favorite horse, but

Batoor's change of name had had nothing to do with horses.

He sent von Strucker an inquiring look across the sprung wooden floor of the training room, but the Prussian moved the fingers of one hand in a way that told Al Borak to carry on with the exercises. The baron wanted to think about the challenge the Yemeni had brought him, and he thought best when the front of his mind was kept busy watching the skills of his crack mujahideen on display. They were orphans or otherwise unwanted outcasts from several Islamic countries who owed their allegiance to none but each other and to the man who had rescued them from poverty and disgrace—a man who, though an infidel himself, had had them thoroughly schooled in the Holy Q'ran. Especially the suras that explained the rightness of jihad.

Now, as the sixteen men positioned themselves in the wide-legged fighting stance and drew their iron-muscled arms and legs into preliminary positions, von Strucker knew again the same fierce pride he had felt, so many years ago now, when he had presented his troop of Iron Eagles to the bespectacled gaze of Heinrich Himmler.

"The *Eisenadler* are the finest soldiers in the world, Herr Reichsführer," he had said. "Stronger, faster, smarter, braver than the legionaries of Rome, the hoplites of Alexander the Great, the Teutonic knights of old."

Himmler had watched the blond young men go through their paces, completing an obstacle course in half the time it would have taken the best squad of Hermann Goering's elite parachute division. He oversaw a demonstration of close-quarter fighting with trench knives and bare hands, with strikes and counterstrikes too fast for the untutored eye to follow.

Then the diminutive man with a neck so scrawny his uniform collars had to be specially fitted yawned and said, "Yes, yes, Herr Baron, but how do you make them last?"

For there was the problem. The baron had chosen the fittest of the fit from the Wehrmacht and the SS, the most fanatically motivated young men the Reich had to offer. He had trained them to their peak, then he had augmented their superb physical condition with a concoction of his own: a mixture of amphetamines, vitamins, and a few rare substances culled from von Strucker's encyclopedic knowledge of what the medical profession called "nontraditional pharmacology"—everything from the curare of the Amazon jungle to the most subtle potions of ancient Chinese herbology.

"How," Himmler said, "do you keep them from burning out?"

The Iron Eagles would only be useful for short-term missions. The baron's stimulants would keep them functioning far beyond their physical limits, giving them speed and power that would swiftly overrun even the most elite troops of the Americans or British. But after two days, at the most three, the Reich's supersoldiers began to shake uncontrollably. They saw horrors at the edge of their vision, started at sounds only they could hear, until they collapsed—sometimes into psychoses from which they could not be redeemed.

"I will find a way," he had told the SS chief, "to make the effects permanent. Then you will have invincible legions with which to conquer the world."

"You mean the Führer will have invincible legions," Himmler said.

The baron had clicked his heels and struck a rigid pose. "Of course, Herr Reichsführer."

But Hitler had never gotten his legions of *übermenn*, though von Strucker could have delivered them. *That is*, he now thought as he watched the Green Fist leap and strike with inhuman speed, *I could have delivered them if only those fools in the concentration camp had kept their hands on that strange little Canadian.*

He sighed. *But at least I got enough out of him to keep me alive*, he thought. *And if I'm alive, then so is he. And one day I will catch him again.*

Al Borak clapped his hands and the sparring instantly stopped, the sixteen mujahideen forming up in two ranks of eight before coming to attention. Their leader had been working them hard, but von Strucker was pleased to see that not one of them was breathing at more than a normal rate. He knew that if he took the pulse of any man in the squad, it would register as lower than forty beats per minute.

Al Borak again sent a look of inquiry toward the baron, and von Strucker signaled his assent. The tall Pashtun went to a door at the far end of the training room and opened it, then gestured to whoever was beyond. Two men clad in desert fatigues and armed with Kalashnikov rifles entered, walking backward, their weapons trained on three men who now came through the doorway, their hands bound behind them. The escorted men were followed by two more guards whose AK-47s were leveled at the prisoners' backs.

Two of the three men were clad in the black combat fatigues of the U.S. Navy SEALs. The third man was in desert camouflage, with a sand-colored beret that bore the winged dagger and motto "Who Dares Wins" of the British Special Air Services. The escorts brought them out into the center of the wooden floor and stepped back. Another guard followed, carrying a small roll of canvas. At Al Borak's unspoken direction, he laid the cloth on the floor before the prisoners and unrolled it. The bundle's contents clanked together, then were revealed as two SEALs combat knives and the black dagger that was traditional for UK special forces.

Al Borak waved the armed guards away and they departed by the door through which they had entered. He bent and took up the dagger, hefted it to feel the balance, then stepped behind the British trooper. A flick of his hand and the man's bonds were severed. The soldier brought them forward, rubbing at the wrists.

Al Borak had come back around to face the SAS man, giving the prisoner the full benefit of his strange eyes. For though his features were pure Pashtun, the skin dark and the brows heavy and black above a prominent nose, the Green Fist's leader's eyes were as gray as a winter sky—undoubtedly the legacy of one of the many European armies—Russian, British, even Alexander's ancient Macedonians—that had left their traces, and usually their blood and bones, on the unforgiving plains and mountain passes of Afghanistan. It was the eyes that had caught von Strucker's attention when he had called the youthful Al Borak out of the crowd at the orphanage in Kandahar. But it had been the youngster's more unusual, and quite deadly, talent that had led the Prussian to bring the boy into his Arabian establishment.

Now von Strucker stepped forward and the three prisoners watched his approach with wary suspicion. The Prussian knew he must make an unusual impression, for he was clad in the clothes that he still found most comfortable: a high-collared tunic and riding breeches, both of field gray, and calf-high boots of gleaming black leather, such as he had worn when he had been Oberführer von Strucker of the Red Skull SS in Hitler's Third Reich. This uniform, however, was without insignia or campaign ribbons; the days when the baron's cap and collar had borne the red skull of Heinrich Himmler's Special Projects Office were long gone.

He lifted the monocle that hung from a black cord secured to a silver button on his tunic and positioned it before his right eye. He hadn't needed the lens for sixty years—his eyesight had become perfect after he had extracted the elixir from the mysterious man who had then disappeared from the concentration camp—but he liked to use the monocle for effect.

"You are wondering why he has freed your hands?" he said in accented English to the SAS trooper, halting a few feet away and standing with legs apart, hands behind his back, in parade rest. "Because you are going to have a chance to win your freedom."

The soldier looked from the Prussian to the Pashtun, then his gaze came back to von Strucker. His mouth twisted in disbelief.

"I see you don't believe me," the baron said. "I give you my word as a German officer. Here is what you must do: pick one of those twenty men to be your opponent. Al Borak here will give you your stiletto. Our man will be unarmed. You have only to kill him, and you will go free."

The prisoner looked to the squad of mujahideen standing immobile, eyes front and unblinking. The baron saw the man's eyes narrow as he examined his enemies. They were a mixed group, most of them Arabs but with a sprinkling of Afghans and Pakistanis, as well as a Filipino and a Malaysian. Each was in his twenties, superbly fit, though none was overly large in stature.

"Go ahead," von Strucker said. "Choose."

The soldier rolled his shoulders and rotated his neck to loosen tense muscles, then approached the squad cautiously. When none of them reacted to his presence, he examined the men closely, then finally shrugged and indicated a man in the middle of the second rank. "Him," he said.

He had chosen Ismail Khan, a Pakistani who was second-in-command to Al Borak. Khan was a little shorter than the SAS man and not quite as wide in the shoulders. At Al Borak's command, the mujahideen slid smoothly between the two men in front of him and crossed the open space to stand before his leader. Al Borak handed the man two gray pills and a canteen of water to wash them down.

The Pakistani swallowed the pills and turned to face the SAS soldier.

"Here," said Al Borak, casually tossing the dagger so that it spun lazily in the air. The SAS man looked surprised but caught the weapon with easy skill.

Al Borak stepped back, as did von Strucker. "Whenever you are ready," the baron said.

The soldier's demeanor had changed the moment he caught the knife. *A good fighting man*, von Strucker thought. He watched with interest as the Briton moved forward in a slight crouch, the weapon held low before him.

Khan stood at ease, arms at his sides, his body loose. His brown eyes dispassionately regarded the oncoming man with the knife. For a moment, confusion registered on the SAS trooper's face as his opponent gave no sign of being ready for what was about to happen. Then the soldier lunged forward, the hand that held the dagger making a short upward thrust toward the place where the mujahideen's ribs joined his breastbone—a killing blow that should have driven the seven inches of razor-sharp black steel into Khan's heart.

But the Pakistani was not there to receive the fatal strike. With eye-blurring speed, he had pivoted on his right heel, turning sideways to present the SAS trooper with a target made of empty air. At the same time, the heel of his left hand came around and caught the Briton at the base of his skull, propelling him down and forward, stumbling and off balance. A burst of laughter came from the squad.

The SAS man rolled and came up smoothly, the fighting knife ready. But Khan was already beside him, a hard-edged hand striking down at the Briton's wrist like an ax. The black dagger flew from the man's deadened grasp, but as it spun away the Pakistani's other hand flicked out like a striking cobra and caught the weapon in midair.

He turned the black metal over, laid it on an index finger to test its balance, then flipped it end over end to catch it by the blade. Now he spun, the knife hand raised to shoulder height, and his arm flashed down with inhuman speed. Almost instantly the dagger was buried in a scarred target hung on a wall thirty feet distant, its quivering hilt and quillions quivering from the force of the impact.

Khan turned back to the British soldier, whose face was now slack with fear. The Pakistani beckoned with two fingers, while a small smile lifted the corners of his mouth. When the trembling SAS man did not come forward, the mujahideen moved, striking with a series of blows so fast that von Strucker could not see them land, but could register only the effects: the eyes popped free on the cheeks, the blood spurting from ruptured eardrums, the sudden slump of the shoulders under the desert camouflage that meant both collarbones had been fractured, the way the Briton's head shot forward that meant Khan's knuckles had crushed his larynx in a killing blow.

Now the Pakistani stood back, looking down at the choking, gargling mess that had, moments before, been a first-class fighting man. Al Borak snapped a command and Khan came to attention, about-faced, and marched back to his grinning squad mates. The front rank parted to admit him.

The leader of the Green Fist turned to the two Navy SEALs, but the prolonged and noisy death throes of the soldier distracted him. He went to where the man lay and knelt on one knee beside him, then placed his hands on the Briton's chest. For a moment Al Borak's face went blank, his eyes looking inward, then suddenly the thick black thatch of hair on his head rose straight up, as did the fine dark hairs on his bare arms and the backs of his hands. Bright flashes of intense electrical energy, like a cascading series of miniature lightning bolts, burst from his palms as they lay upon the SAS man's camouflage blouse. The air filled with the acrid reek of ozone, then came the stench of charring flesh as smoke rose from beneath Al Borak's hands. The dying man's entire body spasmed, his spine arcing so that only his head and bootheels touched the floor, the latter drumming an involuntary death tattoo on the polished wood.

The Green Fist leader drew his hands away. The lightning ceased and the rigid body slumped, lifeless, wisps of gray smoke rising from the corpse's chest, where the cloth of the SAS uniform was marked by two carbonized handprints.

Al Borak turned back to the Navy SEALs. He looked them up and down, then picked up their fighting knives from where they lay on the canvas. He went behind the Americans and cut their bonds, pushing them roughly toward the mujahideen. "Let us even the odds," he said. "This time, we'll make it both of you against just one of ours. Now go and choose."

The prisoners looked at each other and at the smoldering wreck that had been the captured Briton. "Well," said one to the other, "nobody ever said this had to be a long career."

Von Strucker did not stay to watch the inevitable outcome. While he had been watching the mismatched combat, he had felt the first stirrings of an ache in one shoulder. That meant it was time for a visit to the room that only he was allowed to enter.

OTTAWA, CANADA,

THE PRESENT

"THE library will be closing in ten minutes." The halting voice came from a speaker set into the ceiling above Logan's head. It was only when the message was repeated that it registered. He looked up from the book about the Canadian Army in Italy and saw that the place was almost empty. The nervous woman who had helped him was back where he had found her, a microphone in her trembling hand, and from the way her eyes moved away when he glanced at her, he knew she had been watching him.

He turned his gaze back to the pictures in the coffee-table book. Many of them were frustratingly familiar: a narrow street of brick houses, all with second-story balconies of ornamental metal; a wide, cobbled square with a smashed fountain at its center and dead bodies in German uniforms strewn about in the ungainly postures of battlefield deaths; a lightweight, open-topped tracked vehicle—his mind supplied the words "bren carrier" and a strong impression that it was a good thing to stay out of—and a group of men in Canadian battle dress, wine bottles and glasses in hand, sitting around tables in an outdoor café or tavern, behind them a wall whose whitewash was pockmarked by bullets and shrapnel. A pretty girl, her hair covered by a scarf knotted under her chin, smiled into the camera.

The last photo held his gaze. The faces were familiar, especially the square-jawed sergeant who was looking not at the camera but up at the girl. So was the wall. At the far right of the picture some words painted on the wall had been cut off. One word was "Oster—" and just below it was "Gambrel—" Below that was "Orto—" His mind supplied the rest. Osteria was the Italian word for tavern, and the line below meant "of Ortona."

And he had been there. He had walked those streets. He had known some of those men. Unless somebody had somehow managed to plant a false memory of that time and place. But why would anyone want to make him think he had been in Ortona in 1943? Just to drive him insane?

He looked again at the girl and her smile stirred some emotion in him. Wistful. Sad. A sense of something once held precious, now lost forever.

"Five minutes," said the voice above his head. "We will be closing in five minutes. Patrons who wish to check out materials should please bring them to the desk now."

Logan stared at the pictures, willing his clouded mind to pull the scattered memories and impressions into some kind of pattern that made sense. He looked again at the wide shot of the square with the dead Germans in it. The white wall out of focus in the far distance looked as if it could be the tavern where the soldiers had stood drinking wine and saying the kinds of things soldiers always said to pretty girls in between the times that bullets were flying.

But now Logan noticed a detail that he had missed before. At the left side of the photograph was a Canadian soldier in paratrooper gear, a sten gun held loosely in the crook of his arm, his face turned partly toward the camera.

Logan came to his feet so fast that the chair he'd been sitting on shot backward and tipped over. He strode toward the desk, the book in his hand, one finger marking the page with the photo that had sent a shock through him.

"A magnifying glass," he said to the librarian, who had jumped to her feet and looked ready to run away. "All I need's a magnifying glass."

She had large upper teeth that were now biting into her lower lip, but she pulled open a drawer in the desk and fumbled within, coming up with a big lens in a square frame of black plastic. "Here," she said.

He snatched it from her and spread the book on the desk and peered at the man with the sten gun standing at the edge of the photo. The face was in shadow. Both he and the cameraman must have been covered by the shade of a building behind them, looking out into the brightness of the square with the destroyed fountain.

But the image was clear enough. The strong nose, the ridge of bone from which the thick, dark brows sprang, the black hair, swept back but unruly under the paratrooper's beret, the stubble-darkened jaw.

He looked up at the librarian, saw her recoil from whatever his eyes were showing. "I need this book," he said.

"You can check it out," she said, though it took her three tries to get out the third word in the sentence. "Do you... do you have a card?"

"I don't think so," he said. "But I'll bring it back."

She looked at the book as if she were telling it, *Good-bye and good luck*, then said to Logan, "Fine, yes, that'll be fine. You can take it right now."

"And the glass."

"We've got plenty of them."

He turned and moved toward the door, slipping the magnifying glass into his pocket and pressing the book against his chest to button his coat over it against the freezing rain that was still coating the city in a shroud of ice.

But as he hurried through the slick streets all he saw was that harsh face beneath the paratrooper's beret. He recognized that face, even in a dark and grainy photo from sixty years ago.

There wasn't a face in all the world that he knew better. It was the face that looked back at Logan every morning when he shaved.

THE EMPTY QUARTER, SAUDI ARABIA,

THE PRESENT

VON Strucker burst through the door of his private quarters, deep within the bowels of the facility he had had built here in the wasteland of the Arabian desert. Far above, the midday temperature was nearing fifty degrees on the Celsius scale, heat that would kill a man in a matter of hours. Down here, the temperature was always a comfortable twenty-one—about seventy degrees Fahrenheit—but the Prussian's brow was beaded in sweat as he made his way across the spartan sitting room and into the bed chamber with its simple narrow cot.

He parted a set of double doors in the far wall to reveal a rack on which hung spare tunics and breeches, two pairs of boots beneath. Wincing at the pain in his shoulder, the baron swept aside the clothing. The wall behind was bare rock, the hard granite that underlay the desert sands, rough hewn with unsmoothed bumps and still showing the scars of a power chisel.

The baron set his palm on a rounded projection in the top-right corner of the wall. He pressed, and the bump sank into the granite. At the same time, a harsh grating sound came from within the stone and the entire rear of the closet moved back a foot, then slid sideways on hydraulic pistons. Beyond lay a small chamber, lit by a simple overhead light and containing only a laboratory bench. Atop the bench's sterile surface was a sealed cylinder of transparent glass, of a size to hold four liters. Into one side of the container ran lengths of surgical tubing whose other ends were connected to a small machine that whirred and hummed beside the flask. A single hollow filament exited from the other side of the cylinder and disappeared into a hole in the countertop.

Von Strucker entered the room and palmed the control on the inner wall that closed the massive granite door. Only when he was sealed in did he go to the bench and undertake once again the process that had kept him alive and vigorous all these years. First he checked the readings on the whirring machine and saw that appropriate levels of nutrients were entering the cylinder, and that waste products were being cycled out. The small fragment of human tissue that floated on a net of gold mesh suspended within the saline solution that filled the container remained in good health.

Now the Prussian bent, feeling as he did so a twinge of pain in his lower back. *Just in time*, he thought, as he took a compact centrifuge from a shelf beneath the bench. He lifted it to the countertop, then connected it to a power source.

The bench concealed a secure box, made of the strongest steel, its thick heavy door equipped with a touch pad that recognized only von Strucker's fingerprints. He placed his fingertips against the sensors and the door opened. Had anyone else touched the pad, alarms would now be sounding throughout the underground complex and the secret room would be filling with a toxic gas. Within the safe, held in a foam-cushioned armature, was a solitary Pyrex test tube half-filled with a colorless liquid. The filament that led from the cylinder on the bench's top passed through the rubber stopper that sealed the tube.

Carefully, the baron removed the tube from its holder and withdrew the stopper, replacing it with another that had no hole through it. He rose and opened the centrifuge, placed the tube in a groove designed to hold it, and snugged it down. Then he sealed the machine, set its speed control, and pushed a button. A whirring noise rose through several frequencies of sound until the device was spinning so rapidly that its whine was almost at the edge of human hearing.

Von Strucker leaned against the bench, his elegantly tended fingernails tapping fitfully on the polished top. He noticed a tiny discoloration on the back of one hand and even as he focused on it, the liver mark spread and was joined by another. The skin appeared dry and he could see blue veins beneath it. He was aging rapidly.

A chime sounded from the centrifuge. Its high-pitched whirring cycled down through the frequencies and slowed to nothing as the machine stopped. The baron withdrew the tube and held it up to the light to examine the contents. Most of the tube was still filled with the colorless fluid, but in the bottom were a few cubic centimeters of a cloudy liquid.

He placed the tube in a rack and reached below the bench for a flat plastic box that contained a hypodermic syringe with a needle longer than the test tube. He removed the tube's stopper and used the hypodermic to draw off the substance that the centrifuge had concentrated in the bottom. When the reservoir was full, he removed the long needle and replaced it with another that was less than an inch long. He noticed that his hands were now shaking.

Swiftly, von Strucker removed his tunic and found the length of rubber tubing that he used to bind his arm just below the left bicep. He depressed the hypodermic's plunger to evacuate the air from the needle and when a droplet of fluid appeared at its tip, he put the needle to the now distended vein in the crook of his elbow and slid the steel into his flesh.

He unknotted the tube that constricted his arm and let the fluid flow into his system. He put out his hand and watched as the tremor disappeared and the dark-spotted skin regained its youthful elasticity. The aches in his shoulder and lower back faded like distant trumpets.

The Prussian took a deep breath, let it out slowly. He felt renewed strength flowing through him, the power of distilled life force energizing his limbs, filling his being with unstoppable vigor. Quickly, he disposed of the equipment, then knelt on now uncomplaining knees to place a new tube in the secure box and connect it to the filament that came from the cylinder above. He locked the safe's door, then rose and regarded the small fragment of human bone marrow that was contained in the flask and nurtured by the small machine.

Safe again, he said within the privacy of his mind. The injection would repair his tissues and preserve them against the ravages of age. He would remain, physically and mentally, a man in his prime, never aging beyond the day when he had first extracted the elixir from the nameless Canadian. The dark-haired wild man who had growled at him in the office of the concentration camp's commandant, after they had nailed him to the tabletop to keep him still while they investigated why he wouldn't stay dead.

OTTAWA, CANADA,

THE PRESENT

WHEN Logan got back to the condo, a cardboard carton rested outside the door. *I guess it's about that time*, he thought as he unlocked the door and stooped to pick up the box, hearing a *clunk* of liquid-filled glass as its contents shifted. He placed the library book on top of the carton, covering the printed letters that read *Seagram's Seven Crown Blended Whiskey*, and carried them both in, then set the box, as always, on the built-in table in the galley kitchen.

Like the money, a case of Canadian whiskey arrived once a month. Logan didn't know where he had picked up a taste for Seven Crown, but nowadays the thought of drinking any other kind of liquor actually repelled him. It felt natural to sit with a glass in his hand, the smell of the liquor in his nostrils and the sweet aftertaste hardly fading from his mouth before he took another slug.

Normally, he would have opened the case and cracked a bottle. But not tonight. Instead, he left the carton still sealed on the table and carried the book into the living room. He set it on the coffee table in front of the couch, both of them of that characterless breed of furniture often found in midpriced chain hotel rooms and government offices.

He threw his coat and hat into a corner of the couch, then remembered the magnifying glass. He dug it out of the pocket and sat hunched again over *Canadians at War: The Italian Campaign*. He started at the first page and proceeded page by page through the book, examining every photograph through the lens. He noticed that he had a tendency to snap the pages, then let his eyes dart from image to image. *Okay*, he thought, *so I'm not the patient type. But this needs to be done right.* He forced himself to slow down, to go at it methodically. *I don't want to miss anything.*

He found it on page 156. It was another picture of Tommy Prince, walking toward the camera on some cobblestoned street. In the background were three other Canadian paratroopers. The cameraman had used some kind of deep-focus lens that didn't obscure the details of the middle ground. When Logan pored over the image with the magnifying glass there was no doubt: one of the three men coming up behind Prince was either Logan himself or some uncanny double. Same mouth, same nose, same heavy stubble on his cheeks, same widow's peak of dark hair dipping down into his forehead.

He stared at the image for a long time, wishing he could reach into that flat, black-and-white world and grab the front of that paratrooper's woolen blouse, pull him out of the book and into this anonymous living room in Ottawa and ask him, "Who the hell are you? And who the hell am I?"

Instead, he rose and went to the kitchen, came back with a glass and fresh bottle of Seven Crown. He spun off the screw-top lid with an expert flick of thumb and two fingers. *Done that a few times*, he observed to himself, as he half filled the glass.

He took a good mouthful of the sweet liquor, rolling it around on his tongue. He knew he'd done that a lot, too. *The body remembers even if the mind can't*. But another impression came with the burn of the whiskey passing down his throat. He reckoned he must have sat here enough times, drinking a bottle dry, drinking his way into another kind of oblivion than the fog that filled his head. And too many times those sessions with the bottle had given the whiskey an aftertaste of defeat.

But not this time. He screwed the cap back on the bottle. And somehow that small action felt like victory.

And then he wondered how he could get himself to Italy.

THE EMPTY QUARTER, SAUDI ARABIA,

THE PRESENT

SAFE again. But safe for how long?

The thought kept circling in the baron's mind as he returned to the room where Green Fist operations were planned. The morning training session would be over by now, so he summoned Al Borak. While he waited, he mentally ran over the problem of the tissue in the cylinder. When it had been freshly harvested, more than sixty years ago, its output of white blood cells had been enough to sustain von Strucker in perfect health for thirty days. But today he had needed an injection, and today was only twenty-seven days since his last use of the needle.

It was a problem of diminishing returns. The tissue was living marrow taken from the mysterious man's femur and kept in a special nutrient solution that von Strucker's hand-picked team of scientists had developed in the Reich's most secret experimental medical facility, located in a heavily guarded bunker beneath a Berlin hospital that had catered to senior members of the Nazi regime. The solution had been originally developed to preserve limbs severed on the battlefields of the Eastern Front, in the hope that doctors in Wehrmacht field hospitals could reattach them. But as soon as von Strucker heard of its existence, he convinced Reichsführer-SS Himmler to let him use the precious substance for his *übermenn* program.

At that time, von Strucker had been seeking to stimulate artificial mutations in human test subjects. His teams sought out healthy young men and women from the trainloads delivered daily to the camps, but tending to hundreds of breeders would have required a massive establishments of cooks, guards, and head counters, any of whom might be spies planted by the baron's rivals within the Nazi state apparatus. It was so much easier to excise the few parts needed to create embryos, keep them alive in the solution, and send the unneeded tissue—that is, the rest of the test subject—to the crematorium.

While the effort to create mutations was given first priority, the Prussian also had teams of investigators combing the Reich and its conquered territories seeking mutants who had appeared spontaneously. Most of them, of course, were of no use—there is no particular advantage to having six fingers on a hand or an eye that sees ultraviolet—but much was learned from dissecting such subjects.

Rarely, however, a potentially useful mutation appeared. There was a Czech boy whose skin—when he was frightened or excited—was able to divert light. At such times, the outer layer of his epidermis neither absorbed nor reflected light. Instead, it passed the photons "hand to hand," as von Strucker explained it to Himmler, so that it bent around him and made him effectively invisible. But the mutated gene that caused the invisibility effect also suppressed some important factors in the brain's development. As a result, the boy was not much smarter than a chimpanzee.

There was also a Dutch girl who could project her consciousness backward in time, seeing and hearing events that had happened far away and even before she was born. Von Strucker had been working with her to increase her range and improve her targeting ability by meditation and by a diet rich in certain vitamins and plant extracts. Then Himmler insisted on forcing her to attempt to see the future. The girl was still in a coma when the Russians took Berlin and the baron fled.

His mind came back to the problem of the marrow in the vat. It produced the mutated white blood cells that kept von Strucker untroubled by germs, aging, injuries, and systemic breakdowns. But the small piece of stolen flesh was not itself immortal; the nutrient solution in which it lay required a regular infusion of the marrow's own product or it would start to decline. So for more than sixty years, the Prussian had shared its output of life-preserving white blood cells with the tissue that produced them. Shared them, but not equally. In order to have enough for himself, he had short-changed their source, causing the marrow to gradually lose some of its potency.

And now he could look ahead to a time—perhaps decades away still, yet mathematically certain to arrive—when he would need an injection a week. Then it would become an injection a day, then twice a day, until ultimately the fragment of stolen flesh would not be able to produce enough of the elixir to keep the breath of life moving in and out of von Strucker's lungs.

Before that day arrived, the baron needed to find the Canadian again—or one of his descendants, if the mutation bred true. He had no doubt the man was still alive somewhere—he had never met anyone more unkillable—but when his inquiries had yielded no results, he came to the only logical conclusion: the mutant's gift had been recognized, most likely by a government security apparatus, that had done exactly what the baron would have done—yanked him out of his normal life and put him to work.

The door to the planning room slid open. The tall Pashtun stepped through the doorway and the door slid closed behind him. "So," he said, speaking Arabic but with the softer accent of southern Afghanistan, "did our friend from Yemen approve the plan?"

"No," von Strucker said.

Al Borak's gray eyes widened. "Is there a problem?"

The Prussian's thin lips took a wry twist. "More of an opportunity." In a few words he explained the change of target, then said, "We will need a good model of the target area and its approaches."

The Green Fist leader stroked his lean jaw. "It is a hard target. We will lose some men," he said. "Maybe a lot of them."

"That is what they are for," von Strucker said.

"Still…"

"We can always get more."

Al Borak pressed his palms together, then flexed his hands so that only the fingertips still touched. "True," he said. "And their deaths will be glorious."

When he separated his hands completely, the air crackled and blue-white sparks leaped from one palm to the other. He smiled at the baron and said, "Or at least that's what we'll tell them."

OTTAWA, CANADA,

THE PRESENT

I may not know who I am, Logan was thinking to himself, *but I'm pretty sure I haven't led a straight-arrow life*. It wasn't just the frequent dreams full of blood and screaming, of crunching bone and the crackle of automatic weapons fire, dreams that always faded when he tried to examine them. It wasn't just the scars on his hands and whatever it was that people saw in his face that made them decide to cross streets or seat themselves at a table on the other side of a restaurant from him.

It was the fact that he knew exactly the kind of place to seek out if he wanted to get a passport he wasn't entitled to—even knew how much it ought to cost. So when the man sitting at a light table in the back room of the print shop had told him the forged document would cost him six hundred dollars, he had not hesitated.

"It'll cost me three," he'd said, leaning over the table. And the man had looked up into Logan's eyes and said, "Right you are. Come back tomorrow night at six."

"I'll wait right here while you do it."

The man hadn't looked too happy about it, but he got out his camera and got to work, and Logan was satisfied with the results. The passport wouldn't stand up to serious scrutiny—its number was not connected to any file—but it looked real enough. The man had said it was one of a batch of pristine blanks stolen from the Queen's Printer so recently that the passport office didn't yet know they were gone.

Now Logan put the document back in an inner pocket of his plaid coat and collected the ticket from the clerk at the Air Canada counter in the departures area of Ottawa International Airport. He'd paid for the ticket with cash—the monthly envelopes contained more than he needed for food and since his liquor was supplied free, he had accumulated a healthy wad of surplus fifties and hundreds.

The security checkpoint brought a surprise. He emptied his pockets of metal objects and took off his shoes, but the metal detector went crazy when he stepped through. A plump woman with a hand-held wand detector and a Punjabi accent asked him to hold his arms out, then showed him a startled face when the instrument seemed to suffer the same kind of overexcitement as the walk-through gate.

When it was eventually established that the wand was reacting to metal that was not in his clothes but *inside him*, she called over her supervisor. This was a skinny, balding man with an Adam's apple that couldn't keep still.

He repeated the woman's wand motions with the same loud results, then said, "Do you have metal pins in your arms and legs, maybe a plate in your skull?"

"I don't know," Logan said. "My memory is pretty bad."

In the end they shrugged and let him board the plane. He settled into a window seat in coach. Nobody sat beside him and once they were at cruising altitude, the flight attendants came around with their cart full of little plastic bottles.

"Seven Crown," he said. "Give me five of them. No ice."

The badge on the attendant's shirt pocket said his name was Randy. "It's our policy to only sell them one at a time," he said.

Logan looked at him. "It's my policy to buy them by the handful."

Randy decided that Air Canada's policy could stand a minor and temporary change. "But don't tell anybody I did this," he said.

Logan emptied all five of the little bottles into the plastic tumbler and took a mouthful. Outside, it was a late November night and the airbus was thousands of feet above the clouds covering eastern Canada. He looked out at the blackness between the indifferent stars above and the gray blanket below. It could have been anytime out there.

ORTONA, ITALY,

DECEMBER 1943

"HEY, Patch! There's a major from headquarters looking for you again. He was snooping around the mess wagon."

"But you told him you haven't seen me."

"I did, but I don't think he believed it."

Corporal James "Patch" Howlett, late of the First Special Service Force and currently unofficially attached to the Loyal Edmonton Regiment, accepted the steaming mess tin that Sergeant Rob Roy MacLeish had brought back to the basement of the half-ruined house where MacLeish's squad was bivouacked. The red-haired sergeant had gone to collect the rations for both of them because it would have been difficult for Patch to explain to any passing officer what he was doing a couple of hundred miles from where his unit was stationed.

"What's he want with you?" the sergeant asked his old friend. The two of them had come down from the lumber camps in northern Alberta in the first week of the war and joined up together, only to be separated when a colonel had come through the basic training camp looking for volunteers for a newly forming parachute regiment. Both had put their hands up, but only Patch Howlett had been accepted.

"You know officers," Patch said, sniffing the contents of the mess tin appreciatively before dipping in a steel spoon. "They're always wanting you to do things you don't feel like doing."

He changed the subject. "So, Rob Roy," he said, "tell me about the girl."

MacLeish's green eyes narrowed in wary suspicion. In the old days, he'd lost more than a couple of sweethearts to Howlett. Something about Patch's dark, brooding nature pulled them like moths to a black flame. "What girl?" he said in the most innocent tone he could muster.

Patch squinted at an inch-thick cube of grayish meat on his spoon. "Horse?" he said.

"Our artillery caught some Jerry horse-drawn transport in one of those gullies west of town," MacLeish said. "Cookie said it seemed a shame to waste it."

Patch chewed the meat, then dug into the stew for a chunk of potato. "I've eaten worse," he said. "But back to the question—there's always a girl."

The sergeant's face softened. "Her name's Lucia," he said. "Lucia Gambrelli. Her family ran a tavern down by the harbor, until her father was shot by the Germans in a reprisal for a raid by partisans. That made her brother, Giovanni, decide to join the partisans and get revenge. Now he's disappeared."

"Sounds like she brings out your knight in shining armor."

MacLeish blushed. "Maybe a little. She's a sweet kid. Before her brother went missing we were talking about, you know, after the war's over…"

"You've changed," Patch said. "You used to say no girl would ever get you to tie the knot."

"It's the war. It makes you do things you never thought you'd do."

"You don't know the half of it," Patch said.

The rest of the squad trickled in and squatted with their backs against the basement walls to eat their evening meal, casting sidelong looks at the newcomer. If they thought it strange that their sergeant's AWOL friend had attached himself to their squad, they didn't mention it. Besides, the new man's shoulder patch—a red stone spearhead stitched with "USA" and "Canada" in white thread—identified him as a member of the elite fighting unit the Germans had begun calling *Die Schwarzen Teufels*—the Black Devils—for the shoe polish with which they blackened their faces when going out at night to cut throats and take prisoners.

The First Special Services Force, now becoming known as the Devil's Brigade, was a combined unit formed when the battalion of Canadian paratroops in which Patch served had been merged with a unit of U.S. volunteers who had backgrounds as forest rangers, hunters, and lumberjacks. Trained to operate behind enemy lines and as elite assault troops, the FSSF had already achieved legendary status for their successful assault on Monte la Defensa south of Cassino. American and British forces had suffered heavy casualties in repeated attacks that had failed to dislodge German forces dug in atop a mountain that was mostly sheer cliffs hundreds of feet high. The Devil's Brigade had silently scaled the cliffs and attacked the Germans from the rear, taking the supposedly impregnable position in a matter of hours.

"We're going out at twenty-one hundred," MacLeish said.

"Mind if I tag along?" Patch said.

"I was hoping you might."

The corporal scraped a final spoonful of stew out of the tin and wiped out the last traces of gravy with a cob of bread. "What kind of fun will we be having?" he said.

His friend smiled. "We call it mouse holing."

○————————○

ORTONA was a fishing port and prewar vacation spot on the Adriatic Sea, about midway up Italy's east coast. The Allies' theater commander, Field Marshal Montgomery, had assigned the Canadian First Division to take it. The German Army's high command had decided that the elite troops of the Wehrmacht's Third Paratroop Regiment—Hitler's fire brigade in southern Europe—were the perfect force to defend the place. Rushed into the line to reinforce a battered Panzergrenadier regiment already falling back in the face of strong Canadian and British attacks, the *fallschirmjägers* turned the town into a death trap.

With the civilian population mostly fled or carried off to be slave laborers in Germany, the defenders blocked access by demolishing the empty houses at key intersections. They set up machine gun and antitank gun positions in nearby buildings, creating overlapping fields of fire trained on the rubble and the streets along which the Canadians would advance, and spread mines around like confetti. The plan was to lead the assault toward the wide Piazza Municipiale at the center of town, turning it into an escape-proof killing zone.

The Germans had rigged the game, so the Canadians declined to play. Instead of moving through the deadly streets and alleyways, they took to burrowing through the common walls that connected one house to the next, using pickaxes or shaped demolition charges or the PIAT shoulder-fired antitank weapon to blow man-size holes, then leaping through with grenades and small arms fire. It was house-to-house, room-to-room fighting, with both sides rigging explosive booby traps as they withdrew from unholdable positions. It was a mini-Stalingrad of a battle, fought in third- and fourth-floor rooms, the air choking with the dust of shattered masonry and the stink of TNT—a succession of sudden, desperate struggles, fought face-to-face and hand-to-hand.

At 2045, MacLeish's officer, a tired-looking lieutenant, came through the blackout curtain and down into the basement, bringing two canvas satchels of grenades. He saw the stranger sitting in the shadows beside his sergeant and said, "Who's this?"

MacLeish stood. "Old friend of mine, come for a visit. Thought he could come along tonight."

The lieutenant, "Can he fight?"

"Used to be the best bare-knuckle boxer north of Edmonton."

The officer lifted the oil lamp from a rickety table and brought it over to where the special forces corporal squatted on his heels against the wall. He took in the spearhead on the man's shoulder and the VK-42 fighting knife in a scabbard on his hip. "Is that your only weapon?" he said.

Patch rose smoothly to his feet. "I've got this," he said and showed the lieutenant a sten gun equipped with silencer. "All you'll hear is the bolt clicking."

"All right," the officer said. "Just make sure you do what Sergeant MacLeish says."

"I always did."

MacLeish smothered a laugh as the lieutenant gathered them around the table and spread out a hand-drawn map of a street that ran south to north and had six multistory houses along its east side. A house in the middle of the west side had been blown up and tumbled into the street, effectively blocking it. The officer pointed to the house on the northeast corner and said, "The Jerries have a machine gun on the second floor. There are also snipers in at least two of the other houses, but they keep moving around.

"We'll go in through the ground floor of this first house here"—he pointed to the street's southeast corner—"climb to the fourth floor, then mouse hole our way along the row until we've cleaned them out. Grenades down the stairwells, then sweep each room. Watch out for trip wires."

He distributed the grenades, every man taking a few. Two of the soldiers slung their rifles and hoisted pickaxes. Another man hefted a long crowbar, then the lieutenant blew out the lamp and they exited silently into the December darkness.

They went single file along the rubble-strewn streets, Patch falling into place just behind MacLeish. The street they were heading for was four blocks west and they felt their way through the blackness until they came to the final corner, where another squad of Loyal Eddies represented the farthest forward line of the Canadians' advance.

MacLeish's officer spoke to the sergeant of the other squad. "Anything?"

"All quiet, sir," said the man.

MacLeish whispered to Patch, "That means they've either pulled out so they can blow it up once we're well in, or they're waiting in one of the houses so they can jump us as we come through a wall."

"Then we'll just have to get them before they get us," Patch said. "Hell of a lot of fights get won on the first punch."

They went across the street to the back of the first house, one man at a time, at a dead run and crouching low, in case a German sniper with a nightscope was covering the open space. When the last man was across, the riflemen on the other squad opened fire up the street, making a noise to cover the *crack* that came when the long crowbar pried open the house's back door.

"Let me go in first," Patch said.

"As you like," the officer said.

The door led into a kitchen. The air in the room was stale with the odor of moldering food and the ashes in the open hearth where the cooking was done. Patch moved silently across the stone floor, one hand outstretched in the lightless space, found a wall and then a doorway that led to a hallway. The only other room on this floor was the front parlor, the hallway running from the front door to a staircase that rose to the upper floors.

The place was empty. He could tell. In night operations against the Germans, slipping around behind their lines, he'd found that he could sniff them out by the lingering odor of sausage and cabbage that seemed to be such an important part of their diet. He had used to think that everybody could smell faint scent traces the way he could, just as he'd thought that other people could see in the dark, but now he knew different.

He went back to the kitchen and whispered to the men outside, "Ground floor clear. I'm going upstairs."

He heard them coming in, as he crept up the stairs, placing his feet carefully on the outsides of the risers so the old wood would not creak as it took his weight. The floor above held bedrooms: one across the front of the house, with two tall louvered doors leading to a railed balcony; and a pair of smaller chambers probably meant for children. All were empty.

He went back to the stairs. MacLeish was waiting at the bottom. "Second floor clear," Patch said. "Going up."

He quickly checked the third-story rooms and the servants' cubicles in the attic. "Nothing," he told the Loyal Eddies coming up the stairs.

"Right," said the officer. "Picks and pry bar."

The soldiers set to work in the glow of the lieutenant's flashlight, breaking a hole in the wall separating a windowless third-floor room from its counterpart in the house next door. The picks dug through plaster into old brick beneath, chips flying and dust beginning to billow.

Patch spoke to MacLeish. "I can get onto the roof from the attic. I'm going to go scout farther up the block."

"Watch yourself," his friend said. "They like their booby traps, the Jerries do."

Patch went up to the top of the house. A small window opened just below the eaves above the back alley. He put his head out, listening, sniffing the night air. Then he swung himself up and out and in a moment he was crouched atop the roof. He went north, his boots scritching on the terra-cotta tiles. Two doors up, he found a hole in the roof—when they'd blown up the building across the street, a chunk of it had come flying over and punched right through the tiles and rafters.

Patch lowered himself through the opening into another attic, its floor littered with bricks that smelled of smoke. *The chimney*, he thought. *Must've got lobbed over like a mortar bomb.* He found the open trapdoor that led downstairs and made his way through the floors below. Empty. He came back to the third floor and put his ear to the wall that connected the house with its neighbor to the south and heard faint sounds—MacLeish and his squad were already into the second house and would soon be coming through into this one.

He thought he should go back onto the roof and farther up the street, to see if he could locate the German positions. But something was tugging at the edge of his awareness. There was an odd smell about this house, very faint. He went out into the hall and sniffed the air, trying to separate the strange odor from the mixed reek of rotten food and the mold that had taken hold of everything after the hole in the roof let in the winter rains.

Find the Jerries, his training said. *Know where your enemy is before he knows where you are.* He went up to the roof and made his way to the last house on the street, the one that the lieutenant had said concealed a machine gun nest. He found no convenient hole in the roof, but there was an attic window in the same place as in the first house, and taking a grip on the eaves trough, he agilely swung out and down, kicking his way through the thin slats of the wooden shutters.

Sten gun at the ready, he crouched over the trapdoor, listening, his nostrils flared. He heard nothing, but the scent of German rations came to him, along with the sharp smell of gunsmoke produced by the MG-42—the 7.92-millimeter machine gun known as "Hitler's buzzsaw" for its twenty-rounds-per-second rate of fire.

Silently, Patch went down the ladder that led to the third floor, checked the rooms, then descended the stairs to the second floor. Here was where the machine gun would be, in the front bedroom that would be laid out just like that of the first house, with double doors leading out on to a balcony. He slid back the bolt on the sten gun and eased along the hallway to the bedroom door.

The scent of a much-fired German machine gun was strong. Patch stepped into the doorway and sprayed the room with two long bursts of nine-millimeter parabellum. The sten's silencer was so effective he heard only the clicking of its action and the sounds of the bullets smacking into walls and furniture, while its muzzle flash lit up the space.

The empty space. There was no machine gun, no dead and dying German soldiers. He went into the room, saw where a table and chairs had been piled against the doors to the balcony, doors that were opened just wide enough for an MG-42 barrel to poke out. And, in fact, there was a machine gun barrel lying against a wall—the high-speed weapon overheated barrels so often, German machine gun crews always carried a few spares. That was where the smell of gunsmoke came from. But the Jerries were gone.

It took him only a moment to put it all together. This room had been occupied by the Germans earlier today. They had fired their machine gun to let the Eddies know that they were here, but then they had pulled out without being seen. Patch's muzzle flashes would have told German observers that Canadians were mouse holing through the houses. And his animal-sharp sense of smell had picked up that odd odor in the third house.

He swore, then turned and raced for the stairs, rushed up into the attic. He was out the window and onto the roof in seconds. Careless now of making noise, he raced across the terra-cotta tiles to the hole that led down into the third house. He dropped through onto the shattered chimney below, bellowing, "Get out! Get out! The place is booby-trapped!"

He heard a shout from below, recognized Rob Roy MacLeish's voice giving orders, a rush of boots, and men swearing. Then the world exploded.

○——————————○

"CORPORAL Howlett," said a man's voice he didn't recognize. "Can you hear me?"

Patch came out of darkness into more darkness. He tried to put his hand to his eyes, but found that he could not move his arms from where they lay at his sides. He seemed to be in a narrow bed whose covers were snugged down tight.

"He can't talk to you," said another man. "Half his face was torn off."

"Go away," said the first voice, a man's voice speaking in the slightly British tone of an educated Canadian. "And make sure we are not disturbed."

"Look," said the second voice, "I had him moved to the VIP ward, as you asked. But this man is under my care. I have a professional responsi—"

The first voice interrupted, its tone purely matter-of-fact. "If you don't leave, Doctor, I will have you shot."

"Are you insane? This is a Royal Canadian Army field hospital, not some Nazi—"

"I assure you, Doctor, I can indeed have you shot. I could have you disappeared to a place where much, much worse things would be done to you, things that would make you beg for somebody to put a merciful bullet in your brain. And no one would say one bloody word about it."

Patch heard a swish of canvas as the doctor departed and knew he must be in a field hospital of the Army Medical Corps. And from the nature of the conversation, he was in a private section, the kind of ward where they put wounded generals, a place with no witnesses.

"So, Corporal Howlett," said the cultured voice again, "let's have a chat."

Patch said nothing. He heard a sigh followed by a rustle of clothing as the man moved. A moment later, sudden agony lanced through the sole of his left foot. He tried to pull his leg away but found that his lower limbs were as immobilized as his arms. He was strapped tight to the cot at chest, hips, and knees.

"I've just made a two-inch-long incision in your foot," the voice said. "It's bleeding freely, as it ought to. But, what's this? The bleeding has stopped."

Patch struggled but the bonds were too tight. The pain in his foot was already fading, but it wasn't the fear of pain that made him desperate to get free.

"And now the cut is closing," the voice said. "I wouldn't believe it if I wasn't seeing it with my own eyes."

The bound man felt a tingling in his hands but fought to suppress the instinct that the sensation foretold. It was bad enough that someone knew of his recuperative powers. But if he could keep the secret of his hands until his arms were free…

Now the voice was saying, "Sergeant Ken Cashman told me something strange. You remember the sergeant? He's your section leader in the FSSF. He was with you when you made the assault on Monte la Defensa last week.

"He said just as you came over the lip of the cliff a German machine gun opened up on you. He saw you fall, saw the spurts of blood the rounds made coming out of your back. He went on with the attack, but when he came back to collect your identity disks, he couldn't find your body."

Patch lay silently. Nothing he could say was going to help this situation.

"Then," the voice said, in a patient tone, "he saw you walking around, sound as a dollar. Though you weren't wearing a shirt, even though it was early December on top of a mountain.

"Do you know what Sergeant Cashman decided? He decided that he had seen somebody else get shot and, in the confusion of battle, had mistaken that unfortunate soldier for you.

"And that," the voice continued, "would have been the end of it. Except that he talked about it to a couple of people, and one of them talked about it to me. And I remembered hearing something similar when I was attached to the Parachute Regiment."

Patch's mind was racing now. He remembered an intelligence officer who'd joined the regiment shortly before its first battalion had been merged with the U.S. soldiers into the combined special force unit. The man had been there when Patch's company had been conducting an exercise, a night jump in full combat gear, and things had gone terribly wrong.

He remembered the jump. He'd come out of the Dakota's side door all right, and the static line attached to the overhead cable inside the cabin had opened his chute for him. He'd drifted down toward a farmer's field and was coming in for a perfect landing when a sudden gust of wind threw him sideways and into a heap of rocks that generations of plowmen had piled up in one corner of the field.

The impact snapped his right shin, the splintered bone tearing through flesh and the cloth of his jump trousers. He'd screamed in pain as the wind-filled chute tried to drag him across the rocks. A medic had come running and got him out of his harness, shouting for stretcher bearers. They'd strapped him down and hauled him off to an ambulance that had been standing by in case anyone came down wrong, and minutes after he had jumped out of the Dakota he was rolling along a country road headed for the base hospital.

The officer's voice picked up the story. "But when they got to the hospital, the man's leg was fine. He said he'd only banged it on the rocks and that a stick of wood had ripped his uniform. So they sent him back to barracks, and no report was filed.

"The medic was accused of being drunk on duty. He swore that that was no stick he had seen poking out of the man's flesh. It was naked bone. And even after everybody forgot all about it, he used to tell the story when he'd had a drink or two. Everybody got tired of hearing it. They gave him a nickname, used to call him Old Naked Bone."

But not everyone forgot about it. The intelligence officer hadn't. He'd bought the medic a drink or two and gotten the story out of him. Even got the name of the man who'd been carried off the field on a stretcher. Then the officer had a friend at the Loyal Edmonton Regiment back home do some research. His contact had sent him a letter full of tall tales about a man called Patch Howlett who'd been a legendary bare-knuckle cage fighter in the lumber camps of northern Alberta. They'd called him indestructible.

"And then I found myself assigned to the intelligence staff of the First Canadian Division, not a hundred miles from where the FSSF is operating. So I asked your outfit's G-Two to let me know if he heard any strange stories about a Corporal Howlett. And just the other day, he told me about the strange incident in Sergeant Prince's section—and your name came up. So I went up on La Defensa and poked around—and found a corporal's blouse that had matching bullet holes in the chest and back, and plenty of blood in between. Someone had stuffed it in a crack between two boulders.

"I thought I should pay a visit to your outfit," the officer continued, and now Patch could hear his voice moving toward the head of the cot. "But the moment I arrived and began asking questions, the legendary corporal went AWOL. Of course, the place you'd run to is where your old friend Sergeant MacLeish was serving. That was your mistake, you know. If you'd just sat still and played dumb, you might have gotten away with it."

"Wanted to see my friend," Patch said through the layers of gauze that swathed his head. "How is Sergeant MacLeish?"

"Ah, now we're getting somewhere," the voice said. Patch heard a flipping of pages. "And here's another funny thing. Your chart says that your lower jaw and part of your tongue were blown off when the Jerries blew up that booby-trapped house. Yet, here you are talking to me. I think we should take a look at what's under there."

Howlett felt a tug near his jaw, then another as a ribbon of gauze was pulled out from beneath the back of his head where it lay against the pillow. The tugging continued as the officer unwound the bandages. He felt cool air on his revealed flesh.

"Ahah," said the voice. It was meant to be said with quiet satisfaction, but Patch could hear the excitement the officer was trying to suppress. Finally, a thick pad of gauze was lifted from Patch's eyes and he blinked against the light.

The face looking down at him was narrow, the eyes a little close-set behind wire-rimmed military-issue spectacles, but sharp with intelligence, the weakness of the chin offset by a certain cruelty about the mouth. He had a pencil-thin mustache that he now stroked with one finger as he regarded what had been under the gauze.

"I don't have a mirror, but I'm guessing I don't need to show you, do I?" he said. His eyes widened theatrically. "Why, it's a miracle, my boy."

"What happened to Rob Roy?" Patch said.

"Your friend, the Loyal Eddie? The basement of that house was packed with demolition explosives. He and all of his men were blown to pieces, just like you. Except in their case, the effects were permanent." The officer sat on the edge of the cot. "But he was nobody, and now he's a dead nobody. Let's talk about you. About the special contribution you're going to make to the war effort. And, even more important, to my career."

"I need a drink."

"In a minute."

"Now, or I don't say anything."

"Sir," the officer said.

"Or I don't say anything, sir."

He watched the man pick up a scalpel from a nightstand up near the head of the cot on the right-hand side. That must have been what he'd used to cut his foot. "You heal," the officer said, "but first you hurt."

Patch looked the man in the eye and saw what he expected to see: behind the cool confidence was fear. He had fought enough cage fights to know how to use an opponent's fear against him. He said, "Yes, I heal. But I don't always run away when people find out about me. Sometimes I quiet them down another way."

"You're threatening me?"

"Call it setting some ground rules. If we're going to work together."

The officer put the scalpel back on the nightstand. "All right," he said. "We'll play nice."

"Why don't you start by telling me what you want?"

The major sat on the edge of the cot again, stroked his little mustache, then said, "What I want is a career. I want to be on the inside where the big decisions get made, to be the one who makes those decisions, and the bigger the better."

Patch shifted under the restraints but they were too tight. "What's that got to do with me?" he said.

"This war's going to end," the officer said. "We'll roll up the Germans in Italy in another year or so. Then there'll be a second front in France and we'll kick them right back to Germany, until we meet the Russkies coming the other way.

"And when that happens, there'll be a new war, a long war. But not a tanks and bombers war. Everybody will be too worn-out to go right into more of what we've all been getting. No, this will be a struggle waged in the shadows. A war of assassins."

"I'm a soldier," Patch said, "not a murderer."

The major went on as if he hadn't heard him. "There's a place back home," he said, "called Camp X. It's where they train spies and agents before they drop them into occupied Europe. I know some people there. They're developing new programs, already preparing for the next war. One program is called Weapon X."

He broke off and looked at Howlett. "Do you know what a mutant is?" he said.

"No."

"Never mind. A wolf doesn't need to know what a wolf is. He just needs to be a wolf."

"What's your point?"

"Let's just say they're looking for a certain kind of recruit. And an officer who walks in with just what they're looking for can write his own ticket."

Patch looked away, as if giving the matter some thought. "What's in it for me?" he said.

The major chuckled. "Glory, three square meals a day, an opportunity to travel, 'The Maple Leaf Forever'—whatever floats your boat."

"Huh," Patch said. "So I could write my own ticket, too?"

"Within reason. Better than being a corporal."

"Huh."

The major's voice hardened. "And better than spending twenty years in a military prison. You are a deserter, after all."

"Well, then, they can just shoot me," Patch said. "Then we'll shake hands, say we're square, and all go our separate ways."

"Ha ha," said the major. "If that were to happen, some general would scoop you up and deliver you to the same people I would."

"Doesn't sound like I have much of a choice."

"Sure you do. Think about it. Just don't think too hard. Leave the thinking to me and this could be an ideal partnership."

"I'd still like that drink."

"Sir."

"Sir," Patch said. "This healing thing, it makes me thirsty."

The staff officer's eyes grew bright behind the lenses of his spectacles. "Yes, tell me about that. How does it work? How long does it take? What does it feel like?"

"If I could have a drink, sir."

The major got up, went over to a carafe and tumbler on the nightstand. He poured water and held it to the corporal's lips.

"If you would just untie this strap across my chest, I could sit up and do it myself."

Suspicion seemed to draw the major's close-set eyes closer together. Patch said, "I'd still be strapped in from the waist down. Being able to heal fast doesn't make me Superman."

The man put the glass on the nightstand, then squatted down to do something beneath the bed, out of Patch's line of sight. The strap across his chest loosened and the major stood back.

Howlett slowly eased himself up until he was resting on his elbows. He rolled his shoulders to loosen them. "That's better," he said, then reached with one hand for the glass of water, gulping it down. He set the glass back on the nightstand and put the hand that had held it under the covers again.

"Would you mind pouring me another, sir? Can't reach the jug. You know, the healing thing always dries me out."

Another thing Patch had learned from bare-knuckled fighting was that sometimes it helped to show the other man the opportunity he was looking for. You could draw him in close, where the real damage gets done. The major wanted to know about the mystery, because to him that was the door that could open on all of his dreams. He had his eyes on that prize as he moved in closer to pour another glass. And as the man was paying attention to the pouring, Patch flexed his forearms under the covers, felt the pain rip through the scarred flesh between his knuckles, the hot blood running down his fingers.

The officer moved to put the glass down on the nightstand, saying, "When did it start? Were you always like this, or did it come on—"

As the man's hand withdrew almost out of range, the corporal's left hand came out from beneath the covers, so fast it was a blur. Before the major could react, Patch swung toward him and three razor-edged claws punched down, piercing the hand that had held the glass and pinning it to the officer's thigh. Patch felt the shock of impact as his middle claw dug into the heavy leg bone.

The officer's body convulsed in agony, his knees buckling and his head coming forward, mouth open as he sucked in air for the scream that had to come. But the gasp was the last sound the major ever made, for as his face came within range, the corporal drove the claws of his right hand up and under the lenses of the wire-rimmed spectacles, through the eyeballs they covered, and all the way through the brain behind.

The officer twitched and jumped like a gigged frog, a noise like a dry cough issuing from his still-open mouth as his lungs deflated. Patch yanked free both sets of claws and the dead man slumped to the floor in an ungainly heap.

The corporal paid him no heed. He was already slashing with his bloody razors at the canvas straps that bound him to the cot. They parted like tissue paper and moments later he was on his feet, if a little unsteady from being doped up and comatose. He flexed his arms again and the weapons disappeared, leaving the major's blood smeared on his knuckles.

Patch was naked except for a bandage across his chest that he now tore free. A tall cupboard on the other side of the tent yielded no clothing. His own uniform must have been shredded in the blast that killed MacLeish. He turned to the dead man and pulled him by the armpits to straighten him out. He was about the right height, though narrower in the chest and shoulders.

Patch sniffed and said, "Good thing you didn't crap your pants." As he began to unbutton the jacket, he added, "Sir."

———o———o———

THE major's Jeep had been easy enough to spot, thanks to a division HQ tag on the hood. Now Patch steered the vehicle along the waterfront road that led north into Ortona. He hadn't bothered to turn on the Jeep's slitted blackout headlights—his night vision was good enough to guide him around piles of rubble and craters that were gifts from the Germans. They had rained down 88-millimeter shells on the road in a vain attempt to stop the Canadians from breaking through a few days before.

He had to put distance between himself and the hospital. Eventually, the intimidated doctor would want to know what had happened in the VIP ward. He would find the cot empty, its restraints slashed, and a man-size scalpel slit in the outer wall. And when someone thought to look in the cupboard, they would find the staff officer, eyeless and naked as Samson.

Between now and then, Corporal Howlett needed a better-developed plan than a stolen Jeep and an ill-fitting officer's uniform. A mile or so ahead was the town and the harbor. There might be a few fishing boats tied up. Even a dinghy would do. He could row up the coast and go ashore behind the German lines, use his commando training and his old bush skills as a hunter to live off the land and evade capture. He'd heard the hills inland had caves that had been used by shepherds since before Caesar's legions had marched along this same road he was driving.

Ultimately, of course, somebody would want to know how the major had been killed. But at this point, the only people in Ortona who had known Patch's identity were probably still being dug out of the rubble of a row of houses or waiting to be discovered in a field hospital cupboard. If he stayed out of sight for a while, he could come back, tell a tale of being captured by a Jerry patrol and having escaped, then go back to being just another corporal.

He saw a military police checkpoint up the road and pulled the Jeep over beneath a stand of poplars. Nobody would mistake him for a staff officer and he had no papers. He proceeded up the road on foot, then went down onto his belly for the last hundred yards, wriggling his way silently through a grove of olive trees. Past the MPs, he moved stealthily through the darkness until he came to the edge of the town.

He eased himself through the shadows between two little buildings and found himself looking across the road to a seawall, with the masts of ships beyond. He crossed the open space and crouched at the top of the wall. The tide was out, the exposed shore reeking of kelp and harbor sludge. Several fishing boats were tied up below him in a rectangular basin between two stone jetties, but none were small enough for him to get out of the harbor without starting up an engine. He needed something more basic—a rowboat pulled up on a beach.

He recrossed the road and continued north, slipping between houses and shacks, keeping to the darkest spots, and looking seaward between the buildings for the kind of craft that could take him away. A couple of blocks farther on, he came to a broad street that led inland. That was not the direction he needed to take, but he looked up the street and saw that it opened on to a square.

Across the open space he could see the corner of a building, a whitewashed wall with black lettering painted on it: OSTERIA GAMBRELLI. He could see a chink of light through a shuttered window.

A wave of regret washed over him. He remembered Rob Roy MacLeish's face as he'd talked about the girl from the tavern, about the plans they were starting to make for after the war. He wondered if anyone had told her what had happened to her sergeant, or whether she was in there right now, pouring wine and grappa for soldiers and wondering when her Loyal Eddie would come rolling in, twinkling those green eyes.

He hadn't been able to save his friend, but he could do something for Rob Roy's girl—at least tell her gently what had happened, before she overheard it in the kind of language soldiers used when they were in a tavern talking about the newly dead. He could just imagine Lucia Gambrelli's heart lifting when someone mentioned that Rob Roy MacLeish had bought a farm, and he could picture how her face would look when someone explained what those pleasant words really meant.

He turned toward the tavern, sidling along the street on its darkest side. The square was empty when he reached it. He straightened his shoulders and marched across the open space like an officer who had every right to do what he was doing. He angled his approach to bring him to the alley that ran along the side of the *osteria* and worked his way to where a board fence enclosed the yard at the back of the building. He put his hands on the top of the boards and vaulted silently over.

The rear door was unlatched. He stepped through into a kitchen full of warmth and good smells but empty of people. In the center was a long wooden counter, topped in gray stone, beneath a frame from which hung pots and utensils. A black iron range, wood-burning, stood against the outer wall to his right, steam coming from a couple of big lidless pots. He sniffed at one of them, thinking Rob Roy would have got himself a fine cook, would have grown comfortably fat on pasta and cheese sauce. On the inner wall, a pair of double doors painted dark brown led to the tavern's main room. They were still swinging—someone must have gone through them just before he'd come in through the back door.

Patch moved to stand beside the doors and waited. He heard a clatter of crockery, then the doors swung inward and a young woman with lustrous black hair and the kind of perfect face Howlett had seen on statues in Italian churches came through bearing an armload of plates and salvers. She crossed the room to pile them on a counter by the sink and he moved silently behind her. When he put his hand over her mouth she started and struggled, but he held firmly while he whispered in her ear, "I'm a friend of Rob Roy MacLeish."

He had to say it twice before she stopped struggling. He released her and she turned to him. "He not come tonight," she said. "You bring message?"

He saw her big dark eyes moving as she searched his face. Before he could speak, she read what was there and her eyes filled with tears. "Oh, no," she said.

"It was very quick," he said. It was probably true, and it was better than telling her her man had died an agonizing death, crushed by shattered masonry or ripped open by splintered floorboards.

Her shoulders sagged. She clasped her hands in front of her and looked down at them. "First, my father," she said. "Then my brother. Now the man I love." A tear fell onto the back of her hand and trickled toward her wrist.

"Maybe your brother is just hiding from the Germans," Patch said. "Maybe he got stranded behind their lines when the front moved north."

She looked up at him, a little hope fighting its way through the sorrow. "It is what Rob Roy say. But I think it is just to make me not sad. He say he look for him when they push the *Tedeschi* more north."

"A good plan. We're pushing them back every day."

She sighed and another tear came. "Now nobody look."

"Do you know where he would be?"

"There is a *caverna* we play in when we are *bambini*."

"*Caverna*? You mean a cave?"

"*Si*. A few *chilometri* past my uncle Enzo's olive trees. Giovanni would go there. It has water from the rock."

A cave with a spring. It sounded perfect. Patch said, "I will go and take a look. Tonight. Tell me how to get there."

She stepped back and took a good look at him now. "You?" she said. "The *Tedeschi* will shoot you. They have very good *soldati—soldati dei paracaduti*. You know what that is?" Her hands sketched a parachute in the air over her head.

"I know," he said. "But I am a very good *paraca*-whatsit soldier, too."

She looked at the officer's insignia on his epaulets, the uniform blouse that didn't quite fit. He saw a spark of suspicion in her eyes. "Who are you?" she said.

"My name is Patch."

The name meant something to her, but the doubt was still there. "Show me your hands," she said, "like this." She held up two small fists.

He showed her his knuckles. She touched their scars, the old ones and the fresh pink ones, with one small finger. "He tell me of you. Before the war, you fight, he win money on you. Every time."

"That's true."

"You look for Giovanni? Help him?"

"I will go to the cave. If he's there, I will help him, keep him safe until the *Tedeschi* are all gone."

The suspicion came back. "Why? What is Giovanni to you? What am I to you?"

"It is because of what you were to Rob Roy MacLeish. Because he was my friend, and I don't have too many friends."

He asked her if she had a photograph. She went out of the kitchen and came back in a couple of minutes with a black-and-white photo that had been taken right outside the tavern. The man had posed very formally, in the Italian way, one hand tucked inside his buttoned jacket. But his handsome face was broken by a wide smile.

"I make him laugh," she said, "just before Poppi make the *foto*."

Patch studied the image for a moment, then handed it back.

"That is enough?" she said. "You don't forget?"

"I never forget a face," he told her.

ORTONA, ITALY,

THE PRESENT

AT Rome's Leonardo Da Vinci Airport, Logan had changed his Canadian dollars for euros at the currency exchange booth, the pretty Italian girl behind the glass wicket showing a little surprise as he pulled handfuls of paper money from different pockets. "I packed in kind of a hurry," he said.

He had taken a taxi to Stationi Termini, the city's main railroad station, and learned that if he wanted to get to Ortona he first had to take a train east to the city of Ancona on the Adriatic Sea, then transfer to a southbound line. By midafternoon he was in a coach heading down Italy's east coast. He had chosen a seat on the inland side and now he watched the hills and fields roll by, interrupted by fishing villages and ancient towns whose modern inhabitants made most of their living off tourists.

All of it had looked familiar, and yet none of it had. It was a landscape he had seen before, but none of the landmarks leaped out at him and said, *you were here*. After a while he leaned his head against the window and closed his eyes. Images came to him in flashes, mostly of anonymous places—a row of houses, a wooden door in a whitewashed wall, a rooftop seen at night. None of the pictures connected, but he sensed that there was a thread linking them—or that there had been until somebody had carefully and systematically gone through his brain, snipping the linkages away. Leaving him what he was, a man who didn't even know his name.

The train came into Ortona in the evening. He stepped onto the platform and knew right away that all of what he was seeing was too new to be of use to him. Everything must have been rebuilt since the war. He walked into town, turning corners at random, looking at the buildings lit by the modern streetlights. Waiting for some scene to speak to him, but getting nothing.

Then he came around another corner and found himself at the edge of a small square. On one side of the piazza, a short street ran down to an enclosed harbor where fishing boats mixed with pleasure craft. On the other was a small square building with bright yellow walls, light spilling from its windows and music sounding from behind a pair of doors painted red. From an iron bracket that projected above the door hung a wooden sign, on which were carved in curvaceous letters the words OSTERIA GAMBRELLI.

That's wrong, he thought. He couldn't make out what it was about the scene that was wrong, and the harder he tried to nail it down the more elusive it became. Then he forced himself not to try. He stood and just looked at the tavern, even letting his eyes unfocus. And now it came. The walls should be white. The backyard should have a wooden fence, not waist-high iron railings and tables and chairs. The sign shouldn't be over the door but painted on the wall. But the name called up a faint touch of a feeling that fled when he tried to catch it.

He could hear his pulse beating faster in his ears. *I've been here. Not in a dream. Not just somebody telling me about it. Nobody implanted this memory in me. I've* been *here.*

He crossed the square, pulled open the tavern door, stood there letting his eyes roam over what was in the big public room: tables and chairs, tourists and locals eating and drinking, a pair of musicians weaving notes from a mandolin and violin into some happy tune over a buzz of conversation and laughter. Some of them looked up as he stood in the doorway, but quickly looked away again. The full-bellied man in shirtsleeves behind the bar gave him a more searching inspection, then put on a professional smile and reached for a plastic-covered menu.

"Signor?" he said and when Logan made no answer, "you want a table, some wine?"

Logan just wanted to look, to find out if the inside of the place would call up the same certainty as the outside had. So far nothing was coming and he flicked his eyes toward this man who was distracting him, irritating him. The fellow took a half step backward, then Logan got hold of himself and said, "Yes, a table. No wine. Do you have Seven Crown whiskey?"

"*Non*, signor," the bartender said and led him to a table with two chairs near a pair of swinging doors in the inner wall. Logan glanced at the menu. The whole thing was in Italian, but he recognized some of the items. That didn't mean anything, he told himself—he'd find the same dishes offered in restaurants on Ottawa's Sparks Street mall.

He tried the same technique he'd used outside. It was harder here, with the distractions of the chattering crowd and the musicians, but he let his gaze wander at random around the room, seeing but not focusing on the paintings on the walls—ships on the sea and a big stone church on a hill—and the shapes of the windows.

None of it rang that inner bell that he'd heard when he'd been outside. Not until his eyes came all the way around the room to the two swinging doors. They were of dark old wood, slotted lathes with gaps in between, in a simple frame that had been painted more than once. And now the feeling came again, and with it the urge to see what was behind.

He rose and stepped through the door, took in the scene beyond. A mustachioed man in white was at a natural gas range to his left, shaking a skillet full of something that sizzled on the heat. The waiter who had brought his wine was arranging slices of crusty bread in a basket at a granite-topped table in the center of the room. He looked up, startled, as Logan came through the door.

"Signor," he said, "you cannot come here. It is not for the customers."

Logan ignored the protest, ignored the voice of the bartender in the public room behind him, who was also saying, "Signor, Signor," the voice getting closer. He let his mind go, let the sight and, most of all, the smell of the kitchen just come to him, without trying to focus on any one detail. And again, it happened: *The stove, that's different. The counter, that's the same. And the door leading outside, it's been painted, but I know it.*

As he looked at the door that led to the tavern's backyard, it opened. Through it came an old woman in a black dress, her face lined but full of dignity, her dark eyes meeting his with a challenge that left Logan in no doubt that she was in authority here.

The bartender was tugging fitfully at his elbow from behind, the waiter was advancing toward him with a worried look but making shooing motions with both hands, and the chef had turned from his cooking but the expression of outrage that had begun to appear on his face was rapidly dying. Logan did not see any of them.

His eyes were locked on the old woman. The look of resentment that she had first cast at the intruder in her domain had been shattered by an outbreak of astonishment, tinged by superstitious fear—as if she had walked into her own kitchen and come face-to-face with a ghost.

She stood frozen in the doorway, eyes wide and mouth open. Then she brought one pale hand to her lips and whispered, "Patch!"

For all Logan knew, it could have been a word from some obscure Italian dialect, a curse to fend off the evil eye. Yet he could tell right away that it was a name, and that she had called him by it. And he knew that the shock on her face was the shock of recognition.

"My name is Logan," he said.

He saw her react to his voice, saw that its sound only confirmed what she had already decided. She crossed the room, moving briskly despite her age and dismissing the waiter and the bartender with a quick flurry of Italian. She came around the counter and looked up at him. Her eyes on him stirred another memory.

"Your name is Logan?" she said.

He was going to say, "Yes." Instead, he said, "I think so."

"Show me your hands," she said, holding up two closed fists, "like this."

He put up his hands. She touched the knuckles with a slim finger.

"Your name," she said, "is Patch."

ORTONA, ITALY,

DECEMBER 1943

IT helped that the rowboat had been painted black. He'd muffled the oars with rags stuffed into the oarlocks after he'd taken it from the little boathouse where Lucia Gambrelli's father used to keep it. The innkeeper had liked to go out on the sea in good weather, to relax and catch a fish or two.

The boat was now drifting empty on the outgoing tide and Patch Howlett was a couple of miles inland from the big white rock on the shore that she'd told him to look for. He'd skirted a farm abandoned by its owner and which was now the temporary quarters of a German infantry company, crawling and wriggling through the sparse grass of a winter pasture. Then he'd found the goat path that led west and into the hills, well away from the old road that was patrolled by the enemy.

The sky was clouded and the land almost completely dark, but his night vision kept him on track. The higher he rose in these foothills of the Appenines, the clearer he could see the Adriatic flat and gray behind him, where an offshore break in the clouds lit the sea with a pearly light.

There were fewer Germans in the higher country. They must expect the real assault to come on the coastal plain, he reasoned. These steep and grassy hills, cut by narrow ravines that ran east and west, were no place for armor to operate. And tank-supported infantry actions were the mainstay of both sides in this campaign, when they weren't trying to slaughter each other with artillery barrages.

He came to a level area at the top of the goat path, a small plateau planted in neat rows of olive trees. *Uncle Enzo's place*, he told himself. The winter-dry leaves of the trees rustled in a chill wind that rolled down from the higher country, but he didn't mind—the sound would cover any noise he made. He went quickly through the first grove, over a low stone fence and through a second stand that ended where the land began to climb sharply again.

He went up a grassy slope so steep he sometimes had to use his hands. The wind was strengthening so that he didn't smell the wet wool of sheep until he almost stumbled upon a small flock nestled in a hollow. The ewes bleated sleepily and the ram snorted at him, but the animals quieted when he kept on moving higher, glad that there was no dog to make a noisy fuss.

He was pretty sure he was following Lucia's directions, and he became certain when he came to the tall standing rocks with a tree growing sideways out of them. Beyond the rocks, the slope eased and he soon came to the brow of the hill and began to descend the other side. The western slope was even more gradual, and he could make out a stand of poplars down and to his left. He angled toward them and moments later he was among the trees.

It was pitch black here, but he heard the gurgle of water that the woman had told him to listen for. He went toward it, then followed the little stream until he found where it issued from a crack in the hillside. A bush covered the fissure, but he worked his way behind it as Lucia had told him to do, and found that the crack widened a little higher up the slope. He put his nose to the cave entrance, smelled damp earth and blood and something else that he could not quite place.

"Giovanni," he whispered. "Giovanni Gambrelli."

"*Sono qui*," came a faint voice from within. Patch thought it meant, "I'm here."

He squeezed his way through the gap in the rock, his booted foot coming down on the soft earth floor of the cave. In the complete blackness of the interior, Logan could not see anything, but his animal sense told him that someone was nearby. Hands extended, he felt his way forward, sniffing the air. Now he knew what the unnatural smell was: gun oil.

"*Non spari*," he said. The combined special force had been taught a few Italian phrases that might come in handy on a battlefield. That one meant "don't shoot."

He took another step into the darkness and his eyes were blasted by the sudden glare of a powerful flashlight. Logan looked away, but his field of vision was filled with a purple ring of afterimage.

"*Non si muova*," said a hard voice and Logan knew that the words meant "don't move." He also knew that they had not come from Giovanni Gambrelli. The accent was German.

Still half-blinded, he swung toward the light again, flexing his arms and preparing to spring. But whoever held the flashlight was not alone. From the side came a burst of automatic fire and the unmistakable rip of a Schmeisser machine pistol. Logan felt the rounds tear into his legs below the knee, piercing his flesh though missing the bones. Still, the impacts staggered him, and as he toppled forward the brass plate of a rifle butt loomed out of the darkness and smashed into the side of his head.

ORTONA, ITALY,

THE PRESENT

"HOW can you be here, unchanged?" the old woman said. "It is more than sixty years."

"I don't know," Logan said. "My memory is gone. I'm trying to find out who I am."

They were sitting in a small parlor in the living quarters upstairs. She had poured herself a glass of the fiery Italian brandy called grappa—Logan had declined to join her—and now she regarded him with wonder. But she had the kind of mind that does not stand in awe of mystery for long, the kind that has to grapple with the puzzle and make sense of it. When she said, "How can you be here?" she wanted an answer.

"But you remember this place?" she said. "You came here because you remember?"

So he told her what he knew, produced the pictures he had torn from the library book and brought with him. She touched the photograph of the men sitting outside the tavern, and a tear came to her eyes. "I never saw this picture," she said.

"Is that you?"

"Yes. And that is my Rob Roy."

"Rob Roy?" The name echoed somewhere in the fog behind his mind.

"Rob Roy MacLeish." She touched the image of the fair-haired soldier looking up at her long-ago self. "He was your great friend." She paused, then said, "If you are truly you."

"What happened to him?"

She told him. The words went through him like the melody of a forgotten song. He closed his eyes, listening to her, and saw images: a man's face, smeared in blacking; a small window; a rooftop covered in terracotta tiles.

"Do you have a photo of him?" he said.

She rose and went to an ornate credenza, opened a wide, shallow drawer, and reached into a back corner. "I had to hide this from my husband," she said, "all our years together. He would not have understood."

She handed him an old black-and-white photograph, now faded by the passage of time. Logan looked at the smiling face and there was no question. "I knew him. The memory is real." He closed his eyes and let his mind go loose, and more images came to him: MacLeish grinning at him over a mug of beer; MacLeish on the other end of a two-man saw, sawdust flying as they bucked a big spruce log in a lumber camp.

"How can it be?" she said again. "Look at me in your old photograph. And look at me now. Why are you not old?"

"I don't know."

"Did you fall into a hole in time and come out sixty years later? Or did someone put you in a *congelatore* full of ice to keep you frozen?"

"I don't think so. But how would I know?"

"Who was the first man to land on the moon?" she said.

"Neil Armstrong."

"Who is Michael Jackson?"

"A pop singer, kind of weird."

"9/11."

"Planes flying into the World Trade Center."

Her face said, *that settles it.* He had not been catapulted from the 1940s to the early twenty-first century. Nor had he been cryogenically frozen and recently thawed out. "You have lived the same years I have lived," she said, "but something has stolen away the particular memories of your own story."

"Not something," he said. "Someone."

"Ah," she said. "And you mean to find that someone, to ask him who you are."

"Yes, and then I'm going to ask him why he did this to me."

"I don't think," she said, "the answers to your questions will please you."

"That's all right. I don't think he'll like the way I ask them."

ORTONA, ITALY,

DECEMBER 1943

"WHO are you? What is your mission?"

Patch Howlett tried to see past the bright light that shone into his eyes when they pulled off the blindfold, but the figure beyond remained in shadow. He was bound to a sturdy wooden chair, his hands manacled behind him. The room had whitewashed walls, but the white was flecked here and there with the red of blood. There were dark stains on the concrete floor.

A hard hand came from behind the glare, moving fast, to connect with his cheek and slap his head sideways. "Do I have your attention now, Herr Major?" the voice said, giving the last word the German pronunciation, *my-or*. "Or do I need to—" The sentence was finished by the same hand striking from the other direction, the pain of the backhanded blow embellished by a heavy signet ring.

"Let me acquaint you with your situation," the unseen man continued. "You are not a prisoner of war. You are a captured spy, taken in a trap laid for these Italian pigs who cut the throats of our sentries and blow up troop trains."

The interrogator began pacing the floor behind the light as he spoke, and now Howlett saw that the man's uniform was not that of the Wehrmacht, the regular German army. Instead the black collar tabs showed the double lightning-bolt runes of the SS and the single oak-leaf rank insignia of a Standartenführer—the equivalent of a colonel. The heavy ring on his right hand was inset with a black stone inlaid with the SS symbol in silver.

Before the First Special Service Force was deployed to the Italian front, Howlett and the rest of his unit had been warned that if they were captured, the Germans might not observe the rules of war. British commandos taken in raids on German installations in occupied France had been shot by the SS, even though they were fighting in uniform and with proper identity disks around their necks.

"So there will be none of your name, rank, and number nonsense," the SS man said. "No cozy chat with some oaf of a Wehrmacht intelligence officer, then off to a Stalag to sit out the war drinking tea and opening Red Cross parcels.

"You will tell me everything I want to know, sooner or later. If it is sooner, I may send you off to a concentration camp. If it is later, you will welcome the firing squad that relieves you of your misery."

Howlett could see his face now. Young but not too young, with the blond hair and blue eyes that the Nazis liked to think were the unmistakable marks of racial superiority. But this one also probably had brains, or he wouldn't have risen so soon to high rank in the highly competitive rat race of the SS intelligence service. It would not be a good idea to fence with him—and besides, it was easier to tell the truth.

"I was looking for Giovanni Gambrelli," he said.

The statement earned him another slap. "We know that. You called his name as you came into the cave."

With a little training, the German would have made a decent bare-knuckle fighter, Patch thought. He had the natural ability to hit hard. His cheek stinging, he said, "I promised his sister, Lucia, that I would look for him. She's worried."

This time it was not a slap. The SS man's fist landed a short but powerful punch to Patch's jaw, the ring ripping his flesh and drawing blood. "If you want to play games," he said, "I know some good ones."

"It's the truth," Howlett said. He shook his head to quiet the ringing, thinking the Jerry really could have been a contender. "She's worried about her brother and I'm in trouble. I punched out an officer and stole his uniform. Lucia told me about the cave above her uncle's olive trees. I could hide out there until my unit moved on, then I could come down and help her run the tavern."

The blue eyes were watching him closely. "You are not a major?"

"No."

The German touched the collar tags on Patch's uniform. "Not a divisional staff officer?"

Howlett's head came up and he looked directly into the man's eyes. "Do I look like a staff officer?"

The German's eyes narrowed. "Then what is your rank? What is your unit?"

"The Loyal Edmonton Regiment," Patch said. "I'm a sergeant. Sergeant Rob Roy MacLeish."

BERLIN, GERMANY,

DECEMBER 1943

WHEN the orderly opened the door, Wolfgang Freiherr von Strucker strode into the vast, high-ceilinged room in the SS headquarters on Prinz Albrechtstrasse, marched to the ornate desk against the far wall, and stood to attention. With military precision, he threw out his right arm in the Nazi salute and said, "Heil Hitler!" at the same time bringing the heels of his polished boots together in a resounding clack. Then he removed his officer's cap with the red skull insignia, placed it under his arm, and waited for the slight-statured man behind the desk to notice him.

For several seconds, the only sound in the room was the scratching of the gold nib of a fountain pen on a sheet of cream-colored vellum paper. The top of the paper bore a swastika-and-eagle-wings emblem, and beneath it, the title Reichsführer-SS that belonged to the mousy little man in the black uniform.

Heinrich Himmler wrote another line in his spiky, compressed handwriting, then added his jagged signature at the bottom. He recapped the pen and laid it on the desk, took up a rocking blotter, and carefully dried the wet ink before placing the page in a basket at the corner of the desk. Only then did he look up at the Prussian baron standing rigidly before him and say, "Tell me, Herr Oberführer, why are you wasting the Reich's resources and producing no results?"

"I am expecting very good results any day now," von Strucker said. "We are near to isolating the brain chemistry that governs muscular reflexes. When we succeed—"

"If you succeed," said Himmler. His voice was mild, but the baron knew the SS leader could order mass murder in the same tone that he would use to call for a cup of herbal tea.

"We will succeed, Herr Reichsführer. It is but a matter of refining the samples taken from the test subjects' brains. Then we will—"

The little man's round spectacles flashed in the light from the lamps. Now the tone grew sharp. "It is always 'but a matter' of this or that. Yet every time you claim to have overcome one obstacle, I immediately hear that a new one has suddenly appeared in your path."

"The brain is a complex—"

"Yes, yes, very complex. But I am a simple man, Herr Oberführer. I give orders, and I expect results. If I do not get the results I want, the results the Reich needs, I give new orders."

"Yes, Herr Reichsführer," the baron said.

"Will I have to give new orders concerning you?"

"No, Herr Reichsführer."

"See that I don't." Himmler reached for another piece of paper from the stack at this elbow and uncapped his fountain pen. It was a moment before von Strucker realized he had been dismissed.

His Mercedes-Benz staff car was waiting outside. The uniformed SS driver holding the door open for him was almost certainly assigned to report any evidence of disloyalty so the baron kept his face rigidly neutral. He told the man to drive him back to the hospital in what had been a leafy neighborhood of Berlin before the Allied bombers had reduced much of it to rubble. The car drove to a service area at the building's rear and through a segmented door that rolled upward as they neared it. They descended by a spiral ramp to an installation deep below street level, where von Strucker went straight to his office and summoned his team leaders to an emergency meeting.

"Himmler has given us an ultimatum," he told the four men in lab coats. "If we do not produce good results soon, this project will be abandoned. I do not need to spell out the consequences."

The four faces paled. The Reichsführer-SS had personally authorized their project. Their failure would be an embarrassment to him if Herman Goering or Joseph Goebbels, his rivals in the Nazi inner circle, got wind of it. So if von Strucker's team were broken up, the breakage might be literal—Gestapo men in black leather trench coats would come for them and the last sights any of them would see would be the graves they would have to dig for themselves in some isolated woodland, as each waited for the pistol shot to the back of the head.

The most senior of the scientists, Dr. Schlimmer, touched a pale hand to the top of his head to make sure the long hair he combed sideways over his bald crown was still pomaded in place and said, "The Iron Eagles are ready for a demonstration."

"Define 'ready,'" said von Strucker.

"We have delineated the correct dosages for optimum effect."

"And the side effects?"

"Minimal."

"What about the man who became psychotic?"

Schlimmer patted his hair again and swallowed nervously. "An underlying psychological flaw that was not detected in the screening. It was unique to that subject."

"You are sure?" the baron said. "The Reichsführer will want to inspect them closely. We would not want one of them to try to tear out his throat."

"We will screen them all again. Rigorously."

The other three projects were in no shape to put before Himmler for a demonstration. The "invisible boy" had a tendency to throw his own excrement when he was afraid, and since meeting new people usually frightened him, no one could guarantee he would be out of ammunition if he was trotted out to impress Himmler.

The Dutch teenager who could dream her way back through time was better, but von Strucker did not want to produce her until he could deliver a scientific explanation of the genetic basis for her strange talent, so that he could design a reliable breeding program. A corps of spies who could eavesdrop on any conversation within twenty-four hours of its occurring, or read any document that had ever been composed, would be sure to perk up Himmler's interest. But right now all he had was an inexplicable mutation.

"We must bring in more... opportunities for study," he said. "Our people in the camps must examine more prospects." As he spoke, he glared at Bucher, the stocky, pink-skinned man who was responsible for coordinating the search for mutants.

"They do their best," Bucher said, perspiration breaking out on his moon-shaped face. "The camp administrators complain that our examinations slow down their processing of the inmates."

Von Strucker made his decisions. To Schlimmer, he said, "Prepare a demonstration of the Iron Eagles. Give them that unit of captured Red

Guards for targets, but make sure the Ivans are well-fed and rested."

He turned to Bucher. "You will personally visit each of the camps. Remind the commandants that we are working under the expressed authority of the Reichsführer-SS." But to himself, he thought, *At least, until that authority is withdrawn.*

He suppressed a shudder as his staff filed out of his office, Bucher carefully closing the door behind him like a schoolboy who has just escaped an expected thrashing from the headmaster. The Prussian sat at his desk and stared at the portrait of Adolf Hitler that hung on the opposite wall.

I am ruled by a blowhard from Bavaria and a man who used to farm chickens, he thought, *and I am trying to make miracles for them.* He leaned forward to place his elbows on the desk and lowered his forehead onto his spread fingertips. The Iron Eagles demonstration would buy him time, time to intensify the search for mutants. He knew they were out there. His search teams found prospects and fed them back to him, though most of their talents were militarily useless—people who could digest iron or extract the square root of a ten-digit number in an eyeblink.

Most of them turned out to be demented or otherwise unuseful. Still, just going by the odds, there must be others out there—people with valuable inborn talents who were neither insane nor crippled by degenerative physical conditions. But why was he not finding them? Did they learn early to hide their conditions?

If so, he had a solution. He had dissected enough of the useless varieties to believe that he could eventually home in on a vector that would yield a reliable test. The difference would be revealed in the blood, and von Strucker would devise a blood test that would tell their secrets. His searchers would be able to drip a drop of blood into a tube or onto a piece of treated paper and know within moments if the ordinary-seeming man or woman before them was one of the common herd—or one of the precious few.

In the meantime, he could at least make some members of that herd capable of performing amazing feats. He had made a close study of adrenaline and of the neural structures that governed reflex and reaction time. Combining his own researches with those of the Reich scientists who were developing ever more powerful amphetamines, he had produced a formula that stimulated the brain to hyperspeed while providing the skeletal muscles with the energy required to function at their maximum.

The hysterical strength that sometimes allowed mothers to lift automobiles off their pinned offspring could now be artificially instilled in anyone who swallowed one of von Strucker's pills.

But the effects were only temporary. The Iron Eagles were fine soldiers made even finer for a few hours. Then they fell apart, burned out, and were often unusable again. They were perfect for a shortlived blitzkrieg assault. But two years of fighting in Russia had taught even Hitler that some victories could only be won by playing the long game. Now the Reich required supersoldiers who remained super, year after year—and Wolfgang Freiherr von Strucker had sworn to the Reichsführer-SS that he could deliver them.

———o———————o———

"YOU are going to die," von Strucker's translator told the company of Red Guards standing at attention in the broad courtyard of the former military school that had been turned over to the baron for the development of his *Eisenadler*. The place had been used to train cadets since the days of muzzle-loading cannon and unrifled muskets, long before Chancellor von Bismarck and the first Kaiser Wilhelm had assembled the German state from a collection of squabbling principalities.

Not one of the Russians moved or gave any indication that the translator's words meant anything to them. "You will die," the translator repeated, "but you will have an opportunity to die fighting. Like men. Like soldiers."

The elite rifle company's captain took one pace forward, slamming his right foot to the flagstoned ground as if he was on parade before the Kremlin. He looked straight ahead as he spoke. "You have perhaps mistaken us for Ukrainski," he said, in passable German, referring to the black-uniformed Ukrainian SS troops who guarded many of the concentration camps. "We will not fight for you."

Von Strucker waved the translator away and spoke directly to the Russian officer. "We do not want you to fight *for* us," he said. "We want you to fight against us."

The captain's broad Slavic face registered suspicion, but he could not keep a shadow of grim curiosity from creeping into the hard stare he turned toward the baron. He and his men had thought their war was over, that they would be sent to be forced laborers—slaves—in Nazi factories, dying of the diseases that came with overwork and underfeeding. If they weren't beaten to death by guards, many of them with Ukrainian accents, who delighted in dealing out sadistic punishment to Russians. It was not the kind of death that appealed to men of a guards regiment that had twice been awarded the Order of the Red Banner, the second time presented by Marshal Zhukov himself.

The Russian turned his head and regarded the SS soldiers ranged on all sides of the walled courtyard, their submachine guns trained on the prisoners of war. "Bare hands against Schmeissers?" he said. "We might still take a few of you."

"No," said von Strucker. "Here are your weapons." He signaled to an SS sergeant who stood beside a pile of wooden crates marked with Cyrillic lettering. The noncom stooped and upended one of the long boxes, then pulled away its lid. Inside were four Mosin-Nagant bolt-action rifles, slow to fire but as accurate as the Mausers that German troops used. The Prussian gestured again and another crate was opened, revealing two of the sturdy PPSH submachine guns with drum magazines that were standard issue for the Red Army.

"They were taken from your own armories in 1941," von Strucker said. "Still in their factory grease."

"I don't understand," the Russian captain said.

"Two kilometers east of here," the baron said, "is a stretch of woodland. You will be taken there with these weapons. You will find waiting for you an ample supply of ammunition and some entrenching tools.

"You will be left there overnight to make whatever preparations you like. In the morning you will be attacked by a special unit of shock troops. They will give no quarter, nor will they expect any.

"You will die. But you will die as men."

The captain's eyes went to the weapons, then back to von Strucker. "What if we decide to try to fight our way home?"

"Then you will still die. But you will die choking on the poison gas that the Luftwaffe will drop on you the moment you attempt to leave the woods."

The captain's face remained impassive as he received this information. Then a light came into his eyes and he showed the baron a humorless smile. He turned smartly on his heel to face his men. "*Tovarichi!*" he said, then barked a string of Russian.

Von Strucker saw the reactions among the prisoners as they looked to the crated weapons and heard their officer's explanation. The same cold fire came alight within them. Fists clenched and jaws set. When the captain finished by asking them a question, they responded as one man with a harsh cry of "*Da, da!*" *Aye-aye.*

Good, the Prussian thought. *They will do their part.*

———o———————————o———

IN the gray light of a late-autumn German dawn, Heinrich Himmler's luxurious staff car entered the courtyard, followed by two other vehicles full of his aides and bodyguards. Flanked by an honor guard, von Strucker met the Reichsführer-SS as he stepped from the car, the little man's pale eyes passing over the men standing at attention with no more interest than if they were the stones beneath his feet.

"I have prepared a briefing, Herr Reichsführer," the baron said, leading the visitors into the school's main hall, where a sand table display of the operation's terrain awaited. But after the briefest overview of the miniature trees, fields, stone walls, and paper flags which represented the four squads of Iron Eagles, the head of the SS yawned and turned away.

"Here are the pertinent figures," von Strucker said, offering a sheaf of papers bound in a leather cover. Himmler flicked one finger in the direction of an aide whose boots, belt, and buttons were burnished to perfection. The hanger-on stepped forward and took the data.

"Well," said the little man, "we are here, so we might as well see it."

Von Strucker brought his heels together and thrust out his elbows. "*Jawohl*, Herr Reichsführer!" Within the privacy of his head he suppressed another set of remarks and gestured for the party to follow him out of the building. A path led them past the obstacle course to a steep hill that overlooked the exercise area. A bunker had been dug into the brow of the hill, its meter-thick walls of reinforced concrete pierced by narrow observation ports. Inside, von Strucker had made sure that a wooden step had been installed below the slot Himmler would look out of—making the Reichsführer-SS stand on tiptoe would not improve his mood.

The baron took two pairs of high-powered binoculars from a wooden compartment next to the observation port. He handed one to Himmler and slung the other around his neck. "If you are ready, Herr Reichsführer," he said.

The little man in the black uniform made a small sound that von Strucker took for a yes. The Prussian picked up the handset of a field telephone affixed to the wall and spun the crank on the instrument's side. He spoke into the receiver—"You may begin"—then lifted the binoculars to his eyes and adjusted the focus.

It had snowed briefly just before dawn, so the open field below and the evergreen woods it led to were lightly dusted with white. The *Eisenadler*, in their field gray, were clearly visible as they came out of the ditch at the near end of the field that was their start position and advanced toward the Russians. They went forward in four squads of eight men each, crouched low and moving fast.

The Red Guards were dug in at the edge of the woods. The ground was not frozen and they had had all night to dig foxholes and rifle pits and to cover them over with branches and small logs. The snow had helped camouflage their positions further. As von Strucker swept his binoculars over them, he could not easily make out where the enemy waited.

The Iron Eagles were halfway across the open ground now, advancing in open order through dead, knee-high grass, zigzagging constantly. A single shot rang out from beneath the trees, followed by a rattle of rifle and submachine gun fire. The advancing Iron Eagles dove face forward into the snow-covered grass. From von Strucker's vantage point they remained visible and he thought they resembled nothing so much as large gray snakes, wriggling toward the Russians at an impossible speed.

Each man also continued to move at a tangent, changing direction every few seconds, yet covering the distance to the edge of the pines faster than any Olympic sprinter could have managed on his feet and running straight and level. Now an *Eisenadler* abruptly lifted his head and upper torso above the tips of the dry grass, an automatic pistol in his hand.

The observers in the bunker heard two small pops as the enhanced soldier fired twice, but long before the sound crossed the distance, the man was back down again and wriggling sideways to take up a new firing position. Meanwhile, the Russians poured fire into the place where the shots had originated, even as other *Eisenadler* began to pop up and fire before disappearing from sight.

"Our men are armed with Lugers and fighting knives," von Strucker told Himmler, "and each pistol has only eight rounds. The Russians have good rifles and submachine guns, and plenty of ammunition."

"Hmm" was the Reichsführer's lukewarm reply.

"Although they appear to be shooting all along the line, they are concentrating much of their fire at the ends of the Russian position." He drew Himmler's attention to the far right of the Red Guards' firing line. "There you may notice that three of our men are now going into the woods. They will eliminate any command post and reserves, then come at the enemy's forward positions from behind."

Himmler made the same uninterested sound.

The firing from the edge of the woods had slackened.

At the left of the Russian line, four more *Eisenadler* rushed from the field into the trees, moving so fast that they had disappeared beneath the shadow of the dark pines within a heartbeat of rising up from the grass. The men left in the grass snaked closer, still lifting up and firing single shots until their weapons were empty, then abandoning them for the knife as they slithered into Russian rifle pits and covered foxholes. Occasional faint screams crossed the distance to the bunker.

A silence fell on the scene below, broken moments later by the harsh ring of the field telephone beside von Strucker. The baron unhooked the receiver and listened for a few seconds, then reported to his visitor, "The enemy are all dead. We have sustained no casualties except for one man who was grazed by a ricochet."

Himmler lowered his binoculars and stepped down from the observation port. He handed the glasses to the baron and brushed a nonexistent speck of dust from the front of his tunic. "I see," he said. "And what do you believe this means, Herr Oberführer?"

"It means that the Reich has a potent new weapon, Herr Reichsführer."

"Perhaps," Himmler said. "But creating potent new weapons is not your assignment."

"Herr Reichsführer—" von Strucker began, but had to fall silent as the little man held up one finger, then wagged it warningly.

"You have taken ordinary men," Himmler said, "indeed, men who are better than ordinary in strength and coordination, and you have so enhanced their natural abilities that thirty-two of them armed with knives and pistols can cross open ground and wipe out a full company of better-armed enemy soldiers dug in under cover."

"Yes, Herr Reichsführer."

"But I do not want to enhance ordinary men. I want to create new men, a new breed of men whose superiority is not added by chemicals injected from the outside, but is to be found built into their very nature, born in them, in their lifeblood."

"Herr Reichsführer," von Strucker said. "These men can help win the war."

The little man gave him a look that, accompanied by a small shake of the head, meant that Himmler was talking to yet another fool who did not see the grand vision that was obvious to the Reichsführer-SS. He clasped his pale hands behind his back and began to pace back and forth in the bunker, head down, as if working out a problem.

"I am not concerned about winning the war," he said as he walked. "The dunderheads with red stripes on their pants who infest the general staff may worry about it, but I do not. We will win the war, probably next year when the new weapons come into production, but certainly by the end of 1945. We will win because it is our destiny to win."

Now he stopped and turned to face the baron, his spectacle lenses reflecting the morning light from outside the bunker. "My vision goes far beyond this year, far beyond this war. We are creating a thousand-year Reich. And that is not work for ordinary men, no matter how many drugs you may inject into them.

"That is work for supermen. And the task I have set you, Herr Oberführer, is to find those supermen. Find them or create them. If you can't do that, what use are you to me?"

ORTONA, ITALY,

DECEMBER 1943

OF course, the intelligence Standartenführer hadn't believed that Patch was a garden-variety sergeant of the Loyal Eddies. Not at first, and not even after a thorough beating that left the prisoner with a shattered kneecap, a fractured collarbone, and most of the small bones in his feet broken or cracked. The two SS men who methodically worked him over were experts. They stayed away from his head—because that was where any useful information would be stored—and concentrated on body parts that could be struck again and again, causing excruciating agony, but creating no risk that the man in the chair might be rendered useless.

"Tell me again about your years in the lumber camps," the officer said. "What kind of trees did you cut?"

"Mostly poplar and spruce, for the pulp mills—" Howlett began, then screamed as the beefy noncom standing behind him brought his oak truncheon down on the broken collarbone.

"And the red Indians," said the officer. "You said they were of the Blackfoot tribe, *ja*?"

This time, a bootheel came down on his ravaged naked feet, grinding the instep, making the ends of broken bones grate against each other. Patch howled.

"Gunter," said the interrogator, "I am trying to have a conversation with this man." The German corporal lifted his heel and the officer continued, "So, the Blackfoot, no?"

"No," said the prisoner, through clenched teeth. "The Blackfoot are in southern Alberta. Up north are mostly Cree and Métis."

The Standartenführer consulted his notes. "That is not what you said the first two times."

"You're wrong. It's the truth."

The end of the truncheon ground into the broken collarbone. Patch screamed and writhed under the agony. They kept rebreaking his bones before they could knit. But he concentrated on fighting the terrible itch in his forearms, handcuffed at the wrists behind the chair back. His claws would be useless, but if he let them show the interrogation would take a whole new direction. And he would not easily escape. Maybe never.

"Let us come back to Giovanni Gambrelli. How long did you say you have known him?"

"I don't know him. I know his sister." Howlett tensed, waiting for the pain that accompanied each question and response. But the SS were masters of their cruel art and knew that as soon as the subject believed he understood the rhythm of the torture it was time to change the sequence of events.

After a while they took him out of the chair and suspended him by his pinioned arms from a chain strung from a hook set into the ceiling. The noncom and the private would lift him up and then let him drop, so that the full force of his plummeting weight would wrench his arms almost from their sockets. They beat him on the knees, ankles, and shins with their clubs, the bones cracking, until he shrieked and bellowed like a wounded beast.

"What is your name?" the officer screamed into his face as the blows landed.

"MacLeish! Rob Roy MacLeish!"

And then, suddenly, it was over. The officer looked at his watch and said something in German to the corporal. Howlett was unhooked from the chain and dragged from the room, down a damp corridor with brick walls and a concrete floor and thrown into a stinking cell.

For a long time, he lay on his side on the cold floor. At first the pain of the hurt they had done him washed through him like a speeded-up tide set to the pace of his own heartbeat, and he could hardly distinguish the fire of torn ligaments in his shoulders from the ice-sharp ache of his cracked shinbones. Then, gradually, the tide slackened and ebbed, the individual pangs and agonies separating themselves like small islands appearing as the sea went back home. He gritted his teeth as his body exercised its phenomenal power of self-repair. He hated bone breakage worse than when his flesh was cut or crushed—fractures hurt even as they healed.

"Are you all right?" The accent was Italian, not German. Patch took his mind away from his pains and noticed for the first time that he was not alone in the cell. A shadowy figure squatted beside him.

"I've been better," he said. "Who are you?"

"Bruno Tattaglia. You want me to help you? There are some rags over there you can lie on. Better than the floor. I have a little water also."

Patch shifted, drawing himself away from the stranger until he could get a better look at him. The cell was windowless and unlit, but a peephole in the door let in some light from the corridor outside, enough to see that the other man was in his twenties, dressed in a torn and filthy suit, his face discolored by fresh bruises. Patch levered himself to a sitting position, leaning back against the damp cold wall, and the man put a tin cup to his lips. He sniffed, and smelling only well water, drank.

"You are British?" Tattaglia said.

"Canadian."

"How did they catch you?"

"I got lost. What about you?"

"I am the schoolteacher in a village up in the hills. They were rounding up those they accused of being partisans."

He offered more water. Patch took another mouthful. "And are you?" he said.

"Am I what?"

"Are you a partisan?"

The man said, "And did you really just get lost?"

"I was looking for someone."

"Who?"

"Giovanni Gambrelli."

There was enough light for Patch to see the other man shrug. "You will not find him."

"Why not?"

"Because he is gone. First they squeezed what they could get out of him. They are very good at squeezing. Then they put him on a train to Germany. To a camp. They are emptying out places like this, before the Allies get here."

"What camp?"

"Who knows?" Tattaglia said. "Besides, it doesn't matter. Whatever camp you go into, you don't come out."

"How do you know about Gambrelli?"

"Because, until this morning, he was sitting where you are sitting."

The sound of a heavy steel bolt being slammed back came from the other side of the door. An SS man entered and deposited on the floor two tin bowls half-filled with thin liquid, then threw down a couple of husks of stale bread. Before leaving, he spat in the direction of the food.

Tattaglia took up one of the bowls, dipped bread into it, and chewed. "What is that?" Patch said. "What do they feed us?"

The other man swallowed. "Always the same. Some kind of pumpkin soup and stale bread from their own mess. And always they spit. The *Tedeschi* like to turn everything into a routine." He put down his bowl and picked up Howlett's. "Can you eat?"

"I need to keep my strength up."

Tattaglia dipped Patch's bread in the soup and held it so the Canadian could tear off a chunk. While Howlett chewed and swallowed, finding the soup so thin as to be almost tasteless and the bread moldy, the other man ate from his own bowl. Alternating, they soon finished the meager meal.

"That's it until when?" Patch said.

"Another piece of bread and some water in the morning. Then this again in the evening."

"You've been here long enough to know the routine?"

"Yes. Four days now."

Patch leaned back against the wall. His bones had now knit themselves up and his shoulders felt normal again. The bullet wounds in his legs had been healed before the men who had captured him had turned him over to the interrogation unit. Fortunately for him, the SS saw no point in making inquiries about the physical well-being of those they intended to question.

"So," he said, "how far are the train tracks from here?"

"Not far," Tattaglia said, a note of surprise coming into his voice. "If this cell had a window, you could hear them. Why, do you have somewhere to go?"

"You speak pretty good English for a village schoolteacher." As he spoke, Howlett tested the manacles that bound his wrists together, two rings of metal connected by a short chain.

"I had a flair for languages."

Patch pushed against the floor, his knees bent, so that his buttocks came clear of the cold stone. He held his hands as far apart as the chain would let them go, then pulled against the metal bracelets. He groaned as skin and muscle tore, heard as well as felt the small bones in his hands being crushed and snapped like dry twigs, but still he forced them down and down, suppressing a scream that might have brought a guard, until he was sitting on the handcuffs. Then he pulled straight up against the steel rings, blood from his self-inflicted wounds acting as a lubricant, until his hands came free of the restraints.

He sat, his legs stretched straight out before him, hands in his lap, feeling the ache as the bones put themselves back together and the flesh grew whole again.

"What are you doing?" said Tattaglia. "Do you need help?"

It was too dark for his cellmate to see what he was doing, but Patch's night vision showed him a look of genuine worry on the bruised face. "I'll be fine," he said, "in a couple of minutes."

"Listen," said the other man, "Giovanni said someone might come looking for him. I want to know if I can trust you with a message he said to pass on. He said it was important."

"Yeah?" said Howlett. "Well, you can trust me."

"How do I know?"

Patch fought to keep a grim smile from twisting his lips, even though he was pretty sure the other man couldn't see. "You think I might be a German?"

The other sounded uncertain. "Well, you never know. Listen, you tell me how you were connected to Giovanni. And if I think I can believe you, I'll tell you what he said."

"What good would a message from Gambrelli do me?"

"You never know. You might escape, or get a chance to pass it on."

Howlett nodded. "It's true," he said, "you just never know."

As he spoke, he flexed his forearms, felt the sharp pain that always came when his claws ripped through the flesh between his knuckles.

His feet were completely recovered now, his shinbones mended. He was still hungry and a little tired, but he was ready. He bent his knees, leaned forward, and came smoothly and silently into a crouch.

"Tell me," said the man across from him, "what did you have to do with Giovanni?"

"Let me whisper it to you," Patch said. "The guards might be listening."

The man didn't disguise the eagerness on his face as he leaned forward. *He thinks it's too dark for me to see*, Patch thought, but he could see his target perfectly as he brought up his right hand in a brutal uppercut that drove the spikes of his mutation through the undefended flesh of the man's lower jaw, up and through tongue and soft palate, and into the brain of this supposed Italian schoolteacher—this man who claimed to have sat here four days living on pumpkin soup and moldy bread flavored with SS spittle, but whose skin exuded a different odor for Patch's animal-sharp sense of smell to detect, an odor of sauerkraut and fennel-spiced German sausage. The same odor that had clung to the two thugs who had dragged Patch to the cell.

The spy twitched and flopped reflexively, but he had been dead the moment the razor-sharp claws had shredded his neural tissues. Even before he ceased to move, Howlett was pulling the clothes from the corpse. He tore off his stolen uniform and dressed in the filthy suit, then put the staff major's torn khaki on the body. Next he arranged the dead man on the pile of rags, facing away from the door, the arms behind and with the handcuffs positioned more or less as if they were confining the wrists.

Then his plan, made as he had listened to the spy, came up against a sudden barrier. *What the hell's the German word for "help"?* he asked himself. They hadn't taught him that one in the special force training sessions. He'd learned, *hande hoch*—"hands up," and *nicht schiessen*—"don't shoot," and *raus*, the general term for "move your butt." But right now none of those would do him any good in getting the cell door opened.

He squatted on his heels and let his memory work for him. He went back to the assault on Monte la Defensa. There had been a wounded Jerry in a machine gun pit off to his right when they'd gone at the fortified pill box with grenades. What had the man been calling?

And then it came. Patch readied himself, crouching over the corpse with his back toward the cell door, his claws out and ready.

"*Hilfe!*" he shouted, just like the wounded machine gunner. "*Hilfe!*"

Almost instantly, he heard the bolt shoot back. Light spilled across the floor as the door was flung open and then was immediately obscured as two SS troopers crowded into the doorway, one of them saying, "Dieter, *was ist los?*"

Still in his crouch, Patch spun and drove his claws into the throat of the one who was leaning down to examine what he thought was a prisoner in distress. The SS man gurgled and gasped, dying in a rush of bubbling blood from a severed jugular and windpipe.

The second man had been behind the first. Horror and panic swept across his face and he turned to rush from the cell. But Howlett had already flung the first guard from his claws and now he leapt onto the fleeing man's back, knocking him to his knees in the corridor, hearing at least one kneecap snap from the impact of their combined weight. Patch's left arm went around the man's neck, and iron-hard muscles choked off his attempt to shout the same word that had summoned him and his comrade to their deaths. Then Patch's right arm went down and around the man's torso with a blur of speed, his claws striking inward, driven up beneath the ribs to pierce the frantically beating heart. He'd been trained to do the exact same move with the VK-42 stiletto and now, as the man went limp beneath him, he was pleased to find that it was just as deadly with his natural armament.

He flexed his arms, withdrawing the bloody claws, and looked about him. The corridor was empty, the doors to several more cells standing closed. He went to the nearest one, threw back the bolt, and opened the door. A face looked at him, pale and fearful, from within the gloom.

"Come on out!" Howlett whispered.

The fear turned to hope. The man got to his feet and came into the corridor. When he saw the dead SS man, a grim smile took control of his mouth and he grunted something Patch didn't understand, then knelt and rolled the corpse over. The guard had had a holstered sidearm, but in a moment it was in the released prisoner's hand.

The Canadian had already gone to the next cell door, opening it and moving on to the next. The man with the gun joined in the effort, and soon the small space grew crowded with more men, and one woman. All were battered and bruised, some limping on broken feet, squinting through eyes surrounded by swollen flesh, cradling arms that had been wrenched from sockets.

One of them took charge, a big fellow in blue workman's overalls. The man Patch had first freed had acquired another Luger from the dead guard in the cell, and this he handed to the leader. The big man ejected the magazine, checked that it was full, and slipped it back into the pistol's butt with practiced skill. He ratcheted back the weapon's slide to put a round in the chamber. Then he smiled, showing a gap where a tooth had recently been knocked out.

He looked at Howlett and said, "*Grazie*," then turned to the others and followed with a rapid string of Italian that Patch didn't understand. With the two armed men in the lead, the group headed for the iron-bound door of heavy wood at the end of the corridor.

Patch didn't move. "Wait," he called after them, keeping his voice low. "Does any one of you know where Giovanni Gambrelli is?"

The big man turned. "Gambrelli, he go train. *In Germania*."

"When?"

"*Ieri*."

The word meant nothing to Howlett. Seeing his incomprehension, the woman chipped in. "Not this day. Day before."

"Yesterday?"

"*Si*. Ee-esta-day."

So the spy in his cell had told the truth. Gambrelli had been put on a train to Germany a day earlier. So where did that leave Jim Howlett?

It didn't take him long to think it through. He hadn't had many friends in his life, but of the few Rob Roy MacLeish had been the best. They'd worked together, drunk together, fought in saloon brawls together, wenched together. It had been MacLeish's idea to come down from the northern Alberta lumber camp and join the army. Volunteering together for the paratroops but not both being accepted had separated them for a couple of years, but the accidents of war had brought them back together.

But only briefly. Only long enough for them to be separated permanently by a German booby trap. Now his friend was gone. All that was left of him was the girl he'd loved, the girl to whom Howlett had made a promise, in Rob Roy MacLeish's name.

There was nothing that would particularly draw Patch back to the FSSF. He liked the men he served with, respected many of them—like the Ojibway sergeant, Tommy Prince—for their guts and go-at-it attitudes. Their wounds didn't heal in minutes the way his did, but they still stood up and went forward, right into the worst that a skilled and determined enemy could throw at them.

The Devil's Brigade could get along without him. And he couldn't go back to Rob Roy's girl and tell her he had failed, unless he could first tell himself that he had done all he could. Besides, it was probably not all that hard to get into a Nazi concentration camp. The tricky part would be getting out.

"Wait!" he said to the people gathered around the door. He tapped his chest, said, "Commando," and "Me first."

The big man looked at the dead SS man on the floor and his battered face formed one of those eloquent expressions that allow Italians to communicate plenty without speaking a word, an expression that said, "Who am I to argue with an expert?" He moved aside and let the obviously lethal foreigner take the lead.

The door was locked from the inside. Patch eased back the heavy metal bolt that secured it. He gently pushed and it swung silently open on well-oiled hinges. Beyond was a set of stone steps leading upward and curving out of sight. Above the door was a single lightbulb and somewhere up the steps was another.

Patch's feet were still bare and he made no sound as he went up the stairs, his right shoulder almost brushing the curving wall. The others came behind in single file, led by the two with guns.

The steps curved up to an archway. Beyond was a hallway painted in institutional green. When he had crept far enough upward to see that much, Howlett also saw what he had expected. An SS guard stood just beyond and to the side of the arch that led down to the cells, his hands cradling a Schmeisser submachine gun slung from a strap over his shoulder. But the guard was there to prevent people from breaking in to rescue those who were confined downstairs. The man didn't expect death to come at him from behind and below.

Howlett brought out the claws of his right hand. As he came to the top of the stairs, he clamped his left hand over the guard's mouth, pulling him backward into the stairwell and letting the man's own weight drive him down onto the three needle-sharp talons. Patch felt the middle claw briefly grate on bone, then its point slipped into the softer material between the fifth and sixth cervical vertebrae, slicing through the spinal cord and killing the man instantly.

The leader of the escapees took charge of the body, slipping the machine gun from the dead hands and passing it to a man behind him. The big man in the coveralls saw the claws extending from Patch's hand. He looked from their dripping tips to their owner's face. Then his own face said, without words, "How is this any of my business?"

Patch gave him a nod. Then he turned and went without a sound into the corridor, saw that it ran about thirty feet to a door that had the look of an exit to the outside. Above the door hung an electric clock that said it was just going on 5:45. The place had no natural source of light, no windows or skylights, but it had that empty feel that argued for its being early morning rather than late afternoon.

Along the corridor were two doors with glass panels in their upper halves. No light shone from within either. Patch went forward. The place looked to have been the jail of a small town—he'd seen the inside of a couple of such places, northern Alberta style, in his bar-fighting days—that had been taken over by the local SS intelligence unit. So probably he would not find a high wall and guard towers outside. There might be a vehicle yard and some kind of fence, or the door ahead might even lead out onto the street.

Beside the door was a light switch. Patch thumbed it off and, with the corridor behind him in darkness, he cracked the door just wide enough to put an eye to it. A man stood outside, in field gray and a coal-scuttle helmet marked with the SS runes. Moments later he was gasping out his last breath on the tiled floor of the corridor and the freed partisans had acquired another machine gun.

The plaza outside was empty and still night-dark. A shoot-on-sight curfew coupled with the predawn cold of a morning in late December kept the town's residents in their warm beds. Howlett scanned the open space that was lit by only a few dim lamps above doorways, including the one above the door in which he stood. Its glass globe was open at the bottom and he reached up and unscrewed the bulb.

Across the plaza was a large building that must have been the town hall. A red banner with a black swastika in a white circle hung from an upper floor. Two armed soldiers flanked the front door, and Patch saw a brief glow as one of them drew on a cigarette.

He closed the door and spoke to the big man, using sign language to augment the message: "Two guards across the street."

"We go…" the leader said, then spread his fingers and moved his hands outward to show that the escapees would scatter in different directions.

"Trains?" Howlett said. "Where?"

It took three of them to come up with enough English to explain that he had to go left then right after two blocks, downhill toward the sea.

"Okay. Let's go."

"*Grazie*," said the big man, and the woman crossed herself and said, "*Benedicali*." From the way she said it, Patch was pretty sure it meant "bless you."

They went out, one at a time, giving each an opportunity to clear the area before risking motion that might attract the attention of the sentries across the square. Howlett was the last to go, moving silently on cold bare feet. *At least there's no snow*, he told himself. He kept to shadows and stepped into doorways to watch for Jerry patrols, but the town was quiet.

He found the downhill street and made his way toward the sea. Soon he could hear a steam engine huffing and the clack of railcars being shunted in a trainyard.

"IT cannot be done, not even if we throw them all away."

Al Borak leaned over the tabletop recreation in miniature of the Green Zone, the complex of streets and buildings surrounded by impenetrable layers of security that the American forces had built for themselves in the heart of Baghdad. The accuracy of the model was virtually perfect, the data having been acquired from a Russian military surveillance satellite through a series of black market channels.

"The place has been expertly designed for defense in depth," the Green Fist leader said. "Cracking the gate or going over the blast walls only channels us into these confined routes—" he used a wooden pointer to tap the possible avenues of approach, "—that are covered by overlapping fields of automatic weapons fire. The weapons are computer-aimed and -operated, so even if we suppress the perimeter guards with nerve agents, our men will be cut down before they get beyond the first defensive layer."

"What about aerial assault?" von Strucker said. "A high-altitude, low-opening parachute drop, avoiding the outer rings and bringing them closer to the target zone."

"There is no way to keep their approach from being seen. The closest they would get to the inner core would be when they were deposited in the Green Zone's morgue."

"Underground? Sewers and service tunnels?"

"Blocked, monitored, guarded by automated firing systems."

Von Strucker ground a fist into the palm of his other hand. "Our friends are not going to accept 'impossible' as an answer," he said, staring for the umpteenth time at the uncooperative puzzle of little structures and spaces that covered the table. "Beneath their cold calculations lies a certainty that Allah will deliver them victory, by a miracle if necessary." He had worked under people who had that same uncompromising attitude and knew what it led to when it was applied to difficult military situations.

Al Borak said, "If we trained and conditioned a couple of hundred men like the twenty we have now, one or two might get through and reach the objective."

"We don't have the time. This is a once-only opportunity, and the date is fixed," the baron said. He clasped his hands behind his back and paced up and down the side of the table, his eyes probing the model's details. "We will just have to create that miracle."

He left Al Borak to consider the problem and returned to his quarters. In the secret room behind the closet he checked the level of liquid in the Pyrex tube in the safe. It looked to be no less than it had been at the same point in the production cycle last month. But as he resealed the hidden room and stretched himself on his narrow cot, the Prussian had to fight to keep a chill of apprehension from taking hold.

He did not relish the prospect of having to leave this secure place he had arranged for himself, to start again with some other group. The Foundation had been a good find for him, had allowed him to keep out of the sight of those who had hunted him through the wreckage of the Third Reich, who would gladly kill him now if they could get their hands on him—once those hands had twisted and fretted him into explaining in the most exquisite detail how a man who was more than a century old happened to have the well-tended body of a fit and vigorous forty-year-old.

He had come to the Foundation by a circuitous route. In April 1945, with the Russians pounding their way into Berlin and with the Americans and British rolling back Germany's disintegrating armies in the west and south, von Strucker had sent a message to Himmler, telling him that he was taking the remaining Iron Eagles south to the mountains of the Tyrol to prepare for the coming guerrilla war against the Allied occupation. Instead he ordered the last handful of his men to escort him to the Swiss frontier.

Avoiding contact with the enemy as much as possible, fighting only when absolutely necessary, the stimulants in their veins constantly renewed from the last batch to come out of Schlimmer's lab, the burned-out remnants of the *Eisenadlers* had brought the baron to the shores of Lake Constance where he had long since arranged for a one-man submarine to be waiting in a concealed boat shed. He left the former cream of the German forces shivering and hallucinating on the lakeshore and crossed to freedom.

A passport and ample funds waited for him where he had left them in a safe deposit box in Zürich. He became Señor Hans-Klaus Bauer, a prosperous Argentine citizen stranded in Europe by the war, now eager to make his way home to the city of Córdoba in the foothills of the Sierra Chicas. A month later, he was walking its sunny streets and sitting in its outdoor cafés, sipping the surprisingly good wine from the Mendoza region—and planning his future.

The die-hard Nazis who made their way to Argentina and Paraguay, establishing secret societies where they got together and dreamed beery fantasies about someday returning to power, did not interest him. They were a horse he had ridden as far as it would go, and now he looked about for another steed. But he kept in contact with the former gauleiters and SS gruppenführers, because they were assiduously forging connections with groups that might suit his purposes.

And so it was that, after the creation of Israel in 1947, von Strucker made contact with the Foundation, an organization that had recently spun off from the Muslim Brotherhood in Egypt. His first impression of them, after a meeting in Cairo, was that they were a curious blend of religious fanaticism and hard-nosed pragmatism. But they had access to substantial funding from the Middle East's new phenomenon: the oil-rich sheik. The Prussian formed a consulting relationship with the group's operational planners, advising on methods to improve the fighting abilities of their volunteers. As the organization grew in wealth and power, the relationship deepened and when von Strucker suggested the creation of a highly secret research and development center in the wasteland of southern Arabia, the results he had already delivered to his clients made them happy to say yes.

Thus Wolfgang Freiherr von Strucker, hereditary lord of a stately old *schloss* in an East Prussian forest that had been seized and disposed of by an enlarged postwar Poland, had spent decades in underground corridors beneath a searing desert. He who had once debated the ideas of Nietzsche and the strategies of von Bismarck in the bustling halls and high-ceilinged lecture rooms of Heidelberg's schools had spent most of the past fifty years exiled among swarthy fanatics who constantly invoked the will of a God he had long since ceased to believe in.

The isolation and cultural dislocation might have driven another man mad, the baron supposed. But he had something that he could cling to, a shining ambition for whose realization he would gladly endure another century of this barren existence. For what did it matter if a man wasted a hundred years of his life, if that century was but a tiny fraction of a span that was effectively endless?

Von Strucker meant to live forever. All he needed was to stay alive long enough to encounter once more the little man he had had nailed to the table—to crack his bones and extract more of his marrow, enough to let him unravel the eternal secrets that would give him eternal life and mastery of the world.

There would be a way to carry out the mission. He would find it. And then he would continue, through his client's resources, the search for mutants. He had convinced the Foundation that Allah had sent the faithful a deliverer, an invincible warrior who did not know that he was the chosen. But could he but find this *mahdi*, this "expected one," von Strucker had the means to show him the sign that would prove who he was—the sign that was in his blood, and no one else's.

So now von Strucker rose from his narrow cot and set off to study once again the tabletop model of the Green Zone. He would find a way to carry out a successful assault. Whatever the cost, he would keep his clients happy. And they would continue to provide the resources that would allow the baron to seek his personal grail: the savage little man whose veins were filled with the precious blood of immortality.

He would find his grail, empty it—and live forever.

ORTONA, ITALY,

THE PRESENT

"YOUR brother, what happened to him?" Logan asked Lucia Gambrelli.

"He must have died. He never came back."

"And I guess neither did I."

"Not until now," she said.

Frustration was building in him. He had followed a trail to this room, but it had not been a clear path, laid out before him. Instead it had been a series of bright spots separated by darkness—the photo of Tommy Prince, this tavern in an Italian town, the face and name of Rob Roy MacLeish, a friend who was dead sixty years, this old woman who had been a girl to whom he had made a promise.

But now there was no new patch of light beckoning beyond the darkness ahead. After finding a hope that had drawn him forward through the past couple days, after feeling a growing sense that he was finally getting somewhere, to come up now against a dead end was unbearable.

As if she could read his thoughts, she again offered him a glass of grappa. "No more booze," he said. "Not until I find… whatever I can find."

She took the glass away. "I wish I could help," she said.

An idea came to him. "Wait," he said, "did anyone ever report seeing Giovanni?"

"We asked the Red Cross. Years later, we got a report that he had been sent to a camp called Höllenfeuer, and that he might have died there of—I don't have the English word. In Italian it is *tifo*."

She spelled it for him. *Typhus* or *typhoid fever*, he guessed. They used to call it prison fever, because it was spread by lice and fleas when men were crammed together in squalor. Aloud, he said, "Höllenfeuer? Where was that?"

"In Poland, they said."

Höllenfeuer. He repeated the word inside the silence of his mind till it echoed in his head. "It means something to me," he told Lucia. "I think I was there."

HÖLLENFEUER CONCENTRATION CAMP,

JANUARY 1944

WHEN the train of cattle cars finally arrived at the camp, Giovanni Gambrelli was not in good shape. He had been passing blood in his urine and the pain in his lower back was enough to make him scream every time the shunting of cars threw him against the wooden slats that penned in the prisoners but did nothing to keep out the cold. Patch Howlett figured that SS boots had ruptured both the Italian's kidneys.

He heard the rattle of a chain, then the railcar's door slid open. A hard-faced man in a black SS uniform beat on the floor of the cattle car with a heavy wooden truncheon and said, "*Raus!*"

"Come on," Patch said. He knelt and put one hand in Gambrelli's armpit to help him up. The other hand he put over the man's mouth to keep him silent. This was not a place where it was wise to show weakness. He had listened to the conversations among the prisoners during the long train journey out of Italy and across Germany to what seemed, judging by the unpronounceable names of the last few stations they had passed, to be Poland. He had gathered from those who spoke a little English that they were being sent to a labor camp where the only ticket to survival was the ability to work. The day you couldn't do your job would be your last day on earth.

He pulled Gambrelli's arm over his shoulders and, supporting the sick man, led him to the door where they jumped down to the slush-covered concrete of the platform. The Italian groaned at the impact, but the sound was lost in the noise of shouting guards, the puffing of the train's steam engine, the yipping of dogs, and the amplified voice of a man in a black uniform who was barking at them through a megaphone.

Howlett didn't understand much of the German's harshly accented Italian, but all he needed to do was follow the rest of the shuffling mass of prisoners as they were herded along the platform to a wider area. Here the SS men pushed and shoved them into ranks and files. A pasty-faced man wearing a white lab coat over an SS officer's tunic passed along the rows, giving each man a two-second looking over. Some he tapped on the chest or shoulder with a wooden pointer and these were quickly seized by guards and manhandled down the platform and through a gate in a tall wire fence topped with three strands of barbed wire. Evergreen branches had been woven into the fence so that what was beyond remained invisible.

The men who were being removed were the old, the sick, anyone who looked unfit to work. "Stand up," Patch said out of the side of his mouth as the man in the white coat approached. Gambrelli's jaw muscles bunched, but he stood straight as Howlett withdrew the arm that had been supporting him.

The inspector paused before the Italian and looked him up and down, his stick poised indecisively, his eyes narrowing in suspicion. Patch, next along the rank of men, growled deep in his throat. The sound drew the SS medic's attention.

"*Sagten Sie etwas?*" he said.

Howlett didn't know what the German words meant. He shook his head and said nothing. He had decided days before, after he had worked his way into the crowd of prisoners being herded toward the trainyard back in the town where he had escaped the cells beneath the town hall, that the only way he could pass for one of the captured partisans and slave laborers was to pretend to be mute. Now he pointed to his open mouth with two fingers and shrugged.

"*Stummer?*" the medic said, then when Howlett shrugged again, he said, "*Muto?*"

That sounded like Italian for "mute" and Patch nodded. The German sneered and passed down the line, Gambrelli forgotten as he slapped his stick against the chest of an elderly man. Howlett growled again as the black-uniformed guards dragged the old man to the gate in the wire. A stream of people, men, women, and crying children, were being herded directly to this gate from the three cars at the head of the train. Every one of them wore a six-pointed yellow star sewn to their coats. Gambrelli, as well as the half-dozen captured partisans who had been in his car, each had a red triangle with a black letter *I* on his tattered jacket. Those sent as forced laborers were unmarked.

The inspection over, the man with the megaphone shouted more orders and the guards began driving the men down the length of the platform. A flat-faced SS man, his baton held horizontally in both hands, pushed Howlett to move him along. Patch bit back his anger, did not meet the thug's eyes. It would do no good; even if he killed them all, he couldn't escape with Giovanni Gambrelli in his current condition.

He'd had no trouble finding Lucia's brother once he arrived at the trainyards. His first thought was to silently kill the sentries that guarded the warehouse where the prisoners were gathered and lead an escape, much as he had at the town hall. But Gambrelli was in no shape to run.

Patch couldn't abandon the badly injured man. A promise to Rob Roy's girl was as binding as a promise to Rob Roy. There was nothing to do but to go where the Germans were sending the partisan, until he was well enough to abandon the hospitality of the SS.

Shoving backs and beating legs with their clubs, the guards drove the crowd past the rear of the train, then down and across the railroad tracks. Another section of the camp stood behind more wire fencing, though on this side of the rails no woven green branches hid what the fence enclosed. Row upon row of long, low wooden buildings, made of unpainted boards and roofed in tar paper, stretched for hundreds of yards to the left and right. A double gate yawned, flanked by Schmeisser-toting guards with snarling German shepherd dogs slavering to slip their leashes.

The prisoners were driven through into a broad street that ran the length of the camp. Howlett's bare feet slipped in half-frozen mud but he kept going, supporting the injured Italian. They were hurried along past three of the buildings that seemed to be barracks, then around a corner into a wide mud-floored space that occupied the center of the camp. On three sides stood open sheds without walls, and they were herded toward one of these.

The shed contained several rough tables, just planks set on saw horses, with wooden bins and barrels set beside them at intervals. With impartial blows and curses, the guards shoved the men inside and got them lined up along the tables. A man who had been sitting on the end of one of the trestles now climbed atop it and called, "*Attenzione!*"

He was a short but heavy-shouldered. The knuckles of his ham-size hands had been broken and healed more than once. One cheek was disfigured by the kind of scar a broken bottle makes. He was dressed in no better clothing than most of the men who had come on the train with Patch, but he looked well-fed. On his jacket was sewn a green triangle.

A brawler and a thug was Howlett's assessment. He listened to the man's guttural Italian, delivered in an even thicker accent than that of the man with the megaphone. Patch caught only one or two words, but the gestures that accompanied them told him that they would work in the shed, putting things in the bins and barrels. One bin was labeled *Haar*, another *Kleidung/Frauen*, a barrel was for *Schuhe/Kinder*.

"Well," he whispered to Giovanni, "it beats digging ditches."

But the Italian's face had paled even further as he listened to the man with the green badge. He leaned his hands on the plank table and breathed heavily.

"What is it?" Howlett said.

A canvas-covered truck entered the open space from the street they had come along. It turned and backed toward the shed, stopping just short of the roof. Two men got out of the cab and came around to the vehicle's rear. One of them, the driver, also wore a green triangle and looked fit and healthy. The other wore a blue triangle and looked as if he hadn't eaten or slept well in years.

Later, Patch would learn that red badges were for Communists, social democrats, and anybody else whose politics the Nazis didn't approve of. Blue was for foreign forced laborers. And green badges were worn by *kapos*—German criminals whom the SS put in charge of political prisoners, slave workers, Jews, and Gypsies, encouraging these sweepings of the German underworld to give their brutal natures free rein.

The driver grunted something that was probably an insult and signaled the blue badge to unhook the truck's tailgate. It dropped with a crash and two more forced laborers began pushing the vehicle's load out onto the concrete floor of the shed: suitcases, from elegant leather bags to scuffed pasteboard; clothes of both sexes and all kinds and sizes; shoes and boots; toys and books; and big bags of rough sackcloth whose contents couldn't have weighed much because they hit the concrete with scarcely a sound.

Giovanni Gambrelli was shaking. He looked like a man fighting a need to vomit. The two *kapos* were giving orders, clearly telling the men in the shed to get the piles of stuff onto the tables and to start sorting. One of the sacks landed in front of Patch and the man he had come to save. Gambrelli put his hand in the bag's open mouth and drew out some of its contents.

He looked at what was in his hand, then turned to Howlett with a face gripped by horror. "*È la verità,*" he whispered. "*Li assassinano tutti.*" It's true. They kill them all.

What he held in his hand was the freshly shorn hair of a little girl.

———o————————o———

"SOMEONE has to live to remember this. Someone has to tell the story."

The words remained in Patch Howlett's mind. They were almost the last words Giovanni Gambrelli ever said, translated from the Italian by a man named Bertolli, a former language teacher who had been sent to Höllenfeuer after getting caught chalking up anti-occupation slogans on walls in Rome. The teacher had not lived much longer than Gambrelli— both had died in one of the epidemics of typhus that swept through the camp, carried by the swarms of fleas and lice that infested the unheated barracks, where prisoners had to huddle together for warmth on wooden shelves. The teacher had also translated the name of the camp—Höllenfeuer meant "hellfire" in German. Shivering with cold and fever, the man had said, "Somebody in Berlin has a sense of humor."

Patch had lost his. But he had found a mission. He observed and remembered. He watched the trains roll in, tracked the greasy black smoke that rose up to dirty the winter clouds, memorized the names and faces of guards and *kapos*. Filed it all away, for the day of vengeance.

———o————————o———

BUT the mute man would not work. He would not sort the last possessions of the dead, adding one last insult to the fate of the innocents who were hustled from the cattle cars and rushed behind the fence with the evergreen boughs woven through the wire. He would stand in the frozen mud with the rest of the prisoners when the loudspeakers mounted on the watchtowers summoned them to roll call. He would line up for his bowl of thin soup and moldy bread. He would go to his hut and lie on the verminous boards when the last whistle blew. He would even report to the sorting shed.

But he would not handle the loot from the dead.

At first Helmut, the scar-faced *kapo* who had been a pimp and enforcer in the mean streets of Munich, beat him with the lead-weighted rubber truncheon that was his staff of office.

But still the mute prisoner would not work.

Then the guards went at him with oak batons and iron-heeled boots. Years in the camp had made them experts in the science of inflicting painful, humiliating death. After evening roll call, while the whole of the work camp watched, they ringed him in the assembly area, clubbed him to his knees, then kicked him until his face was unrecognizable and his ribs caved in. When he was dead they hung him on a frame of barbed wire and left him there as a reminder to anyone else who did not want to work.

But when the prisoners turned out for the morning roll call, his body was not there. Hauptscharführer Müller, the senior SS noncom in the work camp, raged at the assembled forced laborers. His face turned brick red and spittle shot from his mouth as he strode along the trembling front rank, shoving men at random and bellowing "*Wo ist er?*" Where is he?

"Herr Hauptscharführer," came an uncertain voice from the rear of the formation. "*Er ist hier.*" He is here.

It was Helmut the *kapo* who had spoken. Müller wheeled and went down the side of the block of men. He found the ex-pimp standing behind the last row, his meaty hand gripping the arm of the small man who wouldn't work. The man who showed no sign of the murderous beating that had been laid upon him the evening before.

The SS noncom pulled up short. Confusion struggled with rage in his face but, as it always did, his core of brutality overruled every other reaction. He unsnapped the flap on his holstered Luger, withdrew the weapon, snapped back the slide, and aimed it squarely at the mute's forehead.

"*Uberleben Sie dieses, kleiner mann,*" he said with a cruel smile—survive this, little man—and pulled the trigger. Blood, bone, and brains flew from the back of the prisoner's head, and the small man fell lifeless to the ground.

Müller rounded on Helmut, the smoking gun still in his hand, and issued curt orders.

"*Jawohl*, Herr Hauptscharführer," said the green badge in a voice that shook with fear. He grabbed two men from the rear rank and sent them for a wheelbarrow and shovels. When they returned, he had them load the body and led them out of the work camp and to the open ditch where those who died of illness or abuse were buried en masse.

They threw the corpse on top of three frozen bodies that had lain there since the day before and quickly shoveled earth over all of them. Then they went back to the camp, where Helmut made a point of not letting Müller's eye find him for the rest of the day.

But at the evening roll call, the count was one more than expected.

○────────○

WHEN Karl-Heinz Baumann came to Höllenfeuer in February 1944, it was his last hope to rescue his career within the SS. Obersturmbannführer Baumann had once been a key aide to the Schutzstaffel's golden lion: Reinhard Heydrich, Reich Protector of Moravia and Bohemia, and architect of the "final solution to the Jewish problem," whose headquarters were in Prague. Like his mentor, the man Hitler had affectionately dubbed the "Blond Beast," Baumann combined a considerable intelligence with an icy ruthlessness. He had been delighted to be seconded to Heydrich's staff because it was clear that the man would someday emerge as the successor to the charismatic corporal who was leading Germany to its rightful dominance among the nations. And when that day came, Karl-Heinz, who had once won a prize at the University of Graz for an undergraduate essay on symbolism in Goethe's epic tragic play *Faust*, would be a trusted aide to the most powerful man in the world.

Then, on May 27, 1942, all of his plans were plunged into the pit of despair. Czech partisans, working with the British OSE, had waited where Heydrich's open-topped staff car slowed to take a sharp corner. They had killed him by throwing a bomb into his lap. Reichsführer-SS Heinrich Himmler, relieved to see one of his major rivals removed from the game of power, had appointed a far less competent man—an oversize Austrian drunkard named Kaltenbrunner—to take over Heydrich's duties. Karl-Heinz Baumann, having risen through his dead boss's influence to the SS equivalent rank of lieutenant colonel, found himself facing, at best, an assignment to shuffle papers in some pointless office. At worst, he might be moved over to the Waffen-SS and sent off to fight Russians.

Karl-Heinz Baumann did not mind seeing blood spilled, even German blood. He just saw no point in spilling any of his own. Thus, he used every connection and contact he had developed within the SS to wangle, after weeks of treading water in Berlin waiting rooms, a private interview with one of Himmler's closest aides. Somehow he managed to make enough of a case for his administrative abilities that, after more months of paper shuffling, he was recalled to Prinz Albrechtstrasse and ushered into the presence of the Reichsführer-SS himself.

"Klaus tells me that you know how to get things done," Himmler said.

Baumann stood rigidly to attention before the elegant desk. "I do my best, Herr Reichsführer."

"There is a concentration camp in Poland. The closest anyone could come to pronouncing the barbarous Polish name of the nearby town was Höllenfeuer, and the name has stuck."

"Yes, Herr Reichsführer."

Himmler drew a piece of paper toward him, arranged his rimless spectacles more securely on the bridge of his nose, and said, "Productivity and morale there have plummeted lately. The commandant has committed suicide."

Before he could stop himself, Baumann said, "Why, Herr Reichsführer?"

Himmler looked at him without expression. "I don't care why," he said. "I only care that the problem is fixed."

"Yes, Herr Reichsführer."

"If you fix it, we will talk again."

"Yes, Herr Reichsführer."

The little man removed his glasses, breathed on the lens, and polished them with a snowy white handkerchief.

"If you do not fix it, we will never talk again."

"I will fix it, Herr Reichsführer."

And then he was dismissed. But as he marched across the Persian carpet to where Klaus held open the door, Himmler said, "Heydrich thought highly of you."

Baumann stopped, about-faced, and said, "Thank you, Herr Reichsführer."

"Don't thank me. I didn't think highly of Heydrich. You have a month."

HÖLLENFEUER CONCENTRATION CAMP,

FEBRUARY 1944

THE commandant's quarters at Höllenfeuer had been the home of the local railroad station master until the camp had been built around it. Obersturmbannführer Baumann found it cramped but adequate for a *kommandantur*. A rug had obviously been removed from the office—the floorboards were a lighter color where it had lain—and right next to one edge of the pale oblong was a darker stain.

"Your predecessor's blood," said Hauptsturmführer Otto Schenkel, the plump, damp-eyed SS officer Baumann had inherited as an adjutant. "We have not been able to get all of the stain out. The rug was ruined completely." He had entered carrying a box of books that had been in the baggage compartment of the train that had brought the new commandant. "Shall I put these on the shelves?"

"Yes," said Baumann, sitting at the desk and taking up one of the several files neatly arranged on its top. He opened it and scanned the rows of figures on the first sheet, then methodically made his way through the information as Schenkel supervised the bringing in of his books.

"These are beautiful volumes," the adjutant said, running his hands over the calf-leather binding and gold-embossed spines. "Goethe, Schiller, the poetry of Heine. You must be proud to own such fine books."

"I was, once," the new commandant said. "I prided myself on having absorbed the grand ideals of German civilization, of being able to recite verses and quote long passages."

"And now?" Schenkel said, organizing the Goethe next to the Fichte.

Baumann did not look up from the file. "Now I am proud to have surpassed such folly."

"Yet you keep the books?"

"They are the trophies of my final victory over sentimentality."

An SS guard came in, his arms straining to hold a heavy wooden crate that tinkled musically as he moved. "Careful!" Baumann snapped. "That wine is priceless! It has been in my family for generations. My father handed it to me and someday I will pass it on to my own son."

"The house has a cellar that would do for keeping wine," Schenkel said. He gave orders for the crate and several others to be taken there. Then he said to his new commandant, "Herr Obersturmbannführer, may I sometimes borrow a book? I had only a grammar school education and regret not having been exposed to those 'grand ideals of German civilization.'"

Baumann closed the first file folder and reached for the second. "You would do better to read Nietzsche and, especially, the Führer's *Mein Kampf*. Then you would understand that life is about *will*, not windy idealism and overblown romanticism." He scanned the first page of the new file, then said, "On second thought, you would do better to give more attention to your duties. The organization of this camp is a disgrace to the Reich!"

Schenkel came to an attention with a click of his bootheels. Beads of sweat appeared on his upper lip. "There have been problems, Herr Obersturmbannführer. Unusual circumstances."

Baumann slapped the folder closed. "Circumstances are about to change!" he snapped. "And whatever these 'problems' may be, they will be solved!"

"*Jawohl*, Herr Obersturmbannführer!"

The commandant rose and ordered the adjutant to assemble the senior officers so he could inspect the camp. As Schenkel made for the door, Baumann called him back and said, in a milder tone, "Herr Hauptsturmführer, obviously there are problems here. That is why I have been given this command. Solving those problems, quickly and efficiently, will bring both of us recognition and credit. You do not want to be stuck here forever, do you?"

"No, Herr Obersturmbannführer."

"The war will not last much longer. At your level you cannot know it, but the Reich will soon have weapons beyond the dreams of ordinary men. The world will be Germany's, and men like me—and perhaps you—will be its rulers."

"Yes, Herr Obersturmbannführer," said Schenkel. He saluted, turned, and left to carry out Baumann's orders. The new commandant did not chide himself for encouraging his adjutant to believe a lie. Schenkel would never be a ruler of men, not even of his own meager destiny. But truth and lies were words without meaning, mere empty concepts to be filled by those who had the will to dominate, the will to shape the world to their own liking.

Karl-Heinz Baumann was such a man. And this camp was about to be shaped by his will.

o———————o

THERE was an indefinable sloppiness to the place, Baumann decided as he let his senior officers lead him through a systematic inspection of Höllenfeuer. It was visible in the details: in the way the guards came to attention, without the quivering rigidity that his rank should have stirred in them; in their frayed cuffs and poorly shined boots, the patches of unshaved stubble on their cheeks. Of course, one couldn't expect too much from the Ukrainian SS guards who made up much of the camp's complement. But even the Germans' tunics showed soup stains and tarnished buttons.

The "special handling" facilities for Jews seemed to be adequately run, he noted. His on-site assessment matched the impression he had gotten from the figures in the files Schenkel had laid out for him. The real problem was in the section of the camp where political prisoners and other social undesirables were organized into work gangs to cut firewood, to grow the crops—mostly turnips—that were mainstay of the inmates' diet, and to sort the materials left over from the processing of the Jews. It was here that productivity had fallen off in recent months, and even before Baumann reached that part of his inspection, he believed he had a good idea as to why.

"They are too well-fed," he said. "I have reviewed the figures and we are giving them too much food."

"*Jawohl*, Herr Obersturmbannführer!" said Untersturmführer Krentz, the junior officer in charge of the commissary. He did not tell the commandant that the figures were unreliable. They did not take into account Krentz's unofficial sideline: a hefty portion of the food listed as going to the prisoners was actually sold to local wholesalers.

The party of SS officers entered the zone of the work camp where the prisoners were sorting the possessions of the dead. Baumann's eyes swept over the scene and again he saw evidence of the slackness that had contaminated the operation.

A noncom at the corner of one of the open sheds spotted him and shouted, "*Achtung!*" as he simultaneously came to attention. The motion lacked a proper SS snap and Baumann approached the man.

"Name," he said, slapping his gloves against the side of his greatcoat.

"Hauptscharführer Müller, Herr Obersturmbannführer."

"Are you in charge of this section?"

"Yes, Herr Obersturmbannführer."

Baumann inspected the man closely, saw the bloodshot eyes, the ruddy tint of skin, the puffiness of the flesh. He leaned in closer and sniffed. "Have you been drinking on duty, Müller?"

"No, Herr Obersturmbannführer."

"Why are you trembling?"

"It must be the cold, Herr Obersturmbannführer."

The commandant stepped back from the man. He smelled something unpleasant. He thought it might be the smell of fear. He looked again at the prisoners working at the long tables, throwing items into the bins labeled in ornate German script: "Hair," "Clothing/Women," and "Shoes/Children." The men were thin, shivering in their rags. They kept their attention on their work and not one of them met his gaze.

Then Baumann looked farther down the shed and came upon something that made him blink in surprise. Standing beyond the end of the unwalled building was a small man clad in a ragged dark suit, shoulders hunched forward and hands in his pockets. He was staring directly at the commandant, his eyes a hard, dark glitter, his darkly stubbled face grim beneath a shock of unruly black hair.

Baumann turned to Müller. "Hauptscharführer," he said, "who is that man standing with his hands in his pockets?"

"He is just a mute, Herr Obersturmbannführer. We ignore him."

Baumann couldn't believe what he was hearing. "You ignore him? He stands there doing nothing, and you ignore him?"

Müller's mouth moved, but he said nothing. Baumann rounded on his officers, found them looking anywhere but at him. Or at the little man with the stony eyes.

"Schenkel," he called. "What do you know of this?"

The adjutant's Adam's apple went up and down twice and he stammered when he spoke. "It is difficult to explain, Herr Obersturmbannführer."

"Then I will explain it for you," Baumann said. "You have collectively lost all sense of discipline. You have let this—" he gestured at the small man, "—this *üntermensch*, this inferior subhuman of a mute, place his will above yours."

"Herr Obersturmbannführer—," Schenkel began. "It is complicated. The man—"

"Silence!" the commandant shouted. He turned to Müller. "Bring him. Stand him against the wall of that building."

The noncom looked vaguely ill, but he beckoned two guards. The SS men marched to where the small man stood, seized his arms, and dragged him to the wall. The mute stood where they put him, his hands still in his pockets, his eyes never leaving Baumann.

"Now shoot him!" the commandant ordered.

"*Jawohl*, Herr Obersturmbannführer!" Müller unslung his Schmeisser and aimed at the man's chest. His hands trembled, the muzzle of the submachine gun wavering.

The mute began to whistle, a low tuneless sound that made the hairs rise on the back of Baumann's neck. "Give me that!" he snapped, tearing the weapon from the noncom's sweaty grasp.

"This won't be quick," he told the whistling man. He set the Schmeisser for single-shot action, then carefully aimed at the mute's right knee. The bullet passed right through the joint. Blood and bone splinters sprayed onto the wall behind. The little man groaned and fell over onto his side and the wounded leg shot out from under him.

Then he looked up from the frozen mud, locked his eyes on the commandant's, and pursed his lips. The low whistle came again.

"Swine!" The Obersturmbannführer cursed him as he aimed at the man's left knee. He fired and saw the man's other leg flop against the ground, heard a growl in the mute's throat. Then the eyes came back to his, striking him with the cold stare of a caged beast, and the whistling began again.

Baumann reset the Schmeisser and emptied its magazine into the hateful mute, ripping his torso from groin to throat, putting the final shots into his head. Blood and brains flew, and when the firing stopped, there was no more whistling. The hard black eyes had been obliterated by good German lead and steel.

He thrust the weapon back into the noncom's hands. "Now get rid of him!" he snapped.

"*Jawohl*, Herr Obersturmbannführer," Müller said, but his voice lacked conviction. He gestured to the two guards and they stooped and dragged the ruined corpse away by its bare feet.

Schenkel looked as if he had something to say yet was reluctant to speak. But Baumann had seen and heard enough. "Gentlemen," he said, "you have one week to show me a new camp, an efficient camp. Or I might just shoot one or two of you."

The officers came to attention.

"Dismissed," the commandant said, but he detained Krentz, the commissary officer. "Cut the prisoners' rations by twenty percent," he said. "Tell them they will remain cut until productivity shows a substantial improvement."

"*Zu befehl*," the Untersturmführer said. At your order. He hurried away. Baumann was momentarily puzzled by the officer's happy grin, then he put it out of his mind and strode from the assembly area. A demonstration of will had been necessary, and he was pleased to have given them one.

WESTERN POLAND,

THE PRESENT

THE modern European rail system was efficiently run, Logan thought. He'd caught a train that ran all the way from Ortona to Berlin, crossing the Austrian Alps at night with moonlight shining on the icy peaks. At Berlin's Zoo Bahnhof train station, he'd changed trains for Poland. Not once along the way had he been asked to show his passport.

Lucia had had a book about Höllenfeuer. There were a few pictures, but they were poor quality and grainy, apparently shot by inmates who had bribed guards to smuggle in cameras. But the exposed film, tucked away in hidey-holes, had deteriorated before the rolls could be brought to a lab where the images, some horrific, some just hopelessly sad, were finally printed.

The rural train station that the camp had been built around was gone, along with the village that had stood nearby, destroyed in the fighting that pushed the German armies back to their homeland in early 1945. The nearest town dated from the postwar rebuilding boom and was full of dreary Soviet-era apartment blocks, but in anticipation of Poland's joining the European Union a hopeful town council had established a tourist information center. Logan was directed to it by the owner of the small hotel where he'd found a simple room and bath.

"I'm looking for information about the Höllenfeuer concentration camp," he told the young blonde woman behind a counter on which maps and brochures in several languages were spread for the taking. "I want to go to the site."

Her English was precise but adequate. "There is nothing there. The prisoners revolted and burned it down."

"Still," he said. "I want to see it. Where can I get a guide?"

"Are you sure you wouldn't prefer to visit the sausage-making factory? It has won prizes. They give you free samples."

He leaned over the counter and she stopped talking. "A guide," he said.

It turned out there was a man who tended the site for some organization in Germany. He was willing to show it to visitors.

"Can you call him?" Logan said. "Tell him I will pay him if he can come now and take me there."

The man arrived within fifteen minutes to find Logan waiting outside the tourist center. He was a fat-bellied, thin-haired Pole of mature years who drove a smoky-engined little box on wheels that was left over from before the 1989 collapse of the Soviet bloc. The gears ground whenever he shifted them, but the car got them out of town and down an unpaved road lined with leafless trees. After a mile or so, they bumped over some old train tracks, then came to a closed wooden gate. Behind it was a muddy track winding into a patch of woodland.

"We have to go by foot," the man said. "Car doesn't enjoy mud."

He led Logan along the track, their feet slipping on patches of ice between the frozen ruts that gouged the earth. They came to a place where the trees abruptly ended. Beyond was open ground, marked by several large, low mounds covered in short grass, with stone-flagged walkways between them. In front of each mound was a man-high stone cairn that bore a dark metal plaque.

He went to the marker. The plaque had Polish, German, English, and Hebrew words on it. The English said, "Mass Grave #1. Estimated to hold the remains of four thousand forced laborers killed between June 1942 and February 1943."

He examined all the other plaques. Each told the same tale of the anonymous dead. He turned to the man who had brought him here and said, "What else is there?"

"No-thing" was the answer. "All fired, long ago. Trees grow up."

A dead end, Logan thought. The place evoked nothing. There were no buildings, no watchtowers. The trees were just trees, the grass just grass. All the thousands of dead behind the cairns could tell him nothing.

The fat man had produced a camera. Surprisingly, it was an up-to-date German digital. "I take picture?" he said. "For memory?"

Logan cursed. "No," he said. "This is not the memory I need."

But the man snapped the shutter anyway.

"Back to town," Logan said. "I need to talk to the girl at the tourist center." But when they were in the car, another thought came to him. "Do you keep copies of the pictures you take, pictures of people who come to see the graves?"

"No," the man said. "I not keep."

Logan was grasping at straws. "Who pays you?" he said.

"A German *organizacja*. At Berlin."

"Why? Are they survivors of the camp? What is their interest?"

"I don't know. I cut grass, show visitors."

"What is the organization's name? Where can I find them?"

They had got back onto the unpaved road. The guide lit a strong-smelling cigarette, threw the match out the window, and said, "I have card. I show you."

They drove to his home, a fourth-floor flat in a run-down, faceless apartment block whose concrete façade was crumbling. The elevator in the foyer bore a hand-lettered sign in Polish that must have read OUT OF ORDER because they went up several flights of fire stairs to emerge into a narrow hallway that smelled of old cabbage.

The man's apartment was small and scantily furnished—a tired old couch and a couple of wooden chairs, a battered coffee table covered in empty beer and vodka bottles. In one corner a much-thumbed pile of Dutch and Danish porn magazines looked ready to topple over. "Please to wait," he told Logan and disappeared through a curtained doorway.

Logan looked out of the grimy window at an identical apartment block that stood across an open space paved in cracked asphalt. Anger stirred in him, born of frustration that after coming all this way he had hit a brick wall. He balled his fists and felt the muscles of his forearms bulge. As soon as he did so, a stark and nameless fear took command of his mind, as if the most terrible thing in the world was about to happen to him.

It always happened when he clenched his fists and the fear did not fade until he willed his hands and arms to relax. He brought up his hands and looked at the scars on his knuckles and thought, *What have I done with these, to put such a fear in me?*

The Pole had been gone a long time if all he was doing was fetching a card with an address on it. Logan went to the doorway and eased the curtain aside with the backs of his fingers. Beyond was a bedroom as small and grungy as the living room, with an unmade bed and a musty, mud-colored carpet decorated with unwashed socks and gray underwear.

But against a wall, a small scarred table supported a modern notebook computer, its top open and its screen showing a screensaver of two women who seemed to know each other very well. The guide sat in a wooden chair before the computer. He must have been waiting while it went through its start-up cycle because now he worked the mouse pad, sliding a finger up and down and double-tapping as the image of the women disappeared and an e-mail program's prompt came up.

The man did something with the digital camera that made it click. A moment later the computer beeped. He tapped the built-in mouse again and a window appeared on the screen, then a blue bar rapidly filled its center, moving from left to right. When the bar had gone all the way, the man double-tapped the mouse again and the program closed. He reached to pull down the top of the notebook.

"What are you doing?" Logan said.

The guide jumped, came up in a half crouch, turned toward the door. "Is my job," he said. "Take *fotografía*, send to Berlin."

Logan came into the room. The pot-bellied man backed away, eyes and mouth wide in a face that had suddenly gone pale, and Logan realized he must look like a madman about to attack. He stopped, made a conscious effort to calm himself. "I am not going to hurt you," he said. "I just want to know why you sent my picture to Berlin."

"Is my job," the man said again. "I send *fotografía*, they send euros." He rubbed his thumb and two fingertips together. "Is not make bad thing."

"Where is this card?"

It was on the table beside the computer. The man offered it to Logan as if he were offering a dog biscuit to a snarling pit bull.

The card bore the name Höllenfeuer Erinnerunggesellschaft, with an address on a street called Invalidenstrasse and an e-mail address, but no telephone number. Logan pointed to the e-mail address. "Is that where you sent my picture?" he said.

"Yes."

"Who do you send the pictures to? Who lives at that address?"

"No peoples are living there. Is *organizacja* only."

"Did you meet someone from the organization? Did someone come here and give you the job?"

The Pole was growing more nervous. Logan had the sense that the interrogation was reaching a point where the man would begin making up information just to have something to offer a questioner who frightened him. Even as he recognized that he had to reassure the man, he was wondering, *Why do I know that? What have I been, back in that past I don't remember?*

"Listen," he said, putting some warmth into his voice, "let's go sit down in the other room, just talk a little." He remembered what the man had said, and parroted his words back to him, "Is not make bad thing. Just important to me."

The guide looked to be calming down, some color coming back into his face. "Okay," he said.

"Do you have anything to drink? Maybe some vodka?"

"Yes. In *kuchnia*."

"In the kitchen?" Logan said. "Good. Why don't you get it?"

He went back through the doorway and took a seat in the living room. The man was still scared and might run for the door, so Logan reached into his pocket and said, "I want to give you some money."

The Pole was halfway across the living room, at a point where he could go left into the kitchen or straight to the door that led to the hallway. He stopped. "Money?" he said.

Logan made the same gesture with thumb and fingertips. "Euros," he said and produced a hundred-euro note. It showed a bridge crossing a river and a map of Europe on it.

The man went into the kitchen. Logan heard a *clink* of glasses and a refrigerator door opening and closing, then the Pole returned with two tumbler glasses and a half-full bottle of vodka. "Not make bad thing?" he said with a tentative smile.

"Not make bad thing," Logan said. He handed over the hundred euros and the guide's smile grew. Soon they were sitting across the coffee table from each other, the guide perched on one of the wooden chairs. The thought of drinking the vodka brought a taste of bile to Logan's mouth, but he put the glass to his lips and pretended to swallow.

"Now," Logan said, "this word"—he pointed to the long string of letters on the card after the word Höllenfeuer—"how do you say it?"

"*Erinne-rungge-sell-schaft.*"

"What does it mean?"

The Pole took more of the vodka. "It mean 'remembering.' 'Remembering...'" He added some Polish words, then said, "people who are together, remembering together."

"Good," Logan said. "And this is a street address?"

The Pole was happy to help. "Invalidenstrasse," he said. "*Strasse* is 'street.' *Invaliden* is men who are not soldier, finish being soldier."

"Veterans?" Logan said. "Veterans Street?"

The man nodded encouragingly. "Yes, maybe."

"And this word, *postkasten*, with a number after it?"

"Is for put letters in." He mimed sliding an envelope into a slot.

"Post box."

The guide nodded some more and took another slug of the vodka. It made him smile.

And now that he had the man feeling comfortable, Logan could ask the questions he really wanted answered. "Did people come from Berlin to see you?"

"Man comes, I start work for *organizacja*."

"Did he bring you the camera and computer?"

"Yes."

Logan took the bottle, poured more vodka for the other man, and pretended again to sip his own drink. "What was the man's name?"

The Pole paused with his glass halfway toward his lips, clearly ransacking his memory. Then his brow cleared. "Holzbauer," he said. "Josef Holzbauer."

"And he's the man you send the photos to?"

"I think it so. Yes."

"So he would have photos of all the people who have come here?"

The Pole shrugged.

Logan stood up, drained his glass, and took out another hundred-euro bill, immediately capturing the man's full attention once more. "Can you give me a ride to my hotel and then to the train station?" he said.

"You are betting on it," the guide said.

o————————o

WHEN the crazy rich foreigner was safely on the train to Berlin, Taddeusz Czazinsky took out the two hundred-euro notes and regarded them happily. On the way back from the train station he stopped at the store on the corner and bought another bottle of vodka, this time the best on the shelf. Back in his apartment, even before he took off his overcoat, he poured himself a healthy glassful and drained it, then poured another. It was only then that he noticed a discreet beeping sound from the bedroom.

The sound came from the notebook computer. He flipped it open and saw that he had received an e-mail that was marked with the double chevrons that meant its priority was urgent. He opened the message and read it. It was from Josef Holzbauer in formal Polish, without any of the shorthand that Czazinksy and his Internet contacts used when they traded addresses of porn sites.

It said, "What is the name of the man whose photograph you sent today? What is his address? Do you know where he is now or where he is going?"

Czazinsky laboriously typed out a reply. "I do not know his name or where he lives. But I have just put him on the train to Berlin. He is coming to see you."

Holzbauer must have been sitting at his own computer, because Czazinsky's notebook was beeping to tell him that he had received a reply to the message before he had even had time to get back to the vodka in the living room.

"What train?" said the new message. "When did it leave?"

The Pole typed in the information. He waited to see if there would be another response, but when none came after a few minutes sitting before the little computer, he again heard the vodka sweetly calling him from the living room.

HÖLLENFEUER CONCENTRATION CAMP,

JANUARY 1944

KARL-HEINZ Baumann was disagreeably surprised to discover that the station master's house had never been wired for electricity and that the previous commandant —who was starting to look more and more like precisely the kind of romantic idiot that the German school system all too often produced—had actually preferred to work by the inferior light cast by a coal-oil lamp's yellow flame. He resolved that electrification would be the first improvement he would order, once he had the camp running as it should.

He was at his desk, reviewing through-put figures for the past year. The columns of numbers spoke to him clearly. Höllenfeuer's performance had been consistently on the low end of acceptable until a couple of months ago. Then had come a sharp downturn in the work camp's output. Quotas were not met. Disciplinary infractions had mounted: guards reporting late for duty, failing to turn out in proper uniform, offering insubordinate responses to their superiors' orders. Then the numbers seemed to show that discipline had improved, but Baumann knew better. He knew that standards had fallen even further, so much so that officers and noncommissioned officers had begun to overlook offenses that should have resulted in the offenders being brought up sharp and punished.

A tap on the door drew him out of the web of statistics. "Come!" he barked.

Schenkel entered, closing the door quickly against a gust of ice-laden wind. "You said I might borrow a book, Herr Obersturmbannführer."

"If you must," the commandant said, "but you would be better to study the Führer's book."

"I have of course read it," the adjutant said. "It is a brilliant analysis of Germany's situation."

"Which," Baumann said dryly, "is exactly what is printed on the dust jacket."

"Yes, Herr Obersturmbannführer." Schenkel had taken a thin volume of verse from the shelves.

"You will never get anywhere, Schenkel, until you understand that life is about the exercise of will."

"Yes, Herr Obersturmbannführer."

Baumann leaned back in his chair. "Take this place. It is rife with incompetence and insubordination. Why? Because the officer who was supposed to provide the fundamental strength from which all would draw their energy was a weakling and a coward."

"Yes, Herr Obersturmbannführer."

"He must have been a weakling and a coward because he shot himself right where you are standing."

Schenkel looked down and saw that he was standing on the stained floorboards. He moved a step to one side.

"Will," Baumann said. "It is all about will."

"Yes, Herr—" Schenkel began, but the commandant cut him off, his head cocked to one side, listening.

"What is that noise?" Baumann said.

"I hear nothing," Schenkel said. "Perhaps the wind."

"It sounds like whistling." The Obersturmbannführer rose and strode to the door. "I will not have my men whistling on duty. And I will certainly not have any of those Italian swine..." He broke off, standing in the open doorway, peering out past the overhang of the porch as the wind drove sleet into his face.

An SS guard was supposed to be stationed beside the door, but there was no one there. The yard beyond was dark, only half-lit by the electric bulbs strung along the top of the perimeter fence. Something moved out there in the murk and now Baumann heard again the sound that had caught his ear: a low, tuneless whistling.

He turned back to the lighted room, where Schenkel was studiously avoiding looking at him. "Call out the guard!" he ordered. "A prisoner is loose in the yard."

His adjutant turned a pale face toward him, a tic at one corner of his mouth. "Herr Obersturmbannführer," he said, "if I may advise—"

The commandant's eyes bulged and his cheeks grew red. "You will not advise! You will carry out my orders or I will see you on the next train to the eastern front!"

"*Jawohl*, Herr Obersturmbannführer!" The man dropped the volume of poetry and squeezed past his superior. Outside, he made quickly for the nearest guard post, shouting orders in a voice that cracked with strain. He pointedly did not look at the shadowy figure who stood in the yard whistling.

Four SS men in greatcoats and helmets came running, rifles in their hands, led by Hauptscharführer Müller. They slammed to attention in front of their commandant.

"Don't stand there looking at me, *scheisskopf!*" Baumann said, pointing into the yard. "Arrest that swine!"

The squad turned around and Baumann clearly heard, over the whistling, an involuntary groan from the noncom. The men did not move. "I will have you reduced to the lowest rank," the officer said.

"*Kommen Sie*," Müller said and moved grimly through the ice-crusted snow, the four SS behind him. They marched to where the whistling shadow stood. One of the guards raised his rifle and drove the butt into the small man's face. Bone crunched and the figure toppled over. The others crowded around, their boots and weapons doing more damage. Then, at Müller's order, two of them bent and hauled the bleeding victim to his feet. They dragged him to where the light spilled from the commandant's open door.

Baumann drew his Luger from its holster. "So," he said, "dead and buried will not do for you, *ja?*"

The small man raised his battered face and shook the long black hair from his eyes. His eyes locked onto the officer's in a glare as hard as obsidian. He pursed his split lips and began to whistle.

The nine-millimeter bullet tore through his forehead and blew out the back of his skull. Blood and brains and bone stained the crusted snow behind him.

"Now take him," Baumann said, "to the crematorium."

Müller said, "With respect, Herr Obersturmbannführer, the fires are not lit."

"Then light them!"

Müller snapped to attention, said, "At your order!" Then he turned to the squad and across his face flashed an expression that Baumann knew he was not supposed to have caught. But the commandant had seen that look and the Obersturmbannführer was not a man to let things slide.

"Hauptscharführer! You have something you wish to say about my order?"

Müller snapped to attention again. For a moment it seemed to the commandant that the noncom was wrestling with some inner question. Then his heavy face took on the expressionless cast of an SS trooper and he shouted, "*Nein*, Herr Obersturmbannführer!"

Baumann watched them march off toward the other section of the camp, Müller in the lead, the four SS guards each holding onto an arm or leg of the dead mute.

The commandant turned to find his adjutant standing on the porch, the book of poetry in his pudgy hand, watching the small procession fade into the sleet-blown darkness. "There you see," he said. "It comes down to will."

"Yes, Herr Obersturmbannführer," Schenkel said, "it does."

BERLIN, GERMANY,

JANUARY 1944

"THERE is a rumor at one of the camps in Poland," Bucher said.

"There are rumors at every camp in Poland," von Strucker said. "What does one more matter?"

"This one is interesting," the pink-skinned man said, coming farther into the baron's office and closing the door behind him. "I got it from an SS commissary officer who drinks too much and probably sells half of the inmates' rations on the black market."

"Thieving drunks are not interesting," von Strucker said. He had more important things on his mind, including the tersely worded memorandum on his desk. It was signed by one of Himmler's aides and it demanded an update on the progress of his special projects section. But von Strucker had no progress to report.

"Herr Baron," Bucher said, "you should listen to me."

The Prussian raised his close-cropped head and sighed. "Very well. I'm listening."

"The camp has been in trouble for months. Its last commandant shot himself."

"By accident?"

"Not unless he accidentally pulled the trigger of his sidearm while the muzzle was in his mouth."

"All right. So why did he do it?"

"A prisoner drove him mad. In fact, the man has driven half the SS contingent to drunkenness and desertion."

"Is that also rumor or is there some fact behind it?" von Strucker said.

Bucher leaned in closer, lowering his voice even though the two of them were alone in the office. "I looked around the camp. It was clear there was something wrong. Morale was nonexistent. The new commandant was in a perpetual black rage. And whenever I asked the usual questions about whether there were any 'unusual' prisoners, I kept getting the strangest looks—sideways looks, as if there was a big secret that no one dared talk about."

"But someone did talk about it."

"Krentz, the commissary officer. As crooked as the runes on his collar. But he likes his drink, so I took him to a blind pig in the nearby town and bought him enough slivovitz to refloat the *Tirpitz*. And he talked."

"So what did this alcoholic criminal tell you?"

"That there is a prisoner in the camp who does not die."

The baron sat up straighter. "That is unusual," he said. "Dying is what they are best at."

"This one has been beaten to a pulp, had his brains shot out, been buried alive, burned in the crematorium."

"That sounds like dying to me," von Strucker said.

"But he keeps coming back. Without a mark on him."

"A ghost story? Every camp has its ghost story."

"No ghost," Bucher said. "He comes back alive. They say that he heals. Even from the grossest wounds. That if you throw him into the ovens his flesh heals faster than it can be burned."

The baron put in his monocle. He tapped his fingers on the supercilious memo from Himmler's aide. "What is the name of this camp?"

"Höllenfeuer. Its commandant is Karl-Heinz Baumann. He used to be one of Heydrich's little ducklings, but these days he is swimming for his life."

"Himmler doesn't care for him?"

"If Baumann is a duckling, the Reichsführer-SS is a bad-tempered fox."

Von Strucker made up his mind. "Call the Luftwaffe liaison office," he said. "I want a plane. Now."

BERLIN, GERMANY,
THE PRESENT

IT was past midnight when the train pulled into the Bahnhof Zoo station. Logan didn't think there would be anyone at the Invalidenstrasse address, but he had the taxi driver take him there anyway. *Always scout the objective thoroughly*, a voice said from the back of his mind. *The worst time to find out what you're getting into is when you're neck-deep in it.*

It wasn't his own voice. Somebody, somewhere—some*when*—had drilled strategy and tactics into him. The memory of how he had learned his lessons had been taken from him, but the lessons still remained.

The vodka-loving Pole had been right: no "peoples" were living at the headquarters of the Höllenfeuer *Erinnerunggesellschaft*—"remembrance association," he guessed was a proper translation. The cab stopped in front of a nondescript office building whose windows were all dark. It looked to be the kind of place to house businesses and societies that only required a couple of rooms—import/export firms, insurance brokers, clubs that consisted mainly of mailing lists of like-minded people who got together in hotels for annual conferences at which they reminisced about the good old days.

"Is there a good hotel within walking distance of here?" he asked the cabdriver.

"The Mercure is not far."

"Take me there."

The hotel was clean and not fancy. Logan stretched out on the room's double bed in the dark and stared up at the ceiling. He had no great hopes about what he would find at the Höllenfeuer Remembrance Association's office in the morning. Maybe they would not want to let him look at the photos of those who came to view the grassy mounds and the stone cairns. He intended to insist, and it seemed that whenever he insisted, people became eager to accommodate him. But what were the chances he would recognize a face? And, if he did, anyone he might have known at the camp—assuming he had actually been there—would now be more than sixty years older. Or more likely, dead for sixty years.

He closed his eyes and willed himself toward sleep. That, too, seemed to be an ability he had learned somewhere back in the impenetrable fog that was his past. And as the night wore on, he dreamed. The dreams did not offer him a coherent narrative. Instead, he caught snatches and flashes: a face contorted in pain, voices crying out in agony or shouting harsh words, images of fences and rough wooden walls, of fists and boots coming at him.

The dreams shook him loose from sleep. He awoke with the thin light of a Berlin winter dawn trying to penetrate the hotel room's drawn drapes. He struggled to hold on to the last few images, wanting to make a pattern of them, but they all evaporated from his mind.

THE EMPTY QUARTER, SAUDI ARABIA,

THE PRESENT

"WHAT if we acquired American uniforms and gear?" Al Borak said. "Some of the men could pass for Latinos."

Von Strucker shook his head. "No. The security procedures are tight at the best of times. With the target on the premises, nothing will be left to chance. Not even his own mother could get within shooting distance of him without someone checking her identification."

The tall Pashtun folded his sinewy arms and stared for the umpteenth time at the unhelpful model of Baghdad's Green Zone. "Then we must tell them it cannot be done. It would mean throwing away a fine weapon for no purpose."

"These are the kind of people who are happy to send their children to blow up other people's children, just to make a statement," the baron said. "For them, the fact that an operation is completely futile is not necessarily an argument against carrying it out."

"Well, if we have to smash the Green Fist, then we have to smash the Green Fist. We would only have to start all over again. The madrassas are full of underfed boys that no one wants."

"You don't understand," von Strucker said. "They might not expect an old infidel like me to charge into the muzzles of the Americans' rifles, but they will not want you to miss your chance of being welcomed into Paradise by seventy-two virgins."

Al Borak's pale eyes flickered. "I have never been all that interested in virgins," he said.

"Then we need to think of something."

"If necessary, could we not tip off the Americans?"

A phone on the wall rang. Von Strucker crossed to it, snatched the handset from its cradle, and snapped, "I gave orders I was not to be disturbed!"

The voice of the facility's chief communications officer quavered slightly. "I regret the interruption, sir," he said, "but I am calling pursuant to one of your standing orders."

"Which one?"

"Standing Order Nine."

For a long moment the baron said nothing. He kept the handset at his ear, but his eyes lost focus as if he was staring into the far distance.

"Sir," said the communications officer, "are you still there?"

Von Strucker came back to the here and now. "Yes," he said, "relay me the message."

"It consists of only one word, sir. In German. That word is *kontakt*."

The Prussian realized he had been holding his breath. Now he let it out and found that the smallest smile had taken control of his narrow lips. "Alert the hangar crew that I may want the Gulfstream V brought to immediate readiness for departure."

He hung up the phone on the communication officer's acknowledgment of the instruction. Ordering the plane had brought up a sudden sense of déjà vu, but it soon faded as he turned to Al Borak and said, "Get your men ready to leave," he said. "They will use the visas and identification that will allow them to enter Europe as a soccer team owned by our friend in the United Arab Emirates. We will refuel at his field in Abu Dhabi and fly direct to Berlin. They will need civilian clothing suitable for a German winter, but you will not be staying long."

The leader of the Green Fist was looking at him curiously. "I do not believe I have ever seen you so excited," he said.

The baron knitted his fingers together and touched his knuckles to his lips, almost as if he were praying. Then he opened his hands and lifted them as if praising heaven. He said, "The solution to our problem may be about to walk into an office in Berlin. And more than the solution to just this business." He flicked his hand toward the model buildings on the table. "Much, much more. Now get the men ready to leave at a moment's notice."

The Pashtun departed. The baron went through the door right after him, but as Al Borak hurried toward the barracks and training area, von Strucker went swiftly to his private quarters. With the door closed and secured, he opened a notebook computer and turned it on. Alternately tapping the mouse and the keyboard, he sent a deeply encrypted signal that was received without any record of its reception by an official Royal Saudi government telecommunications satellite. The signal was then relayed through a number of facilities in and above the Middle East and southern Europe, until it ended at a secure terminal in an office on Invalidenstrasse in Berlin.

The response from Berlin was almost immediate. Moments after he sent the signal, von Strucker's notebook alerted him that he was receiving a j-peg file. He waited, again holding his breath, as the download's blue bar passed across the window. Then he touched the computer's mouse. The liquid crystal display filled with an image—a stretch of second-growth woodland, some grassy mounds, a tall stone cairn that bore a dark metal plaque—and glowering into the camera, a pair of dark eyes beneath a forehead into which descended a widow's peak of raven black hair.

The baron found that his mouth was dry, that his hand trembled as he reached to send a new signal to Berlin. With a deliberate effort he took control of himself. He typed a single word and tapped the mouse. Up to the Royal Saudi satellite went the message: RAT-TRAP.

Von Strucker let out another inheld breath. Again, he felt that involuntary smile taking over his lips. But this time, staring back at that face on the notebook's screen, he let the smile spread.

BERLIN, GERMANY,

THE PRESENT

AT 8:00 a.m., the front doors to the office building on Invalidenstrasse were unlocked. Logan went in and found a lobby that was typical for a building whose owners didn't believe in wasting their money on useless decor. Instead of a reception desk and security guard, they had opted for an easy-to-read directory—white plastic letters on a black background—that told him that the Höllenfeuer *Erinnerunggesellschaft* had an office on the fourth floor.

Both the building's elevators were in use. Logan didn't want to wait anymore, so he went up the fire stairs two at a time. He emerged into a bland hallway paneled in fabric-covered pasteboard with doors of dark-stained wood. He moved along the corridor with rapid steps, almost running, his eyes flicking to the plastic plaques mounted on each door at head height.

Six doors from the fire stairs, he came to the office he sought. Its plaque showed the same words as were printed on the Polish guide's card, but underneath, taped to the wood, was a piece of paper with a handprinted sign: GESCHLOSSENE HEUTE—KRANKHEIT IN DER FAMILIE.

Logan tried the door. It was locked. He knocked and waited, then knocked again, louder. No one came. He folded his arms and leaned his back against the wall, waiting, thinking. Of the six words on the sign, the only ones that he was confident of translating were *in der Familie*, which almost certainly meant "in the family." And the only reason he could think of for someone to put a sign like that on a door was to tell people that the place was closed up because of death or sickness in the family.

Still he waited. Maybe the sign was put up yesterday or the day before. Any moment, the elevator's chime might herald the arrival of the office's occupant, back after a brief period of mourning or a course of antibiotics, to open up the Höllenfeuer Remembrance Association for another day's business.

The elevator did not come. Instead, the door to another office opened and a middle-aged woman stepped out, carrying an empty carafe from a drip coffeemaker. She started and stopped dead when she saw the strange man push himself away from the wall with a quick flex of his knees and turn toward her. Logan saw the fear on her face and made an effort to sound unthreatening.

"Excuse me, please," he said. "Do you speak English?"

"Of course," she said, holding the carafe in two hands before her as if she might have liked to take shelter behind it. "How may I help you?"

"I am looking for a Mr. Holzbauer. I believe this is his office."

"Yes, it is." Her eyes went to the sign. "But this says he will not be in today. There is illness in the family."

"Ah," Logan said. "So that sign was put up today."

"It was not there yesterday," she confirmed. A new thought changed her expression. "It is strange," she said, "but I know that Herr Holzbauer is a bachelor and I thought he has said he is without family."

"Do you think he will be here tomorrow?"

She shrugged. "*Geschlossene heute* means 'closed today.' Herr Holzbauer is a very precise man. He would not say 'today' if he meant tomorrow also."

Logan sighed. "I will come back tomorrow then."

"He opens the door exactly at nine," she said.

Back outside, Logan had nowhere to go and twenty-four hours to kill. He walked back to the Hotel Mercure, but when he arrived at its front doors he realized he couldn't spend an entire day and night sitting and waiting.

Restless, he crossed Invalidenstrasse at a traffic light and began to walk at random. He could always find his way back by telling a cabbie to take him to the hotel. He came to a street called Lüisenstrasse and turned on to it. He seemed to be in the heart of Berlin, many of the buildings monumental in style and with a governmental look to them. He hadn't walked more than a mile before he saw down a side street something he recognized—the eighteenth-century Brandenburg Gate—and turned toward it.

He reached the old stone monument and stared at it, waiting to see if something would bubble up out of his damaged memory. But nothing came, and he realized that the fact that he could identify the six-pillared gate meant nothing. He'd recognize the Eiffel Tower or the Taj Mahal if he came upon them, but so what?

He walked on, heading south on a street called Ebertstrasse, and after a quarter mile he came to a strange sight. A whole block of the downtown seemed to have been leveled, the buildings replaced by a maze of gray stone blocks—hundreds, maybe thousands of them—as big as old-time tombs, with narrow cobblestoned lanes laid between them. Some of the blocks were taller than he was, some low enough to sit on. They were not sited randomly but in straight lines, the heights increasing and decreasing so that the whole arrangement looked like billowing waves of granite.

Some kind of cemetery, he thought, and went toward it. But when he examined the first block he came to, there was no inscription. Nor was anything written on the next, or the one after that. He went down one of the aisles and found that the sound his bootheels made striking the cobblestones was muted. Soon he was in a stretch where the blocks rose higher than his head. All he could see was a narrow corridor of gray stone stretching before and behind him, and the cold blue sky above. But there was no need to worry about getting turned around and lost among these stones. He wasn't in a maze—the lanes all met at right angles and any straight line would take him out.

Now something was stirring in the back of his mind, some memory that this strange arrangement of faceless gray granite slabs was pulling up out of him. It wasn't a sense that he had been here before, not in this particular place. It was a feeling that he had been in a situation like this—hemmed in, confined to a place where all the options narrowed down to nothing but the basics, with only cold, hard, unyielding stone to push back against.

He couldn't remember the situation, but he could remember the feeling. And he was sure he had pushed back.

HÖLLENFEUER CONCENTRATION CAMP,

FEBRUARY 1944

KARL-HEINZ Baumann stood on the platform beside the train tracks. He kept his head erect and his gloved hands clasped behind his back, the confident posture of a senior officer who awaits the arrival of his superior. But he knew that when he unclasped his hands they would tremble and it occurred to him that he should have breakfasted on something other than a full bottle of the Montrachet 1878. The vintage was magnificent but the wine had left his mouth sour, with acid at the back of his throat. He was sure that the SS Obergruppenführer—a rank equivalent to that of a full general—who was coming to inspect the camp would smell its fumes on his breath.

Rumor had it that Ernst Kaltenbrunner, the man whom Himmler had named to replace Reinhard Heydrich, also knew his way around a bottle. But even if Kaltenbrunner was a raging alcoholic, it didn't mean he was going to forgive an Obersturmbannführer who had failed to straighten out a camp that was going from bad to worse.

A high-pitched whistle sounded from somewhere off in the distance and Baumann flinched. But it was not the low-toned sound that now haunted his dreams, that had made him open bottle after bottle of the rare and precious wines. They were supposed to have been a legacy for his eldest son, but the commandant no longer believed he would ever have an heir to leave them to. He no longer believed in the future. For him, there was only now—and now was hell.

The whistle sounded again, closer. The first notes of a shrill laugh escaped the Obersturmbannführer before he could suppress it, causing his plump adjutant to turn toward him in concern. Baumann waved Schenkel away, noticing as he did so that his gloved hand did indeed shake. He disguised the tremor by taking his chin between thumb and forefinger, stroking it as if pondering some weighty thought.

Puffing steam and dark smoke, a polished black engine came into view down the track, already slowing to stop at the station. The engine flew twin swastika flags from its frontwork, as well as a pennant that identified it as pulling the private train of the head of the SS security division, the Sicherheitsdienst, or SD.

Behind the coal tender were two carriages, the second of them luxuriously appointed and adorned with an eagle-and-swastika motif in gold paint over crimson-painted wood. Before the special train had even come to a halt, black-uniformed, white-gloved SS descended from the first car and positioned themselves around the platform, submachine guns at the ready. Even here in the depths of a Polish forest, their commander had no intention of suffering the kind of fate that had befallen his predecessor in Prague.

As the train stopped, a junior officer jumped down from the second carriage and placed a white-painted wooden step beneath its stairs. Then, as Baumann and the senior officers gathered around him came to attention, a man almost seven feet tall in his jackboots, wearing a full-length greatcoat of black leather, stepped from the train. As he looked about him, his face, marked by dueling scars from his student days at the University of Graz, wore an expression that said he did not expect to see much that would please him.

The camp commandant and his officers threw their right arms out in the Nazi salute and Baumann was mortified to see that his limb was visibly shaking. He quickly brought it back down to his side, stepped forward, and offered his hand to the Obergruppenführer. But Kaltenbrunner merely raised his own right arm in a half salute and ignored the proffered handshake.

Baumann's heart sank, but he tried to put the best face on it. "All is in readiness for your inspection, Herr Obergruppenführer," he said.

"I hope it is," said the head of the SD. "For your sake."

The "special handling" operations had been suspended for the day, but Schenkel had prepared a full dossier of statistics on daily and weekly through-puts. Kaltenbrunner glanced at the columns of figures, then handed them without comment to the crisply uniformed Standartenführer who was his principal aide. He allowed Baumann to lead him and his party behind the fence with its interwoven evergreen branches and along the narrow corridor that led to the extermination chambers that were disguised as shower rooms.

The Ukrainian SS guards who handled most operations in this section of the camp stood in formation for inspection. Baumann was relieved that their turnout showed no glaring flaws. *Perhaps it will all go well*, he thought.

While the Obergruppenführer walked up and down the rows of Ukrainians, the commandant whispered to Schenkel, "Tell me again."

"Müller took him in chains to the lake," the adjutant said. "It must be twenty kilometers from here. They went out on the ice, broke a hole through it, and let him sink. He is at the bottom."

Why shouldn't it work? Baumann asked himself. *All right, so the monster can't die. So let him live on through the years—in cold mud beneath a hundred meters of water. By the time the chains rust away, I'll be an old man sunning myself on the French Riviera.*

Kaltenbrunner was coming back. Baumann scanned his superior's face, saw nothing to alarm him. The tiny hope he had kindled now flickered a little brighter. "Herr Obergruppenführer," he said, "allow me to show you the labor camp. Then we have prepared a light meal for you and your officers."

They crossed the railroad tracks and entered the work camp. The German SS troopers at the guard posts responded to the presence of general officer rank with reasonable snap and precision. The visitors did not go into the prisoners' barracks—they would have been alive with fleas the moment they stepped inside—but Kaltenbrunner looked through the door of one and nodded his head.

They inspected the equipment and mechanical sheds, where inmates who had useful skills maintained and repaired camp fixtures and vehicles. All was in good order in both places and it seemed to the commandant that Kaltenbrunner's expression was now less severe than it had been when he had stepped down from the train.

"I understand that you are an aficionado of fine wine," Baumann said as they left the mechanical shop. "I would be pleased if you would give me your opinion of my Château d'Yquem 1874."

The SD chief's eyebrows went up. "A Château d'Yquem '74?" he said. "I look forward to it, Baumann."

They went down the work camp's main street and turned into the assembly area with the sorting sheds on three sides. Baumann had ordered work stopped early the day before so that there would be plenty of material to be processed during the inspection. As the visitors came into view, Helmut and the other green-badge *kapos* dug their truncheons into ribs and barked at the starved and shabby men behind the trestle tables heaped with pathetic loot.

The prisoners' frost-bitten hands sorted and folded. The barrels filled with shoes and toys and hair. The stack of empty suitcases rose at the end of the plank tables. And the head of the SD, the man at the pinnacle of the organizational pyramid of which these sheds were the bottom-most layer, stood resplendent in his greatcoat of black leather, his oversize hands snug in calfskin gloves, and watched with evident approval.

"Not so bad," he said over his shoulder to Baumann. "Indeed, much better than I had been led to expect, Herr Obersturmbannführer."

Baumann clicked his heels. "Thank you, Herr Obergruppenführer," he said and was relieved to hear that his own tone had regained some of its old force. "Perhaps you would now care to try the Château d'Yquem '74?"

Kaltenbrunner turned with a smile on his face. He laid a companionable hand on the commandant's arm. "I would like that very much, Baumann. A magnificent vintage. And there is no reason why duty should not also include a little pleas—" He broke off as an expression of puzzlement replaced the indulgent smile. He was looking at something behind the commandant, and not liking what he saw.

A silence fell, broken only by a low, tuneless whistling. Baumann felt a cold sensation run all the way through him, as if someone had poured ice water into his skull so that the chill fluid could seep straight down, dissolving his insides and flushing them through his boots into the dirty slush that covered the assembly area.

"Herr Obersturmbannführer," the head of the Reich's Security Service said, all warmth now fled from his tone, "there is an odd-looking little man glaring at us. Can you explain to me why he isn't doing something to justify his existence?"

BERLIN, GERMANY,
THE PRESENT

THE Gulfstream V landed at one of the private terminals at Templehof Airport and taxied to a waiting hangar. Customs officers met the passengers as they came down the plane's gangway, but the formalities were brief. When the officials had stamped their passports and left, a middle-aged German with a nervous tic in one eye came out of a glassed-in office and approached diffidently.

"Are you Holzbauer?" Al Borak said in rudimentary German.

"Yes," the man answered. "All is in readiness. The van is waiting outside."

"Good. Where are the keys?"

Holzbauer held out a ring and identified the keys that opened the Invalidenstrasse location's front door, the office on the fourth floor, and the loading bay at the back. "The key to the van is in the ignition."

"Very well," said the Pashtun. "You will now go home and stay there all day tomorrow. You will have no contact with anyone. The next day you will go to work as usual. Is that understood?"

It was. Holzbauer left in the direction of a taxi stand. Al Borak waited until he was well out of sight, then made sure that no one else was in the terminal except his own men and the plane crew. Then he went up into the aircraft and knocked twice on the door to the luggage bay.

A panel at the rear of the compartment slid aside and von Strucker stepped out. "All ready?" he said.

"Yes. I will bring the van inside," Al Borak said. He regarded the Prussian curiously, then added, "It must be strange to be back in your homeland after so long away."

The baron returned him a cold look. "I have more important things to think about," he said.

HÖLLENFEUER CONCENTRATION CAMP,

JANUARY 1944

THEY had shot the ragged little man, of course. With the chief of the SD looking on, incredulous that a prisoner was standing around with his hands in his pockets, whistling and doing nothing, there was no choice. Hauptscharführer Müller had shot him and two of his men had dragged the mute away, blood trailing behind them in the gray snow.

Kaltenbrunner's scarred face now wore the same grim scowl that he had showed on arrival. He declined to speak to Baumann again, and left it to his chief aide to announce that the Obergruppenführer would not dine at the camp after all. Baumann could send a bottle of the Château d'Yquem '74 to the Obergruppenführer's private train, which would be departing soon.

But as his party left, Kaltenbrunner could not resist turning back to sneer at the hapless commandant. "You are a disgrace to the SS, to the homeland, to the Führer," he said. "I will see you transferred to a place where you can do less harm—and where your career can come to the miserable end it deserves. You will command a penal company on the eastern front. The Ivans are always laying new minefields to be cleared."

"Yes, Herr Obergruppenführer," Baumann said. His staff had drawn away from him, leaving him isolated before the furious visitor.

"Consider yourself lucky that I do not have you shot out of hand as an example to your officers and men," Kaltenbrunner said. He spun on his heel and strode back to the train tracks, his aides and bodyguards following.

Baumann saw Müller coming back from wherever they had taken the little man. The commandant called him over. "What did you do with him?"

"We put him behind one of the supply sheds," the noncom said. "There didn't seem much point in—"

"Yes, yes," Baumann cut him off. He sighed, then said, "Go and get him. Take him to my office and tie him securely to a chair. I am going to have a little talk with him."

IN the parlor next to the commandant's office, the sideboard was heaped with the buffet that would have been offered to Kaltenbrunner and his entourage. Beside the piles of sausage and sauerbraten, the kugel and *kirschtorte*, were ranked the finest wines of Baumann's collection. A gap in their ranks showed where the Château d'Yquem had been removed by Schenkel and carried off to the Obergruppenführer.

Baumann surveyed the foregone feast for a long moment. Then he swept his arm along the length of the sideboard, sending plates and dishes and all their contents crashing and splattering to the floor. A sausage landed on the instep of his polished jackboot and he flicked it away to splat against the wall. He reached for the nearest bottle—a magnificent Château Haut-Brion 1877—and worked the tip of a corkscrew into its stopper. As he twisted the screw in and pulled the cork free, he heard behind him in his office the sounds of the mute being brought in, then the clank of chains as Müller secured him to a sturdy oak chair.

Baumann did not bother with a glass. He upended the bottle and let one of the most glorious wines of the nineteenth century pour over his tongue and down his throat. He did not even swallow, let alone pause to savor the taste, but just let the priceless liquid fill his belly. He drained half the bottle before he took its mouth from his lips, then belched up the air that had accompanied the wine's descent to his stomach.

"Herr Obersturmbannführer," Müller's voice came from behind him, "your orders have been carried out."

"Dismissed," Baumann said without turning around. He heard the noncom and his men leave, heard the outer door close. He raised the bottle again and drank long and deep, the fumes from the wine rising into the back of his throat and filling his nose. Then he turned and looked at the fate that had befallen him.

The ragged man was slumped in the chair, the chains tight across his chest and arms, his legs and ankles similarly held. His chin was on his chest, his long hair hanging down. The commandant went to the bound man and examined him. He'd never seen what happened after each time the inmate had been taken away dead. Now the commandant counted the bullet holes that had pierced the mute's chest in a burst from Müller's Schmeisser. There were seven.

Not bad grouping, he thought. He reached forward with one gloved hand and poked a finger into one of the wounds. The dead man did not react. When he took it out, the fingertip was not stained with blood—the wound had already cauterized itself.

Now as he watched, the wound filled in from within, the steel-jacketed nine-millimeter round pressed out of the body so that it fell to the man's lap, then bounced onto the wooden planks of the floor. The bullet rolled and came to rest beside the stain they had never been able to get out, the mark of the previous commandant's final defeat.

Another bullet appeared on the man's chest and tumbled down, then one more. *The rest must be trapped in his clothing*, Baumann thought, then wondered at how his mind could be so calmly, coolly analytical when his whole world had come to an end.

Though not quite to an end, he thought. *It could take them two or three weeks to cut my new orders and deliver them.* And while he waited, he would use the time productively.

The man in the chair gasped, a sudden intake of breath filling the still chest. His head came up, his eyes opened, and he looked at the commandant.

"So you know that they call you 'the man who won't die'?" Baumann said. "Too bad." He drained the last of the Haut-Brion, flipped the empty bottle so that its neck landed in his hand, then swung the container against the mute's head. The bottle shattered, shards of the thin glass slashing and piercing the prisoner's face. Blood flowed and one eye was ruined. The man's scream was satisfying.

Baumann waited until the prisoner's remaining good eye focused on him again. He gestured to the stain on the floor. "My predecessor understood only part of his relationship to you. He grasped that his true situation was not that you were locked in here with him, but that *he was locked in with you.* And so he put his pistol in his mouth and freed himself."

The prisoner's torn eye was healing itself even as he watched, the cuts on his face closing, fading. The hard face looked back at him with undisguised contempt and undiluted hatred.

"Too bad," the commandant said again, examining the jagged remnant of the broken bottle that was left in his gloved hand. "Too bad for my predecessor that he lacked the will to break through his despair and see the truth behind the situation. Because the real, terrible truth is not that you are a man who won't die, but that you are a man who *can't* die.

"But," he continued, "you can certainly suffer."

Baumann drew back the arm that held the bottle and swung and slashed. He gouged and ground the weapon into the screaming man's face and neck. And when the sharp points had snapped off, and the bottle was reduced to just a stub of its neck, he went again to the parlor and got another one.

He waited, drinking, not even noticing what he drank, while the ruined flesh knit itself back together. He was in no hurry. He had all day. And all night. And the day after that.

BERLIN, GERMANY,
THE PRESENT

THE efficient young man at the front desk of the Hotel Mercure had identified for Logan the strange grid of faceless tombstones south of the Brandenburg Gate.

"It is a national memorial," he said in almost unaccented English. "To remember the Jews killed by Hitler. Underneath, there is an information center."

Logan hadn't seen the stairs that descended to the information center. He had walked through the array of granite blocks and continued on through the streets of Berlin. Eventually, he had decided that its wide streets and imposing buildings had nothing to tell him about his past. He had found a cab and come back to the hotel, eaten dinner, and gone to bed.

But something was working in the back of his mind, because the night brought dreams. He heard voices speaking in German, harsh voices shouting orders. He did not understand the words and phrases, but with them came ghosts of strong emotion—anger, outrage, pity, and a great sadness that drove him out of sleep and left him surprised to find a tear trickling down one cheek.

He had trouble getting back to sleep. The dream fragments left him confused and angry. He kept thinking about how he would like to lay his hands upon whoever had done this harm to his mind. *We live only in the present*, he told himself, *in that thin membrane between what has been and what is to come. But without our past, whatever joys or horrors it may hold, we have nothing but that flimsy tissue. And it is not enough.*

Yet as he lay on a rented bed in an anonymous hotel room in a city that had nothing to do with him, one welcome thought came to him. The images and voices that speckled his dreams, the faces he had recognized—

Tommy Prince, Rob Roy MacLeish, Lucia Gambrelli—they must still be stored somewhere inside him. Whoever had savaged his memories had not been able to wipe them clean. Perhaps all they had done was to lock his past away in some sealed room in the back of his mind, or to bury it beneath dead layers of fill.

But even the strongest locks can be broken, he told himself. That which is buried can be dug up again and brought back to the light of day. Logan might not know who he was or where he came from, might not even know his true name, but he was becoming increasingly sure of his true nature. *You can lock me away*, he thought, *but I will break free. You can bury me alive, but I will come up out of the earth. And then there will be a reckoning.*

After a while he slept again, without dreams, and awoke to find the room brightly lit by light seeping past the closed drapes. When he threw them back he saw that Berlin had received its first snowfall of the coming winter. The streets and rooftops were coated in pristine white, the sounds of the awakening city muffled.

At five minutes before nine, he stepped out of the hotel and walked the short distance to the building on Invalidenstrasse. In the lobby, two young men were waiting beside the elevator, both olive-skinned and black-haired, bundled up in identical overcoats. As Logan came in from the street, brushing snow from his hair, one of them pushed the button to summon the elevator. Then both separated, as if politely making room for him to be first aboard when the car came.

Logan had no patience this morning. He strode to the fire stairs and went up them two at a time. Behind him he heard one of the men speaking in a language he didn't know, the tone urgent yet controlled. He had heard people speak like that before, he thought—not in that language, but in that way. But when he tried to get a grip on where and when, as always it slipped from his grasp. He let the question go. His business was on the fourth floor.

The hallway was as empty as it had been the day before. When he came to the door of the Höllenfeuer Remembrance Association, the note was gone. He knocked and a voice from inside said, "*Kommen Sie.*"

The office was small and blandly furnished: a utilitarian desk and a couple of chairs, a computer and phone, a credenza and file cabinets against one wall. The wall space above the furniture held frameless blowups of black-and-white photographs: a watchtower above a wire fence, empty train tracks, an aerial view of barrack rooftops and muddy streets, a small house with a swastika flag hanging from a pole that jutted out from the front porch roof.

The last image gave Logan a twinge of memory, but he did not try to reach for more. Instead, he focused on the person behind the desk, a tall man with close-cropped dark hair, a hooked nose, and startlingly gray eyes, who sat with his outsize hands clasped together on the desktop.

"Do you speak English?" Logan said.

"A little."

The accent was odd, like nothing Logan had so far heard on the streets of Berlin. "Are you German?" he said.

"Turk. How I help you?"

"Photographs. Höllenfeuer camp."

The man smiled and rose from behind the desk. "In room," he said, gesturing to a door in the office's inner wall. "Many photo. You open."

Logan crossed to the inner door. When he opened it, there was no light within. He reached inside, feeling for a light switch, but when he found one and pressed, nothing happened.

"The light's out," he said, turning his head to look over his shoulder. Only to find that the gray-eyed man had come silently around the desk and was close behind him.

Then he felt the man's palms on his shoulder blades and he was pushed into the darkness, the door singing shut behind him. He put out his arms to break his fall, but his hands encountered hard, muscular flesh beneath cloth. He couldn't see, but he had an animal sense of people in front of him, around him. He struck out with his fists, tried to get a leg up to swing a kick. But it was as if he were in one of those dreams where he moved in slow motion while everyone around him was fast and unencumbered. Some kind of cord had been slipped around his legs at the ankles and even as it was tightened, another went around his knees.

His arms were seized—it felt as if two or three pairs of hands had hold of each limb—and forced down to his sides. More restraints snaked around him, trussing him snugly from shoulder to wrist. And it was all happening so *fast*!

He growled and struggled against the bonds, surprising himself by the sheer bestiality of the sound that came unbidden from his throat. The muscles of his forearms were bunching and burning, and some part of his mind was telling him that that was a bad, terrifying thing to be letting happen. He felt a searing pain begin in his hands and the pain drove the anxiety to new heights. His pulse was thudding in his ears like the heels of a flamenco dancer on speed. But behind the growing panic he felt an anticipation of impending release, almost sexual in its intensity.

Then another pain registered, a pinprick in his shoulder muscle. He knew that sensation. It was a hypodermic needle going in, and the burning pressure that followed meant that something was being injected into him. A tidal wave of darkness began to rise in his mind, but he fought it down, forced it back. He was thinking, even as he struggled to hold on to consciousness, *I've done this before.*

A voice was speaking near his ear, in a language he didn't know. But Logan could interpret the meaning from the tone: the speaker was complaining that the injection hadn't worked. Another voice responded, giving curt instructions, and now he felt a second stab in his shoulder, more of the cold burning sensation, and again the darkness tried to claim him.

But again, he held it at bay. Like a man facing rising floodwaters, he built a dike of will against the pressure of oblivion, a levee of sheer refusal to succumb. Even as he bent all of his concentration to resistance, a part of him was sensing a familiarity. This kind of thing had happened before and he had survived it. *Because of who I am*, he thought. *Because of what I do.*

The complaining voice spoke again. The voice that gave orders snapped back, then shouted something. The door opened and light not only flooded in from the outer office but from overhead lights in this room. Logan saw that he was in a windowless conference room, its long table upended and pushed back against the wall, the chairs stacked in a corner to leave space for the several young men who swarmed around him, keeping him from falling. They were dressed as civilians but each one wore military-issue night-vision goggles, and they had the look of a team that had been trained to work together.

Except that things clearly weren't going according to plan. One of them, slightly older than the others, spoke and Logan recognized the voice as the one who had been giving orders. He was answered by the gray-eyed man who now stood in the doorway. *Sergeant and lieutenant*, Logan thought. It was there in the tone of voice and the body language.

Another wave of darkness tried to claim him, but he fought it down, shaking his head to clear it. One of the men held up a full hypodermic and asked a question. The man in the doorway spoke over his shoulder to someone in the outer office that Logan couldn't see and received an answer that must have been negative, because the man with the needle put it away unused.

Now the gray-eyed man stepped into the conference room-turned-snatch zone and approached Logan. He examined the trussed man, then said something to the others. The hands that supported Logan fell away and he tottered, his legs bound and his head struggling to remain above the dark tide. Then gray eyes reached for him with those outsize hands. He saw strange calluses on the fingertips and palms before they went past his eyes to touch his temples.

He never heard the sharp *crack*, nor saw the flash of bright light, nor smelled the charred flesh. The world went black and rushed away from him as he fell into nowhere.

HÖLLENFEUER CONCENTRATION CAMP,

FEBRUARY 1944

AS the camp's adjutant, Hauptsturmführer Otto Schenkel had always worked in a small room down a hallway from his superior's quarters in the *kommandantur*. But after Baumann moved the man who wouldn't die into his office, it became too difficult. Höllenfeuer had thousands of inmates, hundreds of guards. That made Schenkel the chief administrative officer of an establishment far larger than the midsize manufacturing company that his father operated in Bremen, turning out fountain pens, mechanical pencils, and similar goods. Keeping the camp running involved a great deal of detailed work, and that work required concentration—a quality that the adjutant found difficult to sustain when he was constantly disturbed by the prisoner's screams and Baumann's own loud drunken rants.

So Schenkel had moved his desk and files to a separate building, bumping Untersturmführer Krentz, the commissary officer, out of his space. Krentz was now sharing a smaller room with Weber, a thick-necked SS junior officer who looked after the camp's transport. Today Weber had come to Schenkel and confided that the commissary officer had been selling camp supplies and using the money to buy liquor.

"Krentz no longer makes any attempt to disguise what he is doing, Herr Hauptsturmführer," Weber said. "He is drunk all the time."

Schenkel had other worries, bigger worries. "So is our commandant," he said. "But there is nothing to be done until a new senior officer arrives to replace him." He gestured to the reports that littered his desk. "And while we wait, this place goes to hell and damnation."

Weber ran a finger nervously around the inside of his shirt collar. "That is what concerns me, Herr Hauptsturmführer." He lowered his voice. "Krentz may be selling pistols."

"He deals with Polish black marketeers," Schenkel said. "They like to shoot each other. What's another dead Pole or two?"

"But I think he may be selling them inside the camp."

"Inside the camp?" The words made no sense to the adjutant. "The inmates have no money."

"They find it hidden in suitcases or sewn into clothes. The *kapos* get most of it, though they have to share with the noncommissioned officers."

Schenkel was outraged. "That is the property of the Reich," he said. "How long has this been going on? We must conduct an investigation."

"With respect, Herr Hauptsturmführer," Weber said, "I think the possibility that the inmates are arming themselves is the more serious problem. There have been revolts at other camps—Sobibor and Treblinka—where the inmates have shot the guards and escaped."

"There have been no revolts. Those are only rumors spread by defeatists."

"Again, with respect, Herr Hauptsturmführer, they are not. I have a cousin who was on furlough from Sobibor when the camp was taken. He returned from leave to find the place a smoldering ruin, the inmates scattered into the forest. He spent weeks rounding them up again."

"Do you think it could happen here?" Schenkel waved away Weber's response. Even as he'd asked the question, he'd known that the answer was a definite "yes"—Höllenfeuer must be the worst-run concentration camp in the Reich.

He rested his elbows on the desk and his damp palms cupped his jowls. What was he to do? The SS worked on the basis of top-down leadership. Decisions came from above and were carried out efficiently by subordinates, each of whom knew the exact extent of his responsibilities. Schenkel's clear duty was to put this matter before the commandant, as Weber had put it before him, so that the superior could decide what action would be taken.

But Baumann had gone mad. He stayed in his quarters, much of the time in a drunken stupor. His waking hours were spent alternately torturing the small man in rags or carrying on one-sided rambling conversations about Nietzsche and the supremacy of will. In doing so, he was depriving his adjutant of the thing a subordinate most needed: a superior officer who would give him orders to carry out. Schenkel envied the men in Berlin who were daily exposed to the clear calm leadership of Adolf Hitler.

"What do you think we should do?" he asked Weber. "I don't know when we'll get another commandant."

"Herr Hauptsturmführer," the transport officer said, "it is not my place—"

"Neither is it mine!" Schenkel yelped, "but someone must do something!"

Weber thought for a moment, then said, "Müller! He's a practical man."

Relief blew through the adjutant like a spring breeze. "Yes, he is. Get him in here!"

But even as Weber opened the door to leave, he found Hauptscharführer Müller just outside, his hand raised to knock for entry.

"What is it?" Schenkel said.

Müller came into the room, deep worry etching lines into his coarse-featured face. "An Oberführer has arrived unannounced at the camp gate, Herr Hauptsturmführer. He is demanding to see the commandant."

"No one sees the commandant!" was Schenkel's automatic response, then his mind focused on the noncom's first statement. "An Oberführer, did you say?"

"Yes, Herr Hauptsturmführer. And with a red skull on his cap."

"*Ach, mein Gott!*" Schenkel said. A red skull meant that everything had just gotten worse. Immeasurably worse. He needed to think. "Where did you put him?"

"In the visiting officers' quarters," Müller said.

"Good." The adjutant turned to Weber, still hovering at the door. "You go and keep him company. Tell him the commandant is indisposed, but I will join him shortly."

Müller came to attention. "If I may speak freely…"

"What?"

"He does not look like a man it would be wise to keep waiting long."

Schenkel waved a hand to shoo the noncom from the room, then buried his face in his fingers. A Red Skull Oberführer, one of Himmler's Special Projects people, and a senior one at that. Oberführer was a political rank, officially equivalent to a colonelcy, but in practice it meant that its holder was outside the rank structure of the SS. He would be the head of a unit, and he would report to no one but Himmler himself. A man who had the ear of the Reichsführer-SS was always a very good man to impress— and always a man it could be lethal to disappoint.

Trembling, Schenkel rose and put on his greatcoat and cap. He went first to the commandant's quarters. Perhaps Baumann had come through his crisis and was clearheaded again. But even before he reached the *kommandantur*'s front steps, he could hear the bellowing. The words were indistinct, slurred by drink and madness, but the commandant seemed to be shouting a single question over and over.

And if he expects an answer from a mute, the adjutant thought, *he's crazier today than he was yesterday*. Still, the madman was in command, and Schenkel's duty was to report to him, to try to get him to take responsibility. Perhaps the news that a Red Skull Oberführer had arrived would shock Baumann back to sanity. Holding that faint hope, Schenkel went up the steps and in to the *kommandantur*.

The office looked like a slaughterhouse at the end of a busy day. Blood had pooled on the floor around the man bound to the chair, some of it fresh, much of it dry. More gore stained the walls, in arcs and sprays of red droplets. Baumann himself was drenched, his uniform sleeves crimson to the elbows, his tunic's front sodden. The commandant was striding back and forth in front of the prisoner, his boots crunching shards of broken glass underfoot, a blood-smeared book open in his hand.

"Do you believe that?" he was shouting at the bound man who, though blood-smeared, was unmarked by so much as a bruise. "You do, don't you? You believe it!"

When Schenkel came through the doorway, Baumann's bloodshot eyes struggled to focus on him. The commandant stopped and took a stumbling step backward as though faced with an apparition. He blinked and stared at the adjutant for several seconds before he recognized his subordinate.

"Schenkel!" he said. "Just the man." He slapped the open book with his free hand and said, "I've been debating von Schiller's famous line with our friend here."

Schenkel came cautiously into the room. "Yes, Herr Obersturmbannführer. Fascinating. But there is an urgent matter I must—"

Baumann cut him off, quoting from the book in his hand, his eyes blinking blearily at the page. "'Against stupidity the very gods themselves contend in vain,'" he quoted, then snapped the volume shut and gave Schenkel a drunken, lopsided grin. "What horseshit!"

"As you say, Herr Obersturmbannführer. Now there is a—"

"It is not stupidity the gods struggle against," the commandant said, overarticulating in the way of drunks who seek to make a point. "It is *will.* Will is everything!"

Baumann threw the book into a corner and leaned toward the other officer, giving Schenkel a gust of foul breath. "This swine here," he gestured at the man in the chair who glared back at him with eyes like black diamonds, "this *üntermensch* thinks he has will. But he has only stupidity. I am showing him, Schenkel. I am showing him will. I am showing him the difference between will and stupidity, but—" and here the drunken madman laughed as if he had just made a wonderful discovery, "—he is too stupid to see it."

"Yes, Herr Obersturmbannführer. But—"

Baumann was paying him no attention. He groped on the floor beside his desk and came up with a half-empty bottle of wine, raised it to his lips, and drained most of its contents in a series of long gurgling swallows.

Schenkel was willing to try one more time, but even as he opened his mouth to speak he heard a thud of boots ascending the outer steps and crossing the porch. Then the doorway was filled by a lean-faced SS officer with close-cropped blond hair and double oak leaves on his collar tab. The adjutant's gaze was drawn to the red skull on his uniform cap as if the symbol had hypnotic power.

The Oberführer's cold blue eyes took in each of the elements of the scene, then came back to Schenkel. "I am Oberführer von Strucker," he said. "Are you in command here?"

"No," Schenkel said. "I am the camp adjutant. Obersturmbannführer Baumann, here, is in command."

"Clearly," said the newcomer, "he is not even in command of himself." He turned to speak to whoever was behind him in the hallway. "Get some men and escort this drunk to a secure place. He is relieved of command."

Schenkel heard Weber's voice from the hallway, saying, "*Jawohl*, Herr Oberführer!" followed by the clump of the transport officer's footsteps and then his shouting for Müller.

Von Strucker came into the room, his attention fixed on the prisoner in the chair. Behind him, Baumann had drawn himself erect, though he wavered like sea grass moved by strong waves. "I am—" he began.

"You are finished," said von Strucker, without taking his eyes off the prisoner. "I am taking temporary command of this facility, by the authority of the Reichsführer-SS. And if you say one more word in my presence I will have you shot."

Baumann cleared his throat, at which the Red Skull Oberführer turned and put his icy eyes on the commandant. Baumann staggered again, as if he had been physically struck, then his shoulders slumped. Schenkel, watching from a corner of the office into which he had backed, believed he now finally understood what the madman had meant when he talked of the supremacy of will.

○━━━━━━━━━○

BUCHER found a vacant office down the hall from the blood-drenched room. Von Strucker had the fat and nervous adjutant summon a couple of guards, who carried the bound man, chair and all, down to the clean space. When the prisoner was set down in the center of the empty room and the guards dismissed, the baron turned to the perspiring Schenkel and said, "Leave us."

But the man lingered in the doorway. "Herr Oberführer," he stammered, "there is a situation in the camp."

"I would not be surprised," said von Strucker, "to learn that there are several situations."

"But—"

"You are now in command of this establishment. Except for this room. But if you do not leave us, the next thing you will be commanding is your own burial detail."

Höllenfeuer's new commandant left and the Prussian immediately forgot all about him. "Shut the door," he told Bucher, and when the pink-skinned subordinate had done so, the baron said, "Now let us see."

He took off his cap and greatcoat and hung them on a hook behind the door. Then he circled the man in the chair, inspecting him from all sides. The prisoner was lean and underfed but hard-muscled. The long hair and heavy beard growth along his cheeks made it hard to precisely define the shape of his skull, but from the facial features and pale skin, von Strucker judged him to be of Celtic stock. Weber had said the man had come on a train from Italy and that he was a mute.

He came around to the man's front and said, "*Verstehen-Sie mir?*" Do you understand me?

The man gave him the same agate-hard stare he had given the drunk, but the baron saw no flicker of comprehension. He tried the question in Italian, with a similar lack of result, then in French. Nothing.

Then he tried, "Do you understand me?" in English and though the prisoner made no voluntary response, von Strucker was a keen enough observer to know that he had been understood. He continued in English.

"So. You speak English. Are you an Englishman? Or a colonial? Not Australian, though." He watched the man's pupils and the action of the tiny muscles around the eyes. "Perhaps Canadian?"

He saw the faint flicker of expansion and contraction. "Ah," he said, "so it is Canadian.

"What about family? Is someone worrying about you somewhere? A mother, a father? Brothers, sisters?"

No, the Prussian saw from the microexpression that the prisoner could not disguise, *no family*. That was a disappointment. He had hoped for the possibility of breeding this one to a similarly mutated mother or sister.

"Never mind," he said. "But let us see what we have." He drew from the inner pocket of his tunic a small flat case, opened it to reveal a dissecting scalpel and some probes. The man's rags had been torn free from one shoulder by the insane commandant's ministrations, and the baron applied the tip of the scalpel to the deltoid muscle. The prisoner's breath hissed inward and he pulled against his bonds as the blade cut through the skin and underlying tissue, deep into the fiber beneath, until von Strucker could see the white of bone. Blood immediately welled, then just as quickly stopped.

The baron put in his monocle and leaned closer. He had made a cut three inches long and an inch deep at its center, but even as he watched, the tissues drew themselves together. He had seen time-lapse photography of plants emerging from seeds to become full grown, a week's growth in ten seconds. Now he was seeing the equivalent before his very eyes.

"Remarkable," he said. He positioned himself in front of the specimen, squatting so that they were at eye level. "Is it all kinds of tissue? Do your teeth grow back? Do your bones heal?"

The black eyes glittered and he heard a growl deep in the man's chest.

"I doubt you're really a mute," von Strucker said. "The Canadian

Army wouldn't have taken a mute. Perhaps you are shell-shocked?" He stroked his chin. "I wonder: If I cut you in half, would each half grow a whole new you?"

The growl deepened.

"Well," said the Prussian, standing up, "we'll have time to explore all of your many mysteries, won't we?"

To Bucher, he said, "Go and find that fat fool. Tell him we'll need some kind of dissecting table. And have him find a generator and rig some decent lighting in here. I want to do a few preliminaries, then we'll take him back to Berlin for a full work-up."

Bucher bustled out. Von Strucker wiped the scalpel clean and put it away. He stared at the bound man and smiled. "How marvelous," he said, "to have found you."

WHAT this situation called for, Schenkel decided, was a damn good report. "If you don't want to be last, get your story in first" was one of the golden rules of bureaucratic systems. After the encounter with the terrifying Red Skull Oberführer, he returned to his office, poured himself a schnapps to fight down his panic, and began to think the situation through. The liquor helped clear his mind, and he realized that the Oberführer's intervention presented a wonderful opportunity.

Everybody knew that Kaltenbrunner and Himmler did not care for each other, but concentration camps were under Kaltenbrunner's authority. If things went amiss here at Höllenfeuer while one of the Reichsführer-SS's Red Skulls was in temporary command, it would be a black eye for Himmler. Kaltenbrunner's position in the Reich's highest political circles would be enhanced. As the officer who dutifully brought the situation to the notice of the chief of the SD, Schenkel would be remembered, at least sheltered, and possibly rewarded.

Of course, he could not write officially and directly to Obergruppenführer Kaltenbrunner. But he could send an unofficial note to the man's aide. Despite what the rulebooks said, Schenkel knew that the world was tied together by back-channel communications. He put pen to paper for a preliminary draft. The right phrases came easily: "disruption of the normal chain of command," "a nonmilitary officer arrogating to himself authority over military forces," "protests ignored." In only minutes, he had the perfect instrument to redirect all blame for anything that now went wrong at Höllenfeuer.

He made a few minor alterations, then copied the finished draft onto official camp letterhead, signed at the bottom, and placed it in an addressed envelope that he marked "private and confidential." He tucked the letter into the inner pocket of his tunic and breathed a sigh of relief. An SS motorcycle courier would arrive early tomorrow morning and carry the letter to the nearby Luftwaffe airfield. By nightfall, the report would be in Berlin and by morning it would be in the in-tray of Kaltenbrunner's Standartenführer.

And then, let the heavens fall, for plump little Otto Schenkel of Bremen would have made for himself an island of safety.

He poured himself another schnapps to celebrate. As he put it to his lips, the short, pink-skinned man who had accompanied von Strucker opened the door without knocking and strode into the office.

"The Oberführer requires a generator and some decent lighting in the *kommandantur*," he said.

"We do not have a spare generator," Schenkel said. "All are in use." They were supposed to have two backups, one in case a regular unit failed and another for emergencies, but the last inventory had found them missing. Krentz's doing, the adjutant assumed.

"Take one out of use and light the Oberführer's room," Bucher said.

"You are giving me an order to do so?"

"Yes."

"Very well," Schenkel said. He would need to revise the report to include this detail.

The man left. Schenkel rose from behind his desk and stood for a moment, studying the map of the camp that hung on one wall. Then he went out and made his way down the hall to the orderly room. The clerk on duty stood to attention.

"Inform the engineering officer that generator number four is to be disconnected and moved to the *kommandantur*, along with wiring and portable lighting."

"At your order, Herr Hauptsturmführer," the man said.

"Make sure that the engineering officer is aware that the order comes directly from the new commandant."

"*Jawohl.*"

And as the man departed on his errand, Schenkel added, "And tell Untersturmführer Weber to have a staff car brought around. I won't need a driver."

Schenkel went back to his office, a smile on his face. He revised his report, then gathered up a few items he didn't want burned and carried them out to where the staff car waited. A minute later, he passed through the front gate and turned in the direction of the Luftwaffe airfield. Personally delivering his urgent letter gave him a perfect excuse for being away from the camp.

BERLIN, GERMANY,
THE PRESENT

"HE'S heavy," Khan said.

"It must be the chains," Al Borak said. "He's smaller than any of us."

"It's not the chains. It's like he has rocks in his belly."

They were in the freight elevator of the building on Invalidenstrasse, the Pashtun and four members of the Green Fist, descending to the first basement parking level where the van waited. The baron waited there, too, in case they needed someone who spoke German to deal with any curious passersby. Their prisoner was tightly wrapped in chains, his head encased in a bag of heavy cloth, propped upright on a two-wheeled dolly.

As the elevator reached the basement, the small man began to struggle against the restraints. "He came to very fast," Khan said.

"That's why the baron is interested in him," Al Borak said. He directed two of the men to go out among the parked cars and make sure no one was watching. When they returned to report that the area was clear, their leader told Khan and the other man to wheel their burden the short distance to where the van waited behind the loading bay door.

The van's rear doors opened and the baron stepped out. He watched as the Pashtun directed the four men to lift the prisoner feetfirst, dolly and all, into the vehicle. Though they were all fit men, they had to strain to handle the weight.

"He is definitely heavy," Khan said, puffing from the exertion.

The baron peered at the prisoner. "He wasn't abnormally heavy when I first encountered him. I wonder what he has been up to."

Al Borak whistled, and the rest of the team came swiftly from all directions, where they had been stationed to warn if anyone approached the operation area. They crowded into the van on either side of the man lying on his back in chains.

Then, before the doors were closed, the baron said, "Just to be sure, remove the bag."

The Pashtun tugged the cloth away. A hard and angry face looked up at him, then the dark eyes flicked toward the Prussian.

The baron spoke to the man in English. "Remember me?"

HÖLLENFEUER CONCENTRATION CAMP,

FEBRUARY 1944

"WHAT do you think?" von Strucker asked Bucher, "systemic, or some special gland or organ?"

"Systemic, I'd say. It's not as if some parts of him heal and others don't. And they all heal at the same rate."

"I agree," the baron said, gazing down at the man on the table. "My first inclination is to look at the blood. The mutation could be in the lymphatic system, but blood constantly circulates through every part of the body."

"A unique blood cell?" Bucher suggested.

"Most likely."

The pink-skinned man said, "It's a shame we can't ask him, he being a mute. He may know."

The Prussian sneered. "No. When Socrates said, 'The unexamined life is not worth living,' he was referring to man-shaped beasts like this one."

The man on the table growled and the baron checked the restraints again. Once they had rigged the lights, they had begun by chaining him to a sturdy oak table from the officers' mess. It had taken six burly SS troopers to effect the transfer from the chair. But even chained, the subject had been able to wriggle, making fine work difficult. The baron had summoned the camp's carpenter and had him nail the man to the table, using heavy spikes driven through wrists, elbows, ankles, and above the knees. The heads of the spikes were then hammered sideways, bending them over to guarantee that the subject couldn't tear himself free.

"If it's the blood, then we should be looking at the marrow. That's where blood cells get made," Bucher said.

"Agreed," said von Strucker, picking up a chisel and a heavy mallet that had come from the camp's metalworking shop. "Slice open his right thigh. We'll remove a portion of his femur."

○———————○

HAUPTSCHARFÜHRER Müller didn't like it. With the number four generator taken out of service, a substantial portion of Höllenfeuer was unlit, including the row of two-man huts that were bachelor officers quarters, before one of which he stood guard. The floodlamps that lined the fence along the east side were out, so that the nearby barracks that housed the political and deviate prisoners were black shapes in the darkness. Even the searchlights in the watchtowers were dead. Who knew what the swine were doing out there in the blackness? He thought again about the rumors of pistols being smuggled into the camp.

He would have liked to be out there patrolling with some picked men, but the visiting high mucky-muck had specifically ordered that the camp's senior noncommissioned officer had to guard the drunken former commandant. *You have the most to lose if he gets loose,* the Oberführer had said and Müller had had no doubt that it was a threat to be taken seriously. He had stared straight ahead, but his eyes kept wanting to go to the red skull on the officer's cap. All kinds of strange tales circulated about the ultrasecret Special Projects units: how they reanimated the dead to fight again, heedless of their wounds; how they had recovered the spear with which the Roman legionary had pierced the side of Christ, a sacred relic that guaranteed victory to whoever owned it; how they had found an entrance to a vast subterranean world beneath the Alps, peopled by dragons and golden-eyed folk, that Germany would conquer and rule once the Ivans were crushed.

Now Müller came back from his dreams to the reality of darkness. Someone should be patrolling while the lights are out, he knew, but no one had ordered it. Schenkel was nowhere to be seen and the Red Skulls were closeted with the weird little mute that nobody liked to think about. Nobody except Baumann, who now thought about nothing else. Müller resolved to do the best job he could at guarding the drunken madman who muttered and raged on the other side of the door against which the noncom leaned his shoulders in the old sentry's trick to save the feet. Perhaps if he impressed the Red Skull, it might lead to his being invited to join those Special Projects teams. Then he could live in a world of wonders, instead of this *scheissebohrung* full of verminous scum.

Shitbox, indeed, he thought, as the icy winter wind swung his way from the east and he caught the odor of unwashed bodies and dysentery that always hung over the barracks. The wind was strengthening. He could hear it swinging the unlit light fixtures against the wire fence. He strained to hear over their clicking and the shuffling sound of the wind. Was something else moving, out there in the dark?

Abruptly the wind died for a few seconds before gusting up again. In those few moments of dead air, it seemed to Müller that the stink of rancid sweat and dried excrement grew stronger. He pushed his shoulders away from the door and stood erect, swinging the Schmeisser that was slung across his body to point its muzzle at the darkness. As he did so, a chunk of that darkness suddenly achieved greater solidity right in front of him. He felt something hard poke against his greatcoat just over his midriff. Then a giant's fist smashed him back against the door as a nine-millimeter slug from a Luger tore through his upper abdomen and lodged itself in one of his vertebrae. The pistol was wrapped in rags to muffle the sound of the shot.

A hand slipped the submachine gun from the Hauptscharführer's failing grasp, even as he slumped to the steps that led up to the hut's front door, but Müller was already far away. As he slid into death, he was hoping that there would be golden-eyed strangers to greet him, but all that came was a blackness even deeper than what lay over the eastern side of the camp.

The man who had shot him tried the doorlatch of the hut the SS man had been guarding, found it locked, and moved on. There was no time to stand still and nothing to be gained in making too much noise too soon. He handed the Schmeisser to one of the scarecrows in stinking rags who came behind him. The man with the Luger was more warmly dressed, wearing a once-fashionable overcoat that had most recently belonged to Helmut, the green-badge ex-pimp. The *kapo* would not be needing it anymore.

○━━━━━━━━○

THE small piece of marrow floated in a dish of sterile saline solution brought from the camp's infirmary. Bucher poked it with a probe so that one end lifted above the surface of the liquid. "What is it now, two hours? And no sign of necrosis."

The baron examined the specimen closely, one eye closed, the other peering through his monocle. "You're right," he said. "The tissue might have been extricated only seconds ago."

The Prussian turned away from the dish on the table in the visiting officers' quarters and paced the room, head bowed, hands clasped behind his back, thinking out loud. "This reconfirms the importance of the blood. It must be a mutated blood factor. The marrow is producing enough of whatever it is—probably borne by the white blood cells—to keep the tissue alive. Probably indefinitely."

"*Mein Gott*," whispered the pink-skinned man, "it's immortality!"

The baron said, "I wish I had not been in such a hurry to get here. We should have brought some of the Iron Eagles for security. I don't like having that priceless specimen guarded by the fools that infest this farce of a concentration camp."

"Shall I have them double the guard?"

"Yes. But first go and get that senior noncom. We'll let him guard our prize. That's more important than keeping a drunken lunatic from wandering loose."

Bucher put on his coat and cap and departed. The Prussian looked again at the fragment. Then he unstoppered a sterile flask that stood beside the dish on the bench and carefully poured both specimen and fluid into it. He pushed the stopper in tight and held the flask up to the light. The fragment floated weightlessly in the clear liquid. Alone now, von Strucker permitted himself an unchecked display of the emotion that had been rippling through him for more than an hour, ever since he had first cut into the mute. A wide smile split his grim face, and an almost ecstatic shiver passed through the muscles of his back.

He shook the flask, watching the tissue bob up and down, and let his mind explore what would come his way: greater power and wealth than his forebears among the minor Prussian aristocracy had ever known; and life that would go on for centuries. The Nazis prattled mistily about a thousand-year Reich. He would see every moment of every year of it, and more, much more.

At that moment, shots came from outside—the *snap, snap, snap* of an automatic pistol, followed by the high-speed rattle of a Schmeisser. Then the lights went out.

○────────────○

PATCH Howlett growled as he heard the footsteps coming down the hallway. He had been lying in the darkness, straining against the bent spikes that secured his flesh to the heavy wooden table, but had been unable to tear either them or himself loose.

The door opened and the lights came on. He craned his neck to see who was coming into the room, but he already knew by the smell it was neither the drunken commandant nor the ice-blooded man with the scalpel. Four emaciated faces looked down at him, faces he recognized. One of the men shook his head in horror and said, in Italian, "*Gesù Maria.*"

Somebody found a pry bar in one corner, where the carpenter had been told to leave his tools. The man put its curved and slotted end to a spike through Patch's right wrist and pulled the nail squeaking from the wood and flesh. A man wearing Helmut's green-badged overcoat said, "*Baumann, dove è?*" gesturing with the Luger in his hand.

Patch shook his head and shrugged. The spike was gone from his right elbow and the man with the pry was working on his left wrist. The wounds in his right arm had already closed and he reached and took the tool from the man to complete the job.

"*Andiamo,*" said the man with the Luger. We're going.

Patch nodded. He sat up and leaned forward to begin work on his ankles and knees as the men went out. Moments later, the putter of the generator outside the building died and the lights went out.

Patch worked on in darkness, feeling for the remaining spikes and fitting the pry's notch to them. Getting them out was not as easy as he would have liked. The spikes straightened well enough, but the carpenter had hammered them deep into the close-grained oak beneath and from a sitting position Howlett could not use his full strength. As he worked, rocking the spikes from his flesh, he listened to the rising gunfire, shouts, and screams from outside the *kommandantur*. The sounds of battle were coming from several directions now. It was time for him to go. He had discharged his duty.

His father had been of the old breed, a yeoman farmer left over from the Victorian age who had transplanted himself to the rangelands of

Alberta. To the old man, there was nothing more important than to do his duty—duty to family, duty to friends, duty to king and country, done without fuss or bravado. It was his measure of what it meant to be a man, and he had passed on to his son the same standard.

Patch had owed a duty to Rob Roy MacLeish that could only be discharged by helping his friend's fiancée. In the kitchen of the Osteria Gambrelli, at her request, that duty had been transferred to her brother Giovanni. Then in the flea-infested squalor of Höllenfeuer's barracks number eighteen, that duty had again been passed forward, had become an obligation to endure the unendurable, to see and remember what had happened in this small, frigid corner of hell.

Now this place was winding up, the inmates taking murderous revenge on their tormentors. They would leave nothing but smoking ruins. That meant that Patch Howlett's duty was done and dusted, as his father would have said. He could move on—though first he ought to pay a visit to his old friend the drunken commandant, then find the men with red skulls on their caps.

He unbent the last spike, set the pry beneath its head, and began rocking it loose. The darkness in which he worked suddenly brightened, though not by much. A yellowy glow came from the corridor outside the open door, accompanied by the sound of approaching, though unsteady, footsteps.

Patch exerted a renewed effort and the last spike came loose from the wood and his flesh. He noiselessly set down the pry bar and slipped off the table, pressing himself against the wall behind the half-opened door. The light brightened as its source neared and then the commandant came through the doorway, his tunic stained and half-unbuttoned, an oil lamp held high before him in one hand. The other held an open bottle of wine.

"*Wo bist du?*" he said, almost crooning, like an indulgent pet owner calling for a strayed lapdog. He peered, bleary eyed, at the empty table, then held the lamp out toward the dark corners of the room. Finally he stooped to look under the table. Patch swept out an arm and slammed shut the door.

Straightening, the German turned as if the slam had been no more than a gentle tap on his shoulder. "*Ach,*" he said, followed by some words that Patch took to mean "there you are." The man put the lamp on the table and took a swig from the bottle, then rocked unsteadily on his feet, bloodshot eyes struggling to hold Patch in focus. He began to mutter to himself, the same words Howlett had heard time and again, that had always been punctuated by slashes from jagged glass.

But the prisoner had heard more than enough of "*Mein Wille*" over the past couple of days. He now told the commandant, in words often heard in Royal Canadian Army barracks, exactly where he could put his *Wille*.

Baumann blinked at him as if Patch were a pet that had unexpectedly performed a new trick. "*Du kannst sprechen*," he said.

"I can do more than *sprechen*," Patch said. He flexed his forearms and, for the first time in weeks, his claws tore themselves free of his flesh.

The SS officer, secure in his drunken arrogance, did not blanch as many others had done at the sight of Patch's armament. He gripped the bottle by its neck and struck it against the table's edge so that wine and glass sprayed in all directions. "*Komme*," he said softly, the jagged remnant of the bottle in his hand, "*komme, kleine üntermensch*."

"Oh, I'm coming," Howlett said. He moved forward and Baumann took a drunken swing at him with the broken glass. The Canadian met the weapon with the claws of his right hand, then twisted his wrist to tear the bottle neck from the commandant's hand and send it clattering into a corner. "Now," Patch said, "let's see how your precious *Wille* stands up to a little of your own medicine."

He flicked one set of claws across the Nazi's chest, shredding cloth and scoring the flesh beneath. Baumann looked down at the welling blood and said something Patch figured was a curse. The pry bar was still on the table and the commandant snatched it up and came at him, the heavy steel raised two-handed above his head.

But Patch easily dodged the drunk's clumsy swing, responding with another flick of a claw to lay open Baumann's left cheek. The officer took one hand from the pry bar to touch fingertips to the wound, but even as he was looking at the red dripping from his hand, a claw ripped the skin on the other side of his face.

"There," said Patch, standing back like a portrait painter considering a work in progress, "now you look like a real Hun. Dueling scars and all."

His remark earned him only more German curse words, delivered in a shriek, as Baumann swung the heavy bar one-handed. The Canadian stepped lightly out of the Nazi's reach, then his claws swept downward to tear the sleeve from the arm that held the weapon, slicing the skin and muscle beneath.

Baumann gave a scream of mingled pain and rage, staggering sideways as he swung the bar backhanded. Again, he missed his target, but this time he connected with the oil lamp on the table, smashing its reservoir and splashing kerosene on the walls and floor. The lamp's burning wick fell into the spreading liquid and, with a *whump* the fuel ignited.

Flames ran across the floor and simultaneously climbed to the ceiling. A few burning drops landed on Baumann's tunic and he dropped the pry bar as he frantically beat them out. Then he looked with horror at the expanding inferno and made for the door.

"Not a big fan of fire?" Patch said, putting himself between the Nazi and the room's only exit. He flexed his arms and the claws withdrew as the other man tried to push past him. Then he put both palms on Baumann's chest and shoved him back toward the flames. "That's a funny attitude for a man who keeps his ovens going day and night."

The SS man babbled something, then began to scream and beat at himself as droplets of kerosene that had landed on his boots when the lamp shattered caught fire and set the cloth of his breeches alight. He staggered away from the worst of the blaze, slapping at his legs, his screams becoming animal-like yelps of pain and panic.

The heat in the small closed room was now so intense that Patch felt his skin beginning to scorch and his eyes drying out. The pain was bad, but he had stood worse. Baumann rushed at him again, desperate to get at the door. Howlett threw the man back at the pool of fire rising from the floor, and now the gray cloth on the Nazi's back smoldered and burst into spontaneous flame. A second later, Baumann's hair was ablaze.

"Maybe that will of yours can put it out," Patch said.

With a sound that was pure terrified, agonized beast, the burning SS Obersturmbannführer threw himself at the door and the man who blocked it. Howlett thought the man looked like a human torch as he caught the shrieking, charring mass of panicked flesh and hurled it back once more into the inferno.

"You're not quite done yet," he said.

Now Baumann was fully ablaze, his body wreathed in flames of yellow and red, and a black greasy smoke already rising from him as he sank screaming to the burning floor. Patch knew the smell of that smoke. It had been clogging his nose for all the weeks he had spent in this place. But this time, it didn't smell so bad.

He turned his back on Baumann's last moans and opened the door. The rush of fresh air into the fiery space was like a draft into a blast furnace. Patch's ragged clothes caught fire and fell from him. He walked out into the hallway, the fire coming along beside him like a faithful, boisterous dog. By the time he reached the front door, it was already playing with the commandant's trophies—the volumes of Goethe, Schiller, and Heine scattered about the office—sending burning pages floating up into the superheated air.

Outside, the cold wind felt good on Patch's heat-tortured skin. Flames shooting from the burst windows of the burning *kommandantur* lit the immediate area of the darkened camp. He could hear screams and shouts and sustained bursts of automatic fire from the direction of the SS barracks. For a moment, he considered going there to help, but the voices raised in panic all carried German accents, while the cries of vengeance and triumph came in other tongues. He decided to find the man with the red skull.

Sprawled in the dirty snow not far from the *kommandantur* he found the body of the short, pink-skinned man, most of his brains spewed out the back of his head. The farther he got from the burning building, the more the icy wind bit, and Howlett knelt to quickly strip the corpse of its gray SS garb. The dead man had been about the same height and build, though the boots pinched a little. The rim of the cap needed cleaning at the back, but a handful of snow did a pretty good job.

His weeks in the camp had taught him the layout. SS officers' country was close by the *kommandantur*. Howlett figured he'd be able to find the Red Skull who'd experimented on him. The man had an unusual smell about him: an odor of chemicals and the harsh soap that doctors used to scrub their hands. When he found him, the Nazi might already be dead from the revolt. But if not, that was an oversight that Patch Howlett could soon set to rights.

○————————○

THE moment the lights went out, von Strucker put the flask into his valise, snapped it shut, and went to the door. He eased it open a little and put one eye to the crack. He could see nothing but he heard the crunch of on-coming footsteps on the crusted snow. He stepped clear of the door, leaving it ajar, and a moment later it swung silently inward. The baron pressed himself against the wall, shielded from view by the door. A beam of light from a penlight briefly swept across the room, then winked out. A moment later, the footsteps sounded again, moving away in the direction of the SS barracks.

The Prussian waited until the night was still again. Then he put on his cap and greatcoat and headed for the main gate. The two-man guard detail that should have been posted there was not to be seen, but when he got close enough he saw two lumps lying in the shadows along the fence. Their throats had been cut and their weapons were missing.

The main gates had a small man-size portal built into them. The baron quietly opened this and slipped out. The car he had acquired at the Luftwaffe station was parked not far from the fence. In moments he was behind the wheel and pressing the starter. The well-maintained engine caught instantly and von Strucker turned the wheel toward the gray strip in the darkness that was the road out of here. A half mile on, he turned on the headlights and accelerated.

o————————o

THE Luftwaffe station was manned around the clock, but at this time of night the duty section consisted of a leutnant and a couple of enlisted men. They kept themselves warm in a small hut that had a coal stove, the leutnant conscientiously going out once an hour to check the guard posts, though Polish partisans had not operated in the area for some time. Sometimes, as the hours of the night dragged on and the conversation with his subordinates grew stale and repetitious, he wished he'd joined another branch of the services—one where he might have seen more action.

When the guard at the station's front gate telephoned to advise the leutnant that the high-ranking SS officer from Berlin who had come through that morning was back and looking for his plane and pilot, the duty officer sent one of the airmen to wake up the flying officer. He sent the other airman to the hangar to tell the flight sergeant to get the plane ready to fly.

He was standing at attention when the Red Skull came into the hut. He saluted and reported his actions, but the Oberführer merely grunted.

The officer's attention had gone to the other man in the hut, the plump and jowly SS Hauptsturmführer from the nearby concentration camp who had shown up some hours before with an urgent message to go out on the morning's mail plane to Berlin.

"Schenkel, isn't it?" the Red Skull said, his brows contracting above eyes of blue ice. "What are you doing here?"

The other officer had seemed nervous before, disdaining to chat with the Luftwaffe leutnant and his men. Now he rose to his feet, mouth opening and closing as if he couldn't get the words past a paralyzed tongue.

"He is waiting for the morning mail plane," the Luftwaffe officer said helpfully.

"Ah," the Red Skull said, studying the now plainly terrified Hauptsturmführer. The cold eyes turned to the Luftwaffe officer and their owner said, "Herr Leutnant, pass me your sidearm."

"Herr Oberführer?"

"Your pistol. Now. I have come away without mine."

"At your order," said the leutnant, unbuttoning the flap of his holster and producing the weapon. The Oberführer put down his valise, accepted the pistol, and racked back the slide to chamber a round.

Then he raised his arm and shot the Hauptsturmführer through the head. Even as the sound of the shot reverberated in the small space and the dead man slumped to the floor, the SS officer handed the pistol back and said, "This swine deserted his post. You will contact the local head of the SD and inform him that there has been a revolt at Höllenfeuer. The prisoners have killed the guards and are escaping."

The Luftwaffe officer's eyes went from the Oberführer to the corpse and back again. "Herr Oberführer—" he began.

"Now, Herr Leutnant," said the Red Skull, "or you can join him wherever he has gone to."

From outside came the sound of an aircraft engine sputtering into life, then rising to a roar. The SS officer's modified Heinkel was warming up on the apron.

"At your order," the leutnant said, and rang the crank on his field telephone. As he made contact with the local office, he saw the Oberführer kneel beside the corpse and slip a hand into the man's tunic. It came out holding an envelope.

The Red Skull made a *tsk*-ing sound as he slipped the envelope into his own pocket. Then he scooped up the valise and departed without another word.

The phone to his ear, the leutnant watched from the hut's single window as the SS officer strode across the concrete apron to where his plane waited. Beyond were the runways and a screen of tall trees, and above those, in the direction of the concentration camp, the sky was lit an angry red.

A voice spoke in his ear. "SD. Who is calling?"

The Luftwaffe leutnant said what the SS man had told him to say, then he added, "and I've got a dead Hauptsturmführer here."

When he finally hung up, he decided that he had seen all the action he needed.

○———————○

THE scent trail of the man with the scalpel faded under the smell of fresh exhaust fumes outside the camp gates. The SS officer had gotten away. For a moment, Patch considered running after him; perhaps he'd catch him at a crossroads, lost and studying a map. But the cold-eyed man hadn't looked the type to get himself lost, and Howlett decided it was time to go back where he belonged.

The Russians were in the east and the only Allied armies in Europe were in the south. There was always talk about a new front in France sometime, maybe in the spring. Patch decided he'd work his way west, until he found an invading Allied army coming to meet him. Perhaps he would fight a private war along the way, targeting the SS wherever he found them.

He'd keep the uniform. From what the man with the scalpel had said, Patch had figured out that the officer was part of some special SS unit that hunted for people like him—mutants, the Canadian divisional staff officer at the Ortona field hospital had called them. If he now made his way west across the Reich, wearing the Red Skull insignia and ripping up Nazis as he went, Patch might be taken for some rogue monster that had emerged from the SS's own laboratories to stalk and haunt them.

He struck out west, into the Polish forest. It felt good to be running through the trees again.

VON Strucker landed at Templehof as dawn was breaking. He commandeered a car and driver and was at the Prinz Albrechtstrasse headquarters demanding to see Heinrich Himmler as the offices were just opening.

"The Reichsführer has a full schedule," said a stiff-necked Standartenführer in Himmler's outer office.

"He'll want to cancel it when he hears of the opportunity I bring him," the baron said. "And he'll want to see you digging latrines in Russia if he finds that you prevented me from doing so."

Minutes later, the Prussian said to the Reichsführer-SS, "Kaltenbrunner is going to have a bad day. I thought you might like to know why before he does."

As he left the building, he was telling himself that this morning's gift to the little man behind the big desk would at least buy him some leeway to continue his research. But what he needed most of all was to find the little Canadian mute.

Find him, not for the Reich, but for the only cause on earth that truly mattered to Wolfgang Freiherr von Strucker: to live, healthy and whole, forever.

BERLIN, GERMANY,
THE PRESENT

"REMEMBER me?"

Logan heard the voice before he saw the face. His eyes were closed and he realized that he must have been dozing—drifting in a half-conscious state, somewhere between true dreaming and true wakefulness. He didn't want to leave this twilight zone. There were images here—faces, scenes, buildings—and he was sure that they were not conjured just from dreams, but from recalled reality. Something had happened to shake loose some of his memories, and they were passing before his mind's inner eye like leaves blown from a tree in autumn.

"I said, 'Remember me?'" Despite himself, Logan opened his eyes and the images fled. He looked up at the lean face that hovered over him. Then his eyes flicked around to take in the rest of the scene: the roof of the van in which he was lying on his back, the swarthy young men squatting on bench seats along the inner sides of the vehicle, the concrete parking garage glimpsed through the gap between the van's rear doors before they closed. He heard the vehicle's motor come to life, followed by the rattle of a segmented steel door as it opened, then they began to move. In a moment they had exchanged artificial light for the cold glow of a winter morning.

His gaze came back to the man who had spoken. He took in the prominent cheekbones, the taut skin along the jawline, the frigid blue eyes, the close-cropped blond hair, and the bloodless lips set in a self-satisfied smile. "No," he said, "and yes. I remember your face, but not where I know you from. Though I think I ought to."

The smile disappeared; his eyebrows arched in curiosity. "Are you trying to play a game with me?" the man said in German-accented English. "You must have remembered Höllenfeuer—or else why would you have gone there? And if you remember the camp, you surely remember me."

Hearing the voice as well as seeing the face was indeed triggering some response in Logan, deep sediments were stirring in the bottom of his mind. He sniffed. There was an odor about the man, different from the miasma of sweat and spice that hung around the others in the van—a smell of soap and chemicals, almost medical. "Are you a doctor?" he said.

"Is that memory," the German said, "or something else? You sniffed at me, didn't you? Is your sense of smell mutated, too?"

"I don't know what you mean," Logan said.

That won him a little laugh from his captor. "Come now, let there be no games between us. It will go easier on you. I am not a sadist, but I will do what I have to do to get what I need."

"Wouldn't we all?" Logan said, playing for time. He could feel memories floating below the surface, insubstantial as layers of cigarette smoke in the air of a closed room. Yet if he tried to make them appear, the effort would just blow them back to nothingness. He sought to keep his mind still, to let the fragile ghosts rise into his consciousness. But it was hard to force tranquility on himself, because he had found someone who knew him—who knew secrets about him.

"The Pole with the fancy camera," he said, "he was working for you."

"Say he works for a man who works for me," said the German. "Which leads me to ask: For whom do you work?"

"I don't know."

"I find that hard to believe."

It was hard for Logan to shrug while chained to a dolly, but he did the best he could. "Lately I've been having to believe a lot of things that are hard to swallow. Like the idea that I'm old enough to have been in a Nazi concentration camp. Or, come to think of it, that so are you."

The German hunched forward on the bench seat, put his fingertips together, and touched the ends of his index fingers to his lips. He studied Logan's face for a moment, then said, "Are you telling me you don't know what you are?"

"Something has happened to my memory."

The man above him cocked his head to one side and pulled at his chin. "How far back does it go?"

"A few weeks. A couple of months. I'm not sure. Behind that it's all fog."

"Then why Höllenfeuer? That was more than sixty years ago."

"I found a clue and followed. That was where it led."

"Then it led you to me."

"Yes. And you remember me. So tell me, who am I?"

The man above him shrugged. "I wish I knew," he said.

o———————o

"WHERE are you taking me?"

"A place where we won't be disturbed. We have a lot to do."

The van had stopped in an airplane hangar and Logan had been hauled into the passenger compartment of an oversize private jet. The plane immediately taxied out and rolled toward a runway. A couple of minutes later they were airborne.

"Are you going to keep me like this?" Logan said.

"It seems prudent," said the German.

"Perhaps we are on the same side."

"Doubtful. My side is essentially limited to me."

"Still, we could be allies."

His captor made no reply, but the lean face showed an amused skepticism.

"At least tell me your name," Logan said.

"Wolfgang, Freiherr von Strucker. 'Freiherr' is a title. The English equivalent is 'baron.' And you are?"

"Logan."

"Is that a first or last name?"

"I don't know. It's the only one I've got."

One of the cockpit crew came from up front and said something to von Strucker in what Logan assumed was Arabic. The German said to Logan, "We will have plenty of time for conversation later. Right now I must attend to something else." He went forward, out of Logan's sight.

Logan was a little surprised by how he was reacting to being taken prisoner by these men. Chained and carried off in a private jet to who knew where, he thought he ought to be feeling fear, or at least apprehension, but he didn't. His captors, except for the baron, were obviously of Middle Eastern origin. They gave a clear impression of being highly trained, like Special Forces or security service officers. When they had seized him in the dark, they had seemed to move with superhuman speed.

He had no idea what they meant to do with him. Logic said he ought to be worried. Yet, curiously, Logan felt entirely at ease. *Like a tiger surrounded by bobcats*, said a voice from the back of his head, *a wolverine among foxes*. But it was not his voice, just a snatch of unconnected memory drifting through his damaged mind. He found that he was flexing his back, shoulder, and arm muscles against the chains that held him, reflexively testing them.

But when he bunched his forearms, he again felt a flash of anxiety—and again wondered where it had come from. The fear clashed with the confidence he had just been feeling and now he wondered which of those conflicting emotions was the right one for the situation. And which one had been planted in him by the mysterious somebodies who lurked in his shuttered past.

Enough thinking. I'll lie back, learn what I can. And when the time comes for action, I'll do whatever comes naturally. With that thought, another wave of confidence came washing through him. *A wolverine among foxes*, he thought, this time in his own voice. He liked the image it put in his mind.

THERE was a private compartment with four seats between the cockpit and the main cabin. Von Strucker put his head out the folding door that separated the two and beckoned to Al Borak.

"I've had a call from home base," the baron said when they were alone. "Our Yemeni friend is waiting for us."

"He was not expected?" the Pashtun said.

"They have been getting anxious about Operation Severed Head."

"So have I. We don't have a plan that can work, even allowing for maximum losses."

The baron smiled his wintry smile. "We do now."

Al Borak cocked his head toward the main cabin. "Because of him?"

"Yes."

"I am your second in command. When will you tell me how he fits in?"

"I am still working it out," von Strucker said. "But he may have more uses than just the one I originally intended for him."

"Why is that?"

The Prussian's icy eyes looked off into the middle distance. "Because he's a man who needs someone who can tell him who he is."

"And you can?"

"Oh, no. I only know what he is." The smile grew even colder. "But I am sure I can think of something to tell him."

o———————o

THE plane had stopped somewhere and refueled along the way, again taxiing into a closed hangar for the purpose. The men had disembarked to stretch their legs. By the sounds of the hand clapping and chanting, Logan thought they had indulged in some kind of folk dance. They looked happy enough when they came back onboard the plane, stepping over him but otherwise ignoring his presence. He returned the favor, letting the thrum of the jet's engines lull him into sleep.

He dreamed of cold, of a place where men huddled together, shivering, trying to keep warm, a place where it always seemed to be dark even when the sun was in the sky. He dreamed of screams and fists and boots, of muzzles of gray steel spitting flame. The face of a madman kept coming into the dream, shouting at him in slurred German. There was pain and blood and shattering glass, then it all dissolved in fire.

He awoke to the sensation of changing air pressure in his ears. A few minutes later, he heard the plane's landing gear lock into place, then the bump of tires hitting a runway and the thrust reversal of the engines. The aircraft slowed then taxied, finally passing out of daylight.

The baron appeared above him again, giving instructions in Arabic. Logan was tilted up on his dolly, wheeled to the plane's door, and handed down to the ground. He was in a sizable hangar, its only natural light coming from windows in the main door that was now rattling shut.

The German said something to the men from the plane that caused them to form a double line and march off. He then called over the tall, gray-eyed man and gave him instructions. Logan heard the click of a lock behind him, then the grip of the bonds that held him to the dolly slackened. He flexed his muscles and the chains fell to the ground. He stepped free.

"If you will come with me, I will show you something," von Strucker said, gesturing toward the hangar door.

"All right," Logan said.

The German led him to a man-size portal set into the segmented steel of the main door. He opened it and stepped outside. Logan followed and immediately the heat of the desert afternoon struck him like a gust from a furnace. Sweat broke out on his face and chest, and he could already feel trickles of moisture running down his sides under the winter-weight clothing he had worn in Berlin.

Without a word, the baron walked along the front of the hangar, then around the back. Logan followed again and soon found himself climbing a gentle slope that was the disguised roof of the building. At its top, von Strucker waited.

"What did you want to show me?" Logan said when he reached him.

"Nothing," the German said. He swept his hands to indicate the horizon in all directions. "Nothing as far as the eye can see."

Logan realized he had just learned something more about himself: he didn't like people who played cute. "Meaning?" he said.

"Meaning that I have decided that you are not a prisoner here. But, if you decide to leave, I don't think that even your peculiar abilities will keep you alive."

"What peculiar abilities?"

The blue eyes studied him. "You truly do not know what you are?"

"'Who,'" said Logan, "the word is 'who.'"

"'Who' is only part of it," von Strucker said. "Let us go in before we suffer heatstroke. We have a lot to talk about. But first I have to meet with a client."

Logan followed him back down the slope. "What is this place? Who are you and what do you do here?"

"All in good time. You have stepped into a complicated situation, but I am increasingly sure that it will deliver to you what you are looking for."

The man seemed to enjoy wrapping himself in an air of mystery. Logan fought down his irritation. If this "complicated situation" could work for him, he could be patient. "I am looking," he told the German, "for myself. And for whoever stole my life from me. Can you deliver that?"

"Yes, I think so," von Strucker said. "Give me a little time to make some inquiries. It may turn out that you were right when you said we could be allies."

○———————○

THE baron met the Yemeni in the planning room. The visitor was studying the tabletop model, one slippered foot tapping impatiently. "Well," the client said, "what have you to tell me? And it had better be good news."

"It is very good news," von Strucker said. "We can carry out the operation."

"And the odds of success?"

"Virtually certain."

"God willing," the Yemeni added.

"Of course," said the baron.

The visitor narrowed his eyes in suspicion. "What has changed? Last week, you were not at all confident."

The Prussian smiled. "Last week, I did not have the perfect weapon. Please return to your superiors and tell them that I will need a local staging area for the operation. A large house, walled and secure, at a reasonable traveling distance from the target."

"There are many such in the Mansour district," the Yemeni said. "Those who grew rich under the Beast of Tikrit have fled to other countries now that the Armies of God are reclaiming Iraq for the true faith. Their mansions stand empty."

"Then let us have one readied." The Prussian clicked his heels and inclined his head. "Now, if you will excuse me, I must tend to our new weapon."

○———————○

WHEN the German asked him what he remembered of Höllenfeuer, Logan said, "Nothing. Flashes of disconnected images. Faces, voices, flames, screams, a bad stink."

"Hmm," von Strucker said, nodding as if Logan's words had confirmed his expectations. "And what do you recall of your more recent life?"

"It's as if it only started a few months ago."

"Tell me about that."

They were seated in what looked to Logan like a well-equipped infirmary. The place had an X-ray machine and full-body scanners, lab benches with computerized equipment he couldn't even begin to identify.

Through the glass panels in two swinging doors on the far side of the big room he had glimpsed an operating room.

The sights and smells of the place put him a little on edge. But, as always, when he reached for a reason why they should have this effect on him, he found himself grasping at fog. He concentrated on what he knew for sure, telling the German of his life in the condo in Ottawa, of the monthly delivery of funds and whiskey.

The baron stopped him. "The whiskey comes to you? You do not buy your own?"

"There's no need."

"And you never feel an urge to drink something different? Another brand."

"No," Logan said, and even as he said it he felt a twinge of anxiety.

The German was watching him closely. "The idea of drinking another kind of whiskey disturbs you, *ja*?"

"Yes. I never realized that until now. How come?"

But the other man just pulled at his chin and said, "Hmm."

Anger flashed through Logan and his forearm muscles tensed. But he fought it down. "What does it mean?" he said.

"It probably means," von Strucker said, "that your mind has been attacked by powerful psychoactive drugs. Whoever has done this has chemically carved out a small part of your psyche. It's the part that you know of as 'just Logan,' the part that's talking to me now. The rest of you is shielded, as if they've built a dungeon inside your own brain and locked most of you inside it. All your memories. Your true identity."

"Why?" Logan wanted to know. Then he said, "No, more important is who?"

The baron held out his palms like a barrier. "Let us come to that in a moment. The important part right now is not why or who, but how." He leaned toward Logan. "They have to keep administering a steady maintenance dose of the memory suppressant. They do so by putting it in the whiskey. Then they condition you to want to drink nothing else."

The moment he said it, it was obvious to Logan—as if it were something he had been seeing constantly from the corner of his eye but somehow at which he had never turned to look directly. "That makes sense," he said.

"We can probably reverse the effects," von Strucker said, "though first we have to identify exactly which drugs, and in what combination and strengths, have been applied to you."

"You can do that?"

"Probably," said the baron. Then, in a self-chiding tone, he added, "No, I am too cautious, always the scientist. I will say, almost certainly."

Logan felt a fierce elation go through him, but it was followed immediately by a sense of caution. He noted the reaction and thought, *So I'm not a guy who believes in the tooth fairy.* Aloud, he said, "And what's in it for you?"

The German turned his cold hard eyes toward him and said, "The same as for you. Revenge."

"Against who?"

But the other man backed off. "You said on the plane that we might be allies. I do not know if that is so. But it is possible that we have the same enemy."

"Who?" Logan had wanted to hear more, but the German held him off. "Premature," von Strucker said, "until we know exactly what has been done to you and how."

Logan could feel the anger building in him. "Don't play games with me. Why is it premature?"

"Because you might be just what you seem. Or you might be a weapon sent against me."

"What kind of weapon?"

"The kind that's programmed to go off at a preset time, or if someone says the right word."

Logan did not think there was any truth in von Strucker's supposition, and yet he couldn't say for sure that the man's concern was groundless. "So what do we do?" he said.

The baron rose and opened a white-doored cupboard, taking out sterile equipment wrapped in cellophane. "We start by taking some blood and seeing what it contains," he said. "I'm afraid I'll need a lot of blood. The drugs we're looking for come in nano-doses."

Logan rolled up a sleeve and bared the crook of an elbow. "All right," he said, "but tell me about Höllenfeuer."

VON Strucker had worked out what he meant to tell the strange little man about the camp. It was a nice mixture of fact and fancy, with a good twist that would deliver to the mutant what he wanted to hear.

"Höllenfeuer was no ordinary concentration camp. It was a real camp, but it was set up to disguise an ultrasecret operation under the personal direction of Heinrich Himmler's Office of Special Projects—the group they called the Red Skull SS. Its goal was to find human mutations that could be developed into supersoldiers."

"Mutations?" the small man said. "You mean freaks?"

"No, I do not mean freaks," said the baron, wrapping a rubber tourniquet around Logan's bicep and tapping the vein in the elbow to make it stand out. He positioned a needle-sharp canula and slid it into the blood vessel. "I mean people who have useful genetic anomalies. People like you. And people like me."

He saw the other man's pupils contract, a micro-movement that would have been imperceptible to most observers, but was plain to the Prussian's trained perceptions. "You don't believe me?" he said.

"I'm not a freak," Logan said.

"Then how do you explain this?" von Strucker said. He withdrew the heavy needle from the man's vein. Immediately the puncture closed. In a moment there was no sign of a wound.

"What did you do?"

"I did nothing," the baron said. "Watch." He took a scalpel from a sealed package and made to set its point to the back of Logan's forearm.

"Hold it!" Logan said, drawing back his arm.

"It will be no more than a scratch," von Strucker said, "and it will heal within moments."

Logan extended his arm again. The scalpel's tip drew a red line, beaded with blood, through the dark hairs. The scratch disappeared almost as quickly as it had formed.

"Now watch this," von Strucker said. He bared one arm and performed the same operation on his own flesh. His wound also disappeared, though not quite as quickly as the other man's.

"Some kind of trick," Logan said. "That scalpel is a movie prop."

"No trick." The baron handed him the scalpel. "Try it yourself."

The man did so, and von Strucker saw his consternation as the wound healed instantly. "This is why they have interfered with your mind, kept you in storage in Ottawa," the Prussian said. "The people who use you as a weapon do not want you to know what you are. They have probably sent you to do terrible things, things you would find it difficult to live with if you remembered them."

He watched the subject's pupils expand and contract, a tiny flicker of movement, and knew that such was at least a subconscious fear of this man.

"It was the same sixty-three years ago in Höllenfeuer," the baron said, then paused for effect before adding, "except for the one big difference between you and me."

The man looked up. "What's that?"

"I escaped from the camp, to become my own weapon. Apparently, you stayed on to continue being theirs."

o————————o

IT was a lot to take in. Logan lay on his bunk in the room the baron had assigned him and thought about it. Some of it made instant sense—the idea of drugs in the whiskey, for example. He was sure his mind had been interfered with. His amnesia was not natural. Now he understood the little rush of anxiety that went through him when he thought about drinking any other liquor than Seven Crown. Or the stronger surge he felt when he made a fist.

I'm a killer, he thought, *an assassin*. He said the words to himself in the privacy of his mind and waited for a reaction. Nothing much happened. He imagined killing some stranger, doing it with a knife or with his bare hands. Again, nothing much stirred inside him. *How many must I have killed*, he wondered, *to be able to contemplate murder as if it were no more than a trip to the corner store?*

He could even accept that he was a mutant. The way he instantly healed was proof that he was seriously different from the rest of humanity. He doubted it was an ability that could be instilled as the result of drugs or mind control. The German had shown him the same ability.

"Mutants are rare," von Strucker had said, "but they do occur. In the camp, there was a boy who could make himself invisible and a girl who could send her mind traveling back through time."

He had described the one they called Al Borak as another mutant, though different from him and Logan. The Pashtun's nervous system contained powerful natural capacitors that could generate intense electrical shocks discharged from his hands. It was how they had subdued Logan in Berlin.

But what about the rest of the baron's story? That, after the war, the Nazi experimenters had built a shadowy international organization, offering mutant intelligence agents and assassins to any government or corporation that paid their exorbitant fees? That Logan was one of those operatives, but had somehow broken through his conditioning, at least enough to set out on a quest for his true identity?

It almost rang true. Yet when Logan thought about Nazis, thought about doing their bidding, killing for them, something deep inside him snarled a refusal. He had said as much to the baron, only to be met with another shrug.

"Of course you hate them," von Strucker had said. "Of course you wouldn't work for the swine. So they edit your thoughts for you, make you think that you're on the side of truth and justice."

They had been struggling to get blood out of Logan's veins. Even with the largest canula, the blood tended to clot in the tube almost as soon as it began to flow. The baron had had to inject Logan with large quantities of an anticoagulant to keep the red liquid flowing.

"You know already that your memories have been stolen," von Strucker had continued. "You suspect that some of your thoughts are not your own. What kind of people would do that to you?"

"Maybe you're right," Logan had answered. "Whoever I've been working for, it hasn't been the Boy Scouts. But Nazis?" He made a sound of disgust.

Again, the shrug. "Well, they're not Nazis anymore, are they? Now they're just businessmen, selling your services for whatever the market will bear."

Anger swelled in Logan, and he knew it was coming out of his true core. "Then putting me back in the warehouse until another customer comes through the door," he said.

"Except now you've broken out of the warehouse. Now you're in business for yourself."

"And you know who these people are? The ones who have been using me?"

"I think so," said the German. "As I say, I need to make some inquiries. I would not want to point you at some innocent parties."

"Are there any innocent parties anymore?" Logan asked.

Again, von Strucker had only shrugged.

○————————————○

ALONE in his secure room, von Strucker poured the mutant's blood from its clear plastic collecting bag into several test tubes and arranged them in the slots of the centrifuge. He activated the machine and waited as it whirred. When it was finished he drained off the unneeded blood components, storing them in a graduated cylinder for later study, then decanted the precious remainder into a sterile flask. He lifted the vessel and examined the cloudy fluid within. It held five times as much as his monthly injection.

"And now," he said to the empty room, "it requires a test." Moments later he was striding through the concrete hallways toward the section where the lowest-ranking members of the facility's staff had their barracks. From the doorway of the open dormitories he saw several off-duty porters, janitors, and kitchen workers sprawled on their bunks reading magazines or seated at tables, hunched over their perpetual games of backgammon. When he stepped unannounced into their midst, they sprang to their feet, scattering their diversions in all directions.

The baron pointed to a pop-eyed man whose face was disfigured by acne, and said, "Come." Then he spun on his heel and led the way to the main laboratory.

"Sit there," he said, indicating a stool, "and roll up your sleeve."

Trembling, the man did as he was told. The baron tied off the underling's upper arm with a rubber hose. When he produced a hypodermic, the man made a bleating noise.

"This will not harm you," von Strucker, filling the syringe from the tube of elixir.

The man rolled his protruding eyeballs and looked as if he wanted to do nothing so much as run, but the baron could see that fear of punishment would keep him seated on the stool. He swabbed off the subject's inner elbow and inserted the needle's tip into the prominent vein. Then he depressed the plunger, removed the spike—and waited.

He did not have to wait long. The bead of blood that had leaked out the moment he removed the hypodermic grew no larger. The baron wiped it away with a swab. The skin beneath showed no sign of a puncture.

"Give me your hand," he said, and when the man did as he was told von Strucker gripped his hand, took up a scalpel, and sliced into one fingertip. Blood spurted and the man cried out in pain, but in moments the bleeding stopped. Even as the Prussian watched, the wound healed, leaving only the thinnest scar.

The baron let the hand go. The man brought his finger before his eyes, rubbing away the blood with his thumb and staring in wonder at the undamaged flesh.

The Prussian brought a small-caliber pistol from the side pocket of his breeches. The man on the stool had only enough time to shriek in terror before von Strucker fired a bullet into his chest. The impact knocked the subject sprawling on the tiled floor. His eyes blinked once, then his gaze lost cohesion. His chest heaved, then was still.

The baron leaned over the dead man. He tore open the shirt, sending buttons flying, to see the hole where the round had penetrated his flesh. The wound bled sluggishly, as always happened once the heart stopped beating and gravity began to rule the circulation system. As von Strucker watched, the bleeding suddenly freshened. The chest filled again with air and the man breathed once more. Now he saw that the wound was filling itself in. A few seconds later, the healing flesh actually forced the slug out of the man's body.

The Prussian caught the bullet as it came clear of the man's recovered body. He looked at the smooth metal object and smiled. The man was sitting up, poking at his chest in wonder, joy and relief plain in his eyes.

"What is your name?" von Strucker said.

"Achmed, master," was the answer.

"Well, Achmed," said the baron, "I have good news and bad news for you. The good news is that your acne is clearing up. The bad news is that you have lost your job."

He stepped outside the lab and summoned a security detail. "Arrest the man inside," he said. "Bind and gag him. Drive him a hundred kilometers out into the desert, dig a hole—a deep hole, mind you—and bury him alive." As the guards set to work, he added, "Do not speak of this to anyone, or you will join him."

Then, as the guards dragged the squirming Achmed away, he called after them. "Mark the spot." It would be interesting to see if the man was still alive in a couple of weeks.

In the meantime, he refilled the syringe with elixir, though half the amount that he had given Achmed. That time the recovery had been too fast. When the needle was filled, he left it on the lab bench and went in search of a second test subject.

o———o

THE gray-eyed Pashtun they called Al Borak had begun life as the child of peasant farmers in a hill-country village in southern Afghanistan's remote Helmand province during the war against Soviet occupation. While he was still an infant, his parents and most of the rest of his village had died in an attack by the Red Army. The Russians had learned that a party of mujahideen were sheltering in the community overnight, after going over the border into Pakistan to collect arms and ammunition from the American CIA.

In the hours before dawn, when all were sleeping, a squadron of Hind assault helicopters had swept in out of the darkness, their rockets and cannons ripping apart the mud-brick houses. As the gunships came back around for a second pass, a missile struck a box of antitank mines. The resulting explosion leveled most of the village, but a corner of Al Borak's house remained standing, and in that corner rescuers later found him in his cradle, sheltered from the collapsing roof by a heavy pole that had fallen against the still-standing piece of wall.

His name then had been Batoor, the Pashto word for "brave," and he would have needed all the courage he could have summoned to survive as an orphan growing up in a country mostly destroyed by military invasion, civil war, and religious revolution. It helped that, as a toddler, he began to demonstrate the peculiar things he could do with his hands—like shocking senseless an older boy who tried to steal his rice cake.

From that day, the other orphans—and their keepers—stepped carefully around the strange little boy with the light-colored eyes. There were whispers about him—that he was possessed by a demon, that his mother had lain with a devil. He was sent to sleep alone in an outbuilding that had a leaky roof. But Batoor was hardy. And he was lucky. When he was eight, a European had come through the town where the orphanage was, a blue-eyed man who said he was a doctor. The man was looking for unusual children, those who did not easily fit within deeply conservative cultures, where the strange were feared and unwanted. Orphanages were a good place to find them.

The orphanage director gladly produced Batoor. Money swiftly changed hands, a document was signed, and the child departed in the infidel's Land Rover. Life immediately got much better for Batoor—good food, a warm place to sleep, medical care when he needed it. He exchanged his Pashto name for an Arabic nickname, Al Borak—the Lightning. Now, fifteen years later, he had grown to become his deliverer's most faithful follower. He had done all that had been asked of him, and more. He was willing to do all that might be asked of him in the future.

But Al Borak was worried. In the days that followed their return from Germany, von Strucker had spent much of his time closeted with the small man. Medical technicians had pulled extra duty running batteries of tests and conducting scans. When Al Borak had sought out the baron to report on the progress of training for Operation Severed Head, the Prussian had brushed him off, eager to get back to his new fascination.

Perhaps von Strucker had found a new favorite. Batoor had seen times when the man would return from one of his mutant-hunting trips with some new prospect. A flurry of tests would follow, high hopes leading to dashed expectations, and the newcomer would be assigned to menial duties or, more often, would quietly disappear.

But this new prospect was no oddball child or teenager from a third-world orphanage. This was a grown man and it was clear to the leader of the Green Fist that there was a history between him and the baron—a history that von Strucker was keeping to himself.

Though preparations for Operation Severed Head continued, to Al Borak's eyes, the problem with the planned assault had not changed. The mission was still suicide and its chances of success were still effectively zero. Yet von Strucker seemed well content with the progress of the training drills, when he bothered to listen to Al Borak's reports.

Lying in his bunk in his private room, staring at the posters and photographs of Bollywood film stars that decorated the walls, the man who had once been the despised orphan Batoor worried and wondered. Had von Strucker found what he had been seeking all these years? Had the

Green Fist and all its predecessors been merely steps toward a goal that the baron now saw as within his grasp?

Did that mean that Al Borak and his men were about to be thrown away in a pointless death charge against an impregnable position? A convenient way of wiping the board clean so that the Prussian could begin a whole new game, with all new pieces?

Al Borak stared unseeing at the image of a smiling plump Indian actress in a flowered sari while blue sparks rippled across the backs of his fingers.

WOLFGANG Freiherr von Strucker had a decision to make. The medical examination of Logan had brought a shock. The routine bloodwork was under way and the man's DNA was being sequenced—von Strucker was sure there would be something interesting in the X chromosome. They had come to the stage in the series of tests when a full scan by the magnetic resonance imager would have been appropriate. But the moment the subject was broached, the Prussian had seen an almost instinctive alarm register in the man's eyes.

"You have a problem with the MRI?" he said.

"I think so," Logan said. "I don't know why, but something in me says that's a bad idea."

A cold wave of fear rose in the baron. The man had been cooperative up until now. Suddenly, he seemed to have something to hide. The Prussian wondered, had someone slipped a living bomb past his defenses? Von Strucker had made enemies, some of them as intelligent as they were ruthless. Could one of them have put together the right clues from his decades-long search for the man from Höllenfeuer, then manufactured a cunning replica with a few kilos of explosives tucked away in its chest cavity? Is that why the man was so surprisingly heavy?

Paranoia, he told himself. *This is the same man I knew in 1944. The speed with which he heals is proof enough*. But then another thought came. Someone else had clearly found this Logan and put him to work, erasing his memories to make him more manageable. Perhaps his handlers had hired him out to some enemy of the baron's, his job to take out von Strucker.

For decades, the Prussian had sought the man he had once had nailed to a table. His desire to find Logan was a vulnerability, and he would be most vulnerable at the moment he achieved his desire. He was reminded of the old wisdom about being careful what you wished for, because you just might get it. *Or it just might get you,* he thought.

But he rejected the idea. If Logan had been sent to kill him, he had already had plenty of time to do it. His reluctance to enter the MRI chamber must come from some other cause.

"Let us take an X-ray," von Strucker said. Minutes later, in the X-ray suite's control center, as the first plate came out of the chemical bath, he said, "*Grösse Gott,* what have they done to his bones?"

"They are sheathed in metal," the technician said. Even the tiny hyoid bone in his throat was coated in a dense metallic substance that bounced X-rays like steel.

"No wonder he weighs so much," the baron said. "He must be carrying an extra thirty kilos."

"Look at this," the technician said, securing a new image to the light board. "There's a great deal more of the stuff in his forearms. It's as if they've inserted a bundle of rods in there, like reinforcing concrete."

"What is it, steel?"

"Something harder, judging from the X-ray reflection. We'd have to drill into it to get a sample for analysis. But it's a good thing we didn't put him in the MRI. It could have torn him apart."

The baron studied the image. "Obviously, he has been rebuilt for unarmed combat. With those arms he could defend himself from any kind of blow," he said. "And he could probably batter down a brick wall."

He rubbed his chin. One thing was clear: his original plan—to get more marrow out of the subject and culture it for permanent production of elixir—had just struck a formidable obstacle.

On the other hand, someone had gone to a great deal of trouble to turn the little man from Höllenfeuer into a devastating weapon. The baron had uses for such an unstoppable killing machine. The question was: Could he control it?

Whoever had been working with the subject had access to first-level psychoactive drugs and biotechnology that could permanently graft metal to bone throughout an entire skeleton. The baron was no slouch at biotech, but he could only vaguely imagine how the metal—*could it be adamantium?* he thought—had been seamlessly attached to living bone. He also had a good grasp of the kinds of drugs that could separate a man from his memories without rendering him insane or incompetent. He suspected that Logan's handlers had mixed a delicate blend of neurochemicals into a precisely targeted cocktail. *Probably arriving at the right formula only after extensive trial and error,* he thought.

Yet however expert those mysterious psychopharmacists might be, their creation had clearly slipped their chemical leash. If he ever found out who had been using him, von Strucker had no doubt that nothing would deter Logan from getting at them. He was like an unstoppable vengeance-seeking missile that was quite capable of curving in flight and arrowing back to the people who had launched it. And his impact would bring them annihilation.

That brought him back to the question that must be decided: How to play the mutant to gain what the baron wanted—then how to dispose of him.

The intercom on the wall buzzed and von Strucker slapped its control. "I said I was not to be disturbed."

"It is Al Borak," said his second in command's voice. "I would like to talk to you."

"Some other time," the baron said, and pushed the button that broke the connection.

○────────────○

LOGAN had free range of the facility, except for the operational planning room. "That is on a need-to-know basis," von Strucker had told him. "I must run a secure establishment or see my clients desert me."

"Just who are your clients?"

"If we end up working together, you will be told. At this point, I can only give you categories. I offer my services to corporations, national governments, and some nongovernmental organizations."

"And the nature of those services?"

"High-end security contracting. Let us say I specialize in threat assessment and threat reduction."

"You're a mercenary," Logan said. He noticed that the thought caused him no concern. Apparently, he inhabited a world in which soldiers of fortune were part of the scenery.

"But a choosy one," von Strucker said. "I do not work for just anyone."

And that was as much as the German would divulge. "But feel free to look around," he said. "We do research, training, and operational planning. I believe you will find a clean, well-run facility. No dungeons, no torture chambers, no mass graves."

Logan had been given a plastic visitor's badge with a data strip programmed to open doors as he approached them. He hung it on a lanyard around his neck and went everywhere. *Know your operating environment*, said a voice from the back of his mind. *Surprises can be deadly.*

The place was big, the equivalent of a spacious ten-story building set underground, with self-contained water and waste systems drawing from deep aquifers left over from the end of the last ice age, twelve thousand years ago, when this arid land had been rich in lakes and rivers. It was also self-sufficient for power, drawing electricity from geothermal heat exchangers spread out over miles of desert. The differential between the baking days and freezing nights at the surface, contrasted with the permanent temperature in the mid-fifties Fahrenheit just ten feet below ground, provided ample generating capacity.

One level down from the barracks and the well-stocked armory he found the training area. In an immense room big enough to contain a mocked-up residential street, he watched a squad of fatigue-clad men practice urban warfare. While weapons teams laid down suppressing fire from two well-placed machine guns, four pairs of riflemen went down an alley using the time-honored "shoot and scoot" tactic—one man firing, while his partner went forward to the next opportunity for cover, then fired as his partner leapfrogged forward.

It was professionally done, Logan thought, and realized that he could make the judgment because he knew the difference between real soldiering and amateurism. As he heard the crackle of weapons fire and the impact of live rounds hitting targets that popped up in windows and doorways, the smell of cordite biting into his sinuses, images came to the inner screen of his mind: racing across rocky terrain, the flash from a machine gun muzzle aimed his way; chips flying from whitewashed brick and the whine of steel-jacket rounds ricocheting away; a bayonet point lancing toward his eyes, behind it a face under a helmet, teeth bared.

I've been a soldier, he said. *I've fought in wars.* He was coming to accept that he was an old man who had somehow never aged. He must have had twice or three times the experiences of normal men—for all he knew, he might be not just decades, but centuries old—and all of that had been stolen from him. The anger came up in him again and he clenched his fists and forearms. With the reflex came again the anxiety, as if he had come in darkness to the edge of a great precipice and dared not take another step lest he fall into... *into what?* he thought. *Why have they made me afraid of my own rage? What is the secret they are keeping from me?*

The training exercise was wrapping up, the men returning to the starting point. They seemed to be preparing to conduct the alley assault again, though to Logan's eyes the first run had looked flawless. But now he saw that the squad leader was distributing a pair of pills to each man. They washed them down with water from their canteens, then resumed their jump-off positions.

The leader's whistle blew, the machine guns opened up, and the two-man teams went down the alley again. This time, however, an assault that had taken almost two minutes the first time was over in less than thirty seconds. The men moved with limb-blurring speed, but their bullets went to the targets with no loss of accuracy. To Logan, it looked like a speeded-up film. He remembered the struggle in the darkened room in Berlin, how his captors had seemed to come at him with superhuman speed. Now he understood.

When it was over, the men formed up and marched off, singing in Arabic. They looked happy in their work, Logan thought, then checked himself as he realized there was an exception—their leader, the tall light-eyed one, sent him a parting look that left no doubt of the man's hostility.

o————————o

VON Strucker wanted to sing, wanted to dance, maybe throw his hat in the air like a schoolboy. But he had learned early the value of maintaining an image of dignity, even when he was alone. So he simply removed his monocle, polished it on a handkerchief, and reset it before his eye. Then he once more read through the results of the DNA analysis while the joy bubbled up in him again.

The mutation was definitely confined to the X chromosome. More important, it was not a particularly complex change—just a different arrangement of the four component nucleotides, like scrambling the letters of a word to produce an anagram. The best part was that the immortality gene was a prime candidate for being extracted and spliced onto a different biological platform. In a matter of months, von Strucker could have a barn full of transgenetic pigs or rats whose marrow would produce Logan's blood indefinitely.

That meant he did not need Logan. Or at least he would not need him once Operation Severed Head had been successfully carried out, as now it surely would be. All he needed was a few more pints of blood from which to filter the cells that would allow the men of the Green Fist to share temporarily the mutant's ability to recover from wounds that should have been fatal.

With Operation Severed Head safely behind him, he could ease out of the assassination business. He would command the funds to build a new facility, in some more livable region of the world, dedicated to producing the elixir in substantial amounts. The planet was increasingly populated by multibillionaires, all of whom would pay whatever it cost to enjoy their wealth through eternity. Other customers might lack wealth but could pay von Strucker in the equally valuable coin called power. And when he had acquired enough of both, the baron would quietly and discreetly rule the world.

He locked the analysis away in the safe in his hidden room. No one but von Strucker had had access to the gene-sequencing lab during the time it had taken to conduct the analysis. No one else knew the secret of Logan's blood, and he meant to keep it that way.

To calm himself, he filled his lungs, then permitted himself one long and shivery exhalation. Then he went to the intercom and called Al Borak. "Meet me in the planning room immediately," he said. "It is time to finalize Operation Severed Head."

"I'll be there," his second in command said.

LOGAN had almost made up his mind about von Strucker. He was certain the German had never been his friend, and he wasn't entirely sure that they hadn't been enemies, back in the long ago. The man's tale about their both having been inmates of a secret Nazi camp for mutants rang both true and false—like hearing an almost familiar song played on a piano that had a couple of notes that were out of tune.

Besides, the more time he spent in the man's vicinity, the more something stirred down deep in the blocked-off parts of his mind. Maybe it was something as primal as the way the baron smelled—Logan had heard somewhere that odor could be the most powerful trigger for forgotten memories. And the German's odor of carbolic soap and laboratory chemicals was making some buried part of Logan cock its ears and bare its fangs.

He had seen all there was to see of the facility. It looked to be what von Strucker had said, a research and training operation for a high-end mercenary outfit. Some of its clients were "nongovernmental organizations," the German had said—that could be anything from the Red Cross to the Old Man of the Mountain. Logan wasn't sure if he himself was the kind of assassin who drew moral lines—if he worked for ex-Nazis, he probably didn't. If von Strucker had fled rather than work for those same Nazis, he might even turn out to be more ethically choosy than Logan.

But somehow that doesn't smell right, does it? Logan doubted that he himself was any kind of Boy Scout. Yet there was a whiff of something about the baron that told him the German was the kind of man who could give nightmares to the world's hard-asses.

He was in the base's main cafeteria, seated at a table by himself. The menu leaned heavily toward Middle Eastern cuisine—rice, lentils, couscous, beef, and lamb, all served with fiery and pungent sauces—but none of it seemed completely foreign to Logan. *If I'm an assassin, I probably travel a lot*, he thought. *Got to go where the work is.*

The men he had watched at the assault exercise were eating at a table on the far side of the big room. He couldn't understand the Arabic, but the way they talked and laughed among themselves said that they were a well-knit unit. *Buddies*, he thought, *guys who know they can trust each other.*

The thought called up an echo of a memory. He reached for it, and this time it did not immediately disappear. He remembered squatting with his back against a wall, eating from a mess tin. A face swam up from below, laughing. Red hair and green eyes, tough but good-humored. *Rob Roy*, Logan thought. *My friend*. And then the image was fading.

But it was good, he told himself. That had been genuine recall.

Whatever had been done to him—the baron's talk about psychoactive chemicals rang true—it was wearing off. At least a little.

Suddenly Logan needed more. He needed to see more faces he recognized, places he had been, moments that had been his before he had been robbed of them. The German had been taking regular supplies of blood—*he must have three quarts by now*—while telling him that the business of isolating the combination of drugs in trace amounts was delicate and time-consuming.

But someone had consumed all of Logan's time, everything except the last few weeks of his life, and he wanted to know who and why. And as the German had said, the first question that had to be answered was "how?" Logan decided he had waited long enough for that answer.

He got up, the food forgotten, and made for the door.

○————————○

AL Borak walked the corridor to the operations planning center and tapped the entry code into the pad beside the heavy metal door. As it slid open with a sound like compressed air being released, a voice from behind him called, "Hey!" He turned to see the baron's new fascination coming his way from the direction of the elevator bank.

"Your security people told me that von Strucker is down here," the small man said, heading for the open door.

"Not for you," Al Borak said. He knew his English was poor, so he reinforced the message by putting a hand against the man's chest.

"That's not a good idea," Logan said. His own hand came up and took a grip on Al Borak's thumb, then he twisted. Suddenly the bones of the Pashtun's wrist were strained almost to the breaking point.

Al Borak let loose a string of Pashto words that touched upon the man's parentage, personal hygiene, and the least valuable types of goats. At the same time, he reflexively sent a jolt of electricity from his palm into Logan's hand.

Now it was the small man's turn to swear inventively, as his grip involuntarily loosened. He took a step back, shaking his shocked arm and giving the Pashtun a thoughtful look through narrowed eyes. Then he said, "Okay, let's see how this works out," and took a step forward.

"Yes," Al Borak said, "we see." Even as he spoke, he was setting his feet and summoning the strange feeling that since boyhood he had called "the spirit of the clouds." He felt the energy rising and crackling through his whole body. He raised his hands and blue plasma wreathed his palms and fingers.

"Stop this!" shouted von Strucker, stepping through the door and putting himself between them. The Pashtun had to lower his hands and step back to avoid an accidental discharge into the baron.

"What is the meaning of this?" the Prussian said, first in English to Logan, then in Arabic to the tall man.

"I need to talk to you," the Canadian said. At the same time, Al Borak was saying in Arabic, "This offspring of a incontinent dog and a diseased she-goat tried to force his way where he is not wanted."

Logan couldn't have known what the Pashtun was saying, yet he had clearly gotten the gist of it. His small, glittering eyes locked onto Al Borak's and he growled—to the tall man, it sounded like a real animal's snarl—and said, "Anytime, pal."

The baron was still between them, his hands raised to keep them apart. "I said, stop this!" he said. "Why are you fighting?"

The question was addressed to both of them. The small man just shrugged. Al Borak began to speak, but then the other man raised his voice to drown him out. He was saying something in English to the baron, something about needing to know, being tired of waiting.

Al Borak spoke softly into the Prussian's ear, "You should let me take care of this one. He is a danger to us. A disruption."

"No," von Strucker snapped, in Arabic. "He is essential to my plans."

Al Borak subsided and said no more, but he had caught the difference between the words he had used and the baron's answer. The Pashtun had spoken of "us," but von Strucker had said "my plans"—and to the man who used to be Batoor, that small distinction revealed the existence of a great chasm, with him on one side and the man who had taken him from the orphanage on the other.

o————————o

THIS is all I need, von Strucker was thinking as he stood between the two mutants and sought to calm the situation. But then he told himself, *My need for these two is only temporary.* The thought brought an ironic smile that he made sure did not reach his lips. The truth was, he would not need either of these two volatile genetic freaks for more than another couple of days—only long enough to complete Operation Severed Head. After that, he would have no further requirements for mutants of any kind. He would surround himself only with normal human beings, and the only genetic qualities he would select for would be that the women would be beautiful and the men would know how to take orders and carry them out.

This vision of his future, soon to be achieved, gave von Strucker the tranquility of mind needed to pitch his voice calmly. "This is no time for emotional outbursts—" he began.

Logan cut him off. "You got the operative words—'no time.' I'm tired of spinning my wheels. You've had plenty of my blood. What's the verdict on the drugs? And what about an antidote?"

"We are almost there," von Strucker assured him. "It takes time for the active ingredients to precipitate out of the blood. They have to form as tiny crystals on an inert medium. Do you understand?"

He saw the mutant frown. Of course the man didn't understand, because there was nothing to be understood. The whole business about identifying the psychoactive drugs had been just a tale to keep him tranquil while the Prussian got enough blood to treat the assault squad for Operation Severed Head, and while he decided what to do with Logan afterward. Von Strucker had enough blood now, and the elixir had been distilled, but he thought it wouldn't hurt to take just a little more. Better to have a back-up he didn't need than to lack one when he needed it.

"As a matter of fact," he told Logan, "I'd like to take one more sample then put the results in front of a colleague of mine. He's more knowledgeable about neurochemistry than I am, and I think he could give us the definitive answer."

He saw Logan studying him from under frowning brows. Even in his good mood, the baron found the man's gaze to be unsettling. It was like locking eyes with a wild beast in a zoo, except that here no bars separated them. The mutant was dangerous, becoming more so as the memory suppressants apparently lost effect. Von Strucker would be glad to be rid of Logan, as soon as he had served his purpose.

"Okay," Logan said. "One more. But that's it. When does this expert get here?"

"He doesn't," the baron said. "We'll have to go and see him."

○━━━━━━━○

THE man's too smooth, Logan was thinking. There was nothing he could put his finger on, but he was becoming increasingly sure that he and the German were not destined to be allies. *He smells wrong.*

As he stared into the man's eyes, smelling his pervasive odor of harsh soap, something was stirring again in the sealed rooms of his mind, where his memories lay hidden. He resisted the urge to grab at the trace. Instead, he let a long, slow intake of breath filter through his nose, allowing that distinctive chemically smell to dominate his senses, to call up whatever it was linked to in the fog that he could not penetrate.

An image came: the German's face looming over him, looking down at him with clinical detachment. There were emotions attached to the image—rage, frustration, hate—and a sense-memory of being pinned down, like a laboratory animal on a dissecting table. Logan felt the echo of a deep ache in his wrists and elbows, his ankles and knees.

By a mental effort, he held his mind back from lunging at these faint wisps of substance in the general fog. He let them swirl past him while, mentally, he stood still and watched.

"What is going on with you?" the German asked. "Are you recovering memories?"

Logan did not answer. He closed his eyes and paid no attention to the distraction of the man's voice, willing his mind to think of nothing, to stand passively while his memories came stealing toward him like timid ghosts.

Here was the German's face again, looking down at him, light flashing from his monocle. Another man peered over his shoulder, fleshy faced, his skin a scrubbed pink. *These are real memories*, Logan thought. He let the image solidify, saw that the other man wore a military cap with a badge on its front: a stylized eagle, wings spread and claws grasping a circled swastika. And below that emblem was another, a skull against crossed bones. And the skull was enameled in red.

So some of what the German had said was true, Logan now knew. He had been a captive of the Red Skull SS. But now the scope of the mental image expanded a little more. He saw, on the pink-skinned man's gray tunic, square black collar tabs with SS runes on one side; on the other, four diamonds were worked in silver thread. It was then that he noticed that around von Strucker's neck was the same kind of collar, the same runes, but with a double oak leaf instead of diamonds.

"Logan!" von Strucker's voice was harsh, insistent. "What is happening to you?"

Logan's eyes had been closed no more than a few seconds. Now he opened them and saw the baron staring at him with exactly the same expression as in the memory, like a scientist examining an interesting specimen. And over his shoulder, the face of the tall Pashtun was filled with anger and suspicion.

"I'm fine," he told von Strucker. "A little dizziness, probably from the shock your friend gave me." He turned his gaze to the gray-eyed man. "We should try each other out some time. Could be interesting."

The Pashtun met his eyes and said something back that Logan understood even though he knew none of the words. The tall man's hostility didn't bother him, he noticed. That told him something else about the kind of man he was: *I don't have a crying need to be liked by everybody I meet.*

He turned his attention back to the German. "When do we leave?"

AL Borak spent a busy hour making sure that the men of the Green Fist were properly outfitted for the first stage of the operation. Again, they would be pretending to be a soccer team owned by the son of one of the emirs whose principalities were combined in the United Arab Emirates. This time they would fly from Abu Dhabi across the Persian Gulf to Basra in Iraq. From there they would transfer to a convoy of ground vehicles that would take them north to the Mansour district of Baghdad, where everything needed for Operation Severed Head would be waiting.

The twenty mujahideen were happy to be making the trip. As they changed into the designer clothes and put on the personal jewelry that fitted their disguise as pampered playthings of a Middle Eastern potentate, their eyes shone and they kept flashing quick smiles at each other. "Paradise," Gassim whispered to Yussuf as he stuffed his travel bag with bright-colored shirts he would never wear.

"*Inshalla*," breathed Yussuf. If God wills it.

"You chatter like women on a shopping trip," Al Borak snapped. "*Imshi!*" Move it!

Two minutes later, the mujahideen were at attention in their barracks, their travel bags at their feet, open for inspection. Al Borak went methodically from one man to the next, distributing the forged passports and checking each detail. When they landed in Basra, they might be looked over by British security forces, and the British had no reputation for being lackadaisical.

But as he did his job, the Pashtun's mind was on other matters. Within him, a great sadness fought with an even greater anger. The baron had been like a second father to him. He had always thought that he and von Strucker would go on together, building an ever more powerful instrument until, in the fullness of time, he would inherit this business. Now he knew that would never be his future. All these years, the man he had looked up to had been looking for someone else. Now he had found him. And Batoor was, once again, to be orphaned.

A tear of mingled rage and sorrow came to his eye and he knuckled it away before any of the mujahideen might notice. Of course, they, too, were about to be thrown away, once their purpose was served. But, as von Strucker had said, that was what they were for. He had not realized that, to the cold-eyed Prussian, he was just as expendable.

He shook off the emotion. *Time to be practical*, he told himself. He had spent all of these years watching von Strucker, learning from him, modeling himself on his second father. So what would the baron do? The answer, when Al Borak thought about it, was obvious: von Strucker would betray those who trusted him in order to get what he wanted. Batoor, known as Al Borak, could do the same.

He swept his eyes over the Green Fist one final time, saw nothing out of place. He ordered them to make for the elevators that would carry them up to the hidden building's rooftop hangar. As he followed them out of the barracks, the plan leaped fully formed into his mind.

They were bound for Baghdad, where they would meet the man who represented their client. In Baghdad, Al Borak would find an opportunity to have a private word with the Yemeni fanatic. He knew how to speak the language of the faithful, knew how to plant a doubt about a blue-eyed infidel. The Yemeni's master, hidden away in his mountain fastness, was a man who prized certainty. Faced with a doubt, he would act swiftly and ruthlessly to remove it.

○━━━━━━━━━━○

THE baron carefully packed the vials of elixir into a small carrying case lined with cushioning foam rubber. He had taken a final pint of blood from the mutant, brought it to his secret room, and spun out the white blood cells that carried the immortality factor. Although it was days yet before he would require a new injection, he prepared a hypodermic and shot a dose of the fluid into his veins.

As the stuff entered his system, he felt a rush of vitality. *Purely psychosomatic*, he told himself. The elixir did not act as a direct stimulant to the central nervous system and the body's adrenal and paradrenal glands, like the formula he had created to speed up the Green Fist mujahideen. Still, after all these years, he had found the grail of endless life—who could blame him if the discovery filled him with joy?

He went into his sleeping chamber and changed into a sedate suit of lightweight gray cotton, with a white shirt and understated tie appropriate to the team doctor of an emir's soccer squad. His false passport and other documents were in the pockets, but he checked each thoroughly. Now was no time to be tripped up by some petty detail, when his life's ambition was within his grasp.

He went to the elevators and tapped the button for the floor that housed the communications center. As the car rose, he was surprised to find himself humming a tune he hadn't heard since his student days. *I must be careful*, he told himself. *The time to enjoy the feast is when the cooking's done.*

In the communications center, he dismissed the duty officer and his assistant. When they were gone, he activated the encryption logarithm that shielded his exchanges with the client, then typed and transmitted an urgent request through the satellite uplink.

The reply came moments later:

Confirm receipt of message. Will have the materials waiting at destination. What is their purpose?

The baron smiled and typed a response:

To confound our enemies.

Never tell a lie when the truth will serve just as well, he told himself and broke the uplink connection. He returned control of the communications center to its staff and went up to where the aircraft waited.

<hr>

THEY hadn't told Logan where they were going. "Need to know" was all the German would say. When Logan pressed for more information, von Strucker said, "I can tell you this much: I've been training a group of special forces troops for the government of a Middle Eastern country. Now I am going to deliver them.

"As it happens, the man I want to consult with about you is also in the region. We will meet him. He will look at your test results. It is very likely that he will be able to pinpoint the precise mix of drugs that have been used to hide your memories. If so, he can provide an antidote."

"And then what?" Logan said.

"Why, then we will know who you are and who has done this to you. We may even know why. Then you and I can have a talk about joining forces."

"Suppose I'm not interested?"

The baron spread his hands, palms up. "Then you will go on your way. But you will remember that I have helped you. You will owe me a favor. A great deal of what gets done in the world is on the basis of favors granted and repaid."

It all sounded plausible to Logan. He nodded and said, "Okay. We'll see how it goes."

But he had noticed that the German had a habit of watching him closely during their conversations. *Maybe that's part of his mutation*, he thought, *he can read people through their eyes, the way I seem to be able to smell stuff.* So he kept his eyes down.

Back in his room, he changed into the clothes they had laid out for him. His bogus passport was back in his room at the Mercure Hotel in Berlin, but they'd made him up a new one, along with other documents that identified him as a Canadian who worked for a soccer team in the United Arab Emirates. Apparently, that was part of the special forces outfit's cover story. They'd also put credit cards and a few hundred in U.S. currency in his wallet. He didn't put much stock in the generosity, though—what was given could always be taken away.

When he was ready to go, he paused a moment before leaving the room. His hand and arm still tingled a little from Al Borak's shock. He looked again at his fists, saw the tiny lines of scars between his knuckles. He accepted now that he healed completely. The scratch he had cut into his arm with von Strucker's scalpel was completely invisible, without even a hairline of scar tissue. *So why the scars on my hands?* he thought. *Have I done so much damage to them that they can't heal without marks?*

Something shifted in the deep sediments at the bottom of his mind. Immediately, he felt a jolt of anxiety. But now he had no doubt that somebody had planted that reaction in his mind, and he didn't give in to it right away. He continued to stare at his knotted fists, bunching the muscles of his forearms. It felt good, even though the artificially induced anxiety sent his heart rate pounding. It felt like something was going to happen, something real, something decisive.

The electric shocks help: the realization came to him all at once. They'd shocked him in Berlin to subdue him. Then, while he was coming to, he had seen a whirlwind of images shaken loose from behind the chemical barrier that divided his mind. And just a few minutes ago, when Al Borak had sent a jolt through him, the fog had cleared enough to give him a true image of von Strucker at Höllenfeuer.

The realization opened up a new option. If this mysterious expert that the German was taking him to see turned out to be a lie, Logan had found another way to crack the wall that separated him from his own life. *All I need to do is give El Zappo a backhander*, he thought, *to get him going*. He filed the thought away for future reference.

o———————o

THEY took the Gulfstream V again. To disguise their point of origin, they skimmed the desert into Yemen's air space, then rose with the mountains that divided that small country from Saudi Arabia. Soon they were headed north along the Arabian Peninsula's east coast, angling down to a private airstrip at Abu Dhabi. They refueled and took off again for Basra.

Von Strucker and Logan traveled in the plane's private compartment. Al Borak and the Green Fist were in the main cabin, the mujahideen singing songs and clapping their hands, the Pashtun sitting by himself in a rear seat, glowering at everything. The baron had noted the man's change in attitude. Clearly, Logan's arrival had upset Al Borak's picture of the world. He supposed he should deal with it, but he was ready to admit to himself that he had had enough of dealing with temperamental mutants. Perhaps when he gave the men the injections that were crucial to the success of Operation Severed Head, he would give the Pashtun a placebo. It would be one less loose end to tie up.

As he mulled his options, his hands absently stroked the carrying case that contained the elixir. He would not let it out of his sight until Operation Severed Head was behind him. Now he cast an occasional glance across the plane's center aisle to where the small Canadian reclined in his seat. Logan slept, or appeared to sleep, with his arms folded across his chest. Occasionally, the overdeveloped muscles of his forearms bulged as he unconsciously flexed them. The baron found the motion distasteful. It looked to him to be not like a human action, but more like the autonomic movements of a python digesting a baby pig.

No more mutants, von Strucker thought. He smiled. It would be a good life, living forever and ruling the world. And after all these years of hiding in a hole in the ground a thousand miles from anywhere, it was no less than he deserved.

○————————○

LOGAN kept his eyes closed but did not sleep. He was finding it increasingly easier to just let the memories come to him. They arrived in a flood now, though they made no coherent sense. He saw faces, streets, forests, and jungles, empty rooms and ferocious battlefields, square-bodied old cars and sleek modern automobiles, all jumbled together. It was as if everything were shaking loose, but coming at him in random order, with no system to organize the information.

But he wasn't worried. He'd decided he wasn't the kind who worried. *If you can do something about a problem, do it*, that familiar voice said from the back of his head. *If you can't do anything, wait until you can. Either way, worrying about it doesn't get anything done.*

From time to time he flexed the muscles of his forearms and noted how it always brought that same flash of fear. But he was now certain that the fear was not his, that it was a reaction that had somehow been planted in him. If he pushed it, it would break and he would step through to the other side. Only one thing kept him from doing so: the possibility that the mysterious "they" might have implanted something worse on that "other side"—maybe some self-destruct mechanism, built around a pound or two of plastic explosive wedged up against his backbone. Or maybe he would be launched into a preprogrammed berserker mode and mindlessly kill everyone around him. Whatever the outcome, the fear had been put there for a reason. He decided to walk carefully around it until he knew why.

Across the aisle, the German was humming a song to himself. It sounded to Logan like something you'd hear in a *bierkeller*, played by a band that would have to include a tuba. He wondered what was in von Strucker's head. Then he thought, *Not too long from now, I'm going to find out. Even if I have to crack it open to take a look.*

BASRA, IRAQ,

THE PRESENT

THINGS went smoothly after the Gulfstream touched down just after dark in a section of the city's airport that was under the control of a militia whose senior officers had been bribed to let slide the formalities of entering the country. The passengers transferred to a canvas-topped truck that made its way north through the city, convoyed with a pair of armored SUVs with tinted windows. The cars carried several rifle-toting militiamen whose fashion sense largely centered on wearing as much black as possible. They crossed the city on secondary roads, then when the outskirts gave way to desert, the vehicles swung away from the main highway onto a dirt road that wound through scattered villages.

The road had not been repaired in many years and the men sitting on the bench seats that ran along the inner sides of the truck were constantly bounced up and down by the endless ruts and potholes. Al Borak soon got tired of having his buttocks battered and stood up beside the raised rear gate, holding on to the steel frame that supported the canvas cover and letting his bent knees cushion the relentless jolts and impacts.

The baron was riding in the truck's cab along with the militia officer who would talk them through any Iraqi checkpoints—their route would avoid any U.S. or British forces, most of whom stayed buttoned up in their bases at night. The small infidel had climbed in with the Green Fist, though he had made no attempts to make friends. He ignored them as they ignored him, and sat on the end of one of the benches at the rear of the truck, leaning forward with his thick forearms on his knees.

But when Batoor rose and stood in the half-open back of the truck, gazing out at the desert night, Logan also got up and stood beside him. They were lit by the headlights of the SUV following them, and Al

Borak could see that the man's face bore a look of condescension. After a moment, he said something to the Pashtun in English. Al Borak caught only a couple of words—"little trick"—but from the way the man gestured at his hands, he knew that the reference was to his power to summon the lightning for which he was named.

"If you want a demonstration," he said in his native Pashto, "I can give you one."

And even as he said the words, the idea came to him. They were both holding on to the same steel bar that arched overhead. Al Borak had but to call down the spirit of the clouds and discharge it into the roof support and the power would shoot through the small man. Then, while he was twitching helplessly, the Pashtun need give him only the gentlest push on the shoulder and the man would tumble over the gate and onto the road. If the shock and fall didn't kill him, he would be crushed under the wheels of the heavy car following close behind them. And whatever plans von Strucker might have had for this interloper would become a thing of the past.

Al Borak set his mind to the summoning. In a moment he experienced the sharp metallic taste in his saliva that told him that he was charging. He looked down into the face of the infidel and smiled, then let a full charge surge from his palms. He held the discharge steady while Logan's face twitched into a rictus of spasming muscle and his heels beat a tattoo on the floorboards of the truck. Wisps of smoke wreathed around the places where the man's hands touched the steel. The Pashtun could smell burning flesh. Then he reined in the lightning and put his hand at the back of his victim's neck. The small man was already slumping forward and it took only the slightest push to send him toppling over the gate and into the road.

They were moving fast and the chase car was not far behind. The body bounced hard and the SUV driver had no time to touch the brakes before the vehicle's reinforced bumper struck the fallen man and threw him forward. Logan rolled along the dusty road in a tangle of limbs, the impact knocking him out of his borrowed shoes. The chase car's driver strove valiantly to stop the hurtling vehicle, but he couldn't prevent the front wheels from smashing into the tumbling body. The front end bumped over Logan, then the rear wheels completed the job.

The truck continued to move down the road at full speed, its driver ignorant of what had happened behind him. Then Al Borak saw a black-clad man get out of the passenger side of the SUV, a hand-held radio to his mouth. The Pashtun had to tighten his grip on the steel rib as the truck slammed to a skidding halt. Its gears ground as the driver found reverse and they began to back up toward the spot where the SUV waited.

Al Borak put on the face of sorrow he wanted the baron to see when he explained how Logan had lost his balance and fallen from the truck. He tried out the words in his mind: *I reached for him, but it was too late.* He would offer to help bury the body beside the road and they would all move on. It was no great loss. The man was, after all, nothing but an infidel.

The truck backed up all the way to where the tragic scene awaited, and Al Borak jumped down to express his sorrow as von Strucker, carrying case in hand, came hurrying back from the cab to see what had happened. But they were met by a grinning little figure brushing dust from his clothing and shaking it out of his hair. He thanked the astonished militiaman who brought him his shoes and sat on the extended bumper of the SUV to slip them back on.

Then he looked up at von Strucker and said, "Guess I slipped. No harm done."

The baron went back to the front of the truck while Logan climbed agilely into the back. Once aboard, he turned and extended a hand to Al Borak. The Pashtun took the offered hand. It felt normal—no blisters, no ridges of charred flesh—and he saw again the same look of condescension as Logan pulled him into vehicle. "Yeah," the small man said, "a good little trick."

○———————————○

LOGAN settled back onto the bench seat, folded his arms, and closed his eyes. He had learned a couple of things from the experiment. One was that, surprisingly, his bones didn't break. The impact of the SUV's bumper smashing into him had been like hitting a brick wall at fifty miles an hour. It had hurt like hell, had torn his flesh, yet nothing had snapped, not even his smallest finger. Nor had his chest been crushed when both sets of wheels had thumped over his body.

That was a bonus. He'd been willing to put up with the pain of fractured bones, at least until the amazingly rapid healing process did its work. Now he found that it was only his flesh that could be damaged, and it repaired itself so quickly that he was practically indestructible. The realization brought no surprise. Although it was news to the part of his mind that thought of itself as Logan, the rest of him took being shocked, smashed, and run over, then bouncing right back up, as no big deal. *No wonder I have this basic self-confidence*, he thought. A wolverine among foxes didn't have all that much to worry about.

He'd also tested Al Borak's power. He was sure that the tall man had meant to deliver a killing shock. But the surge of electricity hadn't even knocked Logan out, although for a long moment as he'd tumbled and rolled he'd felt dazed, even a little drunk. They'd shocked him into unconsciousness in Berlin, but that was after they'd already pumped his system full of some powerful sedative, and that time Al Borak had administered the jolt directly to Logan's head. So even though one of the foxes had a little extra kick, he wasn't that much of a threat.

As he rolled these thoughts through his mind, a new set of images were flickering out of his inner darkness. The electric jolt had worked its accidental magic again, as he'd hoped it would. *I should keep Sparky around for a while*, he thought. *He comes in handy.* Again, the pictures were random, but many of them involved violence. He saw bodies with gaping wounds, bellies and chests ripped open, severed limbs, pools of gore.

Often he saw the faces of people who were on the receiving end of catastrophic bodily harm, saw time and again the knowledge that could fill a man's eyes as he took the wound that would soon kill him. He knew he had seen that look many times, and at close range. The faces he was seeing belonged to people he had killed. Some of them were women. He knew their blood must have drenched him, their guts must have spilled at his feet, their dying screams and moans must have filled his ears.

And how do I feel about that? he asked himself. *Do I really want to know who I am, if it means knowing everything I've done?*

Despite all the damage he had sustained, he went through the world scarcely showing a scar. But maybe all the damage he had done to others had put scars on him where they didn't show. For a moment he even entertained the thought that maybe he had asked to have his memories wiped. But almost as soon as he asked himself the question, something inside said, *Nah, you're not the kind of guy who can't carry his own load.*

He watched the pictures come and go. There were a lot of them. After a while he opened his eyes and turned to look out the opening above the truck's rear gate. The overcast that had blocked the light of the stars was glowing gray. Some of it was the approaching dawn. Some was the reflected glow of lights on the ground, the lights of a city. They were coming to their destination, wherever it might be.

Good, he thought. *Time to get some things settled.*

OUTSKIRTS OF BAGHDAD,

THE PRESENT

AS the small convoy entered Mahmudiya, the southern suburb of Baghdad, they were met by a guide on a lightweight Kawasaki motorcycle. The commander of the militiamen brought him to talk with von Strucker.

"Iraqi Police commandos have sealed off the roads leading into the Mansour district," the guide said. "Something has them stirred up."

The baron knew what that "something" was, but these men had no need to know. "Can we not make an arrangement with them?" he said.

"They are not of our faction," the commander said.

Von Strucker found a map of the city and had the guide show him where the checkpoints were. He chose the most useful one and said, "Take us to within two blocks of here."

The vehicles rolled on through the predawn silence of the city, past burned-out buildings and houses whose windows were shuttered by metal grilles, the doors protected by steel bars. The man on the motorcycle waved them to a stop just before a corner, next to a deserted public market whose ornate façade had been scarred by a recent car bomb. The baron got out of the truck and went to the rear gate.

He spoke to Al Borak. "I want four men with knives."

There was a rustle and a muted *clank* as the chosen four clambered out of the back of the truck and their leader took four fighting knives from one of the equipment lockers. He passed them to the men, then began to climb out after them.

"No," said the Prussian, "they will go on their own."

He brought the four mujahideen to the front of the truck. There he gave them a set of instructions, brief and direct. The men grinned, and the baron knew that there would be no need to augment their performance with drugs from the carrying case. "Go," he said, and watched them disappear around the corner.

He went back to the rear of the truck. Al Borak was plainly unhappy at not being allowed to lead the attack. The Prussian waved away his truculent protest and said, "I have a more important task for you. When we move forward again, keep the stranger distracted. He does not need to see what happens next."

The Pashtun said he would do as he was bid, but von Strucker sensed a lingering resentment. He reminded himself that his days of humoring moody mutants and catering to the wishes of various fanatics would soon come to an end. Cherishing that thought, he went and sat in the cab of the truck with the valise back on his lap, and waited for the men to return.

○————————○

THE second time the convoy halted, the German came back to the rear of the truck and spoke in hushed Arabic to the Pashtun. The latter tapped four of the men on the benches, sending them over the tailgate, then rummaged in a crate at the front of the compartment, coming up with four knives that he passed to the men outside. Then came another whispered exchange and Logan knew, from the way the tall man's eyes flicked toward him, that he was the subject of the conversation.

The German went away and they all sat in silence for a few minutes. Then came a rush of footsteps and the four men were clambering back over the tailgate, handing back the knives to Al Borak. They resumed their places on the benches, and immediately there was a subdued hubbub of conversation that the Pashtun cut off with a snapped order. The truck started up and rolled around the corner.

So much for von Strucker's cover story about training special forces for an unnamed government, Logan was thinking. To his heightened sense of smell, the stench of fresh blood was unmistakable. He could see that none of the four was wounded, so it was clear that they had been out cutting other people's throats, probably to clear a checkpoint of some kind. Legitimate special forces units rarely found it necessary to sneak about the back streets and eliminate sentries in their own countries. Whatever the German had been training these troops for, it wasn't to hand them over to the government of Iraq. He was also pretty sure that Iraq was the country where they had now ended up, though the baron had not volunteered the information. But not too many big cities in the Middle East looked like a war zone. He didn't recognize the streets they were passing, but he had a pretty good sense, as he had had in Berlin, that he had been in this place before.

Less than a minute after they got rolling again, Al Borak was suddenly hovering over Logan, delivering some kind of diatribe in Arabic. The Canadian obliged him by looking up at him and smiling, which seemed to send the tall man into fresh paroxysms of anger.

He's keeping me busy so I don't look out and see what I'm not supposed to see. It didn't matter. Logan could smell the blood and the loosened bowels of dead men as the truck rumbled past the killing ground. He looked away, toward the men on the benches. They were becoming edgy, seeing their leader so worked up. The four who had done the killing were still powered up, their eyes flicking bright in the darkness of the truck. Logan wondered how it would be to fight them, even when they were juiced up—Berlin didn't count; it had been a lot of flailing around in the dark—and decided he wouldn't mind finding out.

That told him something else about what kind of man he was. *Guess I'm not big on speculation. I'm a guy who prefers to get hold of things, give them a good shake, and see what falls out.* Not everything he was learning about himself was good news. He had to accept that he had killed a lot of people, probably including quite a few who might not have deserved it. *Collateral damage*, he thought. But on the whole, he was coming to think that he'd be able to live with himself.

Al Borak wound down after a while and went to sit farther forward. Logan watched the streets of Baghdad fill with the thin light of dawn and looked forward to getting some answers.

MANSOUR DISTRICT OF BAGHDAD,

THE PRESENT

THE sun was just clear of the horizon when the convoy reached the high-walled compound that had formerly belonged to the owner of Iraq's most successful candy manufacturer whose factory had been stripped to the walls by looters during the chaos of 2003. A year later, after his eldest daughter had narrowly escaped kidnapping by a gang that targeted private schools, the man moved his family to Jordan and put the mansion up for sale. He had hoped that one of the countries seeking to open an embassy in the capital of the new Iraq might buy it—the luxurious Mansour district being a favorite for foreign missions—but there were no offers. It was leased for a while to an international security contracting firm (the newly preferred term for mercenaries). But as the city became a hunting ground for Islamist fanatics, Shiite death squads and unaligned but enterprising criminals, even these hardened ex-South African paratroops and former Russian *spetsnaz*, eventually decided that it was safer to operate from the ultrasecure Green Zone.

The commander of the militiamen had a key that opened the tall steel gates. The SUVs and the truck followed a circular driveway made of crushed white quartz and parked with all three vehicles facing the gate.

The carrying case never left the baron's grasp as he made a quick inspection of the grounds while the militiamen and the Green Fist were led across the house's pillared portico and through the main doors. The client's men providing security all had the gleam of jihad in their eyes, but they appeared to know their jobs. As he returned to the front of the mansion, he was met by Al Borak.

"Everything we require has been provided," his second in command said. "Nonetheless, I will have the men field strip the weapons as soon as they have completed morning prayers."

"Good," said von Strucker. He told the Pashtun to carry on, and made to mount the broad front steps. But Al Borak put a hand on his arm to detain him. The baron saw that the man was agitated. "What is it?" he said.

Al Borak cocked his head over his shoulder. "Him," he said.

The Prussian turned to look. Logan was standing beside the fountain, hands in his pockets, gazing about the courtyard with interest. Then his eyes came around to von Strucker and stayed on him.

"I have told you, he is not your concern," von Strucker said. He turned to enter the house, but again felt the restraining hand on his arm.

"What is he doing here?" Al Borak said.

The Prussian stiffened. "You have no need to know that."

The man's grip tightened. "You said he was essential to your plans. Not ours, just yours. Am I no longer a part of your plans?"

"Do you not trust me?"

"Should I?"

The Pashtun was growing more agitated. Von Strucker felt a warning tingle cause the hairs on his arm to stand erect. "Listen," he said, "Logan is not for you to worry about. When we leave Baghdad he will not be going with us. He will remain here, as a decoy. He will lead the enemy astray while we cover our tracks."

"But he knows far too much."

The baron smiled. "In a little while, he will not even know how to tie his shoes."

The tingling stopped. Al Borak took his hand from the Prussian's arm.

"Come," von Strucker said. "It is time for you to learn what Operation Severed Head entails. Then we will deal with Logan."

He waved and smiled at the small man standing by the fountain. Logan did not wave back, but stood with his hands in his pockets, shoulders hunched forward, watching as they went inside.

○———————○

"WHAT about the schedule?" von Strucker asked the Yemeni. "Have there been any changes?"

They were in the family dining room where the candy maker's family used to gather around the rosewood table for the nightly feast in the month of Ramadan. But instead of sweetmeats and fiery sauces, the polished board now supported only a detailed map of central Baghdad.

"None that make any difference," the client said. "God willing, he will arrive at the airport in a little while. Within the hour, we may begin."

"Excellent," said the baron. He turned to Al Borak. "Have the men assemble in the large banquet room, armed and ready for the jump-off. You may have the honor of telling them the target of this great mission."

Al Borak said, "Who is the target?"

And then von Strucker told the Pashtun the name of the man they had come to Baghdad to kill.

o————o

LOGAN watched the German and the gray-eyed man pause on the steps into the house. He couldn't hear what they were saying, but when the tall one cocked his head in his direction, he knew that he was the subject of the conversation. Something about the scene tickled the back of his mind. It was the sight of the German, his back mostly turned to Logan, speaking quietly to another man. *I've seen this before.*

He didn't strive for the recollection. That was not how it worked. He simply stared at the two figures on the step, saw the baron glance his way and return to his discussion. And all at once another scene superimposed itself: a brightly lit room, von Strucker in a field gray SS uniform, officer's epaulets of silver braid on his shoulders, talking with another officer who was round-faced and pink of skin.

Now Logan closed his eyes, letting the memory come. And, out of the past, he heard the sound of their voices, speaking in German. *"Meine erste Neigung soll das Blut studieren,"* von Strucker was saying.

"Eine einzigartige Blutzelle?" the other man asked.

The words meant nothing to Logan. Except, as he listened, he kept hearing the same word repeated, a word that sounded like "bloot."

Now it came again, the pink-skinned man saying, *"Wenn es das Blut ist, dann sollten wir das Mark studieren."*

Bloot. Logan rolled the word over in his mind. A lot of German words sounded like their English equivalent. And then the memory unwound a little further. He saw von Strucker picking up a mallet and chisel, and the other man putting a scalpel to his thigh.

He felt the ghost of that long-ago moment's agony. His fist clenched in his pockets and the muscles of his forearms strained. The motion conjured up the automatic anxiety again and he forced himself to relax.

He opened his eyes. Al Borak and von Strucker had gone into the mansion. *Das bloot*, Logan said to himself. *The blood.*

○────────────○

THE candy maker's banquet room had tall windows and a long mahogany table overhung by a vast chandelier imported from Austria. It also had sixteen mujahideen dressed for battle in Iraqi Army camouflage fatigues, their boots, helmets, and M-16 rifles identical to the U.S. Army's standard issue. They stood at ease in two ranks as Al Borak inspected them.

When von Strucker came into the room, carrying the case that had not left his possession since they had departed Saudi Arabia, the Pashtun called the men to attention. The Prussian nodded to him and Al Borak raised his voice and spoke to the sixteen.

"Mujahideen of the Green Fist," he said, "God is great! He will give us today a great victory. A thousand years from now, the faithful will still speak with wonder of the deeds we will do this day, here in the city of the Caliphs.

"God willing, we will strike the infidel and the apostates who serve them, in the place that is the heart of their power. We will strike a great blow, and all the world will know that God is great!"

As one, the sixteen raised their fists and chanted, "*Allahu akbar! Allahu akbar!*" God is great! God is great! As they did so, von Strucker placed the carrying case on the table, opened it, and spread it wide. Inside, nestled in foam, were the tubes that contained the distillation of Logan's unique blood cells.

"Men of the Green Fist," he said, "I know that you are ready to lay down your lives as holy warriors. I honor you for your courage and dedication. But I am able to tell you that today you will triumph over your enemies *without* making the martyr's sacrifice. For God has granted us a miracle."

He turned to Al Borak and said, "You are their leader. Yours is the honor of preparing them. I must return to our client." He filled a hypodermic syringe from one of the tubes, handed it to the Pashtun, and said, "Carry on."

BAGHDAD INTERNATIONAL AIRPORT,

THE PRESENT

THERE were no longer any gentle, gradual descents into Baghdad Airport. Whether civilian or military, incoming flights stayed high until the last moment, then made a steep, spiraling dive down to the runway, to provide the least inviting target to anyone on the ground who might have one of many heavy machine guns or even an antiaircraft gun that had gone missing from Iraqi armories in the systematic looting that followed the sudden dissolution of Saddam's army. Some flights also fired flares to confuse any shoulder-fired, heat-seeking missiles—quite a few of those had also gone missing in the spring of 2003.

U.S. Air Force Colonel Arlen McKittrick employed both defensive techniques as he brought the white-and-powder-blue-painted Boeing 747 spiraling swiftly down from the overcast skies that were typical of Mesopotamia in late December. He jammed on the brakes a second after his wheels scorched the runway. As soon as the aircraft's ground speed could be matched, it was flanked by armored Humvees and fighting vehicles that came racing along the tarmac on either side, guns aimed outward. The escorts accompanied the plane to a spot less than halfway to the end of the main runway, where more armored vehicles and a half battalion of special forces troops surrounded two Nighthawk and six Apache helicopters, their rotors already turning.

McKittrick remained at his post in the cockpit, ready to slam forward the throttles and put the jet into an emergency takeoff if necessary. Then he heard the *thump* of the plane's lower rear door opening, the exit usually used by journalists who accompanied the single passenger for whose use this customized 747 was always reserved. But this morning, the reporters and cameramen had to stand aside as a fit and compact man in a dark suit descended the rolling staircase that had been brought to the door.

Surrounded by sharp-eyed men with earpieces and automatic weapons, he strode to the waiting Nighthawks, followed by the four pool reporters who were to accompany him on the six-minute flight to the Green Zone. The rest of the press corps would follow in an armored convoy.

As he stepped up to the door of the lead Nighthawk, the man in the suit looked back at the 747's cockpit and snapped off a salute in McKittrick's direction. The colonel returned the salute. Then, as the helicopters powered up and lifted into the sky, heading east into the Iraqi dawn, he reached for his radio mike, depressed the button, and said, "Baghdad tower, this is Air Force One. We require immediate refueling and clearance for takeoff as and when necessary."

"Air Force One," came the reply, "fuel is on the way and the runway is yours for as long as you need it."

MANSOUR DISTRICT OF BAGHDAD,

THE PRESENT

LOGAN believed he had it figured out. He had stayed by the fountain, working it through while the Pashtun and the men who had come up with them from the baron's desert headquarters piled back into the truck and went out the front gate. The SUVs and the handful of black-clad men who had come in them remained behind. The militiamen took up defensive positions around the mansion and the grounds. One or two of them gave Logan looks that told him they were not interested in making friends. That didn't bother him. Neither was he.

The blood was the key. Von Strucker had focused on it all those years ago. He must have figured it contained the secret of Logan's phenomenal ability to heal. That secret was what the German wanted out of him, why he had set up the Höllenfeuer Remembrance Society to find him again. All the talk about helping him, the "I'm a mutant, just like you" and "your enemy is my enemy" was all a smokescreen to keep Logan around and quiet while he got a good quantity of the precious stuff. And now he had gotten plenty.

The German had taken bone marrow from Logan in 1944. He hadn't aged a day since. Those two facts had to be connected. Now he had brought the walking container of the miraculous blood to Baghdad, and Logan had no doubt the German had something in mind. Maybe the idea was to sell Logan to someone else. Maybe to put him on ice and bleed him indefinitely.

Whatever the baron's plan might be, it was not meant to feature a happy ending for one memory-impaired Canadian. *They use you, then they throw you away.* He paused as a growing racket broke into his thoughts. He looked up and saw a flying convoy of eight helicopters passing overhead from the southwest, moving at top speed. Every few seconds, flares fired from the copters. Tiny door gunners looked out and down, the muzzles of their machine guns constantly traversing left and right. On the grounds of the mansion, the men in black shirts and turbans shielded their eyes and watched the machines pass. One of them said something and the others laughed.

The aircraft passed out of sight and Logan returned to his thoughts. It was not an ideal situation to be surrounded by armed guards who were under the orders of a cold-eyed man who meant him no good. But, faulty as his powers of recollection undeniably were, he was now certain he had been in exactly that same position sixty-odd years ago. And he had come out of it all right.

So it was time to deal with von Strucker. His forearms clenched again, and again the same flash of dread filled him. The unwanted emotion angered him. It didn't come from him. It had been implanted. It was like an insidious parasite that lived in his body, and it needed to be dealt with. *But first the German*, he thought. *Time for the truth.*

He turned toward the mansion.

      o———————o

JUST off the family dining room was a cozy den with leather chairs and couches and a wide-screen plasma television connected to a satellite dish on the roof. The set was showing the raw feed from the Baghdad bureau of CNN. The hawk-nosed Yemeni, dressed in traditional Arab robes, sat in the butter-soft leather embrace of a tan-colored armchair, his hooded eyes fixed on the images.

The baron was in the dining room, rolling up the map and preparing for their departure that would come as soon as the client had seen what he was waiting to see. The foam-lined carrying case stood upright on the floor by his feet, closed and locked. The noise of a scuffle caught his attention and he looked up to see one of the black-clad militiamen attempting to prevent Logan from entering the room from the foyer. The guard was bigger, and he was using his rifle like a baton held in both hands, but the small Canadian had hold of the weapon and was steadily pushing the larger man back. Then he twisted it from the other's grasp with an effortless display of strength.

"Stop!" von Strucker cried, then repeated himself in Arabic, adding, "there is no need for this. The man is a guest. He may enter."

To Logan, he said, "I was just about to come and look for you."

"Uh-huh," the Canadian said. He handed the guard's rifle back with a casualness that von Strucker noted and came into the room, shutting the door to the foyer behind him. The baron saw his eyes take in the rolled map and pay attention to the case on the floor, and he thought to himself, *Not a moment too soon.* Whatever Logan had been in 1944, whatever he was now, with or without his memories, he was a dangerous man.

Von Strucker put on a smile and rubbed his hands, saying, "I have had a chance to show your blood work to my esteemed colleague—" he gestured toward the den, "—and he confirms my supposition."

"Is that so?" Logan said. "Just what did he confirm?"

"You have been attacked by a complex of drugs that are collectively known as mnemophages—'memory eaters' is a rough translation of the medical term. Of course, they do not actually devour your memories. They inhibit the electrochemical action of the regions at the ends of your brain's neuron cells. Signals cannot pass from one cell to another. The memories are still there, but they cannot be accessed."

"Uh-huh," Logan said.

"Do you understand what I am saying?" von Strucker said. "Having identified the precise mix of chemicals, we can offer you a countereffective substance that will unlock your mind."

"Hmm," the mutant said. "And did your colleague happen to bring any of that substance with him?"

"He did," said the baron. "He has already prepared an injection for you."

"Well," said Logan, "let's get on with it."

"Indeed," said von Strucker. He went to the door into the den and spoke to the Yemeni in Arabic. "Will you please bring the materials I asked for? This man speaks no Arabic. He thinks you are a doctor who has a cure for his problem."

The Yemeni did not rise, but gestured to the television. "I wish to see the event," he said.

"This will take but a moment. Besides, it is important to the 'event.' This man will lead the enemy astray. They will not know who has struck them."

"But we want them to know who has struck them," the client said. "That is the point of the exercise."

The baron held his irritation in check. Soon he would be beyond fanatics, as well as mutants. "We want them to know that you have struck them, certainly. There is nothing to be gained from revealing my part in the matter."

The dark-eyed man grunted and levered himself out of the embrace of the chair. The baron had the impression, not for the first time, that the client was of that desert-bred type who would ban all of life's comforts and force the entire world to sit on goat-hair rugs. Again, he was glad he would soon be leaving this life behind.

The man felt in the pocket of his robe and brought out two flat plastic cases, each longer than his hand. "Here is what you asked for."

"Which contains the memory eater?"

"This," said the Yemeni, offering one of the cases.

"Good," said von Strucker. "We will not need the other."

The Arab put the other case on a side table next to the chair he had been sitting in. The baron said, "Now, if you would just play along for a few more moments, we will be finished."

The Yemeni snorted. But he put down the remote, leaving the set showing the CNN raw feed. A man in shirtsleeves and wearing a combination headphone and mike was sitting at a desk, talking to the cable station's Atlanta headquarters, giving a rundown on the main stories that would be fed through the satellite that morning, and scheduling a live go-to for the news summary at the top of the hour. Then he broke off as a young woman came to bend over him and say something in his ear. The man listened, then said, "Wait a minute, Wolf. I've got to check something." He pushed the phone away from his mouth and began to talk with the woman.

The Yemeni came into the dining room and made an effort to look not quite so disdainful of the infidels. Von Strucker took the case from him, laid it on the table, and opened it. Inside was a large-bore hypodermic syringe, filled with a green substance.

The baron picked up the needle and smiled at Logan. "If you would roll up your sleeve," he said. As he spoke, he depressed the plunger slightly to remove air from the spike. As a thin jet of the green liquid arced into the air, von Strucker was surprised to see the mutant put out a hand so that the tiny squirt of the drug landed on his palm.

Logan brought his hand to his face. The Prussian saw his nostrils flare as he took a long, slow sniff of the smear of moisture on his palm. Then the hard, dark eyes locked on his and a voice in von Strucker's head said, *Ach, scheiss.*

GREEN ZONE, BAGHDAD,

THE PRESENT

JAN Visser, born and raised in Pretoria, had joined the Fourth Reconnaissance Commando regiment of the South African Defense Forces—later renamed the 451 Parachute Battalion—straight out of high school. Twenty years later, having risen from raw recruit to the rank of captain, he took his pension, resigned his commission, and went to a meeting in a Pretoria hotel room with a former colonel of the British SAS. It was a brief meeting, from which ex-Captain Visser emerged with the rank of major and a salary several times greater than what the Republic of South Africa offered its field-grade officers. His new employer was Strategic Outcomes Corp., headquartered in the Cayman Islands, and one of the fastest-growing security consulting firms in the immensely less predictable world that came unexpectedly into being after the collapse of the Soviet Union.

Since joining SOC, Visser had seen service in West Africa, guarding diamond exporters; in Central Asia, guarding oil drillers; in South America, guarding people who didn't discuss their business interests with the hired help. In 2003, he became one of tens of thousands of "security consultants" who found high-paying work in the chaos of Iraq, guarding everything from pipelines and power plants to foreign embassies and bases full of regular soldiers.

This morning, Major Jan Visser was in charge of the SOC security team that operated one of the main entry points into Baghdad's heavily fortified Green Zone. The actual gate was a heavy steel pipe with a counterweight at one end that could be lifted to allow vehicles in. But that wouldn't happen until Visser's team had checked identification documents, thoroughly searched the trunk, passenger compartment, and under the hood, run a mirror on a wheeled pole underneath the body, and let a bomb-sniffing dog give everything and everybody the once-over.

To either side of the entry point, as well as just a few feet behind it, stood tall blast walls of reinforced concrete topped by razor wire. A vehicle passing through the gate would have to slowly wend its way around these barriers, then pass through a narrow channel, also lined with blast-proof concrete and guarded by machine guns, before emerging onto the wide streets that ran between the Iraqi parliament buildings, the headquarters of key ministries like oil and defense, and Saddam Hussein's sprawling, domed Republican Palace, which now housed the United States Embassy.

The closest a car bomb would get to the softer targets inside the zone would be the first barrier. If a suicide bomber blew himself up there, he might take out Visser, his car-searching soldiers, and their dog. An assault team could get farther, though not much; if they were good, they could shoot their way in, but those who made it past the blast wall and into the channel would be cut to pieces.

Visser had warned his men to be extravigilant today. It was supposed to be a secret that the Green Zone would be receiving a UIP—Ultra-Important Visitor—and certainly no one had officially passed the word down to those who guarded the perimeter. But the South African had seen security "flaps" before in the zone, and the heightened preparations always turned out to be in anticipation of at least a cabinet-level official, if not higher. When the helicopter convoy came sliding down from the gray sky not long after his team started their shift, he nodded to his men in confirmation.

"Okay," he said, "extra tight until we see those copters heading back to the airport."

It was still well before office hours in the zone, and incoming traffic was light. The broad street outside the high walls—still named 14th of July to commemorate the Baathist revolution that overthrew the old monarchy—was empty. Then a canvas-topped truck, the kind commonly used by the Iraqi Army, came at a moderate speed from the direction of Saddam's Tomb of the Unknown Soldier, with its two pairs of giant concrete hands holding crossed sabers.

"Sharpen up," the major told his men. Around him he heard the click of rifle bolts as each man chambered a round.

The truck stopped directly across from the gate. The driver, helmeted and wearing Iraqi Army camouflage, leisurely opened his door and got out. He ambled to the rear of the vehicle, where he unlatched and lowered the tailgate. Now more soldiers got out, with M-16s—one of them handed a weapon to the driver—and stood around the back of the truck like recruits in need of a brass-tongued sergeant who would snap them into formation.

"You there!" Visser called to them. He had acquired enough Arabic to say, "Don't move!"

But the men did move. They unslung their rifles, holding them loosely but with the muzzles aimed in the general direction of the SOC team. And they began to drift across the street.

Visser was thinking, *A bunch of idiot farmboys who've gotten lost*, but he had not survived three tours of duty in Baghdad by taking chances. He brought his own weapon to his shoulder and aimed at the closest man. Around him, his team were doing the same.

"Stop!" he shouted. "Put down your weapons!"

Yet they didn't. Instead, the man the major was looking at over the sights of his rifle fired a shot. It was just one round and Visser heard it *whuff* past him, a foot or more over his head.

"Fire!" he shouted, squeezing the trigger of his M-16 and sending a three-round burst through the chest of the Iraqi soldier. His men opened up and cut down the men who were still coming toward them, one or two of them getting off unaimed shots from hip level.

"Cease firing!" Visser said. "Get the dog and check the truck!"

The truck was empty. No explosives were stacked within or packed in the chassis. Sixteen dead men lay sprawled in the middle of the street. Visser's top sergeant, a red-faced Australian, gingerly examined the bodies for explosives.

"Nothing," he reported, "no ID tags, no paybooks."

Jan Visser pushed his helmet back from his sweating brow and said, "Well, what the hell do you think that was all about?"

The Australian had no answer, except that he reckoned they had just met "the most incompetent bunch of drongos in the whole bleedin' insurgency."

MANSOUR DISTRICT, BAGHDAD,

THE PRESENT

FOR Logan, the smell from the smear of green liquid on his palm was almost enough. It didn't trigger any precise memories, but it rang a warning bell somewhere in the back corridors of his mind. But just to be sure, he said to von Strucker, "How does he know this is the right dosage? He's never even seen me before."

The German was quick with an answer. "I sent him all your information. This is his area of expertise, after all. Now roll up your sleeve."

Logan looked at the Arab. He couldn't have told from the man's appearance if he was a world-class neurochemist or just a particularly successful goatherd. Whichever he was, his attention was being pulled back toward the TV in the other room, where someone was talking in an excited voice.

"He doesn't look like he's all that interested," Logan said. "Is he missing his favorite show?"

Von Strucker said something to the other man in Arabic. The hawk-faced man snapped back at him and his sun-darkened hand made a brusque gesture. "He is not used to having his medical judgments questioned," the German said.

The Arab was half-turned away now, clearly wanting to get back to the TV, where somebody was definitely excited about something, though the sound was too low for Logan to make out the words.

None of this smelled right to Logan. Instinct told him to push the situation. "If he's the expert," he said, "I'd like him to give me the injection."

The baron spoke to the Arab again, and this time the man spewed a stream of what was surely invective at both the German and Logan. He turned his back and made for the other room.

"Tell you what," said Logan, moving forward and plucking the hypodermic from von Strucker's fingers, then catching the Arab's arm in a grip that stopped him short, "how about I inject *you*?"

And he stuck the needle through the sleeve of the man's robe and into the shoulder muscle, depressing the plunger. The German let out a surprised squawk and grabbed for the syringe, but Logan had already stepped back to observe the effects.

The Arab had turned toward him at the jab of the hypodermic, his harsh face forming a mask of outrage. But in less than a second, the man's expression softened. His pupils dilated until scarcely the thinnest rim of their dark irises showed and his grim mouth went slack. He blinked and looked around the room as if he had just woken from a deep dream and hadn't yet shaken its grasp. He said something that Logan would have bet was the Arabic equivalent of "Where am I?"

"Uh-huh," the mutant said. "So that clears that up."

Von Strucker was making for the door to the foyer. Logan caught him by the collar and yanked him back. As the German came backpedaling on his heels, trying to keep his balance, the Canadian cocked the fist of his free hand and delivered a short, sharp punch to the side of von Strucker's jaw. The baron went limp in his grip and Logan lowered him to sit on one of the dining room chairs. The Arab watched, eyes wide and mouth open, like a surprised infant. Then his knees buckled and he sank to the floor.

Logan first went to the case that von Strucker had guarded so jealously. He cracked it open and saw the rows of test tubes nestled inside. Most of them were empty. That was obviously part of the puzzle. He next went to the map on the table and unrolled it. It was marked in Arabic, so he couldn't read it, but he recognized it as a map of Baghdad. Marked with arrows and dark lines was an area of land confined by a bend in the river. *Another piece of the puzzle*, he thought.

He found the third piece in the small room where the voice from the TV was now speaking excitedly. It belonged to a man in shirtsleeves sitting at a desk and scanning a piece of paper in his hand while saying, "… confirm that the president arrived this morning on Air Force One under ultratight security. He flew by helicopter to the Green Zone where he is scheduled to meet the new Iraqi national unity government this afternoon.

"But first he's going to enjoy a Christmas Day breakfast with thirty servicemen and women from all branches of the military. And, Wolf, I'm told he's brought each one of them a Christmas present from their families. This has been in the works for weeks, with all the families sworn to secrecy. It's amazing they managed to keep it under wraps.

"The breakfast is at the U.S. embassy in the Green Zone. Right after that the president's going to visit a hospital that's only a couple of hundred yards away. He will award Purple Hearts to several wounded soldiers and marines—we're getting their names and hometowns now."

The man checked another piece of paper that someone handed him from off-camera. "So, Wolf, this is going to be the major story of the day—well, probably the whole holiday season. We'll need to change the line-up for the top of the hour, and I'm going to reassign Christianne from the go-to so she can interview the troops at the breakfast and in the field hospital. She's on her way to the embassy right now."

The feed didn't carry the audio of the reply the man was receiving from Atlanta, but Logan could see him nodding an affirmative, then he said, "Right, no problem, we were already set up at the embassy press room, so I'll just pull—"

He broke off as a young woman rushed into the shot and leaned over to speak to him. Logan saw alarm appear on the newsman's face. He said to the woman, "This is confirmed? Get a crew there! Right now! I want eye-witness interviews from the security consultants before some PR flack comes and throws a blanket over it."

As the woman left, he turned to the camera and said, "Wolf, we have a confirmed report of some kind of insurgents' attack on a gate leading into the Green Zone. I've got a crew heading there now."

The young woman was back. He listened to her, then said, "No casualties among the guards at the gate. Sixteen insurgents killed by rifle fire. No car bombs. No follow-up attacks. Doesn't seem to have been a diversion."

He listened to the reply from Atlanta, then said, "No, the bodies are being taken to a morgue where army intelligence will take photographs, fingerprints, and DNA samples in case the attackers can be identified. I'm told the insurgents had M-16 rifles, so they'll get their serial numbers. The information might point to which element of the insurgency had sent them on this apparent suicide mission."

He listened again, then said, "I'll have Christianne talk to the intelligence people on the scene. The morgue where they're taking the bodies is in the same field hospital where the president is giving out the Purple Hearts."

And now, for Logan, the pieces all fell into place. He looked back through the door to the other room, where the Arab was sitting dazed at the table and von Strucker was beginning to stir.

He would have liked to have stayed right there in the house. He had a lot of questions to put to the German. But he couldn't.

The TV was connected to large remote speakers in the corners of the room. Logan pulled the wires free and used them to tie von Strucker firmly to the sturdy wooden chair in the dining room. Then he gagged him with strips of cloth torn from the Arab's robe. The Arab had sunk into what looked like a catatonic state. He was lying on his side on the floor, staring at nothing.

Before he left, Logan took another look inside the German's carrying case. Then he went quietly to the door to the foyer and eased it open. The black-clad militiaman was still standing outside when Logan silently opened the door to the foyer. This time, the mutant dealt less gently with him. Before the guard could turn, Logan put one hand on the man's chin and the other on the crown of his turbanned head. A sharp, hard twist and he heard the neck bones snap. He lowered the man to the floor and took his rifle.

He looked back at the baron struggling against the bonds that secured him to the chair. The image tickled his memory with a faint sense of irony, but he didn't have time to let the full picture come. *Later*, he told himself. *There'll be plenty of time later.*

As he closed the door to the small room and crossed the foyer to the main entrance, a voice in his head kept saying, *My blood. My responsibility.*

○——————————○

BATOOR the orphan learned early on not to trust what people said to him. He also learned how to read faces and voices and body language. Even with his power to summon the spirit of the clouds, he would not have survived long enough to be rescued by von Strucker if he could not tell a lie from truth.

The Prussian had told him about the miracle of the elixir drawn from the veins of the man they had brought back from Germany. He had cut his own flesh and let Al Borak watch as the wound healed itself in seconds.

So that much the Pashtun knew was true. But the rest of it? That the mujahideen could die and rise to fight again?

Maybe it was true. Maybe it was not. Maybe what he had shot into their arms was the true elixir that von Strucker gave to himself. Maybe it was not. Or maybe the dose was not enough. And maybe the stuff von Strucker had shot into Batoor's vein was not the real thing, if indeed any of this was real.

Al Borak did not know. But what he did know, with the sensitivity of a third-world orphan to those who held him in their power, was that von Strucker was done with him. Something had changed since the small man had come. Now the baron looked through Batoor, his eyes focused on some future that beckoned the Prussian the way paradise beckoned the sixteen fools who believed in the tales of perfumed gardens and willing maidens.

Whatever the future von Strucker saw gleaming on his horizon, there was no place in it for a Pashtun orphan with a peculiar power in his hands. Al Borak knew that for sure.

And would the baron casually dispose of him, to clear the board for his new game? Of that, Al Borak had no doubt. When they had been training the original thirty men from whom the final sixteen had come, he had helped bury the failures.

So after von Strucker had delivered his little speech in the banquet room, after he had given Al Borak the first injection, then left him to do the others, the Pashtun had done as he was ordered, putting the needle into each grinning man of the Green Fist. But he had not climbed into the truck. Instead he had told the men that he would meet them in the hospital morgue and lead them in the glorious last phase of Operation Severed Head.

"If I am delayed," he said, "Khan will take charge. And you will proceed without me."

Then he had led them in a shout of "God is great!" three times and the men had filed out to board the truck. Al Borak had closed the door of the banquet room, except for a crack through which he spied across the foyer of the mansion at the small room behind whose closed door the baron and his new favorite were now cooking up some kind of plan.

We will see about that, the Pashtun thought. If Operation Severed Head succeeded after all, Al Borak would appear, having survived and escaped, to share in the glory. If it did not succeed, he would still appear—to point the finger at the blue-eyed infidel who had sabotaged the mujahideen.

Either way, Al Borak meant to secure his place with the Yemeni and the man in the faraway mountains who was his master.

He had learned long ago in the orphanage how to wait patiently and he stood and watched as Logan came in from outside, forced his way into the small room, and disarmed the guard. While von Strucker was calming the situation, Al Borak was replaying in his mind the ease with which the small man had taken the rifle away from the militiaman, and the casual contempt with which he had handed it back. He also thought about how the Canadian had survived the shock and fall from the truck on the road to Baghdad.

He was still thinking about it when the door to the small room opened silently and Logan efficiently broke the guard's neck, scooped up his rifle before it could hit the floor, and headed outside.

Al Borak watched him go, then went and opened the door of the small room. When the baron saw him, he began to make noises around the gag in his mouth. But the Pashtun ignored him. Instead he knelt and examined the Yemeni, finding him apparently unharmed, although he had clearly been the recipient of whatever had been in the empty hypodermic that lay near him on the floor.

Von Strucker made noises at him as he rose. Al Borak looked down at him and was tempted to raise the spirit of the clouds. He started to let the warmth grow in his palms. Then came the sound of rifle fire from outside. He turned and ran for the door.

Seven militiamen had accompanied them from Basra. The group's commander had gone in the truck, to guide the Green Fist mujahideen to a point near the Green Zone. Logan had killed the one in the house. That left five, three of whom were guarding the compound's gate, their attention on the street outside. The Canadian had shot all three without warning, firing the dead guard's M-16 with the efficiency of a veteran combat soldier. When the Pashtun came out the front door, Logan was dragging one of the bodies out of the way so he could open the gate.

Al Borak stepped into concealment behind one of the portico's pillars. When the gate stood wide, Logan went to the remaining SUV parked near the fountain and opened its driver's door. He was just getting into the car when the two remaining militiamen, who had been stationed at the rear of the compound where a gate opened onto a service lane, came running around the corner of the house. One of them charged, screaming, at the small man, firing his weapon as he came. The other knelt, put his rifle to his shoulder, and aimed. The shot went true, and the Pashtun saw Logan's head jerk back and blood fly as the bullet struck his forehead.

Then, as if the bullet had been no more than a thrown pebble, Logan snapped up his own weapon and shot the kneeling man through the head. As rounds from the charging man scarred the SUV's bulletproof windows, he calmly fired twice into the militiaman's chest.

So it is true, Al Borak said to himself as the mutant threw the rifle onto the front seat of the SUV and climbed behind the wheel. His mind raced. *Perhaps the mujahideen will truly awaken from death in the enemy hospital and strike their great blow. But who will get the credit?*

Even as these thoughts were crowding Al Borak's mind, Logan was starting the vehicle and the Pashtun was sprinting from the porch to the SUV, summoning the lightning as he ran. As the Canadian put the car into gear, the Pashtun slapped his palms to its metal body and released a full charge. The paint beneath his hands smoked and bubbled as the jolt of electricity shot through the SUV, frying every silicon chip that controlled its state-of-the-art systems. The engine died as Al Borak lifted his hands from the vehicle and he had the satisfaction of seeing the small man jerk and spasm as the electricity went through him.

The tall man rushed to the driver's door and yanked it open, meanwhile summoning a new charge. This time he wanted the Canadian grounded, not insulated from the earth by rubber tires as he had been on the truck. He would see if the mutant's healing powers could cope with flesh that had been cooked to carbon from within.

○————————○

LOGAN found it all worked fine if he didn't think about it. Or if he just thought about what needed to be done, but left the actual doing of it to instinct. *Or habit*, he thought as he lowered the dead guard to the floor of the mansion's foyer and picked up his rifle. Some part of him was highly trained, extremely competent at the business of killing. The fact that he couldn't remember the training didn't seem to matter. When it was needed, it was there.

He went out the front door, spotted the three men at the gate, and put them down with three three-round bursts from the M-16. The weapon felt right in his hands. He had done this all before.

He had cleared the gate and got it open and was getting into the SUV when the other two arrived. The bullet to his head rang his bell—it actually made a metallic clanging sound inside his head—and he marveled again at the strength of his bones. He shot the men and got into the vehicle.

But then as he started its engine, his muscles locked up as a heavy jolt of electricity surged through him. When the electricity stopped, the vehicle was dead and Logan himself was dazed by the shock. His muscles twitched and jumped and he felt as if someone had stuffed foam rubber into his cranial cavity.

As he shook his head to clear it, the driver's door flew open and he was pulled out onto the crushed white stone of the driveway. But even as he rolled, his physical and mental equilibrium was coming back on line. He got his feet underneath him, feeling the muscles bunch in his forearms—and again feeling that sudden alien anxiety. It angered him. He growled, the sound deep in his chest, while his mind was telling him, *Enough of this!* and he knew he didn't give a damn about whatever would happen next.

He started to rise, his hands forming fists as they came clear of the gravel. Then he felt two hard palms slap the sides of his head and a fresh jolt of electricity shot through him like white fire. The soles of his boots smoked, his blood boiled in his veins, and every muscle spasmed as the grounded current raced through him and down into the earth.

His vision darkened around the edges, so that it was as if he were looking down a tunnel. He had been raising his fisted hands in front of him and now he saw them centered in his field of vision. Then, as the flesh of his forearms rippled and jerked, he was astonished to see three foot-long knives of gleaming metal shoot from between his knuckles—astonished, and then suddenly he was not surprised at all. *Of course*, he thought.

He was able to think because the blades had not shot out into empty air, but straight into the flesh of the tall man who had bent to clap his hands to Logan's head. Their points had pierced the Pashtun's pectoral muscles just in from the shoulder joints, ripping through the corded fibers as if they were tissue paper. The man had staggered back, his arms gone slack and his hands falling away from Logan, taking their lightning with them.

In moments, the small man's own tissues had repaired the tears and burns that the jolt had caused and his head had cleared. He rose and looked at Al Borak, standing there with blood pouring from six deep gashes in his chest, his gray eyes full of the long-sighted gaze of a man in shock. Logan raised his right hand, turned it to examine the three deadly claws.

Of course, he thought again. The implanted panic reaction—the alien parasite someone had slipped into his mind—had lost its power, was gone, null and void. Logan still didn't know how he came to have metal sheathed claws, didn't know whether they were part of his mutation or something that had been grafted onto him by whoever had stolen his memories. But his body knew that he had had them a long time. And it knew how to use them.

He drew back his fist to send its claws through Al Borak's chest, but at that moment the man's clouded eyes closed and he toppled to the ground. Logan made a sound that dismissed the Pashtun with contempt and turned his mind back to what he had to do. He resheathed his claws and left the crumpled form in a spreading pool of blood. He went to the second SUV, parked behind the first. Its engine roared and he spewed gravel as he steered the heavy vehicle toward the open gate.

GREEN ZONE, BAGHDAD,

THE PRESENT

JORGE Cardero's lieutenant would not have enjoyed hearing the things that the specialist was muttering as he dug the ink pad and fingerprint forms from his army-issue briefcase in the morgue of the field hospital. The lieu himself should have been supervising the taking of prints from the sixteen dead hajjis, laid out side by side on the concrete floor. Instead, the officer had watched as the specialist had recorded the serial numbers of the M-16s, then he had made some excuse about taking the rifles to storage, scooped them up, and disappeared. Cardero knew that the lieutenant had really just dumped the weapons somewhere, then sloped off to get a peek at the UIP who was scheduled to come through the hospital's front door in just a few minutes. The enlisted man would have liked to have seen the commander in chief—hell, he'd voted for the man, which he suspected the lieutenant had not.

"But rank has its freaking privileges," he said, adding a detailed and inventive comment about what the lieutenant could do with his rank and his privileges. Then he sighed and knelt beside the first of the dead men, taking the corpse's wrist and reaching for the ink pad.

Hey, he thought, *this guy's awful warm for a—*

It was Jorge Cardero's last thought and it was never finished. The hand that belonged to the wrist had formed itself into a stiff-fingered spike that jabbed straight into the specialist's Adam's apple. While he was struggling to get air through his shattered trachea and the swelling tissues of his throat, the hand came back again. This time the heel of the palm struck the base of the soldier's nose, snapping off the nasal bone and driving it straight into the frontal lobes of Cardero's brain. The body would twitch for a while, but the person that had inhabited it was gone forever.

Ismail Khan came fluidly to his feet and crouched as he scanned the morgue. The place was empty. He ran his hands over his bloodstained fatigue shirt, felt bullets shake loose from the cloth. He turned to the man lying beside him and shook him. "Wake up," he said. "Our moment is come."

MANSOUR DISTRICT, BAGHDAD,

THE PRESENT

LOGAN drove hard, swinging the SUV around corners on two screeching wheels, accelerating down the wide, straight avenues of the upscale Mansour district. Occasionally he took one hand off the wheel and flexed its arm, causing the gleaming claws to shoot from his hand, then retract, over and over. Each time he brought them out, they caused a little pain like fire in his knuckles, like being touched by a lit cigarette. But the flesh healed and the pain went away. Then he'd pull them in and flex them out again, and the arrival of the little pain was always like meeting an old forgotten friend. And the reflexive anxiety? That had been reduced to a tiny, squeaking pygmy mouse way off on the edge of his mind. *How did I ever let them take this from me?* he thought. *And just wait until I find the bastards.*

He was coming down a long straight stretch. Ahead at an intersection a white Toyota pickup was angled half across the road, and half a dozen rifle-toting men in Iraqi uniforms were in and around the vehicle. An officer raised his hand at the SUV's approach.

"No time," Logan said to the windshield. His foot pressed the gas pedal down and he hit three solid blasts on the horn.

The officer screamed an order and the rifles came up. Logan saw the muzzle flashes, then the tinted windshield suddenly showed a galaxy of small, white stars as the steel-jacketed rounds chipped the armored glass. Other rounds rang off the hood and reinforced bumper, but none penetrated to the engine compartment.

The Iraqis scattered as the SUV struck the corner of the pickup's front bumper and spun the Toyota out of the way. Logan fought the wheel as the heavy vehicle fishtailed from the impact. Then he got it settled down and hit the gas again.

VON Strucker struggled against the wire that bound him to the chair, but the mutant had done too good a job. The Yemeni lying on the floor at his feet, a pool of spittle forming beneath his slack mouth, could be no help. By now the mnemophage would have so blocked his mental pathways that he was effectively an infant and would not remember how to talk, let alone untie knots.

The original plan had been for Al Borak to send the Green Fist into the zone, then return to the mansion. Von Strucker had amended that plan, without telling the Pashtun about it, and had injected his second in command with a placebo. Now the baron regretted that decision. He should have kept the mutant to sell to someone who could use him. Although that was assuming that the Pashtun would have ever returned from the mission. The baron had no doubt that Logan would make every effort to foil his plan. As he had been tying the baron to the chair, he had muttered through clenched teeth, "My blood, you bastard! My blood!"

Over the course of his extended career, the Prussian had often left men tied to chairs, waiting for him to come and deliver their fate. He had never wondered how it felt to be in that position—he'd always had more important things to think about. Now he knew what those men had known, but he didn't feel that he was profiting from the knowledge.

He heard a noise from the other side of the closed door that led to the foyer. The gold-plated lever that worked the latch was jiggling. Then it rotated down and the door opened inward. Al Borak lay facedown in the doorway, his upraised hand falling from the handle as the door swung in. Behind him, the floor of the foyer was smeared by a trail of blood from the front entrance.

Now the Pashtun levered himself up onto his forearms, like a soldier crawling belly-down under enemy fire. Laboriously, he pulled himself into the small room, and von Strucker could see that the front of his shirt was soaked in red and that his face was ashen pale from loss of blood.

Weak, panting, Al Borak came forward, his legs and belly sliding on his own gore. The baron grunted around the gag in his mouth, but the Pashtun did not look up. He came steadily, slowly on, forcing his way past the comatose Yemeni, his dull eyes fixed on only one thing: the baron's carrying case, on the floor beside his chair.

He made it, weakly pulled apart the hinged case, his bloodless hands fumbling for one of the tubes of elixir, then for a hypodermic. His breath came in shallow gasps as he filled the syringe's barrel, then lay down on his side. With trembling fingers he brought the needle toward the crook of his elbow. But before he could insert the spike, his eyes rolled up in his head and he fainted.

The baron roared in rage and frustration behind the gag. Thrusting his body against his bonds, he tried to scoot the chair across the short distance to where Al Borak lay unconscious in a spreading pool of blood. There could not be much more left inside him, von Strucker knew. Soon it would be too little and then it would be too late for the baron.

The Pashtun's eyelids fluttered. Weakly he raised his head, focused dull eyes on the syringe in his failing hand, and brought its spike to his pale flesh. He pressed the plunger and the cloudy fluid was forced out of the barrel. Then his head slumped again, the needle fell from his nerveless fingers, and again the baron raged against his impotence.

Time ticked by. Al Borak did not move, but he continued to breathe. It seemed to von Strucker that the bleeding had at least slowed, perhaps stopped. More time passed and now the man's color seemed to have deepened. A minute later, the Pashtun took in a harsh, gasping breath. His eyes opened and the lackluster gaze quickly sharpened.

He levered himself half up, then pushed against the smeared floor until he was kneeling. His hands tore away the blood-soaked shirt, touched the wounds that were now closing rapidly. He looked at von Strucker and it was a hard look. Then his eyes went briefly to the Arab on the floor and he said, "What of him?"

The Prussian grunted. Al Borak got to his feet. He seemed to have recovered his full strength. He worked the gag free and the baron said, "Quick, untie me."

"What of him?" Al Borak said again.

"He got the memory wipe that should have been Logan's."

"Can it be undone?"

"There is an antidote," von Strucker said. "Now untie me. We must get away from here."

But the Pashtun's hard fingers came to pinch in the baron's cheeks, forcing his mouth open. The spit-soaked gag was crammed into his mouth again.

"First things first," Al Borak said. He gave himself another injection of the elixir. Then he was gone.

GREEN ZONE, BAGHDAD,

THE PRESENT

THE three-story hospital had been built for Saddam, his family, and favorites. Its administration, imaging, laboratory, and emergency departments were on the main floor; surgery, postop, and ICUs were on the second; and longer-term care wards and rehab were on the top floor. The morgue was in the basement, along with the laundry and storage areas.

Ismail Khan's orders were clear: they were to find their rifles, then remain undetected in the morgue until they heard the hubbub that would accompany the arrival of the target. They were then to wait long enough for the UIPs to take the elevators to the top floor, to make it more difficult for the target to escape. Then they were to swarm up the fire stairs to the third floor and carry out the mission. Any of them who survived should scatter and try to find hiding places, though it was expected that the infidel would hunt them down.

Khan did not care about the consequences. Nor did the others. "Paradise," they whispered to each other as they waited behind the morgue's swinging double doors. They were not worried when they revived to find their rifles missing. In the autopsy suite next to the morgue they found heavy scalpels, knives, and a couple of big cleavers. They tested the edges, found them keen, and smiled at each other, whispering about the glorious rewards to come.

A steel-and-glass door across the hallway led to the fire stairs. Khan had sent a man halfway up the stairs to listen for the sounds that would tell him when to order the strike.

He put a finger to his lips to tell the men to be quiet. It would not be long now.

MAJOR Jan Visser saw the SUV take the corner onto 14th of July Street on two wheels. When it thumped down onto all four wheels and rocketed toward his gate, he did not hesitate to yell "fire!" even as he brought his own rifle to his shoulder and sent a stream of 7.62-millimeter bullets at the vehicle. But the rounds bounced off the scarred paintwork and darkened glass.

"Come on!" the South African shouted to one of his men, who sat behind the wheel of an armored Humvee. The vehicle lurched forward in an attempt to block the gate, but the move came too late. The SUV did not decelerate as it swerved off the broad avenue and slammed directly into the heavy steel pipe, tearing it from its mounts before continuing into the gap between the blast walls, then crashing into the high concrete barrier that blocked the route beyond.

"Down!" Visser screamed to his men, who had scattered at the SUV's approach. They threw themselves face-first onto the sidewalk and pavement, or dove for cover behind anything that could shelter them from the blast they knew must come. Nobody drove a vehicle into a Green Zone checkpoint unless it was packed with explosives. The last time this had happened, a second vehicle—a cement truck whose huge rotating reservoir was loaded with the contents of looted artillery shells— had crashed through the gap made by the first blast, then blew itself up inside the zone.

Face pressed against the concrete, Visser waited for the blast he was sure would kill him. For some reason, he found himself counting the seconds. But when no explosion ripped apart the day, he looked up. The SUV was against the gate's rear blast wall, its front squashed in like an accordion and its windshield popped out and lying on the bent hood.

"Up!" the major ordered. He told the Australian sergeant to check the wreck and set the rest of the men to watching the street for a follow-up.

"Nothing," the sergeant said. The nervous dog was sniffing at the vehicle's open door, but not excitedly wagging its tail as it always did when it smelled what it was trained to find.

"The driver?"

"The car's empty, Major," the Aussie said.

"Remote control?"

"Maybe. It's too messed up to tell." The sergeant passed his hand across his brow, wiping away sweat. "Hell of a day, isn't it, sir?"

Before Visser could answer, they heard the automatically aimed machine guns beyond the blast wall open up. "Check that!" the South African said.

But when the sergeant reported back moments later, he said there were no bodies in the killing ground. "Might have been some drops of blood on one wall," he said, "but if the crash buggered up the electronics and started those machine guns firing independently, I don't reckon on going in there to find out."

Visser weighed it up. First the sixteen idiots offering themselves as targets, now somebody crashes an unmanned vehicle into the gate. "Maybe somebody's just practicing," he said. "Call the techs and get the machine guns checked. And intelligence will want to look at the car."

○———————————○

THE president and his Secret Service security detail, accompanied by embassy staff, military brass, and the media pool, filled all three elevators that came up to the top floor of the hospital. As they emerged from the three cars, an army doctor stepped forward to be their guide to the wards where the commander in chief would present the Purple Hearts. But as he opened his mouth to say "Welcome, Mr. President," they all heard a rattle of distant rifle fire, followed by a heavy crash.

The Secret Service men had left their machine pistols at the embassy. The president's media handlers didn't think it looked good for him to be surrounded by heavily armed bodyguards when he was visiting wounded soldiers and marines. Now they drew their nine-millimeter Glock pistols and positioned themselves around the president. The senior agent, the one the president had called Frank, spoke into the microphone on the inside of his left wrist, "Bluepoint, this is Eagle One. I want the nearest helicopter sent to the hospital roof, right now." Then he turned to the three-star general whose command included the Green Zone and said, "Are there armed troops in this building?"

"Just that Marine Corps guard of honor that saluted in the lobby," the general said. "But they'll only have one clip apiece."

"Get them up here. Tell them to come by the fire stairs."

The three-star looked as if he didn't enjoy being ordered around by a civilian, but then the moment passed and he began issuing orders.

The senior Secret Service man turned to the president and said, "Sir, I think we should go up on the roof. I have a helicopter coming."

But the man in the blue suit said, "Frank, that ruckus sounds like it's pretty far off, and I came to see the men and women on this floor." He turned to the doctor and said, "Doctor, would you like to lead the way?"

○━━━━━━━━○

THE mujahideen in the stairwell heard the commotion above when the target and his party arrived. He reported back to Ismail Khan in the morgue.

"God is great," the Pakistani said.

He crept out into the corridor and put his ear to the concrete wall that ran down toward the elevator well at the center of the structure. He heard the heavy hum of all three electric motors and the sounds that the cars made as they rose in the shafts.

He returned to the morgue and said, "He is here. Make ready."

Each man of the Green Fist reached to the small of his back to tear free a small patch of surgical tape. Beneath were two gray pills. One of them fetched water from a sink and they solemnly took the stimulants. They waited a moment for the drugs to take hold, then, eyes glittering with excitement, they took up their weapons.

"Come," Khan said and led them out into the corridor. He opened the door to the fire stairs and listened. He was about to begin climbing when he heard the sound of distant gunfire, followed by a heavy impact that might have been an explosion.

Then came silence. He paused to think, although the stimulants now coursing through his blood argued for action. But he reminded himself that this mission must not fail. He would take the time to make sure. He listened, but when he heard no more weapons fire, Khan decided that nothing had happened to change his orders. Then he heard boots in the stairwell above him, climbing fast. And then came the *whup-whup* of a helicopter approaching.

"Now!" he whispered to the mujahideen. "God willing, we strike!"

The men of the Green Fist charged up the stairs.

○━━━━━━━━○

THE hospital had two wings extending from a central core. It was only luck that the first ward the president was to visit was at the end of the wing that stood three stories above the laundry instead of the morgue. But it was also only luck that made the marine honor guard choose the fire stairs that were at the end of the wing that contained the morgue. They were between the second and third floors when they heard boots coming up the concrete stairs behind them—coming fast.

The veteran gunnery sergeant in charge of the detail didn't wait to find out if whoever was coming up after him was friend or foe. Friendly fire was a risk a soldier had to take. He turned and fired a three-round burst at an angle down into the stairwell so that the rounds ricocheted off the concrete walls.

The seven other marines in the honor guard turned and leveled their weapons down the stairs while their gunney waited to hear what would come next. If it was "hold your fire!" he would wait to see who came around the corner.

If it was anything else, they would give them hell.

He didn't have long to wait. A shout of "*Allahu akbar!*" came from below, then the rapid clatter of bootsteps.

"Fire!" The marines opened up, filling the narrow well with the blasts of riflery and the whining of ricochets. "Keep firing! Back your way up the stairs!" the gunney said.

The honor guard wasn't geared for real combat, none of them slung around with extra clips of ammunition. The noncom wanted them up and behind a steel fire door they could barricade, before they had nothing left to throw at whoever was coming up the stairs.

⊸————————————⊸

THREE of the Green Fist had died in the withering fire from up the stairs. Four had been wounded, though their wounds might heal if they lived long enough. The baron had warned them that the elixir would probably allow them to rise from the dead only once. He'd said he had had to balance the dosage—giving them enough to recover from the first death, but keeping that recovery slow enough that they would already be in the morgue before they revived.

Ismail Khan did not care whether he lived or died. Paradise awaited. He cared only that he fulfill the mission. "Gassim, Ahmed," he said, "pick up one of the martyrs. Hafiz and Yussuf, pick up another. Hold them before us as barriers. Now, God willing, let us fight!"

"God is great!" the mujahideen cried as the bullets from above thudded into their comrade's dead flesh. They went up the stairs.

○————————○

"FIX bayonets!" shouted the gunnery sergeant as he fired the last round from the single clip in his M-16. A couple of his men squeezed off final shots, then reached for the brilliantly polished blades that were part of any honor guard's gear.

The fight had been too fast. They would not make it through the third-floor door in time. So they would fight and hold them on this side.

"Here they come!" said one of the marines. He spat to one side and set himself.

Below them, two dead men came around the last corner of the stairwell, moving fast. Then, as the men holding them realized that there would be no more rifle fire, the corpses were flung aside and the mujahideen, knives and cleavers flashing, charged.

No guns, was the gunney's thought. *We'll stop 'em.* Then he had time only for, *My God, they're—* before the attackers were upon them, like a ninja movie on fast-forward, flicking aside the out-thrust bayonets and stabbing, slicing, hacking so fast that the gunney's throat was cut and he was falling forward down the steps even as the word "quick!" was forming in his mind.

○————————○

THE three-star general hadn't fired a shot in anger since he'd been a young field officer in Vietnam's Ia Drang Valley, but Baghdad was a war zone and he carried a loaded sidearm. He'd ordered the doctors and nurses to barricade the doors to the wards, then he'd gathered his effectives—three Secret Service agents, one of them a woman, a Marine Corps colonel, and the army captain who was his own aide-de-camp—in the wide space in front of the elevators at the near end of the corridor from which the firing had come.

It was a long, straight hallway with nothing in it but closed doors. Whoever came out of the fire stairs at the far end would have no cover for as long as it took them to run the hundred and twenty feet to the elevators. The general took up a position at one end of the wall, standing and aiming his pistol toward the distant stairwell. The marine colonel placed himself on the other side of the gap and drew his own sidearm, a pearl-handled Colt .45 that was no longer service issue.

The colonel saw the general looking at the weapon. "It was my old man's," he said.

"Good enough for me," said the three-star.

Two of the Secret Service agents knelt beneath the military men, while the third lay on his belly to fire directly down the middle of the hallway.

The captain stood behind his boss. He was unarmed. "One of us goes down, Charley," the general said. "You get the weapon."

"Yes, sir."

And then they waited.

But not for long. The firing from the fire stairs stopped. Moments later, the faraway door to the stairwell eased open and a face peeked out, then rapidly withdrew.

"Ready now," the general said. "Make them count."

The door was yanked open from within. For a moment, the general's heart leaped up as two marines from the honor guard came through the opening. Then he swore as the reality of what he was seeing struck home and he heard the cries of "*Allahu akbar!*"

"Open fire!"

The reek of cordite and the pop of pistols, punctuated by the harsher sound of the colonel's .45, filled the space before the elevators. But the enemy came on so fast, crouching behind the bodies of the American dead held up on the points of their own bayonets. The Secret Service agents could shoot, and the colonel had lost none of his skill, but a charge that should have taken at least thirty seconds, under fire and burdened by corpses, was over before any of those with pistols could squeeze off three aimed shots.

Some of the attackers went down, tumbling and sprawling on the tiles. But the others came on, at impossible speed, to toss aside the shielding corpses at the last moment and fling themselves upon the defenders. And suddenly the general's world was a blur of limbs and blades, of blood and screams, of white teeth grinning in cruel faces. And he was sinking to the floor, holding his ripped belly, and seeing at least four of the killers racing away down the other corridor.

o———————o

"MOVE!" yelled the head of the president's security detail as he and one other Secret Service man pushed their charge up the flight of fire stairs that led to the roof. The man he was raising his voice to was the commander in chief, but that wasn't going to stop him from doing what the job required.

The stairs ended at a trapdoor that damn well better not be locked, Frank was thinking. Below and behind him, down in the long third-floor hallway that ran the length of the hospital wing, he could hear firing—single shots from nine-millimeter Glock pistols—and the screams of men dying. But he could also hear cries of *"Allahu akbar!"* And they were getting closer.

Above him, he could hear the sound of the military chopper he had called for. If it was a gunship with a door gunner, they would be fine. If it was a medivac, this situation could still be too close to call. The Secret Service man in front reached the trapdoor to the roof. It was secured only by a sliding bolt. The man threw the bolt and pushed—and the door opened.

So far so good, Frank thought. The chopper sounded comfortingly louder as he pushed the president of the United States out into the open air.

The helicopter was coming in, and, *dammit, it's unarmed,* the head of the security detail was thinking. *And only the pilot aboard.* He signaled the other agent to be ready to bundle the president through its open hatch the moment it was low enough. Meanwhile, he kept his eye on the trapdoor through which they had come, his pistol ready in his hand.

"Frank!" came the other agent's voice.

The chief risked a quick look in the direction of the incoming chopper. It all looked okay. Then he saw what had alarmed the other man. Someone was clinging to the underside of the aircraft, arms and legs wrapped around one of the skids. As the copter swung over the building, still twenty feet above the roof, the figure let go—legs first, then hands—to plummet straight down to the tarred surface.

The man landed on his feet with a *thump* that Frank felt as a vibration through the soles of his shoes. The impact should have broken both of the man's short legs, but he simply rolled hard and came up blowing air out of his cheeks, as if he'd stubbed his toe and was waiting for the pain to go away. His clothes were full of holes, as if he had been used for target practice by a squad of machine gunners. Smears of blood surrounded many of the holes, but he seemed unscathed.

Then, his hands held in front of him in a gesture that said he was not looking for trouble, the newcomer took a step toward Frank. But that meant he was taking a step toward the president of the United States under conditions that didn't allow anybody to take such a step. So whatever he was or wasn't looking for, what he got was what the training manuals called for: a pistol round in the center of the visible mass.

The slug struck the man's breastbone—Frank was rated expert as a marksman—but it didn't put him down. Instead, he plucked the metal out of his chest and tossed it down. Then he said, "Don't do that. It hurts."

Frank wasn't taking advice right now on how to do his job. He sighted the pistol on point of the widow's peak that descended into the man's forehead and put calculated pressure on the trigger. Behind him he could hear the chopper racketing louder than ever and feel its wind throwing him forward. *I'll have to adjust for that*, he was thinking.

The small man was taking something from a pants pocket and swallowing it. *Enjoy your last meal*, Frank thought.

Then behind the target, the trapdoor sprang open and four men in bloodstained Iraqi Army fatigues swarmed onto the roof and raced screaming toward him—*No, toward the chopper*, Frank thought as he swung the pistol toward them and fired.

He got one, the man went down, but the other three had already closed the distance between the trapdoor and the man who had leapt from the helicopter.

But that was as far as they got.

ISMAIL Khan recognized Logan right away. For a moment he wondered if the baron had sent him here to help, then he saw that that was not the case. As the target's bodyguard turned, so slowly, and fired his pistol at the mujahideen, the small man turned to face the four of them and the look in his eyes left no doubt as to what he intended to do.

But God will not let you, Khan was thinking even as he registered Gassim's taking of a bullet in the chest from the bodyguard's gun. The death did not matter. What mattered was the bloodstained bayonet that the Pakistani had taken from one of the marines in the stairwell. He would use it on the man with the gun, leaving Logan to be disposed of by his two comrades who still survived.

Khan saw it all, knew just how it would happen. He would rip open the one who had just shot Gassim, then he would run to where the helicopter—its blades rotating lazily—was just about to kiss the surface of the roof. He would kill the second bodyguard who was even now, but far too slowly, squatting to boost his master into the aircraft.

Then with a shout of "God is great!" Khan would seize the enemy, throw him down, and thrust the bayonet into his heart. Then he would slice off the infidel's head. He would carry it to the edge of the building where its rear overlooked the Tigris River. Holding it by the hair he would cry out in a voice to carry across the city of the Caliphs, "There is no god but God, and Muhammad is his Prophet!"

Then he would fling the head of the Great Satan into the eternal waters. After that he would sit down and await his martyrdom and then the perfumed gardens of paradise.

His heart bursting with the sacred joy of holy war, Ismail Khan brandished the bayonet and rushed forward.

○————————○

LOGAN would have gone for the one with the bayonet, except that when he moved to do so, he saw that the two coming right behind the Pakistani were now rushing straight at him.

When they had come out of the trapdoor they had been moving quickly, just as he remembered from watching the training exercise. But the baron's pills were also fast-acting. No sooner did they hit his stomach than he felt the effects—a cold ripple seemed to pass through his skeletal muscles and suddenly everything was slowing, the *whup-whup* of the landing helicopter behind him suddenly sounded like half speed, then quarter speed, then as slow as the leaky tap back in his condo in Ottawa that dripped lazily into the bathroom sink all night.

The two Arabs were coming at him, one with a cleaver, the other with some kind of big autopsy knife. Their faces showed a happy expectation of an easy job, soon to be out of the way.

But Logan flexed his forearms, felt the thin pain tear his hands, then fade as soon as it appeared. And when the men came at him, one slashing with the cleaver, the other stabbing upward with the knife, he made no move to block the blows.

Instead, he swept his hands forward and up, palms raised, so that his claws entered their bellies and sliced upward through flesh and gristle and even bone. He cut through them as if they were made of nothing more substantial than Jell-O.

I thought so, he said to himself, even as he was turning to go after Khan. He didn't know what the metal was that came from his hands, but he was getting comfortable with the idea that he could cut his way into and out of anything.

The Secret Service man who had shot him was down on the tarred surface, the hand that had held the pistol slashed to uselessness and his chest laid open by a second wound. Still he was reaching with his other hand for the fallen Glock.

Khan was already at the helicopter, hacking at the other agent. Logan could see a red furrow along the side of the Pakistani's face and half his ear was gone—the Secret Service agent must have got off a shot that had almost done the job.

But now the agent was dead and the Pakistani was dragging the man in the blue suit out of the helicopter's open bay. His face was alive with cruel glee as he threw the victim down and raised the bayonet above his head.

"*Allahu*—" he cried, but the "*akbar*" never came. Logan's claws flashed, sending both hand and weapon spinning off while blood fountained from the stump.

"My regards to the virgins," the mutant said, then he thrust three blades through the side of the Pakistani's neck and sawed sideways. *Like a hot knife through butter*, he thought as the mujahideen's head toppled from the severed neck and rolled to land nose-down on the tar.

Logan flexed and the claws disappeared, the torn flesh instantly restoring itself. He reached down to help the president of the United

States to rise. At least he assumed it was the president. He wasn't sure he recognized the face. *But people always look different on TV*, he thought.

The man in the suit was staring at him. Then his eyes flicked down to Logan's hands. "You better get on the chopper," the Canadian shouted over the noise of the rotors. "This might not be over."

He put a hand on the man's arm and lifted him into the copter.

"I know who you are," the president said. "Code name Wolverine."

Then the chopper was lifting and pulling away, too late for Logan to jump aboard, too late for him to do anything but yell into the wind, "What? What does that mean?"

But the aircraft was going, going, gone. He watched it dwindle in size as it banked and headed toward the big domed building that flew the Stars and Stripes. Behind him, the wounded Secret Service man was saying something.

"What?" Logan said, turning. But suddenly he was convulsing as a lightning bolt surged through his body, the energy bringing a fiery pain that passed from his head down to his heels. Its heat melted the tar beneath his soles.

Two hard hands had gripped the sides of his head. The power continued to pour agony throughout his body. He could smell his hair burning beneath Al Borak's palms. He could feel the saliva boiling in his mouth. Again the darkness was creeping in from the sides of his vision, the light narrowing to a circle that kept getting smaller.

And still the energy kept pouring through him, till he wondered, *How much more of this can I take?* His mind didn't know. And for all the confidence that his body seemed to have in its own power, he had a feeling that he'd never been subjected to sustained electrical shock of this magnitude for this long.

Then he heard, as if from far away, a small *pop* and the hands left him, taking the pain away. He staggered, his eyes not yet able to tell him where the edge of the roof was, so that he almost toppled over into the water below. Then his vision recovered, along with his strength, and he looked to see what had caused Al Borak to release him.

The tall man was reaching over his own shoulder, down the back of his shirt, to pluck something from his flesh. His hand came back with a nine-millimeter round between his thumb and forefinger. He looked at it, then tossed it aside. He glanced at the wounded Secret Service man, but the agent had done all he could do, squeezing off one shot before fainting from shock and blood loss.

Al Borak turned his attention back to Logan.

"It's all over," the smaller man said. He gestured with his thumb to the distant helicopter. "He's out of reach."

The taller man shrugged. "You say, that time, we should try, each one and the other. Could be interesting."

"I remember that."

"How about now?"

It was Logan's turn to shrug. "I got other things to do. People to see."

"After today," said the man who used to be Batoor the orphan, "I got nothing." He spread his hands, and blue sparks danced between them. "Except this, and you."

He crouched, his hands extended before him like a wrestler's, and came forward.

The now familiar little pain lanced momentarily through Logan's hands. He circled warily, then flicked a clawed hand at the Pashtun. Two things happened: he got a solid shock down one arm; and the wound he opened up in Al Borak's forearm closed almost as soon as it began to bleed.

"You've been taking our friend's special medicine," Logan said.

The other man smiled. "I want it to be like you say—'interesting.'"

"Well, then," Logan said, "this ought to interest the hell out of you." He lunged forward, arms straight, claws point first. The six blades tore into the Pashtun's chest and sprang out of his back, slicing flesh and piercing bone as if it were balsa wood. Al Borak screamed in pain and rage, but his arms reflexively closed on the smaller man's neck and the spirit of the clouds burst from him as never before.

Logan's teeth ground against each other and his eyeballs felt as if they might be forced from their sockets as the force of the discharge boiled the tissues of his brain. He had lost control of his limbs but that no longer mattered because the momentum of his rush carried both of them back over the edge of the roof.

They tumbled as they fell, Logan's greater weight putting him on the bottom, so that his back struck the narrow strip of riverbank below. But his claws were wedged deep into Al Borak's torso, and the Pashtun continued to pour his energy into the Canadian, as they bounced, then rolled, then toppled over the top of the stone wall that confined the Tigris.

The water was silty and deep, and the Tigris could get cold in a Baghdad December. But the important thing, Logan thought as they sank into its murky depths, was that this river was no friend to the man who was impaled on his claws. He felt the tall man convulse as he himself had convulsed when Al Borak's lightning had gone through him.

Then the current was bumping them along the bottom, plowing them through silt and waterlogged wood, and occasionally smashing them against blocks of stone that had probably lain there long enough to interest an archaeologist. After a while, the rigidity went out of the other man and he hung limp in Logan's grip.

The Canadian kicked against the river bottom and sent them both rising toward the surface. As the light brightened, he could see that the Pashtun's gray eyes were open, that he was even conscious. Enough of the elixir stolen from Logan's blood was in his veins to have kept him from drowning or from shocking himself to death.

Logan's head broke into the air. He filled his lungs and dove deep into the river, taking the Pashtun with him. He felt with his feet along the bottom until he found a place where there were plenty of stones. Then he freed Al Borak from the spikes that held him. The man tried to swim upward, but he wasn't fast enough.

Logan used his greater weight to hold Al Borak down. He pressed him into the cold ooze of the Tigris, then piled stones on top of the Pashtun until he had made a good-size underwater cairn. A couple of times, he broke off to rise to the surface and fill his lungs, then dove down to continue the work. As he heaped the stones up, a voice from the back of his mind said, *If a job's worth doing, it's worth doing well.*

Logan wondered whose voice it was. Then he got back to work.

MANSOUR DISTRICT, BAGHDAD,

THE PRESENT

WOLFGANG Freiherr von Strucker had fallen asleep in the chair, worn-out from the effort of trying to scoot it across the little dining room and out into the foyer. He had hoped that the front doors might have been open and that he might somehow attract the attention of a passerby. But when he finally got beyond the small room he found the outer doors locked.

He awoke when the gag was pulled from his mouth. But his moment of hope ended when he saw the face of Logan looking down at him. The mutant's eyes were hard and dark as volcanic glass.

"We need to talk," he said.

"I only wanted to help you," von Strucker said.

"Good," said Logan. "You can start by telling me who I am."

"I don't know."

"Wrong answer."

"I never did."

"For both our sakes," Logan said. "I hope that's not true. Because, if it isn't, I'm going to be unhappy. But by the time we establish to my satisfaction that it's not true, you're going to be downright miserable."

The baron swore to him that he could not tell Logan what he wanted to hear. But he promised to drop all other concerns and use all his resources to find out. While he was making these statements, the mutant brought over an end table and set it down near the chair. Then he went into the dining room and returned with the carrying case. There were still several tubes containing the elixir and he filled the hypodermic from one of them.

"The thing about being me," he said as he squirted a jet of cloudy fluid from the needle's tip and bent over the baron's arm, "is that you have to know how to suffer. Being able to recover fast doesn't do anything to stop the pain. You heal, all right—but first you hurt."

He shot the stuff into von Strucker's vein.

"I figure we've got a lot of time before anybody comes to check on the house," he said. "But I'm anxious to get started."

The baron watched in horror as the small man flexed his arms and three gleaming claws sheathed in adamantium sprang from each hand.

As he moved toward von Strucker, he said, "Now, you just won't believe the things I can do with these."

"Please," said the baron.

Logan laid the tip of one claw against the corner of von Strucker's left eye. "What does 'Code name: Wolverine' mean?"

A great wave of relief washed through the Prussian. Even buried in the Empty Quarter, one heard things. He would be able to answer the mutant's first question. "Wolverine," he said, "is a member of a group of mutants known as the X-Men."

○————————○

THE name rang an echo somewhere deep in Logan's being. He withdrew the claw from beside the German's eye, and saw the man's gaze follow the movement of the gleaming length of razor-edged adamantium.

"I've heard he has claws," von Strucker said.

"So I could be this Wolverine?"

"You could," von Strucker said. "You very definitely could."

"And these X-Men, what do they do?"

"They help other mutants, especially young ones. There's some kind of school, run by a man named Charles Xavier."

That name almost called up an image of a face, but the features would not come into focus. Still, an almost animal sense of familiarity welled up from the bottom of Logan's mind. He felt he knew a man called Charles Xavier. And the man was not his enemy, might even be a friend.

Regardless, he now had a new lead to follow.

"Where is this school?" he asked the man in the chair.

"Somewhere in the United States," von Strucker said. "They don't advertise the location."

Logan set the claw back against the corner of the German's eye and said, "You're not being a big help."

Then he saw the man swallow nervously and watched an expression of indecision flicker across von Strucker's face. "Looks to me like you're trying to decide whether or not to tell me something. My advice is to spill whatever you've got before I have to dig for it."

He pressed with the point of the claw, following as the man tried to move his head away from the needle tip.

"All right, all right!" von Strucker said. "I'll tell you!"

The small man eased up on the pressure but kept the claw against the German's face. "I'm listening."

"When we came here," von Strucker said, speaking fast, "I still wasn't completely sure what I wanted to do with you. I asked the Arab to bring the mnemophage that would wipe your memory. But I also asked him to bring the antidote." He swallowed again. "It's in the television room."

Logan stepped back and studied the man. "You expect me to shoot myself up with another one of your concoctions?" He trailed the tip of one claw down the baron's chest, slicing through clothing to score the flesh beneath.

The German twitched and gasped. "Even if it was a massive dose of poison it wouldn't do me any good! Five minutes later you'd be back to normal and I'd still be strapped into this chair!"

Logan thought about it and conceded the point. "But what if it's a superdose of memory eater? What if I lose what few memories I've managed to recover?"

He saw the German thinking hard. Then von Strucker looked up and said, "Write yourself a note and pin it to my chest. Let it say, 'If you don't know who you are, kill this man.'"

The mutant examined the proposition from every angle he could think of. "There's still some risk," he said.

"For me, too," said von Strucker. "You'll remember what passed between us at Höllenfeuer."

"I already do," Logan said, and saw the German's Adam's apple go up and down again. But a voice from the back of his head was telling him, *No risk, no reward.* He sheathed his claws and went into the TV room, found a small flat case on a side table, and opened it to reveal a hypodermic full of a blue liquid.

There was paper and a pen in the family dining room. He wrote himself a note, using the exact words that the German had suggested—except to the phrase "kill this man" he added the word "slowly." He showed it to von Strucker and received only a shrug in reply.

He pinned the paper to the man's chest, then took up the hypodermic, squirting some out of the needle to remove any air bubbles. Then he set the tip against the vein in the crook of his elbow and put his thumb on the plunger.

For a moment he paused. The thought came again that he might have done terrible things. He had no doubt he had killed men and women. For all he knew, behind him lay a bloody trail of slaughter, of the guilty and the innocent both, a heap of torn bodies that were his doing.

Did he want to know? he asked himself. And from deep inside came the answer: *Yes. A man does what he has to and lives with the consequences.*

He pushed the spike into the vein and squeezed the blue liquid into his body. The stuff burned as it surged through his system. He could feel it climbing his arm to his shoulder, now into his neck and now hitting his brain.

And all at once, there it was. All of it. Faces and names, places and events, the dead and the living, the good he had managed to do and the evil that he had been part of. The blood. The pain.

Charles Xavier. Jean Grey. Mariko. Roanoke. Weapon X. Alpha Flight.

It did not come back to him. It had always been there, and now he came back to it.

He dropped the hypodermic on the table and looked at von Strucker. The bound man said, "I told you the truth. Now you know who you are."

"Yes," said Logan, "I do."

"Then will you let me go? This will not be a good place for me in a little while."

Logan remembered the little room in the *kommandantur* at Höllenfeuer, remembered being left nailed to a table.

"No," he said. He headed for the door.

As he left, he was thinking, *I know who I am, and I know what I can do.* He also knew who had stolen his memories and why. And he knew exactly what he was going to do about it.

ABOUT THE AUTHOR

HUGH Matthews is a pen name of the fantasy and science fiction author Matthew Hughes. He has won the Crime Writers of Canada's Arthur Ellis Award, and has been shortlisted for the Aurora, Nebula, Philip K. Dick, Endeavour (thrice), A.E. Van Vogt, Neffy, and Derringer Awards. In 2020, he was inducted into the Canadian Science Fiction and Fantasy Hall of fame. His web page is at www.archonate.com.

X-MEN

MUTANT EMPIRE OMNIBUS

Magneto—the X-Men's oldest, deadliest foe—has taken over a top-secret government installation that houses the Sentinels, powerful mutant-hunting robots. The X-Men must fight to keep this deadly technology out of Magneto's hands and stop him from carrying out his grand plan: establishing a global Mutant Empire. The X-Men must join forces with old enemies to stop him—but in Magneto's brave new world, who can they trust?

X-MEN AND THE AVENGERS

GAMMA QUEST OMNIBUS

When the Scarlet Witch of the Avengers and Rogue of the X-Men both disappear under mysterious circumstances, each team's search leads them to more questions than answers. Desperate to recover their missing teammates, they must join forces to uncover the truth. But their efforts will bring them up against a foe with the deadliest power of all: to make them turn on each other!

SPIDER-MAN
KRAVEN'S LAST HUNT

After years of crushing defeats, Kraven the Hunter—son of Russian aristocrats, game tracker supreme—launches a final, deadly assault on Peter Parker, the Amazing Spider-Man. But for the obsessed Kraven, killing his prey is not enough. Once his enemy is dead, Kraven must become the Spider.

SPIDER-MAN
FOREVER YOUNG

Hoping to snag some rent-paying photos of his arachnid-like alter ego in action, Peter Parker goes looking for trouble—and finds it in the form of a mysterious, mythical stone tablet coveted by both the Kingpin and the Maggia! Caught in the crosshairs of New York's most nefarious villains, Peter also runs afoul of his friends—and the police! His girlfriend, Gwen Stacy, isn't too happy with him, either. And the past comes back to haunt him years later when the Maggia's assumed-dead leader resurfaces, still in pursuit of the troublesome tablet! Plus: With Aunt May at death's door, has the ol' Parker luck disappeared for good?

For more fantastic fiction, author events, exclusive
excerpts, competitions, limited editions and more

VISIT OUR WEBSITE
titanbooks.com

LIKE US ON FACEBOOK
facebook.com/titanbooks

FOLLOW US ON TWITTER
@TitanBooks

EMAIL US
readerfeedback@titanemail.com